PENGUIN BOOKS

SKALLAGRIGG

William Horwood was born in Oxford in 1944, the youngest of a large family. He has a degree in geography from Bristol University and was a feature editor with the *Daily Mail* until 1978. His first novel, *Duncton Wood*, was published in 1980 and was an immediate bestseller. Since then he has published *The Stonor Eagles* and *Callanish*, as well as some poetry. His daughter Rachel suffers from cerebral palsy; this experience led him to write *Skallagrigg*.

SKALLAGRIGG

WILLIAM HORWOOD

PENGUIN BOOKS

PENGUIN BOOKS

Published by the Penguin Group
27 Wrights Lane, London W8 5TZ, England
Viking Penguin Inc., 40 West 23rd Street, New York, New York 10010, USA
Penguin Books Australia Ltd, Ringwood, Victoria, Australia
Penguin Books Canada Ltd, 2801 John Street, Markham, Ontario, Canada L3R 1B4
Penguin Books (NZ) Ltd, 182–190 Wairau Road, Auckland 10, New Zealand

Penguin Books Ltd, Registered Offices: Harmondsworth, Middlesex, England

First published by Viking 1987
Published in Penguin Books 1988

Copyright © Steppenmole Enterprises Ltd, 1987

Made and printed in Great Britain by
Richard Clay Ltd, Bungay, Suffolk
Filmset in Monophoto Photina

For Janet, Rachel and Joseph
with love

CONTENTS

PART I

THE QUEST
FOR THE
SKALLAGRIGG

ONE

If we are going to find the Skallagrigg we must start in 1927 with Eddie, though I had better say immediately that his real name was Arthur.

The boy was seven then. He could not talk, or control his limbs, or do anything without help; not even protest. He was what was then called a cripple. Worse than that, he seemed to be an idiot cripple.

In 1927 they came and finally took him from the little life and love he had. It was his only trip in an automobile, out through the great gates, down Blackhorse Lane, up the hill through Apsham Wood and past the endless wooden fence which he saw that one last time, peering beyond it to the meadows where the grass stood tall and the wind and sun were light and warm. And where that dry summer he had been allowed to lie alone for a time and stare up at the fragile petals of the red poppies whose awkward, crooked stems were like his arms and legs and whose life reached up, as he desired to, to the sky and wind above the swaying grass. Then the wooden fence was gone, the fields beyond it lost from sight, and Apsham Hill no more than a distant rise receding in the square of glass in the back of the shaking vehicle that was taking him away.

By train then, in the care of two male nurses he had never seen, strangers who smelled of cigarettes and handled him roughly. They took him to a towering place of dirty yellow brick and sunless, barred windows whose name he did not know and naturally was not told. He was an idiot.

They stripped him of his clothes, of the blue knitted socks he liked, of his grey flannel shorts, of the whistle round his neck – in fact, of the very last things he knew. They shaved his head in case of lice. They washed him with water that was too cold, with brushes that were too hard. Probably then they filled in the first records (the medical profession is rather particular about records. Of course, that does not stop mistakes creeping in and falsifications being maintained and turned into inviolate truths, like the notion that Arthur was in fact Eddie when the truth was quite otherwise). So they filled in the first records, correctly calling him Arthur at that point but getting the diagnosis tragically wrong: congenital idiot. They did not know the condition of cerebral palsy. How could the pioneering work of an English doctor seventy years before, who had shown that Arthur's kind of deformities were of the body and not the mind, have found its way inside that massive, closed and almost mindlessly self-perpetuating institution?

Having filled in the records and seen that the consultant procedures were properly, if rather briefly, observed, the one in charge (for whom picking up Arthur had been a pleasant change of routine and a nice day out) said, 'We'll put him in Back Ward in Jerry Baxter's old cot. From his kind of home, snobby and that, he'll be too soft yet for any other ward.' So you see, in a kind of way they cared, even if it was the care attendants take of the cattle in a slaughterhouse to ensure they reach the place of death in one piece.

They carried him into a world into which you and I will eventually have to travel if we are to find the truth of the Skallagrigg. At first sight it seems rather quaint and charming since the foyers and corridors of parts of the hospital still retained the wire flower-baskets which the wife of a long-dead medical superintendent had bought for the hospital as a way of 'improving' life for the patients. No flowers now, though. The door frames too, at least in the section of the hospital visitors were allowed to see, had a certain reassuring solidity, being of that Victorian oak and architrave style whose effect is to give those in authority a sense of reassurance, and those subordinate the uneasy feeling that they are always on the threshold of punishment.

But further into the confines of that place, where they had taken the helpless Arthur (as he still was), heavy custodial padlocks defaced the doorways, and keys jangled as they pushed him down nightmare corridor after corridor, then into a ward past cots in which threshing, frightening men-children lay.

They unlocked another door, the riveted padlock as big as Arthur's feet, which led into a children's hell. A place of ugly, subnormal youth which held beings and miseries such as we thought lived on into the twentieth century only in social history books. A rank odour of faeces, urine and polish; rows of dirty high-sided cots within whose confines, dreadful and dim (for the windows were small and high and seemed all to face north), lay lost living things, deranged and crippled children, unloved, forsaken, forgotten; cotted for ever into an isolation that deprived them of touch or contact; their eyes staring out or staring in; some of their limbs and heads moving back and forth, back and forth, in the filth of their beds, which a later generation of medical workers would recognize as the movements of psychotic boredom.

Arthur, sitting twisted in the wheelchair they pushed him in, stared at this infernal scene with a fear made worse by the sight of an empty cot, waiting at the far end of the ward. He stared at the inmates he passed and saw that some were his own kind – congenital idiots! – their limbs constantly moving in an uncontrolled roundel. Past sickening incontinence they took him, through cries and screams. Near monsters enough like himself to make a nightmare live; the bulbous set of their staring eyes . . . the audible slavering of huge tongues and mouths that puffed out spit . . . the red sores upon their legs and backs . . . all real. They lived and stared at him from a world that he sensed would inexorably become his own.

As he passed them by, one only seemed to see him: the face yellow and long, the eyes staring; a hand reaching out towards him through the bars of a cot, and a noise that Arthur knew instinctively expressed interest and curiosity. Arthur would have shrunk away from that cadaverous hand if he had been able, but as its fingers touched his leg the nurse said, 'Leave him, Frank, go on, get down. He's not interested in you.' And Frank, named as a human it seemed, lay down like a dog.

Arthur's own grey eyes were the only mirror of his desolate, frightened mind, but none observed him with charity or kindness. The nurses took his shocked silence for indifference; his indifference for idiocy. So with no thought of offering comforting words or gentle touches, they brought him to that empty urine-smelling cot he had seen, raised him up and lowered him in. They had put him in his place in Back Ward. Then the worst thing of all: they walked away and left him.

On one side was a blank wall that might have been a dingy
green if the light in the ward had been better; on the other side,
within smelling distance, was a creature in an identical cot, tangled
into sheets with only some lank dark hair showing on one side,
and a distorted ever-moving hand on another, the one not seeming
to be associated in any way with the other.

The blanket they put on Arthur was so heavy and he so weak
that it took him more than an hour to free one hand and raise it
towards the window he could just see, to try to touch the lost sky
outside.

He started to cry from homesickness but they did not understand
he was crying. He never made normal sounds. His thorax was not
made that way and his tongue, twisted and thrusting and horrible
if you did not know him, got in the way of genteel sounds and
corrupted them into dribbled grunts and curious horrific sibilants
from a lost and undesirable world.

If they had been told that his whimpered cries were those of a
normal little boy (at heart) deprived suddenly of love and home
and hope and put into a hell he could not understand, they would
have refused to believe it. Homesickness implies awareness, and
awareness intelligence. And intelligence, or the possibility of it, in
those wards, was a blasphemy that was not spoken. So they told
him to shut up.

Hours, days, weeks passed. Only one child in that hell tried to
talk to him: Frank. Pathetically thin yet capable of pulling himself
up in his cot and making a few words, he would stand in his cot
and look towards Arthur at the end of the ward and call out 'Lo,
lo, lo' in an endless plea for a return 'Hello', which Arthur could
not give.

One day in the bathroom they took them to twice daily (usually),
Frank reached out and touched Arthur and Arthur did not shrink
away. Instead he grinned in spastic recognition and made a noise
that Frank took to be friendly. Then Frank, for reasons never
known, said 'Eddie' and though the nurse said, 'No that's Arthur',
Frank said, 'Eddie, Eddie, Eddie', and Arthur/Eddie began to cry.
Terribly.

'Now look what you've done you silly Bugger,' said the male
nurse.

Later, from his cot, Frank said 'Eddie, Eddie, Eddie' on and on until Arthur/Eddie finally let out a call or cry that Frank correctly took to be an acknowledgement. And so a subnormal renamed Arthur 'Eddie', and that name attached itself to Arthur, possessed him and finally by custom and omission displaced his real name.

But the final loss of his identity came later. For now, he still cried. Still they said, shut up. He was hit. He was abused by a patient called Rendel who was useful to the nurses and had the run of several wards. He was subject to the fondling of a young male nurse named Dilke, the same that told Frank to bugger off.

Dilke did not like the boy's hand wandering up towards the sky again and again, as if he knew something was there. And Dilke liked even less the way the boy's grey eyes began to stare at him and followed him about the ward. Dilke was strange, he looked as sweet as pie and he smiled when he hit people and his face was innocent when his hands pinched patients' soft weak arms. Dilke knew people in charge. Dilke was a cunning bastard who got promoted. The wards had an extra smell when he went round, and its name was fear. He took to carrying a stick with a hook in the end – for opening the old windows, officially. Unofficially, even the most backward patient knew that the stick could hurt if you weren't where you were meant to be and things weren't tidy. Sometimes, just for fun, one of the new nurses would take Dilke's stick and carry it into one of the wards and hold it above a patient's head or before his legs. The laugh was to be had in watching the instant conditioned reflex of the patient's cringe.

In this hell Arthur lived. No one knew he was intelligent, not even the patients, and they are usually the first to know. So no one at first made sense of the sounds he made or even considered that he was calling out a name, endlessly; a garbled name to someone he thought would come to help him and take him away back over the fence by Apsham Wood and into the field where the poppies crookedly grew.

That someone was the only person who could have helped him. That someone knew that inside the crippled, unstill body was an intelligent mind, and a loving, sensitive, responsible heart.

So Eddie (as he was becoming) dribbled and threshed in the deprivation of his cot, reaching his hand towards the window and calling beyond the walls in which he was imprisoned, beyond the fields over which he would never run, so that the one who knew

the truth about him might hear and take him back at last to where
he could be loved.

   The name he tried to call was 'Skallagrigg'.

Eighteen months passed before he fell ill and weakened to a point
where he could not even raise that jerking arm or control anything.
One day he cried and cried and cried because he had messed his
sheets and so was no better than the incontinents. No one knew,
of course, that those clean, grey flannel shorts he had entered the
hospital with, and which were now packed away in an orderly
fashion and labelled in a box in the cellar beneath the main
administration wing, had been bought for him to mark the day he
had learned to indicate with a movement of his left hand and jerk
of his eyes that he wished to be taken to the toilet. A moment of
special growing up. Those shorts, along with the whistle that no
one had thought to put in his mouth before taking it from him and
packing it away (duly noted on a sheet for patients' possessions),
had been his things, his very own; his belongings and so his belonging; his identity as (as he was) Arthur. But now, eighteen
months on, he was not only losing his name but also that control
which the purchase of his grey flannel shorts had celebrated. Yet
so weak was he by then that he could not even cry out his misery
at having messed his legs and sheets. He was finally losing even
the strength or belief to call out the beloved name of Skallagrigg.

   No one could know that his 'illness' had come to him suddenly,
a terrible shooting pain that was of the mind and yet was felt in
the body, a silent NO as if the very door of life itself had swung
heavily across his path and shut. Before this numbing pain he felt
the Skallagrigg had deserted him; was not there; no longer believed
in him. He knew it. He could feel it.

   So numb, mindless, staring but no longer seeing, thin, he expressed his wish to die by becoming ill. Some might say, however,
that eighteen months is a remarkably long time for one so young
to survive hell before beginning to crack up. That little boy, who is
one of our helpers towards the Skallagrigg, had in that time seen
so very much that was educational: violence, intense suffering,
sadism, sexual molestation and death (among the patients); and
vanity, idleness, cruelty, hypocrisy and inefficiency (among the
nurses and doctors). Some might even suggest, and as your col-

league in this quest I stress the point, that his survival thus far betokens a remarkable and prophetic resilience and character in one who, at that time, was still less than ten years old.

By then, however, he was sufficiently distrustful not to believe that his hasty removal from his cot to the lost world outside – down a long corridor, past staring adult men in an airing court, into an unbelievable and beautiful light he had not seen for so long (called the sun), and then up some stairs into a different building – might herald release and a return home. Yet some hope for this did still exist and as his grey eyes stared (no longer quite as listless as they had been) he again whispered that unknown word that no one recognized as his attempt to speak: Skallagrigg. But he had no faith in it. His Skallagrigg was dead to him. He had been deserted.

It did not take Arthur long to discover he had been moved to the infirmary and that in this place people turned weak and died. Just like they did in Back Ward. His initial jubilation at the sight of the sun and different things was temporary, for he weakened like the others and drained away to almost nothing as the tuberculosis he had developed – the outward form of that inward loss – grew more serious. The hope he had momentarily felt on his release from Back Ward into sunlight was replaced by a terrible desolation so profound that the discovery that his 'friend' Frank was in the infirmary as well did not seem to interest him. Though Frank, seeing him pass by, had sufficient wit and strength to declare, 'That's Eddie!' at which the strange nurse pushing Arthur said those fatal words: 'Oh, Eddie is it? All right then, Eddie,' and so the name took deeper root.

Arthur/Eddie did not bother to protest. He soon saw what was coming because one night he watched a patient near him die, and understood that in those final minutes the patient was calling for something he would never get. Arthur always remembered the eyes staring sightlessly across at him in the early morning; the dead white of those eyes, unblinking and dreadful, seemed to be the only light. He wanted then to die himself and he turned somehow to stare up at the barred and windowed dawning sky. Pain, even discomfort, had gone. Awareness of his body receded as he retreated to his mind and stared out from it. Yes, his calling to the Skallagrigg had ceased, for the Skallagrigg would not come now. He was alone, forsaken.

He was alone.

He had nothing left to hold on to, nothing but a body he did not want. He was a boy far along the road to death, the only road on which he was able to walk as if he were normal; along which he could now run, and pass the wooden fence beyond which, now black and withered, the poppies bent their heads. And only the dawning sky angled in the window above him gave comfort, and a distant, growing chorus of birds, nearer here than they had been at Back Ward. But their sound began to fade as Arthur reached the very edge of death. And for the last time he whispered the word nobody had ever understood: 'Skallagrigg'.

It was then, in those final fading moments that, for the first time since Arthur had been put away, he heard the Skallagrigg call his name.

But not 'Eddie, Eddie', not 'Eddie', but his very own name, his real name spoken by the voice of his beloved Skallagrigg, 'Arthur, Arthur, I am here I am here I am here I am here, I can hear you I can hear, don't go don't leave me . . . ARTHUR DON'T LEAVE ME I'LL FIND YOU I'LL COME ONE DAY I'LL FIND YOU AGAIN, don't leave me . . .'

And Arthur heard the Skallagrigg begin to cry and he knew that all this time the Skallagrigg had been there and that finally, always, he would hear his call. Arthur's limbs stilled and his arm no longer needed to try to reach the sky, or his mouth to say that impossible name, for the Skallagrigg was there in spirit in that room with him, and his arms were reaching to him and raising him as they always had before, and he Arthur, he Eddie, was needed and must not go away. And he felt again the love of the Skallagrigg, from him and to him, an inviolate love and terrible responsibility and he knew he must be strong, he must survive. It was his duty to be there, and to call out and say he was and would be always, so long as he was needed, until one day, one distant day, the Skallagrigg would learn at last what he would need to know to find his Arthur and take him home.

In those moments Arthur's faith was born again for he knew that the Skallagrigg had not forsaken him, and that one day he would really come; not as a dawning light at the window, or the rising of a morning chorus, but as he was and had been and always must be, a part of Arthur as Arthur was a part of him.

So did the Skallagrigg come to Arthur that first time as he lay dying in his bed, with those eyes of a dead patient staring at him from across the ward and the light growing stronger. Our Arthur turned a little, a great effort for him, and whispered that name he loved and which loved him; and he knew that he must live.

Arthur/Eddie's recovery began from that day. He found his health again. He was allowed to sit out in the sun on the once-fine terrace that overlooked the gardens whose beauty made all the more pathetic the squalor inside the buildings that faced them. Perhaps, then, it was as well that the windows were set deliberately high, so that the patients could not see out of them.

Eddie was now witness to the curious fact that ill patients were better off than the not-ill ones (I hesitate to use the word 'well' of anyone in that hospital). The seven months he was convalescing in the ward next to the infirmary were to be the happiest of his later childhood. Somehow the nurses were kinder and the patients, arrayed in a line of wheelchairs and beds, had the opportunity to communicate with each other.

Eddie began to make friends. But he was still weak, weaker than he knew, and so his memory of those months was confused and inconsistent and he remembered only one of those there at that time: Frank. A young man who, like Eddie, had found that the only escape route from Back Ward was illness.

To Frank, Eddie would owe the revival of the belief that he was, after all, someone on his own account, someone with an identity, someone who could, in spite of his useless body, do something. And what was that? It was a powerful thing: he could make sounds that others could understand and into those sounds he could weave meanings and messages that made people travel outside their crippled bodies.

Eddie's favourite place soon became the terrace with its red and black tiles and round wooden pillars stained by winter rains and bleached and dried by wind and summer sun. Lying there on one of the beds, and graduating later to a wheelchair that mercifully long summer of 1929, he saw colours and wonders such as the sun makes daily in the dew on the grass, and the trees form eternally with their shapes in the haze. From there too he could watch the comings and goings of the hospital's ambulant patients, the less disturbed ones, who were allowed to walk across the grass and among the trees that ran down to a little glen at the distant edge of the hospital's grounds. Sometimes, when the wind was right and the air warm, he would hear laughter and voices from this distant magic place and it became Eddie's dream that one day he might go there, and look back.

Frank liked him and as Frank could make himself understood he usually asked to be put next to Eddie. Eddie did not talk to Frank but lay staring and smiling, warm and lazy, saying only that one word 'Skallagrigg'.

The miracle happened simply enough. One day Frank turned to Eddie and asked, 'What Skallag? What Skallag?' his thin face straining and his mouth slipping over the awkward word.

Eddie said (garbled, rubbish noise to the nurse standing by), 'Skallagrigg is a friend. Skallagrigg comes to me.' Frank looked vacantly at him and said nothing, his gaze wandering towards some mugs of tea that were being brought to them.

Three days later Frank said, 'When Skallag come?'

Then, for the first time, Eddie knew he could be understood. And he began to talk and talk and talk, garbled and not understood except through some miracle by Frank. Who thus became the first person ever to hear the fundamental story of the Skallagrigg; of the fence, of the poppies, of the long crawl to the very centre of the field where, if only you could get there . . . Frank heard it and in a kind of way understood.

Then Frank turned Eddie into his special friend, laughing when he was put nearby, refusing to eat his stew until Eddie had his, staring where Eddie stared. Fortunately the staff were unaware of this, for they frowned on friendships as if, in some way, they could reduce the institution to something flexible, wilful and uncontrolled.

One day Eddie was taken out on the terrace and found that Frank had gone. Nobody understood his questions or why, after two days of confusion and distress (he believed that Frank had died), he fell silent, the smile of that year's summer days quite gone.

Eddie did not see Frank again for many years though later, and by chance, he discovered that his friend was well but had been moved to a ward in the new block away from the older part of the hospital. Then he feared that Frank would die there, taking with him that special secret he, Eddie, had learned at last he could impart: that for people like them there was a saviour who understood and would be there, if only you could get to the wooden fence and somehow climb it and crawl and crawl until you were right in the centre of the meadow fields beyond Apsham Wood.

Eddie grieved for his lost friend but he was tougher now and had been in and out of one grief already. So he started to talk to others, knowing that one day he would find someone else who could interpret his noises, and listen to his secret. He would find another Frank who one day might even make it to the glen where the able-bodied patients walked on Sundays and he could tell them about the Skallagrigg and why the Skallagrigg was needed here, now, to get Eddie and take him back to where he had been Arthur.

So Eddie talked and talked about his faith, but never never never to the nurses whom he feared and did not trust. The Skallagrigg was not for them but for other patients like himself, especially the handicapped ones. Eddie made the Skallagrigg their secret.

Thus did Eddie give birth to the myth of the Skallagrigg.

They kept him in the infirmary for several more months until, when the winter came and they saw that he was stronger, he was put in Elm Ward, which was mainly for adult males. But he was tougher now and that much older and there was a bed for him there.

It was a cot and chair ward as his first had been, but at least the windows were a little lower and could be seen out of when a nurse picked him up to move him. Eddie lived for such moments and often tried to ask Staff to hold him for a bit by the window so he could see out for longer than a second to where the grass was green, and beyond the walls to where, somewhere lost, his Skallagrigg must live. Staff never understood.

Because Elm Ward was upstairs and the weather was always bad they did not get out much to see the grass and trees Eddie had grown to love. In the first six years of his life there he was taken out only four times: church three times, Guy Fawkes bonfire once; that was all.

It was about the time that they moved Eddie to Elm Ward that they got the records wrong and the nickname Frank had given him was entered as his real name and his surname went wrong as well. It shouldn't have happened but it does. Eddie, strengthened by his friendship with Frank, tried to explain that his name was Arthur, but how could they understand? If you know with dogmatic faith that someone is an idiot then you will never even consider that his words might make sense.

But that lost boy's name *was* Arthur, and his courage and his faith would, in time, be as great as any king's.

Month after month Eddie made sounds about the Skallagrigg until gradually, year by year, those very few fellow inmates who had the patience to listen and the common love to ignore the dribble and the threshing face and arms could make it out: SKALLAGRIGG. Eddie began to tell them his stories about a boy called Arthur, who was locked away like they were, and his friend the Skallagrigg who would come for you and help if you believed enough. Some of the patients Eddie spoke to could speak almost normally, not with a vast vocabulary or to much purpose, but they knew words. They told each other of the Skallagrigg. They spoke of Eddie's friend called Arthur. But they were lost, subnormal nothings too and their voices were barely heard. Yet there was something about those stories little Eddie told that demanded repetition and generated a kind of faith. Naturally, most laughed or simply retreated into their own private world. But a few, a very few of the few, did not. They thought of Eddie's Skallagrigg and stared unlaughing out of the windows and over the distant high walls to where, perhaps, the Skallagrigg might be.

Many who shared that grim institution with him died, most in the squalor and loneliness of the wards and the infirmary. Many died within sight of Eddie. The hydrocephalic John died because Rendel tried to pick him off the floor and his big head broke his neck. Eddie saw it and others too but they could not make Staff understand. Joe Ryman nearly died because a new nurse put him in the wrong position in the chair and he turned and suffocated. The whole ward heard him dying. It took three-quarters of an hour, during which time he managed to hold himself up so his throat did not fold and his face go purple. Each of them knew and they called out in their different ways, 'Go on, Joe, someone'll come, someone will see. Please keep up, Joe, keep up.' Even idiots have the will to see that others stay alive.

Eddie watched, and tried to shout as well. Then he could see the shouting was not helping. He tried to think what he could do. He called to the Skallagrigg to help: no reply. Then he fell silent, thinking, desperately thinking, knowing that the pandemonium of the other patients was achieving nothing. They must make the nurse see that Joe Ryman was dying.

Then Eddie knew what to do. He called out, loudly, to the next bed in an urgent voice. He knew that someone would realize he was trying to say something. He called and called until the next bed heard and looked.

Eddie said, 'Silence. All be silent.' And one there who sort of understood, one of Eddie's Franks, said, 'Eddie says be silent. Sshhh. Eddie says look at Joe. Eddie says shhshhh and look.'

Then one by one they stopped panicking and did Eddie's will. A terrible silence descended, and the unnaturalness of it achieved precisely what Eddie had hoped it would: attention. Staff gradually realized something was wrong. Staff saw that Joe Ryman was dying under their noses. Staff got him up in time.

So that day Joe lived, though no one but those few patients knew it was Eddie who saved him. The story went round that Eddie got his Skallagrigg to come and tell Staff that Joe was suffocating. And Eddie did not deny it. He learned two things from that day: one was that he had brains and that was comforting; the other was that you could attach things to the Skallagrigg and make people believe in him even more.

Others were not as lucky as Joe. Frederick Inman died because Dilke, now a charge nurse and powerful, pushed him too hard in the washrooms where the cap on the radiator was missing so there was a spike. He hit the soft part of his head on the spike and he died. Dilke said it was an accident. Of course it was.

Through the decades that began with Eddie's coming, the wards, the desolate corridors, the infirmary, all stayed much as they had always been, untouched by time, unseen by the world outside, and unknown to it.

Yet through the squalor and death Eddie lived on, sustained by a pathetic faith. The older he got the more he interwove his stories about the lost boy Arthur and his saviour-to-be with the only reality he knew – the hospital and the places and people inside it: the light and the darkness of the wards, Rendel, Dilke, the sun in

the airing courts, the birds, the images and ideas some of the
nurses gave, or which he saw aslant in the pictures in papers and
magazines they brought in. He wove his own rich mythology of
Skallagrigg, a saviour who would come, and he repeated and
embellished it in his own threshing idiot spastic way to the few,
the few of the few, who would listen.

For Eddie had a plan and it was this: if he told enough people
then surely one of them would get out of the hospital one day, and
somehow get the Skallagrigg to listen, and then he would come
and take him home again.

Yes, the Skallagrigg would come, and the legions who were
Rendel, and the armies that were Dilke, would quail before his
anger and his power and his strength, and they would bow down
before the love that he, Eddie, could command. And when that day
came, Eddie would be taken back and shown how to climb over
the wooden fence past Apsham Wood, over into the meadows
beyond which the Skallagrigg lives, and there he would be helped
to stand at last and feel the winds, warm and soft, cold and violent,
on his cheeks.

Yes, one day, one day the Skallagrigg would hear his cries, and
come for him, to take him out of hell.

This quest of ours is that boy's story, and we will discover how
the love he carried into that grim place survived and his faith and
persistence was rewarded; and how at last Eddie (real name
Arthur) found again the Skallagrigg he loved.

TWO

But 1927 is an eternity away and to lead us back there we need someone's help. Her name is Esther Marquand and we first meet her in circumstances which make her no less helpless than Arthur was when we first found him over half a century ago.

It is 1982. She has fallen and cannot get up without help. Time was when she, too, would have been a 'congenital imbecile'; but now they call her cerebral palsied.

We are in the grounds of a private school in Oxford, in the far corner of a football field next to a canal. It is early summer and yet the wind is strong, violently strong, and there is evidence across the fields that it has been strong for days: broken branches, a fresh scatter of young leaves across the grass; a desolate air to the hedges; a race of high dark cloud on the horizon.

Above Esther Marquand the branches of a great tree bend in the squalling wind as if to reach down and raise her, but they never will without breaking. She struggles to turn over, the wind cutting at her face and uncontrolled hands, and so strong that it turns the heavy wheel of her wheelchair where it lies by her on its side. Those hands of hers are twisted, and they jerk in that same way we saw half a century before in Eddie's hands and those of some of his fellow inmates. We do not like them much but here, on the windswept chilly grass, they seem to hold less fear for us than once, so long ago, they did. Familiarity makes abnormality seem less strange.

Esther has fallen because her wheelchair was left by someone called Tom (a Down's syndrome boy whom, despite appearances, we shall have reason to learn to love) in the wrong place. It has rolled forward on the sloping grass, hit a fallen branch and tipped over. Fortunately, the straps that held Esther have broken, otherwise she might have been crushed or hurt under the heavy social security-funded chair. Now the strap buckles tap in the wind against the metal of the chair.

Normally so cheerful, she cries out her garbled words in anger
and bitterness. The mud of the playing fields is on her knees and
oozing between her bent fingers, and caked in her hair. She is
alone and without help and feels a fool. Her tears, now ceased,
were for the stupid indignity of it rather than from any physical
hurt.

She turns her head with her cheek in the muddy grass to look
over towards the canal and beyond it to the wooden fence around
the distant meadow fields. One can see that she is in some ways
rather more attractive than Eddie. Not just because she is a girl but
because her body is not quite so distorted and ever-moving as his,
though there is something not quite right about the power of the
muscles in the neck and throat. No doubt they compensate in
some way for a muscular weakness elsewhere. Conventions of
normality, we are beginning to see, hinge on harmony – but whose
idea of harmony? Not evidently the Skallagrigg's or else young
Eddie would not have had such trust in him.

The wind shrieks in the tree above and whines dismally as
together we go and look more closely at her, bending down to
stare into her eyes just in time to see the natural fear and dismay
we might expect replaced by something more promising: surprise,
insight, intelligence (in its older meaning of news arrived, information received). And we feel that even if she could see us
fictional beings, she would be more interested in the sound she can
hear from across the canal, carried on the great wind, and the
meaning it conveys.

Note how, in contrast to our meeting Eddie where we lost our
heads and showed our hearts, with Esther we are able to be cool,
calm and analytic. Strange that. At seventeen she does not inspire
us with human warmth and tender loving care of the kind that
Eddie began to engender in us in spite of the ugly shell he first
presented. There is something unfortunately off-putting about the
intelligence touched with smugness that masks young Esther's
face. We had best remember that even for physically able people
seventeen can be a terrible age.

From the muddy, uncomfortable ground she is staring towards
the direction from where the wind comes and her mouth is opening
to it to try to say a word. Not long ago, being unfamiliar with
spastics, we would not have understood it as a word at all. But

now we know it might be and we even know what we are listening for, as that word she tries to say begins with harsh familiar consonants: 'Sk'!

Skya!

She literally spits out the word, her legs jerking with the effort.

Skayag! But now we too are excited and we follow her stare over the canal beyond the wooden fence in awe as we begin to think that we can hear, as she knows she can, a crying on the wind, a calling, a message, that carries an awesome and terrible insight, the full import of which now fills her eyes before our own. And her insight has flowed with the wind to us, able-bodied though we are and . . .

SKYAGREE!!

. . . privileged though that knowledge is; intended once, fifty years before, only for spastics and their kind. The excitement of this moment is that you and I are witness to, are the subject of, that unique point at which knowledge of the Skallagrigg moved from the lost arcane world of spastics to the different and far more vaguely defined world of able-bodied folk. Yet how hard for us to feel the same excitement and awe as Esther felt about something so far removed from our experience. How far into the journey shall we have to be before we can begin to feel the inconceivable, namely what it must be like to be Esther herself.

To be heroes, to be romantically loved, to be afraid, to be adventurers on a quest, to be almost anything but what Esther and Eddie both are, is easy enough to imagine. But to be *them*! To *be* them? I fear the Skallagrigg may ask it of us if we are to know him.

So . . . at that accidental moment when Esther Marquand, left for a time by a friend, was caught in the wind, slipped and rolled and then toppled over, thrown into mud churned by the boots of little able-bodied boys, she had the insight that would change her life, and that of so many others including (we hope) our own: she finds herself suddenly understanding that those stories she has heard through the years from other spastics, of a saviour called the Skallagrigg, contain *reality*. They are not *stories*. They are about somewhere and someone real. The Skallagrigg *exists*. In Esther Marquand's mind that greatest of imaginative leaps has occurred, an insight of overpowering strength, as the Skallagrigg moves from fiction to reality and makes his own reality come alive in her, and gives her faith and purpose and the beginning of a power dreadful in its zeal and quite suited to her so-far humourless and rather selfish face. A purpose that will not rest until it finds out the Skallagrigg.

In the face of this massive insight, the discomfort and embarrassment of her fallen position beneath a tree in a storm fades away and is replaced by restless impatience. For it seems to her that with the understanding comes a sound on the wind, manufactured by her mind, of course, but real to her, and external. It is a calling from far beyond the wooden fence, far beyond that strange stormy day we are witnessing when Esther Marquand first began to appreciate the true nature of the Skallagrigg. It comes over decades of faith and its sound makes Esther want to rise to her feet and run and shout the news.

Unable to do this, she is whispering instead her version of the word 'Skallagrigg' into the violent wind hoping it will take it up and make it whole and strong so that others may hear it as she, now, herself, hears it, for the first time truly.

As her mouth struggles again and again to say the word her understanding of its meaning burgeons rapidly and she affirms (though she does not know this then) what no other has ever understood: Arthur, the boy in the story, is real, and his call to the Skallagrigg is real, it is real, it is not just stories after all. Arthur made them so the Skallagrigg would hear. He did he did, yes he did oh he did. Arthur 'Arthur, Arthur' and Esther Marquand, over fifty years later, seventeen years old, cursed by the same malfunction of body as Arthur but better blessed by circumstances, changed attitudes and a local council that cares for the disabled, begins to answer Arthur's call, and to believe that one day her answer will be heard.

But we already know something she does not and can shake our heads sympathetically at the basic mistake she has made. She thinks *Arthur* is real! But we know, don't we, that Eddie is the 'real' one now; Arthur died before the twin armies of subnormal Frank's renaming of a little spastic boy, and errors in record-keeping. So unless she finds out that Arthur has become Eddie and that Eddie is what the records call him then she will never find him, not ever.

Back to Esther who now, evidently, knows what she must try to do. And she lies still and waiting in the mud knowing that Tom will come and find her soon, and set her chair aright and lift her back into it so that at last she can start out to find a way to reach Arthur and help him find the Skallagrigg. For she has managed to understand that that, in essence, is what his stories have always been about . . . She's right, of course, and it will not be the only time that Esther Marquand is far ahead of us.

THREE

That was Esther.

Now, finally, we come to the last of your helpers: me.

We started with Eddie in 1927, travelled forward to meet Esther in 1982, and now move on again to ... but the dates no longer matter.

Why *me*? (The very question, incidentally, that people like Esther Marquand ask as they gaze from their wheelchairs on a summer's day at the pretty girls they will never be, walking under the blossom by the playing fields.)

The prosaic reality is that I am a systems analyst and formerly a computer programmer. But I was just twenty when I was first introduced to the game of 'Skallagrigg'. I come from a boring background in grubby Dradely on the outskirts of Birmingham – my father was a works foreman in a steel company – and I had switched from my home city to Essex University to complete a Masters Degree in computer sciences. It was not going well. I had begun to drift. And in my case that meant playing and creating ever more complex and exotic interactive games on my micro-computer. It was a whole subculture. We dedicated players did not drink, smoke, sniff or even have much sex. No time, you see. We played games. You just name it – Philosopher'sQuest StrangeOdysseyLabyrinthofFearKragoCastleNukewarLegionnaire VCEmpireoftheOvermindVolcanicDungeonCamelotDragonquestLo rdsofKarmaTheCrystalChaliceofQuorumTheHobbitAdventureQues tWarlordNightflite3DMazeStoneofSisyphusAbyssTimeMachineTre asureTombeKeysoftheWizardMinesofSaturnKeysofRothCastleofblo odyRiddlesDeathSatelliteIntotheLabyrinthKraal'sKingdom – we played it. We felt like pioneers, but it was an escape from reality into a cliquey, clubby safe world just the same.

Fortunately, kids mostly grow out of this kind of thing, some-times slowly, sometimes with a sickening jolt caused by any number of different things – lack of money, pressure of final examinations, parents, etcetera and so on.

My jolt came suddenly too, and simply. A fellow games nut who had been doing a brief job in America came back and asked me the question that changed my life. He said, 'Have you played "Skallagrigg" yet?' Try to remember, please, that at that point I knew nothing of what you and I have already shared: of Arthur/Eddie or Esther Marquand.

I remember clearly being asked the question, the memory of it still sends an icy shiver down my spine. Just that one word, 'Skallagrigg'. My world fell silent about me and even my fellow gamers noticed that something was wrong.

I did not know the game but, dear God, I knew the word. It was the one single word, the only clue, until then quite meaningless and without any connotation or link, that I had to who or what I was.

Please listen. I have told no one until now, but if we are to travel on together I had best make you understand. In Dradely, where I was brought up by my father alone, we never mentioned family. My father was not secretive about my mother: she left him, she lived at such and such a place, she lived with someone else and had a new family by him. She visited us twice, none of us had much to say, and that, more or less, was that. No problem.

No, my interest and curiosity, and finally my obsession, was with *his* side of the family, which (if it existed at all) he would not talk about. His parents for example, my grandparents: uncommunicative silence. Who were they? What had they been? He would never say a word about them.

Then one day, when I was thirteen and beginning to get aggressive, I said to him, 'Why won't you tell me about the family, Dad? Haven't I a right to know? What about your Mum and Dad?' He stared at me and shook his head. He could be frightening.

Do you know, in all his life he only spoke about it once to me, though that was enough to convince me that he must have often thought about it.

It happened two years later when I was fifteen, at a New Year's party in, of all places, Dradely Comprehensive School. There were a lot of parents there, and grandparents too, and I saw that he was distressed and getting drunk, which I had never seen before.

'Show me your classroom,' he said finally.

So, hoping he would calm down a bit, I took him to 21E whose door was open. He went straight in, sat down at a desk and stared at the blackboard.

It was then that he talked about his childhood and my grandmother for the only time. It was a rambling, tearful and familiar story: a girl who had got pregnant, a man who had deserted her, according to a neighbour, a mother who brought up a child – my father – alone. She was not a well woman according to his account, but she seems to have done her best for him. He was bright, brighter than her at least, and he left home as soon as he could. In her final years my grandmother lived with him, and he always wanted her to tell him about his father – my grandfather – but she never would. Towards the end, however, she did say a few things and that 'her man' had not been bad as people said. Not at all. He was a good man but couldn't help himself. My father said he had asked her again and again to say more and to let him get in touch, but she never would. But right at the end she had spoken strange words, and even spelled one out, again and again. The nurses said it was senility but my father did not believe that. He said that when she said the word she had pride in her eyes. 'I can spell it,' she would say, 'with an S and a K and an A and an L and another L and an A and a G and an R and an I and two G's,' as if someone had taught her. He asked her what it meant and she would say only that Skallagrigg was where his father would be.

When he had finished my father got up from the desk he was sitting at and took a piece of chalk and wrote right across the blackboard the word SKALLAGRIGG. I might have forgotten it, but when we came back for a new term the word was still there.

So when, a few years later, someone said, 'Have you played "Skallagrigg" yet?' you can understand why I reacted as I did.

I could hardly believe that such a strange word could exist outside my family. I had even begun to think my dad invented it to fob me off; but I remembered it because it was strange, and the answer to the question I had asked was so fundamentally important to me.

With some difficulty I got hold of a copy of the game (it was US-originated) that was configured for my system and started to play it on my computer, curious but confident and self-assured. After all, I was an expert at those games and it was going to be just another one ... except ... except from the very first option it offered a player, I knew it was not going to be the same as the others.

Most games begin something like this (from 'Empire of the OverMind'): YOU ARE IN A FOREST, YOU SEE MANY TALL TREES, A PATH. YOU ARE HOLDING NOTHING SPECIAL 〉 You then key in something simplistic like GO ON PATH and the game is programmed to respond to this with OK YOU ARE ON A HIGH PLATEAU, and so on.

Some games offer options: ... YOU CAN GO NORTH TO THE CAVE OR EAST TO THE BLACK MEGALITH and an 'N' or 'E' on the console effects the option chosen. This is all pretty basic stuff.

But the first situation and set of options that 'Skallagrigg' offered was so shockingly different and alarming that I simply stared at the strange words on the screen for a very long time before I remembered that the computer was waiting and that I must key something in to get going. But when I did so the program aborted. Again and again until I was convinced there was a bug in it. But then I had an idea and keyed in something more ambiguous in response to the first shocking question, and the program did not abort. I had started.

When I entered into its world I was fascinated but afraid, because right from its start that game dragged me back, as it does every player, to the moments of the very origin of my independent being. And from there it seemed to make me grow, and change, and find a way that led, years later, to ... well, among other things, to this shared moment between you and me.

How slowly and painfully I played that game! Time after time I gave up in despair of ever finding my way through mazes of a quality quite different from those I had become a master at navigating. There, in the world of 'Skallagrigg' I was nothing or worse than nothing. I grew progressively weaker and (it seemed) more handicapped. It took me more than a year to reach the objective that the quest slowly led to: the Skallagrigg.

Yet when I had, one last mystery in the game haunted me. If

you reach the final frames the screen transmutes into that now
famous series of graphics based on a wild passage through the
electronic waves of a fantasy sea near a mythical place called 'The
Racks', which finally shows that you have found the Skallagrigg.
And you stand on a beach watching that great sea, lost in it,
marvelling at the reflections and shapes in its curling depths of a
wooden fence and a meadow, as the colours of that massive sea
seem to change from green and blue to poppy red. For the briefest
moment. And you need help to reach forward, help even to crawl,
for you must reach that sea and enter it to find the fence. You need
help to climb it, and help is there on the beach at your side.

You are about to end your quest in a place where pastoral and
marine images mix and where if you look again, and again, and
again, at that final sequence of graphics, I hope *you* at least (unlike
a single one of my friends at that time who were convinced they
had completed the game) may see the hint of a mystery, of a
question that throws doubt on whether or not, after all, you have
reached the end. That was the mystery that left me dissatisfied at
the 'end' of the game.

I came to understand that the question I was left with led on to
the very heart of the game. In short, that 'Skallagrigg' the game
was merely a disturbing prelude to an altogether more serious
game whose rules and materials lay out there in real life; a game
you and I are entering into now.

I grew rather angry at this discovery and felt cheated, dissatisfied.
So I shelved 'Skallagrigg' – and I shelved the idea that was forming
that I might research further into it – though not in favour of
other games; playing that one had cured me of them. No, I started
a career, took responsibility, began to mature. Yet sometimes at
dark moments, when I was under pressure, when I could not
sleep, when a relationship was awry and I felt lonely and alone,
the sense that really I had never finished the game despite reaching
the 'end' returned to haunt me, and seemed to link itself to that
tale my father had told me about his mum and what she said. It
welled up in me, one big question mark, inarticulate, massive,
demanding and pointing in a direction I feared, and adamantly
refused, to take. Sometimes I would take the game down from the
shelf where I kept that kind of software, and access it, watching
the screen fill with the light and colour of the game's unique

graphics, entering into its challenge ... but leaving it always dissatisfied, feeling that I had not had the courage to form that last question in a way I could confront.

Years later, nearly twenty years, in fact, at such a moment of self-doubt, I took my first step forward since the night my father had talked to me. I wrote to the copyright name on the software and asked if they could tell me anything about the person who programmed the game. I had no reply. I wrote again. No reply. I grew persistent. And finally, indirectly, I found the name of the original programmer.

She was a young athetoid spastic born in England in the mid-sixties. Her name was Esther Marquand.

I found out that the game was not just a game, but described a fundamental part of her life – her search for the true genesis of the stories other spastics told her and which for decades they kept to themselves, in their own subculture. Stories able-bodied people did not then know about, for the very good reason that when spastics passed them on to each other they expressly forbade their retelling to able-bodied people. Stories of the Skallagrigg thus became arcane knowledge.

And what were they? They were stories to shock, and stories to love; the mythology of a life few ever touch. The declaration and affirmation of a love that sustained a stricken life through many years of loneliness and deprivation in an institution almost too terrible to describe.

Esther Marquand was the first to want to find out who created the stories of the Skallagrigg. She was to write these words on to disk on her word processor: 'I had to find out who first called out for the Skallagrigg, and why. I came to believe that the Skallagrigg may not have heard those terrible cries from a hell – cries which only a very few could understand.'

She found the Skallagrigg, and from the experience told us how we might as well, in the only language over which she had complete command: machine code. With it she made a game that we cannot forget.

Now for the bit no one has known until now. Esther Marquand created her game within constraints of a strange and mysterious kind. For in making a profound game out of the love of Arthur and

the Skallagrigg, and with the help of that great love she found
with Daniel Schuster, she was yet handicapped. There was one
fact, one possibility, she was not allowed to reveal within the game
or out of it, because to complete her quest she had had to agree to
withhold for ever information which she thought should be
known.

But though she had promised never to reveal it yet she was
unsure; the very nature of what she was made her unsure. She did
not know if she had the right, *despite her promises*, to keep silent.
And so, caught between a promise and her sense of truth she made
the only compromise she could: she wrote into that subtle classic
game a special puzzle, a message really, a pointer, knowing that
only one person in the world could ever interpret it. Knowing,
moreover, that the chances that this person might do so were
nearly nil. That person would need to play the game, would need
to make a series of associations so seemingly random that only he
could make them. And he would need to *want* to go the way she
pointed.

I do not think she felt that programming this opaque clue was a
betrayal of her promise. Rather that it gave that someone a distant
chance to find the truth to which he had a right.

That someone was me. And the message she was sending was
really intended for my father. 'What does Skallagrigg mean?' he
had asked from that depth of anguish and self-doubt that must
affect anyone who does not know the truth about himself. In the
game she created, Esther Marquand quite deliberately provided the
answer, though she equally deliberately weighted the odds against
it ever being found.

But that someone whom she never knew *did* get to play the
game called 'Skallagrigg', *did* read a hidden clue, and in it *did* find
a question, a terrible terrible question, that pointed – just as Esther
intended it should – away from the keyboard out into the real
world, which is where Esther finally wanted it to be.

So now you know. Our journey's purpose is to transmute the
clues in the game suffered and created by Esther Marquand into
some kind of life or truth, or history if you will, and to find a means
of telling it.

Perhaps you are beginning at last to understand my fear, and to
share it just a little, for the way to the Skallagrigg is going to take

in experiences that neither of us wants, and lead us into places
where the sunlight does not easily shine . . .

. . . until we reach a wooden fence over which, with luck and
help, we may climb, and then crawl, handicapped as we shall be,
to the centre of a meadow with the grass swaying above us, to find
him at last, and ask him to reach down and raise us up.

FOUR

It's hard to say exactly when 'Skallagrigg' began to be seen as the most remarkable and profound of the computer games that were created in the eighties and nineties.

It crept slowly and unnoticed into the collective consciousness until one day, perhaps in the late nineties, people began to talk of it familiarly as part of the general cultural scene, and it gained that curious negative attribute that attaches to some books, music and art: an unwillingness among people who are supposedly in the know to admit that in all honesty they do not know much about it and have not read/seen/heard or (as in this case) played it.

'"Skallagrigg"? Oh, *"Skallagrigg"*! Yes as a matter of fact I've got the IBM version with the complete original graphics. Longer of course but quite extraordinary and so far ahead of its time . . . It's not really difficult once you get into it . . . Of course, the key question is [nodding of heads and knowing glances], *what* is the Skallagrigg?'

Appreciative silence until some bold mind adds subtly, 'Or *who*? Must have been incredible, the person who created it.' More silence.

Mmm. Perhaps I had best say something more about the nature of the game 'Skallagrigg' itself. I'll keep it brief since we are about to travel far beyond the game.

'Skallagrigg' developed out of the role-playing fantasy games which became computerized in the early eighties after starting as complex, though popular, dice and paper fantasy games in the mid-seventies. These were controlled by one of the players, dubbed the Dungeonmaster, who knew all of the game of which the players knew only a part.

The first attempts to computerize these dungeon and dragon games were crude text-only affairs in which the essence of the role-playing games – the interaction with other characters, the creation of imaginative worlds, the omnipotence of the Dungeonmaster – was lost. It was too complex a job to program them and they were often reduced to mazes and puzzles in which the pleasure was in solving problems rather than in creating worlds.

Even so they were popular – still are among kids – and created huge new markets. And though the rules were, to the outsider, seemingly complex they were in truth infinitely easier than the rules that we learn in order to conduct our day-to-day living as 'normal' people.

What was missing was the kind of freedom the original D&D games offered which could, with the right Dungeonmaster and fellow players, be truly experiential. It was Esther Marquand's achievement to create a game that did this with a computer, creating a world of such subtlety that it offered real choices, real freedoms, and ways and avenues for feeling and growth as, step by step, you made progress in the quest. And she resisted the temptation, which must have been especially real to one so handicapped, to cast herself in the role of Dungeonmaster and so project into power the kinds of frustrations about normality which she must have daily felt.

She preferred to program the game in another way, deliberately creating tricks like the notorious moment at the beginning of the game when the keyboard does not respond to a person typing in the letters of the word 'Skallagrigg'. She thereby made players feel what it was like to exist as she and Arthur existed, and so gradually gave them the experience that would enable them to find the object of the quest.

Nevertheless, every work of art has its origins and it was evident that 'Skallagrigg' had been created by a person, or persons, who had lived through all these role-playing and puzzle games, and was a grandmaster of them. The game Esther Marquand created uses their free structure and methodology; but its essential purpose was radically different: it was not to provide a game that was an escape from reality, but to create a game that would lead the player from the comforting fantasy world he seeks to a reality he finds hard to confront. What is radical about 'Skallagrigg' is that it seeks to destroy all need for the kind of escapist fantasy on which it is based. It prepares the player for the real world and finally, ruthlessly, pushes him out into it.

And yet, anyone who has played the game, or even only just begun to do so, recognizes soon enough that whoever created it was not ruthless, or 'radical', or cunning, but filled with a love and a sense of magic born of honestly facing the very world so many seek to escape in so many ways.

So I began to want to know more about Esther Marquand, the gentle powerful person who had created the so-called game, and made that first pioneering journey to find the Skallagrig. For one thing was very clear to me, frightening though its implications were: the game was based on reality. The journey to the Skallagrig had really taken place. Esther must have been there in real time, in real places, and alone faced the demons she later turned into a terrible and moving fantasy. She must have been terribly vulnerable for she did not have dice or weapons or kitsch magical enchantments to win her struggles for her, but only herself, and her courage, and her faith. But it was worse, far worse than that, though I did not know it then. You see, she had not had even the most basic attributes – advantages – that you or I have. She was disadvantaged in a way that, as those who knowingly nod about Beethoven's deafness might blithely say, does not bear thinking about. As a professional programmer I knew enough to realize that such a complex suite of programs, with verbal and graphic programming techniques which, in many cases, broke new ground, must have involved more than one person. Yet by then too I knew enough about life to see that such an original and powerful statement as 'Skallagrig' confronts us with could only have come from one mind. Original statements, especially ones as creative and humane as 'Skallagrig', rarely come from committees.

My starting point, as you know, had been a letter to the copyright address listed on the game itself: © 1992 GraphicSoft 8929 East Thomson Boulevard, Los Angeles, California, in white letters on a deep and rich blue background. The name behind the holding company was, to my surprise, Daniel M. Schuster, the quiet, un-assuming founder and majority stockholder of the world's biggest specialist graphics software corporation: GraphicSoft Inc. of Hanniman Beach, Southern California. Daniel's son Robert, incidentally, is much better known: he was for a time one of the world's top five or six windsurfers and star of a Pepsi Cola advertisement. So I knew the name.

There came a day when I stood beside Daniel Schuster on Hanniman Beach watching his slight but wiry nine-year-old granddaughter, Mary, sailboard jumping across surf whose roaring white force completely dwarfed her. He made me stand there in the wind to watch her laugh across the frightening seas, and turn and turn again over the surf, her sail (though several metres high) dipping out of sight behind the rolling waves to reappear triumphantly as her body leaned out from the board, her harness strained, and spray flew into the sun.

Schuster was a loving man and made me stare out at her, sharing his pride. And that day, after many attempts to get him to talk about 'Skallagrigg', he said with deceptive irrelevance and with a startling Englishness about his voice, 'My granddaughter only really conquered her fear of the surf this summer. She asked me, and not her father, to help her because she knew that once when I was a young man, in the eighties, I could windsurf as well as anybody and that I understood why she might feel afraid. Trouble with her father is, he's so damn good that he's a bad teacher.

'I stood here one day,' he continued, 'and saw a marvellous moment of discovery as at last she successfully water-started the board through the surf, rose up with the sail filling above her, and suddenly relaxed into total enjoyment. I swear, though the surf is too noisy for it to be possible, that I heard her laugh with pleasure.

'But in my mind that laugh was really someone else's, the laugh of the person you want me to tell you about. It was what Esther Marquand's laugh *would* have been had she ever been able to windsurf as my granddaughter does. And I stood here on the beach, the surf racing up the beach and its foam dying on my bare legs, and I saw Esther, I saw her again as she was, as she *really* was in spirit though never in body – lithe, and happy, and totally lost in whatever it was she was doing. I began to cry with a mixture of pleasure and sadness, with the rushing surf at my feet.

'I think that Robert, who was up on the beach in one of the huts, must have been watching, and must have seen that I had seen that moment of growth in confidence in my granddaughter, his daughter, though he could not have guessed the memories it triggered off. As I struggled with my tears and watched her out at sea on her board oblivious of me, jumping, tacking, gybing over the waves, he came from behind me and put his arm round me. I could not look at him.

'"You asked me so often what she was like," I remember saying to him "and I could never tell you, Robert. Not to my satisfaction. Well, *that* is what she was like. That was all I saw in her and her mind was as committed, as graceful, as joyous, as *that*. And if she had been able to windsurf that is how she would have been . . ." and we both stared out at little Mary on the board, the sea water shining on her tanned body which that summer had begun to become a woman's, and my son whispered . . . "I know, I know, I've always known. You made me know without saying anything." Two grown men, standing on a Californian beach, both crying and listening to laughter we could not hear!

'You want to know about Esther and how I came to help her make "Skallagrigg" and you've come from Europe to ask me. I admire that, though I don't know you. But you've played her game and I think you understand something of why she made it and someone ought to tell her story at least. So I will help you.'

Daniel Schuster took me back up to his great white house fronting Hanniman Beach and into the studio where he works. It is full of computers and screens. It is ordered and tidy. After a long pause of seeming doubt he resolutely took me to a room at the back of the house, took a large cardboard box marked 'Rank Xerox (UK) Ltd' from a cupboard, and opened it. It was an old and worn Sadler keyboard, the kind designed for one-hand use and developed originally by Leon Sadler for use by handicapped people.

'It was her keyboard,' Schuster said matter-of-factly. 'She wrote most of the "Skallagrigg" programs on it. She could never lift her hand high enough to clear the edge of the console so it got worn down where she dragged it over to the keys.

'And these,' he added, reaching up to take down one of many boxes of disks, 'are the disks she used.'

I looked curiously at them. They were old-style eight-inch floppies and I hadn't seen any like those for years. Schuster gave me a box of them to hold and open and as I did so I had the feeling that he was relieved, as if, after a very long time keeping a secret, he was glad to be sharing it. I saw that each of the disks was neatly labelled in a curiously wayward and childish script with dates, places and file names.

I remember Schuster leaned forward and touched one and smiled as he looked at the writing. 'That's Tom's writing, you'll have to get to meet him. He knew Esther. He understood . . .'

And for a brief moment I asked myself 'Why me?' and I immediately smiled, because that is the question every player of 'Skallagrigg' is forced to ask again and again and again; and which I have already suggested is so often asked by a quite different group of people, in a quite different way: the severely handicapped.

Why me?

I could hear the sea roaring in the distance; a large Old English sheepdog ambled into the room and rubbed itself against the chromium legs of a draughtsman's table; someone whistled in another room. Even as I felt Schuster's relief, I sensed that I was taking from him a burden that might prove hard for me to carry.

'Tell her story,' he said. 'Tell them how she made "Skallagrigg". It's all there . . .' and he waved his hand into the dark recesses of the cupboard, with its box after box of floppy disks. 'You see she always wanted to be doing, but there was so little she could do but sit with the console before her and write, and write. She put it all on to disk, how she pursued and found the Skallagrigg, and I should long ago have called it up and read it for myself. But . . . going back to that would need a special courage I don't have. It's all there, she put it all down . . .' and he waved warily at the boxes of disks and was glad to pass the job of making something of them on to me.

But it wasn't all there. And the burden I so lightly took that day in Schuster's studio proved a heavy one, and one beneath which I would very nearly sink. It is one that only now I feel I am beginning at last to bear fully. It took me to places I needed all my courage to visit, and to people before whose goodness I would feel ashamed, and before whose evil (how old-fashioned these words seem, like out-of-date floppies!) I would shrink.

At that first meeting Daniel Schuster gave me a list of people and places I should follow up. We ran through them and he gave me more help than I could ever have expected. He kept saying, 'It's time her story was told; it's time now.' He looked younger by the minute.

But then I asked a simple question and suddenly I saw a harder side to Schuster, tough and uncommunicative. The very qualities.

perhaps, which had enabled this so far smiling and cheerful man to create one of the most successful software houses in America.

All I asked him was: 'Does Esther have any living parents?'

What I got from him was that she had a father, called Richard Marquand, and that under no circumstances was I to attempt to trace him or interview him. *Under no circumstances.* He stood up and paced around, breathing heavily and looking angry. It was an undertaking I then naïvely gave, and was to break later when, as I have tried to explain, I realized that my task was to serve Esther's purpose, not Daniel Schuster's.

FIVE

Richard Marquand was not easy to trace; not easy, that is, if you did not know where to look. A computer marketing man I got talking to about 'Skallagrigg' and who had once worked for Fountain Systems, the computer servicing group, knew the name immediately and told me how to find him.

Sure enough there was Richard Marquand, sitting on a shelf next to my desk inside the current *International Computer Yearbook*, page 673, under Australia. He was listed as the honorary president of Fountain Systems (Holdings) Pty, an Australian-based computer service bureau, one of the biggest servicing South-East Asia. He was also listed as majority shareholder in ComputaBase, the computer retail group, which put him solidly in the billionaire class.

Richard M. Marquand BA (Hons), BCS: an entry complete with professional qualifications (mainly selling and marketing), a Sydney address and what turned out to be an office telephone number.

Instinct and (in view of Schuster's attitude) the need for discretion suggested that I persuade another Fountain contact to write to Marquand on my behalf. 'Skallagrigg' was not mentioned, vague personal business was. A reply came eventually: '. . . Mr Marquand retired now . . . never travels . . . unlikely to be of much help . . .' and a polite final sentence to the effect that if the inquirer was ever in Sydney it might be possible to arrange an interview.

Two years passed before I was in Sydney, or rather in Melbourne on a business trip for a European client, when I took the opportunity of tracking down Richard Marquand.

It was not easy. He was a rich, well-protected old man. And given Schuster's warning, even after so long, I was still not willing to write ahead and explain myself in detail as I feared this would only invite rejection. Having traced his address I simply arrived at his house and knocked on the door.

I was lucky. Nobody else seemed to be at home and he opened the door himself.

'Yes?'

He had an English accent. He did not look friendly. Old and scraggy round the neck and with that slight staring to the eyes and bias to the mouth that suggested he had suffered a mild coronary.

I stood staring back, finding I did not know what to say, the more so for having come, in a way, so far.

But even as I introduced myself he started to close the door.

I panicked and spoke the first words that came to me, 'I think your daughter wrote one of the great computer games programs of the twentieth century.'

This histrionic statement served only to make him close the door yet further. The road to my past was being blocked before my eyes. Then, as if from a distance, Esther called and told me what to say. And even as I spoke the words I knew where they were from: for there is a key moment in 'Skallagrigg' the game when these are the words needed, or something very like them, if a player is going to progress.

'Sir,' I started for a third time, the term of respect taking me by surprise, 'I need your help to find the Skallagrigg.'

The man before me stopped closing the door and seemed suddenly to age. He leaned against the door frame, his blue eyes looking beyond me as if back into a past which still called out to him, and from which he could not escape because he could not come to terms with it.

Sensing an opening I pressed on: 'I need your cooperation, Mr Marquand, to help me find the real purpose of your daughter's work.'

Richard Marquand began to open the door again and finally he said, 'I wonder what I can do to help?'

He invited me in and led me slowly to a large elegant living room, leaving me there for a few moments. Its furniture was quality antique and on the walls were many paintings. Most were original but I was drawn to one that was not, a reproduction of a painting by Andrew Wyeth, the realist American painter of the mid twentieth century. It showed a woman in a plain pink dress, in the middle of a field, unable it seemed to get up, and straining to look at and perhaps to reach a farm on top of a gaunt rise in the land.

'Do you know Wyeth's work?' asked Richard Marquand, returning.

It happened that I knew this painting.

'He made paintings of things he knew. That one's in the New York Museum of Modern Art. It's called "Christina's World". The farm is Olsons, where Wyeth did much of his best work. Christina Olson could not walk, you see, but she would drag herself out into the field and look back at the buildings that were her life.'

He stood staring at it for a moment or two and then added: 'Some people see this as a painting of triumph, others of tragedy. I . . . I don't know, myself. I just don't know.' I knew he was talking of his daughter. He turned from the picture and sat down with great care as the old and frail often do. He was neat and tidy and gave me the impression of being well looked after, much cared for.

He was also evidently intelligent and clear thinking, for all his old age and frailty, and he asked me what I was trying to find out. He conducted the meeting as the president of a large organization would, and I found myself sitting on the edge of my chair as if I was explaining my budgetary over-spending to the financial director. I talked, he listened.

Eventually he said something. 'It's only a computer game she made, only a game,' he said.

'Have you played it, sir?' I ventured, daring at last to ask a question.

He was silent for a long time. My eyes flicked round the room searching for clues to Esther and I felt like an old-style private detective. I found out nothing about Esther, but a lot about Richard Marquand. The room was curiously spartan, devoid of personal knick-knacks of any kind. Neat and passionless. There was a framed photograph of his wife on an otherwise empty bookshelf and a matching one of him, both perfectly polished and in old-fashioned black and white. At the far end of the room, on a smaller bookcase in which he had encyclopaedias or something of the sort, was one other photograph. It was set at just such an angle to me that it caught the image of the window to the garden and I could see nothing but reflected white light.

'Tried to play the game once,' he answered finally. 'Not good at that sort of thing . . .' he began. Then he added softly in a very different voice, 'No. No I couldn't. I did not know how.'

He did not give anything more away, he merely listened to me. He warded off any personal questions and then looked at his watch, almost discreetly.

I grew suddenly desperate, feeling again that a unique chance was slipping away. I thought of similar moments of trial and doubt in the games I had so often played. I remembered such moments in 'Skallagrigg' when one had all the clues, all the information, and yet I could not seem to resolve a puzzle and move on safely from a situation. Sometimes taking a risk offers the only way forward.

So I mentioned Daniel Schuster's name. He suddenly grew cold and his eyes took on that callous hard look that some old men are masters of. Passionless anger. His was mixed with bitterness.

'I do not want you to mention his name again.'

'But . . .'

His anger or bitterness or whatever it was died away and he stared at me blankly, his mouth opening a little.

'Why are you researching Esther's game?' he asked. As I formed a careful reply – for I had no intention of revealing the belief I had that Esther Marquand had inserted special clues for me alone – he seemed to sense that I was avoiding the truth.

'I . . . I . . .' but as I struggled to find a convincing answer I was saved by the opening of the front door and the arrival of his wife. When she saw me she said nothing but simply regarded me coldly.

'My wife Kate, Mr . . .' I had to repeat my name myself for this chilly introduction to be completed.

But with Kate Marquand's arrival the interview, if that was what it was, seemed to die with me having told him almost everything, and Richard Marquand saying nothing.

But as I left with various empty promises that he would help more if ever he came back to Britain and similar nonsense, he said with reference to nothing in particular, as if he had been sub-consciously thinking about it, 'Is it really so great, "Skallagrigg"? The game she made?'

I nodded saying, 'Yes, I think so.' I felt suddenly relaxed as if, having lost the play, all pressure had gone. So I added, 'Esther Marquand has given enormous pleasure to many people, and I think she may have changed some lives as well. I think that the people who play her game would like to know something about her as I do. Mr Marquand, many people have learned to love her through the extraordinary programs she wrote.'

'Have they?' he said, and he stared away from me through the front door, which was already open for me to leave.

'I am very proud of Esther you know, Mr . . .', he hesitated over my name for a moment and made a noise that he hoped was it. 'It is very hard to bring up a handicapped child, you know, so very hard. But Esther . . . was my only child.'

He tried to smile, but something in him stumbled and needed support, and his wife moved closer and seemed more concerned. And yet she made no attempt to stop him remembering and talking, nor any to rid the house of me. I waited in silence, vulnerable, and making no attempt to control the situation – just as his daughter Esther had taught me to through the game of 'Skallagrigg'. For the handicapped – perhaps in a sense therefore for all of us – it is, finally, the only way forward.

Then, reluctantly, as if it had come a long long way and was unsure of itself, a smile lightened his eyes and hesitated on his face. 'So she created a game and people want to know more about it and her?' And he looked at his wife as if to say, 'There, I knew she would do something, I knew that really she could.'

Then his eyes filled with tears and he mumbled, 'Sorry,' turned from his wife and disappeared to the back of the house. His wife turned to me and said far more gently than I had the right to expect, 'It's a hard memory for him, you see. What Esther did was so very hard on him.'

Eventually Richard Marquand came back down the stairs, carrying a file with the logo 'Fountain Systems' on it and a buff envelope which, a brief look confirmed, contained a quantity of photographs. He disappeared into the living-room and came back moments later carrying the framed photograph whose image I had been unable to make out because light had been reflected in its glass.

'This was Esther,' he said simply, holding the photograph for me to see. It was black and white, and she sat in a wheelchair, straps round her waist and shoulders to hold her in place, and a most lovely open smile on her face. Her eyes were clear and piercing, like her father's, and her hair straight and shoulder-length. Her legs were angled strangely, and on her feet were curious boots resting on protruding footplates. Her hands were raised and her fists oddly clenched as if she was signalling to her father, 'No, no don't take a photograph of me.'

Behind her, holding the handles of her chair, was a young man, obviously Down's syndrome. He wore glasses and was looking down at Esther in front of him. He was grinning.

'That's Tom,' said Richard Marquand, 'and I took the picture in the garden of Harefield. It is my favourite.' I noted his wife Kate's hand tighten on his arm. We all stared at the picture in silence for a few moments and then he sighed, smiled at me in a hurt, crooked sort of way.

'Please take these other things for the time being,' he said, indicating the file and the envelope of photographs he had already given me. 'You may find a use for them. Return them when you can Mr ... um ...' He *had* forgotten my name, barely having looked at the card I had given him.

'Thank you, sir, I mean, I ...' I flustered my thanks in surprise.

'Promise me not to show them to Schuster.'

With such precious things within my grasp, I would at that moment have promised almost anything.

I made to look at the file and envelope but he stopped me.

'No, no,' he said. 'Not here. In your own time. Not here.' He looked at them with something like fear in his eyes and I knew these things had been hidden away for years until this moment, and that he had no wish to look at them. Then he reached for his wife's arm as if suddenly tired, and began to look bored. While Kate had that distant hurt in her eyes of a woman, living and good, whose desires and dreams of children have never come true, and whose reconciliation with childlessness has been long, and slow, and hard. Now she reached out and held her husband's hand.

'I'll return them safely,' I said of the things he had given me.

Then, at last, I had an insight that made me feel I understood better than before the nature of help Esther Marquand wanted me to give when, and if, I found the Skallagrigg.

Holding those mementoes of her life in my hands, looking at her father and his second wife whom by then I knew he had married after his 'difference' with Esther, the daughter of the first, I felt an overpowering sense that I was Esther's emissary, and her father's final happiness was part of the task she had left me.

It seemed to me that at that moment she was saying to me, 'I can't help them now, but you can. You can.' And yes, I think she also said to me, 'Lead them when you can to the Skallagrigg.'

I thanked them both for their trouble, apologized for my intrusion, and repeated too many times that I would return the things Richard Marquand had given me, whatever they were, quite safely and that I would keep in touch and tell them how my researches were going.

They nodded their heads non-committally and Mrs Marquand smiled politely as if she did not expect to see me again. I sensed in them that same feeling I had in Daniel Schuster, as if like him they were passing a burden to me they no longer wished to carry.

Later I did go back, and that time I did get Richard Marquand to talk, though only about the earlier years that led to the discovery of Arthur and the Skallagrigg. He would not talk about some aspects of Esther's life which I had to find out about in other ways, and he would never speak about her programming partnership and relationship with Schuster. But he wanted to hear, as they both did, all about what I had discovered, and he was not averse at least to listening to what I said about Hanniman Beach and the life Daniel Schuster had made for himself there.

So my research proceeded until one day I found myself back at Hanniman Beach in Schuster's Californian studio, despairing about the cul-de-sacs I seemed always to reach. Not of fact so much as of feeling.

At some low point, then, and due shortly to leave, I suddenly confessed to him that I had met with Richard Marquand not once but twice, and that here in my luggage I had copies of that envelope of photographs and file of writings he had given me.

Schuster was angry, forbiddingly so, and I reached my lowest point in that part of the search. Like a naughty schoolboy I produced the goods, and thus I was guilty of breaking promises to both men.

He looked at them, glowering, and I grew suddenly angry.

'Dammit,' I said, the role of guilty researcher too heavy to bear,

'I think it's what she would have done. How can I find out about her without talking with everyone involved?'

He said nothing, thumped the material on the table, and grew increasingly angry. I had seen his toughness before but never this level of anger.

'You had no right to do this,' he said. 'None. You don't understand any of it, none of it. It isn't as you think . . .' and then he stormed out of the house to the beach, the Old English sheepdog following after him after throwing me a shaggy, contemptuous glance.

Upset, I followed after him but he was off down the beach, while the dog, too lazy to cope with sand and the strong wind that came from the south-west, sat down and watched him.

It was a strange moment. I had a feeling of déjà vu, the kind that I had often had doing my research into Esther and her game. So I asked myself about it as I watched Schuster.

He was not young any more but still remarkably fit, and he had in his day been a very good windsurfer indeed. There were a couple of rigged boards down by the surf, and two or three people he knew. He went up to them, talked briefly, and took one of the boards. One of the group followed him and pointed at the surf. It was heavy and grey, as if it had suffered a storm out at sea, and there were clouds on the horizon that might be that storm approaching. The wind seemed stronger and colder by the moment. The sea uninviting.

Whatever the friend said Schuster seemed to ignore it, turning away with the board under his arm, and going down to the shore. He came back for the rig and with white surf running right up to his legs he fitted the rig to the board, looped the dagger board in the crook of his right arm, pulled up the sail loosely towards him, placed his left foot on the board, eased it forward into an oncoming rush of surf, and then with one expert powerful move, pulled the sail hard to the wind, leaned back and surged off through the surf straight towards an impossibly high wave.

A lost memory was suddenly triggered inside me and I involuntarily stepped forward and knew I was seeing the source of that famous graphic of waves with which the game 'Skallagrigg' begins. I stared immobile, sitting high up the beach, my legs and my arms no longer my own but someone else's, a girl's, as I knew that I saw a scene that Esther Marquand had once seen. Not here, perhaps, for so far as I then knew she had never left England, but sitting on a beach, watching helpless, as great seas engulfed a man on a board – *her* man, her only-ever man – and great troughs between waves engulfed even his mast and sail for long frightening periods, and wind ruffled at her hair and tugged at clothes she could not put on and at straps she could not undo. I saw the source of the imagery that roars through the game of 'Skallagrigg', the moving force to the great impossible heights of a fence, wooden and old, whose failing struts and bars could not be climbed without help.

Up and through the roaring and whiteness and then on to the next great surfing wave went Schuster, assured, angry, still a master of the same medium in which his son Robert was so famous. And in which I had watched, over the years of my research, his granddaughter Mary begin to grow up.

Then Daniel Schuster was beyond the worst of the surf, powerful and strong, and the sky darkened above him and the wind was colder still as he began a wild passage through electronic waves that, I began to see then, was to him a fantasy sea near a mythical place called 'The Racks' where finally, finally, in a game called 'Skallagrigg' you find the object of your quest.

And watching Schuster then I felt I had finished my research and had now only to find you, my unseen companion, and ask you to listen and join me as together we go back to Esther's beginnings, and then further back to Arthur's, until we have the wisdom and the knowledge to climb at last that wooden fence whose image was in the dark reflections and curling depths of the sea Daniel Schuster sailed . . .

The moment faded and I got up and returned to the house. Schuster came back an hour later, in a towelling robe and dog-tired. He grinned to make up with me, to show his anger was gone.

'So what's bothering you?' he asked with that smile of his. His grey hair was salty wet.

'Where shall I start?' I asked him, though I already knew. We stared at each other in silence. He poured us both a bourbon.

'If you're asking that question then you've probably finished your research, but for the details,' he said slowly.

'Where would Esther have started?' I asked suddenly.

'Where *did* she start?' he asked in turn, referring to the 'Skallagrigg' program.

'With that famous first question . . .'

He nodded, and I saw the way forward at last.

With you as witness, I turn on my computer and boot in the 'Skallagrigg' program for one last time.

The familiar logo and copyright line comes up, with the instruction at the bottom of the screen: PRESS RETURN . . . but surely my journey is beyond the game now, we don't need to go back to the game, I've done it before.

You insist that I do, and I know you are right. And your presence frightens me a little for I feel vulnerable before you.

I press RETURN and after the briefest of pauses that first terrible question, before which so many players stumble and fall, comes up and you ask that I read it out, as if you cannot read it perfectly well yourself. But you want me to start again, right from the beginning, and I feel as alone as she must have done, so terribly alone; as Arthur/Eddie must have done.

So now, with the question Esther chose to start her game, we ourselves begin this final quest for the Skallagrigg:

YOU ARE A PARENT AND YOUR DAUGHTER HAS JUST BEEN BORN. YOU STAND WITH THE DOCTOR STARING DOWN AT HER WHERE SHE LIES BENEATH A DOME OF PERSPEX, TINY AND PREMATURE AND ON A RESPIRATOR. HER SKIN COLOUR IS YELLOW. HER ENTIRE TINY BODY MOVES MASSIVELY WITH EACH BREATH. THE DOCTOR SAYS, 'IF SHE LIVES SHE MAY NEVER WALK, NOR TALK, NOR PICK UP AN OBJECT FREELY. SHE MAY I'M AFRAID BE BLIND. SHE MAY BE SUBNORMAL. I'M SO SORRY.' HE WALKS AWAY AND YOU ARE ALONE WITH HER. IMAGINE YOU HAVE POWER OVER HER OF LIFE OR DEATH. YOU

LET HER LIVE	Type L for Live
LET HER DIE	Type D for Die

Experienced games players always type 'L', for a 'D' can lead nowhere; they know that death is not a good beginning to a game.

However, 'L' for LIVE was not the solution either. 'Skallagrigg' was different from other games. The options it at first seemed to offer on-screen were not all the options that existed, nor all for which it was programmed. The correct response to the first question, or rather the one that will lead you forward through the program towards the Skallagrigg, is: 'Don't know.' So why don't you key it in?

DON'T KNOW

PART II

ESTHER AND
RICHARD
MARQUAND

SIX

The night Esther was born her father, twenty-five-year-old Richard Marquand, made a prayer so dreadful in its arrogance and implied disrespect for life that later, when his eyes had softened with age and his shoulders were just a little bowed, he would shudder at its memory.

Esther was premature, born six weeks before full term and weighing only two and a half pounds. Normally not disastrous, except that Esther had had to be delivered by Caesarian section, her mother having been mortally injured in the car accident that led to the whole tragic business of Esther's birth. The problem with Caesarian deliveries in babies so premature is that the incision in the mother can only be quite small, and brain damage can occur as the baby is removed. Nobody's fault really, and, like an earthquake, an avalanche or a flood, just an Act of God.

So that night Mr Marquand, shocked by the sudden death of his wife Sheila and the grim overnight transformation of his life from steady success to stark tragedy, stood tired, numb, confused and terribly alone, staring into a plastic dome in an intensive-care unit. Inside it, horribly tiny, desperately (as it seemed to him) breathing, with legs no bigger than his fingers and a head that seemed barely human with veins coursing black and blue across it, lay the thing they called his daughter.

Neither education nor life had prepared him for this moment; nor indeed for the marriage that might now be seen as the tragic precursor of his situation. He was simply a young executive in an office equipment firm, he had recently moved from a flat to his first house, he had (as it seemed to him) a large mortgage, and he had been intensely ambivalent about the thought of their having a baby. He had wanted to wait; she had not.

Though he did not know it, as he stood in shock before the plastic dome beneath which the as yet unnamed Esther lay,

Richard Marquand was a man in change. But the shocked are often impassive, and he stood there looking like the tired, mid-twenties young executive which was all, so far, he was.

Then anger began to mix with shock and loneliness, an anger the more virulent because the deceased Sheila had left him to cope with this mess alone. Muddled in among it all as well was grief – for himself, for his dead wife and for his daughter; and it was this grief and a nascent fear that led him into a petitionary prayer to the very God the result of whose Act he was now staring at.

For he had asked the doctor, 'Will she be all right?' and the doctor had been suspiciously non-committal. The matron in charge of the intensive-care unit was kinder, and more forthcoming. The APGAR ratings on Esther were very poor, meaning that the prognosis was not good, and, ah yes, there had unfortunately been traumatic distortion of the head at delivery. The matron had looked at him and said: 'I'm sorry, Mr Marquand, but it does not look too good. She is very weak and the birth . . . was in the circumstances very difficult. We'll know more in a few days; ask to see the doctor then.'

She had thoughtfully started to leave to let him stay alone for a time at his tiny daughter's side but had turned back and said, a little hesitantly, 'Mr Marquand, we were wondering if there was a name . . . for the child . . . for our records.'

Richard stared numbly down at 'the child' and the only name he remembered Sheila talking of was 'Esther' after her great-grandmother, Esther Mary Ogilvie. She had sat in bed one night reciting a whole list of Christian names, and then their surname. Elizabeth Marquand, Ruth Marquand, Jane Marquand and finally Esther, over which she had paused before repeating it: Esther Marquand.

'I think my wife wanted her to be called Esther . . . Esther Mary, after her great-grandmother.' Between them Esther Mary Marquand, yellow and damaged, so tiny she might have been another life form, gulped another desperate all-embracing breath.

'Lovely,' said the matron. 'Those are very nice names.' Then she left the father with his daughter.

It was some time after that, still staring numbly down into the incubator, that Richard said his prayer. It was long and rambling, but the gist of it was this: If she's brain damaged let her die; let her be free. Only let her live if she is normal. *Please* God, only let her live if she'll be normal.

A prayer, one might think, the majority of people would sympathize with, and perhaps even applaud. But a few might have asked questions of this prayer before giving it their support. What is 'normal'? What is 'living'? Should anyone, even God himself, have the right to take life once that life is made, in whatever form?

But in fact something altogether more prosaic and unpleasant now occupied the conscious mind of Richard Marquand. The anger that had replaced the shock and self-pity now suddenly burgeoned inside him for, physically separated from his daughter as he was, by fear and plastic, the bonding that might naturally have taken place had he been able to hold her close and protect her (as unconsciously he wished to do) did not occur. Instead of unthinking healing touch there was dreadful destructive thought and it said: Is not this thing the cause of my wife's death? For where had she been going that same evening? Sadly, on baby business: to an ante-natal relaxation class. And she had been late and hurried . . .

Was it not then his daughter's fault, in a way at least?

Or, perhaps his own, when he thought further about it. Should *he* not have driven her?

He was to see that same pointless question in the eyes of more than one of her relatives when, four days later, Esther's mother was buried in her home village of Charlbury, Oxfordshire, with half the village attending.

'So young, isn't he?' they said to each other as he walked past them in a black suit to stand with the family, but terribly alone. Staring at the broken sandy soil of Oxfordshire, unable to bear the accusing eyes of Mrs Ogilvie, his always proud but now bitter mother-in-law, who had not spoken to him when he first came and probably would not now.

'Could I have a word?' It was Martin Amey, the vicar who had married them three years before, taking Richard Marquand's arm and guiding him back into the darkness of the church.

'I know there is nothing useful I can say that I did not say in the service but, well, I wanted you to know that many here are thinking of you. Yes *you*.' And if Richard cried then, for the first time, and if the vicar waved away nosey Mrs Ofrett who came

back into the church (seeing as the vicar had gone back in there
with the bereaved), what did it matter and who cared?

'I know it's a cliché, Mr Marquand, but time really does change
the way we see things. Perhaps because *we* change. Please remember that if there is ever anything you feel I can do, or anything
you might like to discuss then get in touch and come and see me.'
The vicar waited quietly while Richard composed himself.

'How is your daughter?' he asked, trying to look to the future.
Richard simply shook his head and looked at the flagstone floor of
the church. Very stoic, very British. Very silly, for he needed to
talk. It would be a need unsatisfied for numbed years yet to come.

Later, when he arrived at the Ogilvie family home, Sheila's father
Brian came up to Richard and said, 'I'm sorry, old fellow, I'm so
very sorry,' and for a moment the two men held each other on the
porch of the family home. Then Mrs Ogilvie had come and the
intimacy that Richard so desperately needed was gone.

Yet that embrace and the young vicar's few kindly words at the
church meant much to Richard Marquand and bore him through
the rest of the day. He might have wished his own father was still
alive or that his mother had come. They had both of them been
only children.

At a little after two o'clock he left Charlbury as he had come;
alone. The child who was the sole result of the marriage, and who
still lay prostrate and tiny beneath an incubator shield, was barely
mentioned throughout the day, as if her familial world was waiting,
knowing she might be damaged, to see how great the damage was
before deciding what position it would take.

Richard Marquand never had Esther in his home, not then at any
rate. The weeks she was kept isolated in intensive care cut him off
from her and the toughness that had taken him rapidly through
the company for which he worked reasserted itself into a hardening
position: he could not look after his own daughter. With the travelling he did, the future he had, the so-many-things a man may
fabricate to rationalize the easiest course . . . no, it would not be
fair on Esther.

And so Esther, when she finally came out of hospital, was
fostered by a Mr and Mrs Dillard in Surbiton. But not for long.
Complications. Operations on her stomach. She went from here to

there, to hospitals and foster homes; residential centres, specialists, and eventually to the Dale Centre in a west London suburb, a home for damaged children and geriatrics.

Yet, for all his seeming care-lessness, Richard Marquand could not keep entirely away. He came from time to time to see his slowly growing daughter, staring down at her in her cot, and occasionally, if encouraged, picking her up.

But, yes, she was damaged. He could tell that. Less from the way she looked, which was so far normal enough, since the spasmed muscles had not yet had time to contort her, but rather from how clumsy her limbs were compared to those of his friends' babies who were all of a piece when he picked them up. Yes, she was going to be – she already was – spastic, through brain damage at birth. And the chances were high that she would be mentally subnormal as well.

Sometimes, rather awkwardly and feeling vaguely fraudulent, he would push her out from the Dale Centre in a pram into the streets of Ealing, enjoying for a second the stares of others who did not know that she was damaged or that that lovely smile was five months late according to the normal stages of child development. And those grey-blue eyes, an echo of her mother's, that would have been so beautiful in a normal face, might, if the tests were right, be only partially sighted.

Yet, as the years began to pass, colleagues at work would catch him, as he caught himself, staring out of a window at a drifting sky and thinking, not entirely unhappily, that he had a daughter, and her name was Esther. And he would go and see her again, soon.

He would never agree to adoption, though the literature had been sent more than once and various social workers had assured him that it would be in the child's best interests. But some deep instinct, as yet untutored and inarticulate, told him that it might not be in *his* best interests and because of that, finally, not in Esther's either.

Promotion, passing years, moves, an eighteen-month stint in Germany, and letters from Mrs Dillard, the foster-mother who seemed to have grown most attached to Esther, just to tell him how Esther was getting on. Sometimes, too, little presents. One year she 'made' him a calendar – a red card with a little cheap printed calendar stuck on to it (the glue daubed more or less

unknowingly by the guided hand of Esther) and 'To Daddy for
Christmas, from Esther' neatly written by a teacher in a blue felt-
tip pen at the top. He stared at this little thing and could only
think, again and again, 'She will never write for herself, never ever
write.' Or that she would never cut paper with scissors, or reach
forward and choose a coloured piece of card like this from a sta-
tioner's shop, or actually *say*: 'It's for you, Daddy, from me, for
Christmas. With love.'

He lived alone, benumbed, not even knowing he was grieving,
not seeing the sterility in his life, an automaton's life whose only
passion expressed itself in his job in which he was methodical,
effective, aggressive and successful.

Yet as time went by he found that involuntarily, inexplicably (to
him!) he would do what in those first months and years he had not
been able to: he would weep for the suffering he felt because his
daughter Esther had been born so wrong.

Then he continued living the life of a demi-father who when he
looked in the mirror in the morning could not yet perceive the
lines of weariness that were beginning to form, nor the loss settling
slowly beneath his eyes; nor guess that sometimes prayers such as
the one he made at her birth are answered strangely, years and
decades after they were first uttered, and far more wisely than we
know.

SEVEN

When Esther was seven and a half Richard Marquand had a letter from a Miss Eileen Coppock, the new full-time social worker at the now expanded Dale Centre. Could Mr Marquand find time to arrange to come in and see her, preferably during weekday office hours?

On the phone she sounded, if anything, a little curt, certainly less kindly than the previous social worker. He had the feeling that he had better wear a suit, and be precisely on time, and he found himself a little nervous as he drove through the centre's gates.

Reception, who knew him and appeared to expect him, showed him immediately into the social worker's office.

'Ah Mr Marquand, I am Eileen Coppock.' The woman stared at him. She was perhaps a little older than his thirty-two, though not much, and her face did not have that vacuously sympathetic counselling look that invites the troubled to talk about their woes but can plunge the aware into yet deeper despair. If Mr Marquand had woes it did not look as if they would get much of a hearing from Miss Coppock. Problems yes, but self-pity no.

She was tall and, as social workers go, elegant. There was a clipped no-nonsense look to her, and her desk (which as an office equipment marketing man Richard Marquand was long trained to notice first) was tidy. There was only one bulging buff file in sight and that, evidently, was his daughter's.

'I am, as you know, the new social worker here. What you may not know is that our structure has changed somewhat and our approach is now rather more multidisciplinary than before. I will not at this stage bore you with the details unless you really wish to know –' she hesitated as if to give him the opportunity to ask what these details might be while making it perfectly clear that she had no great wish to go into them. Richard Marquand remained silent.

'. . . but this has involved a review of all the clients we have here, including, of course, your daughter Esther. My job is to familiarize myself with each case and arrange future reviews with my colleagues and that's one of the reasons I asked you to come in and talk. There is another, but first perhaps you could help me by telling me something of how *you* see Esther's future.'

It was not a question Richard Marquand was articulate about nor one he had ever really been asked, least of all by the very people who were meant to know so much about it all. He started, and faltered, and started again until Miss Coppock quietly said, 'I think it might be best if you begin right at the beginning.'

'What, at the birth?'

She nodded and smiled gently, and suddenly, and for no reason that he then understood, Richard Marquand felt extremely vulnerable. For he saw in her eyes the look not of a counsellor but of a human being who cared as an adult should for others around them, and who understood, profoundly understood, that for all his smart clothes and refusal to take his daughter home, for all the rarity of his visits, for all of everything that he seemed to be, he cared too and was still struggling to face the shock of a damaged daughter.

Seven years and more of isolation, seven long years of struggling alone with unexpressed feelings, grappling with a tragedy of which he could make no sense, seemed suddenly sharable, suddenly no longer his alone. There, on the far side of a desk from a rather severe-looking new social worker, those defences he had erected from the moment of Esther's birth began, like walls overtaken by time and circumstance, to crumble and fall. And in their dust, among their ruins, the useless shaking limbs that were his daughter's seemed to be his own, and the mouth that twisted in movements she could not control, was his. And what he felt to be her agony, he suffered too.

'Well, it's a long time ago now. It was all very sudden, you see, because Sheila, that's Esther's mother, she was . . . we were living . . . there was only a few weeks to go . . . I'm sorry I . . .'

He found himself beginning to cry as he had not cried in the years since the funeral; deeply and angrily and speaking out with bitterness that it should have happened to Esther at all and that it was 'Not her fault' and 'Her grandparents couldn't give a damn and 'How can I plan when no one will tell me what her future will be?'

'Having Esther is like having something you made wrong but can't put right. Sheila died before she even knew she had a daughter, let alone a handicapped one. She left me to cope with it all and I've tried, I've tried to understand why.'

He paused, searching Eileen Coppock's face for evidence of some kind of response but seeing none, not even sympathy or lack of it, his frustration before the unanswerable question he had asked caused him to get up from his seat and go over to the window which overlooked the recreational gardens of the grounds of the Dale Centre. At this particular window, at least, the sun had succeeded in entering, and it fell now at his feet and on to his black shoes.

He leaned against the casement and said, quite loudly, 'I wish she had died at birth. I wish she were dead.'

Miss Coppock let him recover himself and then walked over to the far end of her office saying, 'I think we've missed the morning tea, but it is rather thick and institutional and I prefer coffee so I brought in my own kettle. Would you like a cup?' He nodded and sat down again while she made it.

Much later she said, 'Well now, Mr Marquand, you've been coming to see her here, and occasionally at her different foster homes, since the beginning. The records suggest to me that you care and you care deeply. And I think where a great many fathers in your position might have simply retreated you have come forward again and again. It must have taken courage.'

Richard Marquand could only nod non-committally, but he felt a deep reassurance. Perhaps he had not done so badly after all.

Her tone now became more businesslike. 'As a matter of fact, there is a particular reason I have asked you here. Esther is now seven and a half and she appears to be trying to communicate verbally in some way. She chatters, though her range of sounds is severely limited and there seems a delay between what she may be thinking, and what she actually "says". It may be, of course, that she is not "saying" anything. She is still so young . . . for children with her degree of damage are always much slower to reach the different stages.'

Miss Coppock paused, turning over the papers in the file, and then said, 'The speech therapist saw Esther again on the 28th, that's three weeks ago, and her report is, well, undecided. So far as we can tell Esther is trying but her best communication remains the simple yes and no indicators which she does with her head and eyes.'

Richard Marquand sat silent, but he was increasingly excited by what Miss Coppock was saying. It was the first time since his daughter had been born that anyone he had dealt with, whether doctors, therapists, welfare or social workers, had dared even to hint that she might, after all, have a spark of that without which there can be no 'normality': intelligence.

She poured two more coffees and sat down again, this time in an easy chair adjacent to his.

'Well! Where had we got to?'

For the first time since he had arrived Richard Marquand realized that he was in the middle of a highly structured and careful interview. He smiled.

'What is it you want me to do, Miss Coppock?'

She smiled back, one equal to another. She had read the case notes, talked at length with all so far involved, and had had to make a decision about how to talk to Mr Marquand. She began to feel she was right.

'I understand your daughter enjoys your company and looks forward to your visits. She is generally rather unsettled and difficult after you have gone and, while some see that as a Bad Thing, frankly I see it positively. It means she has a relationship with you. Now, if she *is* beginning to try to communicate, then your closer involvement now may speed the process. I know all the ties you have and that your job involves travel; I know, or can guess, the difficulties. But I would like you to think about it.' She paused and then continued, 'The books say that someone like me should shut up and listen so maybe I've said too much. It's such a difficult business this . . .' Miss Coppock waved her hand around the room, at the charts on the walls, at the file drawers, at her in-tray. At the telephone.

Then she fell silent, waiting, observing. It was difficult to read Richard Marquand. Obviously he felt deeply about Esther – dammit, who wouldn't? – but he was cautious, sipping his coffee and thinking, his slight smile surely hiding a lot.

But he hesitated before the commitment that he thought Miss Coppock wanted from him and which really he wanted from himself. For seven years the image of his daughter had been slowly becoming clearer to him and now something rather obvious yet very startling occurred to him. Esther was *his* daughter, no one else's, with her smile and jerking, wandering limbs, her slump and the way her hands and fingers stuck forward.

That was true. Yet as he thought of her so clearly he saw too a distant landscape beyond her, which was green and sun-filled and where the weight of her did not exist. There might be a different Richard Marquand there who did not have all this to think about. And self-pity soured the new hope and he did not want to say 'yes' to whatever it was Miss Coppock was asking of him.

'Can I see Esther now?' he asked. And immediately felt guilty because he felt he was about to put his daughter on trial. He wanted to see her again before deciding to give her more time, more commitment.

Miss Coppock nodded and softly said, 'Of course.' She had tried her best and she saw the hesitation in her client's eyes.

'No need to do more than think about what I've said,' she began. But he got up smoothly, charming, smiling, and distant now, to end the interview by going to his daughter.

'Look who it is, you know who it is. It's your Dad, isn't it!' The helper's voice was too loud and coaxing.

Esther lay in a bean-bag, her head trying to stay still as she stared blankly towards the three adults by the door. They seemed hazy. She looked at them for clues to identity. Blue shoes: Miss Coppock. Black shoes shining: a man.

As the shoes came towards her across the wide parquet floor a male voice said, 'Hello, Esther.' It was this that first told her it was her father.

Esther's body jerked into joy, her face all smiles, and she let out a scream of delight. She was wearing a blue corduroy dress, thick red tights and red sandals.

'Esther's been talking, haven't you, Esther? Esther's been saying things!' declared the helper.

Richard Marquand bent down to his daughter who was nodding

and smiling, and he wished Miss Coppock and the helper would go away. He wanted to pick up Esther and kiss her.

The room, which had once been the main library of Dale Hall, had several other children in it. Another girl, wearing a grotesque padded head-gear, was staring across at them from a wheelchair, a great board over her lap on which there were pieces of bright plastic. Two boys, both handicapped, were listening to a radio that was softly playing over by the bay window. An older boy, older than Esther, was in a bean-bag like hers, near the two boys. His face was terribly thin and pale, gaunt as a dying child in a famine relief poster. But his hair, his eyes ... blond and blue, so penetrating. He stared at Richard who recognized him as one of Esther's friends. Richard said 'Hello, Peter,' and Peter jerked in the way Esther did but he was more damaged and his head twisted and his hands contorted and spasmed as he made a desperate trapped sound that was his hello.

'We'll leave you for a while then,' said Eileen Coppock meaningfully, taking the helper's arm and leading her out of the room. 'I'm sure Mr Marquand can manage by himself. Call if you need any help.'

Richard picked Esther up, her weight awkward against him until he had his right arm under her and her head was nestling into his shoulder.

He kissed her cheek. Her skin was soft and brown as her mother's had been. Mrs Dillard, the foster-mother, had once said frankly that he was lucky 'his girl' was an 'attractive little thing': 'Makes all the difference to the way the world treats them. All the difference!'

He walked with her through a shaft of sun towards one of the great library windows and saw their joint reflection approaching.

'They say you're trying to talk, Esther,' he said to himself in the window pane. The body in his arms jerked and laughed.

'Skyagree.'

'What?' he smiled, holding her from him so he could look into her face.

'Skyagree,' she said.

He stared at her and saw that her face had an unusual earnestness about it.

'Skyagree,' he said copying her nonsense.

There was a long pause. Her eyes wandered and she lost concentration. Then suddenly she looked at him again and shook her head, staring.

'Skyagree.'

'*Are* you trying to talk?' he said softly, as if speaking to a stranger. His heart was thumping in his chest.

'Skyagree.'

'Skyagree,' he repeated. Another long pause. Another shake of her head.

'Something like it?' he asked.

But this she could not understand.

'Skagagree,' he tried.

A pause. She suddenly nodded, smiling.

'Skagagree,' he repeated. This time she shook her head and whispered, 'Nah.'

'Something like it again?' This time she understood and nodded. He laughed. It was a nonsense game.

So he held her by the window, him looking out and she looking over his shoulder into the room, and played the game.

It was six attempts before he got the 'Skalla' right. And many more before he realized that 'Skallagree' was nearly right.

Once or twice he tried to get her interested in something else but though she seemed sometimes tired and dispirited yet she persisted, saying 'Nah, Skyagree' to bring him back to the game.

So he said, trying again, 'Skalla . . . skalla . . . skallagridd.'

Her silence, her earnestness, would have stopped an army in its tracks. He sensed that they were sharing something important. A faint, a very distant, 'Nah,' came from her.

Then he began to go through the alphabet's consonants: 'skallagrib, skallagric, skallagrid, skallagrif, skallagrig, skallagrij, skallagrik, skallagrill, skallagrim . . .' and suddenly she was power and electricity in his arms.

'Skallagrim!' He said triumphantly.

'Nah,' came back the whispered negative.

So he started working backwards realizing that her response time might have been slow.

'Skallagrill.'

'Nah.'

'Skallagrik.'

Shake of the head.

'Skallagrij.'

'Nah.'

'Skallagrig?'

'Yeh! Yeh! Yeh!' The power of her shout took him by surprise.

'S–K–A–L–L–A–G–R–I–G.' He spelled the word slowly, not that he believed she knew the letters but that he wanted to spell it for himself.

'Yeh . . . Nah!'

A slight negative.

She tried to say something, her lips hissing feebly at a word. And then something extraordinary happened, though only later did it seem strange, for at the time their conversation was little more than play to him, and though he felt he was communicating yet he did not really believe it.

He said, almost without thinking, 'Two "G"s?'

There was a pause. Esther's eyes wandered about the room and she strained back in his arms as if looking for something. Then she said, 'Yeh.'

'Skallagrigg with two "G"s on the end,' he repeated.

'Yeh!!' said Esther giggling, as if she knew the difference, even knew what a 'G' was.

Then after a final slow pause and a wandering look around the room again she relaxed in his arms and very gently her head nodded complete affirmation. And he saw that she was tired as if she had been making a great effort of concentration to play the strange word-game.

'But what is it?' he asked rhetorically, in exaggerated surprise, 'Skallagrigg?'

She could give no answer, and anyway the room behind him was in a sudden turmoil as the girl in the chair had knocked her Lego to the ground and Peter in the bean-bag was crying, or at least making terrible noises, and the two little boys by the bay window were beginning to call out for attention.

Miss Coppock and the main helper appeared at the door.

Urgently, conspiratorially, hoping she could understand, Richard Marquand whispered in his daughter's ear, 'Do you want to come and see my home, Esther?' Was it his imagination that her head, and soft hair, nodded tiredly against his own?

'Soon then,' he said as he kissed her goodbye.

From the Marquand Collection: Disk 2, file 'MARQ03'*

That afternoon at the Centre was the first time I ever really talked to my father. But he did not really understand anything of what happened.

The boy in the bean-bag was Peter Rowne. He was an athetoid like me in long-term care. His mother never wanted him. Peter was the first person who ever recognized my intelligence. He once told me I was the first person he could ever really 'talk' to. He used to tell me Tom and Jerry cartoon stories with his feet and nobody ever understood why we laughed so much.

He could talk better than me and when I didn't understand I'd say 'Nah' and he'd stop and say, 'Is it this you don't get?' I'd say 'Nah.' 'Or this?' and I'd say 'Nah.' 'Or this?', and I would nod my head, or just smile when he got it right.

Ask the right questions and a 'Yes' or 'No' in answer can reduce the whole world to a specific in a short space of time. It's the basis for the game Twenty Questions. It's the binary way we spastics find easiest to talk when our speech is so bad that sentences are an effort to articulate even though we can understand everything people say to us.

Computers work this way as well, using positive and negative indicators in a logical tree to move from the most general to the most specific.

That was the method I used to get the story out of Peter, and it was the way he found out things I wanted to ask.

It was very simple though I was so slow at it then that it took me over three weeks to get the story from him. This was my first ever Skallagrigg story.

> There is a great field and around it a wooden fence, very high and strong. If you try really hard you can get to it. But then you must find a way to get over it. The grass in the field is full of lovely flowers, but it is high, higher than you, so you can only see the sun above on the flower and grass tops, and watch the wind play there. If you want to stand up, which

---

* The Marquand Collection is held in the electronic media and disk library of Berkeley University, California. All copyrights to this material and similar material used in 'Skallagrigg' are vested in Daniel M. Schuster of Hanniman Beach, California.

you do, you must crawl all the way to the centre of the field
alone. You'll find a man there. If you can get to him he will
help you stand up.

It took me a long time to make Peter understand that I wanted to ask
a special question.

He was very patient and he used a logical tree to find out what I
wanted to know.

'Is it about the fence?'

'Nah.'

'Is it about you?'

'Nah.'

'Is it about the flowers?'

'Nah.'

I don't know how many questions Peter asked before he reached
what I wanted. Naturally he didn't speak those sentences out because
there was no need. Once you've established that the nature of the
question is 'Is it about?' you need only indicate the subject. We developed our own language to short-cut our speech difficulties, partly
from things other children taught us, partly from our own imagination.
Until now, Peter has been the most expert at our language I have ever
known. He was so intelligent, so able to adapt his language to another's
limitations. I miss him so much.

'Esther, is it the man in the middle of the field?'

I nodded.

'You want to know something about him?'

I nodded.

'You want to know his name?'

I just stared at him.

'He's called the Skallagrigg,' said Peter. 'He'll help you or me if only
we can get to him.'

'Is he real?' I wanted to ask.

'And he's real,' said Peter, who needed to believe it even more than
me.

I could not say the word Skallagrigg. I shall never be able to say it.
Nor in fact could Peter. But he knew it because he, like me, had been
told it. Another spastic had passed the story on. Someone, some time,
had known how to say it and Peter had guessed how to spell it. He was
good at spelling.

I practised saying it again and again, and I got as far as 'Skyagree'.
On a previous visit I had tried to say it to my father but he didn't
understand. He thought it was just a noise.

When he came on that visit he asked me home for the first time, I could tell he had changed. He held me especially close and I felt really safe. So I said it again and again until he understood I was trying to say it. Except, of course, I didn't know how to spell it or anything. I only knew the few letters and numbers Mrs Dillard had taught me.

When Daddy started to try to say it I was so excited. But I had to look over to Peter to see if he was saying it correctly. I watched Peter and he said yes or no with his eyes. Right was yes, left was no.

Slowly my father worked towards the correct word. Sometimes Peter didn't seem sure. Sometimes my father moved so I couldn't see Peter. I wanted to go to the toilet but I knew I mustn't. It was too important.

Until at last my father said it in a way that satisfied Peter: Skallagrigg. And I heard for the first time in my life the name of what I then thought of, as I did for years to come, as a sort of god. I believed that somewhere was the Skallagrigg and that he made the cerebral palsied walk.

Then it all broke up because Peter started to cry. He was twelve. But that moment when my father said 'Skallagrigg' was the first time in his life that a normal adult person had done something that *he* wanted. Not something simple like making them know he was hungry, or needed to be toileted or moved somewhere. But something in the mind, something intelligent. So he started to cry, because it proved it was possible.

EIGHT

Richard Marquand lived at that time in a modest terraced house in Haven Lane, Ealing, a prosperous west London borough. It had a tiny paved garden in the front and a narrow, walled long garden at the back with a defunct outside toilet. The house interior had been gutted, rewired, replumbed, redecorated and now, if ever a home mirrored a man's soul, Richard Marquand's did.

It was curiously barren and bare of personality or emotional life. No family hearth here (the chimney breasts had been removed); no saucer of milk for an aged cat (Richard did not like animals in the home); no family photographs on mantel or by bed (Richard's few photographs were neatly labelled in an album stored in a cupboard); no familiar old rugs, stained, worn and loved (Richard had bought the perfectly fitted green carpets along with the house and saw no reason to change them).

Instead there were clean and dust-free surfaces (Richard being orderly), and a fridge with a limited range of carefully wrapped or boxed food, and newspapers folded and TV magazines exactly where they should be: by the television set. And a pad and a pencil by the dark blue telephone, and a digital clock set exactly right, and a calendar on the kitchen wall that hung in silence, marking out the endless days of Richard's emotional numbness.

One Saturday in June 1973 Richard Marquand stood in the front bay-window awaiting Esther's arrival. She had been twice on brief visits since that day months before when he had first met Eileen Coppock and promised Esther a visit, and now it was her birthday, and she was to stay with him for the night for the first time. She was eight years old.

The house had been systematically organized for her visit, so that Esther need not be carried upstairs. He would bring down a mattress from upstairs so she could sleep in the lounge, and a builder had made the outside toilet working and presentable.

Esther and Nasim, a Pakistani girl from the Centre who was her favourite helper, had enjoyed themselves writing out invitations to the few people Esther could invite: Eileen Coppock, her friends Peter Rowne and Karen Gee, both resident at the Centre, Nasim, and . . . and . . .

'What about Tom?' Nasim had asked.

'Nah,' said Esther dismissively. Tom was a mongol boy at the Centre who liked her but whom she always rejected. He was three years older than she was.

'He'd like to go. He'll see Peter and Karen's invitations.'

Esther's mouth turned down sharply, ready to cry. She felt she was under pressure.

'All right, all right, Esther,' said Nasim. Not Tom.

Esther got excited.

'Someone else?'

Yeh. She had thought of somebody . . . but it took Nasim a long time to find out who: Esther's grandparents. Eileen Coppock had to telephone Richard for their address.

'But she's never even met them,' he said, surprised.

'It shows she's aware of them, anyway,' said Eileen.

'Yes,' said Richard, giving the address.

Esther seemed to enjoy 'making' their invitation best of all, insisting on scattering two fistfuls of silver glitter on a glued part of it, and making a random shape in red felt-tip pen. Nasim wrote the words, 'You are invited to my eighth birthday party', and then the date and the address.

But after all that their reply was a brief letter to Richard in Brian Ogilvie's handwriting saying that no they couldn't come on the day but they hoped the enclosed two pounds could buy Esther a present.

'Can I come?' asked Tom the day before, when he heard where the others were going.

'Nah,' said Esther.

'Okay, Amh,' he replied, dropping his head sadly. He called her 'Amh' because he heard Eileen say that her second name was Mary and he liked the name Mary, which he pronounced 'Amh'. Esther ignored his hopeful staring at her, but when he turned to go away and she knew he could not see, her eyes followed him.

Just before three o'clock a blue and white Ealing Borough Social Services Department van drew to a halt outside Richard's house and he went outside to meet them.

Esther was craning round inside the van to see Richard and when she did so, and heard his welcoming voice, she squealed with delight, her legs spasming straight out and her arms flailing as her head bent into the effort of her noisy happiness. Richard made a fuss of her and watched her descent on the hydraulic lift from the back of the van to the pavement.

Next down was Peter. His blue eyes stared intently at Richard, whom he recognized, but as his fingers tangled tensely with his shirt and his body paroxysmed into some kind of hello, Richard, unknowing, turned his back on him to push Esther's wheelchair forward. Peter subsided into his unstill silence as he reached the pavement, his hello recognized only by Nasim, who laid a gentle hand on his shoulder.

Finally, Karen insisted on coming down on the ramp though she was ambulant. Richard had not met Karen before and he stared at her with some distaste. She was a tubby, gawping sort of girl who had a frown and stared stupidly up at him. She was mentally handicapped and physically slow, her mouth hanging wet and open, and she seemed to merge a gulping swallow into each word she tried to speak. She seemed at that moment grumpy. Eileen was bending over her whispering cajoling words to which Karen replied with angry gulps.

Nasim, who usually wore practical jeans and a blouse, was dressed that day in a sari and had gold bracelets on her arms. She carried presents in a bright plastic carrier bag. Even Peter, whom Nasim was adjusting into the chair which held his small and twisted body as if it were cocooned in a giant's hand, was looking smart: he wore a white shirt and grey pressed trousers from which his feet, blue socked, poked and pointed. His head bent this way and that, and his mouth was open, the upper lip seeming out of harmony with the lower, and his tongue shooting here and there as he made the wet thin noises that were his only speech.

All ready and the van locked, with Karen's hand in Eileen's, and

Nasim taking charge of Peter, Richard led them all up the tiny garden path pushing Esther's chair and whispering down to her the birthday delights to. come. The adults were smiling but the children gazed a little apprehensively into the rectangle of shadow that was Richard's open front door.

It would be hard to say quite why the party was not, to begin with, a success. Perhaps the three children, and especially Esther, had been looking forward to it too much, and perhaps Richard was a little too nervous, a little too anxious to please, a little too quick to serve the food and drinks and a little too slow to sit back and let the children find their own pace.

But inexperienced party-giver though he was, some deep instinct told Richard not to give in to Karen's bad-tempered demands that it was time for the cake. 'Why? Why?' (Gulp) 'Why?' (Gulp) '*Why*?' she wanted to know, sniffing and assuming a huge hunch of misery. The cake, which Richard had ordered specially from a local baker who had iced the words 'HAPPY 8TH BIRTHDAY ESTHER' on it, and a female figure made of sugar in a white eighteenth-century dress, was to be the climax and he had no wish to play his trump card too early. They could wait for the cake a bit longer, if only to give them something to look forward to.

'We could try some music, Richard,' said Nasim. He jumped at the idea.

'Haven't looked at any of these for a long time,' he said, opening the cabinet on which the turntable sat and taking out some records. 'These are just ones that Sheila and I had. Old pop records, Beatles, the Rolling Stones, and some jazz . . .'

No one saw Peter trying to speak, his hands threshing and his head turning to look at Esther, who looked at him then spoke herself.

'Yeh!' she said. She was making a request for Peter.

'I think Esther would like to choose a record,' said Eileen.

'Of course!' said Richard. He ran through them slowly and she stopped him at the Rolling Stones. She glanced again at Peter and then said, 'Yeh!'

The hard, deep music of the Stones began and Peter relaxed, grinning and frothing, and suddenly at that moment, for reasons none of the adults understood, the party at last began.

Later, when the atmosphere was much improved, and Richard,
out in the yard with the children finding 'giants', was beginning to
enjoy himself, the doorbell rang: once, twice, three times and then
a knock, before they heard it over the music. As Richard was
preoccupied with the children Eileen opened the door.

An elderly man stood there, quite tall and with a warm, creased
face. He was holding what was obviously a present, though it was
badly wrapped in previously used wrapping paper.

'I was wondering if this was Richard Marquand's house? Um . . .
Esther . . .?' He indicated the present with a smile.

He seemed diffident and rather reluctant to come in, but Eileen
got him through the little hall into the lounge and went to fetch
Richard whose mock roarings (he had begun to enjoy finding
giants in the garden – one behind the shed, another down an old
chimney pot and a third lurking in the darkest back corner of
perimeter fence) could be heard even inside the house.

Richard broke off and came back into the house in some puzzlement. No other guests were expected, and seeing the man he
stopped still with surprise.

'Good heavens! Why . . . Brian . . . I . . .'

It was Brian Ogilvie, Esther's grandfather.

The two men said a muddled hello, shook hands, and Brian
explained that he had after all been able to come, that, no, his wife
. . . Margaret . . . Esther's grandmother . . . had not come, but
somehow an eighth birthday *had*.

Eileen Coppock stood in the background. She guessed what had
happened: how a bereaved couple had received an invitation from
a granddaughter they had never seen, how Brian had felt he should
reply negatively to it but had sent two pounds for a present, how
that invitation had stayed on a mantelpiece in their cottage in
Charlbury, and how this good man had taken it up sometimes and
looked at it, and wondered about the little girl who was his only
grandchild.

'Eileen, I'd like you to meet Brian Ogilvie, Esther's grandfather,'
said Richard. As he turned to her, she saw pride and some relief in
his eyes as if, after so long alone, he had family to share the fact of
Esther with.

'Esther's in the garden,' said Richard leading the way.

'Esther, it's Bri . . . it's your granddad,' he said, using the name
he had always used with his own grandfather.

For a long moment Brian Ogilvie's old eyes surveyed the three children, trying to relate what he saw to the smiling face in the photograph which Richard had once sent.

But if he had doubts about whom to address and wish a happy birthday to, never having seen her in the flesh before, they were dispelled by Esther herself who, seeing him and hearing Richard say the word 'Granddad', herself fell into a silent and shy smile, her head averted but her eyes looking up at him, as he came towards her and said: 'Hello, Esther, I've come to wish you a happy birthday, my dear.'

His wrinkled hand went out to her shoulder and he bent down slowly, and with some difficulty, and gave her a rasping kiss on her cheek. And there, for a moment or two he stayed, for her right hand came slowly up to touch his ear clumsily then run into his white hair as she made, with the gentlest of sounds, the little noise that was her kiss to those she chose to like.

'Did you get a card from granddad?' asked Richard, prompting her to communicate.

Oh yes! No mistaking the nodding of the head and the excited stiffening of the legs, and the laugh. Nor was there any mistaking Esther's immediate attachment to the present he had brought with him, and which with his and Richard's help, and a few rough sweeping motions of her arms, her fingers unable to grasp the paper but her fists able to press one part down on her chair-tray and the other to rip it away, she finally opened.

Old, worn, an eye loose, but with an expression protective, loving and certain, it was a once-loved teddy bear.

'It was your ... Sheila's ... your ... mother's ... your mummy's ...' said Richard finally, the word strange to him, 'and now Granddad is giving it to you.'

'Mama,' said Esther, her arm and hand laboriously tightening round the teddy bear and a look of seriousness suddenly on her face. Then a smile.

'Perhaps it would be a good idea if we ...' Richard stood in the doorway of the kitchen wondering how to arrange people round the table, but Brian quite misunderstood and said, 'Draw the curtains? Jolly good idea. That's what we used to do for Sheila ... um ... pull the curtain to, you know, she liked the candles in the dark.'

'Yeh,' whispered Esther. '*Yeh!*'

While Eileen closed the curtains, Richard withdrew to the kitchen to light the candles without Esther seeing. He was just beginning to realize that a birthday party has a life of its own which it was possible for him to enjoy.

The party fell silent in the half light, watching for the kitchen door to open. Peter stared round and his mouth winced as his head shook with excitement.

Karen said, 'Oh I gh-like cake!'

Then the kitchen door opened and the cake and its magical lights floated towards Esther, whose eyes and hair caught its flickering golden flames, and settled on the tray that was fitted to her wheelchair. Eight pink candles! A circle of eight flames to stare at in wonder and with awe.

So beautiful did the cake look, so entranced by it were they all as they stared at the candle flames and at Esther's wonder-struck eyes, that not one of them noticed that a stranger was watching them through a gap in the curtains, his eyes round behind thick National Health spectacles, his hair untidy over his forehead, and his nose pressed against the glass of the street window. He ran a wet tongue over thick lips, frowned, and then sniffed and strained forward to see better, his breath steaming the glass.

Meanwhile, Richard read out the words on the cake. Someone said, 'You've got to blow out the candles, Esther' and they began to sing, 'Happy Birthday to you,' and as they reached the end their faces came down from all sides around her, grotesquely lit by the candlelight, seeming to shout at her, confusing her, for they were saying, 'Blow out the candles, blow out, out, go on, Esther, now, now, blow them at once, all at once . . .' and their cheeks puffed and their lips strained to encourage her to do what they wanted (which she couldn't do easily, and couldn't do at all in a set direction), to blow out the candle flames which were magical gold before her. And since she seemed unable to do it, they blew for her, robbing the struggling flames of their shape and identity until they were conquered one by one and driven back into darkness to leave behind only the black wicks that gave them life. Helpless, Esther stared disconsolately at the eight dying and now acrid memories of the beauty they had been.

Quite unnoticed, the eyes behind the glass at the window blinked, and disappeared.

Esther seemed suddenly tired and hardly ate any of her cake. Eileen looked at her watch and the adults began to exchange glances that said that the party was nearly over. The surprise guest had come, the nicest present had been given, the cake was all but finished and now it was time for the others to go.

Eileen Coppock was already standing up, and waiting for the right moment to say they must go and how lovely it had been when suddenly, unexpectedly, there was a knocking at the front door. Thump thump untidy thump. And then the bell. And then another thump.

Richard opened the door and was forced to stand on one side as a boy, a mongol boy, in glasses and carrying what looked like a bouquet of stolen flowers, pushed past him and went to stand on the threshold of the lounge. He thrust the flowers before him as if they would smooth the troubled path that he obviously felt lay directly ahead and said rapidly, 'I love Amh happy birthday.'

It was Eileen who responded.

'Tom! What are you doing here?' There was genuine shock in her voice, though it was tempered with such obvious good nature and concern that it was hardly a reprimand.

Esther uttered one word, 'Nah!'

Karen said, 'Silly Tom.'

Peter stared, his blue eyes travelling from Tom to Eileen and then to Esther.

'He must have come all the way from the Centre!' said Nasim, 'but how?'

They worked out that he must have taken Peter's invitation and shown it to passers by. Nasim had explained that Tom had wanted to come but Esther had said no. It was *her* party and she wasn't having Tom muscling in on it like he did everything else.

Tom stood wide-eyed, trying to look innocent. His eyes travelled to the remnants of the cake, and shone.

Esther said, 'Nah' and her mouth turned down. Tom broke ranks and gave her a kiss, dumping the stolen flowers on top of her teddy.

The party began again as Eileen made a quick telephone call to the Centre telling them that Tom (not even missed yet it seemed) was here with them and they would be coming back soon.

'I like cake.'

'Nah,' said Esther.

The adults watched amused, uncertain which side to encourage, or how to avert a battle.

But Tom seemed to sense just how far he could go in outright confrontation, and realizing he was on a loser he tried another tactic. He went back to Richard put his arm around his waist and briefly laid his head against him.

Then he stood clear and addressed Esther: 'Can I have some cake? Please.' To Richard and perhaps to Brian Ogilvie what was startling about the question was that it was asked at all, in complete seriousness. They were seeing somebody relate to Esther as an equal, as a person in her own right and not as someone to be ferried, helped, to receive passively what others thought to do.

Esther gazed coldly upon Tom and considered his request. Finally she said clearly, '*Nah!*' and that was that.

If Richard was about to intervene he was stopped from doing so by Tom who, obeying it seemed some code of conduct recognized by the children, meekly said, 'OK.'

The moment over, Nasim suggested that Richard put on a record she had brought, which Esther especially liked, of rock-and-roll versions of children's nursery songs.

'There can't be a party without wheelchair dancing,' said Nasim as, the music beginning, Esther and Peter were whisked about the floor and the others, in their different ways, joined in. The favourite turned out to be 'The Teddy Bears' Picnic'. So evocative was the tune and rhythm, so loud the sound, so jubilant the singing, that only one person noticed Esther's head falling, as her mouth suddenly turned down to a cry. Only one saw her hand reach blindly for her grandfather behind her; only one saw her mouth a word that was as silence against the wild singing all about.

It was Tom, at her side, who saw it, Tom who bent down to her and seemed to listen to her, seemed even to understand her, though her face grew longer as he retreated, beginning the semblance of a dance to the final tune. The dance led him by degrees to the patio door and, on a table nearby, he found what he was looking for.

When the song finished, they heard at last that Esther was crying, and began to ask what was wrong.

Tom said, 'It's all right, Amh, I got it.' He pushed through them to her side. 'Ahm wants this,' he said firmly, and he held out the teddy bear that her grandfather had given her. 'She wants teddy singing.'

The wreaths of smiles that came then to Esther's face were summer bouquets. Eileen barely had the chance to say to Richard, 'But how did he know? How could he know?' and Richard to shrug in disbelief, before Nasim had started the track all over again for the sake of Esther's bear. And Esther, her father to one side and her grandfather to the other, clutched her teddy to her and beat and sang with the melody.

While Tom, unnoticed, laughed and laughed and hugged Eileen to make her forgive him his trespasses and not mind if he helped himself to a slice of birthday cake.

Late that night, long after the others had left and Esther was in bed and meant to be asleep, she called out and Richard went to her.

Ever since Nasim had gone, having stayed behind to help Richard bathe and toilet Esther and get her ready for bed, he had felt profoundly nervous and ill at ease. Never before had he had a child in his sole charge.

So Richard stood at the door, looking across the hushed and darkened room, and wondering what Esther could want.

She was trying to tell him something and he could not understand. Then she began to make a blowing sound with her mouth and he guessed and he guessed until he could think of nothing more. He knelt down by her side in weariness and said, 'I don't know what it is, Esther, and really you should try to go to sleep.' Whatever it was it did not seem urgent, for Esther looked up at him gently, and her body was quiet beneath the duvet he had bought specially for the occasion.

She made blowing noises again. Then she did struggle, just enough to free her hand and raise it up and, with difficulty, point a finger towards the kitchen door. Richard looked round.

'You want a light on in the room?'

'Nah,' whispered Esther.

A drink? Something to eat? Esther's eyes screwed up against the light from the kitchen and she blew again.

And then Richard understood, oh yes, it was obvious what she meant. 'You want to see the candles alight again, don't you?'

She nodded. They were learning to understand each other.

He found the candles in a heap on the silver board on which the cake had sat. Only a third of the cake remained, but he carefully stuck them back in as best he could. Then he got some matches and took them and the cake with its candles, unlit, to her bedside. He propped her up with pillows so she could see.

'I'll turn off the light on the landing so you can watch the candles being lit.'

Which he did, and her face gradually grew brighter and brighter as each candle lit up and flickered before her, her hair shining brown in their flames.

'Do you want to blow them out?' he asked.

'Nah,' she said, shaking her head and staring in fascination.

They stared together into the flames, his arms round her, and an insight came slowly to him.

'You didn't want to blow them out at all this afternoon, did you?'

'Nah,' she said again, more softly.

'I should have understood,' he whispered.

But she was silent, lost in the free and gentle dance of the flames, her eyes shining and her lids beginning to droop with sleep.

After a time she made her blowing motion again and he said, 'Now?'

She nodded.

Then one by one he blew them out for her, and as he gently rearranged her pillows she began to drift into deep and contented sleep.

NINE

Over the next two years Esther's visits to Richard became increasingly frequent. He learnt to cope with her alone, and Eileen told the Centre that he should be encouraged to, though in practice he found it was so tiring that he preferred to pay one of the part-time helpers at the Centre to come in and give a hand. Usually this was Nasim, who had a special affection for Esther, and seemed to understand her needs more quickly than anyone else. Sometimes Tom accompanied Esther on these visits, for she seemed calmer when he was there and they 'talked' together, taking the strain off the adults for a time. Occasionally Tom seemed to understand what Esther wanted more quickly than Nasim, getting her a drink or unbuckling her straps in preparation for toileting.

'Ahm's ready now, aren't you?' he would say.

Esther, her eyes wandering as if they could not quite see, would nod and whisper, 'Yeh.'

It was during this period that Richard's trust in life began to return. He was already beginning to think that change for the better was possible as he realized the limitations of his house in Haven Lane, that it would be good to have a larger garden where he could play with Esther, and she and Tom could romp'about a bit.

'Esther, we're going to have to move somewhere bigger!' he said one especially beautiful autumn afternoon in 1975.

Richard always spoke to her as if she could understand, though just how much she took in was unclear. Eileen Coppock continually warned him against hoping for too much – parents of the handicapped tended to want to think their children brighter than they were, and to mistake the yes/no signals for deeper comprehension. It was one thing to recognize familiar words like shop, walk, food, bath, and familiar people's names – even quite backward children eventually learn to do that – but it was another to apply the information intelligently, to make deductions and to communicate ideas.

But Esther did not show much intelligence, that was the truth of it. She seemed to lose concentration, she seemed to like only the same endless repetitions: the walk to the shops, the buying of little gifts for Nasim or Eileen, the scribbled drawings ... oh yes she could nod her head when these things were suggested and smile happily doing them. But intelligence? Richard longed for some sign of it from her.

That autumn, there was a case meeting about Esther at the Centre and it was decided that she could usefully go back to the Spastics Society for an assessment. She had had one before, when she was three, but it had been inconclusive and the new multi-disciplinary Centre staff were sufficiently impressed by her to feel that a new assessment might prove valuable in highlighting the best areas for future care and training.

On the day itself, in chilly December, Esther's mouth turned down in a stubborn misery that was close to violent tears. And when she got to the Assessment Centre she did not perform well. It seemed to be, as Eileen put it, one of her off days.

The mask slipped only once. A session involving looking at a light to check her visual range was interrupted by another consultant, a young man, who came in and said, 'Sorry, but have you got our teddy bear?' The consulting rooms had a number of fluffy toys for younger visitors and it seemed that one of them, in an adjacent room, wanted a teddy.

Esther immediately looked round inquiringly as one of the assistants found the teddy bear.

'You've got a teddy, have you?' the consultant asked Esther.

Esther nodded.

'Do you like him?' The mask of non-cooperation settled back. But as it did so, the younger doctor took the toy saying light-heartedly, 'Ah, but does Teddy like *her*?'

And Esther, for the first and only time that morning, allowed herself to laugh. At which the consultant, to his eternal credit, added a note to his notes, a fact remarked by Eileen Coppock but not by Richard.

By lunchtime they were all exhausted and entered the canteen with relief. It was a bright and cheerful room, with pictures on the wall and the smell of more imaginative cooking than some in-stitutional canteens. Richard wheeled Esther to the service area to choose some food. She was still being negative, giving a 'Nah' to everything except the shepherd's pie, before which she at least stayed silent. He chose it for her by default.

They sat down to eat and since Esther was unsociable Richard let her get on by herself, strapping her special bent spoon to her right hand and ignoring her while he talked quietly to Eileen. Esther ate slowly with long pauses between each mucky mouthful when she would gaze about the canteen and at the people at the other tables.

The room was laid out spaciously to accommodate the passage of wheelchairs, and there were about twelve handicapped people among the thirty or so diners.

Of all the diners there, the happiest and most relaxed were two older men, one about sixty and very disabled, and a younger man in his mid-forties who was feeding him, though he himself also seemed slightly cerebral palsied. They both wore suits, but of an old-fashioned cut and with shirts that were white and too big for them. One had a blue V-necked pullover on. Their hair was military short and looked as if it had been cut by the same institutional barber.

As Esther watched, another man came into the canteen, looked around, saw the two men and walked over to their table.

'Mrs Vaughan says we'll be through here by three p.m., Jack, so we can go back tonight all right. King's Cross isn't that far and they're laying on the minibus.'

He addressed the older, more disabled man who replied: 'Awrrwiathh!' All right.

'I'll leave you then,' continued their helper, 'because I've to sort a few things out with the library while I'm here. Right? I'll come and fetch you when the doctor's ready, at about two.'

The older one nodded again.

Jack's friend offered him more of the sweet he had been finishing but seeing that he did not want it put the spoon slowly back into the bowl. He jerkily found a paper napkin and wiped Jack's mouth and said something and laughed.

Jack seemed to think for a while and then began to speak, and there followed a conversation of such good humour and evident fun to themselves that several people looked over at them and smiled.

Not that the words they spoke were English as she is spoke by the able-bodied; for though the younger man seemed capable of relatively normal speech, it was Jack who was doing most of the talking, and his words were made up of contorted consonants and veering vowels all his own; and it was soon apparent, too, to anyone who, like Esther, was watching them, that their language included gesture as well as speech, though of a strange and subtle kind. For the twisted and spasmed hands of the old man moved as if each was a different character, one young, one old, and his legs, though thrust out on one side and twisted in on the other, seemed to move in tune with the hands, though gently, like an echo to footfalls in a church.

Two or three minutes into this dialogue Esther suddenly jerked upright, stopped eating, and began to pay rapt attention.

From the Marquand Collection: Disk 3, File 'MARQ05', page 5, starting line 38

The only knowledge I had had of the Skallagrigg myths before that December was through my friend Peter at Dale Centre in Ealing, who had told me about the field beyond the wooden fence where the Skallagrigg waits for us.

Peter didn't realize it, but he missed out a key element in the initial story he told me. He did not mention Arthur, the boy who most wanted to get to the wooden fence, the boy who was the Skallagrigg's special friend.

Then on December 12th, 1975, I went for assessment at the Spastics Society in London and heard about Arthur for the first time.

Daddy didn't realize that the two men in the canteen were telling me a story to cheer me up. And he couldn't know the story was about the Skallagrigg.

The old one, whose name was Jack, saw I was scared of the assessment and said, 'Well, I thought Christmas was coming in a couple of weeks until I saw *her* face!'

His friend, Eric, turned around and looked at me and grinned. He was nice. Jack was a bit frightening. I didn't know what to say.

Jack said, 'Can you understand me?'

I nodded. He was easy to understand if you watched his hands and listened carefully to his voice. He seemed pleased.

'You must be intelligent because half the time I can't understand myself! So why are you scared?'

I was too shy to answer.

'She's nervous,' said his friend.

'She ought to laugh a bit more,' said Jack.

'Maybe she's got nothing to laugh about. Tell her a story.'

It's a pity non-spastics can so rarely make sense of spastic talk because it can be a beautiful language. The nearest most normal people get to it is signing among deaf people. I've seen enough of that to understand quite a bit and to know that each signer is different, just as ordinary speakers are each different. And each signer has a different range and ability, just as speakers have. Some have wider vocabularies than others, and sign with great subtlety and beauty; some are naturally funny, others always serious. Some are tight, some open.

It's the same with spastic talk, though there are far fewer of them and it's rarely developed to its fullest range because there isn't the opportunity. Daniel, you asked me once how it was done and I put it like this: imagine being by the sea and the sea can talk to you. How does it do it? By sight, by sound and by smell; by presence and by silence, in a thousand ways. Well people talk like that really but normal people only hear their words because normally they don't have to bother to learn the other ways they speak, the non-verbal ways. But intelligent spastics develop an ability to interpret the non-verbal and so talk between them can be far subtler and more fulfilling than an able-bodied onlooker hearing only the (to him) garbled sounds and unable to interpret the movements or understand the references might think.

This is the story Jack 'told' me at the assessment centre.

It happened a long time ago when no one but Arthur believed in the Skallagrigg. That was when Arthur was a boy about the time Dilke first came.

Well now, Arthur was in a ward for men because there was no other place for him, the hospital having had a fire and there being rebuilding going on.

They all knew about the fire because two patients died and another was affected badly by the smoke. In the ward where Arthur was they smelled the smoke and heard the screams and the fighting and they were scared and panicked. Dilke had to come and beat them with his stick before they would shut up and settle down and maybe he was right. Who knows?

Then several months later and blow me but one afternoon
about quarter to five, just after the lads have been put to bed
for the night, Arthur smells smoke and he says, 'Aye, aye,
that's the beginning of a fire, that's what that is.'

Some of the other lads said the same and they got restless.
Dilke says, 'Shut up, there's nothing to complain about. It's
probably leaf burning. What's more I don't want you lot
moaning, there's been enough of that for my taste and that's
why this ward for one isn't going to the dance.'

There was a dance, you see, and Dilke was a great one for
springing nasty surprises. Others' disappointment was bread
and butter to Dilke. A lot of the boys had been looking
forward to the dance as it was a chance to meet others and
have a laugh. It only came once a year. If Dilke stopped them
going like he had the previous year then that would be two
years since they met anyone different. He knew how to get
obedience and silence did Dilke, he was that cunning. Then
he went off to investigate, leaving a young nurse in charge.

But Arthur says, 'Leaf burning, my eye, it's February and
the leaves are rotted or too wet to burn. That's the same smell
as last time.'

And despite Dilke's threat some of the lads were beginning
to panic in their cots, rattling the bars and saying, 'Get us up,
we want to be ready to get out, we don't want to burn!'

Then they heard a fire bell and worse pandemonium starts.
Even Arthur starts to shout. He doesn't want to turn black
and die in the orange flames of fire.

Then the nurse says, 'Shut up shut up shut up, you heard
what Mr Dilke said,' and he waves Dilke's stick, but even that
had no effect. So he goes off to see what's happening and
leaves them all alone. Then they heard shouting outside and
staff running and the smoke was getting thicker and Arthur
began to shout more. He believed he was going to die helpless and all he could do was look along the polished floor to
the gap beneath the door and wait for the orange flames to
show. Then above all the shouting and the panic and the
rattling of cot sides and the banging of desperate feet on the
beds and mattresses Arthur heard a voice that was calm and
quiet; it was the Skallagrigg.

'You'll be all right, you'll be all right, Arthur, if you just
keep still. It's no good panicking, that won't save your life.
You better tell the others that, because there's no one else
can calm them down but you.'

So then Arthur relaxes, and when the Skallagrigg speaks to him like that his body is in better control and his limbs don't shake.

'Sshh!' he says to the next cot. 'Shh.' And they seem to sense his calm and one by one they calm down.

'Listen,' says Arthur, 'there's no point shouting. They know we're here. Best thing I can do is tell you about the Skallagrigg.'

'What's that?' said someone.

'He's there to help the likes of us. Outside, beyond the walls, but he knows we're here, really he does and . . .'

'What's he look like?'

'He's strong, he could pick all of us up and set us straight if he had a mind to, but he won't if you make such a noise. He . . .'

Then Arthur spoke about the Skallagrigg, and kept their mind off the fire, and kept them calm, or as calm as they could reasonably be.

Later the medical superintendent came round and stood at the door and stared in. You could see smoke in the air. He was breathing heavy and . . .

At this point Jack's helper came back and he had to stop. But at the canteen door he got his chair stopped and turned back for a moment: 'We'll wait to tell you the rest. It's got a happy ending. We'll find you again.'

I don't remember anything more about the assessment. But when we left at three p.m. the two men were in their chairs in the foyer. They had their helper with them. When he saw us he came forward and said, 'I think my friends want to say goodbye to your girl.'

Daddy seemed surprised but he took my wheelchair to them. Jack continued exactly where he had left off:

. . . he was sweating, but when he came into the ward and saw everyone there was calm he calmed down himself. He said, 'There has been a small fire and no one is hurt. Charge Nurse Dilke has been helping put it out but your second will be back shortly.' Then he went away but after a moment came back. He said, 'Thank you for keeping calm. This has been the most orderly ward in the hospital.'

Next day he came back when Dilke was there and thanked us again. Arthur thought, 'Right, this is the only opportunity

we're going to get.' He said to one of the lads, 'Ask him if this
ward's going to the dance. Go on, ask him. That'll put Dilke
in a fix.'

So the lad did: 'Please, sir, are we going to the dance? This
ward. All of us.'

'Yes I should hope so!' says the Super. 'No reason why not
and that's the least they deserve, eh, Dilke?'

Arthur was pleased to see the frustrated look on Dilke's
face and hear Dilke forced to say, 'No need for them to ask,
sir, that was our intention. They're good boys, sir.'

'Very good, Dilke, I'll look out for them there!'

When the Super had gone Dilke came straight to Arthur's
cot and looked down with hatred in his eyes.

'Was that your clever idea, Arthur?'

Arthur's trouble was that Dilke was the only one in the
hospital who knew he was bright. Dilke didn't like intelligence. It's a threat to order is intelligence. He was always
getting at Arthur and stopping others finding out the truth.
Arthur didn't know that then, but he knew he didn't like
Dilke.

'No,' says Arthur, 'it wasn't my idea but the Skallagrigg's!'

But of course Dilke couldn't understand Arthur's speech,
never could. So the lads who could and who heard had a
laugh though they were careful not to show it.

When the dance night came the lads were got ready specially with nice shirts and that. They liked wearing something
different from pyjamas you see. But Dilke had a card up his
sleeve. He let Arthur be got ready as well so he was all
spruced up and clean as a new pin. Then when the lads were
ready in their wheelchairs and were taken to the dance across
the hospital one by one, he left Arthur till last and went back
especially for him. Arthur was alone in the ward sitting in his
chair, waiting. He was excited to be going to the dance.

Dilke stood at the door and said, 'You're not going, my lad,
because you talk when you shouldn't. You're too clever by
half, but not clever enough.'

And with a cruel laugh Dilke closed the ward door and
turned off the light so Arthur was all alone.

Arthur cried a bit. Then he heard music and he stopped.
From all that way he could hear the sound of the dance. He
knew the lads would miss him but none would dare ask the
Super about him because Dilke would punish them later.

Then he thought, 'At least my pals are there and that's something.'

Then the light went on even though no one opened the door and Arthur saw that the Skallagrigg had come. And he said, 'You're having your own dance, Arthur, specially for you.' And that music swelled into a band, and those distant shouts became people and laughter and pretty girls and orangeade in jugs and cakes for everyone. And the ward had balloons in it and Arthur was helped out of his chair by the Skallagrigg and he was shown dance after dance until he got that tired he said, 'It's time I got off my feet, I can't go on!' And he laughed, and so did the Skallagrigg, because they were together again at last and enjoying themselves at a dance that no one ever knew took place.

That was a long time ago that was, when Arthur wasn't so very much older than you.

That was the end of the story and I asked a question. I asked Jack, 'How old is Arthur now then?'

He said, 'No one knows because sometimes he's old and sometimes he's young. It all depends who tells what story.'

'Are there other stories then?' I asked.

Eric said, 'There's lots, didn't you know that? Lots.'

On the way home Eileen said a strange thing about me to Daddy. I was in the back of the van, but I heard them when we stopped at traffic lights.

'The report won't come through for a bit. But the consultant did say something interesting that makes me think that even if she didn't seem to do well today he is thinking positively. He said, "One good thing is that she's got a sense of humour. The teddy bear incident which made her laugh showed that. If there's one sure way in these cases of severe disability that we can get a clue to intelligence it's through humour. It implies a capacity for cognitive association."'

Daddy said very seriously, 'What was so funny about the teddy bear incident? I don't know what you mean by that.'

He didn't see me grinning in the back of the van.

TEN

Some months after Esther's assessment at the Spastics Society, Richard Marquand at last had the opportunity to move out of the Haven Lane house to something larger. His company, Fountain Systems Limited, which specialized in office equipment systems, had put him in charge of a small venture in systems analysis for clients seeking advice on computer applications.

The job was to be based in Fountain's office in Slough, twenty miles west of London, and because of the travelling he decided to move outside London to nearby High Wycombe which was just a short drive from the Slough office and near the motorway that went straight to Ealing where Esther lived during the week.

It was a move which would also make possible a development of Esther's relationship with her grandparents, Brian and Margaret Ogilvie, who lived only forty miles further west, near Oxford, and from whom she had been estranged except for the diffident and tender visit of Brian Ogilvie on her eighth birthday.

Since then, and despite letters from Richard suggesting that they visit, 'Granddad' had resisted all efforts to develop the contact because, as he explained in a letter to Richard, 'Margaret is not very well and reminders of the past always upset her.'

Richard was now increasingly concerned to find the right home for them in High Wycombe: one that could accommodate Esther on the ground floor since, month by month, she was getting larger and more tiring to handle. The problem was that houses in the High Wycombe area were expensive, especially the detached ones with the right space and a large garden. To raise the money he knew he would need the support of his company. Richard had joined Fountain Systems in 1963 and was under the control of the company's rising star, marketing director Edward Light. The two men had an instinctive trust and understanding and it had been Light's hope that Richard would rise rapidly in marketing, for he quite clearly had an immediate and wide grasp of sales and marketing problems. So far as Richard Marquand had close friends in those days Edward Light was one of them.

After the death of his wife and the birth of Esther, Richard continued to do his job well but Edward Light had seen the change, and so did his colleagues. Subtly, so subtly, Richard Marquand had aged. He could turn on the charm, win the orders, achieve more visits than anyone else but he had no ambition to do more than fill the slot in which he happened to be when Sheila died.

Yet Edward Light continued to believe in Richard and resisted pressures to ease him to one side, the more so because he had been the one person in whom Richard had confided about Esther. He had asked Edward Light not to mention this to any of his colleagues, a request that was honoured, and this shared secret forged a strange bond between the two men.

Once or twice a year Edward Light had an informal lunch with Richard, to keep in touch with the man rather than the executive. Richard enjoyed these lunches and was relaxed at them. Edward invariably asked after Esther and had seen, these last years, a slow softening in Richard's attitude towards her.

So it was that Edward happened to have one of these lunches a few weeks after Esther's eighth birthday, when so much had changed for Richard.

The moment he came into the restaurant Edward could see something was different, better. And Richard did not have to explain what because on the bag he was carrying was printed a familiar logo and the single and telling word: MOTHERCARE.

'Pregnant?' smiled Edward Light.

Richard laughed, a real warm laugh for a change.

'Just shopping,' he said. And he took out, with unaffected pleasure, a pair of blue woollen tights and matching leather shoes. 'For Esther,' he said. 'They need them at the Centre.'

'Do you think she'll like them?'

From that day, Edward Light knew that Richard might begin again to find his true worth in the company. When the job of managing the market research department fell vacant he made sure Richard took it. Then, before Richard Marquand's department even started suggesting that they should be getting into the

computer market. Edward Light had marked him down for the job
of managing the project.

So when the opportunity in Slough arose, and the timing seemed
right, Edward persuaded Richard Marquand to take it.

'What do you know about computers?'

'Enough to know the potential, but not enough to program one.
If we're going to get into systems analysis properly I'm going to
have to go on a few courses.'

'It'll be money well spent. If I'm right, and the trends in America are any indication, then mini- and microcomputers are
where the growth in our kind of markets is going to be. It'll be
all about selling, cost control and systems – and you're the right
man. I'll be sorry to lose you from headquarters but anyway I
suspect the whole lot of us will be out in Slough within a few
years so you'll have a head start in the house market on us poor
suckers.'

Richard began his search for a home to suit Esther's needs as
systematically as ever, writing to all the estate agents in the areas
he was interested in and spelling out his needs.

But it was some months, during which time he started the
subsidiary company in Slough and was commuting daily from
Haven Lane, before he at last found what he was looking for.

Abbey Road was tree-lined and the houses were all substantial
Edwardian or Victorian villas, a little run down, their hedges
overgrown. They stood dark and mysterious, hidden away down
old gravel drives on which were parked expensive cars that had
seen better days.

Richard drove slowly down the road looking out for the house
name, though it was no good hoping Esther would see one – she
could not read, nor it seemed did she wish to try.

The first clue they had was a 'For Sale' sign (not the agent's), its
paint peeling, half blown over by long gone winter gales into the
depths of a laurel hedge. Beneath it, in the shadows, was a wooden
gate, half open and hanging uncomfortably from one remaining
hinge; and on the gate, its black letters faded grey and its white
background mildewed green, was a painted board which read
'Harefield'.

'I'll just have a quick look,' he called to Esther, whom he had no

wish to unstrap and get out, if the whole thing was going to be a
waste of time.

He advanced a little down the curving, gravelled drive, the house
coming into clearer view. A magpie, dark blue and cream white,
flapped suddenly above his head from out of a beech tree, flew
towards the house and was lost beyond the chimneys.

It was a substantial property but it was also old and worn,
tired and waiting as if it had served its time and now, fearing
nothing and with no one having further use for it, it wanted to
die.

There was evidence of vandalism. A downstairs window was
boarded up and an upstairs one broken and open to the elements;
while at one end of the roof house martins seemed to have set up
home, their mess dropping to the window ledges beneath.

Richard shook his head and began to turn away. But then he
paused, the weight of years upon him, and he turned back to look
again as if he was looking not so much at the house as at himself.
He had waited so long for someone to reach out and touch him
again. He felt tired and he heard Esther call, but he ignored her.
The house before him seemed to call more loudly than she did and
he felt his feet firmly rooted on its ground. For a moment he looked
down at the gravel in which tiny shoots of grass and shepherd's
purse grew, and he lost track of himself, of time, and felt for a brief
moment the strangest thing: that this place was solid and secure
and a place for a traveller to stop and rest and feel at last that he
had come . . . home. Home. Richard looked up, shaken by the
thought.

He sighed and turned back. 'Come on, Esther, we're going to
take a look.'

The gate had to be lifted and heaved open to let the wheelchair
through. The house ahead of them came more fully into view as
they passed overgrown brambles and a brick garage covered in old
ivy and with a pile of rotting planks up against one wall.

The downstairs rooms had bay windows, of red brick, lintelled
and faced here and there in a mellow stone. The paint on the
window woodwork, the doors, the old-fashioned cast-iron drain-
pipes and gutters to which ivy clung, even on the woodwork of the
old porch before the door, was all of a faded dark green. The
windows themselves seemed blank and unstaring, and here and

there Richard could see old-style roller blinds half down inside, yellow now and stained.

The prospect of wheeling and levering Esther up the three awkward steps into the porch was too much for him.

'Let's go round the back and see the garden first,' he said.

Pushing her over the gravel path, avoiding the taller weeds, they rounded the side of the house. It seemed surrounded by garden, or hedges, with no sign at all of the adjacent property. A world of its own. There was an old boiler house, a coal bunker, and then a passage through to a wilderness of grass that must once have been a lawn, or lawns, but was now grown waist-high into hay. Beyond an uncut and unruly hedge that formed a wide semicircle at the back of the house he could see the tops of old and well-established fruit trees.

There were rambling brambles in white and pink flower over-grown on to the 'lawn' in front of the hedge and he was about to attempt to push the wheelchair further down in the garden towards the fruit trees when, for the first time that afternoon, Esther seemed interested in something. She reached out her hand.

'What is it, Esther? Do you like the grass?'

She said, 'Nah.'

The garden?

Mmm. Nah. Not that.

The flowers? There were quite a number when Richard came to look beyond the first impression of undergrowth and overgrowth. Some were the remnants of faded spring flowers – daffodil stems with dried petals, coltsfoot leaves, rose bay willowherb, and the clocks of dandelion.

But others were now in full bloom: yellow crucifers of mustard, a riot of purple-blue upright vetch entwining at the wheelchair spokes, and on what seemed a half-buried wall, some way off, and catching the pale spring setting light, two solitary poppies, their petals soft as a kitten's step.

The poppies?

She laughed, nodded and reached out again.

It was then, as Richard struggled to push the chair over the high grass of the old lawn, as they tried to reach the poppies, that from somewhere around them – perhaps in the flowers at their feet, perhaps from the old bereft back windows of the building – the old house and gardens found their voice at last and began to sing a song of home to them which, as if hearing it, the friendly sun itself seemed to make an effort to shine on each plant they saw, each windowsill and handle, each brick and every piece of mortar: to warm it, to make it glow, to make it seem the home they sought.

So that by the time they reached the poppies, and Esther touched their petals with her slowly untangling fingers, her eyes seeming to travel up and down the hairy crooked stems and settle on the drooping heads of other poppies not yet open, that modest hopeful song was heard, and Richard and his daughter were beginning to feel that perhaps they had found a home.

So they turned towards the house, to open the back door and explore inside.

The inside of the house was dry. In only one room upstairs had the roof leaked badly, and in the room with the broken window the damage was slight. True, the plaster was cracked here and there, but the old mouldings in the rooms were secure; the paint dulled to a depressing brown but the woodwork it protected was good and solid and well turned, well matured. And the floor! Downstairs it was oak parquet and at the same level throughout so that, provided they could avoid the detritus of newspapers and broken objects strewn about, Esther's wheelchair ran smooth and swift.

Better yet, the 'extension' was a library judging from the shelves, all wood and warm and light; and the kitchen, old though it was and in need of renovation, was large enough to have a big table of the sort Richard had always wanted; a sitting room, a conservatory, and even before he mounted the stairs to investigate the bedrooms, the house was in song all about him, each room, each corner, a hive of thronging possibilities that made light of the rewiring needed and the lack of central heating and so much more.

Later Richard unstrapped Esther, and took her in his arms in the great library which was to one side of the house, overlooking the side and rear gardens.

'Well, it's a distinct possibility, isn't it?' he said. Her head was soft against his chest.

He walked with her towards the garden side of the room, going to the great windows that went almost to the floor. Sun slanted across him from the other window on the far side of the room, and he could see their reflection in the window he was approaching. He remembered standing like this once before when, at the Dale Centre, for the first time he learnt to talk to her and she told him the word 'Skallagrig'.

'Do you like the house?' he asked softly.

She nodded.

Richard took a deep breath and, still holding her, turned about the great room.

'And this room, would you like it as a bedroom?'

'Yeh,' she whispered.

'Then we'll buy the house,' he said holding her close as if to protect him from the decision he had just made.

That evening Richard phoned Edward Light at home. He told him that he had made an offer for a house at a price that was substantially more than he could afford. The agent would, no doubt, be checking with his bank on Monday morning to make sure that he could go through with the deal.

'What can I do to help?'

'Tell the bank that the company guarantees the loan.'

There was a pause. Edward Light was thinking.

'How long have you been running the new company now, Richard?'

'Three months.'

'Is it going to work?'

'Yes, Edward, it is.'

'All right. I think we can do better than a guarantee. I think we can do a share deal. I think you should indeed have part of the new company and that can be your collateral with the bank.'

Richard thought quickly. A share of the equity was not a free gift, but would be paid for out of his future bonuses and shares in profits. It was Edward's way of giving him motivation, and it carried the risk that if the new company failed to get off the ground he would still be left with a substantial loan to pay back to the company.

Richard said coolly: 'That's fine, but I'm left with the problem of where the purchase price comes from. So set a precedent, Edward; make it a company loan. I'd like to keep the bank out of it.'

Edward laughed. 'Well, actually, that's not a precedent, it's precisely the arrangement I've got myself.'

Richard thought of the old untidy house, and Esther, and himself, and he took a deep breath. There was a pause.

At the other end of the line Edward Light smiled and said, 'It's a deal.'

A bargain, in fact. Harefield, bought on the eve of escalating property price rises in the London counties, became the foundation on which Richard Marquand was able to build a fortune.

ELEVEN

The purchase of Harefield went through quickly and Richard's plans for it were systematic and thorough. Within a few weeks the conversion of the library into a simple suite for Esther, and the opening up of the kitchen area into one big practical room, had begun. The interior was now a mess of builders' things, and the gravelled front drive the temporary home of a skip, two pallets of breeze blocks, a cement mixer, and the dusty tip of two ceilings and three walls that had been demolished in the kitchen.

The gardens stretched raggedly about them, overgrown from years of neglect, and they were for the most part still unexplored and mysterious. At this very moment, somewhere in their jungle depths, a herd of elephants trumpeted and moved unseen – and Esther laughed, for she knew that Tom, who had come with them for the day to visit the house for the first time, was out there somewhere playing games.

Behind an old red brick wall to one side of the house, on which those poppies that had first attracted Esther had been growing, lay a walled vegetable garden. The particulars to the house referred to this merely as a 'vegetable garden' which understated not only its dimensions (nearly an acre) but also its magic. Among the grass and undergrowth, the old patterns of planting could be seen – a cluster of enormous rhubarb, the tall spikes of several rows of onions, and cabbages and brussels sprouts, their plants long gone to seed and now bold and enormous and unreachable through the rising and prickly walls of raspberry canes.

To one side of this great abandoned square were the red-bricked and roof-tiled outbuildings, their doors staggering and ajar, their depths full of old gardening tools and supplies – rotted hessian bags, a rusting spade entwined with white bryony that had climbed through an open window and colonized the sunny side of a shed interior; an old and massive watering-can, its copper funnel pitted with holes; and greenhouses, turning green with lichen and ivy, and sundry other sheds (where the herd of elephants seemed now to have reached, judging from the rattlings and mulching silences that came to Richard and Esther, sitting on a blanket in the long grass with a picnic ready and waiting). But there was more, far more.

The sides of the Harefield property were bounded by shrubs and hedges even higher than those demarcating the main lawn, and though the houses either side were homes like his own, so far away did they seem, and so spacious was the feeling the summer greenery gave, that they might have been living alone on an island; though sometimes there came the sound of a distant dog barking, the soft rasp of a saw, the purr and crunch of a car on gravel, and the calling of children's voices.

Tom had grown rapidly in the three years since Esther's eighth birthday and, though smaller than average for fourteen, he seemed enormous by comparison with Esther, and a worthy guardian, protector and, yes, slave, against the savage world beyond her wheelchair.

The truth about Esther was that none of the assessments, the speech therapists, the experts at the Centre gave much hope for her future development. The key factor was Esther herself and it seemed evident that if there had been a real intelligence she would already have revealed it, however mutely. Eileen Coppock was more hopeful than some, saying that sometimes children in Esther's position blocked off their wish to communicate as an angry protest about what they were. Perhaps something would help her break out and start making an effort . . .

From the Marquand Collection: Disk 4, File 'MARQ12', page 2, starting line 1

Tom and I explored the garden and never found its end. There were red-brick walls with yellow ragwort and valerian growing on them and so many flowers whose names I later learnt. Daddy got a flower book and I so wanted to turn its pages. It was thrilling to see living plants that had their pictures in a book as if, somehow, the evidence of the picture made the living plants more real.

Later we went through the orchard and Tom said suddenly, 'I want to climb the tree. I want you to come.'

I said I would watch him, but he dropped his head and shook it. 'No, you too.' He had never climbed a tree before and didn't dare go alone.

I said I wanted him to climb it, **for** me. But he said no.

He said, 'Can't you never climb?'

I said no never.

I remember Tom sat on the grass and was sad. I wanted to put my arms round him like he did me and Daddy. Tom was thinking about my handicap.

Looking back I remember 'conversations' as if we had spoken to each other, but of course I mainly signed, being able to say only a very few words then. So for 'said' read 'signed' where I'm concerned. I was lucky in Tom: he was slow and had patience, and often instinctively understood what I needed or was getting at much faster than so-called quicker people ...

'You know I can't climb or walk,' I said. He was silent and didn't look at me. 'Tom, you **know**.'

He looked up at me and up at the tree and then he said, **'Never?'** He was upset and I had never seen him like that.

It was a lovely warm afternoon and I was quite happy. I waited for him to come out of it.

Then Tom was suddenly afraid and I understood he was thinking about tomorrow and the next day, understanding I wouldn't climb with him then.

'What's wrong, Tom?' I asked.

'I'm scaredy, Amh,' he said. He called me Amh.

'What of?' I said.

'Of never,' he said, his head bent low and his fingers running miserably across the spokes of my wheelchair.

Looking over his head I saw the wooden fence at the end of the orchard and I had an idea.

'Maybe I'll walk one day,' I said.

'When?' he said.

'When I get to the Skallagrigg ...' and as I said that all the fear about the future in him came on me and I really was scared.

'Tom, I'm going to tell you a story. So you'll know not to be scared, not ever.' He looked up at me, his mouth open, and his eyes wide.

'Yes, Amh?'

'See that fence?' I began. He stood up and looked at the fence. Then, for the first time, I told someone else the story of how the Skallagrigg was beyond the wooden fence, and if you could find out how to get to him he would help you to stand up and walk.

Tom listened in silence.

'Sk . . . Sk . . . will help,' he said. 'You?'

I nodded.

'Me?' he said, and he thumped his chest.

'You can walk,' I said.

Ha ha ha. He laughed.

'Help you now?' he asked.

Then I explained not now, not yet. Things weren't ready yet. We'd have to learn about the Skallagrigg first . . . but I lost him then. He didn't understand, except it wasn't going to be now. Then he pushed my chair near the fence and he stood on tiptoe to try to look over and through it. It was made up of slats of wood, cut to a point at the top, but with ivy and things on it. Here and there it had fallen in but Tom didn't think to go to those bits. He chose the highest, strongest-looking bit to look over. I think he understood that the fence was an idea, so he chose the strongest part.

'Skalg!' he shouted. He never did learn to say the word properly. Then he waited, but there was no reply, only the high rustling of the dark copper beeches above and beyond us. And parting the creeper he peered through the fence and waited there for a long time, as if he thought the Skallagrigg would come.

The building works on Harefield were finally completed in October 1976 at the same time that the Haven Lane house was sold, and Richard was able to move in.

The strict budgeting that Richard's lack of funds had forced on him meant that no decoration was done upstairs, except for the necessary central heating installation and rewiring. When guests came they were shown the ground floor with the beautiful parquet flooring which extended right through to the kitchen and was the perfect surface for Esther's electric wheelchair which she was now able to use, if a little jerkily. The control was a simple joystick, stiff enough to respond only to her clear and more positive hand movements, and the chair was set on the lower speed, for her reactions were too slow for her to cope with the 'faster' option.

Richard and Eileen had both been concerned at the silence into which Esther seemed to have fallen since late summer. Reports from the Centre school were not encouraging: she was less cooperative than before, and less willing to try the simplest things. Her attention seemed to wander, and she did not want to do anything for anybody.

It was clear that something in her had changed and Eileen fell back on the simplest and most obvious explanation, and perhaps the correct one: Esther was growing physically self-conscious, sudden pallors of the skin, a loss of baby-ness about her cheeks, and even . . . a red spot!

'But she's only a girl,' said Richard. 'She's only eleven.'

Eileen Coppock laughed at his shock.

'It'll come, Richard, in time it will come. Probably later than most but she will grow up. This is just the beginning.'

This only increased Richard's longing for some sign from Esther that she had a mind, could deduce, and was intelligent. Without that, much as he loved her, he feared there would be nothing in the future but endless rounds of taking care, of warding off others' sympathy, of pretending that little achievements were more than they were, and coping with womanhood for a girl who, it seemed to him, could never be a woman.

As autumn deepened and the weather got wetter and colder, it became harder to keep Esther occupied. She seemed bored with his attempts to interest her in reading or simple play. Sometimes nothing pleased her except sitting in front of the television to watch programme after programme, little of which, presumably, she could understand. She watched with equal interest comedies, talk shows, news and Open University programmes on Saturday morning. Sometimes Richard turned them off halfway through to see if she protested, to indicate to him that she was understanding what she saw; but she never did. There was something profoundly distressing about the sight of his daughter, slumped in her wheelchair, her legs sometimes moving involuntarily, her hands at strange angles, her eyes staring, her mouth open and often dribbling, staring at the rubbish on the television.

The neighbourhood in which they now found themselves was quiet, middle class and professional and without the character of Haven Lane. People were polite, but a little distant. On one side was an elderly couple living in a house far too big for them; on the other, the home from which children's voices sometimes came, lived an architect. The children were apparently his visiting grandchildren.

So it was that, having got into conversation with a mother and her five-year-old daughter at the end of Abbey Road on the way back from some local shopping with Esther, and finding she lived in one of the newer houses on the main road and that she was divorced, he invited her and her daughter Lizzie for tea the following weekend. A prospect that neither girl, staring at each other without expression, seemed happy at.

This was not simple neighbourliness, and nor was it the result of a sudden urge in Richard to find a mate. The fact seems to have been that it was his birthday and as no one knew except for Eileen and the two children (so far as they understood) and his mother, Richard did not intend to celebrate it.

Yet no one feels nothing on their birthday, so he had issued the invitation to young Lizzie and her mother.

On the day itself, Richard received two cards through the post – from his mother and from Eileen – and one from each of the children. Tom had come for the weekend and brought Esther's and his own card with him. They had been made, under supervision (Nasim's probably), at the Centre, one saying 'Happy Birthday Daddy' and then signed with a random squiggle (Esther's 'signature') and the other reading 'Happy Birthday from Tom and all at Dale Centre' with signatures of Tom, Nasim and many others.

Tom presented this to Richard at breakfast, along with a present from Esther – a telephone book for the kitchen – and one from Tom – a picture cut from a tomato packet and crookedly mounted. Richard no longer consigned such gifts to drawers and, giving Tom a hug, he stuck this one on the sideboard. And that, or so it seemed and Richard thought, was the extent of his thirty-sixth birthday.

Esther's 'guest' arrived with her mother promptly at a quarter to four, clutching a present for Esther.

It was a colour-and-shape game in which the letters A to Z, the numbers one to nine, and some basic shapes like a star, a square and an oval in different-coloured plastic were to be put in their matching holes on the board. It was clear that Lizzie had been rehearsed before she came and with suspicious politeness that did not hide her fascinated dread of Esther, she placed the toy on the tray attached to Esther's wheelchair.

Esther, after a period of sulks in the morning, started out in a good mood and did her best to pick up one of the pieces. But Lizzie's mother had overestimated Esther's physical abilities and all she did was to knock three of them on the ground.

Tom patiently picked them up and put them back in front of her to let her have another go. But try as Esther did they scattered to the floor again, to Lizzie's evident disgust.

'That's wrong,' said Lizzie finally, '*I'll* show you.'

While the two adults talked over a cup of tea, Tom and Esther watched as Lizzie, who was pretty and blonde, furrowed her brow and bent over the board, carefully trying to fit the pieces, warding off Tom's good-natured attempt to help her with a firm, 'No, not you.'

She was painfully slow, trying each piece in the wrong hole before arriving at the right one.

Esther stared.

It was when the girl attempted to place the four in the hole cut for the seven that Esther seemed suddenly to lose patience.

'Nah,' she said suddenly. 'Nah.'

'I want to,' said the girl.

'*Nah.*' Esther was upset. She attempted to raise one arm to the board that Lizzie was so laboriously working over and to push it off her tray, but long before the message reached her arm and it began its malevolent intent the girl very firmly put her hands on the board. Esther could not move it.

'Nah,' screamed Esther, her mouth turning down and her head and eyes averted.

'Now, Lizzie, leave it alone. Let Esther play with it. You've given it to her.'

'Esther can't do it,' said Lizzie, 'but I can. Look!'

She picked up the board and showed her mother as Esther vainly tried to control the heaves and sobs that were racking her body.

'Esther . . .' began Richard warningly.

'Lizzie, be nice please,' said her mother.

Lizzie pouted and looked smug, rose to her feet, pulled the two sides of her party frock out, and performed a balletic step or two around the kitchen floor.

'La, la, la, la,' she sang innocently.

Tom got up and tried to get Esther to play the board game again but she pushed the board on to the floor and stared a terrible heaving stare at Lizzie.

Realizing that the two were not going to get on Richard got up, opened the patio doors, draped a pullover across Esther's shoulders and pushed her out into the garden with Tom, to separate her from the girl for a short while.

'Calm down, Esther, for goodness' sake,' he said quietly to her. 'I'll make some more tea and you can come back and have some, politely I hope.'

'Walk and explore!' said Tom.

'Not too far,' said Richard. 'I'm making some more tea. Five minutes at the most!'

He closed the doors as it was cold, and Lizzie, good as gold now that she had got rid of Esther, sat neatly on the floor and tried to draw on some paper her mother had brought, her neat blonde head the very model of ingenuous spitefulness.

Then she said, 'I'll tidy up I will,' and very deliberately began to pick up the scattered letters and numbers of the game, sneaking an occasional look outside to see if she could see the others. But they had disappeared.

A few minutes later Richard opened the patio doors and called the children back. There was no sign of them. Responding with that special sense most parents have if their children are in danger, he went out into the garden and called them more urgently.

Esther's wheelchair had gone from the lawn, and Tom was gone too. As Richard headed across the lawn for the orchard Tom came running out from among the wilderness of brambles at the bottom of the garden looking as if he hoped the eyes of the world would be anywhere but on himself at that moment.

'Where's Esther, Tom?' asked Richard, trying to sound calm.

Tom stared at him. He was frightened.

'Ahm's with Skalg!' he said, to Richard's puzzlement.

Then a scream swamped everything else and Richard ran past Tom through the orchard into the terrible sound of his daughter's pain. As he ran on, while behind him Tom put his hands to his ears and turned away, he saw Esther, beyond the fruit trees, beyond the thick grass, among the withered remnants of the virginia creeper, hanging by her two thin wrists from the highest part of the wooden fence. Her wheelchair stood upright nearby, the straps loose and flapping in the wind.

Her wrists were caught between the uprights of the fence leaving her feet swinging loose and clear of the ground. Her face was hard against the fence and the moment she heard Richard's cry of 'Esther!' – a mixture of alarm, surprise, and anger – her cries gave way to gasping whimpers. One of her legs was bleeding and her dress had ridden up, caught on the brambles.

She hung helpless and hurt, her legs thin and bent against the strong uprights of that part of the fence. Her head fell back so she could see him coming, her mouth was open in a scream of pain and distress that rose up into the copper beech heights of the world beyond the fence.

As Richard lifted her off and took her into his arms he shouted savagely, 'Tom! *Tom!*' but no Tom came. Only a shout from Lizzie's mother, 'Is everything all right?' at which Richard, sensing that it was better that Esther was not fussed, called out, 'It's all right, it's OK. It's nothing much, just a little tumble.'

Esther was heaving and gasping for breath but not crying now. One of her wrists was raw where the fence had cut into it.

'What was Tom doing?' asked Richard. 'What . . .'

'Me,' said Esther, trying to convey with a look and her tone that she wanted the blame. 'Me!'

She began now to cry, terribly, safe in his arms, her body battered and bruised.

'Tom made you?' said Richard. She cried, her whole body shuddering with grief.

Behind them, where the lawn became the orchard, Lizzie and her mother stood staring. Lizzie was white-faced and subdued. Richard, protective of Esther and angry at their staring, became suddenly very calm and controlled.

'You had better leave me alone with her for a while,' he said in a voice that made them leave at once.

'Why did Tom do it?' said Richard, the control in his voice belying the anger he felt at Tom, and the dark tidal wave of a deeper rage whose source was the great seas of guilt and self-pity, frustration and hurt at Esther and all she was, and would ever be.

In his arms Esther struggled to find words to answer, but none could ever come.

'Toh,' she said, and her voice cracked into terrible cries of anguish. But Richard misunderstood them, for they were cries not at Tom but for herself, that she could not explain. She could not speak. Richard believed she was saying it was Tom's doing and that her tears were tears of betrayal.

At this moment of terrible misunderstanding Tom chose to reappear, coming quietly up to them and staring at Richard trustingly though a little ashamed and afraid.

Richard turned on him savagely and, had Esther not been in his arms, might easily have hit him.

'Never leave her again, Tom, do you hear? Never ever ever leave her or let her get hurt. You should protect her and not run away, you should look after her, you must never ever do that again as long as you live.' His voice was thunderous, and Tom turned white before it, for how could he understand that Richard's anger, finally, was with himself and his violent shouting the only violence he could express about the horror that he felt the fact of Esther made his life?

'You should protect her. Never leave her again. You should look after her.'

From that day on Tom always protected her, always looked after her. Tom took on a responsibility which would become his strength and his purpose. Tom gained a role in the face of Richard's despair.

'Sorry,' said Tom putting out his arms to them. 'Sorry Amh.' And before his love Richard's anger turned to sobs and the three of them clung as one in the shadows of the wooden fence.

From the Marquand Collection: Disk 4, File 'M A R Q 12', page 30, starting line 18

I can't remember that girl's name now but she was spoilt and had prissy little eyes and she was so pretty that I wished I'd been able to spit at her. Of course I couldn't. She was also stupid.

She gave me a game – it was a moulded plastic board with alphanumeric impressions on it, letters and numbers you put into the right holes – and she wanted to show she could do it. It wasn't very difficult. You put the square in the square and the circle in the circle, the 'A' in the A, the 'B' in the B, the 'C' in the . . . it was so boring!

I had given up trying things like that but I was insulted that that girl could do something so simple and get praise when, if I had been physically able, I could have done it faster than she could. It was a good example of how being disabled makes people think you're stupid as well.

It was when she came to trying to put the numbers in the holes that I got really upset. I like numbers. They have a special feel to me and beauty and order of their own. If someone says two and two makes five I feel uncomfortable. It just isn't **right**.

I suddenly got very upset, very frustrated, and I began to show it and Daddy put me outside with Tom and that was unfair because it meant that she had Daddy to herself and I wasn't allowed there until tea was made. But it wasn't just jealousy.

Tom could see I was upset and asked why.

'He doesn't know I'm Amh,' I said. Then I began to cry.

Poor Tom, he hated me crying. It was torture to him.

He said, 'Skalg will tell Daddy.' Then before I realized what he was doing he pushed my chair to the wooden fence, ran forward, peered through it, shouted 'Skalg! Skalg!', unstrapped me and hauled me out of the chair and pushed me up the fence.

'No, Tom, no.' It was cold and the brambles hurt my legs and my dress was getting green lichen on it from the fence. **'No!'**

But sometimes Tom wouldn't listen, even to me. He thinks he knows best.

'Skalg! Skalg!' he shouted and then he pushed me higher up the fence as if he thought me looking over would help. But I was too heavy to hold and my arms shot forward, my wrists caught between the slats and I slipped out of his grasp and then I was hanging there and hurting and cold. He couldn't free me.

Then Tom started to cry and ran away to hide. He felt he had done wrong and would be punished. When Tom was young his parents often punished him. They hit him. Eileen told me that once.

Yet when I began to scream in pain I made Tom understand: 'Dada.'

DADDY. GET DADDY, TOM. GO AND GET HIM.

That was one of many things he did for me when my life, and yours too Daniel, depended on it. That time he braved Daddy's anger and went out to find him. Poor Tom: he must have felt so frightened of the consequences.

Once Lizzie and her mother had gone, Tom and Esther calmed down and watched television. It was late afternoon and Richard, who was converting one of the bedrooms into an office for himself, had some shelves to put up.

But the children did not watch for long. Esther lost interest, her head slumping sideways as her hands jerked and fidgeted and she stared vacantly around the sitting room; while Tom sat on the floor by her chair intermittently watching television and playing with three model trucks he had.

Esther suddenly jerked to life.

'Toh!'

Tom looked up at her. She wanted him to do something. She was pointing with her hand over the far side of the room. Book? Shoe? Telephone? Game? He went through the list and she nodded at game.

He got the letter game. He opened it upside down. All the pieces fell over her tray and on to the floor. Sometimes she hated his clumsiness.

'Do it,' she said.

Tom shook his head, put his chin into his chest and returned to his trucks.

TOM!

She did not speak his name as clearly as that, but so sure was the authority in her voice that he got up immediately and stood dutifully at her chair looking at her.

DO IT.

He stared, pig-eyed and hesitant before the granite rock of her purpose.

PICK UP THE PIECES, TOM. PUT THEM ON MY TRAY. START.

Tom scurried around, laboriously gathered together the pieces and the board, his big thick fingers at sixes and sevens with the different colours and shapes.

A square was a square and went in the square.

A small circle was a small circle and didn't go in the big circle.

PUT IT IN THE SMALL CIRCLE.

He did so.

The 2 was like the Z but that was wrong.

PUT IT IN THE 2.

'NAH!'

THE 2.

The star was a star and he liked it and held it up.

PUT IT IN THE STAR SHAPE, TOM.

Reluctantly he stopped playing with it and put it in the star shape.

Richard came in, stared at them, said he was getting supper, said he was glad Tom was helping Esther with the game and began to leave.

'Me!' said Esther trying to tell him she was doing the game. Tom was doing what she said. It was *she* who was doing it. But Richard was preoccupied with chores and did not hear the entreaty in her voice or understand that she was showing Tom what to do. Instead he watched them for a brief moment at their curious chatter which was a world of its own, saw that Esther was still upset, and went out to the kitchen.

PUT THE 3 IN THE 3. THE RIGHT WAY ROUND.

Tom did so.

Then he picked up the 6 and tried it at the 9.

IT'S DIFFERENT, THEY'VE MADE IT DIFFERENT. TURN IT THE OTHER WAY UP. NOW PUT IT IN THE 6.

Slowly he was getting there.

The troublesome 4, the last few letters and eventually they reached the end, both completely tired. Tom took the board into the kitchen, carrying it carefully as if his life depended on it. He presented it to Richard.

Esther could hear them: 'Well done, Tom! You and Esther did it did you? Well done Esther . . .' his voice came through to her, pleasant, dutiful, non-comprehending. He really thought Tom had done it. He did not understand.

Alone, the grey light of the television flickering and shining blindly on her chair, Esther's head slumped down. 'Dada . . . me,' she whispered, unheard. She wanted to be there, she wanted him to know it was her.

'Supper won't be long,' called Richard from the kitchen as Tom came back, looking sheepish.

Immobile, mute, weak, Esther stared at him. He put his hands out to hug her, to say sorry for taking the credit. She turned her head from it and the face was grey in the flickering light of the television. Tom slunk back to his toys. But her mouth kept moving, whispering, 'Me, me, me, me.'

ME. TOM.

Tom jerked to life at the sudden force of her command. He came and stood by her sensing an energy and purpose in her that he had never experienced before.

GET THAT PENCIL.

By distorted slurred words and struggling gestures she told him, and the message was directly understood, the order behind it instantly obeyed.

'Yes, Amh,' said Tom, terrified of her.

It was in a box with the other toys and some paper they had been drawing on, or rather paper on which Esther's hand, forcibly wrapped around a crayon by Tom, had been dragged, to make Daddy a birthday picture.

'That's nice, Esther,' he had said, but these days she was beginning to recognize the sadness in him at the lie implicit in the things she 'made'. For they both understood that she could not really be said to have made them. Not really, not with her own mobile hands. They both understood that she would never make them.

GET THE PAPER.

Tom got it.

BRING THE BOARD GAME BACK HERE.

Tom almost ran to get it. The urgency in Esther's voice that drove him on came from her knowledge that supper would soon be ready and then the chance she wanted to take would be gone.

PUT THE PAPER ON MY TRAY. GET THE LETTER D. NO NOT THE B THE D. DRAW ROUND IT THERE. NO THERE. THAT WAY UP.

'Esther, Tom, supper in two minutes!' Richard's voice called out but Esther put it out of their minds . . .

QUICKLY, TOM.

He pored over the paper with a pathetic and desperate concentration using the letters as stencils to Esther's command. Hesitant, unmanageable, clumsy, wilful, the struggling pencil held in his right hand crept around letter after letter held in his left. The colour changed twice because Tom broke the points. The paper was crumpled and torn beneath his elbows and over the edge of the tray.

NOW A NUMBER, TOM. THE THREE.

In despairing bondage Tom started on the three.

GOOD. ONE MORE. YOU CAN DO IT, TOM.

'Come on you two, tea-time.' Footsteps approaching.

RIGHT ROUND THE SIX NOW TOM. YES YES. NOW . . . HIDE IT
TOM. DON'T LET HIM SEE. DADDY MUSTN'T SEE YET.

Tom was capable of simple cunning. He let the paper fall on the
floor, as if it was just another drawing.

Richard came in and pushed Esther through to the kitchen,
unaware of the paper on the floor. Tom followed terrified that he
would give it all away, though quite what the secret was he did
not know. But Esther was doing something important, something
very important, and he was there to help her all he could. It was
part of protecting her, part of never leaving her.

Towards the end of the meal Richard said, 'I've got a surprise. I
got a nice cake, just a little one, to end my birthday with. For you
two really.' Then he added in the hope that it might cheer everyone
up – the children seemed so subdued, 'I can probably find candles
as well.'

The cake was put on the table, the few cards Richard had
assembled around it, the few candles he had left from Esther's last
birthday stuck in it and – 'Where's the matches?' Not where they
should be, that's where!

It was then, as Richard searched the drawers at the far end of
the kitchen, that Esther decided to act.

GET THE PAPER, TOM.

'But, Amh . . .' Tom had been taught never to get down from
the table until he had permission of an adult.

GET IT.

Tom got down from the table and went out to get it and then
returned as quietly as he could. The paper was in his hand, Richard
still foraging through a drawer.

PUT IT ON THE TABLE. BY DADDY'S PLACE IN FRONT OF THE
CARDS. YES. THERE.

'Found them!' said Richard.

Esther's face was white with tension. Her perception of herself in
the world had changed already that day but now she waited to see
if her father's perception of her would change as well. She wanted
him to understand that she had a brain. She wanted to begin
standing up at last.

The paper was glaringly obtrusive on the table, but Richard did not immediately see it.

'Here we are! I'll light the candles and then Esther can decide whether she wants them blown out or not.' Ever since Esther's eighth birthday it had become a family habit, shared by Tom, that Esther chose when the candles were blown out. It gave her great pleasure. Richard leant back and turned off the room lights and the room fell dark.

Outside, at the patio doors, the November wind fretted. There was a rattle of matches as Richard said, 'I've stuck the candles in so we can cut at least half the cake without disturbing them . . .' A match flared in his hands, and one by one the candles were lit, increasing the strength of the flickering golden light they cast on the cake, over the table, on their three faces, on Esther's entangled tense fingers, dimly on the walls behind and powerfully, as if that was the candles' sole purpose and intent, on the crumpled and battered piece of drawing paper which Esther had planned and over which Tom had been forced to slave. It lay in front of the four birthday cards.

Esther willed her father to see it, and to understand.

Knife in hand Richard smiled and said, 'Well, Esther, shall we blow them *all* out!' in a voice that knew perfectly well she would not agree to even the smallest being blown out yet.

'Nah,' she whispered.

'Well then I suppose . . .' As he leaned forward to cut the cake his eyes fell on the paper and read the brief message on it. His hands stilled and the smile in his eyes faded to surprise. Tom stared silent and terrified. Esther waited.

'I . . .' began Richard, his hand leaving the knife half in the cake as he reached towards the paper.

'What?' he said softly as he finally picked it up. 'What . . . is . . . this?' He simply stared.

'You, Esther?' he said at last. 'You?'

'Yeh,' she whispered. 'Me.'

Stencilled on the paper, untidily in different colours, was a simple statement of truth: 'DADDY 36' it read.

DADDY 36.

The candlelight flickered across Richard's face as he read it and reread it, and layer on layer of understanding came through to him, first that the paper was put there while his back was turned, then that Tom must have put it there, then that Tom could not possibly have thought to write it himself, then that there was only one person in the world to whom he was Daddy, then, layer on layer, he understood that Esther could spell, that Esther knew his age and could make sense of numbers, that it was his Esther and not Tom who had done the alpha-numeric game that Tom brought into the kitchen, that Esther was upset earlier because he had not realized she could do it better than that silly girl: Esther was reaching out to him with her mind and in her own way, of her own accord, clearly and categorically, wishing him a happy birthday; Esther could think and make things clear. His Esther had a brain.

As he looked around to her Tom whispered, 'Amh did it, Amh made me do it. Amh can spell.'

'Can you, Esther?' said Richard softly. The candlelight caught her hair, and glowed in her eyes as she nodded briefly and said, 'Yeh!'

'And numbers?'

'Oo yeh!' she said, her eyes never leaving his.

'Is it a birthday card?' asked Richard.

'Yes,' she said with a triumphant smile.

But it was more, far more; it was the first real thing that Esther had ever created which was as she wanted it to be. For it was not the characters on the paper that mattered but what they meant, the many many things they implied. And Daddy understood what she meant.

'Oh, Esther,' said Richard, and he got out of his chair and bent down to her, his cheek to hers and a relief flooding into him so great that in a moment he would start crying and laughing at once, as Esther slowly raised her arms, the spoon still attached to her right hand, and did her best to hug her father back.

TWELVE

Esther's breakthrough into literacy in the winter of 1976 was accompanied by an acceleration of those physical and emotional changes in her that had already alarmed Richard Marquand, and which now began to cause problems for Eileen Coppock and the other staff at the Centre.

The roundness in her face had already gone, but now her hair, auburn until then, seemed somehow to grow darker. The smile was still there but it was no longer simple, nor always polite, and it could change now into coldness and impatience.

She had been growing steadily heavier and, though never overweight, her helpers had to make sure they were positioned correctly to lift her, and needed help sometimes from a second person in the more awkward moves in and out of minibuses and cars.

Her voice was strange and distant, as if calling from a place it did not wish to be. It distorted the vowels and consonants of the few words she could manage, as a fairground hall of strange mirrors distorts a face and makes it seem at once funny and a little frightening. Her 'O's were long, the 'S's sibilant, the 'f's frothy, and the timbre of the whole was inclined to make unfamiliar listeners strain and smile awkwardly, and look away.

It was about then, at the turn of 1976 and 1977, that the seeds of a deep anger about her disability were sown in her, an anger that was exacerbated by her natural intelligence and which robbed her of the innocence that put a magic circle about Tom. An anger fuelled by a sudden growth of self-consciousness, and the discovery in the world at large that appearance mattered, despite what everyone said.

It was then – though this was unknown to the Centre staff or to Richard – that her relationship with Peter Rowne, who had first told her of the Skallagrigg years before, deepened. For she alone knew he was even brighter than she was, far brighter, and that she could learn from him things she would let no one else teach her, about herself and what she was. For Peter was the most severely handicapped person at the Centre with no motor control in any of his limbs and unable to help himself at all.

But instinctively she saw the strength of his mind, and in all her life he was one of only two people with whom she could share the arcane and abstract processes of thought sustained by her love of numbers and (later) algebraic logic. A love that took her, as it might have taken Peter had he had the chance, out of a body that was a prison to a world of intellectual elegance and delight.

Eileen Coppock knew that Esther was intelligent, and suspected that Peter might be too, but what could she do? The Centre did not have the staff or budget to provide the special education such children needed. So they had to be lumped in with the Karens and the Toms and left to struggle, slowly to discover that kindness and functional help is all most of them can hope for, unless they make sufficient fuss for the world to listen and act.

And this, ironically enough, is precisely what Esther's distressing, awkward, disruptive and bloody-minded behaviour at the Centre now did. For though the wheels of the multidisciplinary team turned slowly, the more slowly in Esther's case because of the generally negative report she had had from the Spastics Society, turn they did at last and won for her the acquisition at the Centre of its first typewriter for the disabled.

From the day Esther first put her fingers to it and learned to cope with its simple controls, she felt she had been given a weapon as wondrous and powerful as Excalibur; though she did not then suspect that of all the battles she would fight with it the most important would be on behalf of a man, by then quite old, as disadvantaged as she was, whose calls and cries she had unknowingly heard already, as whispers on a breeze that came from far beyond a wooden fence and spoke the strange name 'Skallagrigg'.

The typewriter was a Patient-Operated Selector Mechanism – happily abbreviated to 'Possum' for its Latin meaning, 'I am able'. It was set up in a corner of the day-room watched by an excited group of youngsters in wheelchairs, and some curious older folk who did occupational therapy in that room. It consisted of an electric typewriter, sturdy and black, with a big white light board above it, divided into squares by black lines, each one marked with a number or a letter of the alphabet, plus a few basic typewriting functions – space, back space, tab, carriage return. In addition, there were sets of controls on a long lead which were put on the tray or at the feet of the operator whose wheelchair was brought up to the Possum.

'It's operated pneumatically,' said Mr Schott, the man who came to set it up. 'That means by air. Some people suck and blow because they have no dexterity, but in your case you can operate it with one of your fingers, and you'll get better and better at it. You position the cursor on the light board first horizontally and then vertically, to get the right square. Then you can press a key to print that letter.'

But Esther was barely listening, for already the cursor was on its way to square 2,3 and the 'S' . . . and then the 'T' on square 2,1. E–S–T . . . Esther paused and tried to relax before taking the light in the grid to 2,4 and 'H'. Then 'E' again and finally along to column 3 and all the way up to row 4 for the 'R' to spell her whole name. E–S–T–H–E–R.

Esther waited.

'Let's see how it looks then,' said Mr Schott.

He leaned over the typewriter and took the paper out of the carriage. He held it up and most of the watchers leaned forward to see the name printed, in capitals, on the right side of the paper: ESTHER.

The world seemed silent about her as she stared at her name, printed for the first time in her life by herself. And a look of purpose stole into her eyes, purpose and intense excitement.

'Do another one before I show you other controls on the machine,' said Mr Schott.

'Do Tom,' said Tom.

'Me!' said Karen.

Others shouted too.

Esther seemed paralysed by the demands on her to write another name.

'She can't do you all,' said Eileen Coppock, laughing above the noise.

Esther turned her wheelchair to look at everybody, her face excited and triumphant. For once she was the centre of something positive, something happy . . . and yet as she looked around the day-room her eyes became serious. Through the hubbub and pushing she saw Peter, immobile though ever-moving, staring at her, trying to speak, trying to be heard as well.

Then giving that up he began to jerk his eyes, one of the few controls he had, left left and then right right right right right . . . five times . . . and alone of all of them there Esther knew he was speaking numbers. He was sending her code. The Possum code. He was saying square 2,5.

Even before she turned to look she knew what letter it was and of whose name it represented the first letter.

'P' for Peter.

Then she started to move the light to his command: 2,5 for 'P', square 1,2 for 'E', the letters printing out each time. As she did so Peter moved his eyes behind her, racing ahead of her, coding the squares: left left, right for 'T', then right right, left for 'E' again and finally left left left left, right right for 'R', unseen by anyone, not even now by Esther for she knew that that was what he was doing and what he meant. Until at last the name was typed.

A pause while Mr Schott tore it from the typewriter roll, and read aloud what Esther had typed: 'PETER'.

Then he looked about him in a kindly way and said, 'Which one of you lads is Peter?' And Peter jerked and pulled and fretted in the cage that was his body, pale and thin and weak, and his mouth spasmed and his teeth clicked as, in his own lost way, he attempted words that were unrecognized except by Esther.

Peter was trying to say, 'Me, it's me.' And Esther was looking at him and jerking her hand right right right right, left left left left for Y, and then Peter was eye signalling right, left left for E and both of them signalled together right right, left left left for the S.

Y–E–S.

Yes, it's your name, Peter.

Yes, Esther, it's me. We've found a new way of coding, don't you see, it's a way we can develop you and I and we don't need to make a sound so long as we have sight of each other, though we could use sound if we wanted. Oh, Esther, can you see?

Yes, Peter.

We're going to be able to talk more now, and work things out and develop our own talking further. It's so obvious. A grid system! I should have thought of it before. Do you understand Esther? If we just memorize the grid . . .

Yes, Peter.

'*This* is Peter,' said Tom.

And Mr Schott looked at the pale and intense eyes of the boy, a spastic of fourteen but with a face that looked older, pale and racked, and he held up the piece of paper.

'Hello, Peter, Esther's spelled your name.'

Peter tried to speak, but couldn't. His feet pressed and tangled at each other, his arms jerked. 'No, I spelt it,' he failed to say.

Tom took his name for him, and poked it between Peter's strap and pullover. He knew Peter would want to keep it. It was his name and no one else's.

The Possum opened up a new language for Esther and Peter and made it possible for them to talk when talk might otherwise have been impossible – like across the dining-room in the Centre.

They did not bother with the Y–E–S in Possum code, it was too cumbersome for their purposes. But they used it to shortcut their tree method of asking questions, and borrowed from it the idea, which Esther was later to perfect with a computer, of encoding complex notions into a simple form, of which the final triumph would be the game 'Skallagrigg'.

THIRTEEN

One of Esther's discoveries with the Possum was that she could write letters to her father. The very first Richard received, undated, but probably written when she was eleven, illustrates some essential points of her style and the nature of her ability. Here it is, exactly as written and sent:

> Der Daddy,
>
> Im writing this on teh Possum machine in the Centre. I am loking forward to the weeked. Tom has a cold.
>
> LoveEsther

Some of her mistakes arose out of inexperience with the machine, others from a simple ignorance of spelling, yet others from an inability to read as writing what she had written. Her habit of missing the second 'o' in words with a double 'o' stayed with her always, as did her curious inability ever to agree with anyone else that there ought to be a gap between 'Love' and 'Esther'. She always had trouble too with the word 'the' – spelling it in every combination of its three letters.

Significantly, Esther made light of these mistakes and was impatient with helpers and teachers who, then and later, would remonstrate with her and try to make her write correctly. For her, provided the message got across, its form was unimportant: communication was the essence, not the minutiae of its codes. Later, much later, she would begin to argue that her spelling and verbal structures sometimes conveyed more, as, for example, her habit of signing off 'LoveEsther'; for why, she would ask, should grammatical convention be allowed to create a divide or break between her feelings and herself in her relationship with, say, her father when no such divide existed. Love Esther? Never! Love Esther.

Despite himself, Richard was depressed. Somehow he felt guilty that he could read in only a few moments what took her two or three hours to type, and he felt duty bound to praise in her something that by able-bodied standards was only an average achievement. Nevertheless, such an achievement would have been reached more slowly but for the imagination of Eileen Coppock who, seeing Esther's obvious educability and aware that it would take a year or two before they could get her a placement at a special school for spastics, took a personal interest in her and encouraged her to read. There was more to Eileen's increasingly urgent interest than there seemed: she was herself planning to leave the Centre to do some research in America, and felt so strongly about Esther's potential that she wanted to see her educational future secure before she left.

Since most of the books at the Centre were picture-orientated, or large-format children's books, and since Esther displayed a hostile boredom towards these after one reading, Eileen began bringing in some of the books she herself had been reared on – Enid Blyton, Noel Streatfeild, Louisa M. Alcott – and would sit with Esther and read them with her until after several months it was clear that Esther wanted to try on her own. At this point Eileen (to whom Esther later acknowledged she owed so much) obtained through a contact (the budget not being available) an electrically driven page-turner which could cope well with hardcover books.

So successful was this device that soon Esther insisted that it accompanied her home at the weekends and it was added to that lengthening list of special equipment that was now part of Esther's impedimenta: manual wheelchair, electric wheelchair, removable strapped seat, standing frame, bath float, toilet seat, wide bent straw for drinking, non-slip food plate, and spoon strap, all brought home at the weekends when she was staying at Harefield.

Esther's letters were not just the voice of one growing girl but of a community, a ghettoed people, whose voice had been silenced too long and whose cries were only now beginning to be heard. A voice that had not yet quite found itself.

Take the letter dated 14 April 1977 as an example and see how much it does not tell!

Dear Daddy,

I hope you are well. Tom is ill with a cold again but
sends his love. He has a new pair of boots for football and
cant wait to try them out. Yestrday four of us went in
the minibus to Brighten to a Spastics Day Out. We were
Peter, Karen, Tom and me. It was cold and rained.

    There were stories and a play in the confrance centre I
liked I was scared. Later Nasim took me alone to the sea
and I saw big waves. I was scard also.

LoveEsther

  Esther was later to give a much fuller version of this day out,
and one which better shows its significance in her search for the
Skallagrigg.

From the Marquand Collection: Disk 15, File 'MARQ06', page 5

Daddy always filed my letters away and even though he won't write
personally to me now, at least he has sent copies of them all so I can
use them for this.

  The letter dated April 14th, 1977 is about the daytrip when four of
us were invited to go to a Disabled People's Day in Brighton. There
was a group of spastics down from the North of England, staying a
week in Brighton, and we were invited to go as part of a group from
the London area, mainly to be an audience at a play production they
did specially. When we arrived we were each given a name tag.
Peter's said MY NAME IS PETER ROWNE and he was very proud
of it.

  I told them that Peter and I wanted to be independent and left alone
for a bit to 'explore' – there were various activities going on, demonstrations and things. So they took us at our word and parked us in
the hall near a group of other spastics, telling one of the helpers there, a
man, to keep an eye on us.

  Then the helper who had been told to look after us came over and
said, 'My name's Maurice. Your helper Nasim said to watch out for you.
They're going to be rehearsing the play, would you like to watch?' I
nodded and when he asked Peter I nodded for Peter as well.

  The rehearsal was taking place in a separate room, which had an
auditorium with seats and stage just like a theatre with great red velvet
curtains going right up into darkness.

Maurice said, 'You sit here and don't make any noise. That man's the author, Andrew Moore. He's from Manchester and a friend of mine. I'll tell him you're going to watch.' He pointed out one of the people in wheelchairs in front of the stage. He wore a green pullover and had a board with paper on it in front of him and held a pen, so obviously he could write.

I can't remember that much about the play now except it was about a spastic boy called Arthur and a girl named Carolyn and how their love triumphed against the odds! There was more to it than that and Peter seemed to understand it better than I did because at one point he signed me to shout out 'YES!' for him to the actors on the stage: audience participation I think. At the end Peter said, 'Thank you, Esther.' He was crying again and he said what no boy had ever said to me. He said, 'I love you.' I think he felt that play was about him.

Then he added, 'And guess what I'd do if I was able?'

I said shyly I didn't know. Though of course I did.

He said defiantly, 'I'd kiss you, like they do on telly films.' Then he laughed and so did I and I was near enough that my hand could touch his face.

I always say that that was my first kiss.

Then the lights went up and the author came up to us from the front in his electric wheelchair. His head and hands were big but the rest of his body was wasted and shrunken.

He said, 'Thank you!'

I said, 'What for?' Or tried to. He seemed to understand.

'Because you and your friend made it worth me writing the play. My name's Andy Moore.'

He was very serious with a permanent frown and he stared at me with dark unfunny eyes in a way that made me feel I had to think about what I was trying to say. But because he was spastic himself I did not get tied up as I did with able-bodied people I did not know and he did not find it too hard to understand me.

Peter's legs shook and he tried to make a sound. Dribble came from his mouth when he tried to say something. I had never seen him try so hard. But it was no good.

I said, 'Peter can't talk easily but I can understand what he's trying to say. He's asking if your play is about the Skallagrigg.'

Andy Moore seemed surprised that Peter was aware of such a possibility. After a moment he said, 'That's right. You've probably heard of him. He's a fictional character. Like Arthur, he's a myth.'

Peter and I looked at each other. I think that even by then he did not seem like a myth to us.

FOURTEEN

That same sea-swept day at Brighton (of which her first letter to her father was such an inadequate account), Esther Marquand heard another Skallagrigg story, and one which much later Daniel Schuster had reason to be especially interested in. The story tells of The Racks, an idea and image she was to use in the final passages of the game of 'Skallagrigg'.

From the Marquand Collection: Disk 25 (Miscellaneous 2), File MISC102, page 1

I persuaded Nasim that I needed some fresh air despite the stormy weather outside the Conference Hall.

So we went out near enough the edge of the sea wall to get a view of the rough sea.

The waves were building up a long way out, all grey and white and threatening, and for a time we watched them coming in, breaking on the shingle and their surf and foam surging up it, right to the foot of the sea wall below us.

The air was full of spray and smelt salty and you could feel the power of the waves as they hit the beach. We stayed there for a while just watching it in awe.

After a while I said to Nasim that I wanted to be pushed along the promenade. At that moment we saw Maurice, the helper from Manchester, pushing someone else out into the storm. I saw him wave and smile. Nasim started pushing me in the same direction along the promenade and we joined them.

Maurice had a friendly grin on his face and I saw that the man he was looking after was one who I had seen at the front of the theatre with Andy Moore at the rehearsal. He was about fifty and a spastic, though not too bad by the looks of him.

Nasim said to Maurice: 'I've never seen a storm by the sea before.'

They started pushing us up the paths of the garden by bushes which were worried with wind.

'Where do you come from then?' Maurice says.

At this point the man Maurice was pushing turns to me and whispers, 'I get the feeling he likes your helper.'

I nodded.

The man said, 'Well he better make it snappy because I'm going to get cold dawdling along like this while these two introduce themselves.'

Maurice waited.

Then Nasim said, 'I'm a Muslim.'

Maurice was silent and I was too innocent then to know why.

Then she added, 'But I'm a modern girl.'

The man whispered to me, 'That's a relief! Our Maurice thought he'd backed a loser there. Ha ha.'

After that we got to the top of a mound which turned out to be a ruined eighteenth-century lookout tower knocked down that had been turned into a council garden. It was higher than the sea wall and the front of it buttressed out beyond it, so the sea broke right on to it and sent up plumes of spray.

The man and I agreed we wanted to go as near to the edge as we could, for the excitement, and Nasim said, 'All right Esther, but only for ten minutes or so.'

The man says to me, 'That's not for your benefit, my girl, but theirs. It'll give them time to chat each other up.'

We watched the sea for a bit.

After a while the man turned to me again and says, 'You're Esther aren't you?'

I nodded.

He explained: 'I saw you at the rehearsal. Andy Moore the author was very pleased you and your friend shouted out. He said you understood the play.'

I said, 'It was Peter my friend who wanted to shout first.'

He said, 'All right, Peter then. Andy was surprised you understood about the Skallagrigg being part of the story.'

'I know about the Skallagrigg, I've heard about it before. I like the Skallagrigg.'

The man said, 'My name's Bill, I come from Manchester and that's why I know Andy. I'm in Overdale Centre but he's lucky enough to be in Holmewood. That's a good centre and very modern.'

Behind us Maurice and Nasim were talking.

Bill said, 'They're getting on all right so it looks as if we're stuck here for a bit.' He laughed so nicely that I couldn't help smiling. Helpers sometimes think we're idiots but we know what goes on. Nothing wrong with it, though. We all need the comfort and love of another.

Bill asked, 'Have you got a boyfriend then?' His knee nudged at mine and I was embarrassed.

I shook my head.

'I had a girlfriend once, she was normal,' he said. He was not smiling now, and his eyes stared out at the rough sea. 'She had to go away,' he said. Then he laughed and said, 'All good things have to come to an end so enjoy them while you can.'

Suddenly he said, 'Do you want me to tell you a Skallagrigg story I know?'

I thought, 'If Bill tells me then I can tell Peter something for a change.' So I nodded.

Bill had an interesting way of talking though he was not always clear. But he knew that and sometimes stopped and said 'Eh?' just to check you were keeping up with him. His head was near mine and he smelled of coal tar soap.

'It's the one about The Racks and it's most appropriate to the occasion of us being by the sea and that's what made me think of it. Do you know it?'

I said no I didn't, please tell me. So he did.

One time Arthur went to the sea. His only time. It was during the war and there was evacuation. This was long after he was put away. Most of the lads were taken that day to the beach but Arthur had offended Dilke so he was punished by being left in his chair on a cliff overlooking a bay. Below him great swells of sea stretched out. This was near big cliffs and he's sitting on top of one looking down at the sea. He couldn't see straight down on to the beach because he was set back a bit on the cliff, but off to his right there was a bay and he could see people and pleasure boats on the bit of beach in view.

Arthur didn't mind being left like that because at least for a bit he was free of Dilke and other nurses like him. From the moment of evacuation when they had gone down the window-corridor past the baskets and the black court outside to the front of the hospital and the sun hit his face he had felt free and he knew he was on holiday and he better enjoy every moment because it was all he was going to get for many a long year. So why should he mind being stuck on the cliff alone for a bit?

To the right side of the bay the water was troubled because

there was rocks and things just below the surface, or just breaking it. Sometimes they showed up when a trough of water between two swells went past and the water was low enough to let the submerged rock show through. There were no boats out there. Too dangerous by half.

But Arthur got worried. He kept thinking: 'Suppose a boat got out there, what could I do to help?' He knew he could do nothing, not even warn anyone.

As the afternoon wore on the tide came in some and the water seemed to grow rough, especially in that area of submerged rocks. Then he remembered something. He had been told there was a very dangerous area of rocks just near there and they were called 'The Racks'. The moment he recalled that he knew he was looking straight at them and he got really scared and had a feeling that because he couldn't stop himself staring at them something terrible was going to happen. It was as if he would make it happen from his mind, and he didn't want that. So he tried hard to look elsewhere. But it was no good. He hadn't learnt to control his mind then, Arthur hadn't.

Sure enough a little sailing boat appeared round a headland. It was drifting out of control towards the racing water of The Racks. He closed his eyes and tried to think it wasn't there but when he opened them again it was, and getting closer to the dangerous rocks.

Arthur said to himself, 'I'm making that boat head for disaster just looking at it. I must do something.'

But he could think of nothing he could do except watch the inevitable. He soon saw that the boat was in trouble because the wind was getting stronger and driving it straight on to The Racks.

The nearer it got the more clearly he could see. There were two men in it and one was trying to bale out while the other was trying to row the sailing boat out of danger but the wind and current seemed against him. From high on the cliff top Arthur could see everything – most of all how futile their efforts to escape The Racks were. By the minute the little boat was getting near the white broken water. He looked round and there was no one there. He had been left completely alone. Then he was really scared for the boat and for himself. He wouldn't be able to live with himself if an accident did finally happen.

So then suddenly Arthur knew what he must do: he must

call out to the Skallagrigg for help. So he did. 'Please, can't you see what's happening? Can't you come and help them?'

The wind got stronger. The sky got darker. He saw the two men in the boat stop rowing and baling and standing instead waving towards the shore. But from where Arthur was he knew there was no hope of them being seen, the water between was too rough, and the rocks were in the way. Only he could see.

'Please come and help,' he called, 'Skallagrigg, please come.'

Then he felt a peace behind him, and knew the Skallagrigg was there.

'I could feel you calling my name, Arthur. Is something wrong?'

Arthur explained what was happening.

'You must tell me what to do,' said the Skallagrigg.

'I think you should help them by warning someone,' he told the Skallagrigg.

'I will,' said the Skallagrigg. And then he was gone.

Now all Arthur could do was watch.

The boat continued to drift on to The Racks until he lost it among the waves and the foam. Then he heard a loud bang, and another, and saw a puff of smoke in the sky and a brief flash of a light. It was the lifeboat rocket. Then far along the beach where there were fishing huts he saw people running. There was a lifeboat being launched. It went out into a darkening sea towards The Racks. It was so dark now that hardly a thing could be seen. Then the people looking after Arthur came for him. They talked about the lifeboat being launched. They said a boy on the beach had seen the boat in distress and alerted the lifeboat but Arthur knew that really it had been the Skallagrigg who got the message through. He knew it was because he summoned the Skallagrigg's help. Then they talked more and he learnt that the rescue was not entirely successful. The boat was lost and one of the men was missing presumed drowned.

Arthur started to cry because he felt it was his fault. By looking at The Racks he had made the accident happen. If they hadn't put him on the cliff the boat would probably never have got into trouble in the first place.

Then they hit Arthur and told him not to cry and he was being a nuisance. He had nothing to cry about. That wasn't his place. He felt it was right they hit him because it was his fault really. But he shut up until they put him to bed. Suddenly he felt peace around him and knew the Skallagrigg had come. He was at the side of the bed but Arthur didn't dare look.

'It's not your fault,' said the Skallagrigg. 'You told me to warn them in time to save a life. That man is living because of you, so don't cry. It doesn't matter if no one knows. *I* know.'

And that's the story of Arthur and The Racks.

I stared out to sea after this thinking about Arthur's friend the Skallagrigg and how lucky I was to have friends like Peter. It was almost dark and towards the end of the story I had felt Nasim was a little restless though she was talking to Maurice.

'Where does the Skallagrigg live?' I asked Bill.

'Everywhere,' said Bill. 'He lives wherever we handicapped people are.'

'Where does he come from?'

'The past,' said Bill. 'Right out of the past.'

'Where was he first of all?' I wanted to know.

Bill looked out at the sea, his eyes remembering his own beginnings.

'He was in a cot and he couldn't stand up.'

'That was Arthur,' I said.

'Was it?' he said strangely.

FIFTEEN

Soon after lunchtime one Sunday in early December, the last exeat before the Christmas holidays and a day so wet that Richard had decided that Esther must stay in, the doorbell rang.

It was Brian Ogilvie, his old Austin Cambridge looking rather stylish on the gravel drive of Harefield, but somewhat worn like his Harris tweed jacket and the thick stick he leaned on.

'Well, what a surprise,' said Richard ushering him in. 'This is unexpected!'

'I've been playing the Fool for the Charlbury Morris Men,' said Brian with a laugh, at the sound of which Esther, her head turned intently round as far as it would go to listen out and identify the visitor as she sat in her chair in the kitchen, let out a squeal of delight, and thumped her legs forward against the table legs.

'Hello my girl!' said Brian, going in to give her a kiss and as much of a hug as the straps and encumbrances of the wheelchair allowed. 'And how are you? Bored with the bad weather I expect!' Esther nodded.

'You're doing well at school, I hear. Your father wrote and said you'll be going to a special school in the New Year and that you can do arithmetic now . . .' and she nodded and garbled some half words together but he shook his head and said, 'It's no good with me, I never understand except for your laugh. I know what that means, Esther! It means you're enjoying yourself!' And she nodded and stopped trying to speak.

The news about the school was finally true – after two years of trying, Eileen Coppock had succeeded in getting Esther a place in a special school where she could have the skilled teaching necessary to push her much further than the Dale Centre could.

Esther was now twelve and a half. The puppy fat had gone, the face was longer, the eyes more wary, more watchful; but the smile

– when it came – was now bright and broad and won the hearts of helpers and friends. Just as the moods, which came more frequently, upset people and created disharmony, for Esther's personality was strong, her desires always stated.

The building work on Harefield had long been completed, and the tight financial position Richard found himself in initially had eased – helped by the rapid establishment and move forward into profitability of Fountain-Marquand, the computer services company which he ran for Fountain Systems. The computer market was growing exponentially, and Richard was realizing that, almost by chance, he was in a strong position to profit from it.

Brian's visits to Harefield had become something of a delight to all of them, though they were irregular and never pre-planned. He just came – rather as in Esther's childhood Richard had 'just visited' as if in response to an inner need which later – as it now had – would find its full expression.

So that December Sunday in 1977 as Richard made some tea and Esther fell silent, Brian sat down comfortably at the great pine table in the open-plan kitchen. Brian was explaining his lunchtime activity and why it was that old Fools, it seemed, never die.

'I *used* to dance with the Men regularly up until the end of the sixties. But I don't know . . . I got older, the Men got younger and some of the dances were getting a bit rough for me. They've got a regular Fool of course, two in fact, but both were indisposed and they had an engagement over at The Plasterer's Arms in Beaconsfield so they asked me to step in. I've done it before but I'm a bit stately to be a Fool. Still beggars can't be choosers,' and he beamed as he drank his tea, his eyes shining more than Richard had seen on previous visits and his large hand reaching out to meet Esther's searching one.

'Sheila once said that Morris dancing was your "true delight",' said Richard. 'Her words.'

There was a pause. 'Anyway,' said Brian, 'I just thought I'd, er, well come over and . . .' Brian always made light of his visits but Richard had come to understand that they followed a pattern, and the pattern started and ended with Margaret Ogilvie. Probably the two of them had been stuck in their cottage in Charlbury over the weekend by rainy weather just as Richard and Esther had been stuck in theirs, and probably too the endless bitterness of Margaret had oppressed Brian again and the trip with the dancers had given him the chance to visit High Wycombe. But, of course, he always had to get back . . .

'Yes yes, I've got to get back . . .' But he relaxed back for another cup of tea, evidently reluctant to leave.

'Mama,' said Esther clearly, fixing her grandfather with a stare.

He did not seem to understand, so she said it again, straining forward towards him: 'Mama.'

There was a very long silence. Richard had got up to make more tea and while he did so, his back to them, Esther waited expectantly, putting all her effort into maintaining a stare at Brian. There was no doubt what she had said and what she meant: her mother. Sheila. Once wife, once daughter, of the men who were now avoiding Esther's look.

Eventually Esther's head wandered a little, the effort of holding it in one position too much, and her look became uncertain, a little defeated. She had said that word before sometimes, at the Centre and here at home, but responses were never very fulsome. She sensed that her father did not want to talk about it.

But *she* did. She wanted to talk now.

More weakly, as if she had no great expectation of any real reply and that person who had been her mother was unobtainable even as a memory, she repeated, 'Mama', and she looked down at her angled feet, and beyond to the kitchen floor.

Karen Gee had a mother, a mother who sent her things. Peter had one, but she never came. Tom didn't have one. Karen laughed at Esther because she didn't have one. Esther wanted to know why she had gone. She knew where: to death. But *why* had she?

Then suddenly she was distressed, her chest heaving and heaving to try to control the sobs that would come out and could not be controlled.

In that moment, when two fathers were faced by the past and the present, it was old Brian who found the strength to respond most truly. A rasp came from his throat that might have been, 'Oh dear,' or 'Oh, my dear,' or even 'Oh, my darling,' and a look of real distress came over his worn face. He put down his cup of tea clumsily, half got up with some difficulty, and put his hands and arms out to comfort his granddaughter.

And what he said was, 'I know, I know,' as if he did know what troubled her so deeply. And then he said it, the word as clear as she had spoken it. 'You're thinking of your Mama, aren't you?' And she nodded into his tweedy shoulder, sobbing, sobbing the deeper for knowing that there somewhere in that smell of him, of tweed jackets and tobacco and age, was the girl who had been her mother.

Behind them, leaning against the clean, shiny and ordered surface of the kitchen units, Richard Marquand stared bleakly, unable to move or speak.

'Esther wants to know about Sheila,' he explained simply.

Brian Ogilvie stood up straight, his face rather angry.

'Well of course she does, Richard, it would be damned unnatural if she didn't.'

They stared at each other blankly, and Esther was silent, her sobs suddenly under control as she listened.

'I think it's time we put a stop to this nonsense,' said Brian, his voice a lot younger and more assured than it had been when he had first knocked at the front door. 'Esther not having a mother, I mean. I think it is time she met her grandmother.'

'Well, of course, I agree,' said Richard cautiously. 'But I think that . . .'

'Now,' said Brian. 'Not tomorrow, not next year, now. We must do it now because . . .' and in that fall of his voice, that look out into the garden was the sense that once long ago he had wished to see Sheila again but it had been too late by then; and the chance was gone for ever with the skidding of car tyres.

Now was the time. There is no time. Or if there is it is too short to waste. A family's resource of love cannot be frittered away by one woman's bitterness and loss.

'It's a long time ago since your mother died, Esther,' said Brian sitting down heavily and staring at the still tea in his cup. 'Let me see . . .' he seemed almost to be talking to himself, 'How old are you now, my dear . . . you'll be eleven, no twelve. It was 1965. That's how long ago it is since I . . . since your mother . . . since your mother died.'

He got up slowly from the table and stood at the closed patio doors looking out at the garden. Richard and Esther stayed silent. He was remembering another garden where once he watched a little girl run.

'Sheila was a very good runner. She won a sports cup for it and I've still got the little replica they gave her. The big one had to be returned for the next year. Actually, she . . .' and Brian turned back to face them, and sat down again as Richard poured him an encouraging cup of tea, 'she liked dancing too. Country dancing, barn dances in the parish hall. I used to take her on a Saturday night when she was your age Esther. Dear me, she flung herself about too much for me!'

'I never knew that,' said Richard.

'Oh yes. But of course young girls get sophisticated and go to London and put those things aside for a time. But they come back to it. Everyone comes back to the dance eventually. Even old Fools like me!' He laughed, and so did Esther, sharing the emotion rather than any understanding of what a Fool was.

'Have you still got that teddy I gave you?' asked Brian. 'That was your mother's.'

'Toh,' said Esther.

'Yes,' said Brian, not understanding. He got up as if he felt he must go, but wisps of memory drew him back to the patio doors and the view of the garden.

'Esther calls him Thomas,' explained Richard.

'Another summer gone,' he said, 'and time's running on. What time we do waste. I really think, Richard, it is time Margaret knew Esther,' he said firmly.

'But I'm not sure that Margaret would really want to,' began Richard, 'and I don't want to risk a scene for Esther.'

'You mean Margaret's damn foolery has rubbed off on you my boy, that's what you mean. Take her by storm! That's what I did when I first met her before the war. Surprised her. Before she could say no she found she had said "yes".'

He paused and then added in a gentler voice, 'She doesn't really mean it, you know, but she took Sheila's death so hard, so very hard. For some reason she blames you, and well . . .' and then he looked for a moment meaningfully at Esther and then at Richard again.

'Look, my dear chap, I've played the Fool all afternoon and I might as well continue playing it for a couple more hours, though Margaret might not see much to laugh at. I would like you to come to Charlbury now. Now.'

And as Richard's hesitation was overwhelmed by Esther's vigorous and excited nodding, Brian looked at his watch, pronounced that they could all be there in less than fifty minutes, fetched his stick and opened the front door in readiness for their departure.

Then as Richard agreed, and pushed Esther out to the hall while he got a few things together, old Brian Ogilvie grinned as he had done when he first came in and said, 'Would you like to dance, my dear? Your mother's favourite dance which I taught her myself?'

'Yeh,' said Esther.

So using her chair for support he pushed her about the hall, though carefully lest he fall down, as behind her on the floor his feet lightly stepped out the patterns of an old dance called 'Lord Raglan's Daughter'.

And there, in that hall, on an afternoon in December, an excited Esther took note as she was whirled in her chair and made to laugh. She felt the patterns in an ancient dance, and the seeds for the free and joyous structures and rhythms that run through 'Skallagrigg' were sown.

'Arise and pick a posy, sweet lily pink and rosy, it is the finest flower that ever I did see . . .' Brian half sang, half hummed and finally muttered to himself.

'Yeh!' said Esther, wanting more.

But Richard was becoated and ready and pushing her out into the cold wet December afternoon to a meeting that might not be sweet or rosy. Yet from which might bloom as fine a flower as ever they would see.

SIXTEEN

It took less than an hour to reach Charlbury, but by the time they had, the afternoon light had faded to twilight gloom, and the village streetlamps were already on; warm light, yellow light, over old doors and in windows lintelled and framed by mellow Cotswold stone, through streets that rose and turned in the darkness past shops that were closed for the Sunday but lit up with Christmas decorations.

They parked the cars and began to get Esther out.

'Now, Richard, Margaret may be a bit surprised . . .' began Brian doubtfully, pulling the collar of his coat tight against the cold and appearing at last to falter a little.

'A bit!' exclaimed Richard as he heaved Esther into her chair and strapped her in.

'And she may be a little awkward, but it isn't really her fault. Don't stay too long, not this time anyway!'

'Probably be the last time,' said Richard.

Esther herself was silent and staring with apprehension, her hands were clenched tight as Richard eased her chair up the steps in the front garden of the Ogilvies' double-fronted stone house which was more than a cottage but not quite a farmhouse. But for a single room upstairs, the house was in darkness.

Brian Ogilvie fumbled with keys, opened the door, and switched on a light just inside the door so that Richard could see to tip the wheelchair back, push the front wheels over the threshold and heave Esther inside to the hall.

There were red rugs over floorboards, good quality but worn, and a grandfather clock next to a telephone on a little period table. The clock ticked deeply and steadily, and Esther, nervous, stared at its pendulum swinging slowly back and forth behind glass.

The two men stood like conspirators. The house seemed deserted.

'Hello, dear?' Brian called up the stairs, then down the corridor in the general direction of the kitchen, 'It's me. I've brought someone to see you.'

Richard waited, his knuckles white on the handles of Esther's wheelchair. Esther's head was on one side, her eyes staring: she was trying to hear the direction from which her grandmother would appear.

There was then, from somewhere upstairs, the opening of a door and the hollow sound of shoes on a boarded floor. Brian slowly started to climb up the stairs.

'I've brought someone . . .'

They heard her voice, whispered and tight and out of sight. 'Who is it? I'm really not prepared for visitors Brian. I . . .' They heard her falter and stop, they heard Brian say as brightly as he could, 'It's Richard; Richard Marquand. And we've brought . . .' and Brian's voice dried up before someone they could not see.

Finally they saw her shoes, brown brogues descending the stairs, then her legs in old-fashioned stockings, her tweed skirt, her waist, her arms and her hands on the wooden banister, a worn wedding ring, hands gripping and slow; and finally they saw her face: impassive, severe, staring down at them. Terribly pale. The eyes cold. The hair nondescript grey. The whole effect strained and tense.

'Oh.' Her voice was surprised and a little shocked.

Richard had decided long ago that if ever this grim reunion came and he should have to address her, it would not be as 'Mother' as once it had been, but as 'Margaret'.

'Hello, Margaret,' he said. And suddenly he was calm, suddenly quite unperturbed. Another's bitterness can wither one's soul, but facing her again after so long and after so much, Richard felt for the moment at least that his soul was strong and more sure than it had ever been.

'We've brought Esther to see you,' he said simply, a father now with a daughter to cherish and protect; facing a mother, a grand-mother, who was lonely with a loss of something dear and irre-placeable.

'Oh!' said Margaret Ogilvie again as her eyes travelled coldly

from Richard's to Esther's. The two stared at each other, Esther
quite expressionless.

'Esther,' said Margaret. 'Yes, I see.'

After an uncomfortable pause she came down to the hall, Brian
turning and following behind her. They stood awkwardly, the
smiles sparse.

'I haven't much in the way of tea, I'm afraid. Some biscuits
perhaps?' said Margaret, gathering her strength and establishing
her distance with meagre social grace.

Richard sighed inwardly. He thought the years might have
changed her as they had him. He wanted to break through the
bitter ice but did not know how to. So that soon, within moments,
he found that that initial sympathy for her was fading as he slipped
back inexorably to the part he had always played in her presence:
dutiful, polite, tense, uneasy.

She was older and thinner, and the grim angularity of her face
contrasted with the warm red affability of Brian Ogilvie's.

'So you're Esther,' she said to Esther standing and staring at her.
There was not the ghost of a concession to friendliness, not the
slightest attempt to put Esther at her ease. Esther stared back,
hostile, legs stiff and her hands angled and tense. Reluctantly, she
nodded.

Some unused and half-forgotten social rule reminded Margaret
she should smile at children and, for a moment, the most distant
corners of her face did accommodate a smile.

Then Margaret's cold awkwardness seemed to invade all of them
as they uncomfortably made their way with creaking small talk
down the back corridor and into the kitchen, leaving the grandfather clock to heave and click behind them, rather out of joint
itself for a moment or two before its regular steady ticking overtook
the rugs and the lovely polished floorboards, marking time before
the day (which seemed distant and unlikely) when love, harmony
and good humour would return to this old house.

The kitchen was much as Richard remembered it, without heart.
The good taste of the rest of the house was inherited not personal.
The paintings, the polished wood, the rugs, the traditional
bathroom and the guest rooms, these things Margaret knew how
to provide only because they were ingrained in her by class and
upbringing.

But the kitchen had to be her own, and it failed. It combined modern with old in a way that did a disservice to both. Some units, once new and smart, were so tatty and worn that they disfigured the garden end of the room, quite ruining the elegance of the leaded windows behind. There was a modern electric kettle next to two battered and ugly saucepans; a row of uncomfortable and half-used utensils on a rack on one wall, the rack a decayed red against the yellow paint. The curtains were not drawn but had they been they would only have made things worse: their heavy floral pattern was out of keeping with the drying up cloth that had been carelessly thrown to dry across the back of a chair. On one side of the room was a heavy mantelpiece over a solid fuel boiler, the latter spluttering a few forlorn flames.

There was the smell of dutiful, unimaginative cooking about the place, and though there was nothing untidy or dirty about the stacks of plates, the cupboards of provisions, the old-fashioned refrigerator and the brand new dish-washer (which did not look at one with the gas cooker next to it), yet there was a sense of decline and sadness.

Whether or not Esther was aware of this emotional dereliction was hard to say. The only signs of disapproval she made were a stubborn ungiving silence and stares that attached themselves to Richard like balls of stone round a prisoner's feet.

'Would you sit down or perhaps we ought to have it in the sitting room. I'll make . . . yes you make . . .' Margaret Ogilvie said, as Brian began the process of making tea. Kettle, water, switch, tray, milk bottle, jug, tea caddy . . . the stages seemed painfully slow and clumsy, made more so by Margaret's half helping of Brian as she uttered inanities about sugar and Richard sat watching and depressed. She was building towards something: a scene. Dear God, he suddenly knew why Sheila had left for London as soon as she was old enough.

'I really think,' she finally began, her voice no longer hesitant and undecided, 'that you should have phoned if you were coming, Richard. We have no tea biscuits, Brian; yes, the digestives will do. I would have liked to have been prepared for . . .' her eyes could not help glancing briefly towards Esther in her chair by the table, 'everything. I really think that would have been right. In the metal tin, Brian. The tin.'

Anger rose in Richard and he opened his mouth to reply, to shout out his feelings, but at the end of the kitchen by the awful work surfaces Brian had turned round and was mutely pleading with him.

In the brief glance they exchanged Richard sensed again what he had sensed in him that distant day when Brian had bravely come to Haven Lane for Esther's eighth birthday: the suffering for a lost child. The two of them had lost so very much, it wasn't for him to be angry. He had no need for anger now, for he had something to prize and to love, the very thing they had lost. He stood up and went closer to Esther, his hand on her shoulder and she relaxed because she felt him relax, his hand warm, loving and comforting.

'Esther wanted to see where Sheila was brought up. I know it must be difficult, Margaret' – a look of distaste ran over her face as he dared use her Christian name again – 'and I'm sorry if it's a bad time but it might have been even harder if we had phoned. Esther just wanted . . .'

Then Esther spoke at last.

'Mama,' she said quietly and questioningly, and Richard, following her eyes, saw that she was looking at a little framed black and white photograph of the three Ogilvies propped up on the mantelpiece above the boiler. Brian's eyes followed Richard's. He put down the tea towel he had, for no good reason, been holding.

'That's right, old girl,' he said, 'that's a picture of your mother.' He took the photo down and held it in front of Esther. Richard pushed her to the table and Brian put the photo down.

'It was taken in the garden, wasn't it, my dear?' said Brian as he turned back to the tea making, and his right hand reached out and touched Margaret's arm for a moment, as if to say, in the private and complex language of a couple who have lived much of their life together, 'It's all right, it's all right, nothing worse can happen now. They mean no harm.'

But still Margaret stood awkwardly, unable to cope with Richard's simple apology and the sudden shift away from confrontation brought about by Esther's curiosity about Sheila's picture.

'Well, I think we will go into the sitting-room,' she said eventually, still severe and cold, 'I think it more appropriate to the occasion.'

Whatever she meant by the word 'occasion' it imposed formality and the opportunity for a more familial cup of tea was gone by the time the wheelchair, the tray of tea things, biscuits and fruit cake, and all four of them, had traipsed back up the corridor past the grandfather clock to the formal terrors of the big cold front room into which, Richard remembered Sheila telling him, Margaret had never normally allowed children.

The high soft chairs, the polished tables, the gleaming fireless thirties brick fireplace, quite out of keeping with the eighteenth-century house, stiffened the back and froze the spirit, making the fingers clumsy in the contorted gilded handles of Margaret Ogilvie's china tea cups. The talk was desultory – of gardening, of house repair, of Charlbury's shops, and of the Austin Cambridge.

Esther tried a mouthful of the cake but it crumbled and stuck to her lips, the left-over part scattering over Richard's fingers and down on to the carpet. The tea was too milky and drooled down Esther's chin to her chest. It was made all the more embarrassing by Margaret's upright frostiness.

No further mention of Sheila was tried, nor did Margaret address or look at Esther directly. So Esther sat stiffly and then became bored and reverted to the kind of social distress that she had not displayed for two years or more.

'What are you doing at Christmas, Richard?' asked Margaret believing that 'misbehaviour' in children should be ignored.

'We just stay at home and have a good time, don't we, Esther?' he said. Esther managed glum accusatory assent.

'Last year, Tom, one of Esther's friends, came and stayed. We had a great time, but this year he's going on a special camp.' But the memory of the 'great time' withered before Margaret's evident boredom. Her face was pale and pinched and she looked tired. Nor did Esther back up Richard's claim for the previous Christmas: instead she stared at the digestive biscuit he had placed on her tray and uttered little heaving breaths from a down-turned mouth, her head lolling this way and that as if she was deliberately playing the part of an idiot.

When Richard felt he could safely say that time was going by and they had a long drive home there was a general feeling of relief.

'I'm glad you came, old boy, it wasn't half as bad as I expected,' muttered Brian as they said a final goodbye at the kerbside. 'Margaret probably enjoyed herself more than you might think.'

They clasped each other's hand and said goodbye.

'See you at Harefield soon I hope,' said Richard.

As he drove away and Brian stood in the doorway to raise a hand in farewell silhouetted against the bleak light of the hall behind him, Richard felt he was leaving him in some kind of purgatory. Then relief mixed with a profound and impotent depression overcame him, and Esther sat in reproachful silence all the way back through the evening to High Wycombe.

Yet, finally, it was not Richard but Brian Ogilvie who knew Margaret best. A few days later Richard received a letter postmarked 'Charlbury, Oxon.' in an unfamiliar hand.

'Dear Richard,' it began and his eyes travelled quickly to the end of the small tight handwriting to see that it was from Margaret.

> I was, as you know, somewhat surprised at your visit
> last week, but feel it was well meant.
> I have been thinking about what you said about
> Christmas and have discussed the matter with Brian and
> we feel it would be only right if we invited you to spend
> the two or three days over Christmas here. That is your-
> self and Esther. It is not perhaps any longer a house for a
> child but we had good Christmases with Sheila in the
> past and perhaps Esther could enjoy herself.
> You may well have other plans which I will quite
> understand but please let me know as soon as you can
> so I may make the correct preparations.
>
> My kind regards . . .

The blue paper, the neat repressed handwriting, the memory of that tea in the sitting room – why should they? Why *should* he impose it all on Esther, and for the whole of Christmas? And yet, he had to admit that the days of the holidays sometimes dragged with no other adults. His life was really work, and Esther and he had few real friends. Well, none in fact. Sometimes he felt terribly lonely. Christmas was going to be without Tom this year and Esther was going to be away from the Centre and her friends for nearly three weeks; he was not looking forward to it.

There was, too, the sense of wanting to respond to Sheila's mother in a positive way; she was making an effort, at what cost he could barely imagine, and he felt he should not turn his back on her, nor take the let-out about 'other plans' that she offered.

Yet Esther would not like it . . .

He impulsively picked up the phone. Brian answered. The clock ticked as usual in the background.

'It's Richard. I'm phoning about Margaret's letter.'

'Yes, old chap,' said Brian gloomily. He was not looking forward to Christmas either.

'Yes,' said Richard. 'Well, we'd like to come . . .'

'Good heavens!' said Brian.

Pleasure, delight, warmth, surprise, and above all gratitude, as if he, Richard Marquand, had done the Ogilvie household a great favour – these were the ingredients of Brian's response.

Eventually Richard was able to put down the phone. Well, someone was happy at any rate and Esther could damn well put a brave face on the worst moments. It would be good for her.

Then he wrote against 23 December in the house diary he kept in the kitchen, 'To Charlbury for Christmas', making a mental note to set time aside with Esther to buy Christmas presents for her grandparents.

SEVENTEEN

Esther did not like it.

She demonstrated against the very idea of it with her voice and expression; she resisted being bundled into the car and strapped in her seat; on arrival at Charlbury she protested loudly at being put into her wheelchair and pushed along the pavement and up to the Ogilvies' door.

But she fell suddenly silent when the door opened, and her father's heart sank to see that Margaret, while finding it possible to write an invitation letter, had found it impossible to present them both with a Christmassy smile of good cheer and warmth that might, just might, have disarmed Esther.

So they installed themselves reluctantly on that evening of 23 December. They had eaten at home so, after a desultory hello, Richard took Esther upstairs for a bath. The water was only warm, the cast-iron bath high and cold, the floor of unyielding linoleum, the towels old and harsh to the skin. It was going to be a disaster.

Lying naked on the floor Esther seemed to sense Richard's dismay: her anger gave way to misery and she started whimpering.

'Esther, you're a big girl now and you're going to have to learn that there are occasions when you have to do your duty, and this looks like being one of them.' His eyes cast about the old-fashioned bathroom for diversion and, finding none there, settled on the warmth and pattern of her nightdress. '*You* look nice at least.' His flattery did not work. Reproach stayed in her eyes and he could find no easy answer to her mute question: Why are we here?

Then as she lay beneath him, her legs stiff, her feet pointed and strange, her hands slow and weak, her hair wet and clinging, she began to cry, great gulps of misery, fuelled by a growing self-consciousness that she was a big girl and shouldn't cry and they could hear downstairs, they could all hear, and she couldn't stop,

and they didn't want her and she was a nuisance to Daddy, and
and and . . .

'Come on, Esther, we'll get you to bed and in the morning . . .'
She was tired and floppy in his arms, heavy in her heaving misery,
and shook her head when he offered to tell her a story. She *was* a
big girl now and felt a loneliness he could not understand or easily
assuage.

At least Esther did not wake once she was asleep, though Richard
himself barely slept. The strangeness of being back at Charlbury,
doubts about the two days to come, and troubling confused
thoughts and memories of Sheila kept him tossing and turning
uncomfortably. Esther was sleeping in Sheila's old room, and he in
the formal guest room next door.

His thoughts circled and recircled until he was exhausted, and
then he drifted into an uncomfortable and troubled sleep, waking
much later to a sound in the corridor; one of them going to the
toilet. A soft cough: Margaret Ogilvie. So she could not sleep either.

The slow chimes of four-thirty came from the grandfather clock
in the hall below. Esther would wake in another two and a half
hours, and need him to come in and say hello half an hour later.
The chimes faded as he drifted back to a last and slipping memory
of Sheila, stopping by the door in this room on her way out early
one morning after illicit pre-marital sex and turning back to look
at him as if looking at a stranger. Then the grandfather clock had
chimed another quarter, Sheila had gone and he had turned into
sleep, as, so many years later, he was now doing . . .

Christmas Eve. Brian Ogilvie's good-hearted attempts to bring
mirth and cheer to the house with warming seasonal drink and
cheerful chat were swamped by the sea of his wife's coldness. It
was not that she had not tried, since preparations had, in a sense,
been made: a turkey burdened the larder, a bag of chestnuts
imposed itself on the sideboard, a Christmas pudding stared
mournfully out of the fridge, cheeses waited miserably in their
plastic wrappings, Christmas crackers lay mute in their box, decorations hung lifeless from beams and walls which gave them
scant welcome – no, it was not for want of material effort. It was
simply that the heart essential to the enterprise, her own, was not
in it. It seemed that that same dutiful impetuosity that had made

Richard accept Margaret's invitation and had made her send it . . . but her gesture had been without feeling or spiritual foundation.

Yet, somehow, the four of them managed to fill Christmas Eve with this and that: a walk to the shops, a drive to see the decorations in Chipping Norton (Margaret declining to come so she could 'deal with the chestnuts'), a tasty but cold lunch (Margaret being too busy to prepare a hot meal), and a 'treat' – an intimidating one – still to come.

This was to be tea at Nancy Petrie's house in the High Street just near the church. Mrs Petrie was vice-chairman of the local conservative party and a do-gooder if ever there was one. Hearing that the Ogilvies' handicapped and probably backward granddaughter was coming, she had nobly offered to open hearth and home to the 'poor child' for tea, an offer Margaret Ogilvie (despite the weak protests of Brian who could not stand Nancy Petrie) accepted as it filled up time which, she greatly feared, would drag.

But before that, at three in the afternoon, father and daughter had an inviolable date to wrap their presents to the sound of the King's College Nine Lessons and Carols service from Cambridge. It had been something Richard had done by chance on Esther's first Christmas with him when she was eight, and was now one of the few family rituals they had.

Richard lit some candles he had brought with him – he had left nothing to chance – and put them over the fireplace in the front room. He wondered whether he could light the fire . . . the room was cold, after all, but then the whole damned house was cold. But he feared Margaret had laid the fire ready for the morrow and turned an electric fire on instead, and fiddled with the lights that Brian had draped over the little Christmas tree they had installed by the window, the box of tree decorations at its side still only half used, as if the task had been interrupted and not resumed.

The lights came on suddenly in Richard's hands as he systematically tightened up the bulbs and Esther, for the first time that day, made a sound that seemed like pleasure. She always liked candles and lights. Outside the afternoon light was dull and already beginning to grow dim as the first carol carried them away from the place they were in.

Once in Royal David's City
Stood a lonely cattle shed
Where a mother laid her baby
In a manger for his . . .

It was the traditional start, a soaring solo boy's voice echoing
about the fan vaulting of King's College Chapel, and slowly, powerfully, it was joined by the massed deeper voices of the main choir.

To this lovely sound they began their wrapping and began for a
time to relax, the tension going from Esther's fingers, feet and legs
as she helped Richard choose the right paper from the sheets he
had, and in her own way fisted the bows and ribbons into place.

There was a bottle of red wine for her grandparents with 'Happy
Christmas to you both, Love Richard and Esther'. A tea cosy for
Margaret from Esther. A framed picture of Richard, Esther and
Tom for Brian Ogilvie, which Esther particularly liked. Richard
held her hand and made it scribe the words on a label to be stuck
on the back: 'Happy Christmas, with love from Esther and a Happy
New Year.'

With the soft light of the candles about them, and the fire beginning to warm them at last, they could not know that just then, in
the kitchen, old Brian Ogilvie had gone up to Margaret where she
slaved so pathetically at the preparations whose work she was
unable to share with any of them, and put his arm around her
angled and forbidding shoulders, and said, 'My dear, I'm sure it
will be very nice, very nice. She's a sweet girl, our Esther.'

As he turned away from her, knowing she would not respond,
he heard the distant sound of the carols from the front room, and
he turned on the brown bakelite radio they kept for morning news
in the kitchen, and found that same service to which Richard was
listening. Then, leaving it on, without another word, he let the
carol fill the kitchen as once, in happier times when their Sheila
was a little girl, it had filled the whole house.

Then he silently closed the door and left Margaret to it, putting
on his overcoat and scarf and taking up his stick . . .

'Brian, you will be back in time for tea,' called out Margaret
opening the kitchen door after him and fixing him with a stare.

'Yes, dear,' he said, quietly leaving.

He did not see her stand then, knife in hand, untidy kitchen behind her, and stare after him, her eyes softening as, untroubled by people, she listened to the carols on the radio and let herself relax thinking more fondly than anyone knew of Brian and what he was doing, because she knew where he had gone on this day every year since, since *then.*

Brian Ogilvie had a ritual on Christmas Eve. It took him first to 44 Adnam Lane where Mr Allen Parsons, old friend, fellow country-dancer in years gone by, chess companion, and once a special favourite with Sheila, waited for him.

The two old men walked to the High Street and there, from one of the shops, and without much said, they bought some flowers: arise and pick a posy, sweet lily pink and rosy, it is the finest flower that ever I have seen . . . Some years early daffodils, some years roses, this year, this soon to be so special year, sweet-smelling freesias.

They walked down the High Street to the church, through the churchyard gate, round to the southern side of St Mary's where they went off the path and over to a grave, the stone paler than most, but just now beginning to green with algae and winter damp.

They stood together, overcoated arm to overcoated arm, sticks into the wet grass, and they stared and remembered, just for a little they remembered. Sometimes Mr Parsons might speak, saying, 'She were a good lass your Sheila, good at heart', or 'Another Christmas come then, Brian, another year', and Brian stared down. Then he would lay the flowers on Sheila's grave, the black yews dark about him, the older gravestones tilted and lichened, the flowers bright for now, to fade and be lost with the New Year as the life they remembered had been lost.

'It would be nice if you came in for a sherry on Boxing Day to meet Esther,' said Brian. But Allen Parsons only sighed and shook his head and stared at the grass, for they both knew that Margaret would not approve. She had been rude once to Allen who used to come to the house to play chess with Brian on a Sunday, and he had preferred not to go back since then. That was the year Sheila died. Why, she did not even say hello to him in the street now.

'Maybe,' said Allen non-committally beginning to move away.

'She's a good and bright girl you know,' said Brian. 'Oh yes, quite bright. And with a wicked sense of humour like her mother.

Oh yes, just like Sheila.' He stood still a few moments before turning away to join his friend.

Then the ritual was finished for another year, and they started back up the High Street.

'We're having tea at Nancy Petrie's,' said Brian.

'Better you'n me, Brian me lad,' said Allen.

Brian laughed and took his friend's arm; two old men who had nearly lived their lives and knew, despite everything, how to take pleasure in the simplest things.

'Brandy,' said Brian. 'Must buy some. For the brandy butter. Do it later.'

'Full works then for the meal, is it?' said Allen Parsons.

They passed the lighted and decorated window of the butcher and heard, somewhere, a Salvation Army band playing carols.

Margaret decided that they should walk the few hundred yards to Nancy Petrie's, which they did, properly dressed and feeling on show. They were a few moments late as Richard had ignored Margaret's worrying and insisted on listening right to the end of the carol service.

Well, at least there was a festive wreath of holly, ivy and fern on Mrs Petrie's well-polished door; at least there was a coal and log fire once they had got past the yapping dogs; and at least there were candles, red and green, for Esther to concentrate on during the worst moments of being carefully looked over, judged and (as it seemed to Richard) found embarrassing by Mrs Petrie's three young, sombre and overly polite grandchildren.

Richard bore it well. He knew it was not that people were cruel or malevolent, it was simply that they could not cope with the affront Esther made to normality. To believe that such a being, so out of control, so unable to send signals, could *think* was barely thinkable. For to do so was to imagine what it must be like to be her, and to do that was harder even than knowing oneself. And so they sat having tea, politely, pretending not to notice that Richard had to help Esther eat a biscuit, and push the globules of saliva-softened crumbs back into her mouth; no one seeming to hear the gulps and choking gasps as she drank the cup of tea, cooled to a ghastly whiteness with cold milk, and the dribbles that followed the removal of the cup, and the fine linen napkin that was so soiled it might never be quite the same again. Yes, the smiles were as pale and brittle as Mrs Petrie's expensive tea set.

The only thing that could be said was that the older Richard Marquand got the thicker his skin became. But the social cuts still hurt him deeply, the pain would never go away. The sense that he could do nothing for his daughter, nothing ever, nothing to make her right, would never really leave him.

So the tea was, finally, a strain and they were glad when five to six came and Margaret gave the signal that they should leave.

After that, and light-hearted as if they had just come out of the dentist, it was back up the road to watch the tail end of a good old English Ealing comedy on television while Margaret prepared a supper she correctly described as 'only a scratch meal'. It was tinned soup and spam salad and Esther's face said, Yuk!

As soon as she decently could, Margaret drove them all from the kitchen so that she could get on, and from there came bangs, and silences, and smells of steam, as she soldiered on, a martyr, through her Christmas meal preparations.

Gloom was descending like sleet and no amount of discussion about the prospect of the morrow could lift it from the shoulders of the house. Esther, dog-tired, was bathed without demur, towelled without protest, tucked in with scarcely a murmur, and fell into the escape of sleep. And later, towards ten-thirty, by which time Margaret and Brian had retired, Richard crept up to her bedroom and put by her bed the red Christmas stocking that she would not, without help, be able to reach. Standing there in Sheila's room, looking at her Alison Uttley rabbit books all in a row near the old washstand, the wardrobe still hung with two of her school dresses, and a hockey stick propped in a corner where more than a decade before . . . no, no . . . nearly twice that, she had left it, Richard wished he had the power to call up Father Christmas, the power to bring light and love, laughter and music to this old hurt house. But he had not. He felt powerless as he sat down for a moment on the edge of Sheila's dressing-table chair and looked at their daughter, and at the stocking he had decorated alone in the front room downstairs.

He went back downstairs and sat by the dying fire until nearly midnight. Then he put on a coat and gloves, and walked down to the High Street.

He was not alone. As he walked in darkness he saw others walking too, and heard the sound of St Mary's bells, chiming cheerily into the night, announcing that the midnight service would begin soon. He did not go on, but stood in black shadows, watching others go to form a congregation. The church bell stopped, silence fell, and he started back the short distance to the house again.

Decades later Richard Marquand remembered stopping a final time before going back into the house, for he had heard, tolling out of the darkness, a single bell, on and on and on, as if some solitary being somewhere wished to tell those few lonely souls who wandered homeless in the night that Christmas had come, and would always come to those who heard and believed.

Later, when Esther Marquand became the first to collect the stories of the Skallagrigg together, there was one of special significance for her which she loved to read again and again. This is her final version of it.

One Christmas, just before the war, a new chaplain came. He was young and inexperienced and his name was Father James Freeman.

Until then Arthur had refused to go to chapel. He said to one of his friends who repeated it, 'I don't believe in God the father almighty or in Jesus Christ only son of God or the Holy Catholic church. But I believe in the forgiveness of sins.' So they let him not go.

It was December and the new chaplain came to the Back Ward and sat down among the boys who didn't go to church. There were about ten of them. Father James was in black with a white collar. He looked neat and clean and Arthur looked at him and waited.

The Father was young, not much older than he was. He said, 'I understand that most of you have decided that you would prefer not to go to chapel.' He waited for a bit and some nodded and some ignored him. He was right to say 'most' since Dilke had ordered that a couple of them shouldn't go because they couldn't shut up and keep still which is what you should do in chapel.

Father James said, 'I respect your views and would not try

to dissuade you from them. But I am going to do my best to conduct the services here in a way that will make sense for believers and non-believers alike. We all of us suffer a loss of faith sometimes. All of us.'

Arthur thought to himself, 'Well, that's a turn up for the books! A Man of God who has doubts! I'll have a go at this!'

So when Father James was leaving them Arthur called out as best he could. The Father didn't recognize this but one of the boys said, 'Arthur says he'll go.'

Then Father James came over and sat by Arthur's chair and looked into his eyes.

'Do you want to?' he asked.

And Arthur found he could nod. He was that relaxed.

'There we are,' says Arthur to himself and the Skallagrigg, 'we've done it again. Though God knows what I'm letting myself in for. Ha ha ha.' Arthur liked a good joke.

The great day of Arthur's visit to the chapel was Christmas morning as it happened. Arthur was wheeled in and was surprised to see how full the chapel was, the patients nearly outnumbered by people from outside, all wrapped up against the cold.

The patients didn't take communion at the golden brass rail long and strong beneath the altar. The few who took it had it served to them where they sat. Some wanted to go up but Dilke said, 'No, one starts and all the buggers'll start and what do we do then? They don't do it for God, they do it for something to do.'

Arthur sat and stared. He was thinking: 'I'm glad I came. This is better than Back Ward.' Even so, Arthur was feeling low that Christmas. He always missed the Skallagrigg then, though he knew he was especially near. But he needed a friend. He lost the best friend he had years before, his name was Frank. Tall thin Frank, thin as a bar to a cage. They moved him without thinking to tell Arthur and Arthur (who was just a kid then) thought he had died. Later he learnt he hadn't. He had gone to a different ward in a different block, so Frank might just as well have been dead. Whom God hath joined together let no Dilke put asunder, Arthur was thinking as the service began with loud vibrations in the wheels of his chair from the organ. After the last 'normal' person had finished communion and turned back up the aisle to the pews, someone among the patients slowly stood up.

'Sit down. You, sit down,' whispered Dilke harshly.

But the patient stood there. People were pretending not to notice, but were as quiet as mice, waiting to see what would happen. The patient said, 'I want to. I want it up there. I want the drink and what they eat. I believe in God. I want to drink of His son's blood, and eat of His son's flesh.'

That's what he said, or something like it.

Father James said in a firm voice, 'Yes, of course. Help him come forward, please.'

And before the whole staff, the whole hospital, and in the silence of the staring children and the visitors, the wives, the retired staff from the village – before them all the patient made his way along his row to the aisle, and down it to the altar rail. And wasn't Arthur surprised! That brave patient was none other than his lost friend Frank. So Frank went down to the Father and all watched as he knelt down and put his arms on that golden bar that shone with Christmas lights. Father James came to him with the white biscuits on a tray and he offered them to Frank and Frank took one. Father James said the words over him.

But Frank wouldn't eat the white wafer he held and those hundreds behind in the pews watching could see his legs shaking.

'Father, I'm scared,' he said.

The whole Christmas congregation waited, and even the children were quiet.

Then Father James looked down at Frank and saw that he was scared and frightened of God, and of the bread and wine, the flesh and the blood.

And Father James did what no Father before him had done in that church. He knelt down facing Frank and spoke to him, and he took the wafer and he broke it, and he showed Frank it could be eaten, and Frank ate. And the Father talked more and took the golden chalice and showed Frank it could be supped from. Then Frank bent his head and the Father spoke a blessing for him alone and you could feel that blessing like it was a fire that had been lit and would never go out.

Then the Father turned to the altar and took the bread and then the wine and Arthur saw that he did not twist the chalice like they do between people, nor did he wipe it. He supped it from where Frank had supped it, his spit to Frank's spit: and he was with Frank and they were with Christ. From that moment Arthur began to love Father James and to tell the Skallagrigg about him.

Frank knelt there for a time with head bowed and then got up. He turned back to face the whole congregation but he wasn't scared any more. His eyes were alight like they had never been.

He came back with head up, up the aisle. But it didn't end there.

From the back Arthur called out loud and clear, garbled words that no one understood except one, and that one was Frank. Frank stopped and stared, his face puzzled. Then he saw Arthur, his very old and very dear friend. And his face was a Christmas present to the whole world because it was filled with joy. And he walked slowly like he always did, straight past Dilke and he said, 'Lo, Arthur. Lo. It's Christmas. Happy Christmas. I took Communion up near God and he found you again for me.'

And Arthur said some more and Frank nodded and said, 'Yes, Arthur.'

That was how the friendship between Arthur and Frank came into being again, on Christmas Day before the war. And when they said prayers after that for the rest of the service, or sang songs and thanked God for this and that, Frank stood holding the handles of Arthur's wheelchair and wouldn't be budged, not ever again. Ever after that all through their long lives, that was where Frank chose to say his prayers.

The night fades to Christmas dawn 1977. The tolling bell has long gone and Esther has slept through the deep of the night. Now she is stirring and beginning to wake.

Margaret Ogilvie is already awake and fretful, and wondering why despite herself, despite everything, she has woken thinking of Esther. Esther, her granddaughter. Only with difficulty does she manage to suppress the uncomfortable, unfamiliar and alarming feeling she has woken with. Because it really is quite absurd. Oh no, it cannot be. She will not let it be.

Love? Esther?

But, once born, such love does not lie down and die. It waits, as it waited for Arthur and the Skallagrigg, until the time is right. Then it calls out its name as God called out to Frank that Christmas Day, and it is heard.

EIGHTEEN

At three-thirty on Christmas afternoon, after the broadcast of the Queen's Speech had ended, and while they were still sitting round the remnants of dinner in the dining-room, the crisis that had loomed over the Ogilvie household for the previous thirty-six hours finally broke.

Until then Christmas Day had, in fact, been a moderate success. The presents had been exchanged over a pleasant breakfast in the kitchen, supervised warmly by Brian Ogilvie, and Margaret had, for a time, seemed moderately relaxed, though she fretted about when, exactly, to put the turkey in the oven.

But that done, and the table laid in the dining-room ready for the Christmas meal, they had all gone off to a morning service at St Mary's which Esther seemed to enjoy, joining in the singing of the carols as best she could, and looking about during the readings and the prayers.

Christmas dinner was not as bad as it might have been – though the turkey was not ready until an hour later than planned, the vegetables were overdone by three-quarters of an hour as a result, and the stuffing oozed wet and mysteriously uncooked in the middle of the bird.

Nevertheless, by five to three they had pulled all the crackers and put on paper party hats, and even Margaret was flushed with sherry; by three Brian Ogilvie was mellow and relaxed and nearly past paying interest in anything much except to say 'Hear, hear' to those parts of the Queen's Speech which seemed to demand it.

Then the radio, specially brought in, was switched off and Richard made them all tea. But when he sat down again, and their tea was ready before them, Esther stiffened, looked about her and said with that same forbidding authority which until now she had inflicted only on her friend Tom: 'Mama.'

For a moment or two this did not seem like crisis. Brian mumbled an 'Of course, m'dear', and wandered off to the kitchen to fetch the photograph she had seen on her first visit, thinking that that was what she wanted.

But it was not. She stared at it and then, staring round at all of them in turn, once more said: 'Mama!'

Her meaning was quite plain, and her dismissal of the kitchen photograph underlined it. She wanted to see more photographs of Sheila, and damn Christmas.

Her unsmiling stare, her intelligence, her purpose, cut through the silly hats and the facile small-talk. It cut through Brian's elderly and genial haze. It had no patience with Richard's resigned paternal plea for her to shut up; it did not waver before the clearly hostile alarm in Margaret's eyes.

The three adults were seeing an Esther Marquand none of them had seen before. She wanted – no, she *intended* – to see photographs of her mother and she wanted to do so now. *Now.*

Richard drew his sword and stood ready to do battle for his daughter: 'Esther would enjoy seeing some photographs of Sheila as a girl,' he said. 'Have you any?'

Margaret drew herself up into a strange tight posture, took the green tissue paper hat off her head and patted her hair before saying, with a severe and forbidding stare at Brian to silence any disloyalty he might be harbouring (a stare which had, though no one in the room noticed it, not a little of the same steel that already glinted from the opposing eyes of her granddaughter across the table), 'I really don't think we know where they are, do we, Brian?'

Then, the transparency of this lie being so obvious, she added without a trace of guilt and in a voice that brooked no denial, 'I mean, it would really be quite difficult to get them out.'

There were fortress walls of silence all about, but over their ramparts and among their turrets strange sweet spirits began to fly up, circling, making their presence strangely felt. Esther's eyes seemed electric blue-grey and confronted old Brian over the table; Richard glared for a time but then relaxed back with a sudden smile of paternal pride as if he had discovered that Esther had no need of a champion, and could fight this one herself.

But most powerful and benign of all was that good spirit, warlike yet kindly, that settled about Brian Ogilvie and made him seem to shed a pall of years. By some alchemy his affable resolution to avoid a scene that had kept him smiling for two days, and in a sense for more than ten years, suddenly seemed decidedly shaky.

He stood up and for the moment his confidence and good-natured sureness were stronger by far than the bitter fears in Margaret's eyes.

'I'm sorry to contradict you, Margaret, but you see I think it would be a very good idea if we showed Esther some more photographs of her mother, if that's what she wants. Especially on the day that Sheila always loved so much.' With that he left the room, the echoes of the man he had once been and was now again reverberating so strongly that Margaret remained in her chair in pained suffering, and stared helplessly after him.

Silence reigned while on the floor above them, in one of the spare rooms, Brian creaked about and opened drawers. Then he fell silent for a time before coming back down the stairs.

He came in with a large cardboard box which he put on the table between himself and Esther. He cleared more space and then began to take from it album after album of photographs, and yellow and red envelopes in which film developers had returned photographs which had never been sorted.

'Perhaps you could make some more tea now, Margaret,' he said with a firm smile as he began to go through the photos of the Ogilvie family, one by one.

Great-grandparents, uncles, friends, and black poodles; the garden of their first house in London; snaps of a walking holiday in Wiltshire – black and white photographs all, which showed different moments in the life of the modest middle-class family into which, in the early thirties, Brian Ogilvie, a young civil servant attached to the War Office, had married.

'Three hundred and fifty pounds a year I earned,' said Brian looking at the only wedding photograph they had: Brian as a young man and a young Margaret all in white, and shy, and perhaps a little plain beside her elder sister and mother.

Margaret returned with a tray of tea things and sat down at the table. She was pale, and had been crying. Brian reached over and touched her arm. 'It's for the best, my dear, it really is. Esther and Richard are family, they'll understand.'

Margaret managed a brief and fragile smile, and then poured them each some tea and, with a sniff and a quick dab at her nose

with a handkerchief, looked at the photograph Brian was holding:
her own wedding photograph.

Esther stared at it too, for a long time, and then over at what
that bride became, a bitter woman, tense and lost, sitting now
quite subdued, with red eyes and unable to protest.

Then came a photo of a London garden: the garden to a flat they
had on the borders of Kensington and Notting Hill Gate; a cat on a
windowsill in the sun; the childless years of a marriage on which,
in a kind of way and judging by the smiles, the sun had at least
gently shone.

'But we decided that it would be best not to have children, you
see, not for a time, until we were more secure,' explained Brian.
'Well, old boy . . .' he began to continue apologetically.

Margaret leaned forward and interrupted. 'Perhaps you cannot
imagine how little money we had then, Richard. Brian was lucky
to have that job, a good job, though it was hard to manage on the
money. I took work as a part-time secretary/book-keeper to a
wholesale florist in Bayswater.' She paused and a moment's smile
came to her face at the memory. 'He was a . . . kind man. I was not
perhaps a good secretary. He had a Christmas party, you know,
every year, and all the husbands and the fiancés were invited. It
was surprising how many of the girls suddenly had fiancés, surprising how many engagements were broken off after the New
Year!'

Richard laughed to encourage them both, and refilled their tea
cups.

Brian pulled out another photograph. A baby on a blanket in a
garden, a pram with high-spoked wheels and a white frilled
awning.

'Sheila?' asked Richard.

'No. One of my sister's children. She, she never had any difficulty
having children.' Margaret's voice was sad. 'I, er . . . well, we had
thought . . . it would be easy. We were told . . .' Margaret cast a
quick glance at Brian and then away into that place on the table-
cloth where she seemed to see the past. 'I wanted a child, you see,
but there were problems. And then, in 1940, after over two years
of trying, I . . .'

'Margaret had a miscarriage, I'm afraid,' said Brian. 'I was away
in the army by then. She was alone. It was a hard time for her.'

Margaret continued the story: 'It was late into the pregnancy. He was . . . I was told it was a boy. A little boy. After that I was told I might not have a child. The doctor simply said I might not have another child. I . . .' And her hand reached out for Brian's and held it as, perhaps, it had not been able to then when it had so needed to.

'I was ill, you see, after that, not really able to cope.' Margaret looked up, her eyes clear and a little angry. She looked at Richard. 'I was ill, upset, but we didn't have the same help or understanding as your generation has now. We coped alone. Brian knew nothing, and I didn't think it right to tell him, to worry him. He knew only we had lost the child.'

Esther listened, quite still. She was staring at Margaret.

'Mama,' she said.

'Yes, my dear,' said Margaret looking directly at Esther for once, 'I expect you want to know how your mother came. Well it was a miracle really. Brian came home on leave in 1942 and we took a short holiday in Wiltshire where we had been before our marriage. The weather was good and we walked and Brian was so kind and well . . .' She managed a fond smile which for a moment transformed her face, and then added, 'Well, you know!'

Brian searched through the photographs and came across one of a baby wrapped up in a white swaddling blanket. He showed it to Esther.

'That's your mother, old girl. That's Sheila.'

'She was born in a private ward at the Radcliffe on September 25th, 1942. The sister had a friend in the army and quickly got a message to Brian for me. You were in Kent I believe.' As Brian nodded Margaret sniffed again and got up to make yet more tea. 'The consultant told me afterwards that I probably would not be able to have more children. It was a difficult birth, you see, very difficult. There is a history of that in our family.' There was a pause and she looked at Esther. Margaret's eyes were blank again and she left the room quickly.

When she had gone Brian said, 'They say the pity of war is on the battlefields, but you know it is at home as well. We didn't know what civilians suffered, you see. They had experiences they could not share just as we did. I simply was not there the first time and nor the second, when Sheila was born. That was very very

difficult it seems, and rather touch and go for Margaret. How can a
wife forgive her husband not being there when he is most needed?
Nobody's fault, but the fact was I *wasn't* there. She nearly lost her
then, and all Sheila's life Margaret's greatest fear was that she
really would lose her.' Brian paused before adding, 'And then she
did, you see. She did. It really happened.'

Brian looked over at Richard and smiled bleakly as if to explain
why, all these years, he had stayed loyal to Margaret and loved
her; and why she might have found it so hard to meet Esther.

Both men had almost forgotten the presence of Esther, who sat
still and listening throughout, a little pale and shocked, and watching now for Margaret's return.

She came back with hair neater and eyes clearer, seeming
resolved not to let emotions get the better of her any more that
day. She sat down and said firmly, 'I think perhaps that's enough
of photos and memories now,' as if she had been practising the line
in the kitchen.

'Yes, of course, yes.'

But Esther had not had enough and her legs stiffened and a look
of annoyance crossed her face.

'Later, you can see some more later.'

Esther seemed to relax at this. Perhaps she had had enough of
sitting and wanted a walk. She would keep them to that 'later'.

But then as Brian stacked the photos back into the box, rear-
ranging those inside to accommodate them all more tidily, he took
out a few packets of a different size and shape from anything else
they had seen.

'Cine film?' said Richard.

'That's right. Used to have . . .'

'Mama?' began Esther hopefully.

Her hand tried vainly to reach out as she stared at those boxes of
film.

'Mama?' she said.

'What is it, Esther? The boxes of film?' asked Richard, interpreting for her. '*Are* they of Sheila, Brian?'

Margaret suddenly stiffened into panic and hostility.

'No, Brian, not those. That's enough now,' she said. 'Can't you
see it's quite enough!'

She stood up, took the box, removed the remaining packets of photographs and put them on the table. Picking up the box with the cine films still inside, she began to leave the room.

'If Esther must see the photos she may, but not the films.'

The dining-room grew suddenly cold about them. Its austere oak furniture, whose formality and darkness had somehow been submerged by the festive spirit and opening of hearts, imposed its presence once more, and the bland cream wallpaper seemed suddenly able to reject the colour and light-heartedness of the few decorations Margaret had contrived to put up. The spirit of Christmas was in retreat.

'Me,' said Esther, glaring at Margaret, and pathetically reaching out for the boxes that Margaret was taking. '*Me!*'

'No, Esther, you can't have everything your way. *No.* These are mine, they're ours and not for you,' said Margaret. Her face was white, almost grey with strain and upset, and she was beginning to shake with imminent tears. 'Can't you understand that, Esther? Can't you see how hurtful you're being?' She almost shouted the words.

Then Esther began to cry, terribly, her legs stiffening out and her arms slowly rising in a gesture of hopeless impotence. 'Well, I don't know, Margaret, I don't suppose there's any harm . . .'

'Brian!'

And if, earlier, Brian's past youthful strength had briefly shown itself so now did Margaret's, and it was infinitely stronger. She spoke his name with such savage control that it seemed as if the very letters of which it was comprised should march off to the detention block in disgrace.

Then she was gone, with the box and the films, back upstairs where a drawer was opened and firmly closed, and a bedroom door was shut.

Esther was inconsolable. Neither Richard nor Brian could find anything to amuse her, and nor was she interested in Richard's attempt to explain that some things are difficult for older people and if she was only patient then in time she would get to see the films; but it was no good, and even a walk, normally the sure antidote to tears and misery, had no effect. She continued to cry and to complain. So that Christmas Day, which had started at least moderately well, declined irritably and sadly around them until each one guiltily longed for the time when Esther could be put to bed.

But even when that time came she did not stay quiet, her cries
of protest going on and on until it was gone nine o'clock before she
fell into a kind of sleep.

At ten they all thankfully retired leaving a day of emotional
disarray behind them. At eleven Esther woke again and began to
cry out her continuing protests loudly. Richard went to her. She
would not be quiet. 'Me' and 'Mama' were the words she spoke.
After three-quarters of an hour Richard lost his temper and did
what he had rarely done: he shouted at her. She cried more. He left
her, slamming her door and then his own. For a short time she
was quiet, staring at the closed door and breathing heavily, but
then it was as if she made a decision. She began to scream out in
impotent rage. Through closed doors, her muffled cries were
chainsaws on the mind.

At ten to one Brian Ogilvie, now quite sober, could stand it no
longer. He would have gone to Esther before but for Margaret's
orders, entreaties, threats and whispered reasons as to why he
should not.

But finally he said, 'Oh please shut up, Margaret, it's all your
damned fault anyway,' put on his dressing-gown and went into
Esther's room. She fell as silent as she was able, given the violence
of her anger. He sat on the bed and let her settle down.

He had learnt a thing or two about her.

Finally he spoke. 'Something's wrong, is it?'

She had the good grace to manage a weak grin at this under-
statement.

'Do you want me to get Daddy so you can go to the toilet?'

'Nah.'

'Do you want a drink?'

Silence.

'You know that I know what you want, don't you?'

She nodded and, miraculously, giggled.

'You want me to show you those films.'

'Yeh,' she whispered.

'You're as stubborn as your mother used to be,' he said.

She stared at him.

'Esther, my girl, it's one o'clock in the morning!'

She stared at him.

'You ought to be asleep.'

'Nah,' she said.

Then he did something that he had not done since Sheila was a little girl. Lowering his voice to a barest whisper, he said, 'If . . .' (Esther nodded) '. . . I were to show you the films . . .' (Esther nodded again) '. . . would you . . .' (Esther said 'Yeh?') '. . . go to sleep?'

Esther stared at him for a long time.

'Nah!' she said finally. And then she laughed so much that he had to shush her. So loudly indeed that in the next room Richard heard it and felt relieved. He had heard Brian go in and now that Esther was quiet thought it best he leave Esther to him. And with this thought he turned on his side and drifted into real sleep.

In Esther's room, Brian Ogilvie sighed, tightened his dressing-gown cord, and rather creakily bent down, putting his arms around his granddaughter to lift her out of bed and take her downstairs and give her a film show all her own.

From the Marquand Collection: Disk 7, File 'M A R Q08', page 2

Granddad carried me downstairs and put me in the front room and turned on the electric fire. He said, 'You won't make a noise and wake everyone up?' But I wouldn't have, not for the world.

Then he delved into the bottom drawer of the oak sideboard and got out an old projector. Then he went and got the film from wherever my grandmother had put it after lunch.

'The screen's in the loft and I'm not getting it because it'll wake Margaret and we can't have that. But we'll do what I did when Sheila first saw these because the screen hadn't come. I showed them on the wall.'

He put the projector on the table and took a picture off the wall. Then he said 'Damnation' because he had not used it for so long that the house had been rewired to square-pin plugs and the projector had an old round-pin one on. He got a new one from the understairs cupboard and changed it.

When he was ready he wound the first film on. It crackled and was in an old-fashioned reel like the big grey metal ones they used to have for feature films at the Centre before they got a video. He turned all the lights off except for the ones on the tree, so the room was in semi-darkness.

Then suddenly the bright projector light went on and he directed it to the wall and adjusted it back and forth until the edges were sharp. He had to put two books under the feet to get the right angle. He pushed the sofa I was in to face the square of light. I hoped no one would wake up to disturb us.

Then he said, 'Luckily the wallpaper's bland so you'll just get a few pale stripes on the picture.'

He turned on a motor and there was a whirring and sudden darkness and some numbers 7 6 5 4 3 . . . and then a black cross and a black and white image, but it was all fuzzy and unclear. He turned the focus and then we were there, back in the past.

It was mountains. It was a Swiss holiday, I knew that from some of the photos he had shown me earlier.

'This isn't the one with Sheila in it,' he said. 'But we'll run it through just the same and then run it back. It's not long, only about five minutes.'

It wasn't very interesting and he made comments as it went through like, 'Well! Long time since I saw that! This was 1958 and Sheila was away in France that year. Our first holiday without her.' But there were too many mountains and he didn't know their names like Daddy would have done.

Then the film was over, wound back, put in the reel again and I waited for the next one.

He held the boxes up to the light.

Then he said, 'I think this is the one. Oh, and this. Yes, it's these two. One's by the sea and one's in the garden. Mainly. But I don't know which is which. We'll have to find out, won't we Esther?'

He threaded one into the projector and turned on the motor and then the light. Sudden white light, a flicker of numbers into the film black and white, and there, the grass of the garden a little pale, the initial image a little out of focus because she was skipping towards the camera: my mother as a little girl.

She wore a gingham dress and had white ribboned plaits, and her cheeks were chubby. She was conscious of the camera. You could tell because she kept looking at it, her eyes smiling and her head still as if she did not quite know how to move it.

I kept thinking, 'That little girl's my mother!' Sheila Ogilvie. She picked up a ball and threw it up and caught it, her legs skinny and one pigtail coming over her shoulder while the other stayed behind. The projector whirred and from the side of the image came another person, young and in an elegant dress. Margaret Ogilvie! She was so different, so much younger and gayer, I was shocked to realize how she had changed. She walked over the lawn and joined Sheila and, putting her arm around her shoulders, turned to the camera and stood still, all prearranged. They stood smiling, my mother's hand going up to protect her eyes because they were facing the sun to get the best light.

Granddad began to talk softly over the whirr of the old projector.

'She was six then, no older. Margaret didn't want to be in the picture but Sheila said she wouldn't pose for me if Mummy didn't come in. She . . .'

The image cut to a view towards one of the trees in the garden. Mummy was on a makeshift swing. I noticed her shoes and her feet. She had pretty feet. Then I saw mine, stretching out stiffly into the flickering light reflected off the wall. Pointed and twisted.

Back and forth she swung, at first all formal but she seemed to grow used to the camera and she relaxed and started to laugh and you could see her teeth and the little girl face and almost hear the laughter as if it was still alive.

My grandfather said, 'I put a swing up for her. She used to love that. Even when she was older. The rope's still there.'

Then a shot of a car in the street, some pavement where the camera was on at the wrong time and my mother the girl, no older than me but pretty and smiling, so sunny, on a path and behind her on the road, a little fuzzy but recognizable, was Margaret with some cases by the car.

'We were going on holiday. That was us about to leave. We . . .'

The film finished, white light flooded our eyes, and a loose end rattled in the spool.

The second film was that little girl, my mother, standing on a sunny beach, waves at her legs. She was shouting with pleasure at the camera. No voice though, no sound. I shouted back, warning her of what was on the horizon. Clouds . . . me. Too late for her to hear.

'Mama!' I shouted, beginning to cry, 'Me.' Me. She just smiled and laughed and didn't hear. Then I knew whose name to call, because her shadow was on the beach, yes it was. She could hear and help me. It was to her, my grandma, I must call, as if my mother was refusing to hear but surely Margaret Ogilvie would hear, and would know how to protect her daughter from the future which was my fault, all my fault.

'Nana! **Nana!**' and I shouted her name, the name I was able to call her, loudly and louder, ever louder not caring if she woke, wanting her to wake out of that film, from out of her room, come to me and help me stop being what I was.

Well, I didn't know it but she did wake. I didn't know it but she came downstairs, I didn't know it but she had stood at the open door behind us, silent and herself distressed, watching as that second film came on, her face caught by its flickering black and white silence as mine was, as my feet were, as Granddad was.

'Nana! Mama!'

I shouted for them as the film ran on. She did not seem to hear me calling, that little girl. My mother was sitting now, her back to the sea, and the horizon far far away and vague on the wallpapered wall, and mother Margaret helpless among the distant stripes of the wallpaper.

'Mama!' It was as if I was trying to run foward towards her but I couldn't run or even crawl because my legs and arms wouldn't move the right way.

Then I sensed that my grandfather was crying too, his hand ever tighter on mine as we both stared helplessly at where Sheila, the girl, my mother, was in that distant place where she was still safe, free and oblivious of us; both of us needing her again and me calling because only she could stop me being what I was, unable to ever go to her, unable ever to reach forward to touch her.

'Mama!' and then 'Nana!' and I was crying to her and to them both, confusing their names in my tears, and my whole body in grief and no longer caring if the noise woke the house, but turning round because something, the Skallagrigg, something, was coming, turning with the grey light flickering on my crying face as I saw standing there, staring at us, watching us, silent and still and watching us watching Mummy, Margaret. And I cried out to her for help.

Then it was as if her body cracked, and she came forward with her arms reaching towards me, towards us both, caught in the slow flickering light, and I was crying towards them that I didn't want this present, this place, where I was what I am, unable to run, unable to be myself. I wanted to run from her, but I could only turn back to the little girl on the wall and cry out without caring what effect I had on anybody, 'Mama, help me help me help me' but the girl that was to be my mummy was so beautiful, so perfectly formed, and her legs could hold her body as she stood up on the sand, turned to the sea again and walked out into it. And she would not hear my cries.

'Mama!'

But then I couldn't see any more, for my face was screwed up against the loss and the world around it and I could only call out her name garbled, not even say it right, and reach out for help.

Then my grandmother reached me.

Her arms were round me, her lips were to my cheek, her love and warmth were encircling me as Margaret, my grandmother, who had cried in the kitchen for so long came to me at last and accepted me for what I was and I found that those weak arms could hold, and that mouth could softly speak those same loving words that, years ago, when that forgotten film was made, they had spoken then; and her hurt eyes could weep, her head against mine and her arms around me as my grandmother whispered, 'It's all right it's all right it's all right, we understand, my dear, we understand, my darling.'

And I felt the protection of a mother's arms encircle me for the first time in my life and I could cry into them not caring any more, crying with my whole body, my legs against hers, my head to her shoulder and my mouth wet and open and screaming for the mother that I never had and saying Skallagrigg, Skallagrigg Skallagrigg as if that word was the passport to a freedom between ourselves.

When I opened my eyes again and stopped shaking, though my breathing was gasping and violent and my mouth drawn down by the effort of it, Granddad had gone out of the room and the projector was off. It was just the lights of the Christmas tree red and green and I looked, I really looked, for the first time into my grandmother's eyes, and saw they were not yet so deserted that she could not weep, nor her mouth so bitter that it could not smile at me as once, so long before, she had wanted to smile at my mother, her daughter, but had been unable to for fear she would lose her. She had not dared to love freely, as if such love risks losing all.

But now she was free to love me, she had lost all and found that when it all was gone, quite gone, somewhere there was something left of her, for her to love. 'Yes, dear,' she smiled, 'yes yes yes, darling, you're safe you're safe. I'm sorry I'm sorry I'm sorry. I love you, Esther. Esther, I'm here . . .' and I closed my eyes and slipped into the love she had held back so long, so long and bitterly, held back perhaps even when my mother was alive.

She had finally allowed life to rain its tears in her, and flowers had come out across the desert of her heart.

Early morning: A pot of tea by the Christmas tree and the three of them talking as if, at last, they knew each other: Esther, Granddad and, as she instantly became, Nana; a word that became as much loved by her as by Esther herself. And they got the rest of the photographs, talked to her of Sheila, and told her silly things, old stories that neither had spoken of for so long: of the day when . . . and the party where . . . and the school trip during which . . . and all the silly happy things that make up a family's memories. And when they had talked enough, Margaret Ogilvie, straightening her hair and just a little self-conscious again, said, 'I would like to see the films again please, Brian. Wouldn't you, Esther?'

Esther nodded, and they ran the films through once more, and this time they shared their memories with pleasure. Their grief had sweetly gone, for in its passing they discovered that they had a granddaughter who was theirs, and who could understand, and who in her way could talk to them. And as a parent loves a new-born child and does not see any ugliness, so Margaret then began to love Esther, not seeing strangeness or handicap in her at all. And from this full love, won with difficulty, came much that later made Esther what she was and helped her find the support she would need to reach the Skallagrigg.

And though Margaret was never truly relaxed with the world outside, nor less than forbidding to others on first sight, to Esther she was for ever special and beloved after that Christmas night's discoveries.

Richard Marquand had slept through that night.

But in the morning he knew that something had changed. Margaret brought him a cup of tea, with a smile of all things, and though she was still formal yet she was infinitely softer, and able to talk to Esther, and of her, as if she was her own.

Then Granddad Ogilvie staggered in with Esther in his arms and dumped her on Richard's bed, and Esther, by saying 'Mama' with a smile, got them to tell Richard what had happened, or a part of what had happened. But that was enough, more than enough, to understand why, that year, the Gregorian calendar suffered a strange and magical hiccup in one home in Charlbury, near Oxford, England. For Boxing Day mysteriously became a second Christmas Day and all that day the lights of the family Christmas tree in Charlbury shone with a power greater than electricity could provide, while the old grandfather clock seemed to stir and tick with a new vigour, as if eager now to march on to a happier New Year than many of those past.

NINETEEN

A fortnight later Esther Marquand left the Dale Centre in Ealing, and all her friends there, to start at Netherton Manor School for the Disabled.

Netherton Manor is set in deep countryside in Hampshire, ten miles from the coast. When Esther Marquand was there, it was still a privately funded residential school with an atmosphere established by the strict, paternalistic Christian ethic in which it was set up in 1928. A rambling Victorian building with the shields and insignia of the Whitaker family stuck over every archway, doorway, fireplace and ceiling, it was the proud creation of Sir Patrick Whitaker, a Bristol engineer who as a young man invented Whitaker electrical pumps and made his fortune. In 1928 Sir Patrick's successors endowed the building and grounds as a school for the disabled, and so it remained to the end of the century.*

The school's finest feature was, or had been, its gardens and grounds – two hundred acres of woodland to the north and east, a large area of playing fields to the west, and to the south a lawn that sloped suddenly down past a dilapidated French garden to a tiny and charming chapel used originally by the staff of the manor and its attached farms, of which there were four.

By the late 1970s, when Esther Marquand arrived, the buildings were in considerable disrepair, which is evident from any of the official and unofficial photographs taken at the time. The oak panelling in the main rooms was chipped and unpolished, while the black and white stone tiles along the corridors of much of the ground floor were cracked and missing in places – and a source of difficulty and danger to children in wheelchairs.

Somehow the spirit of the legendary Dr Perry-Wilcox, first

* Today (2019) Netherton is one of the staff training centres for the European Commission's Special Education Needs Unit, having closed as a school in 2008. This change of use was funded by the Fountain-Marquand Foundation.

headmaster, disciplinarian, scholar and autocrat, still lurked, a memory passed on by each generation of Nethertonians. His severe portrait still hung outside what had been his study (by then a common room), and stared self-importantly out of the succession of black and white school photographs that spread along the main corridor and round past the kitchen towards the boot room.

Study of those photographs reveals the changing nature of the school through the years before Esther's arrival – all male at the beginning except for some young staff helpers; few wheelchair-users at the start, mainly boys suffering from rickets and mild poliomyelitis. Collars and ties and gaunt subdued expressions. Then the war, and a young plump man in uniform appearing in the 1946 photograph: Ronald Warburton, BA (Cantab.), the mathematics teacher who was later to help bring out Esther's talents. Staff come and go, the male staff age and become less smart through time and the number of women increases, and they smile where once they frowned. In 1957 a new man takes Perry-Wilcox's place: the thin and ineffectual-looking A. W. Wright MA (Oxon), formerly deputy headmaster who had sat so dully at Perry-Wilcox's side for many years past.

Sadly, Dr Perry-Wilcox left behind him an inadequately trained teaching and administrative staff on which A. W. Wright made little impression, and the school went into decline.

Then the photographs (which have significantly been rehung so that the newest now occupy pride of place by the main door and the oldest are relegated to the kitchen corridor) show a change of personnel. In 1976 A. W. Wright disappears and in his place, and now in colour, with the pile of the school rising behind him and the pupils in ranks with staff and helpers, appears the young version of a man who, very much later, was to become a minister of education in a Liberal/SDP government in the 1990s, Clive Imray, BA Hons (Manchester), Dip.Ed, DMS. Two years after that, to the left of the picture and among the pupils at the end of the second row, Esther Marquand appears for the first time. She does not look happy.

Esther's first two terms at Netherton Manor were so disastrous that had Richard Marquand known about the internal reports, he might have felt rather less sanguine about Esther's future than he did.

From the start her attitude was negative and uncooperative, and though the staff of the school made allowances for new students it was very soon a problem, which affected not only staff assessment of her, but also isolated her from other students. She seemed to combine a smug arrogance with idleness and indifference.

Her level of performance in all subjects except mathematics fell far short of what the school might reasonably have expected given the assessments it had made, and the recommendations of the sponsoring local town council and education authorities. Only in maths did she hold her own, and then only just.

All this was exacerbated by puberty. Her physical development was far behind that of normal able-bodied twelve- and thirteen-year-olds. Naked she was a little girl still, her breasts unformed, her skin pale and hairless. She was, Richard and her helpers knew, continuing to grow bigger and heavier by the month, but there was no physical sexuality at all, unless it was a rare giggle and flash in her eyes. Those grey-blue eyes were perhaps the only feature of all her twisted and angled body which hinted at the possibility that one day Esther Marquand might be transformed from the undeveloped girl she still was into a young woman.

But for all her physical immaturity, her mind was distressed, wild and impatient (in other words, quite normal) and found fault with almost everything.

During those first months at Netherton, too, her mental insecurity and emotion confusion were laced with the sudden loneliness and distress that any child would feel for having left behind the only friends she knew: Peter, Tom and Karen, the last an enemy-friend whose mean hostility and unkindness Esther now found, oh confusion, she missed.

But there were other feelings emerging, and one of them (or a whole ugly range of them) related to her father and other women. She had never thought of the possibility of his having a girlfriend before – in those few relationships Richard had had he was very discreet and had never brought anyone home. But that year he had met someone, Evelyn Cafferty, an executive with an office systems group, to whom (and with justice) Esther had taken a dislike on the single occasion they had met. Beyond that she knew nothing, but it was enough to undermine her innocent confidence that Richard would always be there to protect and look after her. The beginnings of sexuality in Esther made her realize that it was possible, indeed very probable, that this would not always be so. And so jealousy about her father and what he was doing on those weekends when he was 'too busy' to come and visit her, mixed with a natural insecurity, made her worried and restless, and added to her present tendency to be uncooperative.

Her handicaps only increased these sufferings for they meant that she had no escape into physical action. She had to wait, and wait, and wait for others' help and did not have those outlets – such as tears, or browsing, or flicking through radio stations one by one – that privacy provides. Almost everything was done for her. So the days and weeks of the first term went slowly by as she learned that the place to which she had fought so hard to get, and which others had helped her to reach, could not change the stark fact of her handicap, though there was hope that somehow, some time, something might change; there was always hope, for without it there is nothing.

But the day that might bring change was a long time coming. The Easter holidays passed, and then the summer term. Then came the long holidays, overshadowed by her dread of another term at Netherton. With autumn came the new term, and Esther sank deeper and deeper into non-achievement as her un-cooperativeness continued and her silent protest deepened. As the days passed, the school knew that soon now it would have to say that it had failed with Esther Marquand.

One day in early November Richard Marquand had to visit clients on the south coast, and arranged to take Esther into Southampton to see a client's computer. Quite why we do not now know, nor could Richard later recall. Perhaps the school felt that a day out with her father would be good for her.

That evening Esther wrote a letter.

> Dear Peter,
>   Today I saw something that you would like. Maybe
> you've heard of them on telly: computers. Daddy took

me out for the day to Southampton to meet someone
who owns an engineering company there. He was very
nice. His cousin is handicapped so he said he was
interested in meeting me.

The computer was in a room by itself and quite big. It
is a lot of grey desks and metal cupboards, and quite
boring to look at. But he helped me press a key just like a
Possum except that the numbers and letters came up on
a television screen, in green. I explained through Daddy
that I liked doing sums. It wasn't easy to get it going for
that but he did and I added 2 and 2 (you know the
result!!). Then I multiplied 2 by a number like 578 and
the result came immediately. Then I did a really big one
and it worked out the answer to lots of decimal points.
But what it also did was print out the results on paper
nearby IMMEDIATELY. Lots faster than a Possum. If
you could only have one, Peter, you could play maths
with it. All you need is thousands of pounds! But I bet it
would be possible. He gave me the 'printout' and I
enclose it with this for you to see. I don't understand
the other numbers and letters.

Is Tom well? I would like to see him. I hope Karen isn't
being a pain. My school is as bad as ever and I want to
leave. See you in two weekends.

                                        LoveEsther

That this letter happens to record in her own words what we
believe to be one of the twentieth century's most remarkable
computer programmers' first experience of a computer is interesting, but it is not the reason we remember it. It is because it is the
only one of her letters to Peter Rowne to survive.

It is collected among those letters Richard Marquand so methodically preserved, with another shorter one attached to it whose
heading is that of the Director of Ealing's Dale Centre. It reads:

We enclose this letter written by your daughter to Peter
Rowne. Unfortunately Peter died last week in Ealing
General Hospital and in Ms Coppock's absence I am
writing to inform you. We have not written to Esther

about this as, knowing she might be affected by the
news, we felt that perhaps you would prefer to inform
her yourself. If you would like to discuss the matter
with me I may be reached on extension 241.

The letter was signed, rather formally, by a Ms Kathleen Allen,
'Social worker, Ealing Dale Centre'. Richard read it several times,
uneasily; not because he did not understand its implications but
because he was that day packing his bags to head north on a brief
snatched break with Evelyn Cafferty.

He stared at the letter but did not see it. Rather, he thought of
the options: cancelling the trip to get down to Netherton to see
Esther, writing to her . . . yes, that was best. No. Call Margaret.
She might take on the task of consoling Esther. Anyway, the harsh
fact was that Peter Rowne was probably best out of his misery.

TWENTY

Margaret Ogilvie instinctively understood the significance that Peter's death would have for Esther, and realized it offered an opportunity for creating a change in her attitude at Netherton.

As soon as she heard the news, Margaret travelled with Brian to Hampshire. She spoke briefly to Clive Imray, the headmaster, and explained what had happened. He, sizing her up, said, 'I would be grateful for a little time with you later, Mrs Ogilvie, if I may . . . to talk about something quite different, but very much concerned with Esther. We are worried . . .' Margaret's face showed real concern. Yes, she concurred, they must talk later.

Esther was brought out of class and, leaving Brian with Mr Imray, Margaret took the handles of her chair and wheeled her across the lawns to the dilapidated French garden where they would have privacy. It was cold and damp underfoot, and a misty haze softened the trees and hedges of the garden which dropped, in a series of balustraded terraces, towards the church.

Margaret's face was purposeful and Esther was silent, knowing something was terribly wrong. Margaret had been careful to say, 'Your father asked me to come down . . .' partly because she feared that Esther would think that something had happened to *him*, but also because she knew that Esther might, at this moment, feel deserted by him.

As soon as she found a bench far enough from the school buildings for privacy, Margaret sat down facing Esther. 'I'm so sorry, Esther, but I have come with bad news, my dear.' She moved closer, loosening the straps a little because the school seemed inclined to make them tighter than Esther liked. Esther looked terribly afraid.

'I'm afraid your friend Peter has died,' said Margaret simply. 'I'm so sorry.'

Esther went white and her eyes stared into Margaret's. Margaret reached forward for her, undid her shoulder straps completely and knelt down by her chair and took her in her arms. Margaret held her as she had held her once before, but this time Esther was stiff and silent and in shock.

Then Esther tried to speak, to ask what had happened, and the question that ends in a cry from the void in which the bereaved is left: *Why?*

Her body strained in her chair, her mouth open and struggling with the word, her eyes desperate with grief and appeal, her legs jerking this way and that and her hands rising in slow contortions as if to protect herself from the knowledge that there was no answer to the question.

'I think you knew he had had bad flu in September and then bronchitis,' began Margaret. 'Well, his condition grew weaker and last week he went into hospital with suspected pneumonia. He did not suffer, he . . .'

But then Esther began to cry terribly, because she knew he must have suffered and could imagine him there alone, so alone, and afraid; only she would have known how to talk to him, to tell him someone was near, he wasn't alone. She knew he must have wanted her, and must have called out, but no one would have known who he was calling for. She should have been there.

WHERE WAS EILEEN COPPOCK? WHY DIDN'T SHE . . .?

Margaret held Esther and understood the questions she was trying to ask, understood her grief.

'Eileen has been away on a course these last few weeks, in preparation for her stay in America I believe. But she phoned me to send you her love. She is so sorry. She wished she had been informed because she would have called you. People don't always understand, Esther. People don't know.'

But Esther was seeing Peter again, lying in a white clean hospital, with none of his things near him and staring out of that shaking head, staring and alone while she was here at this place, doing nothing, nothing.

WHEN? Her body spasmed.

'It was Sunday night. Peter died in the early morning.'

Esther wept uncontrollably in Margaret's arms, her legs riding up against Margaret's knees and her mouth open and wet to Margaret's shoulder, her gasps of grief interspersed with words

Margaret could not understand. Then she was screaming, her whole body shaken and shaking, and they were cries from a prison in which Peter, whom she loved so much, had left her alone. The loneliness of Netherton she could bear, for that was outside her; but this, the sense there was now no one and there would never be anyone ever again who could understand, who could reach her, who could talk to her as Peter had, who was her equal, her kind; this loneliness was inside. From her cage of twisted sinews and misplaced limbs she cried out and screamed, and Margaret held her the closer and the more powerfully because she too knew of loss and loneliness, and remembered a time like this when she had needed to cry out and should have done so.

At last, when the afternoon air was chill, Esther began to talk, her 'words' interspersed with sobs and terrible gasping cries, their meaning and intent gradually becoming clear to Margaret.

Esther was talking about Peter, as any mourner for a friend does and must. She was remembering. Then she was crying again. Margaret understood.

'Are you crying because he was so clever, is that what you're saying?'

Esther nodded.

'It's because you think he was cleverer than you, isn't it?' This was not really a guess. Esther had once written to Margaret about Peter and said as much. It was just that . . . 'Peter didn't have a chance, did he?' And Esther's eyes filled with tears again, and her face screwed into hot grief and her mouth trembled with the single word 'Nah' again and again. Peter was so clever, so much cleverer than her, and he had never been able to talk to anyone but her. She was crying for the life he never had and for the isolation he had suffered.

It was nearly dark when they returned and had tea and sandwiches. Brian tactfully took Esther for a walk around the grounds while Margaret spent some time with Mr Imray. When they joined her again Margaret was looking very thoughtful. She had learned just how badly Esther had been doing at the school. Now was not the time to talk to Esther about it. She would have something to say to Richard first.

'We shall be coming down at the weekend, Esther, to see you again and make sure you're all right.'

'But, Margaret, there are . . .' began Brian, thinking of things he had planned for the weekend.

'Brian!' Margaret was at her most powerful, a single stare was enough to tell Brian that she knew something he didn't and that any plans he had for this coming Saturday were irrelevant since he would be needed to drive her to Netherton.

Yes, Margaret.

On the way back to Charlbury Margaret told Brian what Mr Imray had said about Esther's school performance and how near she was to being asked to leave. Brian saw Margaret's eyes filled with purpose, and her cheeks, normally pale, flushed and her spirit strong. She was going to see that Esther did not fail.

Brian was pleased, for he had not seen this kind of strength in Margaret for years.

In the three days before her return to Netherton, Margaret was busy on Esther-errands and Brian was forced to become her chauffeur. They went to the Centre and talked with the social worker. They contacted Eileen Coppock. They tracked Richard down on holiday and talked with him on the telephone. They wanted Richard to come straight home but he was reluctant to do so. 'Surely . . .' said Margaret, but Richard felt that she was being over-dramatic. However, Margaret rightly sensed that she was fighting for Esther's life and she used every bit of energy and intelligence she had. She spoke with Mr Imray again, on the telephone, and she realized that Esther would not be given a second chance. Netherton might not be exactly right, but everyone she talked to convinced her that there was nothing better. Time, and sympathy, were against Esther.

Margaret kept asking everyone she could, 'Who are Esther's friends?' And their answers came down finally to two names: Tom and Karen.

'But she can't stand Karen,' said Richard over the telephone.

'That is not the point, Richard. Karen is one of the two people of her own age she knows and who knew Peter. You don't have to like someone for them to be your friend, and to need them at certain times. Yes, yes . . . Karen it must be.'

'Be what?' asked Richard.

'It must be whom Esther needs to see,' said Margaret cryptically.

And she put the receiver down, her face alive and vital as if, after so many years, she had finally found a purpose.

The following Saturday morning Brian drove her first to London where, at the Centre, they picked up two extra passengers.

Knowing her grandparents were coming, Esther waited at the main entrance for them. She saw their car arrive and was surprised to see not just the Ogilvies but Tom and Karen as well.

They stared at her for a moment across the black tarmac drive before Tom ambled over and gave her a hug; Karen, seemingly reluctant even to say hello, eventually went to her and stared malevolently at the ground. Both reactions made Esther feel loved, and that she belonged to someone.

Margaret had arranged with Clive Imray to have lunch with the school, which he encouraged because it made a change for the staff and students to have visitors. It was Karen who made friends, and Tom for once who was silent, staying as near to Esther as he could, wearing a new jacket and on his best behaviour. He had grown since she had last seen him, and his hair was longer, and the colour of his spectacles had changed from black to brown. They slipped down his nose and he pushed them back carefully with a finger, his mouth open and his tongue on his lip.

After lunch Margaret explained that she wished to talk with Esther, and talk she did. Kindly but firmly, she told her exactly what Mr Imray had said and what was going to happen unless a miracle of effort now took place.

Esther stared at her (they were in Mr Imray's room which he had loaned for the occasion) and protested, cried and complained.

'You can be as angry as you like, Esther, but that does not alter the fact that you are not doing the best you can. If you want to be treated as an equal by everybody else you had better start behaving like one. And you had best not forget, my dear, that since you are handicapped you are going to have to work harder than ordinary people just to be considered their equal.

'Mr Imray has been extremely frank with me and says that facilities for your particular kind of handicap are not ideal here – for example the difficulty of using a Possum whenever you want because of the staffing problems. Well I'm sorry, Esther, but have you any idea of what the conditions in ordinary schools are?'

Esther stared.

'Do you know why you got here?'

Esther was silent.

'The assessments *showed* that you were bright and intelligent.'
Margaret paused and turned the screw finally where she suspected it might hurt most: her vanity. 'But, my dear, perhaps
we can be forgiven for beginning to doubt that. Now, you have
a few weeks of term left in which to show that you have any
brains at all. If you do not, then I will still love you and so will
your father because that has nothing to do with what you do.
But you will have been stupid and the thought of that disap-
points me. And my respect for you ... well, I'm sorry, Esther,
but it is simply not good enough. Nor is the fact that you are
unpleasant to people and, it seems, ungrateful for what you
have.'

Margaret got up and Esther remained silent.

'Now, you have time to spend an hour or so with Tom and
Karen and then we must go and I think you had better spend the
remainder of the weekend preparing yourself for the hardest period
of work you have ever faced.'

There was no smile, no hug; nor was there anger or rejection;
but rather a loving disappointment which thrust deep into Esther's
soul and made her feel selfish, idle, indulged and guilty all at once,
and left her with nothing to say.

It was therefore a subdued Esther who was pushed around the
grounds by Tom and Karen, the one effervescent now that he had
escaped the pressure of having to behave properly, the other deter-
minedly silent since she had met a boy she wanted to be friends
with and didn't at that moment want to walk; but she hung on to
Esther's chair all the same.

They went to the woods, over to the playing fields; they looked
at the geese and talked briefly to Henry Barton who gave Tom the
errand of fetching some feed for the chickens. Never once did they
talk of Peter, or even mention his name.

They raced precariously down the sloping lawn, veered off to
look at the French garden until finally, as if their meanderings had
had this as their sole objective, they found themselves tired,
breathless and with nothing to say, outside the door of the school
chapel.

Tom, normally diffident about going into a building he thought might be officially out of bounds, did not hesitate. He pushed Esther's chair before him and Karen followed them inside.

The light was dull, and the walls rose dark between the nineteenth-century stained-glass windows. There was a little organ to the right, beyond the front row of pews, and the polished quarry tiles were sometimes loose under the wheels of Esther's chair.

Tom liked churches and he would normally have wandered off and explored, but not this time. The moment he came in he became subdued, and Karen, silent now and uncomplaining, moved even closer to Esther. They grouped, silent, and faced the window above the altar.

Esther stared at the crude yellow radiants of the stained-glass sun that shone out above Christ's head. Salvation, and the promise of heaven. But Peter did not believe in heaven. Nor in Christ. He said numbers were more mysterious and more beautiful and delivered more.

Now he had gone, and left them. So they were together in the gathering gloom, close for comfort, with thoughts that led nowhere, staring at a window. Staring.

Tom said, 'Peter's died.' His voice shook a little. He wanted to cry.

In the silence that followed Esther understood for the first time that just as she had needed Margaret, so now her two friends needed her. She knew things they did not. Karen missed Peter too, just as she did; and Tom missed him as well, though differently, less miserably. But each one knew their friend was gone, and Esther knew that their group was diminished by his going. Margaret had instinctively known the importance of bringing the three children together, and letting them mourn in their own way.

'Amh?' Tom said. She looked at him but he was silent.

Tom wanted Esther to speak. To her right Karen moved closer, not looking at Esther or giving any sign that they could be friends, but closer and closer at her side, her fat arm to Esther's, and then her hand on Esther's leg for comfort.

Around them the little arches and bays of the church darkened into twilight, and the light faded; outside a kindly silence fell, an evening stillness, and the grass began to grow wet with evening dew.

Inside the chapel Esther stared at the darkening windows. It

would have been easy to tell them that Peter had gone to the
Skallagrigg and was all right now, but it wasn't like that; the
wooden fence and the Skallagrigg were not for the dead but the
living, it was for now, for her, for each of them.

But as she thought of the fence and visualized it, it seemed to her
that she knew that Peter was beyond it because he had got there
before he died, and she knew that he had found a way over it
because there was a way, there was. And though he had fallen
and been unable to go on he had called out to her to tell her that
she could learn to climb the fence as well and go even further than
he had. Yes, in those last moments he had not been in pain, and he
must have known she loved him and cared, and he must have
seen the way over the fence and found the strength for it . . .

Then in her own garbled way she began to tell them there was
hope, that beyond a fence a sun shone all yellow and warm as it
did up there above them in one of the stained-glass windows,
seeming to get warmer and bigger in the window as they stared at
it while the darkness gathered about them. Tom understood some
of what she said, Karen very little, but it did not matter, for her
voice was an invocation and prayer, of greeting and farewell, to
Peter their friend who had gone before them and learned to climb
the wooden fence.

'. . . and so he's there calling to us and he'll always be there
waiting, and he'll help us find the way towards the Skallagrigg.
Peter's only ahead of us, that's all, and we'll go on trying, won't
we, Tom? Won't we!'

Karen nodded and sniffed, understanding in her own way that
Esther was saying things Tom understood and which were a
comfort to them all, and that Peter was not all gone. Something
was left.

'Amh,' said Tom. 'Amh?'

He came round and stared into Esther's eyes and he was grinning, his eyes happy behind his new glasses.

YES, TOM?

'Amh, you're clever,' he finally said.

If Margaret's words of warning and command had begun to
push Esther towards a change, so now Tom's simple and unques-
tioning faith in her did what it had done so often before: it set the
seal on her determination. Suddenly she felt impatient, as if there

was hardly enough time for her to do the things she had to do. So much work, so much effort, to live up to Tom's belief that she was what he would never be: clever.

Before they all left, Margaret, still forbidding – Esther was unable to look her in the eyes so guilty did she feel about her lack of success at the school – said, 'Eileen Coppock sends you her love. She asked especially that you have this.'

It was a simple white paper bag. Tom presented it to her, held it so she could fumble at it until with a roll and a spin something fell out on to her tray.

It was a badge upon which were typed those words that its former owner had treasured. MY NAME IS PETER ROWNE, it said.

As Esther reached to touch it Margaret saw her work was done, and well done. There was a look in Esther's eyes that spoke of a determination to work as she had never worked, to strive to do things that, had Peter been alive and able, he would have taken pride in doing himself. But in his absence, and perhaps because of it, Esther would begin to work at last.

'Goodbye, darling,' said Margaret finally, unable to maintain her aloof disapproval to the last. 'You have till end of term.'

'Nana. *Yeh!*' said Esther, her eyes alight.

Then the car moved away on the tarmac and, as Tom turned to wave through the rear window, it was lost in the dusk but for two red rear lights disappearing among trees.

'Yeh,' said Esther to herself, her fingers rising slowly to Peter's badge which Tom, without being asked, had pinned to her dress.

TWENTY-ONE

That Esther Marquand's new-found intent to work hard found direction and effect was due mainly to two teachers at Netherton. The first, Ronald Warburton, was her maths teacher; the second, Marguerite Gatting, was her form mistress in that autumn term.

Ronald Warburton MA(Cantab) – or 'Warble' as the children called him – was perhaps the most remarkable of Esther Marquand's many teachers, and the first to recognize her mathematical ability and develop it. He was one of those lovable, eccentric teachers once so characteristic of the British private school system, who left an indelible memory in those they have taught.

Warble's plump and jovial face, his twinkling, enthusiastic eyes, his delight in the cunning solution to a mathematical poser, his grubby shirts which were never properly buttoned, his habit of coming into classrooms and muttering incomprehensibly before going out again because he had forgotten something . . . these were what Nethertonians recalled with affection and laughter when they met again and remembered him.

At the time Esther first came to Netherton in 1978 Warble was fifty-five and had been at the school all his working life. His passions were mathematics and music, whose patterns in his mind might well have been one and the same thing. In the two homely, untidy rooms he occupied in the west wing he spent a lifetime of private study of certain of the classic problems that had preoccupied mathematicians for centuries past. Prime number theorems, the Riemann hypothesis, the four colour conjecture . . . these arcane mysteries were food to his soul, and he pored over the literature of their solutions (or more often their non-solutions) with no less avidity than a gastronome over a great soufflé, or a fan over his team's championship game.

The second teacher to have a lasting impact on Esther was

Marguerite Gatting, who had been at Netherton nearly as long as Warble. She was single, referred to herself as 'Miss' Gatting, but had lost or mislaid her husband mysteriously before she came to the school. She had a son, now grown up, who appeared occasionally at her side at public school events like the Carol Service and Sports Day. She was slender and fine featured, with pale delicate hands on which, the wrong one, she wore a thin wedding ring. She taught English and Geography, and, in the classroom at least, her face, normally delicate and vulnerable, became animated and suffused with passion.

Romeo was never more romantic than when brought to life by Marguerite Gatting, Heathcliff never more strange and fearsome, Miss Haversham always succeeded in inspiring a nightmare of horror or two among more impressionable students; as for the great Mid-West, and the Russian Steppes, not to mention Yorkshire and Longshore Drift . . . they were places and processes she inspired students to wish to see, though it was hard to imagine her slim form out in wind and rain and battering sea.

She was the very opposite of Warble in dress and manner: neat, ordered, clipped, usually unsmiling, and her clothes, though always dark and subdued, often had about them some detail – a blood red belt perhaps, a modern silver brooch, a hint of lace – that suggested passion beneath the cool exterior. A passion that she allowed, it seemed, to emerge only in her teaching. She rewarded imagination and effort with a smile of such charm that students immediately wanted to earn the right to another and she had a habit of returning work not publicly, with comments to the whole class, but more discreetly, the books closed, and her comments written in green ink, sometimes harsh, often encouraging, rarely effusive.

It was Esther's good fortune that two days after she had decided she was going to work, and work hard, Marguerite Gatting set her English class an essay: 'Why I like my favourite fictional character'.

CAN WE WRITE ABOUT ONE WE HAVEN'T DONE IN CLASS? Esther asked, via her Possum.

This was the kind of question Miss Gatting liked, since it showed an imagination and wider reading than she usually found, and she liked it the more for coming from Esther Marquand who until then had never asked a sensible question and had shown no enthusiasm at all.

'Yes,' said Miss Gatting simply, 'you may, if you know one.'

This posed Esther a problem, since she did not in fact have a character in mind: she simply wanted to be different. But she accepted the challenge and that week reread one of the books that had enthralled her two years before when Eileen Coppock had encouraged her to read Frances Hodgson Burnett's *The Secret Garden*.

The book's heroine, Mary Lennox – 'the most disagreeable child ever seen' – was the one Esther chose to write about, but she wrote about her in a way that made plain to her teacher that Esther identified with her subject.

> I like Mary because she gets over her deformity of
> character by beginning to think about other people,
> which isn't easy for someone like her. I like her because
> she has a dream which is the walled garden, but she isn't
> afraid to try to make that dream reality. If I had been the
> author I would have described Mary in more detail, like
> what she wore and how she did her hair, and what she
> did first thing when she woke up in the morning, and
> why she was so horrible and twisted in character that
> all she did was to think of herself. As for Dickon (the
> country boy in the story who knows about nature) I
> think he was a bit too good to be true, and I think Mary
> would have said so, or at least thought so, but the
> author couldn't say that otherwise it would spoil the
> story. But I bet she didn't have much patience with
> Dickon when she grew up! But most of all what I like is
> the fact that Mary learns that no one can help her but
> herself, and she's lucky, because she's in a place where
> she's left alone enough to get on with it without
> interference, except from Ben the gardener. So she finds
> the key to the garden and one day she opens the door to
> it and her life begins to change. And I think she senses
> more than any other character the presence of the
> woman, her guardian's dead wife, who made the garden
> and loved it, and I sympathize with Mary because I
> understand why she might think or hope that when

she grows up she'll be able to make a thing like a
garden, and put her love into it, so that even if what
she is isn't obvious to the world as a whole at least it
will be to those who come, like Mary did, and see the
garden that she made.

Marguerite Gatting read this unusual essay several times, her
pen poised over the foot of the last sheet of Possum paper, hesitant
about what to write. It was not a question of the scale of the mark
– the piece was not only the best Esther Marquand had ever done
for her, but the most felt, and the most effectively critical, of the
class. No, it was rather that Miss Gatting understood that this was
a breakthrough which required the right response.

In the event she gave back the essay with a smile and a rare
public comment, softly spoken but loud enough for others to hear:
'This gave me great pleasure, Esther,' she said. Pleasure, the one
commodity Esther might well have felt she gave nobody. Pleasure!
And Esther blushed, looked down at the sheets on her tray, and
read again and again the words Miss Gatting had written in green:
'Quite excellent. It is a good book isn't it?' And so began Esther's
first success. Having gained approval she would never again lightly
throw it away. Very soon she would establish herself as one of the
best in Miss Gatting's classes, in both English and Geography.

It was during those same few weeks, between hearing the news
of Peter's death and the end of that autumn term, that Warble
became aware that in Esther he might have a student with unusual
aptitude in maths.

Sometimes in that period her sense of loss would overwhelm
her, and it happened one day during an art class when she was
finger-painting. Her face contorted into misery as she raised her
dripping hands to her face and slashed it with blue poster paint as
she tried, unsuccessfully, to stop herself weeping.

Matron came and she was taken out. Unable to make anyone
immediately understand what was wrong – though most sensed it
must be to do with the recent death of her friend – she was taken
to a classroom where there was a Possum and asked to type out
the problem. It was then that Warble came by and, hearing her
weeping and seeing that Matron was having trouble understanding, came in and asked what was wrong.

Esther fell silent.

Matron explained.

Warble pulled up a chair and sat down by Esther.

'Oh we know what's wrong, don't we?' Warble's voice was gentle and a little sad, and his warm eyes soft. Esther stared at him, her face still blue in places where Matron had failed to get all the paint off.

'You miss your friend, don't you?'

Esther stared, her face strained and her eyes flooded with tears as she started to nod and weep. 'Yes, Esther, I'm afraid it takes a long time for such a pain to go, a long time. It was like that when my mother died, you see. But is it better to have had such a loss than never to have had friendship or love at all?

'Type his name, Esther. I don't know your friend's name.'

Slowly she did so between sobs, and with tears on her cheeks as she hunched over the controls of the Possum.

P–E–T–E–R R–O–W–N–E

Warble looked at the name and then spoke it. 'Oh dear,' he said, his comfortable presence so sympathetic and benign that Matron nodded meaningfully at him and silently retreated from the room, leaving Esther to his good care, 'I'm so sorry, Esther. It's a terrible thing to lose a friend.' He touched her arm, which was unusual for him, and said, 'Perhaps you'd like to tell me something about him.'

For a long time Esther was silent, sniffing sometimes, gulping, heaving and in tears, staring at the Possum as if it might tell her what she could say.

Eventually she typed out a sentence that surprised Warble: HE LIKED NUMBERS. HE WAS BETTER AT THEM THAN ME.

'Are you good at them then?' asked Warble. 'You haven't exactly shone at Netherton, have you? Not like a star in the firmament. More like a dim thing caught behind cloud perhaps?' Esther managed a smile.

Warble mumbled a doubtful, 'Mmm,' and then said, 'What did he like about numbers?'

Esther immediately typed: HE LIKED THE PATTERNS THEY MADE. HE SAID THEY WERE BEAUTIFUL. THEY WERE LIKE MUSIC TO HIM.

'Are they like that to you?' Warble's voice was suddenly hushed, as if he dared not hope to hear what he hoped he might. His eyes were serious.

Esther hesitated. Then she typed: I DON'T KNOW SOMETIMES I PLAY GAMES WITH THEM IN MY HEAD AND THEY CAN BECOME BEAUTIFUL.

'What games?'

Esther smiled.

PETER TAUGHT ME A GAME. HE CALLED IT SERIES. HE GOT THE IDEA OFF A MATHS PROGRAMME ON TV. THEY WERE SHOWING HOW NUMBERS INCREASED IN STEPS LIKE 2,4,6,8, OR 2,5,8,11 OR 2,4,8,16. HE HAD THE IDEA OF WORKING OUT DIFFERENT WAYS TO INCREASE NUMBERS. FOR EXAMPLE YOU CAN THINK OF A NUMBER SAY 123 AND THEN YOU ADD THE LAST DIGIT TO IT (THAT'S 3 TO MAKE 126) THEN TWICE THE LAST DIGIT (THAT'S 12 TO MAKE 138) THEN THREE TIMES 8 AND SO ON. SOMETIMES HE WOULD CHALLENGE ME TO GO FOUR STEPS IN A SERIES, MAKING IT ESPECIALLY DIFFICULT WITH A COMPLEX CALCULATION. SAY START WITH 123 AND IN-CREASE IT EACH TIME BY ADDING THE SUM OF HALF OF IT PLUS THIRTEEN DIVIDED BY FOUR AND SO ON.

Esther stopped typing and Warble was silent.

Then he said: 'One hundred and eighty-seven.'

Immediately Esther said, 'Nah!' with a giggle.

'All right, one hundred and eighty-eight, Miss Marquand, but you didn't say I was to round the result up.'

They both laughed.

Then a gleam came to Warble's eye.

'Have you heard of my brother Barnaby?' he asked.

Esther nodded. Warble's non-existent brother Barnaby was the subject of many of his best mathematical posers, the person to whom strange and quirky things to do with numbers happened, and who appeared in end of term lessons when everybody was having fun.

'My brother Barnaby once took some friends to a restaurant. It was a long time ago when prices were lower than I'm told they now are. Personally I never eat in restaurants, except for the buffet on Southampton railway station. Barnaby is different, being very rich, though, as you will see, careful with his money. Anyway they had a good meal and the bill came to twenty-five shillings.

That was the days of old money. They each put ten shillings on the plate and when the waiter brought the change back they told him to keep two shillings, taking back a shilling each. On the way home Barnaby had a perplexing thought and shared it with his friends: "We each paid out nine shillings (that's ten shillings less the one we got back) making twenty-seven shillings in all. The waiter had two shillings as a tip making a total of twenty-nine shillings. But we originally paid thirty shillings: so who stole the remaining shilling?"'

Triumphantly, Warble stared at Esther for a moment, and then got up and wandered over to the window, whistling. A bell went in one of the corridors and there was an opening of doors and whirring of wheelchairs and sliding of slow feet as classes ended for the day. 'Dum di dum do dum di di,' sang Warble who was never so content as when someone else was silent and struggling with one of his problems.

Esther was indeed silent as she pondered the inescapable fact that twenty-seven and two did not add up to thirty. Then her hands and legs relaxed as she began to review the problem systematically. Three men, a restaurant, thirty shillings, that was the key to hold on to. Thirty shillings. Forget the twenty-seven and the two. No don't forget. See them in relation to the thirty shillings. Twenty-seven and two was a false sum, it was irrelevant. The thirty was split twenty-five for the food, two for the tip, three back to the men: thirty. Twenty-seven and two is a false sum, a red herring.

She leaned forward and typed on to the Possum:

$$25 + 2 + 3 = 30$$
$$27 \quad + \quad 2 = 00$$

Over twenty years later, by then a retired old man on the south coast, Warble remembered that moment quite clearly. It was, he said, the moment when he realized Esther Marquand might have mathematical talent. More than that, he understood that there was a quality to that kind of thinking which relaxed her for he saw her transformed from an upset child to a person focusing absolutely on a problem, and a problem which he knew sometimes baffled very good minds indeed. He saw her normally fretting hands go still, he saw in her eyes a look he recognized as that of someone intelligently concentrating, and he saw the moment of release when she had solved the problem and typed out her solution.

Her explanation of the paradox was succinct, clear and purely mathematical. Warble appreciated its elegance and understood that she had solved not only the problem but also defined and solved the secondary problem of how to communicate its solution efficiently, which is what can differentiate a good mathematical mind from a mediocre one. She could not have done it better if she had been able-bodied.

He remembered asking her, 'Why aren't you doing better at maths, young woman?'

And her reply, typed out after a moment's pause to look up at him: I WILL NOW.

TWENTY-TWO

The winter holidays came and, the previous Christmas having been such a success, it was decided that the family should be together again, only this time in Harefield, with Tom joining them from the Centre.

They all recognized it was to be a time for work and quiet – Esther had come back loaded with assignments to help her catch up the ground she had lost, while Richard was busily coping with the rapid expansion of Fountain-Marquand while, at the same time, beginning to lay plans for developing his own chain of retail outlets to sell computer equipment.

Richard had found a helper through a local paper, a quiet and rather plain girl called Marion who, at her interview in Richard's front room, had said rather shyly, 'I always wanted to help handi-capped people, especially children.' She had no experience and few qualifications, but there was a friendly strength about her that he liked, and as she lived locally with her parents she was able to come in early in the morning to help get Esther up.

She started at seven-thirty on the morning of 18 December, the first day of the holidays, and there was something about her methodical and quiet way that gave the house a certain calm, and established normality as if she had always been there.

Tom arrived and liked her immediately, giving her a hug and repeating what he had said to Esther moments before after his 'Lo, Amh!' greeting: 'I got a big bike now. Red and white and shining bell. Which rings ding ding ding.'

Marion said, 'That's good then,' and carried on with whatever task she was doing, absorbing Tom's hugs, Esther's calls and, later, a period of Margaret Ogilvie's coldness, with equanimity.

Esther's ability to work was greatly increased by Margaret's close involvement. Together they planned out each day as if they were fighting a battle. Margaret found that she was needed – to place books in Esther's page-turner, to sort out sheets on which Esther had typed, to ensure that the Possum was properly aligned and working. She began to read to Esther, and occasionally to write brief notes for her in such a way that Esther could memorize them easily. At the same time she discussed things with her, asking her questions, pushing her harder and harder to show that she understood.

Richard did not get involved in any of this, becoming a remote figure who appeared mainly at mealtimes carrying buff folders full of papers and computer printouts and who seemed content that the house and the people in it functioned more or less without him.

There was a regular walk with Tom before lunch and tea because Margaret had decreed that Esther needed the fresh air; and there was relaxation in the evenings with Brian who liked to listen to serious music on the radio, or read bits of the newspaper to Esther and Tom.

Long afterwards, when she recalled that Christmas holiday for Daniel Schuster, Esther remembered it less for her sudden assault on school work than for a surging inside her of an interest in music.

The radio broadcast a lot of religious choral music for the Christmas period and Esther remembered always those hours of listening with her grandfather, and Tom quiet nearby playing with some toy or object of his own, not wanting to wander far, as great choirs filled the living-room with the sounds of Bach, of Handel and of Beethoven.

Margaret, the day's work with Esther done, would rarely sit with them, liking the relative comfort of the open-plan kitchen and a chance to read a little, her reading glasses halfway down her nose and the door open, for she liked to hear the sound of the music, and the children. Since her reconciliation with Esther the previous Christmas she had begun to find she had the peace of mind to enjoy reading.

It was then that Esther discovered the beauty of Bach and the Toccata and Fugue in D Minor for organ became her favourite piece for a time, with its recurring patterns of notes which mind and imagination could follow but never quite master.

Sometime then Brian drove back to Charlbury and found again

the old HMV wind-up gramophone that he had put away in the attic, and some old 78 records, and even a tin of rusting chromium needles, whose special guardian Tom became.

Together, the three of them, ignoring Richard's stereo hi-fi equipment, explored the old records which once, Brian explained, Esther's mother had on special occasions been allowed to listen to.

'Remember "Lord Raglan's Daughter", my dear?' Brian asked, for he had among the records a number of country and Morris dance pieces. It was the dance he had briefly performed for her on the day they had gone over to Charlbury for the first time.

Esther nodded. She remembered most things.

'Ah, but do you remember the steps?'

'Nah.'

So there, by the Christmas tree one evening, Brian went through music he loved, and with Tom's help showed Esther how the steps went. And when Tom became bored and confused by the regular time of the dance, Brian went out to the kitchen and persuaded Margaret that perhaps, just this once in all their years together, she might partner him 'for Esther's sake, my dear', so she could see how these ancient dances went.

Sometimes, afterwards, when Esther Marquand found the peace to reflect on and remember things that were barely old enough yet to be called memories, she regretted that her father was not there that evening to see Margaret, for her sake, taking Brian's hand and being first talked and then led through two or three of the dances.

Margaret was a little stiff and shy at first, but there is something in that music which makes a girl and a boy forget themselves, and a woman and a man feel like children again and remember when life could be all play, and play ended in laughter. So, Margaret danced and Esther watched smiling, as, 'Lord Raglan's Daughter' over, Brian finally showed her his favourite, 'Upon a Summer's Day'.

And when, in the second part – the dance being for a longways set of six people – an arch was formed, an elegant arch for the music was sweet and slow, Esther ordered Tom to push her out on to the floor, and together they went under the arch formed by the arms and hands of Brian and Margaret. At that moment, the music full about them, they might all have been in a village barn, a band playing, and beer flowing, and crowds about them young and old, so that Brian led his Margaret forwards once more, and she, with a skip to her step and her face a little flushed, danced at his side, and they all of them swirled and turned and ended in a muddle of a huddle, and Margaret was kissed on the cheek and old Brian had to sit down.

Such moments make a family's life worth living; such moments live on in the dance. And if upon that winter's night 'Upon a Summer's Day' was danced, who cared that the set of six was incomplete and the dancers lost their way? Certainly not the spirit of the music, which went on and on, until the record hissed and hissed and Tom with great care lifted off the needle and asked if he could put another one on.

'Bedtime!' announced Margaret, embarrassed by the intimacy of it all. But the mask of her severity had been pulled aside and nobody could take from Brian the pleasure those moments gave him.

A few days later Brian suggested Esther might like to listen with him to some Bach he had on the hissing old 78s. It was the gentle and sweet adagio of the First Brandenburg Concerto she heard, and she now instantly recognized the melody, so sweet and gentle. The record's brief duration seemed a lifetime.

'Let's listen through again shall we, old girl?' said Brian, getting up yet again to rewind the gramophone and turn the record over. 'A bit different from records and tapes now, eh!'

One afternoon she declined the walk because she wanted to listen to some music in her room.

Tom appeared.

'C'mon, Amh. Walk.'

I'M JUST GOING TO MY ROOM BECAUSE I WANT TO PLAY SOME MUSIC. YOU'LL LIKE IT.

'No, Amh.'

YES TOM. IF YOU DON'T WANT TO, GO AWAY. Her face turned sour. She liked being harsh to Tom sometimes. At least on him it had an effect. But not this time.

'No, Amh. Want to go for a walk. In the garden with you.'

NO TOM, NOT NOW. Her face was unsmiling.

But Tom too had changed that year. Tom was growing up.

He went off and opened the patio door on to the cold reality of the early January afternoon outside and he said, 'You're coming, Amh. We're going to the garden.'

Tom was uncertain of this new Esther, something wasn't right about her. Tom wanted to take his friend, his beloved, the person he would die for, to where he remembered she had been normal. So he did so.

And the new Esther barely protested: NO TOM, that was all. As he pushed her out into the afternoon air, the ground hard and frosty enough for the wheels not to sink into the lawn, he said, 'Amh, I'm glad I'm here.'

Oh well . . . Esther relaxed into her chair and let him push her without further protest, and she felt tired and that she had been a long way away and had come back to a place she liked with a person she loved. She had almost forgotten them. Tom had changed, he was stronger, he was bigger; but she felt safe, protected, and loved as no one else loved her.

TOM?

'Yes Amh?'

She pointed through the pergola in the hedge towards the wooden fence where they had played when they were children, 'Which seems,' thought Esther, 'so strangely long ago'.

Down to touch it they went, Esther in her chair. They looked through the winter-bedraggled ivy over the churchyard towards the church. A dim light shone in the great lancet window.

LISTEN, TOM.

'What, Amh?'

From beyond the wooden fence, from where the Skallagrigg was came the sound of an organ. Somebody was practising in the church.

MUSIC, said Esther in the sounds that only Tom easily understood.

'Can't hear, only old trees,' said Tom. He could hear the crumbling sounds of winter, where twigs turned and snapped to a blackbird's scurry, and silence was broken by a wood pigeon's wings.

'No mooski, Amh,' said Tom.

NO TOM, said Esther now getting cold, but not so cold she could not feel needed by him and how much that meant.

'C'mon, Amh, you're going in now.'

And she smiled as he pushed her, purposefully and ever careful of his awesome charge, beneath the leafless apple trees back towards the house.

TWENTY-THREE

Within weeks of Esther's return to Netherton Manor for the spring term it was clear to her teachers that the positive change of attitude she had shown towards work at the end of the previous term was taking effect.

She had done all her holiday assignments and reading thoroughly and was working hard at every subject. At the first academic assessment meeting of the term, in mid-February, Ronnie Warburton expressed the view that she should be moved up into the higher maths stream – one which aimed to take 'O'-level maths in the summer of the following year, which would be a year early for someone of Esther's age. She began, too, to be open to other students, and it was at this time that she began to write in her diary of one of her contemporaries, Graham Downer, as a 'friend'. Graham was paraplegic and confined to a wheelchair, but he had speech and dexterity and shared Esther's interest in maths and her liking for Warble. Through him she became involved with *Outside*, the school magazine, of which he was one of the editors. Its spring issue for that year lists her as one of the editorial team, and carries two of her poems, and a report – 'An Evening with Bach' – of a school visit to a performance of the B Minor Mass at Christchurch in Oxford. Esther and two other students were taken in the school minibus by Warble. Her account is brief and to the point and, like many of her letters, understates the true impact of the experience upon her.

They were given places by a pillar near the pulpit with the good view that Warble had hoped for, though more exposed than Esther would have liked since they were facing others across the aisle only a few feet away. They had to look to their right to see where the orchestra and choir would be, in the chancel in front of the altar. The choir was already assembling, the men in dinner jackets and the women in long black skirts and white blouses, some in full dresses, and several with woollen shawls. But in the aisle between them empty chairs and music stands waited for the orchestra.

Then the choir fell still and silence travelled like a wave to the darkest recesses of the complex aisled and chapeled building. Expectation. The orchestra came in from a side chapel and sat down. It was much smaller than Esther had expected, and there was a rustling of music and a playing of notes and tuning which was new to Esther. They didn't do that on records.

Then the conductor, an attractive man, much younger than Esther had imagined, since conductors on record sleeves all had grey hair and lined faces, came in, raised his hands – one held a white baton – and before Esther had time to catch her breath the choir rose and the Mass started into the Kyrie Eleison: Lord have mercy on us, Lord have mercy . . .

That sudden soaring moment was when Esther Marquand first consciously confronted the possibility that there might be God. She felt her soul rising up with the music into the compassionate majesty of his arms in which she felt an awe and wonder. It was far far more powerful than listening to the records at Netherton. Oh oh oh, she cried out in her heart, unaware of the people opposite, her eyes rising with the arches and timbers to the highest parts of the roof. Oh Lord have mercy, and she knew, she knew, she *knew*, there was something big and bigger than them all, ablebodied and disabled alike: the Lord, who had mercy.

It seemed to Esther that her perception of God was, that evening, a pattern or shape becoming clearer only slowly, a road sign emerging out of mist.

The Kyrie came to its magnificent end, and after a moment's dead silence (in which Esther's gaze dropped from the heights to the people opposite) there was a rustling and a coughing, and a shifting of chairs as the musicians got ready for the next movement and then the music took off again.

But Esther was not carried away again at once and she stared about her and saw someone sitting among the people opposite, in something uncomfortably familiar.

There was a man, and his name . . . Esther never knew his name. He sat opposite, and like her in a wheelchair. But he wasn't spastic, he was ill. His face was grey and his white hair limp over his forehead. Prematurely white. His chin was sunk in his chest. As he looked involuntarily down at the flagstones of the old floor the transept arches of the cathedral rose high above him, powerful and eternally strong against his failing weakness.

He sat next to a woman and a boy and Esther worked out that the boy was the son. The man seemed to have Parkinson's disease, for his hands shook though they were pressed tightly together. Sometimes his wasted legs inside his hanging trousers would start to shake, more and more, faster and ever faster and then the boy would lean across and put his hands on his father's knee and the legs would slowly grow still again, as if the touch of the son was healing.

The man never raised his eyes, staring only at the floor, and Esther watched him, the music flowing upward in her, wondering if he felt awe like she did. He had a son and a wife, he was loved, but that had not protected him from a wheelchair.

The wife had a lively sort of face, her hair was up, and occasionally she smiled sideways at the boy; there was colour and warmth in her face and it contrasted with the weary illness in her husband's.

Esther could not get back into the music as she had with the initial Kyrie Eleison. The ill man blocked her path on that glorious escape.

As the evening and the performance went on Esther began to see that there was a pattern to the man's shaking episodes. Every twenty minutes or so he would start, and then gently, so gently, the boy would reach across and calm him by putting a hand to his thigh or knee, and occasionally a hand to his thin hands: and his body's shaking would stop for a time. There was something deeply loving and accepting about the boy's behaviour. He was not embarrassed, indeed he seemed hardly conscious of what he was doing. It was a long time before Esther noticed that the man's feet were strapped to his wheelchair.

At the interval, which came after the Credo, Esther wanted to shout and clap, and for a moment she saw the man look up and sideways down the aisle towards the choir. Perhaps *he* would have liked to clap. But even had he been able, this was not like a concert on television. It seemed that people do not clap in churches . . .

The music took Esther under its wings and she soared up towards

God with it; the only thing on the ground that kept her in touch with reality was that strange hurt man, his limbs shaking, his eyes downcast.

Then as the choir began the final lines of the Mass Esther was filled with a sense of spiritual triumph and healing which is the Mass's great glory. But what of her body? Would that ever be healed?

She saw the man in the silence made by the music so loud about them, his head beginning to rise, and his eyes were open and clear and grey, and they looked not at the choir, nor the orchestra nor at anything else: They looked at *her*. And saw her. And knew her.

They stared across the aisle to her with pity and compassion and appeal and she knew, she knew as the choir was in its final ascent, that she wanted to ask God that, even if she could not be helped, not ever, then at least she might help others, yes, others like him who suffered worse than she, far worse; life had been taken from him and he did not know how to fight except by sitting and listening to this music and believing its words.

The man's knees and legs began to shake once more, more and more as the crescendo swelled, and Esther gazed across and into his eyes and prayed for him to be still, for his body to be at peace, for his hands to rest, to believe that in spirit if never in body now *sanabitur anima mea*. He was not alone, his gaze had told her that, and that she too need never be alone: God was there.

Even as his son's hands came across, the man's knees stilled, his hands relaxed and, slowly, as if slipping away and drowning beneath a sea, his head began to slump again leaving his gaze upon her until the very last, until he could hold it no more. He gave her a smile, distant as hope and lost memory, a smile that said there were things more important to a person than their body; oh, weren't there? Oh God.

'And did you enjoy it, Esther?' asked Warble on the way through the cold back to the minibus.

'Yeh,' she nodded, her head laid low.

Then she did not know how much it meant. But later, when Daniel Schuster was in her life, she told him that that dark night she began to see the light of God and His darkness too.

TWENTY-FOUR

The girl who was to become Esther's best friend arrived at Netherton without warning halfway through the spring term, right in the middle of one of Marguerite Gatting's English lessons. Mr Imray showed her in, though she drove her own chair, and the form looked at her, as any form does, assessing her. That was the only time she looked even slightly meek. Her nature was bold and lively, and a few strange kids in a classroom weren't going to suppress her for long. Her name was Betty Shaw.

Marguerite Gatting said she could go next to Graham who could show her how things were. But it was upon Esther, sitting nearby, that she bestowed her first and soon familiar friendly grin. Esther grinned back, and in the mysterious instant way that some people become friends, so those two became a complementary pair. One (Betty) bright and extrovert, the other (Esther) plain but for her eyes, and introvert; one impulsive, the other careful; one emotional, the other apparently cool; one non-intellectual, the other academically successful; one always brightly dressed, and Esther never sure of herself with clothes.

The lesson continued and Esther looked shyly at her. Betty's hair was short and very fair, her eyes sparkling and her cheeks healthy, and she had a pert quick look and dark eyebrows that went up and down in surprise, doubt, laughter, scepticism, worldly knowledge. She had spina bifida.

At break-time Graham tried to introduce them.

'This is Esther, er, Betty, Esther . . .'

'Marquand,' said Betty. 'It's on her book there. You CP?' she asked directly, looking into Esther's eyes and ignoring Graham. CP: Cerebral Palsy.

'Yeh,' said Esther.

'My Dad . . .' began Betty in a flood of words that rarely stopped, 'comes from Sheffield,' and she explained why she had an accent of sorts, different from the others. Her father had been suddenly posted south to oversee a building contract and he insisted that she came to a school near him. Netherton provided a place. She didn't have a mother . . .

Esther went into a sudden jerking movement of head and hands, her right hand going towards her chest, her way of signing mother, as her left pushed out and away from her body at an odd angle.

'You don't have a mother neither?' said Betty quickly, understanding almost immediately what Esther was signing and then only waiting a brief moment for Esther's nodded acknowledgement before continuing, 'So we've got something in common then. I'm fourteen. I've got a boyfriend called Alick, he'll write to me I expect and if he doesn't I won't write to him I . . .'

Esther, laughing, signed again and said, 'Me.'

'You will!' said Betty. 'Haven't you a boyfriend then?'

Esther was suddenly shy since Graham was with them. Betty laughed, looking at them both. Then she said, 'You're welcome to write to Alick if you want to. I'm no good at letters anyway. He likes brunettes.' Esther shuddered, though Graham, an innocent, seemed unaware of the significance of any of this.

'Third lesson starts at 11.15,' was all he managed to say.

Within three days Betty and Esther were old friends – the first girlfriend Esther had truly had – and within three weeks they had shared memories: of the kissing of Betty by Paul Wilnaughton in the boot room; of the question to Miss Gatting about sex in *Othello*; of the evening Betty put make-up on Esther's face when Graham blushed to see it, going all strange and stumbly with his words, and Esther felt strange and stumbly with hers.

And of the Skallagrigg.

For Betty knew of the Skallagrigg. You could invoke his name in the choosing ritual of the game of It when players were eliminated by recitation of the rhyme:

> Charlie Chaplin
> Sat on a pin
> How many inches
> Did it go in?
> . . . *Four*

One, two, three, *four*!
You're not It, play some more.

But not Betty, that wasn't the way she played. When a boy who did not like her triumphantly pointed at her on a seven count, she riposted:

If you don't spell it quick
You become It.

'What? What?' shouted the others, instinctively knowing the way to develop the challenge.

This one's big
It's Skallagrigg!!

'Spell it, spell it, spell it or be It!' shouted the others at the boy, who was never their favourite.

But he couldn't, and nor could anyone it seemed, and Betty made him It, and he was furious.

Just memories between friends.

One quiet evening when the two girls were reading, Esther drove her chair over to the Possum and typed: THIS ONE'S BIG IT'S SKALLAGRIGG!!

'You didn't say you could spell it, Ess,' said Betty.

NO TIME, typed Esther. They both laughed, remembering the boy's discomfiture.

'I thought you didn't know about the Skallagrigg down here,' said Betty.

I KNOW ABOUT ARTHUR.

'And?'

THE RACKS THE WOODEN FENCE.

Betty was silent. She stared out of the great windows into evening dusk. Their two reflections stared back: Betty's image bold and upright, Esther's a little slumped.

'Ess, is it true you're going to get confirmed?'

Esther nodded.

'Do you believe in God then, or is it the bread and booze?'

They giggled.

Esther managed to enunciate 'B . . . B . . .', though it came out more like 'Mba . . . Mba'.

But Betty became serious. 'I don't believe,' she said.

They were both silent.

'Skyagree,' said Esther.

'You want to tell me a story?'

'Nah,' said Esther.

'Me tell you one?'

Esther nodded.

As evening fell Betty Shaw told Esther Marquand the first version of how Arthur and Frank made a friend called Norman, with the help of the Skallagrigg.

The story is number XIV in Esther's collection of the stories, where it is told less innocently than in Betty's version . . .

Norman would have scared you if you didn't know him. He was big and strong like a giant and his mouth hung open and was wet. He tried to speak but it didn't make much sense until you learnt what it was. It was always the same. He was asking you to give him something to write with and something to write on.

What Norman wanted to write was always the same, all his life it was the same. It was his name and address. It was the only thing his Mum taught him because he used to wander off and get lost as a kid, so she taught him to write his address. He learnt that when he was a young lad so it proves he wasn't all stupid. And he thought after that, that if he was lost all he had to do was write down his name and address and they'd take him back to his Mum where he was safe and loved.

When he was nine, about in 1920, his Mum was ill and couldn't cope no more so he went to the Institution or the Workhouse which is what some people still called it.

The first thing Norman did after his Mum left him there and didn't come back soon was to try to take the warder's pencil out of his breast pocket. He didn't get far with that. He got desperate when nobody understood. He wanted to give his name and address for them to take him away from that ward, back home to his Mum. After a few days it got so bad he tried to write his name and address in his own pee

on the floor. They said he must go to the 'dirty' ward for
that, so he went in with the shitters.

His Mum came to see him once a month until 1924 when
she was ill and she could come no more. By then Norman
was different and his face was thinner.

In 1926 the Workhouse was closed and he went first to
one hospital and then to another until he got to the hospital
where Arthur was. After that he lost touch with his Mum
and his brothers and sisters.

The first year was all right but in Norman's second year
there Dilke came. Until then most nurses were willing to let
Norman use their pencils sometimes, he would be docile for
days if he knew he would get a chance to write his address.

But Dilke had a genius for finding out what hurt people.
The first time Norman tried to take his pencil out of his
pocket Dilke threatened him and told him to bugger off. The
next time, even though the other nurse tried to explain it
was harmless enough, Dilke said, 'If you try that again, lad,
you'll regret it.' That was early days before anyone knew
that Dilke meant exactly what he said. Dilke had not got
power then, and was only just establishing his rule of fear
by making examples of some of the lads. Innocent Norman
tried it on again so Dilke said, 'Come with me.'

'Hurt him, that's the way, sir,' said another patient. That
was Rendel and that was the first time Dilke and Rendel
worked together. Rendel was vicious and he liked anything
to do with male sex. He was a queer. He was also strong,
though not so strong as Norman.

'You come as well,' said Dilke to Rendel, sensing he might
need help punishing Norman. Norman was scared. A human
being senses when he's going to get hurt just as an animal
does.

They took poor Norman to the toilets. 'Do you want my
pen?' asked Dilke, holding his pen up. Big Norman nodded,
hopeful.

'Kneel down then,' said Dilke. 'Not there,' he added, when
Norman tried to go down by the window where the floor
was dry. 'There.'

Dilke pointed to a place between the latrines where there
was a puddle of piss and vomit and where Norman's
movements would be restricted.

'Do you want my pen?' asked Dilke again.

'Yes,' said Norman his knees in piss.

'Bend forward so your head's just off the floor then,' said Dilke. Norman bent forward so his nose was almost in the pee and gob.

Then Dilke turned to Rendel and said, 'I know what I'd do if I wasn't a nurse. I wouldn't tolerate someone who kneels in piss and puts his face in gob-shit. I'd kick him, Rendel, that's what I'd do.'

Rendel wasn't slow to take a hint. He kicked Norman in the face. Norman was kicked again and again like that. But he didn't get violent because he thought it would mean he would never get a pen. He cried for his Mum. Then eventually Dilke gave him a pencil and Norman took some lavatory paper and wrote his name and address on that.

'There's no such place,' said Dilke. 'I'm right, my lad, this place doesn't exist, you made it up, you're a liar and not even worth kicking.'

Dilke turned away to go back to the ward.

'*No no no no no no no no no*,' cried Norman pointing at his paper. Dilke slowly went back to him with a smug look on his face. He took the paper out of Norman's hands and said, 'This is what this is worth, you filthy bastard,' and he wiped it round the dirty bits of the latrine where there was shit and piss, and then he put in the toilet and pulled the chain.

Most who heard Norman's cry then would never forget it. It was a cry of loss.

Norman went back to the ward but was silent for several days after that. Then suddenly he went mad and attacked a patient and then another and there was pandemonium. It took four nurses and Rendel to strait-jacket him. The Medical Super came and took one look and said, 'He's being naughty is he? Ward 18 then.' Ward 18 was ECT where they put a shock through your head. That was the first time Norman had that but not the last.

As the years passed Norman went in on himself. Once he smiled. Now he never did. Once he had hope, now it was gone. Only sometimes, when a kindly nurse let him write his address down and said, 'Yes, Norman, that's where your Mum is only she's too busy to have you now but she's there all right and I expect she loves you,' only then, and that was rare, did a distant look of hope come back to Norman's eyes as he remembered the place where he had been happy as a boy.

Years passed like they do behind those yellow-brick walls, no one knows where they go. Norman aged.

One day, after the walks in the glen started, Norman found himself near Frank and Arthur who he did not know. As it happened Frank had the Vestry pen on him and Norman saw it. He tried to get it off Frank and Frank resisted. Dilke saw the fight and came up, window stick in hand. Arthur spoke, to stop the fight in time and Dilke rounded on him and raised that stick. He always liked an opportunity to hit Arthur. *Crash!* came that stick down and brought blood to Arthur's wrist. Arthur's body went into spasm because he was hurt.

Then a strange thing happened. A shape loomed behind Dilke and big Norman was there and his arm was out and round Dilke and pulling him away, firmly and gently.

'No,' he said.

Dilke couldn't do a thing. He was lifted off his feet and Norman did it so cleverly in the group that the other nurse didn't see a thing and you couldn't tell if he wasn't just having fun. The boys played round like that sometimes. But for a moment, for once, Dilke looked really scared. Norman had never shown real purpose before.

'Not Arthur,' said Norman.

Then Arthur spoke and Frank said, 'Arthur says put him down, Norman. Now.' And though Dilke began to raise his stick again there was something about the way Norman moved forward protectively again that stopped him.

After that Norman was always with Frank and Arthur on their walks, and because Frank wasn't always strong enough Norman helped Frank lift Arthur in his chair when occasion demanded. Norman could have lifted three Arthurs with one hand. Sometimes he lifted Arthur and his wheelchair together up the steps into the hospital, and that saved time and soon the nurses encouraged it.

Some time then Arthur spoke and Frank asked the boys a question: 'Arthur wants to know what Norman wants the pen for?'

The boys looked at each other. All that was a long time ago and Norman's past was forgotten. But one there knew. A day or two later he started laughing, laughing so much you wanted to kill him. That's the way Eppie was. Eppie said, 'Norman wants the pen to write to his mum, ha ha ha ha ha ha ha ha ha.' So Arthur found out the truth: Norman knew his address once, but maybe not any more.

It was a month or so later and Arthur was in church thinking about nothing much when suddenly the Skallagrigg was there behind him saying something. He said, 'It's time you did Norman a good favour.'

'Like what?' asked Arthur not looking round.

'You work it out,' said the Skallagrigg.

'Will you help?' said Arthur. He knew he would.

Then Arthur knew what he would do. The next day, in occupational therapy, he said to Frank a revolutionary thing.

'We're going to write a letter to Norman's Mum.' Frank looked blank. Arthur was the brains. 'You're going to ask the Father to write it and Norman can sign it and do the envelope. I hope he can remember what his Mum taught him those long years back. Now's the time for it to be useful.'

Arthur had heard about letters from the radio. He had never received one or seen one with a stamp on, but he had seen envelopes. The nurses had brown ones once a week with money in. That was an envelope. You put the writing on paper in the envelope and put it in the red box in the Front Hall. Mr Postman took it personally to where it was sent.

The Father agreed to help, bringing pen, paper and envelope to where the boys were.

'Arthur says you write,' said Frank.

'All right,' said the Father with a smile.

So then Arthur spoke to Frank, a word at a time, carefully, and Frank said the word, and the Father wrote it out properly.

This is what that letter said:

Dear Mum
Please come and visit me.
       With Love from

Then Frank said, 'Arthur says that Norman's to write his name.'

They fetched Norman and Frank put the pen and paper in front of him and said, 'You write your name.'

For a long time he just stared but eventually he remembered: first his name, then to write the address on the envelope.

Then when it was done Arthur looked at the Father and said something and Frank said, 'He says put it in the red box for Mr Postman to take.'

But the Father decided to take the letter himself on his day off. He travelled by train and bus the long way away where

Norman had lived as a boy. An old woman answered the door.

'Please don't get alarmed,' he said, 'but are you Norman's mother?'

She looked worried and upset.

'Is he dead?' she said.

The Father shook his head. 'No. No, he's very much alive. In fact I've got a letter for you . . .' and he gave her the letter.

'You best to come in then,' said Norman's Mum holding the letter like it was a bomb.

He went into her little house. The first thing he saw was black and white photographs on the parlour mantelpiece.

The woman said, 'Those are all my family. They're all gone from home long ago now. That's Albert, that's John, that's Benny, that's Dick, that's Moira and Jennie.' Then she pointed to a little photo of a young woman and a boy, a big boy with a wide wet mouth holding her hand in the street. Even before she said anything the Father knew it was Norman and that young woman was now this old woman. Then he realized how much time had passed.

She said, 'That's my boy Norman.' And even after all those years her voice went soft and tears came to her eyes. 'He was a good boy, he never hurt anyone. But I couldn't cope and it wasn't fair on the others.' She was silent for a long time and the Father knew not to say a word.

Eventually she looked at the letter and said, 'What's it say?' The Father said it was best for her to open it and read it herself.

When she read it she said, 'I will come. Benny's the one with a car, he'll drive me. Yes, I'll come and see him one day.'

Then the Father explained about how the letter came to be written and how Norman had two good friends, special friends, whose names were Frank and Arthur. The letter was really Arthur's idea.

'Frank and Arthur, they're his friends are they?' said Norman's Mum. 'Well, I'm pleased he's got friends. He deserves friends.'

'Will you come?' said the Father.

'I will try, it isn't easy after all this time,' she said.

'No,' said the Father, 'no, it wouldn't be.'

It was three months later on a Sunday afternoon that a nurse came and found some of the boys, including Norman, sitting on the grass in the sun.

The nurse said, 'You've got a visitor Norman.' Norman thought he had been naughty and was scared. The Father found out what was going on and went to the visitors' room to see who it was. Well, it was Norman's Mum come at last after so many years, with a middle-aged man.

'This is not such a bad place then,' she said when she saw the Father. The visitors' room had a green carpet and up-holstered chairs and even had pictures on the wall and proper curtains. Visitors often said the hospital was good because of that room and the fact that the boys came out in clean clothes all washed and scrubbed. It doesn't cost much to create a false impression.

'Yes,' said the Father.

'Is Norman coming now then?' said his old Mum.

'Do you want me to go and see?' said the Father. He was pleased when she said yes because then he had an excuse to go and find Norman himself and not leave him to the tender mercies of the nurses who would be cleaning him up ready to be seen by the outside world. The Father went and found Norman safe with Arthur and Frank. But he would only go and see his Mum if they went along too.

So all four of them went to the visitors' room and Norman had a reunion with his Mum and his brother Benny after nearly twenty years. It was a happy hour and Norman looked like paradise had come. He held his Mum's hand and said words he had last spoken as a boy. He said, 'I love my Mum.' There were tears that afternoon in the visitors' room, and not just from those with Norman. Others saw and they could tell it was a special day for Norman and his friends.

At the end Norman's Mum said, 'Give me the parcel, Benny.' He had a parcel wrapped up in brown paper inside his jacket. Their Mum opened it.

'I knitted these for you and your good friends,' she said.

'There's a scarf for you, Norman, and gloves for you, Frank, and a bobble hat for you, Arthur.' They were made of lovely green wool which had red flecks in it.

Norman took his scarf but didn't put it on. After that he carried it with him whenever he could and showed it to people. It was his treasured possession.

Frank took the hat and put it on Arthur's head and Arthur laughed. Then Frank put on the gloves. He always made sure Arthur was settled before settling himself.

Then Arthur spoke and Frank said to Norman's Mum,

'Arthur wants to know how you knew we were Norman's friends.' So then she explained about the Father's visit.

Frank said, 'Arthur says thank you. He says Norman is a good boy and does you credit. He says that sometimes without Norman to help he doesn't know what he'd do. He says Norman has suffered a lot over the years but he kept going because he always knew that his Mum loved him. Arthur says he'll watch over Norman and see he comes to no harm.'

Norman's Mum thought for a bit and then she said, 'Benny, help me up out of this chair.' She got up and looked at Arthur and his useless limbs and his head that went from side to side and into his grey eyes that saw so much. Then she put her hands on Arthur's chair and leaned down as best she could and kissed him on the cheek.

Norman's Mum said, 'I don't know much but I do know this: my Norman's lucky to have you as his friend.'

Norman said, 'No, no, the Skallagrigg.'

Arthur laughed and when the Father said, 'What is the Skallagrigg?' Frank said quickly, 'Arthur says it's nothing, that's just Norman saying something he doesn't know.'

Then Benny shook each of them by the hand and he said, 'You're better than family to Norman and I feel ashamed. All these years and . . .' and then Benny couldn't speak. Norman stood awkward and then came forward and he looked down at his brother Benny and he put his hand gently on his face and touched his tears. His eyes showed he loved his brother and there was nothing to forgive.

The boys all said that the Skallagrigg had turned up trumps again by bringing Norman's Mum to see him. Arthur didn't deny it.

It wasn't long after that that war broke out and things changed. Norman's Mum came again at Christmas but after that Benny went in the army and she could come no more. By the end of the war she had died, so Norman didn't see her again.

But he kept that scarf and his happy memories and looked on Frank and Arthur as his best friends and he helped them all he could. His strength was there to help Arthur who had none.

This is one of the longer Skallagrigg stories that Esther Marquand collected. But an important one. One day that good turn Arthur and the Skallagrigg did Norman would be repaid more than enough, enough for a whole lifetime. One good turn often makes another.

That story was the first of several Betty told Esther about the Skallagrigg. His name most often came up in their conversations when Betty wouldn't talk about God and Esther wouldn't talk about no God. They both had anger and God discussions seemed to provoke it. But they were friends and found a way: the name of the Skallagrigg provided a common peace between them. Betty explained that in her previous home, Leendern House, Sheffield, the Skallagrigg was often mentioned among the kids. Older patients who visited told stories about him and Arthur.

Together they looked at the big map of Great Britain, on the wall of the common room, pointing out places they had been. Esther saw exactly where Sheffield was.

BETTY, she typed one day, WHAT'S IT LIKE WHERE YOU COME FROM. OUTSIDE. Then she stopped typing and spoke a bit and Betty understood a little. Betty was clever enough to do so.

'It's not so soft and green as Hampshire,' said Betty, 'and they talk different.'

Esther got excited and nodded. She remembered the way Jack and Eric from Manchester, who had told her about Arthur, had spoken; with an accent different from her father's or grandma's. Like people in 'Coronation Street' on television.

Manchester was one of the places on the map. There was also a map of the world. Yet Esther's eyes would wander over the map of Britain, ignoring the romantic delights of farther-off places. She would look at the places whose names she knew and say to herself, 'I know someone from Manchester, I know Betty from Sheffield, Peter came from Leeds originally, Daddy has been to Edinburgh, Stafford is where Anna of the Five Towns was, Haworth near Bradford is where the Brontë sisters were,' and one by one she would tick off the places she could claim acquaintance with by proxy.

'I'd like to travel,' said Graham one morning break-time that same term when snow was on the ground and they stayed indoors.

'I would go to Africa and see the lions, to India to see the elephants, and Australia to look at kangaroos,' said Betty.

'I would go to Russia,' said Graham, 'if they'd have me temporarily, to see the Kremlin and Lenin's body.'

They looked at Esther. Where would she go?

Esther looked at the world map on the wall and said, 'Nah.' Then she raised a hand towards the British map, higher and higher.

'You'd go north in Britain,' said Betty.

'That's just to be different,' said Graham.

'Nah,' said Esther. 'Skyagree.'

'You won't find him or Arthur anywhere there,' said Graham. 'Find them in the sky more like!'

'Yeh,' said Esther.

'So where would you go for real?' asked Graham again.

Esther's eyes reluctantly left the British map and travelled over towards the outline of the world.

'Ahmc,' she said.

'Ahmc?' said Graham with a laugh. 'That's great that is. Very well known.'

'She means America,' said Betty.

'I know, dimbo,' said Graham. 'They won't know what's hit them the day Esther Marquand arrives. There'll be TV cameras and nationwide interviews and they'll say "Why have you come to Ahmc, Miss Marquand," and Esther will say . . .' and Graham turned to her and extended a hand as if to invite her comment.

Esther tried to say something but began to laugh.

'Thank you, Miss Marquand, that's very enlightening for the viewers.'

'You should go on telly as an interviewer,' said Betty Shaw, 'you sound stupid enough.'

Graham grinned. 'And what are you going to be when you grow up?'

'A model,' said Betty. 'For wheelchairs.'

They all laughed.

But in their laughter was fear. Each day brought them nearer to that day when they would leave the protection of Netherton. There was a sombreness to their frequent jokes about the future.

'And what about you, Esther?' said Graham.

I want to help people like the man in the cathedral. I want to help others but I don't know how. I want to do something that Peter would have been proud of. I . . .

Esther was silent. She looked at her hands.

'You'll do something,' said Betty gently, bringing her wheelchair closer. 'You're cleverer than any of us.'

'Wha?' said Esther, looking up boldly into her eyes. What can *I* ever do?

'Don't know,' said Betty quietly. 'But something.'

Esther turned her chair from the maps to the big windows and looked out at the snow-covered lawns. Across them the groundsman's two children ran, hurling snowballs. One had a blue scarf, the other a red one. They wore mittens and started tumbling each other in the snow. Suddenly, for a moment, they stopped and looked back at the school building. Probably they had seen something or heard someone shout. But they looked as if they were staring right at the window where Esther was staring out into the uncertain future.

Abruptly she turned away, drove her chair across the room to the Possum and typed: IF I COULD OPEN THAT WINDOW IT WOULD MEAN THE WHOLE WORLD WAS MINE.

Betty came over, read it, and said, 'That's beautiful, Ess.' The two friends, backs to the window, the air full of the hum of the Possum, stared at the paper. 'I couldn't do that,' said Betty. Esther was silent. Then she typed: I WONDER IF THEY'LL REMEMBER THE FACES AT THE SCHOOL WINDOWS, STARING OUT, OR EVER KNOW THAT ONE OF THEM WAS MINE.

'Who, Ess?' asked Betty.

Across the window behind them, far over the lawns by the big tree down the slope, the groundsman's children ran out of sight.

TWENTY-FIVE

'You can hold this, Esther, and this, and . . .' and Richard Marquand, on his knees among Tom's burgeoning tomato plants and runner beans, laughed as he heaved more uprooted weeds upon her lap and the whole lot slipped from her striving grasp and fell in a heap on the ground.

'Dada!' she protested, laughing with him, as he piled them back on top of her, so much greenery and growth and dust and hairy foliage that she could hardly see. She wore her red gardening dungarees and Marion had put a straw hat on her head to keep out some of the ashes and dust from the bonfire that was the climax to an afternoon's gardening.

Richard pushed her chair down past the rows of vegetables to the end of the walled garden where Tom was tending a roaring fire of dead branches from the orchard and waste vegetation from the garden.

The air was warm and scented with applewood smoke, as white and black ash rose and hung among the foliage, and the tin tray of mugs and a chunky teapot that Marion had brought out an hour before rested at an angle on a verge, the cups used and forgotten, one solitary ginger biscuit left.

Tom was lost in wonder, staring at the bonfire which he prodded occasionally with a rake, watching in delight as sparks and ash billowed into the air above him.

A happy and busy year had passed and it was the late afternoon of an August day. The bonfire was a celebration. Esther had heard that day that she had passed her 'O'-level maths and everything suddenly seemed possible. She had been tried and tested by the standards of the 'normal' world, and been passed. But more than that, they were together, all of them, with Marion again in the house, and the Ogilvies coming at the weekend, and Graham Downer (who had also passed his 'O' level) coming to stay in a couple of days' time.

There was a garden table and sun umbrella on the lawn, the garden was full of flowers and scents and the fruit was setting on the orchard tree. And today, now, the summer sky was a soft violet-blue, with high cirrus cloud off to the south and the sun beginning to settle down behind the trees at the bottom of the garden.

The old house, too, caught its light, its chimneys now soft red and pink, as it looked benignly upon each of them, and their garden. Indeed, if ever a house that summer could have smiled its pleasure at the happy growing life to which it gave shelter, Harefield was that house.

The key to it all was Richard Marquand, and his decision to distance himself from the daily running of Fountain-Marquand, now a successful business computer consultancy, to make time for the idea he had been toying with for some time – a chain of high street computer shops aimed at the small business and domestic user.

He had thought initially that he might have to leave Fountain Systems altogether if he was to start a business on his own. But Edward Light had given him a directorship on the group's main board with strategic responsibility for Fountain-Marquand, and found an able young man to succeed Richard in the day-to-day running of the company.

The new company, ComputaBase, was incorporated in April 1980, with Richard holding eighty per cent of the shares and Edward Light, who was the second director required by law, privately holding the rest. Richard had begun to hand over the supervision of Fountain-Marquand in May, planning to start full time on the new operation at the beginning of September with a skeleton staff of his own. He knew that this summer was the last extended holiday he was likely to get at Harefield with Esther for a long time.

Richard organized the holiday carefully, with Tom there from the start and Esther's friend Graham to come later in August. Marion was living-in this time, and glad to: she said little about her personal life or parents, but it was understood that it was now easier for her to live away from her parents. She was good with all of them, including Tom.

'We going out?' Tom would ask.

'Yes, we will soon, as soon as I've done the ironing. Down to the shops and the T S B,' Marion would say. The Trustee Savings Bank was where she put her savings.

'Post a letter,' Tom would reply, grinning, his glasses rising at an angle on his face, the gums showing above his teeth.

'Yes, and post a letter. And you can put it in yourself.'

'Going in to Amh.'

'No, Tom, not now. Esther's working at her school work. You help me.'

'Want to,' Tom would say, looking longingly towards Esther's room.

'Here, hold this for me and let's see what's on radio.' Marion knew how to handle Tom and keep him occupied. Sometimes they would work quietly together, almost wordlessly, for Marion was so quiet that Tom, always responsive to others, fell silent with her: a peaceable, companionable silence.

Not that Marion was especially quiet in what she did: keeping Esther organized made noise, and she liked to have the radio on for certain programmes like 'The Archers', and some pop music. But conversation was not her gift.

She liked routine and order. She always listened to the 'Morning Story' with tea and a biscuit, followed by the quiet interlude of the 'Morning Service' when, though she got up from her elevenses and worked, she rarely spoke, listening to the reading and the prayers, and sometimes humming the hymn and psalm. Like Richard she was naturally tidy, putting things away, folding up tea cloths, wiping surfaces and putting chairs straight without thought or apparent effort.

In the afternoon she always made a proper sit-down tea, just as she had at home, with a little ham or cheese on toast, followed by bread and jam, or a cake. One day when Richard had been out he came back late afternoon to find his house full of the warm sweet smell of baking, and Marion in the kitchen with an apron on, a cookbook open and baking cakes.

'Mmm!' he said.

'Mmmmyum,' said Tom, eyeing the creamy yellow mixture into which she was stirring raisins.

'Off you go!' she said, daring to laugh, daring to include Rich-ard in that dismissal. She watched them and smiled at Esther, who was 'helping' her. She turned to her baking and Richard stared for a moment at her back, and her hips, and her cheap but neat flat black shoes before he went off into the garden humming to himself, the comfort of her presence in his house and kitchen barely articulated. Marion helped make it that kind of summer.

The only shadow had been Evelyn Cafferty, Richard's girlfriend – though it seemed a relationship of convenience rather than affection. Recently it had been getting warmer, and he had mentioned her tentatively more than once.

IS SHE COMING TO STAY? Esther had asked on the second day of the holiday.

'I'm not sure,' Richard had said, evidently reluctant to talk about it.

A day or two later Marion, who did not like answering the phone, had taken a call while Esther was in the kitchen.

'Um. Yes?' said Marion.

'Is Mr Marquand there?' The voice was cold.

'Shall I call him?' Marion had asked. 'He's in the garden.'

'What a good idea,' said Evelyn. The sarcasm was lost on Marion who put the phone down carefully, went to the patio doors and called out, 'It's the telephone!'

'Who is it?' he asked.

Marion went back to the phone, picked it up again, and said, 'Um. Who are you please?'

'Evelyn Cafferty,' said Evelyn shortly.

'Evelyn Cafferty,' called out Marion.

Reluctantly Richard came. Their conversation was brief and Esther watched, her eyes shining darkly. She listened to her father arranging to meet his girlfriend. Esther was not nice to him that day.

Richard went up to London the next evening, and the following day he was dark and broody, and tired.

WHEN IS EVELYN COMING? asked Esther, watching for reaction mercilessly.

'She's not,' was all he said.

Years later he remembered the final chillingly civilized conversation with her.

'No, Evelyn, no. I'm spending the whole time at Harefield with the children. It's really the least I can do and I'm only sorry you won't join us.'

'You've got to get your priorities sorted out,' she had said quietly. Richard saw before him two people – Evelyn, elegant, sexy, fun, interesting; and Esther, his daughter, vulnerable, a strain, hard work. Yet his conflict with Evelyn over Esther suddenly evaporated before a simple reality: he loved Esther and wanted to spend time with her. As she grew up she was slipping away from him and he felt guilty about that. For every time he had seen her this last year, he had seen Evelyn Cafferty ten times; for every time he had held her, he had held Evelyn twenty more. For every . . .

So when the question of time alone with Evelyn in the holidays came up, a moment Richard had been putting off because of the uncertainty about when ComputaBase might be got going, he had suddenly and clearly seen where his desire and his duty lay.

'No, Evelyn,' he said.

Something irreparable arises from the first firm 'No' a lover gives his beloved. And the beloved had best recognize that there will be times when he or she must take second place.

Evelyn had stayed silent. It often produced results. Faced by her cold presence, men usually wilted and compromised and she was able to bind them to her again.

Richard said irrelevantly, 'Esther's taken her "O" level maths this term.'

'That's nice,' said Evelyn, 'but we were talking about us, Richard.' It was a reply she immediately regretted.

'No we weren't, Evelyn, we were talking about my responsibility to Esther. There just won't be time for us this summer unless you come to Harefield.' Then he added without much conviction: 'You *will* be welcome, you know. You'll get to know Esther better, and it's no good pretending she doesn't exist.'

'*You* have to have a life, Richard, you can't just . . .'

'Esther is part of my life, anyone who has a relationship with me must accept that. She's my daughter, Evelyn, and I feel I've neglected her this last year or so. But . . . it's not just that. I want to spend time with her. I miss her, Evelyn. But you probably don't understand that.'

'No, to be honest I don't. You've got to understand that I'm not a damn nanny, Richard. I leave that to the professionals, though

I'm not sure that that young girl you've got is professional. Does she have a proper qualification? I don't see why you have to have all of them . . .'

'Who?' Richard demanded, suddenly angry. That young girl, he was thinking, got up at 7.15 this morning and got my daughter dressed. That young girl laid breakfast for me without my asking. That young girl . . . and Richard turned his eyes coldly on Evelyn's cool summer suit and the line of her thighs beneath her skirt, and the red shoes of expensive leather. 'Who are "them" exactly?' he asked acidly.

'Esther and her friend Tom. And that boy from her school who's handicapped as well I expect. It's not that I mind that it's just that, frankly, it's not my idea of a holiday.'

'Maybe life isn't about holidays,' Richard said quietly. 'Or about evenings out. Or sex. Maybe my life this summer is about my daughter and her friends.'

There had been a silence then, and a few final polite words, and finally a strained and disbelieving farewell.

They never talked as lovers again.

For a week after that he was horribly tired, and Esther was especially solicitous. She knew instinctively she had won a battle and felt generous. But beneath that adolescent smugness was a deeper instinct, and one that struck fear into her: she knew that one day her father would find someone against whom she would not be able to battle and that she would lose him and be alone.

For several days Marion took care of things while Richard slept and rested, and on the third day Margaret came down with Brian and stayed for two nights, taking the children up to London.

About the tenth day of the holiday, at the end of July, Richard had a sleep in the afternoon. When he awoke the house was silent. Esther and Tom had gone off for a walk with Marion. Richard lay on his bed and looked at the sun streaming on to the wallpaper of his room, feeling its drowsy warmth, and hearing the sound of birds and distant bells. His tiredness was gone, and with it the distress caused by Evelyn. That was over. He felt rested and excited at the day still left, the holiday still to come. He got up, drove down to the shops and bought an almond cake for tea.

'It's our birthday,' he had said to them all when they got back and they had taken the tea things down to the lawn and had a tea-

time picnic, Marion relieved to see Mr Marquand so, so ... so
relaxed.

That was the moment the holiday really began.

Richard and Esther made a plan of the garden and the work to be
done but somehow, delightfully, the garden overcame their
schemes and organization, leading them up seductive byways. A
day that started out determined to see the trellis finally in position
might be side-tracked into smelling the roses and tackling the
overgrown bed beyond the old oil tank to the east of the house ...
whose clearing revealed the treasure trove of ferns and lilies which
had escaped their notice before.

A day that started off with a brief trip to a garden centre just to
buy some green plastic-covered wire to tie back the quince on the
western wall, turned into visits to two other centres and a trip
round a private garden open for charity and tea and rock cakes in
the sultry shadow of a topiary garden.

There had been a time when Esther had tried to get physically
involved in all of this, Richard laying her on the ground by a
flowerbed to pull out a few weeds. But she did not want that any
longer, it was simply pointless. What she did like was sitting near
her father as he worked in the garden, the sun on her bare legs
and arms and glinting through the crevices in her straw hat. She
would talk in her strange way, and eventually set off exploring
down the asphalt paths that ran round house and garden, which
Richard had built wide enough to take her electric wheelchair.
Usually she ended up finding Tom in the vegetable garden where
his tomato plants were beginning to set, the tiny yellow flowers
abuzz with insects and bees.

Sometimes Tom put her into her lighter manual chair and took
her on a tour away from the asphalt paths, in among the laurel
hedges and privets where ants scurried and cobwebs clung, and
where the sun fell in pools on quiet corners of earth. Together they
would listen and watch the life of the soil and vegetation, smelling
the summer air. They found old plants and bushes long since
submerged under weeds. Tom had a sure eye for what could be
nurtured, what discarded; like the raspberry canes they found in
the vegetable garden lost for a decade or more under the tangled
embrace of white bryony and bindweed. Sometimes Tom would

undo her straps and heave her down on to the ground, so that she could see and smell the life there among the scent of stalk and roots, the rough leaf of woundwort and ground elder, and where the shiny cardinal beetle crawled.

'Toh! Toh!' she would call out, giggling, her hands never quick enough to brush the foliage from her eyes, and his hands gently dusting the odd ant or grasshopper from her legs.

'That's good, Amh,' he would say, grinning and pointing heavily at what she saw, his head bowed as he pressed his glasses back on his nose. 'Ant. Earriewig. Bumbles.'

But when it was over, and she was back in her chair, and Marion was calling them indoors, they would make a final ritualistic visit to the wooden fence that overlooked the back of the churchyard – the same church where Marion now went on Sundays, taking them with her sometimes. But there, just beyond the fence, they never ventured, preferring always to leave it as hallowed ground: for there the Skallagrigg was, or might be found. One day.

'Amh?'

'Yeh? Toh?'

Tom would stare to that verdant place, enshadowed, the day drawing in, Marion's call on the breeze and his hands on the handles of her chair, always always always protective.

'Skalg coming?'

ONE DAY, TOM, WE'LL GO TO HIM.

'When?'

DON'T KNOW DON'T KNOW.

She did not know whether to feel excitement or fear at that coming day.

TWENTY-SIX

Graham Downer was delivered to Harefield by his father in the last week of August on yet another day when the sun beat down and the sprinklers were watering the lawn and vegetable garden.

But for all the sunshine Graham looked pasty-faced, and soon disappeared inside the house with Esther.

'It's "Pong",' said Tony Downer.

'Pong?'

'Yes. That's right. As in ping-pong. The new craze. Dammit, Richard, I thought you were in computers.'

'Oh, the computer game. The one you plug into the television set. "Pong from Atari".'

Tony nodded, adding: 'If you don't know it now you soon will. Where's the television?'

Tony and Richard were on the patio overlooking the garden. They were both in shorts and T-shirts, and were sipping beers.

'I *am* in computers, but business computers,' said Richard.

'Don't you believe it, mate,' said Tony. 'Where I come from even the business computers are being used for games.'

Richard smiled. 'Well, yes. Actually you're right. But with us it's mainly the engineers. They test installations with games and play them at lunchtime.'

'And the rest,' said Tony. He stood up and went into the house. A minute later he came back, grinning. 'Just as I thought, they're playing "Pong". Come and look.'

As Richard Marquand stood up Tony grabbed his arm with mock urgency. 'Be warned, my friend. If you gaze directly into the eyes of Pong you will be turned into its slave for ever.'

Richard laughed, and they went through to the door of the sitting-room.

It may have been bright sunshine outside but the room was in semi-darkness, a gloom accentuated by the black and white glare

of the TV screen before which were Graham and Esther in their
wheelchairs with Tom standing behind them.

'Pong' was a black box with two joysticks which, when plugged
into an ordinary television set, displayed on the screen a version of
an electronic ping-pong table. The 'ball' – a squarish pho-
sphorescent dot – was batted back and forth by the joystick-con-
trolled paddles on either side of the screen. Simple, but addictive, it
was beginning to bring to both commercial and public consciousness the potential of home computers.

So it was that on a hot August afternoon in 1980 'Pong' arrived
in the sitting-room of the Marquands' house and two of the people
who watched it being played by Graham Downer would be profoundly affected by the revolution it heralded.

One was Richard Marquand who, though aware of the game
from trade shows he had visited, now saw for the first time its
addictive qualities. Beside Tony Downer he watched in silence as
Graham struggled with the controls, the mindless tedium of the
little moving dot, possessed by the possibility that next time he
might do better with it. Next time . . . Richard was later to report
that within moments of seeing the game in a domestic setting he
realized its potential for his own retail operation. Within days of
this introduction to the game he had not only gained an agency to
sell 'Pong' through his ComputaBase operation, but commissioned
a programmer to create a similar game based on tennis . . . and the
first of his several fortunes was about to be made.

The second person in that room whose life was changed by the
game was Esther. Graham had given her the controls and, though
she could not do much with them yet, she had an overwhelming
sense that before her, for the first time, was something she could
control. SHE COULD CONTROL IT. Up and down, up and down, the
paddles on the screen went where she told them to go via the
joysticks. And to this was added a simple question whose answer
would change her life, and through her, that of many others.

HOW DOES IT WORK?

Later, after her father had had a go and been (to Tony Downer's
great amusement) immediately hooked, she turned to her Possum
and typed up the bigger question: DADDY. HOW DOES A COM-
PUTER WORK?

And when he told her, or tried to, drawing a schematic computer on a piece of paper over tea in the garden (a tea made by Marion, carried out by Marion, and eaten almost alone by Marion, since the others were so reluctant to emerge into the sunshine from their TV game) she became excited, confused, and eventually had to go indoors to the Possum and ask another question.

COULD YOU BRING A COMPUTER HOME FROM THE OFFICE? PLEASE? SO GRAHAM AND I CAN HAVE A GO?

The next day he called his office and a young engineer delivered one to the house: a Minion 570 which had been on trial at Fountain-Marquand.

The children watched the man, who had a nice smile and wore jeans, jogging shoes and a baggy blue-grey shirt, set it up in Esther's room where extra wall sockets had been installed during the original conversion. They listened to the incomprehensible talk he had with Richard, about consoles, disk-drives, booting, VDUs, error messages, command files.

'Playing *that* are you?' the engineer said to Graham, eyeing the game plugged into the television set.

'Yes,' said Graham, eager to talk about it.

'Want a game?'

Graham flicked a switch, pressed a control, and the television screen displayed the paddles and moving dot almost before the man, smiling, said, 'I shouldn't really, I mean ... Mr Marquand ...'

Graham looked hopefully at Richard who grinned and said, 'It's all right Leon, we're all on holiday in this house.'

The engineer took one of the joysticks and Graham the other, the 'ball' began to move rapidly between them. Graham lost a succession of points.

'Have you played this before?'

'Me? Play this? Certainly not. Got better things to do with my time.'

Graham was not sure if he was serious; Richard was certain he was not.

They played a little longer before the man stood up.

'Must get on ...' he began to say, but Richard saw his eyes linger on the screen as if unwilling to leave it, and then on to Esther's Possum.

'How does it work?' he asked her. She was pleased to show him and he watched without comment as the grid screen light worked its way from point to point and she laboriously spelt out a question: WHAT'S YOUR NAME?

'Leon Sadler,' he said.

Esther keyed up his name and printed it out: LEON SADLER.

'Esther's very fast with the Possum,' said Graham.

'Is she?' said Leon. He looked serious and rather thoughtful for a moment, then got the computer working.

He keyed in various things to test it and then said, 'I'm leaving all the manuals so you should be able to work it out for yourselves. I'm also leaving a copy of a disk I've got of some games I've collected here and there. Strictly unofficial, of course.' He winked at Richard who smiled.

'The operating system's conventional CP/M,' he said, as if they would understand.

Richard nodded.

'But I'll just do this one for you as there's a slight variation with the Minion 570.' He took an eight-inch floppy disk up and quickly put it in the disk-drive. It all seemed simple. He wrote 'Games' on the disk and gave it to Graham.

'Has it got "Pong" on it?' asked Graham.

'As a matter of fact no, I don't think so. But there's a primitive version of "Pacman" which is the kids' current favourite. Same people came up with it as made "Pong".'

The eyes of Graham and Esther lit up. Pacman? Their gaze fell to the floppy disk, black and inscrutable, their eyes were greedy.

Before he left, Leon talked with Richard by the front door. They heard him say 'Esther' and 'Possum' and 'calling some in'. They looked at each other: they liked Leon Sadler and felt somehow that he was on their side.

He came back in to say goodbye. 'See you!' he said, as if he meant it.

For a day or two Richard succumbed to an addiction for 'Pong', playing Graham repetitively until he lost to him every time and his interest waned. Marion had a go but found it boring and said she had better things to do.

So it was left to the children to play, or rather for Graham and Tom to play and Esther to watch. Occasionally she had a go with Tom's help against Graham, but her movement of the paddles was a sorry thwarted affair compared with Graham's dexterity. Once or twice Esther played against Tom, but the two of them were so clumsy, and the speed of the ball so relatively fast, that they had no chance of stopping it, or of scoring points against each other except by chance.

Tom was not seduced for long. Like Marion he became bored with it: the game was too fast for him, and though he did better at it than Esther, he could not feel the same fascination. He preferred the reality of outdoors on a summer's day.

'C'mon, Amh,' he said finally, lingering reluctantly at her side, yet equally reluctant to leave her.

NO.

'C'mon!!'

NO, TOM.

'Please, Amh.'

NO!!

Eventually she had to shout it because Tom was spoiling their concentration. Tom left after that and stood miserable and inactive in the garden. Then he went back to his tomatoes, alone.

Graham and Esther remained fascinated. Hour after hour they were drawn to watch that moving white point, inexorable and certain, which could be successfully patted back and forth if only ... if only the paddle could be got quickly enough to the right place.

To Graham, so long employed only passively by any television screen he saw, it was a magical freeing of the spirit. He had control for the first time, and though his kingdom was but a two-dimensional version of a ping-pong table and his solitary subject but a point of electronic light, yet it was the greatest freedom he had ever had. They began to keep scores and set targets, Esther working out figures in her head and taking pleasure in calculations about Graham's performance which involved building in a time factor.

Meanwhile, next to them, the Minion 570 computer waited, silent and untouched, along with the manuals and games disk. Long afterwards, Esther Marquand was to report to Daniel Schuster: 'It was the strangest thing – my father never once tried to show us how to use it and typically he left us to our own devices. We soon picked it up and one day that holiday I first began to realize the potential of computers for me.'

Years later Richard recalled: 'They did not want to learn any-thing from me. Esther was just getting to that awkward adolescent stage of pretending that she needed no one to help her. I tried a couple of times to show her how to use the manuals but I remember she and Graham said they were more interested in a game they had just discovered. But, anyway, our experience at Fountain-Marquand was that some people, especially bright children, learn about computers at least as fast if they have unlimited hands-on opportunity and the right manuals: guidance rather than teaching. Part of the process for them is that they are *not* taught, but feel like explorers in an unknown country, each discovery being exciting and an obstacle passed successfully.'

The fascination for 'Pong' soon began to pall and they began their exploration of the 570, turning to the manuals for guidance.

Graham, long used to Esther's desire to be involved, propped up the manuals one at a time on her tray, and then flicked through them, and they entered the portals leading to the arcane world of commands, of files, of PIP, of STAT, of ERROR MESSAGES and even of FATAL ERROR MESSAGES.

Days passed. Sometimes they gave up exploring the computer for a time, lured out into the garden, to play with Tom, or wander here and there among the plants, blowsy and dry now with the passage of a hot summer, the grass beneath their wheels dry and yellowed, the soil cracked except where Tom had watered his tomatoes day by day.

But in the shade, beneath the apple trees, the grass was greener, and in the shrubbery near the wooden fence the air was almost moist, darkened by the dull greens of the ivy, and the interlocking of branches above their heads.

Still, they stole glances back at the house, feeling that the computer was waiting and waiting for them, yielding its secrets slowly, but fast enough now to keep them coming back for more, as if there were something there beyond that grey and shining eye that must soon be shared with them.

A few days after their first attempt to understand the CP/M operating system, Graham and Esther turned from the sterile pages of the CP/M manual to another entitled *DB Applications Manual*. DB was DATABASE. Database was something big; something very.

very big. It was a way of manipulating facts and figures together. It was a mountain whose summit was so far shrouded in mists.

Minion 570 Word Processing was another manual, and easier. They learned to switch from Disk-drive One to Disk-drive Two. They discovered they could bring up a directory of the files on the disks they had.

But they could not call up the games. Nothing happened when they tried.

WHY NOT? Esther eventually and reluctantly asked her father.

He agreed to look at the screen where the directories had come up and said, 'Have you tried calling up the programs?'

'What's a program exactly?'

'The instructions to a computer.'

Graham called up the file for a game called 'Orbit'.

```
2     PRINT  TAB(33); "ORBIT"
4     PRINT  TAB(15); "CREATIVE COMPUTING
MORRISTOWN, NEW JERSEY"
6     PRINT  : PRINT: PRINT
10    PRINT  "SOMEWHERE ABOVE YOUR PLANET IS A
               ROMULAN SHIP. "
15    PRINT
20    PRINT  "THE SHIP IS IN A CONSTANT POLAR ORBIT.
ITS"
25    PRINT  "DISTANCE FROM THE CENTER OF YOUR
PLANET IS FROM"
30    PRINT  "10,000 TO 30,000 MILES AND AT ITS
PRESENT VELOCITY CAN"
31    PRINT  "CIRCLE YOUR PLANET ONCE EVERY 12 TO 36
HOURS. "
35    PRINT
40    PRINT  "UNFORTUNATELY THEY ARE USING A
CLOAKING DEVICE SO"
45    PRINT  "YOU ARE UNABLE TO SEE THEM, BUT WITH A
SPECIAL"
50    PRINT  "INSTRUMENT YOU CAN TELL HOW NEAR
THEIR SHIP YOUR"
55    PRINT  "PHOTON BOMB EXPLODED. YOU HAVE SEVEN
HOURS UNTIL THEY"
```

```
60    PRINT   "HAVE BUILT UP SUFFICIENT POWER IN
ORDER TO ESCAPE"
65    PRINT   "YOUR PLANET'S GRAVITY. "
70    PRINT
75    PRINT   "YOUR PLANET HAS ENOUGH POWER TO FIRE
ONE BOMB AN HOUR. "
80    PRINT
85    PRINT   "AT THE BEGINNING OF EACH HOUR YOU WILL
BE ASKED TO GIVE AN"
90    PRINT   "ANGLE (BETWEEN 0 AND 360) AND A
DISTANCE IN UNITS OF"
95    PRINT   "100 MILES (BETWEEN 100 AND 300).
AFTER WHICH YOUR BOMB'S"
100   PRINT   "DISTANCE FROM THE ENEMY SHIP WILL BE
GIVEN. "
105   PRINT
110   PRINT   "AN EXPLOSION WITHIN 5,000 MILES OF
THE ROMULAN SHIP"
111   PRINT   "WILL DESTROY IT. "
114   PRINT   . . . . . . .
```

'How does it work exactly?' asked Graham.

Richard explained, 'It's the program for a game written in BASIC, the best known simple programming language. If you want to play one of the games you need to have BASIC operating and put the program into memory.'

When her father had gone Esther typed up, GET THE BASIC MANUAL THEN!!

It was the fourth and it had *BASIC-X78 Reference Manual* printed on the spine. And on the title page it carried this unpromising message: ALL USERS OF BASIC-X78 ON THE 570 BUSINESS SYSTEMS COMPUTER MUST HAVE FIRST READ AND FULLY UNDERSTAND THE CP/M MANUALS, BE CONVERSANT WITH THE OPERATION AND HAVE PRIOR KNOWLEDGE OF THIS PROGRAMMING LANGUAGE.

'Amh?' it was Tom, at the door. Importunate.

NOT NOW, TOM, GO AWAY. NOT NOW.

Tom slunk away into the sunlight and the garden, down the path to his tomatoes and sat staring at them. He had stuck one of

the original seed packets on a green stick: 'Moneymaker, Bees
Seeds,' it read. The packet rattled dryly against the stick. There
was the slightest of breezes, and far off to the south there were
clouds gathering in the blue summer sky.

Behind Esther and Graham, unnoticed, the curtain suddenly
stirred, rose, and fell back. Wind. The sun that had shone in the
gaps between the curtains was fading; twilight had deepened in
the room.

Graham leafed through the manual again, reading it in the
gloom with difficulty, went past the commands and statements
section and on to pages headed 'Functions'.

SPC SQR STR$ STRING$

Esther tried to speak: IT SAYS 'EXAMPLE' SO TYPE THAT IN.
Her words were grunts.

'Shall I type it in, Ess?' suggested Graham after a moment listening to her.

She nodded.

Graham worked out what she had said and read down the page
under the function STRING$.

'Example,' he read:

```
10   X$ = STRING$ (10, 45)
20   PRINT X$ ''MONTHLY REPORT'' X$
RUN


- - - - - - - - - - MONTHLY REPORT - - - - - - - - - -

OK
```

Graham typed in the first two lines but hesitated before typing in
RUN. He knew it was a command. The curtain stirred again,
whipping out. Esther half turned to look at it, catching a glimpse of
one of the flowerbeds, its vegetation stirring before a summer
squall. Graham was too absorbed too notice.

'I saw that somewhere,' he said turning back through the
manual. 'Here it is: "Run, to execute the program currently in
memory." So that means . . .' his voice faded as he looked at Esther.
They both understood what it meant.

It means that the first two lines are a program and that means that typing them out is programming, and it also means they're in memory, whatever *that* means, thought Esther. It seemed that every time they learned what something meant, something new presented itself.

Graham typed RUN and miraculously, so it seemed, the screen was filled with a column reading:

```
- - - - - - - - - - MONTHLY REPORT - - - - - - - - - -
- - - - - - - - - - MONTHLY REPORT - - - - - - - - - -
- - - - - - - - - - MONTHLY REPORT - - - - - - - - - -
- - - - - - - - - - MONTHLY REPORT - - - - - - - - - -
- - - - - - - - - - MONTHLY REPORT - - - - - - - - - -
- - - - - - - - - - MONTHLY REPORT - - - - - - - - - -
- - - - - - - - - - MONTHLY REPORT - - - - - - - - - -
- - - - - - - - - - MONTHLY REPORT - - - - - - - - - -
- - - - - - - - - - MONTHLY REPORT - - - - - - - - - -
- - - - - - - - - - MONTHLY REPORT - - - - - - - - - -
- - - - - - - - - - MONTHLY REPORT - - - - - - - - - -
- - - - - - - - - - MONTHLY REPORT - - - - - - - - - -
```

On and on it went, the whole column jolting up the screen as each new line appeared at the bottom, for ever and ever. For a moment they both felt trapped again, but then simultaneously remembered what to do, and as Esther reached forward again as if she had for a moment forgotten that she was not dextrous enough to operate such keys easily, Graham pressed Control and C and the run of for ever unwritten and for ever unread monthly reports stopped.

There was a silence. Triumphant silence. They had made the computer do something. They had programmed it.

'Gosh,' said Graham. 'That was brilliant!'

But Esther was silent, her limbs still, her mind focused, her eyes glittering and dark.

'Gr . . .' she said at last, pointing at the keyboard and then the screen. 'Graah!!'

She wanted him to type out the program again with different words.

'What words?' he said, staring blankly at the invitation of 'OK'.

'Me,' said Esther, thumping her tray. 'Me'.

Graham turned to the keyboard but Esther shouted, 'Nah, *me*.'

'Oh, you want to type it, you mean. You want me to put your fingers in the right places?'

'Yeh,' she whispered, suddenly shy as Graham took her right hand in his.

With some difficulty, since their chairs got in the way of each other and the legs of the table on which the computer had been placed, Graham began to push down the keys with Esther's fingers:

```
10   X$ = STRING$ (10, 45)
20   PRINT X$ ''ESTHER MARQUAND'' X$
```

As he raised his hand to begin typing R U N she stopped him and said 'Me' again.

Then with infinite care, her eyes staring at each key in turn and her left hand clenched firmly on the tray to keep her body as still as possible and stop her right arm wavering about, she brought her right hand over the keyboard.

R, typed Esther.

The curtains stirred one last time, feebly, and then hung dead still. A glowing darkness fell outside as the first huge drops of rain of a storm began to fall.

U typed Esther.

Heavy rain began to drum on the paths of the garden, on the walls of the house, on the distant roofs, and nearby on the windowsill, spilling inside and on to the parquet flooring.

Graham turned and saw it but looked back to the screen. Esther's hand was poised and her face was shining, grey and fascinated in the light of the computer's eye.

Then her finger, straight and controlled, came down a third time to complete a command that marks the true beginning of the career of one of the twentieth century's great games programmers.

N, she typed.

There was a brief moment of stillness filled with the roar of rain outside and, somewhere near, somewhere rolling massively above, the first crackling of thunder, the roar of ancient gods, as the printer broke out into sound, fast violent sound, clattering at speed

over and over and over again, louder than the rain, as loud as the
thunder that crashed outside as it began to print:

```
- - - - - - - - - - ESTHER MARQUAND - - - - - - - - - -
- - - - - - - - - - ESTHER MARQUAND - - - - - - - - - -
- - - - - - - - - - ESTHER MARQUAND - - - - - - - - - -
- - - - - - - - - - ESTHER MARQUAND - - - - - - - - - -
- - - - - - - - - - ESTHER MARQUAND - - - - - - - - - -
- - - - - - - - - - ESTHER MARQUAND - - - - - - - - - -
- - - - - - - - - - ESTHER MARQUAND - - - - - - - - - -
- - - - - - - - - - ESTHER MARQUAND - - - - - - - - - -
- - - - - - - - - - ESTHER MARQUAND - - - - - - - - - -
- - - - - - - - - - ESTHER MARQUAND - - - - - - - - - -
- - - - - - - - - - ESTHER MARQUAND - - - - - - - - - -
- - - - - - - - - - ESTHER MARQUAND - - - - - - - - - -
- - - - - - - - - - ESTHER MARQUAND - - - - - - - - - -
- - - - - - - - - - ESTHER MARQUAND - - - - - - - - - -
- - - - - - - - - - ESTHER MARQUAND - - - - - - - - - -
- - - - - - - - - - ESTHER MARQUAND - - - - - - - - - -
- - - - - - - - - - ESTHER MARQUAND - - - - - - - - - -
- - - - - - - - - - ESTHER MARQUAND - - - - - - - - - -
- - - - - - - - - - ESTHER MARQUAND - - - - - - - - - -
- - - - - - - - - - ESTHER MARQUAND - - - - - - - - - -
- - - - - - - - - - ESTHER MARQUAND - - - - - - - - - -
- - - - - - - - - - ESTHER MARQUAND - - - - - - - - - -
- - - - - - - - - - ESTHER MARQUAND - - - - - - - - - -
- - - - - - - - - - ESTHER MARQUAND - - - - - - - - - -
```

The printer thundered on as outside the rain fell savagely,
bouncing in a white haze from the paths. And outside too, staring,
Tom stood drenched, his flesh white-pink through his T-shirt,
staring at his tomato plants which bent and bowed under the rain.

Then he knelt in the darkened soil, mud forming beneath his
knees, and eyed an ant close to the ground which scurried through
the devastating floods among the sods and stalks, and sought out
and found shelter beneath one of the tomatoes, still green, which
had sagged with its stalk down on to the soil.

Tom stood up with his hair shiny wet, a drenched figure in the

rain, and turned down the path into the shrubbery. High above
the rain roared on the canopy which wavered, stirred and parted,
and rain came down to the most sheltered part of the wooden
fence, falling on its uprights and turning their lichen a livid green.
Tom put his hand on them and looked over the fence, his big wet
mouth dripping wet, his glasses smudged with mud where he had
tried to clean them, and he stood as high as he could and over the
fence he shouted, loud loud and LOUDER to combat the great rain
and the thunder that was in his ears.

Tom shouted: 'Skalgskalgskalg', again, again, and again.

He fell silent, exhausted. Finally, he made one last effort, and
whispered, 'Skalg, please come.'

And still the print thundered and rain fell as a girl watched the
eternal printing of her name, and saw at last there was a way
towards freedom and to the climbing of the wooden fence towards
the Skallagrigg.

TWENTY-SEVEN

'Amh's not coming. Not here. Amh's *there*.'

Tom spoke matter-of-factly, the sun on his red face and his hands grubby from the work he had been doing in the vegetable garden, where he now stood talking to Richard.

He said the word 'there' with a vehemence which carried his fear of something he could not understand, something which threatened him. His voice dropped uncharacteristically low.

'Get Amh, please.'

Richard patted Tom on the shoulder, curiously moved by this appeal. He could not put into words why it was so potent and so pathetic, but never before had Tom asked anyone to get Esther for him. He had always felt he had a direct line to her, the right to go to her even if it meant occasional rejection. But somehow now he felt he had no such right, and the computer which had been such an excitement in the first days, with that strange moving light, now seemed an enemy that had taken Esther away from him.

'Well, I did say they could carry on with the computer this afternoon, Tom. And you did go for a walk with them this morning.'

'Yes,' said Tom miserably, looking towards the curtained window of the room where the computer was. There was Amh, with Graham and the tellything.

'Do you want to help me in the orchard?' said Richard.

Tom looked down and shook his head.

'Well, if you do you know where I am, don't you?' Tom did not reply.

Uneasy but feeling helpless, Richard wandered off alone down to the orchard holding the curved steel of a brand new pruning saw. He had bought it with Esther at one of the garden centres and she had been going to help him. But now she preferred to compute with Graham. After only a week they were getting deep into BASIC and in all honesty Richard could not think of a reason they should not. As for Tom ... well, they must sort out their own relationships.

Anyway, the sun was shining, and after nearly six weeks of holiday, with another ten days to go, Richard felt rested and relaxed. He had been looking forward to pruning the apple trees for months, and even if this was not, according to the books, the right time to do it, it was going to be the only chance he had. He began to whistle to himself as he arranged the ladder.

Left alone Tom wandered off and sat down among his plants. They had set well and little green tomatoes nestled among their hairy leaves. Their smell was sharply pungent and Tom sniffed them, caressed them and then smelt his hands. He had lost a few tomatoes in the storm, but most had survived well and the plants, which had sagged under the rain, were now upright and proud. No one but Esther had been allowed to touch the unripe fruits, and he had hung over even her to make sure she did not try to pick any before they were red, which would be a long time yet.

He had found another empty packet reading 'MONEYMAKER, BEES SEEDS' with an illustration of a fecund tomato plant to replace the one ruined by rain, and stuck it on a stick near the path where everyone could see. He had got the idea from a horticultural display garden they had visited. Once Tom got an idea he stayed with it. All his life he would mark out his vegetable rows that way.

'When they're red like that I'll have tomatoes 'n' toast,' he would tell visitors.

But now, disconsolate and lonely, Tom sat staring at the fruit. Occasionally he would stand upright and peer towards the house as if hoping that the curtains in Esther's room would be drawn and Esther was at last going to come out.

'Amh,' his open mouth, mouthing a name, seemed sometimes to say. 'Amh.'

Then he sat down and sniffed, and then began to cry.

Ants crawled in the dry-again earth, a blackfly staggered over the stem of a tomato plant, lost among the spiky hairs, a blue-black shiny beetle paused on a piece of soil by Tom's hand, and then moved off.

The sound of sporadic sawing came from the orchard and as the afternoon slowly passed by Tom sat still, miserably thinking. Eventually he came to a decision, wiping his nose on his sleeve as he did so. He picked eight or nine of the green tomatoes saying, 'Sorry, sorry, sorry,' to each one, cupped them into his hand, and set off wearily towards the house.

In the few days since Esther and Graham had started exploring the possibilities of BASIC they had got a surprisingly long way. It helped – indeed it may well have been the major element in their speedy learning – that they were able to call up all the programs of the games on the disk the engineer had copied for them. There were some thirty games listed and they were working their way through them, Esther being the one who insisted that they play them first before looking at the programs which created them. Most were simple alpha-numeric games, some so simple that a single play was enough. Others were more complex. All of them had been plagiarized by the Minion engineers and rewritten for its specific form of BASIC.

Now they were looking at a program called Litquiz, another from Creative Computing, which asked a series of simple literary questions which neither of them could answer:

```
40  PRINT  "IN PINOCCHIO, WHAT WAS THE NAME OF THE
CAT"
42  PRINT  "1)TIGGER, 2)CICERO, 3)FIGARO,
4)GUIPETTO";
43  INPUT A: IF A = 3 THEN 46
44  PRINT  "SORRY . . . FIGARO WAS HIS NAME.": GOTO
50
46  PRINT  ."VERY GOOD! HERE'S ANOTHER. "
```

Having failed to get many of these right they had now listed the program itself and were studying it. BASIC was not hard to understand once the more common commands were mastered, and the on-screen effect during the running of a program recognized. Each line had a number, building up in series of five or ten to allow the insertion of new lines where the program demanded it.

Looking at the Litquiz program it was obvious that ...

The door of Esther's room opened and unwelcome light fell across the screen.

'Amh!'

Silence. The tellything glowed. Tom was studiously ignored.

He pushed his glasses harder on to his snub nose and nervously wrinkled his brow.

'*Amh!!*'

Tom waited hesitantly at the doorway, shy to step forward into the shining world of silences and codes, concentrations and indifference. '*Amh*.' There was an agony of waiting in his voice.

Esther looked round and then back to the screen. NOT NOW TOM NOT NOW. LATER MAYBE.

'When, Amh?'

NOT NOW.

Graham hunched forward irritably, as if to cut Tom out of his consciousness. They had better things to think about.

'*Amh!*' and Tom came up and put a hand on the handle of her chair.

'*Toh!*' Esther was angry. It was the voice that Tom could never gainsay. He knew he must not touch her chair.

'These are good, Amh,' he said finally, having stood in silence behind them, staring without comprehension at the screen.

Then he came forward round her chair, and dropped his handful of small green and hard tomatoes in a heap on the keyboard where some stayed and others rolled off all shiny grey in the light, a cascade of bouncing movement around the static computer before rolling into stillness. Tom stared at Esther hopefully. The screen images jumped and went haywire. The screen went blank and then printed up: OK.

Dead. The previous screens lost. A couple of key strokes, a pause, a couple more, and Graham could easily get them back again . . . but the sudden abortion of the program by Tom's intervention seemed more serious than that, and emotionally it was. They had been lost in a world and forcibly, by Tom's intrusion, dragged out of it and back to reality.

'*Tom!* Look what you've done! Go away Tom. *Go away,*' shouted Graham, anger mounting.

'Yeh,' echoed Esther.

Their grey-green faces were violent and angry at him in the gloom.

'Take these with you,' said Graham, pushing the tomatoes on to the edge of the table where some of them rolled on and over the edge to the floor. Tom scrabbled about in the half-darkness on the floor picking them up and getting tangled with their wheels and the computer's electrical wires. He was slow, uncertain, humiliated.

'Yes, Amh, yes yes,' he muttered, his mouth wet as, chastened and guilty, he scrabbled about trying to find the fruit of his labours. Most he found, but some fell from his hands again and rolled across the parquet flooring and under chairs and the sofa. Scared to stay longer he tiptoed away, leaving the two of them staring once more at the screen in their strange and impenetrable world, Tom quite forgotten.

Outside, in the kitchen, Marion found him standing by the sink, putting the offending unripe tomatoes into the waste bin. Tom was always tidy now.

'Oh, Tom,' said Marion, 'what *are* you doing? They won't be ripe for a good few weeks yet.'

'No,' said Tom. 'Don't know,' he added mysteriously. He looked distressed and lost, hopping clumsily from one foot to the other.

'Is it because Esther's not out in the garden?' she asked, guessing correctly.

'Yes,' said Tom truthfully. His head dropped and he turned to Marion to hug her sideways on.

'She won't be long, Tom,' she said comfortingly. She hugged Tom back. When she had first come he had frightened her, for he was big and his arms strong. But now she was used to him, and smiled.

'Go on, Tom, go and help Richard. He's cut big dead branches down in the orchard. You can help him clear them and make a bonfire. I'll make a cup of tea for everybody soon,' she said.

Tom went to the vegetable garden instead where he walked round its walled perimeter, feeling the red bricks with his fingers. Sometimes he looked back up towards the house. Sometimes he stared at his plants, but he did not go near them.

Then by degrees he left the vegetable garden, steering clear of Richard and making his way into the shadowed shrubberies behind the vegetable garden and beyond the orchard until, timorously and as if he was trespassing to be there alone without Esther, he came to the wooden fence.

He stood there humbly, quite alone, the green shade of the trees around him and the chill of the shadows bringing goosepimples to his arms. His big mouth opened and closed several times, as if he was trying to find courage to speak. The anger that had made him shout 'Skalg!' during the storm was long gone and now he simply shuffled slowly right up to the fence and looked timidly over it. He stared into the deep shadows of the trees and their branches above for a long time.

'Skalg,' he said finally. 'Please get Amh.' And as he stared his face creased slowly into tears and his mouth tightened into a cry and his teeth showed and he said, 'She won't come. Amh won't come here now.'

He stood there waiting. Light faded into late afternoon and Marion's voice called out by the house: 'There's some tea made. Richard! Tom!'

Richard's voice penetrated the shrubbery.

'Can you bring me a mug, Marion? I'm up a ladder.'

Tom shrunk in the shade by the fence as if their voices could see him.

Their voices played about him.

'Oh, I thought Tom was with you,' said Marion.

'Haven't seen him.'

'He wasn't very happy. Esther . . .' their voices faded from Tom's consciousness. He slunk away, sniffing. He went back to the vegetable garden and was there for a time; savagely busy.

Then he walked round the house purposefully, past the curtained drawing-room, to the front garden and down the short drive to the road, and then turned left by himself to walk in the general direction of the shops.

'Going to find the Centre. Going home,' he said to himself. 'Ealing Council.'

They missed him an hour later when high tea was served in the kitchen. It had grown grey in the garden and a little cold. The summer was fading towards autumn. They called and called and finally, exasperated, Marion went off to find him. She came back running and said, 'You had better come, Richard.'

Her expression was enough to get him running down to the vegetable garden.

'Look,' said Marion, shocked.

Tom's tomatoes had been laid waste. Plant after plant was pulled up, unripe tomatoes scattered and crushed as if the plants had been kicked and stamped upon. Not one was left standing; only the stick with the empty seed packet showed what ripe fruit on well grown plants should look like, a red flag over desolation.

'Where's Tom?' Richard's voice was urgent. As, urgently, the telephone rang some minutes later.

Tom had been recognized by a shopkeeper who saw him standing by a bus stop, looking at each one that passed as if he hoped to find one with 'Ealing Broadway' marked upon it. But seeing none, he had stood there as impatient people walked huffily round him to get on their buses, until the shopkeeper, watching from behind his shining window, picked up the phone and called the police. Who, after a talk with the young man and a talk among some of their patrols, worked out where he came from. He was usually seen with that spastic girl and her name was known: Esther Marquand, Abbey Road. Mr Marquand.

'Sorry,' said Tom grinning when he was delivered back. He was thrilled with a ride in the police car. 'But I won't again.'

'Sorry,' he kept saying, not looking at Esther. Richard gave him a hug, welcomed him back.

'*Toh!*' said Esther. 'Toh.'

'Sorry, Amh,' said Tom.

It was cool outside and getting dark, but Esther insisted that Tom take her out. She had been chastened by the whole thing and felt guilty. She understood well what had happened and why. She never wished to hurt Tom, but the computer had . . . had lured them. She would go back to it, both of them would, but she'd watch over Tom more carefully.

OH WHY DID YOU PULL UP THE TOMATOES, TOM?

'Don't know, Amh,' said Tom, only half remembering his misery.

COME ON, TOM.

'No, Amh.'

WE'RE GOING OUT THERE, TOM.

'No, Amh,' said Tom.

The adults did not interfere and Marion, understanding, drew Richard and Graham away.

YES, TOM. NOW.

'Yes, Amh,' he said obediently.

He slowly took the handles of her chair and pushed her past them all and out into the garden.

'Where, Amh?' they heard him ask, as if he didn't know.

YOU KNOW, TOM.

Tom pushed her down to his vegetable garden.

They stared at the plants, wounded and fallen like soldiers.

OH, TOM.

Esther looked at him and did her best to reach out to him. His hand came to hers.

TOM, she began. TOM NEVER HURT THINGS LIKE THIS AGAIN. THEY WERE LOVELY, TOM, THEY WERE RIGHT AND THEY WERE GROWING BIG AND STRONG. THEY WERE PERFECT, TOM, and it seemed as Esther stared at them that she saw herself, or something like herself, and she began suddenly to weep, great tears of misery on her face and Tom was wild with distress to see her.

'Don't, Amh. Please. *Don't.*'

WHY DID YOU DO IT?

'Couldn't stop. Don't cry, Amh.'

IT'S MY FAULT, TOM. I'M SORRY I'M SORRY. But her sounds faded away as Tom went down on his knees among his plants and started picking over them saying, 'Don't, Amh, please please please don't.' His lips were wet with grief and tears but his hands were gentle and his concentration began to focus.

'Watch, Amh. Watch, don't cry.' And with his hands he cleared the bed and sorted out the plants that still had whole stems and some tomatoes on them. He got up and went to the out-buildings and came back with a trowel. He put it down and thought for a bit and then went off again, returning this time with some canes left over from the sweetpeas Richard had put in by the house.

He methodically replanted the plants that still had life in them, propping them up with the canes, breaking off the broken parts to leave the rest standing battered but proud.

'OK, Amh. Water now. Plants come back. Every year they come back.' His hands rested on her leg and he looked at her with terrible appeal as if waiting for her response.

'They come back better.'

Still he waited.

YEH, said Esther finally. THEY COME BACK BETTER.

He went and turned a tap and pulled the running hose over to

Esther's chair, careful not to splash the water on her. Water glistened darkly in the wheels of her chair. Dusk was falling fast. He helped her train the hose along the bed, watering the six plants that had survived.

'Better'n tellything,' he said.

When they had finished he took the broken plants down to the compost heap, and tidied away the trowel and the hose.

'I said to the Skalg to get you,' he said.

DID YOU, TOM. Esther felt drained but content. Her world and Tom's was to rights again, though different.

I would like to go with you down to the wooden fence, she thought.

'We'll go there, Amh. Now.'

YES, TOM.

Tom pushed her down into the darkness of the wood, not seeing Richard among the apple trees quietly watching to see that they were all right. Tom was not murdering Esther, they were making friends again. He watched them go into the shrubbery talking quietly in the strange way they did. Why always the wooden fence? Richard left them in peace.

Tom touched the fence in the twilight.

'Thanks, Skalg,' he said, his hands protective on Esther's chair.

Esther smiled.

'Skalg can do anything,' he said.

'Yeh,' said Esther, wanting to believe it. Understanding that in a way it might be true.

'Skalg come for you,' said Tom. 'One day.'

'Yeh,' whispered Esther in the dark.

'Then you'll come back better.'

Oh no no, Tom, she thought.

'Yes, Amh,' said Tom quietly. 'Skalg can do that.'

HE'LL COME FOR YOU AS WELL, TOM.

'He'll come for you first and you'll be OK.'

OK!

Esther smiled.

OH TOM. Esther could sense the full meaning of his love for her, the responsibility he felt for her. He was saying that one day it would be over, he wouldn't have to worry about her any more. He didn't mind now, she was his life; but one day, when the Skallagrigg came, he would be free.

'Toh,' she whispered up to him.

''s OK, Amh. Don't be scaredy. Skalg's not scaredy. I spoke to him.'

They stared into the silent darkness of the grass and the trees beyond the wooden fence.

'C'mon, Amh. Going in now. Bye-bye.' He said this farewell simply, over his shoulder, as he heaved Esther round and back towards the house.

In the silence of the dusk and Tom's protective love, Esther wondered about the Skallagrigg; and about the computer whose secrets she and Graham were penetrating, which she sensed she could never now turn away from, but which she must reconcile with this real world where Tom was and where she was too.

TWENTY-EIGHT

Tom's outburst and the resolution into peace and deeper trust with Esther that followed, heralded a strange and purposeful contentment at Harefield for the final days of that summer holiday.

Richard was as relaxed as any of them were subsequently to remember, lazing in the garden and taking them all off occasionally for trips into the country, something he was never to do again.

Marion too was content, the more so after Richard had suggested that she might like to stay on at Harefield as housekeeper after Esther had returned to Netherton. He liked having her there, got on well with her, and was beginning to realize the advantage of having someone to look after the place so that he would not come back from business trips to a cold and empty house. For Marion it was the opportunity she had been unknowingly waiting for, and she seemed to blossom with the security and status it gave her.

Then one day Richard had a phone call from Leon Sadler inviting Esther and Graham to his flat in London.

Neither was keen to go as they had reached a critical point with their computing and did not want to leave Harefield for a whole day.

'Half a day,' said Richard. 'Anyway he's done you a favour, Esther. He thinks he's found an improved keyboard for your Possum, and he wants to see if there are any other ways he can speed up your typing for you.'

'Yeh!' said Esther.

'You know, Leon Sadler is an exceptionally talented man and I'm lucky to have his services at ComputaBase. When he saw how slowly you key up words he felt he could come up with something better.'

'That's what the engineer at Netherton said,' said Graham, 'but he hasn't done anything about it, has he, Ess?'

She shook her head.

'Nah,' she said more softly, eyeing her fingers. Fighting hope.

*

Leon Sadler lived in a cavernous ground-floor flat in Notting Hill.
Only three rooms were presentable – the kitchen, a back living-
room and a bedroom – for the rest were given over to the chaos of
his only interest: models, machines and devices, preferably electrical or electronic.

Sadler was dressed in nondescript brown corduroy trousers,
bright pink trainers, and a girlfriend's lurex pullover with a
magnificent streak of pink. His hair was cropped and black, and he
had a day's growth of beard.

He was pleased to see them and after a cup of coffee he gave
Esther and Graham a tour of his home. They both fell silent as they
saw that every space in Leon's flat, every corner, every open
cupboard, had been taken over by the electronic gadgetry of sound,
vision and, more recently, the computer. The floors trailed grey
and black wires which got in the way of their chair wheels; tape
reels lay untidily on shelves, tables were chock-a-block with
equipment.

Leon had been in turn a model-maker, a radio ham, a hi-fi
enthusiast, a calculator freak and a computer hacker. The detritus
of these successive phases began in a back bedroom and led progressively and chronologically through to computers in what had
been the main drawing-room. It had a magnificent ceiling rose
and splendid mouldings, but the walls were undecorated, and at
waist height on each wall were rows of three-pin sockets off a ring-
main.

Leon's computers were not liveried and beautiful like the ones in
showrooms. He was not interested in appearances, but stripped
things down to essentials. Not that he left them unusable. On the
contrary, he seemed able to convert his machines to do new things
by emendations, removals, transplants and graftings of transistor,
tube, chips and controls.

In the mid-1970s, with the arrival of the cheaper minicom-
puters, Leon had come into his own, and his eccentric and once
isolating hobby had transformed him into a much sought-after
electronic engineer and programmer who, from his contracts with
Fountain-Marquand alone, was now earning big money. He was
now recognized as one of Britian's more original and innovative
computer designers, and indeed, was then working on the design
of the first of the ORCK range which was not only to make the

fortune of IDC Computers, which commissioned it, but to establish Richard's own ComputaBase operation. At the same time ORCK would make Sadler himself a millionaire.

Now he led Esther and Graham through into the biggest reception room of the flat.

'This is where the computers are,' he said said waving a hand at monitors, one of which was on and flickering numbers and letters which they immediately recognized as a program, though not in a language they recognized.

'Your father asked me to think about alternative keyboards for you, Esther, and I've called in a couple designed for people with special needs. One by a friend of mine and the other a simple reduction of the conventional keys to eight numbered keys operated in different combinations to give the same scope as a conventional keyboard.'

He waved towards a table in one corner of the room. An ordinary keyboard was ranged alongside several others, some of them very odd-looking indeed.

'Before we try the new ones let's just see how you get on with this ordinary keyboard.'

Esther directed her chair to the table, expertly straightened it, and faced the keyboard. She leaned forward against her support straps as Leon booted the computer to bring a word-processing program on-screen.

She raised her arms and brought her hands forward, the right one first. Her left hand touched the table and pressed against it, her weight leaning on it to steady her other arm. Her index finger, crooked and bent and thrust out from the others, aimed towards the keys and hit the E as the middle finger lowered itself on to the S. Slow motion. Her fingers jerked up, poised shakily, and descended to the T, The remaining two letters of her name were no problem as they were adjacent to the T. ESTHER had appeared on the screen with no mistakes. But it took over a minute.

'Esther always says that she's lucky that the letters of her name are together in a cluster on the keyboard,' said Graham. 'I don't do badly with mine as a matter of fact,' he added, 'except for the M.'

They tried another keyboard, Leon measuring its position rela-

tive to her chair and body and taking notes. For a time he simply
stood to one side and studied her.

'Right, that's enough for me to work on, Esther. It'll probably
take several goes to get it right but I'll get my friend to work on it
as well. He might have to come and see you to take more meas-
urements. Could you just try this one as well, just so you can see
how it works.'

He took up the third keyboard, with eight numbered keys,
cleared the table and placed it before her.

'This one works by translating letters and some of the more
common words into numbers of which, on an eight-key board,
there are potentially over forty thousand,' explained Leon.

'The problem here is one of memorizing what combinations
represent what letters or words,' he said. 'The single keys represent
the common letters like E S and D, while the combinations have
been preserved for long key words which the computer will type in
full for you if you initiate the combination: 475, for example is . . .'

Leon typed it and the word WEDNESDAY appeared.

BIT CLUMSY, typed Esther.

'Could you think of a better code?'

She paused before answering and then looked at Graham.

YES, she typed.

'Good,' said Leon, 'then do so and I'll see if we can find a way of
getting a screen display that's attachable to your wheelchair. Instant communication. Not before time.'

'Yeh,' said Esther.

'Now then,' said Leon changing the subject, 'we've got about an
hour before Richard comes back. He said you were interested in
games and I've got a few things to show you . . .'

Later they retreated from the electronic chaos of Leon's biggest
room, back through his years of hi-fi and radios, into the dusty
graveyard of the aeroplane models and train-sets of his youth, into
the third and smallest room adjacent to the corridor that led to the
kitchen and more normal and acceptable part of his flat, a room he
had not bothered to show them. Esther caught a glimpse of something that made her call out, '*Yeh!!*'

LOOK, GRAHAM. LOOK AT THAT.

'What is it, Ess?' said Graham. She was making excited noises
and trying to point into Leon's smallest room.

'Is it the train station set I made for my Hornby Double-O when I was a kid?' said Leon, pushing the door wide open and advancing towards a shadowed dusty railway line and station, its platforms long disused, its tiny ticket office murky, its old-fashioned porters and station master waiting for ever on a platform to which, perhaps, a train would never come again.

'Nah!' cried Esther.

'It still works, you know.'

'Nah.'

Leon looked behind him at the old models piled on a table and shelves above it to the toy tractors, figures and machines that seemed almost to burst from a half-open cupboard in one corner of the room. There was an old-fashioned blind hanging from the window, blue-black, which he had seen no reason to change. The window was murky with dust and grime, the light grey and without any hint of sun or warmth.

There. That. THAT!

Esther gesticulated wildly and they followed her gaze and the thrust of her hands to the shadowed nook between cupboard and side wall in which was a shape like a tallboy, only glazed and darkly painted, on top of which, its colours now faded, was screwed a board on which were painted the words 'The Enchanted Castle' and beneath that, written in gold and encased in an arrow that thrust its way towards a brass slit embedded in the wood, 'One Penny'.

'Oh! That!' said Leon with a smile. 'That's a penny slot-machine. Do you want to see it?'

A glow of excited expectation came over Esther's face, and Graham's as well, as Leon busied himself with clearing a way through to the slot-machine.

Leon had got 'The Enchanted Castle' from an amusement arcade sale in Blackpool. He had done it up and got it into working order, the mechanism being almost as easily repaired as the simple system of small electric bulbs which lit up successive parts of the scenario as they came into play.

Once it had occupied pride of place in his flat, and he had had a supply of old pennies so that visitors could have a go. He had spent three months getting it working, sorting out the lighting, and repainting the figures and the set. He touched the mahogany facings of the old machine lovingly, and eased it clear of the wall and cupboard. At its rear was a flex of old brown electric wire and attached to that was a black three-pin plug of old design. Leon put the plug into a socket, took an old painted cigar tin from the top of the cabinet and opened it. It was full of worn black pennies.

Esther and Graham looked at them: pre-decimal coinage. They had never seen such things before and they seemed to hold a history and a sense of past which affirmed that general sense of past wonders which Leon's apartment managed to combine so well with present delights.

'Right, now I think Esther gets first go. What you do is put your eye to that hole there and when I put the penny in the flap will go back and you'll get a look into the Enchanted Castle for about a minute. There's a timing mechanism so that when it runs out the eye-flap drops back and you've had your penny's worth.'

He manoeuvred her chair to the cabinet and by loosening the straps and tilting her chair forward a little was able to position her left eye level with the peep-hole.

'When you're ready I'll put the penny in,' he said.

Esther pressed her face to the glass and her eye to the blanked-out hole.

'Yeh,' whispered Esther, her breath misting the glass for a brief moment. And they watched her as there was a click and a whirr, and a light went on in the cabinet, though all they could see was a thin slit of yellow light along the top edge, where the set had the smallest of gaps along a corner. Esther, her eye caught now in yellow light, the rest of her grey and subdued in the dim room, stared in rapt silence.

From the Marquand Collection: Skallagrigg Tales. Disk 30, File 'Skall07' (This version is attributed to Frank Jessop, resident Corley End Hospital, Lancashire, 1911– 81.)

> Some of the boys was awarded a treat for good behaviour at Coronation time. They got a trip to Blackpool to see the lights. Arthur says, 'I'm going!' but Dilke says 'No you're not. You're a frigging pain and be a right nuisance.'

Later Arthur says, 'I been to Blackpool before and I would have liked to go again.'

'Come off it, you never said you'd been there,' say the boys.

Arthur says, 'I'll tell you what I saw there so when you go you see if I'm not telling the truth. How would I know about it if I hadn't of been?'

'Tell what?' say the boys, who liked Arthur to tell them things.

'There's a promenade with lights, and a metal tower with lights, all up every corner and shining in the night tall and straight. That'll take your breath right out of your body. There's a pier that goes out to sea so you can look down on the waves without getting wet. I looked over and saw white foam climbing up towards me. But the best bit is the penny peep shows. There's the murder one and the butler one and the ship at sea one and the enchanted castle one . . .'

'Goin' to tell us what happens or not?' says one lad, his eyes wide.

Arthur says, 'Listen. You put the penny in. In my case someone put it in for me, and you put your eye to the glass. After a moment there's a hole there and a light goes on and then the magic starts.

'It's a castle struck dead, everybody struck still and unable to move. There's servants sweeping the courtyard, there's a king and queen sitting at the top of some steps, there's guards by the big keep gates, their hands raised like they're about to open up to someone outside.

'There's something terrible in the courtyard on a raised square stone table. It's a beautiful princess with blonde hair and in a white dress, like for a wedding. She's got golden shoes on. She's been cursed to sleep and you can tell who by because he's there isn't he, up on top of the tower, looking down with a dilke smile on his face. The wicked wizard in a black robe with bad red writing on. Evil spells. Mind you he gets his comeuppance in the end.' Eppie laughs, ha ha ha ha ha ha.

'As the clock strikes twelve and the wizard thinks he's won,' continues Arthur, 'at that very moment as the clock's bell chimes the prince turns swift and sure and he bends down to the princess and he kisses her red waiting lips.

'Then the enchanted castle awakes into joy. The guards turn and raise their arms in triumph, the servants form a circle

and dance around the young couple, the king and queen
stand up and come down the stairs to welcome the prince
with open arms, and the princess sits up, opens her eyes, and
sees her nightmare is replaced by a dream come true.'

The lads are silent, wondering. Then one says, 'What about
the Skallagrigg?' Arthur isn't one to tell a story without the
Skallagrigg in it somewhere.

'Yes,' says Arthur, 'I needed him like we all do. That penny
peep-show was on the pier where the salt wind blew and
caught at my hair while I was held up to look into the magic
box. In that box where the castle was I forgot about my body
for a time, didn't I? You know that prince?'

The lads nod.

'I was that prince with a princess to kiss and I didn't want
to go back to me in a chair again. So I didn't let on the show
was over even when the flap came across the peep-hole and
I was staring at darkness. I started to cry and call out for the
Skallagrigg to help me stay in that castle where there was the
joy of love and I was a prince for all time. I cried and made a
fuss and I called for him.'

'Did he come?' asks one of the lads softly. They saw that
Arthur was distressed remembering it for them. They knew it
was hard sometimes for Arthur to tell them his stories, but he
did it because he cared for them.

'Yes, he came,' says Arthur. 'He'll always come. Didn't I
ever tell you that one day he'll come and take me from here
when the time's right and he's ready. He's not ready yet so
I've got to wait patiently. I'm learning patience and that's
hard that is. Harder than the hardest of Dilke's blows with his
window stick.' Arthur looks at the lads, his eyes soft with
remembering. 'Yes, he came when I called. I felt his hands on
me and his arms round me and heard his voice saying,
"Arthur, Arthur, I'm here, come back from there. It's only
make-believe it isn't real and I know you want it real but you
won't find me there because I'm here where you really are,
always here where you are. I always will be, whatever happens." And he pulled me back from that false place of dreams
and I felt his arms round me and saw his eyes looking into
mine and they held more for me than any enchanted castle.'

Sure as eggs is eggs Dilke saw to it that Arthur didn't go
on the trip to Blackpool, but one of the lads did a kind thing.
He refused to spend the penny they gave him for the peep-
shows. He got some Blackpool Rock with blood-red letters

saying 'Blackpool' shot right through it and he didn't touch one bit of it. And when the charge said 'Aren't you going to eat it then, Frank?' ('cos that's who the lad was: Frank, who was Arthur's best friend), he just shook his head and kept it out of harm's way in his jacket. Some say he took it back to Arthur but some say different. Some say that when the charges weren't looking he left it on a penny slot-machine he saw. When he got back to the ward he said, 'I got you a present Arthur and I left it in Blackpool. It was some rock.'

Arthur asks a question and Frank replies: 'I left it on the enchanted Castle peep-show so the Skallagrigg would find it. It was to say "Thanks, pal" for rescuing you that day long ago.'

From the moment Esther Marquand experienced Leon Sadler's Enchanted Castle penny slot-machine she seems to have become a creator in search of an idea. And though the idea turned and turned again about her and her world, whispering to her of its massive simplicity, she did not then know how to reach out and grasp it.

'I was so impatient that my chest heaved breathlessly as I watched the others,' she wrote later for Daniel. ' "Do you want another go?" Leon asked. And I'm sure I was brusque and rude in saying no because I had better things to do than watch a made-up world. I had learnt what I needed to from it: I wanted to make such a world myself. But better, richer, bigger, and that afternoon when Leon Sadler first showed me a keyboard that would work for me I understood that I could do it with a computer.'

So they left the room and Leon turned off the light and the peep-show was left in darkness once more, its characters eternally waiting for life to be granted them. Near the floor, barely visible in the gloom, was a maker's stamped metal plaque on the front of the Enchanted Castle booth. It read, 'Made by T.R. & J. Reynolds, Apsham Road, Blackpool.' There was no mention of the county, Lancashire, for in those days who in Blackpool would have doubted where they were?

For Esther, this visit turned out to be the unexpected highlight of the summer, and to it she returned on her last evening of the holidays when she chose to sit alone in the garden to watch the sun set on the summer; to think about Tom and Graham, to remember the days at Harefield, to be excited about the discovery of programming and the computer, and the possibility that inside it she might create a world similar to, but far richer than, the Enchanted Castle. Her world, into which others could come. She wanted to lead them to where they would know for ever that she was not what she seemed.

So Esther sat, until Brian came slowly out and said softly, 'May I sit with you, old girl?'

'Yeh,' she whispered.

He bent down to kiss her.

'Thinking, eh?'

'Yeh,' she whispered, even more softly. As soft as the pink in the evening sky.

'The future? The past?'

'B . . . b . . . sth . . .' she said.

'Both?'

She nodded.

'They're the same in the end, the poets say,' said Brian.

He reached out a hand and put his old one on hers and together they watched darkness take over the sky.

By the patio doors behind them Margaret watched and smiled that smile of love and gentleness she so rarely permitted others to see; while in a bedroom above Marion set a list on the bed and methodically packed Esther's cases for the new school year.

TWENTY-NINE

'How do I get someone I love to ask me out?'

The question was Betty Shaw's and it was asked during a class given by a new teacher, Mrs Elizabeth Fyfield, on a new subject: Liberal Studies.

Mrs Fyfield's method was interactive, and her subject was indeed liberal, for her brief was simply to get the 'O' and 'A' level candidates to talk more openly about their hopes and feelings; and, inevitably, because of their age, their feelings were increasingly sexual.

Few of their parents had broached sex with them and they were concerned and confused about it, the more so because all of them were becoming conscious of the disadvantages their handicaps were likely to put on them in the sexual marketplace. The worries and fears that came up – masturbation, sudden erections, menstruation, the mysteries of the opposite sex, in fact precisely the issues that came up in any such class among any maturing students, able-bodied or handicapped – she dealt with clearly and without embarrassment, emphasizing that all such feelings were normal and acceptable.

The most successful class was when everybody was asked to write two questions on a piece of paper without putting their names on them and these were read out by Mrs Fyfield, answered and discussed.

Esther's questions, typed on the Possum, were: 'Is kissing hygienic?' and 'What proportion of handicapped people ever get married and have children?'

But the most discussed question was the one about dating blurted out by Betty without concern for anonymity: How *do* you get someone to ask you out?

That there might be a hidden agenda in this was not lost on Mrs Fyfield and she might have been forgiven for thinking, judging by

the arguments which raged about the question and the heat generated, that a surprising proportion of the class was in love with
someone who was slow in coming forward.

Esther Marquand, being Betty's best schoolfriend and confidant,
knew perfectly well the real truth behind that simple question:
Betty fancied one of the boys, Stephen James, a kyphotic, and was
hoping that if she stared meaningfully at him when this question
was asked, dim-witted male though he was, he would get the
message.

'It's not the same if *I* ask him because then he won't respect me,'
Betty moaned privately to Esther. 'Respect is very important.'

Esther grinned. Betty was her passport to a knowledge of boys
since she herself did not yet have any experience of them. Betty
was always getting up to some kind of fun and had now kissed five
boys, if only briefly, at parties.

Although their opportunities for such harmless exploration were
very limited they were there, and though Esther, like any self-
conscious adolescent, chose to blame her lack of experience on
circumstances and her seeming unattractiveness, the fact was that
her mind, unlike Betty's, was not preoccupied that term with
boys, but with something far more intellectual: a faster way of
inputting words to her word processor through her keyboard. It
was her work then that, along with the Sadler keyboard, ultimately
allowed her to type as fast as, indeed faster than, able-bodied
people.

At that time she was mainly concerned with her diary which
she did with Betty who helped her with the paper in the Possum
and who was the only friend she could trust not to read what she
wrote or not to laugh if she did. Privacy was a real problem, and
the knowledge that Betty might read her words sometimes restricted what she said.

So, fired by the dual need for privacy, even from Betty, and a
desire for greater speed, she began to abbreviate the words in the
diary, developing by trial and error a system based on frequency of
word usage. She started by shortening the key pronouns to a
single letter and some common words as well: Netherton 'N',
lessons 'l', work 'w'. Frequently used proper names she reduced to
one capital letter – 'B' for Betty, 'G' for Graham, 'D' for Daddy, 'N'
for Nana, 'S' for nearby Southampton.

But this soon exhausted the stock of single letters and she began then to abbreviate longer words to two or three letters, and to modify her existing list. 'And' for example changed from 'a' to a plus sign, though the plus being at the far end of the Possum grid took her a little longer to reach than the letter A. But that had other uses.

Soon she discovered that context made meaning, and frequently there was no need to indicate tense once the general tense was established. A sentence beginning 'I went' established that many verbs thereafter would be in the perfect tense and have no need for 'ed' or 'en' on the end.

So a typical entry (for 12 November 1980) read: 'B + I went to Bth n a grp ystdy, to se t flm "A Clockwork Orange", G cme too b did n tlk to me. Am hvng a shpoo tonite b dnt lik the hlpr cald Flicky. Hp she dnt do t' 'Betty and I went to Bournemouth in a group yesterday to see the film *A Clockwork Orange*. Graham came too but did not talk to me. Am having a shampoo tonight but don't like the helper called Flicky. Hope she doesn't do it.'

The key stroke savings with this method ran to about thirty-five per cent, but Esther quickly realized that the method was unsystematic and, ultimately, limiting. For one thing she could not remember all the abbreviations when she came to read back, and for another she found that she began to think in cryptic terms, with her sentences, which were naturally flowing and long, becoming shorter, her vocabulary limited to words for which there was a known or easy abbreviation.

'I bet there is an easier way of doing it more effectively,' she wrote to Margaret Ogilvie, 'but I can't work out what it is. It keeps nagging away at me that there could be a system like the Pitman's shorthand they learn in the commercial class.'

This jogged something in Margaret's memory, something that stretched back thirty years to the time she had been a secretary. She had herself never really mastered Pitman's but she remembered, or thought she remembered, mention of another system, one that used the conventional alphabet. On the day she received Esther's letter, she drove into Oxford to visit the librarian at the prestigious Oxford and County Secretarial College in St Giles who confirmed Margaret's memory of a long-forgotten text, *Dutton's Speedwords*, and found some discarded copies in a stock room, two of which were given to Margaret, who sent one on immediately to Esther.

Esther never forgot the excitement of looking through *Dutton's Speedwords* for the first time and realizing that someone else had long ago thought as she was trying to think, and had worked out a system of abbreviation which, unlike Pitman's shorthand, could be typed on a Possum. Esther quickly learnt it, and soon afterwards began to write her diary in it and letters to Margaret, who wrote back in Speedwords: 'Za Esther, j at v r e ato ce c le yri i' saying that she was so intrigued to see Speedwords again that she was relearning it herself.

Esther wrote a Speedwords letter in reply. It included the comment that 'Now I can write as fast as anyone, the problem is what am I going to write about?' Perhaps she had in mind the idea that had already crystallized round Leon Sadler's Enchanted Castle peep-show, that one day she could create a text-based game for a computer.

But about what? Esther Marquand's life was very largely about discovering the answer to that question, and acting on it. And just as the exeat started and she was due to be picked up at Netherton by Margaret Ogilvie and Brian, she was unexpectedly pushed on through the maze that would lead her to the Skallagrigg, and the main achievement of her life.

That weekend, when most of the students were going home, Netherton Manor School was host to the British Association (Education Branch) seminar entitled 'Special Needs Education in the British Isles in the Eighties'.

The choice of Netherton was quite deliberate, the organizers wishing to expose delegates to a real special needs environment. For Clive Imray, playing host to the conference was something of an achievement. For Esther Marquand, who most fortunately did not leave until the Saturday afternoon as she was required to demonstrate some computer equipment and the Sadler keyboard in the conference workshops, it was to be a turning point.

There had been a certain excitement about the school for several days before – all rooms had been specially tidied, and the back part of the main school hall had been partitioned off in preparation for a photographic exhibition. Some sleeping arrangements had been changed so that three girls who slept in different dormitories were moved into Esther's dormitory for the weekend, leaving their own for some of the advance organizers.

The morning of the Saturday when the conference was due to start was grey and drizzly and Esther had nothing much to do but wait until early evening when Margaret and Brian were arriving to collect her. Nobody seemed to mind where she went after the delegates had split into three smaller groups and gone off to various classrooms for seminars and discussions (according to the programme, of which Graham had boldly obtained a copy from the registration desk).

She found something exciting about being alone in the empty corridors of the school, the morning light shining coldly on the black and white tiles which made up most of the ground floor. She loved the sound of different noises from different rooms all echoing and melding in the empty gloom. The step of someone overhead, the hiss of an unseen wheelchair, the call of women's voices from the kitchens.

At such moments Esther Marquand usually found her way to the back corridor, to stare yet again at the old school photographs and puzzle over the identity of some of the unnamed sitters. And wonder about the girl – whom she had dubbed 'Laura' – who appeared at the side of the masters in three successive years through to 1938, and was then seen no more. Her eyes were dark and mysterious, her dresses rather too bright and well made for a mere member of the helping staff.

Sounds came from beyond the back corridor in the direction of the main hall; sounds of chairs being unstacked, of a film sound-track being tested, of hammering. Esther went to investigate.

She drove her chair as quietly as she could through the double doors into the hall. It seemed deserted, with loose conference papers left untidily on the chairs ranged at the front of the hall below the stage, and a film projector standing tall, black and silent behind the chairs and facing the stage. The curtains on the stage were half drawn and someone was working behind them, the sounds sporadic. Esther knew there was a screen that could drop down out of the space above the stage, and indeed she could see its white bottom edge as if it had been in use earlier in the day.

But it was the exhibition at the back of the hall that interested her, and towards which, since she had not been stopped and no one seemed to be about, she drove her chair. She felt a curious excitement as she drew near the grey blank panels on metal stands that formed the external wall of the exhibition. To one side there was a gap with a table near it on which there were some green leaflets. The entrance. Esther headed for it.

One of the screens had been half pushed across this makeshift entrance and beyond it she could see the display of captioned photographs, on cardboard mounts and with printed captions.

There was a big banner headline across a free-standing screen which faced visitors as they went into the exhibition area: '150 Years of Special Education in Britain: 1830–1980.' And then a smaller sub-title which read, '150 years of failure'. Although the screen clearly meant 'No entry', Esther was curious, and since the gap was just wide enough for her wheelchair and no notices actually forbade entry she slipped in to get a better look, a delicious sense of exploring the unknown, of being where she should not be, coming over her.

At first it seemed boring. 'Special education for the handicapped in Great Britain is of relatively recent origin,' she read. 'The first separate educational provision for physically handicapped children was made in 1851, when the Cripples Home and Industrial School for girls was founded at Marylebone. A training Home for Crippled Boys followed at Kensington in 1865. Both institutions set out to teach a trade, and education as such was rudimentary . . . Little further was done until 1890.'

Her eyes wandered from this brief history further along the panels to a montage of photographs of what looked like big dark buildings. 'Categorization of mental handicap was very rudimentary and many children, some quite normal, were confined to the institutions for the mentally ill and handicapped that were created through the years 1850–70, often in conditions quite unsuited to proper education or training, though schools were frequently attached to them.'

Each gaunt grim building photographed, the images taken some-times from etchings and lithographs, sometimes from early photographs, had a name under it and Esther read them one by one, staring up at the images as if they were gravestones on a path to-wards the darkness of a mausoleum: Bethlehem Hospital, Bride-well Hospital, Lincoln Asylum, Broadmoor, Maudsley Hospital,

Rorpeton Asylum . . . black and white, an architecture of custody, of walls and turrets, narrow barred windows and desolate brick.

Esther manoeuvred her wheelchair past the big montage of buildings to other photographs, of people this time. A line of eight boys in old-fashioned wicker wheelchairs on a veranda, a pot plant and two female nurses on either side. She looked expertly at the children to diagnose their condition – cripples, not spastics. She did not recognize rickets, but Down's she diagnosed, and a mild hydrocephalus. The children stared at her, as the nurses stared, their hair heavy and greasy; all uniformed, all dutiful, all defeated.

Another photograph showed an old classroom, backs of heads of children staring at a board which had written in chalk upon it the symbols of pounds, shillings, and pence, £.s.d., the old currency. In the photo the children were learning about it, in a corner two girls were sewing.

A ward . . . her eyes fell to the caption: 'Even as late as the sixties, some mental handicap hospitals still confined these children to cot wards for many hours each day, with no serious provision for education or even recreation.' She moved on to read the caption spread under two similar pictures: 'There is a difference of forty years between these two photographs – but which one is the earlier?'

Esther stared hard at them and, indeed, it *was* hard to tell. The beds were the same in each, being of heavy metal, rounded and curved like the lines of pre-war motor cars. The windows were high and graceless ensuring that the view outside was officially unavailable to any poor soul trying to look out, even if they could stretch that high. In the cotbeds were what seemed to be children, some standing staring over the high sides, others lying prone and helpless but, bizarrely, dressed in those same grey school shorts that she had seen in photographs of her father as a boy.

The doors of the two wards were the same in each photograph as well – big, solid and wide enough to take wheelchairs; and painted some institutional colour in a heavy gloss, which coldly reflected the harsh lighting.

The only difference was in the curtains – absent in one, patterned in a modern style in the other. And then too, as she looked closer, she saw that the lampshades were different, the ones in the curtainless ward being of that inverted pyramid type she had seen in offices in old black and white films on television. That was the older of the two pictures . . . and a later caption proved her right.

But the wards were, substantially, the same and so, too, claimed the captions, were the attitudes. One seemed to be a quotation from a survey:

> The children's wards we visited at —— Hospital reflected the attitudes and preferences of the dominant nurse in charge. Some were friendly and created the rudiments of a learning environment, others were very strict and authoritarian. One ward had been under the rule of a nurse for over thirty-five years who ran it in a highly regimented and strict way, punishing untidiness, discouraging any 'aberrant' behaviour by a system of subtle rewards and punishments involving food and the withholding of affection. The children were generally apathetic and uninterested in life around them. There was no evidence of play at all, and our observer saw little interaction between the children at 'play' times.

She moved on. A picture of spastic girls at 'play'. One stared bleakly out at her, her hands clenched, her legs thin and bent, in a chair that offered no visible back support. Under her eyes were shadows and her mouth was thin, turned down and unhappy. But in her eyes, dear God!, there was intelligence. And Esther saw an image of what she might have been in another place at another time. She stared and stared and saw suddenly how lucky she was. Nineteen fifty-two. Only twenty-eight years ago. That girl was still alive, perhaps thirty-five to forty now. This was not history, it was now. One of the girl's hands stretched stiffly out to one side of the chair. Under its wheels was an old sock, round which some string was tied to form a head. On the head, crudely marked, were two eyes and a smile. The girl had dropped her 'doll'. No one had seen to pick it up. Esther moved on and left her behind.

Esther was always to remember the growing distress and horror she felt as she looked at this exhibition. It was her first introduction to the fact that there were others like herself but less fortunate, some who had never had any opportunities; some who, perhaps, had never once had their intelligence or feelings recognized, except in the most elementary ways.

She sat quietly, time forgotten, staring about her until her eyes were caught again by the montage she had seen at the beginning. One photograph was a blow-up of a hospital sports day, with patients in the foreground at the start of a race over some wooden benches. In the background were many spectators. There was a group in wheelchairs, one on a curious cart propped up with blankets. The sun was shining, the scene calm and summery.

Next to it was a smaller picture and she could tell it was the same hospital for, though an interior, the neo-gothic outline of the window was distinct and identifiably the same as in the bigger photograph. Both images too were bordered in a thin black line as if, perhaps, they had been taken from a magazine. She saw a recreation room, with adult males standing in abject, inactive postures, fists clenched and arms curled in front of them. At the end of the room, not immediately obvious, a man in a white jacket stood, feet apart, his muscular size a contrast to that of the patients. He was a charge nurse. In one hand he held a stick which had a hook in one end. Why, that's a window stick, said Esther to herself in horror.

A window stick, as in the Arthur stories. As wielded by Dilke. She was looking at her first image of a dilke and, fascinated, Esther moved her chair closer to examine the photograph.

Beyond him in the corner of the room was a canvas wheelchair, its back to the camera. Protruding from the left side was a twisted and spasmed hand which Esther recognized immediately as a cerebral palsied hand. It was stark white against the dark wall. It might almost have been her hand.

Peering round the back of the chair, though slumped and below its top edge where a normal person's head would have been, was the twisting strain of a face, trying to see, mouth open, one eye visible. A man with grey hair was straining round as if to observe all others in the room unseen. He was a spastic, like her, and his head was turned as hers was sometimes, but that one eye had that same look from a cage that Peter's had had; an eye, or eyes, that spoke of intelligence and observation, and hopeless impotence.

Involuntarily there escaped from Esther Marquand a sound of sympathy, and her hands reached forward as if to comfort the man she saw. Her eyes filled with tears. She was, perhaps for the first time in her life, confronting her full nature.

Esther could not afterwards recall quite how long she sat there
staring at the man staring at a camera lens. Nor was she ever
certain whether the sense she had of closeness to Arthur, subject
of the Skallagrigg myths, was real or later imposed. Finally she did
not care. The truth of an image lies in what it evokes.

But she did not imagine that this man, staring at her, *was*
Arthur — at that time she conceived of him as younger, barely
more than a boy, something like herself perhaps in age. In any
case she did not yet perceive him to be real. What she saw then
was rather an image of that staring, spastic man, trapped in a
chair, that became the key which opened a door to her of the
possibility that in such a place, and in such a state, Arthur might
have lived. Until then she had never had an image of his environment, or only a vague one, and whatever it was it was not so
harsh, so shabby, so dustlessly cold, as these shining, swept wards
and corridors on which the camera dwelt. Nor did whatever image
she had allow for the possibility that here and there (as in the
photographs) plaster had fallen, cisterns leaked, and further down
the shadowed corridors, past doors which had locks on, lay places
which no camera ever saw.

Afterwards Esther said she stared at that man and then at a
nurse attendant in the foreground, a man, strong in the shoulder,
round and rather chubby in the face, and with dark wide trousers
and a white jacket. Never did a man look so in charge. On his face
was a smug expression, a slight grin for the camera, and in his
eyes was menace. His hands hung strong at his hip, hands used to
giving blows. Another man, standing in pyjamas, stared at him
with eyes unnaturally wide and his body angled and wrong. His
bare chest was showing and it was hollowed, with a shadow of
hair over his nipples. His hair was so short that it must have been
cut with a razor.

Behind them the spastic man looked on, even this pathetic world
beyond his reach.

Then a curious and frightening thing happened. She heard a
sound in the ward in whose image she was lost, as of a wheelchair
coming. She literally started back in fear. For a brief subliminal
moment she was there among those people.

She turned her chair and found herself facing another in which
a man sat, a man she knew.

'Well well,' he said coldly. 'Just the wee girl I was looking for.' The 'wee' was sarcastic, he was not a Scot. Nor was his voice pleasant, but rather hard and accusatory, as if whatever she did, whatever she said, whatever she felt, would be wrong. She made a sound as she tried to remember who this was blocking her path.

'We met in Brighton but you've forgotten,' he said with a sneer. 'My name is Andy Moore.'

The writer, the play, the day by the sea, the play Peter spoke out at. The play about Arthur. Afterwards Nasim had walked her along the seafront and she had met that man who told her the story about The Racks.

'Oooo yeh,' said Esther, her path still blocked, Andy bringing his wheelchair alongside so that his head was almost indecently near hers. She felt constricted and confined and was afraid of him. She thought wildly that if he got any closer he would be touching her. She could see the hairs on his chin and in his nostrils. She could smell him, smoky, oily. There was no room to back off.

'I thought this hall was out of bounds to you kids,' he said.

'Nah,' said Esther. Nobody had actually said anything. But her denial covered more than that: it covered the fact that she was not a 'kid'. They didn't use language like that at Netherton. Student, pupil, person, young man, young woman; never 'kid'.

'I heard you were at Netherton from Eileen Coppock,' he said. He stared at her questioningly. There was a kind of contempt to his mouth. Was he in touch with Eileen then, and she with him?

'Privileged place Netherton,' said Andy, continuing his assault, his mouth open so she could see his fillings, his lips big. 'All the best handicaps come here, I'm told. Quite a little hothouse of talent, but then they draw on a better class of family in the south than they do in Manchester where I come from.' There was bitterness in his eyes and his skin was bad. She could think of nothing to say.

'Enjoy the exhibition?' His voice was suddenly much more friendly as he looked past her at the photographs.

She adjusted to his change of mood, and then nodded. To her surprise, and despite his attempt to hide it, she saw a look of pleasure cross his face.

'Yes, well, it's one of the things I do. That, and writing plays, and speaking at seminars like this, and showing films.'

The photos are very interesting, Esther tried to say.

Andy Moore looked at her and then behind her.

'Yeh . . . if you're saying you like the pix,' she nodded, 'you're not meant to. You're not meant to *like* them.'

'Nah,' said Esther quickly, trying to indicate it wasn't liking she was expressing but interest.

'And don't tell me they're *interesting* either because that's what they all say. They're *shocking*, not middle-class wet liberal *Guardian*-reader fucking interesting.'

'Nah,' said Esther, now genuinely shocked.

He stared at her saying nothing and she stared back.

'What did you feel there?' he said, leaning forward, his right shoulder rolling forward and his legs kicking sideways as he stretched a hand out and touched her on the chest firmly and without embarrassment, right where her bra was, where her nipple was. It was the first time a man had touched her, except sometimes when she was being picked up but that was always different. After he removed his hand she still felt it there as if it would never go away again.

'I . . .' she could say nothing.

He smiled suddenly, his smile lulling her into security as if, for a moment, a wild and dangerous dog that had seemed about to attack had lain down and gone to sleep.

'Mr Clive Imray tells me, Miss Marquand, that you are a very bright student. High hopes he has of you. You got an "O" level in maths in record time and you're expected to get an "A" level maths this year and some more "O" levels.'

He waited and she nodded, slightly smug.

'What are you going to do with your education? Find a job? Do more studying? Live as normal a life as possible?' This last thought made him laugh. Esther noticed that his nails were black with filth, his hands engrained. Esther was suddenly close to tears.

Quick to sense what she was thinking, he held up his hands. 'Printer's ink,' he said. 'The hands of a revolutionary.' Then he was silent and looked away from her as if he had seen one of the pictures for the first time and was absorbed by it. His head shook slightly. His hair was black and wild, his shoulders hunched, his hands large. His eyes were big and formidable, combining beauty and gentleness with anger.

'Do you know what I wanted to do?' he said suddenly. 'I wanted the kids at Netherton to see this exhibition. I wanted them to see some of the films as well. But it's "not allowed" . . .' He said this last with a southern upper-class accent and his nose in the air. 'Oh no, this is very much an adult seminar; oh yes, we do not feel it would be suitable.'

He grinned, Esther grinned. He scowled, Esther scowled.

'Do you know what it means?'

By now Esther was used to such rhetorical questions and said nothing, hoping her expression combined concern, doubt, surprise and certainty in one impossible whole.

'It means you're not allowed to see the film I'm about to run through.'

He paused and then said, 'Doing English literature "O" level are we?'

'Yeh,' said Esther safely.

'Let's see now, bit of Shakespeare, a smattering of Chaucer's Prologue, one of the shorter Dickens novels, some poems by Browning, Milton's *Paradise Lost* Book 1, I expect, some worthy novelist like Thackeray and something a bit more modern . . . don't tell me . . . Conrad! *Lord Jim*! Maybe even that great new wonderful discovery Malcolm Lowry and his boring "Under the Fucking Volcano".'

Esther did not know how to react. Several of these were indeed her set books. She had never heard of 'Under the Fucking Volcano'. She grinned involuntarily.

'Well now, that's fine able-bodied literature, but let me show you a classic they won't use as a set book. Not literature you see.'

He swung his chair viciously round and shot off to one of the tables in the hall. Esther took her opportunity to escape from the exhibition and hovered uncertainly outside its little entrance.

Andy Moore stopped his chair at a table on which there was a pile of books and papers and came swiftly back up the hall. He put a thin book on her tray. She looked at it. It was called *A Useless Life?* and was by Harry Barr.

'That man,' said Andy, 'has written as great a book in its way as any by Dickens and all of the rest of them. That man . . .' he shot forward past her into the exhibition area and stopped his chair as somehow Esther had realized he would, before the picture she had stared at so long.

'That's Harry,' said Andy Moore quietly, staring up at the turned head cut off by the wheelchair arm in that recreation room she had stared into for so long.

'Andy! Ready when you are!' Shouted a voice from the front stage.

Then he turned briefly back to Esther and said, 'You staying, or going like a good girl?' The sarcasm was biting and Esther stared at him nonplussed.

Indifferently, he turned his own chair away, went out of the exhibition area to the projector and pressed a switch. It started into light and life, so that after a brief trailer of numbers the same image shone on the screen as stared at her from the stand. The film was about Harry Barr.

With a look at the back of Andy Moore's head as smouldering as she could make it, Esther decided to stay.

THIRTY

That film begins with a man in a recreation room in Sturrick Royal Hospital, Manchester, a mental handicap hospital [*wrote Esther Marquand later.* **See the Marquand Collection: Disk 3, File MARQ07.**) The room is full of adult males standing in abject inactive postures, fists clenched and arms curled in front of them as if protecting themselves from something unseen. At the end of the room, not immediately obvious, a man in a white jacket stands ... beyond him in the corner of the room is a canvas wheelchair. Protruding from the left is a spasmed hand, a cerebral palsied hand, the fingers pulled into permanent hooks and angles by muscles that could never unwind and relax, white against the dark wall. And peering round the back of the chair, though slumped and below its top edge where a normal person's head would have been, is the twisting strain of a face, trying to see ...

I knew what it was. It was the photograph I had seen earlier, which must have been a still from the film.

Then the camera moved to a close-up of the hand, a hand I knew well because sometimes mine spasmed like that, and the hand began suddenly to move, back and forth, back and forth. It wasn't just a photo any longer, it was for real.

I stared, shocked. As it moved the soundtrack came on and you could hear strange moans and wailings like those recordings of whales under the sea. Staccato shouts and long drawn out pleas for help in unearthly voices ... and in the background a television comedy show at which no one laughed.

Then a voice: 'My name is Harry Barr and my hand is as good a place to start as it's useless like the rest of me.' Then the camera moved back to get the whole of the wheelchair and the man in it, and occasionally a blurred figure moved right across the frame as patients in the recreation room moved back and forth.

'This room is where I spend most of my waking hours. Sitting here I have often thought of my life and now I have been invited to tell it you by my new friend Andy.'

The camera swung nearer and round the chair and I saw the man's face full on. He was about forty-five I suppose. I could tell he could never have talked so normal people would understand.

'I was born on January 12th 1938 and because I was a funny boy and something wrong my mother could not look after me and I was sent to Granten Hill Hospital. Then I was moved to Sturrick Royal during the war because it was further from the bombs. So I was in one hospital or another from the beginning and cannot remember my parents.

'My first real memory is sitting in a chair having tea. I must have been four and it would have been in what was then Thames Ward – all the bigger wards were named after British rivers: Thames, Severn, Tyne, Humber, Ouse, Mersey, Trent, nine in all. Thames was the children's ward and had eighty-five children in it. You couldn't expect staff to remember all those names so we had numbers. Mine was sixty-three. The first possession I remember having was a toothbrush with 63 on it. Ever since then it's been my lucky number.

'The hospital is a big place and was all the world to me. I remember being allowed into the laundry room to watch the big dangerous calender machines pressing the clothes and seeing the staff playing cricket.

'Young lads got a bit more freedom than the older "boys" – once you were grown up a bit they had to confine you more, otherwise the place would have been chaos. I haven't seen the calender machines since that day. I would like to go back and take a second look. I've often seen the steam, though, from the laundry block. A lot of the women worked in there and that was nice for us boys as few of us were visited by our mums.

'So I saw more of the hospital in those early years than I did later on when I was moved to other wards – first Tyne and then my last big ward under the old system, which was Mersey.

'Another early memory is when I was seven and the chapel bells were ringing because the war was over. That Sunday we had a special service of thanksgiving and I remember thinking that I would have liked to be a soldier and dress up in khaki and go off in a ship. Ever since then my dream has been to go in a ship working as a jolly sailor and see the world. But I am a realist. I know it will never be . . .' and the voice trailed off as the film cut to a sequence of Harry being pushed outside in the hospital grounds by a white-coated male nurse, and stopping to watch two staff girls in white sportswear playing tennis.

The film was jerkily made, the cuts between scenes clumsy and the 'actors' who were in early scenes with Harry as a young man in the hospital were a bit stiff and formal, amateurs I expect. But I sat through it captivated and horrified at the same time, the feelings of despair and anger and a new self-awareness that had arisen that morning now returned a thousand times stronger.

The film shows how, when he was over thirty, a kindly charge nurse decided Harry must be bright and said one day, 'Harry, I'm going to try to teach you to read and write. Do you want to learn?' In the film Harry says, 'I thought, this is my chance and I must take it. But I knew it would be hard. And it was, trying to remember the letters of the alphabet. But I persisted until I could spell things out by pointing my right foot, the only part of my body over which I have some control, to the correct place on the letter board my good friend made.

'Then one day he got me a typewriter and fixed a peg to my shoe so I could type for the first time. I looked at it long and hard and he said, "Go on, type something." I thought, "It'll take time so it better be important." So I thought some more and he said, "What about your name?" So that was the first thing I typed out, "Harry Barr". That was a proud moment.

'One day he said, "Why don't you ask me a question, Harry, and I'll do my best to answer it." I nodded and thought long and hard. I decided it better be a good one. But what did I want to know? Then it came to me and I typed, "Where is the river Trent?"

'I asked this because it was one of the three wards I had been in and I had deduced from TV where the Thames and the Mersey were. But the Trent never got a mention, and had me stumped. So my friend got an atlas from the hospital library and I spent a whole morning looking through it, finding out where the places I had heard mentioned so often really were. That was one of the most interesting mornings of my life, finding out about my own country.'

There was a final shot of Harry out on the grass in the grounds with some of his friends. Most were in wheelchairs. They sat near each other, with the nurse who had taught Harry a way to write sitting on a chair with them. He was reading Harry a book. Some were listening and some were talking to each other, their voices and laughter strange.

But then I saw something that made me sit up straight and pay attention. It was Harry's face as the titles came up. Harry's head drifted and looked at one of his friends and he laughed and his mouth tried to speak. His friend nodded and said a word, repeated a word.

ANDY ANDY ANDY. I wanted him to show me that bit of film again. That was a hard thing to tell him but he understood. I never trusted or liked Andy Moore but he did understand me better than most.

I watched that final sequence and looked at the others off centre instead of at Harry Barr. One of them, in a chair but with his back to the camera, was telling a story – that's what the others were talking about. And the word that Harry was saying, repeating, was one I knew well: Skallagrigg. Only he said it similar to me, "Skyagree". I could lip-read it off the film. The story they were being told by the man I could not see was about the Skallagrigg.

When the film was over Andy Moore had not quite finished with Esther.

'You'd better get back to the comfort of your education,' he said. 'Forget all about Harry and the likes of him. What do you have to care? You've got it made!'

Esther stared at him, very upset. Her mouth opened and shut and she wanted to cry. But not in front of him!

'Nah!' she said fiercely.

'You've got fight, I'll give you that,' he said, his face coming close and his eyes intense. 'But will you use it? We need people like you to speak out for us. You're the future, Esther Marquand, and you're going to have to make these people listen.' He waved a hand at the hall of empty chairs.

'Here, take one of these and read it. *Do* something.'

He gave her a pamphlet with a green cover, on which was printed, 'HLF. What We Stand For.'

Esther took it and left, the clock over the door showing that she should have been upstairs fifteen minutes ago.

'HLF' she discovered later stood for the Handicapped Liberation Front, and that its chairman was Andy Moore. Its purpose was militant: to establish rights for the disabled, especially their right not just to have a say in their future, but to have the *final* say . . . it was Esther's first exposure to the politics of disablement which, then, were just beginning to emerge. There was a form which prospective supporters and members had to fill in and a request for a membership fee of one pound minimum – 'more if you can afford it'.

After Margaret had collected her, Esther was quiet on the drive back to Charlbury, not responding to Brian's good cheer from the front passenger seat. Margaret said, 'Ssh, dear, she's always tired at this stage of the term; aren't you, darling?'

In the back Esther nodded, saying nothing. But she was wide

awake, staring out at the passing north Hampshire and Wiltshire scenery and thinking, endlessly thinking, of Harry Barr in his canvas chair and the ward in which he had spent most of his life. And the one word she had lip-read him saying: Skallagrigg.

THIRTY-ONE

At the end of that term Mrs Fyfield brought a friend of hers, a professional make-up artist, to show some of the girls how to use make-up. The event was timed for the afternoon of the end-of-term senior disco. Betty, who used make-up already, wanted to try some glitter on her cheeks; Esther wanted to try different lipsticks.

Mrs Fyfield's friend, Davinia, was very tall and glamorous, with a bag full of equipment and make-up. She gave them a talk on its history and the current trend for the natural look. She demonstrated how make-up had changed since the war, deftly using three of them to show the differences so that Betty, who was given the fifties' look, ended up powdered and rouged, and Clare, who was rather thin and pale, was given the full eye make-up treatment of the sixties and looked like Cleopatra. As the afternoon wore on, the room gained a delicious warmth and scent, and the special professionally lit mirrors Davinia had brought along gave an air of theatre and excitement to the proceedings. Biscuits and tea were brought in on especially pretty china, and someone put some music on.

Later they all had a go with different make-up samples, and Davinia said she would work on Esther herself as she could not help herself and her face had 'possibilities'. Possibilities indeed!

'You've a good bone structure and lovely eyes, and an excellent skin,' said Davinia. 'Now . . .' and Davinia pursed her lips and began expertly working on Esther, bit by bit. Esther began to get nervous as she saw 'her' face taking shape in the mirror.

The girls gathered round, laughing and clapping as Esther was shown the final result. She raised her eyebrows with a degree of hauteur, and they all laughed. But she kept the look up, indeed it wouldn't go away, and she felt confident and radiant.

She kept her make-up for the party and when Graham saw her

he couldn't believe it. He blushed and stumbled on his words, just like a bashful hero.

I want him to kiss me, Esther thought. But he did not, even during the last wheelchair dance when most of them paired off with boyfriends, or the nearest they had to one.

'I wanted to,' he told her later, 'but I was scared. You looked so perfect – so I didn't dare!' I want to be loved for me, thought Esther; oh, I want to be loved.

The holidays came once more, and Christmas passed uneventfully at Charlbury. Richard Marquand came for only three days, as he was very preoccupied with ComputaBase. The manager of the Bristol outlet telephoned on Christmas Eve to tell Richard the sales figures. They were good, very good. Three more shops were scheduled for opening early in the new year.

Richard was changing, subtly. His eyes carried authority and Esther felt that when he touched her he was preoccupied with other more important things. Now Margaret and Marion were more like her parents than Richard.

The relationship between Margaret and Esther entered a new and conspiratorial phase, as if everything they did was a womanly secret. Esther chose to be a little aloof with her father, sometimes not deigning to smile upon him and not answering his harmless questions.

'Don't worry, Richard, it's just a phase she's going through,' Margaret explained smugly, the defender of Esther's female privacy. Marion, on the other hand, discouraged this kind of exclusiveness and when she was solely in charge Esther tended to be more open.

On the first Sunday of the new year, after the service at St Mary's Church, Esther received an exciting and quite unexpected invitation. There was, as usual, coffee, and Esther had become a familiar member of the congregation. Jean, a local smallholder's daughter, usually got Esther a cup and helped her drink it. Jean had a brother, Robert, who, though not a churchgoer, used to pick his sister up after the service on his motorcycle.

Esther had often admired the way Bob kick-started the machine, purred off up the main street and swung out of sight towards Chipping Norton. She liked him because he was relaxed and smiled a lot and always said hello. One Sunday he had even pushed her chair up the hill for Margaret and had been careful not to bump it over the kerbs.

That first Sunday of the new year, he was there as usual, coming in out of the cold after the service to have a coffee. They were talking about the barn dance on the coming Saturday night and someone asked Esther if she was going. She had been twice now with Brian and they were getting used to her being there.

'Nah,' she said. Margaret explained: Brian had had a cold and would not be able to take her though possibly Mr Parsons might.

'Tell you what,' said Bob impulsively, '*I'll* take you. If you'd like me to, that is. I mean, well . . ,' he suddenly stalled and stumbled and looked at his sister for support. She nodded and smiled.

'Would you like that, Esther? He's a terrific dancer!'

'Yeh!' said Esther, and the agreement was made.

Perhaps it would have mattered less if Margaret had not made such a thing of it. But, well, Esther's First Date! The first time she was to be taken out by a boy, and one they knew of. He would pick her up, walk her the half mile to the Parish Hall, look after her for the evening and bring her back. By 10.30 at the latest, Robert! At the latest!

'Yes, Mrs Ogilvie.'

So it was arranged.

Optimistic and buoyant feelings got her through the first half-hour of waiting for him the following Saturday evening when, all made-up and dressed up, and with Margaret instructed not to hover nervously, she sat in her chair near the lounge door waiting for his arrival.

'A chap often leaves it a few moments late, like a dinner party, you know,' explained Brian helpfully, glancing nervously at his watch. 'Never arrive exactly on time, eh, Margaret?' he added.

Eight o'clock struck and no one came up the garden path. Eight-fifteen, and for the first time Esther began, subtly and silently, to lose something of her spirit for the evening. Perhaps responding to this Margaret said, 'Well, maybe he's been delayed but I think he might have phoned.'

'Young chaps now don't know the meaning of time,' said Brian. He looked decidedly unhappy, staring towards the fire, his mouth clamped tight shut. They watched the television mechanically.

The minutes dragged on and, as they did, Esther's suffering

began. Her head slumped a little, and her good looks, her spirit,
her very life, seemed to sag in the chair to which she was strapped.
Until suddenly she said, 'Nana', and there was such a look of
humiliation and hurt in her eyes that Margaret said, 'Do you want
to wait in the hall, my love? I mean, you'll hear him better there.'
And she pushed her out to sit by the grandfather clock, helpless
before Esther's misery, and came back in and whispered to Brian,
'I think she wants to be alone for the time being. Oh, where has
the wretched boy got to?'

'Nana?' It was Esther's call. Perhaps he had been in a crash? she
somehow got over to Margaret.

'Well, it's possible, I suppose. We'll leave it until nine and then
call his home.'

'Yeh,' said Esther.

'Coming in by the fire, Esther?'

She shook her head and looked towards the door, her freshly
washed hair catching the light, and her face pretty and prepared.
But in her eyes and the set of her mouth was a look of such
despair that it cut into Margaret and made her feel angry and
helpless.

'Esther, I . . .' but there was nothing to say, only hope he would
still come, even now, and have an explanation Esther would understand.

At nine o'clock Margaret rang Robert's home number. She spoke
briefly and listened without expression.

'So he's not coming for Esther? He's gone into Chipping Norton.
I . . .' but Esther did not hear the words of her angry protest, only
the silence of her own distress, rejection and humiliation. She sat
helpless in her chair, her face pointlessly made-up, her dress bought
especially for the occasion, her helplessness and frustration total.
As Margaret put down the phone and turned to her, Esther began
to cry and in her body were the spasms and anger of a short
lifetime of being for ever different and the belief that she would for
ever be unwanted and unloved. At last, her sobbing ceasing,
Margaret became aware that she was saying a word, a name.

'What is it, my dear?' asked Margaret.

'To . . . ooo . . . ohhh . . .h!' Esther tried to say.

Tom. She wanted to hear Tom's voice.

'But, darling, it's so late.' Yet Margaret made the call and got through to night staff at the Centre in Ealing. Yes, Tom was up, watching TV probably, they'd fetch him.

'Here he is,' said a different voice a few moments later. 'Shall I say who it is?'

'Tell him Esther wants to talk to him.'

There was a pause and Tom came on the line.

'Hello,' he said. He sounded scared.

'Tom, it's Margaret, Esther's grandmother.'

'Lo,' said Tom.

'Esther wants to speak to you.'

'Why?' said Tom.

Margaret held the phone to Esther's ear.

Esther formed the word 'Toh' but it was weak and aspirant. Her breathing suddenly speeded up and her face crumpled. She could hear Tom breathing at the other end.

'Toh,' she said finally.

'Lo, Amh. This is Tom. Why?'

'Toh, *Toh*,' and she began to cry and cry, the sound filling the hall and drowning out the clock, and then seeming to fill the house, terrible cries until she could hardly catch her breath. Margaret held the phone for her, saying nothing. Behind them both, in the living-room, Brian watched. There were tears in his eyes and on his wrinkled cheeks.

'Amh, don't. Don't,' said Tom at the other end. 'Don't, please.'

But she did and he listened. Until Margaret gently took up the telephone to say, 'Tom, it's Nana again. Esther's sad and she wanted to hear your voice. It's because you're her friend. Sometimes she's sad, Tom.'

'Where's Amh?' said Tom.

Margaret put the phone back to Esther's ear.

'Don't cry, Amh, I went to football today. Tottenham Hotspurs v. Arsenal. Spurs won. Amh, please don't.'

'Nah, Tom.'

'Amh, you're my friend. Amh . . .' and then, at the other end of the line, Tom started to cry. Perhaps nothing could have comforted Esther more than that, for he rarely did and she understood it was in sympathy.

'Toh,' said Esther more clearly.

'Yes, Amh,' said Tom stopping. 'Why?'

But she couldn't explain that.

There was a long silence, each listening to the other's breathing.
Tom said, 'I'll tell the Skalg, that's best.'

'Nah,' said Esther, her eyes drying. IT'S NOT WORTH IT. TOM.
'Nah!'

'OK, Amh.' They both sounded happier.

'Sth . . . sth . . .' thanked Esther.

'OK, Amh?'

'Yeh, Toh,' she whispered.

'Bye-bye-bye,' said Tom and the line went dead.

'Bye,' said Esther softly. Then she turned her wheelchair to the
living-room and raised her hand to her mouth.

'A cup of tea will do you good, old girl,' said Brian, going off to
make them all some.

Margaret came in and sat down near her. 'There'll be others,
darling, better ones than that Robert. There will, there really will.'

Esther looked utterly disbelieving and waved her hand as if to
indicate her body and herself.

'Nah,' she said.

'Yes, Esther,' said Margaret fiercely. 'Oh yes! It won't be easy,
but it's never easy at your age, even for the able-bodied. But there
will be others my dear.'

YES BUT HOW DO I GET SOMEONE I LOVE TO TAKE ME OUT? typed
Esther a day or two later when she was talking with Marion about
it all. She liked the elegance of echoing the question Betty Shaw
had once asked. Life was full of satisfactory circlings.

Marion thought for a bit and then fingered the crucifix at her
neck. She was very calm.

'I think you just ask him,' she said simply.

THIRTY-TWO

Time now, for Esther, was beginning to race. One moment her page-turner was taking her through the material she needed to absorb for the coming summer exams, and the next, when she looked up, the weather had changed and weeks had gone by.

The keyboard Leon Sadler had discussed with Esther months before had been more fully developed for her and, after several trials, was working well, its strange ergonomic shape a source of fascination to anyone who saw her using it. Richard and Leon, realizing the commercial potential of such a product, were developing something even more adaptable and sophisticated, while Leon was now creating a portable 'clip-on LCD screen' for Esther's wheelchair which would enable her to communicate with anyone.

Perhaps because of the speed with which Esther could now key in data, her interest in games rapidly developed, though at that stage her main interest was in transcribing published programs taken from computer magazines. Leon Sadler encouraged the school to subscribe to some of the American computer magazines which, catering as they did for a bigger and more advanced market, were much better than their British counterparts. These began to find readers at Netherton, most of whom belonged to the school's newly founded Computer Club of which Warble was the staff organizer, Graham Downer the chairman, and Esther the honorary secretary. The very first set of minutes, which Esther herself word-processed (the first material of hers retained on floppy disk), record a special vote of thanks to Leon Sadler for his advice to the school, and invite him to be the club's 'Honorary Consultant', a position which, by the next committee meeting, he had accepted.

Esther has left no record of her feelings at this time. The diary has few entries, and these are mainly concerned with work. But one for 3 May that year is of interest. It simply reads: 'Got the idea for Prittenden all of a sudden. Laura. Obvious. Won't even tell Betty until I've done it.'

The school's Prittenden essay prize, donated by and named after a former pupil, was something every senior student had been encouraged to enter, with Easter always the time to think about it. Throughout the holiday Esther's mind was blank about what to do. But when she got back for the summer term she found herself, as she often did when she wanted to be alone, running her chair down by the kitchens and looking at the old school photographs.

She had long since made up life histories for the pre-war staff members, and especially for the young woman who mysteriously appeared with other staff so powerfully dominated by the for-midable Dr Perry-Wilcox in the years 1935 to 1938, and whom Esther had decided to call Laura.

A few days into the summer term she had gone to the photo-graphs, stared at them, and the idea for her essay had come. It would not be an essay, it would be a story, the story of Laura as she imagined it. She would make a life for Laura. She would create a past, and without more ado she did so.

The significance of the composition for us now perhaps is what it reveals about Esther and her own inner being, apart from the immediate consequences it was to have for Esther and Margaret. Its beginning can be taken as an evocation of Esther's own mood at that time.

Angry, but determined not to show it, Laura Markham picked up the heavy suitcase and set off on the mile walk down the drive from Netherton Manor School to the main road. She wore her best black shoes and black stockings, and the grey dress she usually wore to teach in. She had no coat, and the only money she had was the five gold sovereigns her much-loved grandfather had given her when a child.

'I will never *ever* return,' she had told her uncle, the school bursar. Yet, as she walked past the familiar trees, the great beech tree whose grey soft lines she loved and the oak trees of Knaller Wood, she could not believe in her heart that she would never come back.

'I won't! I won't!' she said bitterly to herself, 'and I

won't look back, not once.' For she knew he was watching her from the main porch, and if she looked back she
might weaken, and he would come for her and she
would go back and never escape.

Yet ahead of her! What lay there! No hope, only a
sense of loss at what she had to leave behind. For he was
still there, her brother Ross, so young and vulnerable
and she was leaving him behind!

Tears streamed down her face as she thought of him
that morning. She had gone to him and put her arms
around him and he had sensed she was leaving, and also
that he must not cry.

'One day when I'm settled and have a job and money
I'll send for you,' she had told him, 'but I can't yet and
you're too young to understand.'

'Will you come back?' he had whispered fearfully.

'No, Ross, I can never come back. But when you are
older you will come to me. You will find me and I will
make you understand.' He had stared up at her, his
hands trying to reach up to touch her. She had leaned
down to him because he could not reach up that high.
He was handicapped and would never be able to.

It began, then, as a dramatic, emotional story, much in the vein
of some of those Esther had always loved to read, but it turned into
something evocative of Esther's own life, telling of Laura's attempts
to escape the hold of a place that seems now to be a cross between
Netherton and Harefield. Indeed, in the end Laura does not escape,
staying on at Netherton in spirit until the day came when Esther
Marquand stared at those yellowing photographs and saw her
young face and seemed to hear her calls. It is a strange story, full
of echoes of Esther's life and revealing things which would later
have significance, like a fear of heights and cliff edges. The brother
we may interpret as Peter, perhaps, or as Tom; the uncle as her
father, and so on.

The composition was not only well written in a florid, dramatic kind of way but clearly showed that Esther had done some
research into the period to get the dates and clothes right. She
dedicated the story to 'The girl second on the right in the seated

row in the Netherton Manor School photograph dated 1937/38.'
She chose that one because it was the last in which the girl
appeared.

She handed in her entry for the Prittenden Essay Prize, and then
got on with her final exam work. Grim seriousness fell over the
senior school. Silence came to the studies. Psychosomatic illness
afflicted a few students; most of the others looked pale and
strained.

Then the exams during long exhausting weeks in June, until
finally they were over, to be followed by a carnival atmosphere
and sunshine, daytrips to the seaside, and a sense of release.

One day, a week before the end of term, Esther was summoned
to the headmaster's study to be told she had won the Prittenden
Essay Prize, and a couple of others as well. Graham Downer was in
the corridor when she came out; he had won the school's Science
Prize for his presentation of the data of three years of Netherton
weather.

The prizes would be presented on Open Day, the last day of term,
which was to be especially grand this year since all sorts of people
had been invited

Saturday 18 July 1981 dawned dreamily. The frailest of layers of
mist hung over the Netherton lawns and playing fields and
whispered at the guy-ropes of the two great white marquees which
arose on the east side of the main building. The sun rose, already
warm in early morning, the mist suddenly gone, and the school
was bustling, getting ready for the busy day to come.

By nine in the morning the notices were out – CARPARK,
TOILETS, MAIN MARQUEE THIS WAY – and caterers were setting
up long tables in the marquee with white linen tablecloths, while
florists put red carnations and ferns arranged in silver-plated vases
on each one. A green baize table had been set up on a dais in the
other marquee with chairs behind it and rows of chairs facing it
for the prize-giving. The day was so warm that the walls of the
marquee were rolled up and tied on three sides.

Esther attended a morning briefing for the prize-winners organized by Warble, but by eleven she was already waiting, with others,
at the front of the school for the arrival of parents, though she
knew that her father, grandparents and Tom would not be there

before twelve. She was in a light summer frock and looked tanned.

She watched the comings and goings until Betty's father came. When they went off to look at the classrooms she drifted off by herself down the corridors towards the kitchens, past the older photographs and into the old boot room, staring out into the back courtyard.

Time passed. She looked at her watch, slowly but expertly pushing her wrist against her chair's tray so that the sleeve of the light cardigan she was wearing rucked up and she could read the time. Twenty to twelve.

She turned and headed back, stopping at the Laura photograph to say goodbye to her silent, monochrome friend.

'Goodbye for this term,' she intoned to herself. And then, since no one was listening, she started to say it aloud: 'Goh ahd aaahd . . .' and there she stopped because someone was coming. Esther turned her chair back towards the boot room and scurried into the shadows. There she stopped lest the electric engine of her chair be heard, and turned to see who was coming.

A woman turned the corner at the far end of the kitchen corridor and stopped. She was a woman of about sixty, and she was looking at the photographs one by one, leaning towards them, her hair dark grey, her suit new-looking and a pretty red, a matching patent leather handbag on her arm. A parent, no . . . a grand-parent.

Esther's heart jumped: the woman halted in front of the very photograph she herself had been looking at moments before. The woman leaned forward and let out an audible sigh of relief as if she had found what she was looking for. She read the caption which Esther knew by heart: 'Netherton Manor School Staff and pupils, 1937/38: Headmaster H. R. F. Perry-Wilcox, M A.' No other names as in the post-war photographs. Just anonymous faces of forgotten people.

The woman stared at it for some time, and then leaned forward to examine it more closely. Her handbag slipped forward on her arm and swung awkwardly, but she did not seem to notice. Then she seemed to sigh again as she reached out a hand to touch the glass of the photograph as if, as if . . .

The woman seemed suddenly to sense Esther's presence and turned her head sharply. Esther was transfixed. She had not been seen, but she suddenly had a sense that she was watching something she had no right to be privy to. This sense struck her so hard that she almost let out a gasp involuntarily and gave herself away.

The woman's eyes seemed to stare unseeing into hers. They were black and her face was anciently familiar. It was the face of Laura, Laura grown old. The woman was her Laura.

THIRTY-THREE

'What's Amh's prize?' asked Tom.

'B . . .' said Esther, trying to say the impossible word.

'Oh. Books. Yawntime,' said Tom.

Esther grinned as Tom, dressed in a neat jacket and ironed jeans and looking self-conscious, his eyes screwed up against the sun, took her chair and began to push it ahead of the others round the outside of the main school building. He wore a sweatshirt underneath his jacket which had a logo on the front with the words 'BOOMTOWN RATS RULE OK'.

They had arrived soon after twelve and Esther had been just in time to meet them. Both Richard and Margaret kissed Esther and fussed her for a few moments, from which she recoiled, fearful that others in her year might see.

Brian did not bend down to kiss her, but patted her arm and turned to look around vaguely at the school. Esther noticed that the back of his neck was thin, and his white hair rather untidy; and that Margaret took his arm as if to direct him.

'We had better find some seats,' said Richard, restless, eager to get out of the sun.

In the hot marquee most of the seats were already taken and people were fanning themselves with their programmes, but Richard found them some chairs at the back on the shaded side. Esther left them, guiding her chair down the aisle to where the prize-winners were assembling.

As silence fell among the pupils first and then spread among the parents, Esther sat apprehensively, the weight of her position as one of the six special prize-winners upon her. Warble came on to the tiny dais and tested the microphone.

'One two three,' he said. 'All right? Can you hear me at the back?'

There were a few cheerful calls of 'Yes'.

'Quite right,' said Warble.

From the side of the tent the various governors approached the platform and sat down. Men and women, grey-haired and important-looking, smiling and talking quietly among themselves. Then in came Mr Imray, followed by the guest speaker and presenter of the prizes, whom the programme named as Miss Helen Perry-Wilcox, daughter of the legendary founding headmaster.

Esther saw her first in profile, a woman of about sixty, wearing a red suit and carrying a red patent leather handbag over her left arm; a bag Esther had seen before. Esther stared and leaned forward. It was the woman she had seen looking at the photograph; Helen Perry-Wilcox was Laura. Laura come back! Oh, oh and oh there was a singing in Esther's ears and an eerie feeling that she was seeing the past come alive. Despite the heat she felt quite cold.

Mr Imray showed Miss Wilcox to her seat. She sat down quickly with a brief nervous smile and locked her fingers in her lap. Then she raised her head and looked down the marquee and Esther saw those dark eyes again.

Esther stared at her, and continued to stare during the speeches. Finally the headmaster's speech started: 'It is a special pleasure and privilege that our guest of honour should be someone who remembers the school from its early days – Miss H. M. Perry-Wilcox, the daughter of the founder and first headmaster, Charles Perry-Wilcox, who . . .' but Mr Imray did not say anything about her that satisfied Esther's curiosity, like what she did and where she lived and what she had been doing with herself since 1938.

Miss Perry-Wilcox eventually stood up, looking ill at ease and nervous so that a tight silence fell on the summery crowd, one that Mr Imray, Warble and the governors did their best to ease by smiling broadly, looking up at the speaker's profile, and nodding at what she had not yet said.

She did not start well. A few words about how honoured she was, a brief memory of the distant days, a reference to the war years, nothing personal. Nothing about her. Then she suddenly paused as if she had lost her way. She looked down at the notes she was reading from. She hesitated. She began again with 'I . . .' and then stopped. She looked back through her notes.

Then she looked up from her notes, stared round at some of the students, seeming to think of things other than prizes as she looked

at one of the more handicapped of the juniors. Then she started to
really speak and told them what the school had been like to live in
– cold, Victorian, not nice at all! Everyone relaxed; Miss Perry-
Wilcox even managed a smile. Then, charmingly, she gave away
the prizes.

In the moments of seriousness between the smiles and hand-
shakes of the prize-giving afterwards, Esther thought she saw remnants of the sadly brave young woman she had seen in the school
photographs.

Those who could manage it shook Miss Perry-Wilcox by the
hand, others just nodded and grinned, the books being placed on
the chair-trays or in their laps. To all she said, 'Well done', 'Congratulations', or, 'I hope you enjoy it'.

Then finally only the six special prize-winners, including Esther,
were left. At the back Margaret leaned forward with a proud look
on her face and Tom stood up to get a better view. Amh was
getting her prize and he wanted to see the moment.

Some parents had cameras, including Tony Downer who was
about to take a photograph of Graham receiving his year prize.

'Shall I take one of Esther getting hers?' he asked Richard.

'Yes, please do,' said Margaret. Richard nodded.

The prize before Esther's was Graham's science prize, and even
as he took his books from Miss Perry-Wilcox and shook her hand,
Esther, her heart thumping in her chest, started her wheelchair
forward. Then Warble announced the prize and her name.

'The winner of the Prittenden Essay Prize is Esther Marquand of
Va for a fictional composition based on Netherton entitled, "The
Life of Laura Markham".'

As he finished saying these words Esther found herself arriving
at the dais and looking up into the eyes of Miss Perry-Wilcox for
the first time. She smiled and stepped forward, which she had not
done before, and bending down to be close spoke softly to Esther
through the clapping, saying, 'I would very much like to talk to
you about your composition when this is over. May I?' Esther
stared and then remembered to nod her head. Miss Perry-Wilcox
put the two books on her tray. 'What a good and interesting
choice you have made.'

'The prize for . . .' but the event was over for Esther, who turned
her chair round, did not dare look into the crowd to see her family

as, blushing, she returned to her position in the line next to
Graham.

'What did she say, Ess?' asked Betty immediately afterwards,
when everyone was going. 'She spoke to you longer than anyone
else.'

'L . . . LLL' said Esther. She wanted to tell Betty that *that* was
Laura.

Tom came.

'Lo,' he said. He looked uneasy because Esther was with her
intelligent friends. His hand went to the handles of her wheelchair.

'Toh!' said Esther. 'Toh me Toh.'

'Where, Amh?'

Esther looked through the crowd towards the important people.

Tom leaned down and put the engine into neutral so the wheels
were free and he was able to push her away from her friends out
into the bright sunshine. There was a trestle table with rows and
rows of plastic cups full of ice-cold orange squash. Mr Imray and
one of the governors were talking earnestly with Miss Perry-
Wilcox. But her eyes were on the crowd and when she saw Tom
pushing Esther she smiled politely at the two men and withdrew
towards them.

'I am glad to meet you, Esther,' she said, reaching out and
taking Esther's right hand. 'I read your composition. You know, I
mean . . .'

'Yeh,' said Esther.

'I'm Tom,' said Tom.

Esther heaved and thrashed, her mouth sliding sideways and
her eyes strainingly concentrated on Miss Perry-Wilcox. She was
saying something.

Tom said, 'Amh wants to know.'

'Then I must tell you,' said Helen Perry-Wilcox. And before the
several people who were hovering ready to speak with her and
before Margaret Ogilvie and the rest of the family could catch up
with them, they set off the short distance into the school, down the
cool deserted corridors, and back to the picture which had inspired
Esther's story of Laura Markham.

For a few moments the kitchen corridor seemed dark after the
outside sunshine, and shivery cold as well. There were goosepimples on Esther's legs. Having got her there Tom switched on

Esther's chair, made sure her hand was on the control, and then hung back to look in the kitchen door at the neat silence of stainless steel pans and huge catering gas hobs.

Esther went automatically to the Laura picture.

'I was very touched by your essay,' said Miss Perry-Wilcox. 'My name's not Laura though. It's Helen, Helen Monica. I understand you cannot really speak Esther but if you could I would prefer you to call me Helen.'

Esther nodded.

'Yeh,' she said. '. . . ehl . . . ehl.' There was spittle on her mouth from trying to say the name.

Helen Perry-Wilcox took a tissue from the sleeve of her cardigan and gently wiped Esther's mouth. Esther relaxed.

'Why I wanted to say something was because some of the things you said about Laura were true about me . . .'

She looked up at the photograph and studied herself when young for a few moments. There was silence.

'I hated my father,' she said suddenly with terrible emphasis.

The word 'hated' hung harshly about them and seemed to echo painfully about the school corridors. Helen needed no encouragement to talk.

'My mother was dominated by him and her escape was to look after my cerebral palsied aunt, her sister-in-law, in Eastbourne. Today we would call it a separation but then it was not spoken of. Mother was not here, that was all. I think she wanted me to live with her but he would not let her have me. There was one day, a summer's day like today, when she came. She wore a lovely white dress and her cheeks were a little sunburned.

'Of course he had not told me she was coming. He believed that children had no right to know organizational matters like that. He was an insensitive man and somehow your composition reminded me of the past.'

So Helen talked about those days until, eventually, Esther tried to speak.

'Me?' said Helen understanding at once. 'What happened to me? I became a librarian. I never married. I live in Oxford. I am retired and am comfortably settled. I go to church. I play bridge. I do voluntary work in the local community centre. I am taking an Open University degree and . . . but I would have liked, I would

like, to do something more. I don't know what.' Her hand settled
on Esther's shoulder and seemed possessive, making Esther feel
sympathetic and involved.

'Well now,' continued Helen, 'I have talked too much and told
you things I should not have.' She laughed and the darkness of her
past was gone. From outside they heard clapping. One of the events
must have started. 'I hope you did not mind us talking?' Her voice
was tired now, but soft and friendly.

Esther reached a hand out and tried to touch her.

'Are you afraid of leaving Netherton?' she asked looking right
into Esther's eyes. Esther said nothing. 'I felt you might be. Your
composition, you see; it's about leaving.' Then she added all in a
rush, 'If ever I can help you, I don't know how . . . I would like to.'
That hand was on her shoulder again.

Esther suddenly felt tearful and her mouth turned down,
thinking of leaving Netherton.

She nodded bleakly and might, indeed, have started to cry but
then, as if from nowhere, as if he sensed she needed comfort, Tom
was there.

'Got to go out again now,' he said.

'I would like to meet your father,' said Helen Perry-Wilcox.

'Nana,' said Esther.

'Nana?' repeated Miss Perry-Wilcox.

'Margaret,' said Tom. 'Brian. Richard. Eileen. Karen . . .' his
fund of names associated with Esther, which he offered to Miss
Perry-Wilcox, dried up for a moment. Then it resumed. 'Graham.
Eileen. Peter. Skalg.'

'Skalg?' she asked, picking up the only word that didn't sound
like a name.

Esther's legs spasmed and she looked annoyed.

No Tom, shut up. SHUT UP.

'Nothing. Nothing. Didn't mean anything,' said Tom.

Then he looked ingratiatingly at Miss Perry-Wilcox, put his hand
in hers and changed the subject.

'What's your name?' he asked.

'Helen,' she said.

'C'mon Helen!' and with Esther driving her chair herself they
slowly set off to find the others.

THIRTY-FOUR

Margaret Ogilvie was standing by the boot of the old Austin Cambridge, handing out the various plastic containers and carrier bags which formed the Ogilvie equivalent of a picnic set. She turned, yet again, to see if Esther was coming back and saw at last that she was, accompanied by Tom and that interesting woman who had been the guest speaker. At that same moment, Helen Perry-Wilcox, conscious that she ought by now to have joined the Imrays over by the pavilion, and uneasy about interrupting Esther Marquand's family, saw Margaret Ogilvie staring at her.

Two women, both in their sixties, both with troubled lives behind them, both shy and awkward with strangers; yet, as their eyes met, there was that instant and inexplicable sense of accord that becomes, for no clear reason, a deep, trusting and lifelong friendship.

'This is Helen,' said Tom. Then to Helen: 'Here's Amh's Nana.'

At that moment of meeting Margaret Ogilvie would, normally, have looked flustered, and wiped back her lock of grey hair nervously and said something inconsequential to Brian. On this occasion she did no such thing. Seeing the woman whose speech she had liked coming forward behind Esther holding Tom's hand, she sensed that she was quite uncritical and non-threatening, as vulnerable as herself, and she smiled and nodded her head, saying simply, 'Will you have a glass of wine? Well, plastic cup of wine, I forgot the wine glasses.'

Helen Perry-Wilcox seemed touched at this informality, any unease she had felt quite gone, and, in any case, she could see in the distance that the Imrays were preoccupied with parents. Both women felt light-headed.

'Let me help you with that,' said Helen, coming forward and taking the tube of plastic cups still in their wrapper from Margaret's hands. Then she began to open it as if the two of them had planned to make the picnic together.

'I really just came over to say how very much I enjoyed your granddaughter's . . . Esther's . . . composition,' said Helen Perry-Wilcox. 'They sent it to me to read, you see. I have been talking to Esther about the past. I am the girl whose picture she . . .'

'Oh! Brian. This is . . .' and they talked as Esther and Tom looked on.

Richard Marquand was a little way off talking with Graham and his father, Tony, but now they all came over. Richard wanted to go back to his car and get the wine glasses *he* had remembered to bring, but Margaret seemed strangely at ease and forceful.

'Oh don't *worry*, Richard, it will taste the same. And I want you to meet Helen Perry-Wilcox who has read Esther's composition. She was the girl who . . .'

But it took some explanation, both women chipping in, until it became clear that Richard had not yet had time to read Esther's composition. There was a shared moment of dismay between the two that he had not done so.

'I am surprised at you, Richard,' said Margaret. Then, changing the subject, she added, 'Miss Perry-Wilcox, I wonder if you would like to join us for lunch.'

'Oh, I don't think I should, really. I've been very rude leaving the Imrays for so long . . . but perhaps . . .'

'Later?' said Margaret. The two women nodded and smiled. Helen left, but nobody noticed the intimacy, or understood why Margaret was so relaxed that afternoon.

Brian raised his plastic cup and said, 'I shall propose a toast of congratulations to Esther and Graham, our prize-winners.'

'To Esther and Graham.'

Tom raised his mug too, high and towards the sun, as if he was a druidic priest at an altar offering the wine to the heavens. Then he went around to everyone, touching his mug to theirs as he had seen people do when they made toasts. He gave Esther some of his own before he sipped it himself.

'Yuk!' he said.

'I never won a prize at school and I know you didn't, Margaret,' said Brian. Margaret shook her head gently and said nothing. She felt woozy. 'What about you, Richard?'

'I got a form prize for maths.'

'Oh.' Brian contemplated this gloomily. 'And you, Tony?' he asked finally.

'Scripture and middle-school shotput.'

Graham Downer laughed. 'Dad, you never told me that before,' he said.

Brian looked round at Margaret, who lay flat on a sun-lounger with her eyes closed, and said, 'We're the only ones who never won a school prize, dear.'

He nudged her. She opened her eyes. He raised his plastic cup quietly to her, a private moment.

She raised her own, and they touched cups and she said softly, 'Darling,' and smiled. There was a smile in Brian's eyes as he turned back to talk with Richard, while in the distance, Helen Perry-Wilcox turned from the more formal group she had now joined, just in time to see this Ogilvie exchange, thinking perhaps that there are things other than prizes which take time and effort to earn, and are worth infinitely more.

The lunch hour extended drowsily to two-fifteen when the 'sports' began. Nothing too serious since the range of ability was so great and the numbers so small compared with a conventional school that a 'real' sports day was not possible.

More important for the pupils was the opening of the classrooms for the parents to see representative work and various demonstrations of arts, crafts, music and computing – the latter a new interest utilizing the several computers the school now had, showing the programs some of the students had made and some commercial games as well.

Graham had written a program using data collected at Netherton to make simple weather projections. Esther had developed one of the creative computing interactive games, though she was dissatisfied with it, and discouraged her father from looking at it.

At four-thirty, the school bell rang to summon everyone from their various pursuits and a cream tea was served in front of the main marquee. Then there was a sudden bustle.

A wooden dancing surface had been put down on the grass in front of the marquee and the colourful Morris men of Blackstone Quarry, a north Hampshire village, were gathering. One had a melodeon, another a violin, and all wore black breeches, white shirts, red and blue ribbons across their chest and bright floral hats, and good cheer on their faces.

The Blackstone Men were, that weekend, making a number of fund-raising visits to Hampshire villages, schools and pubs, one of which was their appearance at Netherton.

The sun shone, the sudden sound of leg bells carried through the air, and Warble appeared carrying a tray of beer mugs from the smaller of the two marquees, as the rhythmic and appealing strains of the melodeon began the catchy tune of 'The Quarryman's Daughter'. With a few shouts and laughs, the Men lined up, raised their right hands, waved the red kerchiefs they each carried, and danced over the grass and on to the wooden dais.

Brian, who had been resting in the sun-lounger, was helped out of his chair to go and get a better look, while people began to gather about, clapping, smiling, pointing out this and that, and after a few dances, willingly dug their hands into their pockets to drop coins in the box that the Fool presented to them. The Men had set up a table and a high stool at one end of the dance area – the table to hold their beer and the stool for the musician to sit on.

Even Margaret, who had stayed with the picnic things, let her feet waggle and tap to the music, but though she realigned her chair so she could see in the general direction of the dancers it was in truth more to keep an eye on Brian than to enjoy the dance. Yet her pleasure these days was his pleasure, and she recognized the lightness in his step and the happiness with which he turned to Richard or bent down to Esther to point out features of the dance.

There was a sudden lull as one of the Men came on to the dance floor. 'Is it a hot day?' he asked.

'*Yes*,' everybody called out.

'And are there any nice people here?'

'*Yes!*' confirmed the Netherton parents, teachers and pupils all at once.

'And does anybody want to dance?' As he said this the musician stood up, and started what sounded like the very beginning of a rhythmic dance which, just as its beat invited people to get going, stopped and started all over again.

Parents and relatives were forming a simple circle of people and wheelchairs but Brian, after whispering to Esther, shook his head and declined. She did not want to.

The Men had chosen the simple 'Summer Mill' chain dance which requires very little more than walking in a circle to the beat of the music and doing a dosey-do at the right moments. No changing of partners, no complex formations, no arches.

When all seemed assembled the Man shouted 'We need just one more able-bodied man to assist this lad here,' pointing to a junior in a wheelchair who wanted to join in. 'Just one more able-bodied man; come *on*, gentlemen. Sir?' He stared at Richard but Richard shook his head. Then suddenly, with a chuckle, Brian went forward, a little doddery perhaps, but no one cared, least of all himself; he could never resist the dance.

'I'll just help out, old girl,' he said to Esther, 'You can have the next one. But I'll just . . .'

'Go on, Brian,' said Richard. Margaret, in the distance, leaned forward looking worried; Brian was too old for dancing now. He had been so tired after that one he had gone to the previous December with Esther, though he had refused to say anything.

But too late. With his white hair catching the bright afternoon sun, Brian went on to the boards and ranged himself behind the boy in a wheelchair to listen with the others to the brief instructions for the dance though the 'Summer Mill' chain was one of the first dances he had learned. Then they were off and there was nothing Margaret could do to stop him.

Round and round, the crowd clapping, the children laughing and some whirling so fast that those in wheelchairs were held in only by straps, and the large broad backs and strong legs of the Men, their red ribbons crossed on their white shirts, and the flowers on their straw hats all the colours of the rainbow and Margaret relaxing back in the sun as she caught sight again of Helen Perry-Wilcox who, freeing herself from a governor and his wife, came over to say hello again. Margaret looked away down the sloping lawns towards the church and wondered why she felt so relaxed and happy, as the cheerful music came over the grass and Esther raised her hands and seemed to try to clap as well as she watched her grandfather.

'What a lovely day, Mrs Ogilvie,' said Helen Perry-Wilcox.

Margaret looked up at her, shielding her eyes with her hand against the sun.

'Oh, please call me Margaret.'

'I'm Helen,' said Helen. She sat down.

They said nothing, both looking towards the dancers. Then they began chatting amiably, smiling, getting to know one another. Talking mainly of Esther and how bright she was. The sun shining, a small warm breeze rising, Margaret helping Helen to just a little more wine, and their eyes half closed in sun and peace, as their lips smiled. The sounds of the afternoon and the Morris music were fading as . . . as . . .

As suddenly Margaret was wide awake and staring at Esther, where she sat with her back to them watching the dancing. Margaret started forward and out of her chair as she saw that Esther's hands were no longer clapping with the music, they were trying to draw attention, her head was straining round to catch sight of Margaret, her mouth mutely screaming QUICKLY! SOME-THING IS WRONG. PLEASE NANA NANA NANA!

Margaret was up with the name 'Brian' on her lips, and, Helen at her side, she quickly went over the grass to Esther and followed her gaze to the dance area where Brian was pushing the chair of the boy. But he was not pushing, he was leaning, and his face was set in a smile, a brave smile but his colour was fading grey.

Richard, who was standing nearby laughing with the crowd, had not noticed a thing.

'Richard, get Brian off now. *Now.*'

Then he did see, and was on to the dance area, propping Brian up with one arm and easing the boy's chair off with the other and out of the rush. So entrancing was the dance that no one seemed to notice Brian's plight, or his sudden removal.

'It's all right,' Brian was saying as Richard brought him the few steps to Esther and Margaret. 'It's all right, I just just I just . . . the dance . . .' His colour came back but in his eyes there was a frightened appeal to Margaret who took his arm with one hand, and put her right arm round his back, and led him protectively back to their chairs, where he slumped and for a moment seemed to have difficulty breathing.

'Is there pain, my dear?' said Margaret.

'No! Nothing of that kind. I'm not having a stroke dammit,' said Brian with some irritation. 'Just a bit tired, couldn't keep going; the boy's chair's damned heavy. Couldn't keep going.'

It really did seem as simple as that, but later Esther heard

Margaret whisper to Helen, '. . . once before. He got tired like this once before, must have another check-up.'

Later, when all was well and Brian had got his breath back, Margaret declared, 'I knew because Esther saw it, didn't you, darling, you saw his distress. Oh, he's too old for dancing now aren't you, Brian?' Brian sat in the sun, looking better now, normal, in fact, but deep in his face was the set of fatigue and intimations of mortality.

'Yes,' he said, adding to Esther, 'well done, old girl.'

Esther looked round for Richard but he had gone off, a little embarrassed by the fuss, and was talking with Tony Downer about cameras. Then he came back and said cheerfully, as if to re-establish the previous good cheer of the afternoon, 'Well, Brian, you're not going in the granddad's race then? You gave us quite a scare for a moment.'

Brian smiled, tired now. Esther Marquand saw the distant fear in his eyes and fancied, as the intelligent young sometimes do, that she was the only one who did. But Helen saw it too; and so did Margaret. While Tom, who had rejoined them from one of his adventures, hugged Brian and then stood quietly, his hands on the grey metal of Esther's chair.

Only Richard seemed not to see, leaning back in his chair, and relaxing as the afternoon wore to its close.

Weeks passed, the summer holidays had come again, and Brian Ogilvie was sitting in a wicker chair in the garden of Harefield. His hand – his old pale hand which even the hottest sun seemed unable now to turn brown – reached out and touched Esther's arm.

Brian's mind seemed to wander now when he was near sleep, which he often was in the afternoon, his breathing becoming heavy and his eyes drooping, his thin knees seeming almost to stick through the fabric of his light summer trousers.

Today they sat, as they had seemed to sit every afternoon that summer at Harefield, under a faded sun umbrella around a slatted teak garden table on which, as usual, was the chessboard. The whole family was there, drowsy, in the late afternoon warmth of an English summer.

'More tea, Esther?'

Brian stirred at the sound of Margaret's voice, opening his eyes

and contemplating the board, yawning. The pieces were in some
final checkmate position, the lost and taken ones piled into the
wooden box. The late sun slanted across the table, and though
Brian had won once again, yet it was the shadow of Esther's
defeated black king that was cast now across Brian's white pieces.

Brian never had any compunction about beating Esther at chess,
and that was one reason she loved to play him. Some people let
her win because she was handicapped, but never Brian. Chess, like
the dance, was something he took seriously. A player, like a dancer,
had to earn her spurs the hard way.

'No quarter given and none received, my dear, that's the only
way to play this game.'

His games with Esther had been one of the charms of the summer
and were the stuff of which memories are made: the two of them
under the umbrella, the fruit trees ripening in the orchard behind,
Margaret calling, Tom doing something with plants, and Richard
coming home as early as he could from work, which was often
long after the children had gone to bed.

In the background, now quietly organizing the house and seeing
to Esther's needs, was Marion, who had been working full-time at
Harefield for a year now. Never flustered, never involved in the
friction that sometimes existed between Richard and Margaret,
and Richard and Esther, never giving in to Esther's occasional
moods, Marion gave the home unity and, perhaps, a soul.

When Esther was home she took her to St Barnabas's, the church
whose deserted ground lay at the far end of the Harefield acreage,
beyond the wooden fence. It was sombre and dark, and the vicar
was elderly and (to Marion) uninspiring, and she missed the more
lively hymns she was used to at the Pentecostal church she usually
attended. But Esther liked tradition and was used to the older
hymns. Brian sometimes came with them, and the walk was just
within his range. It was understood that on such Sundays Marion
would take the evening off, to have a late service among her own
people.

She very occasionally brought a girlfriend home, invariably
when no one was going to be in, and though Richard told her she
had no need to ask permission, she always did so.

It was a puzzle to Richard that she seemed to have no boyfriends,
for she had become attractive, with healthy cheeks and a nice,

simple appearance. True, she said little, but she was happy, and projected happiness.

That summer, Richard, with Marion's help, took Esther away for a fortnight to Devon at a centre near the sea organized by the Spastics Society. The trip was mainly to help her pass the time until her five 'O' and one 'A' level results came in. She wrote to Betty Shaw:

> Having an OK time thanks very much. Your warnings were wrong!! There's some nice male helpers here only they all go for Marion worse luck! She won't have anything to do with them outside the social life of the Centre and we laugh about it. Daddy seems to be enjoying himself, sort of. Fortunately there are other parents he can talk to and he's getting quite brown. Personally I think he's here out of duty to me and really I sometimes wish he had someone with him if you know what I mean. I feel quite sorry for the parents as it's all organized for us. If I had a child with CP I'd run a mile!!! Well, crawl ten yards!! Joke. Obviously the sun's getting to me.
>
> I bet you're as nervous as me abut the exam results. Only another eight days to go. I think I'm all right for Eng. Lang. and Eng. Lit., History and Geography, but I made a mess of the Religious Studies. Graham and I both think we did all right in the maths, and so did Warble, but I lie in bed at night worrying about it. Graham's written and said he's going to see if he can do Computer Science for 'A' level next year by correspondence as there's no one to teach it. Don't you think that's brilliant? Maybe I should as well.
>
> Seven and a half days to go!! Phone me when you get your results, I won't dare phone you.

But Esther need not have worried. She, like Graham, had passed everything including the maths 'A' level, for which she had a Beta against Graham's Alpha. Indeed, the only failure among the three friends' results was Betty Shaw's Religious Studies which she failed.

'Will your God reject me from heaven?' Betty asked Esther over the phone on the day the results came through.

'Yeh,' said Esther. *'Yeh!'* They laughed. And when Graham phoned he said he would send the computer science syllabus to see what Esther's father thought of it.

After this news there came over all of them at Harefield a sense of calm and relaxation, as if they had all been carrying the burden of Esther's public examinations and could now relax into the long days of summer.

Brian and Margaret joined them from Charlbury after the return from Devon as Harefield was better adapted to Esther's needs, and the garden to wheelchairs and exploration. It meant too that when Richard did manage to get away early he could join them for tea, and see them more easily on the short weekends he allowed himself.

But it was not like the previous summer. There were tensions in the air, subtle and unspoken; frictions between father and daughter, worries between grandfather and grandmother. The future for each of them seemed somehow in doubt, and decisions, most obviously about Esther, were going to have to be made. Even about Tom who, though he had a place at the Centre in Ealing, ought now perhaps to be directed to some kind of work if it could be found.

But there were still cloudless, sun-filled, happy moments and the most regular of them was Brian and Esther having a game or two of chess before tea was brought out. The sight of the two of them starting their game seemed a signal for everyone else to get quietly on with their own things, which in Tom's case meant working out of sight in the vegetable garden and in Margaret's, an afternoon nap. While Marion, the dishes done and the washing hung out, would take her Bible and sit out under the shade of the apple trees and read.

Esther's chess had improved enormously since Brian had first taught her the game a year before, and she now knew all the openings and a good bit about the end game. She had read some books, and had a computer chess game which she could play successfully to its higher levels. Brian could beat it at all levels. Esther was weaker with black than white, being by nature an attacking player, and she seemed stronger on the queen side. But her best education in chess came from Brian, who accompanied their games with a commentary full of chess references which she had no trouble understanding though Margaret, when she heard it, grumbled that it was all double Dutch to her.

Sometimes, between games, he would take up her fallen king and place it carefully in her hand, closing her fingers around it. 'You lost this because you *forgot* the pawns. They're only the common folk but you can't have a king without people, just as you can't have a queen without giving her courtiers to scheme with. Develop your pawn structure right from the start and get it right, then you'll be all right.'

Esther nodded and began yet another game in whose closed system she could lose herself. Game after game . . . but always she lost, always Brian was stronger than she was and she would be forced finally to raise her hand to signal her resignation.

Sometimes after those games Esther turned the chair from the table and drove it slowly down the path away from the house, down to the edge of the orchard.

She stared up at the trees beginning to silhouette in the evening sky. The game was over once more and she was back in reality, and feeling scared. The protection of this garden and her family would not always be hers: the time was coming, she knew, when she would have to go out into the world.

THIRTY-FIVE

On the day before Tom and Graham were due to come for the Bank Holiday, Esther got into a temper because she was refused permission to go shopping in London. It had been half promised, the plan being for Margaret and Marion to drive up to London and take Esther to fashionable Bond Street to look at the expensive shops, and then on to Oxford Street which contained the shops they could afford. Esther wanted to buy something special for the Bank Holiday, and a few clothes for school which started again in three weeks' time.

But no, suddenly it was not allowed. Margaret made the decision giving as her reason the IRA bomb that exploded in Oxford Street that same week which, though it damaged only buildings, was deemed by the television news to be the possible start of a new wave of bombing in London to coincide with the holiday.

Esther could not help thinking that if she was able-bodied she would simply have gone. Being dependent was always frustrating but sometimes . . . she sulked, glowered, pouted, glared and stayed in her room. The weather seemed to match her mood for it was oppressively hot, with a hint of thunder in the air.

Brian went out to the garden but was restless, unable to nap. He hated to think of Esther alone and miserable in her room. Eventually he went to her door and knocked. Silence. He knocked again. More silence. He quietly opened the door and looked in.

'Esther?'

She was staring straight at him, her chair turned at an angle to the table as the page-turner whirred on at her side turning page after page, unread. The curtains were drawn on the sunny world outside.

'Esther, do come out into the garden.'

'Nah,' she said unpleasantly. 'G . . . gawa,' she added, turning her chair so her back was to him, and pretending to read the book.

'Well I'm out into the garden if you do want a game. I'm not feeling sleepy. I would like a game.' His voice faded before her rude silence. Then he left her.

Half an hour later Esther came out into the garden. Her chair came steadily down the tarmac path and over the lawn towards him.

'Yeh!' she said without smiling. She raised her hand to indicate the chess pieces.

'Yeh.'

Her eyes were angry and ungiving.

'Good, good,' he said. But the good nature in his voice withered a little before her gaze and in silence he set the pieces up.

'You're white this time,' he said.

She immediately signed e4, the opening he had defeated her with in their previous game. Brian responded conventionally with e5, and Esther signed for her king's knight: Nf3.

'Ruy Lopez?' he said. It was not an opening she normally chose to play.

'Yeh,' she said. And there was suddenly no sun, no day, there was nothing between them but the board and the conflict of the game which started with an eternity of options and would end, most likely, in a final forced move with defeat for one of them.

That afternoon, that game, the strange chilling anger Esther's mood was generating seemed to make her chess pieces larger and more forbidding as the sun inexorably swung round to catch them in its light. Behind Brian, from one of the branches of the apple trees, a great green apple slewed on its stalk and tumbled to the ground.

Then the Ruy Lopez moves began to flow impatiently from Esther, one after another: inexorable, powerful, fearsome, until it was Brian who, unusually, paused first to take stock.

He tried to keep calm and was tempted by the conventional to bring out the queen bishop's pawn which would reduce Esther's white initiative and tie her to the sort of game he was best at. But . . . but . . . he hesitated. His eyes looked away from the board, he sat back for a moment, his hands felt uncomfortable; *he* felt uncomfortable. Under attack, yet no attack was evident on the board. The pawn, the pawn, the pawn, and his eyes followed the lines that might develop. No, better the queen's bishop. Bring it across to the b row. Yes. Yes.

Esther did not move, just stared. The sun was golden in her hair and her eyes dark and concentrated. On the horizon, beyond the orchard, a dark bank of rain clouds gathered.

Brian moved. Rain started to patter heavily down.

Then there was a strengthening in Esther, a maturing, the sudden casting and sloughing off of an old skin and the emergence of a new and better one. She could see her attacking line and it was, as her grandfather had always told her it should be, based on a strong centre. Tighten the grip on the centre. Secure it. But not directly, more subtly than that. She felt the powering of her mind over the patterns present and patterns future on the board, the beautiful pattern. And oh, she remembered Peter, as if his mind was in hers, and she wished he was here to feel as she did the power that did not come from the body but the mind, a power that filled the spirit and conquered the oppression of the body, for it was greater, so much greater. Her mood of angry despair was giving way to triumphant exultation.

As the game wore on and for the first time Esther felt the power of advantage and winning, around them, barely noticed, the rain drummed, dripped and splashed. The light dry soil of the flowerbeds was turning dark and sopping wet. Puddles formed in rucks of soil. Water ran dripping down the great hedges, herbaceous plants fought the rain, struggling up again and again against the weight of water that fell upon them until one by one the aquilegia, the leaves of the woundwort, the rose, the delphinium, the lowly marigold, lost their strength and sagged.

Each, in their way, would rise again; but not in flower again this year, nor some in fruit. This year's summer was dying in the rain, and an autumn of fruits and change, of stirring and hidden growth, an autumn leading to the winter that sees the death of one year and the secret birth of another, that autumn was coming.

A drop, and then two, and then a third fell now from the um-brella on to the table, just missing the board. The rain had found a weakness in the covering and had worked its way through. Brian wiped the spot dry with a folded handkerchief.

32 . . .?

He no longer knew. Whatever option he took led to the capture of his old beloved king round whom Esther's great white pieces loomed, threatening, powerful, interdependent, unyielding.

Brian leaned forward and made his final move. He picked up his black king, held it for a moment as if to say goodbye, and then gently and with a respect that Esther never forgot, laid it on its side on the board.

32 . . . Black resigns.

Then he looked at her, and smiled, and nodded his head in acknowledgement not just of her victory but of what it meant. She had won not through his mistake – though in a sense all victories are won on the back of mistakes – but rather through the superiority of her play. He had played his best but Esther had played better.

Brian got up slowly, moved from the protection of the umbrella out into the rain, which immediately began to soak his linen suit, and leaned down to kiss Esther, his hand squeezing her arm.

'Yes,' was all he could say. 'Yes, my dear. It is your game at last. Well done, well done.'

With that, and without hurrying, he took the handles of her chair and pushed her back over the sodden grass towards the house. As he did so Esther leaned her head back as far as she could and opened her mouth, and stared up through the rain that drummed on to her face to the black and rolling clouds, whose massing darkness was lit by lightning, and whose heights echoed to the sound of thunder.

'Gr!' she said. And her face was shining pink and laughing. '*Gr!!!*' Granddad!'

Oh yes, and Brian looked up too, at that great sky which had watched over him all his life and which would continue to watch over her when he was gone.

TURN ME ROUND TO LOOK DOWN THE GARDEN.

He seemed to understand her excitement and her shouts. The game was over and the world was different, felt different and she wanted to look at it.

So he turned her round and together, getting more and more drenched, they stared down the old garden, past the umbrella where the board and the pieces still were, to the orchard. Beyond even that, for the rain had flattened and parted the undergrowth, they stared at the wooden fence whose verticals stood black and wet against the dark green of the churchyard's vegetation.

Then Esther shouted, loudly, as loud as she could, a shout of excitement against the rain and the great storm, against whose might, for the time being, she felt she had the strength to fight.

'Skyagree!' she shouted. 'Skyagree!' And she felt his power in her, as she had sometimes before, and she knew that there was no wall, no wooden fence, over which, somehow, she would not find the strength, and skill, and courage, one day to climb.

'Skyagree!' And she laughed again, the rain running into her mouth as Brian Ogilvie, the white-pink of his legs showing through his sodden trousers, heaved her chair round and pushed her the final few yards towards the patio doors which Marion opened as they arrived, with great striped towels ready, waiting to welcome them in.

Five days later, the rain gone and the sun returned but the garden still battered, Brian Ogilvie said he felt tired and fell asleep in his wicker chair, over by the hedge. As his sleep deepened the garden stirred on about him.

Tom was humming over by his rhubarb. Margaret was talking with Marion in the kitchen. Esther and Graham were at the front of the house with Richard who had come back for the Bank Holiday and was discussing how to repair the front gate with them.

But where Brian sat, eyes closed, hands together in his lap, head bowed, these sounds grew distant and faded. Where he sat there was only the sound of a bumble bee, drowsy now and late-summer-old, struggling to escape the leaves of the hydrangea into which it had flown. Struggling then still.

Perhaps Brian heard them all, sitting there so tired, his eyes closed. Perhaps he had time to think there was good young life about him, of his making, and that Margaret had learnt from Esther these past years that she had something left to give for both of them. Perhaps he listened for a time to those about him, out of sight beyond his closed eyes, but their voices soft in the afternoon and melding now into these nearer sounds in the garden where finally he had found real peace and family content, and into which he was now drifting . . . Harefield, his Margaret bless her and give her peace; Richard, Sheila long gone now but her daughter Esther with her young man Graham, behind him in the orchard. No, no that was yesterday. Today, now, they're out at the front with Richard, poor Richard, and that distant whirr is the sound of their wheelchairs, no no no, my dears, it is a dying bumble bee. Oh, dear Margaret, I . . . I . . . and perhaps he looked up and saw his king and queen and courtiers, and Esther's, set neat and ready for another game.

Then Brian, unseen, but at the centre of the family he loved . . . Brian's breathing grew slower and fainter, and his right hand loosened in his lap and slipped slowly over his thigh and down, down, to hang still by the chair in the evening warmth and grow slowly cold.

Later Tom came by and seeing Brian went up to him.

'Where's Amh?' he asked.

Brian was quite still. Tom stared at him. Then Tom bent down and stared up into his face, and down at his hanging arm and hand.

'Brian?' he said.

Tom stood up and looked wildly round, beginning to cry.

'Amh,' he said. 'Where's Amh?' And he ran from Brian up to the house, and then around it, because he remembered where she was.

'*Amh!*' he called as he rounded the building to the front.

And Esther looked sharply round and knew from his voice that something had happened.

'*Amhamhamh,*' cried Tom terribly, as the others, understanding too, went quickly back to the main garden where Brian had been, leaving Esther and Tom alone at the front.

'Amh,' said Tom, 'are you scaredy?'

Then as they heard Margaret's cry, terrible and sharp, and the deeper voice of Richard, Esther reached up as best she could and held Tom to her and whispered, again and again, 'Nah, nah, nah,' as Tom cried.

Then Marion came and said, 'It's your granddad, Esther, best not to go.'

But Esther knew better.

TAKE ME, TOM.

'No, Amh.'

TAKE ME.

'Don't want to.'

TOM!

Then, together, slowly, Esther in front and Tom holding the

handles of her chair, they went round the side of Harefield, to see what Brian had become, and to say their last goodbye to the loved man he had been.

TOUCH HIM, TOM.

'*No, no, Amh.*' And he would not.

But Esther did, even before the doctor and the ambulance came, she touched his hanging hand. Curious about death, strangely removed, icy calm. But beneath all that was a passionate fear that the future she feared was beginning now to come upon her.

They did cry finally, Esther and Margaret, together in Esther's room the following night.

Margaret said as if to herself that there had been no warning, unless the discomfort he had felt at the Prize Day during the country dancing should have been taken as one. Only in June he had his six-monthly check-up, and come through just fine. But he was over seventy and such things can happen, do happen, oh Esther, it had happened, it had.

Only from Esther did Margaret accept comfort; Esther who could say nothing but who had grown to love them both and to under-stand their love. Only with Esther did Margaret now seem to have purpose, obsessively taking over the tasks that Marion was employed to perform, in a house that was now shocked and hushed, quiet but for the bird call in the garden and the life there that Brian had watched and loved.

Graham went home, subdued and upset, the Bank Holiday he had come for barely started. He preferred to go, and he and Esther said hardly a word. Somehow their relationship changed in the moment of Margaret's first mourning cry as if, in a way, Graham had gone too far into the secrets of Esther's life and she now drew back. They were not girlfriend and boyfriend again, and never really had been. As Graham left Esther thought, 'He kissed me only three times.' And then, 'I'm glad he's gone.'

Tom stayed, it seemed best that way. He was upset, and cried, and then went out into the garden or hung around Esther saying little as they waited until the funeral, which was delayed for several days because of the holiday.

THIRTY-SIX

They made the slow drive from High Wycombe back to Charlbury behind a shining black hearse in whose side, before it had left, Tom found his bespectacled reflection and touched it.

They passed through countryside that was dry and honey-coloured from the sun, as if, but for patches of flattened corn, the rain had never been.

The little cortège had to stop near Woodstock, where a farmer was burning stubble and clouds of dark grey smoke drifted over the road. They wound up the windows and watched as the smoke enveloped the hearse ahead.

Once upon a time Brian had wanted to be cremated, but lately, said Margaret, he had expressed a wish to be buried next to their daughter in the churchyard of St Mary's, the parish church of Charlbury.

All so sudden, and nothing much to say. Margaret, Esther, Richard, Tom and Marion, formally dressed and in the church sitting with a few others in its pews, not knowing quite where to look but at the flowers or at the coffin; or to listen to the vicar's voice as he ran through the old service and the organist played a piece of Bach Brian liked.

Then they trooped outside, the sun still shining on the Cotswold stone buildings all about, and gathered round the grave for the final words. Esther had freesias to put on her mother's grave, the first time she had ever done such a thing. She was able to hold on to them only because Richard had wound some wire right around them and looped it over her wrist.

Tom stood in grey trousers and a light blue anorak. He knew where he ought to look – at the hole in the ground where the others looked – but sometimes his eyes wandered. There was a blackbird under a yew tree scurrying in the undergrowth, and a green house roof just over the churchyard wall.

Margaret was shaky, her face grey and thin. She leaned on
Richard's arm wearing a new grey coat, black shoes and stockings,
and a new black leather bag over her arm. Richard was in grey,
with a black band on his arm. A few others were there – Marion
who had been crying; Mr Parsons, Brian's chess friend; and several
of the older Men of the Charlbury Morris and a few neighbours;
not many. And a relative stranger: Helen Perry-Wilcox, to whom
Margaret had written a brief note of Brian's death and who had
responded not only with a kind and charming letter (as Margaret
put it) but added that she would be coming to the funeral.

When the words by the grave were finished Tom watched
carefully to see what he should do. He stayed near Esther, whose
chair was pushed by Marion up and down the grass verges. Tom
saw Margaret and Richard pick up some soil from the neat pile by
the grave and throw it down into the dark rectangular hole where
it clattered; down there, where they put the coffin and some
flowers. Down there. He stared, his hand holding soil, and then he
scattered it, watching and listening. Esther spoke.

'Yes, Amh?' Tom found he was suddenly close to tears and was
sniffing, his cuff to his nose.

Esther raised one of her hands.

Then Tom picked up some more soil and, touching it to Esther's
hand, threw it down with a clatter for her.

The family stood to one side while others did the same, one after
another, sombre and dark in the summer morning. Then they
came and paid their respects to Margaret and Richard, some
smiling down at Esther, some serious, some not looking at her. Mr
Parsons touched her, taking her by the wrist and patting her
hand: 'I'm so sorry, Esther. He was very proud of you, you know.'

Helen Perry-Wilcox, dressed smartly in black, came to Margaret
with a natural sympathy and understanding and as the two briefly
held each other Margaret had to wipe tears from her eyes.

'I'm so glad you came,' she said.

'But of course I would come,' said Helen.

'Hello, Esther,' she said bending down quite naturally and kissing
Esther on the cheek. 'And Tom!'

Tom nodded, grinning at the assembled gravestones with embarrassment and delight at being remembered.

As they began to walk away Esther looked up at her father.

'Amh's got the flowers for her Mum,' reminded Tom.

So they all went back the few yards and stared down at her mother's grave. The stone, once pure white, was beginning to stain grey.

Esther spoke.

'Me,' she said, raising the arm to which the flowers were tied. They swung loose and two freesias fell to the ground.

Tom picked them up, stuffed them back into Esther's bunch, made sure she was holding them properly, and then, without saying anything, undid her straps and pulled her out of the chair.

Esther was lowered on to the ground and, with Richard's help, placed the flowers on her mother's grave.

'All right, Amh?' said Tom, protective. He never liked to see Esther defenceless on the ground.

'Yeh,' she whispered. Then she turned her head and stared along the ground towards Brian's grave. Her hand reached out and her fingers weakly clasped some loose soil the diggers had thrown up.

'Me,' she said.

Tom pulled her half up and she held her hand over her mother's grave and one by one her fingers released the little soil they held, which fell down on the flowers before the stone.

'Mama,' she said.

They stood staring down, Margaret weeping, Richard unable to say anything, and, over by the church tower, tactfully waiting out of earshot, the vicar.

'C'mon,' said Tom eventually. 'C'mon, Amh.'

'Yeh,' said Esther. And, the moment of silence for Sheila over, they gathered themselves to leave, to shake hands with the vicar. They each, in their own way, began to accommodate a life without Brian.

Some drove, many walked the short way up the High Street to the Ogilvies' home. There was a great luminous orange notice outside the Village Hall announcing the Charlbury Men's first dance of the winter season that evening at eight. A coach party of end-of-season tourists were taking photographs. Three boys carrying a football headed down a side street towards the green. Life continued.

By three in the afternoon everybody but close family and Helen

Perry-Wilcox, who had somehow become one of them that summer, had left, and Richard was about to go as well. It had been decided that Esther would stay overnight along with Marion. The ticking of the grandfather clock in the hall had never seemed so slow and unsure in its life, minutes and hours of bleak emptiness.

At five Helen made them all another pot of tea. At five-thirty Margaret expressed regret that she could suggest nothing much for them to do; Brian would not have wished them to be miserable. At six they watched the television news. At seven they had a light supper and Margaret said she felt tired and would go to bed early. At seven-thirty Helen left.

And at a quarter to eight there was a knock on the door. Margaret went to open and found standing there, somewhat diffidently, old Allen Parsons, Brian's friend.

'I hope you don't think I'm intruding but . . .'

Margaret ushered him in, glad to see a warm and friendly face. The past when she had been cold to him was finished.

When he was inside he came straight to the point: 'I was just on my way to the dance because it's the first of the season and Brian would have wanted me to go, I'm sure of that. But . . . er . . .' and his mouth seemed to tremble a little and he looked down at his gnarled hands and twisted them and paused.

'Well now, I haven't been to that first winter dance without Brian for more'n twenty years. I . . .' and he looked into Margaret's eyes, '. . . and it's an odd thing going on my own. I was wondering if . . . well I'd be obliged if Miss Esther would accompany me. I think Brian would have liked that.'

Margaret stared at him in absolute silence and Esther, who had come out to see who it was, sat staring as well.

'Mr Parsons,' began Margaret, her voice only just under control, 'I think my . . . I think Brian would have liked that very much. I am most grateful to you for thinking of it.'

'Oh no, it would be doing me a favour!' he said, more easily.

'Well then, if Esther . . .'

'Yeh!' said Esther.

'She'll need to get ready.'

'Yeh!' And while Marion changed her out of her formal clothes into something more comfortable Margaret and Allen Parsons had a sherry and without saying anything other than inanities managed somehow to bridge a gap which should have been closed years before.

Esther was to remember that dance with particular fondness. Not so much for the music and the laughter and the natural good humour, though it was the antidote she needed to the previous days' grief, but for that ritual first dance which the Men danced: 'Upon a Summer's Day'.

When it was time to perform it there was the inevitable awkwardness: Brian was no longer there to take part in what, for most of them, had never been done without him. It was like summer without the beech leaves shimmering in the sun. So that after the Fool for the night had made a short speech in Brian's memory and the old Men began to form the set, they found they were a man short. No one there felt it right he should take Brian's place, and as no one seemed quite sure what to do and the younger Men looked uneasily at each other, old Allen Parsons put down his pint of ale, took his pipe out of his mouth and put it on Esther's tray for safekeeping, and stepped slowly out on to the floor.

'I expect I'll do,' he said. 'Seen it done often enough.'

No laughter, no comments, just the melodeon beginning the rhythms of the good tune and hush in appreciation of the love and friendship Allen's gesture expressed.

Then, 'Aye, well done, Allen!' said one Man, and there were nods from the others as the set was completed by Allen, right hand to left hand, right foot placed ready. The music of a dance whose pattern stretched back through the decades, and would lead forward to the future, began its ancient way as Allen, never once out of step, danced a dance of celebration and mourning for a friend all had loved.

Esther was quiet and quite still as, after that, dance after dance whirled by and she saw their patterns, subtle not random; patterns on patterns on patterns through space and time, and she sensed she was near to seeing something between the Skallagrigg and Arthur; something like a dance. Something in the stories that linked them inevitably, as Brian and Allen were linked, as the members of a dance set were linked, as the years turned and turned, pattern on pattern.

Then everything seemed to bear on her thoughts as the band
played and the Men sang:

> There will come a time of great plenty
> A time of good harvest and sun
> Till then put your trust in tomorrow, my friend
> Why yesterday's over and done
>> And the storm falls
>> And the wind calls
>> And the year turns round again.

She seemed within grasp of something about the Skallagrigg, something about that. The year turns round again. A pattern, oh there
was a pattern, and it was to do with the past that was them and
the future that was her.

OH, THERE IS A PATTERN BUT I CAN'T SEE IT.

'What is it, Esther? Is anything the matter?' Allen was asking.
But she shook her head and smiled at him.

'Nah,' she said eventually touching his arm.

Yesterday's over and done but the year turns round again.

THERE IS A PATTERN, OH THERE IS SOMETHING IN THE
SKALLAGRIGG, SOMETHING IN THE STORIES SOMETHING I
CAN'T SEE BUT IT'S OBVIOUS BECAUSE I CAN FEEL IT RUN-
NING LIKE THE PATTERN THROUGH A DANCE. I DON'T KNOW
I CAN'T REACH IT I JUST DON'T. IT FEELS LIKE PLAYING
CHESS WHEN I WASN'T AS GOOD AS BRIAN AND I KNEW I WAS
PLAYING WRONG AND I COULDN'T SEE WHY IT FEELS LIKE
THAT. OH I JUST CAN'T SEE IT I . . . AND THE PATTERN IS IN
THE STORIES OF THE SKALLAGRIGG AND IN ME AND IN BRIAN
AND IN THE IN THE IN THE IN THE IN IN IN IN IN
ININININININ . . .

WOODEN FENCE.

Peter help me climb it now, help me get over it.

>> And the wind calls
>> And the year turns round again.

She heard his voice in the song, she fancied he was out there
somewhere in the crowd, healed now, all right now, out there in
the dance in which her grandfather had danced, and danced still.

Arthur. Arthur told the stories. Arthur was like her. Arthur's hands were like hers. And his head. And his stories.

HIS STORIES, OH THEY ARE HIS STORIES. THEY ARE ABOUT THE SKALLAGRIGG. BECAUSE BECAUSE BECAUSE HE LOST HIM, HE LOST HIS SKALLAGRIGG. BUT HE THINKS HE'S ALIVE.

That night, in the unreal reality of a village dance, sitting with Allen Parsons, Esther Marquand for the first time began to hear clearly the voice that lies behind all the stories of the Skallagrigg, whoever tells them.

The voice of a child handicapped and laid low, the voice that whispered into the night of a stricken ward in 1927 and spoke out a name to a high-barred window in the hope, the desperate hope, that one day, somewhere, someone would hear who could understand.

Now Esther was beginning to understand and she sat quite still with the surprise of it. *She* was the one who would understand, *she* was. Her eyes no longer saw the dancers or heard their song. But in her body she felt a pattern she could not quite grasp and it was beautiful and lovely and it had balance and a rhythm she had never felt before.

WHAT IS THE PATTERN? SHOW ME THE PATTERN SHOW ME SHOW ME.

She knew she would not rest until she saw it truly and could follow it to its end. And at its end she too would dance, and that would be her Summer's Day.

THIRTY-SEVEN

Esther Marquand began her search for a pattern in the Skallagrigg stories within a few days of the dance at Charlbury. And she did it systematically.

She started by making a compilation of the stories she knew, typing them on to disk in Dutton Speedwords on a Minion computer at Netherton. This was to be the first draft of *Stories of the Skallagrigg* and it is the primary source for these stories, many more of which have since been collected by others and published in different versions and fully annotated and documented.*

The original work, now in the Berkeley University of California Collection, consists of the thirty-two complete stories and fragments she recorded over a period of eleven months. After that, until her work found its culmination in 'Skallagrigg' the game, *Stories* was continually updated by her, new stories being added as her research produced them, and new versions of ones already collected were catalogued as well.

Before the book was finally published (by Cambridge University Press, 1996) it underwent many modifications, but Esther Marquand, and later Daniel Schuster, never altered the wording of the very first story she heard from Peter Rowne in the Ealing Centre. She referred to it, as most spastics who tell the story always have, as 'The First Story'.

In most cases we are able to date when she first heard the stories by the name of the source, since the diary which she sporadically kept with Betty Shaw through her school years makes mention of many of the people who told her Skallagrigg stories.

Her decision to write down the Skallagrigg stories was accom-

* See Nesbit and Fuller, *A Skallagrigg Bibliography*, Random House, New York, 2017; and P. J. Hemingway, *Skallagrigg: A Modern Oral Tradition*, Cambridge University Press, 2014.

panied by a more active attempt to collect them, initially by badgering anyone she met who might know them and later, and more systematically, by advertising for material in magazines aimed at handicapped people.

This was a busy period for Esther Marquand who was then in the first half of her two-year 'A'-level course in which she studied History and English Literature. The school records show that in addition to her normal school work she represented the school in chess (subsequently entering the Chess Federation Junior Championship in which she reached the regional quarter-finals) and edited the school magazine. She also informally followed a correspondence course in computer science with Graham Downer.

Esther, now over sixteen, was much concerned at that time with a medical problem which is common among cerebral palsied females of her age: she had not started her periods. Her weight was still only ninety-eight pounds and her height was measured at five feet two inches, making her relatively thin – a state of underdevelopment quite typical of her condition. Because they often have involuntary muscle spasms, spastics seem much less prone to putting on weight than some other handicap groups.

Yet she had quite a full face and one might have expected a bigger, plumper girl. The only physical abnormality in looks was in her neck which, from childhood, had been thick and strong to compensate for weak musculature in her chest and back. The severe deformations resulting from muscle spasms familiar in older institutionalized spastics were fortunately absent from Esther and most of her generation because of the very active physiotherapy they had received from an early age.

Most of the girls she knew at school had already started their periods and, despite the potential difficulties and possible embarrassments, this was something she wanted; it was one more way in which she felt abnormal and a non-woman.

She had no boyfriend at this time, the relationship with Graham, never very passionate, having somehow evolved into a sisterly one after Brian's death during the previous summer.

Yet . . . we may guess there were yearnings.

She always remembered her second meeting the previous year with Andy Moore. His name recurs in her diary and he is always mentioned rudely, a sign perhaps that she rather liked him. She seems to have asked him for help in locating people in the north-east who might be able to tell her some Skallagrigg stories. He agreed, in return for her persuading her father's company to take part in an exhibition of computer aids for the handicapped in Manchester.

ComputaBase did take a stand at the show, demonstrating, among other things, the keyboard developed for Esther by Leon Sadler and a prototype version of the portable LCD screen that from then on was to make communication for her (and later many others) so much easier. It was light and durable, and could be attached to a wheelchair so that people with speech difficulties but able to handle a two-way control could key up what they wished to say. Esther went to Manchester with Margaret and demonstrated Leon's new equipment, and collected some key Skallagrigg stories.

One of them she heard from a couple Andy Moore introduced her to at a party held after the exhibition.

'I don't know where Jimmy is,' said Andy, 'but he knows he's to tell you a story. Go and talk to his girlfriend. Her name's Amanda. Hey, Val!' He summoned his own girlfriend, a large able-bodied earth-mother type whom Esther did not like, called Val Dove, and she took Esther to meet Amanda.

She was standing staring at the crowd by a door to a back room where the lights were lower and from which came the sound of the Rolling Stones and people dancing, some of them in wheel-chairs.

She stood defensively, her arms folded across her chest and leaning forward slightly, her face thin, pale and strained, and her eyes dark and staring. She turned when Val Dove called her name, and Esther saw that her hair was lank and badly cut in a lop-sided fringe across her forehead.

Val Dove gave her an automatic peace hug – Esther noticing that Amanda's expressionless expression did not change, and that her arms did not unfold to return the hug – and asked, 'Where's Jimmy?'

'Getting a ciggy,' said Amanda.

'This is Esther who you're going to talk to.'

'Lo,' said Amanda automatically. 'Pleased to meet you. Don't know where Jimmy is. Jimmy's my boyfriend and I'm his girlfriend and we go out together.'

'You work together as well, don't you?' said Val.

'Yeh,' said Amanda.

'Tell Esther where you work.'

'I do envelopes for the Campaign of Nukely Disarmerment. Ban the Bomb. Look!' She suddenly unfolded one arm and pulled back the collar of the blouse she was wearing to display, briefly, a small black and white CND badge.

'Why don't you wear it so everybody can see it?' asked Val.

'Cos it's not pretty.' Then she bowed her head and looked up quickly at Val Dove. 'Anyway, you don't,' she said, reasonably.

After some chat like this Esther got bored.

'Skyagree,' she said.

Immediately Amanda responded.

'Wha?' she said.

'Skyagree.'

'We seen him,' said Amanda. 'He came to us. Ssh.' Her voice lowered and she bent down to whisper in Esther's ear. 'Jimmy and I got married like Arthur. Just the same it was.'

'Yeh?' said Esther encouragingly.

'Jimmy said it was the best thing. I had my dress and these shoes and I had a white handbag from my friend. We did it in the chapel building by the Nukely Disarmerment HQ. I got a ring but I don't wear it all the time. Want to see? Look!'

Amanda picked up a brown handbag and delved into it. She talked to herself as she did so, and so deep and earnest was her delving that Esther almost fancied that she might disappear into the handbag and not be seen again. But eventually she surfaced, holding what did indeed look like a wedding ring though worn thin by use and time, the ring of an old, old woman.

'Like it?'

Esther stared at it and reached out a hand as best she could. There was on Amanda's face a look of real pride. One of Esther's fingers reached the ring and, touching it, felt suddenly strange, a strangeness that travelled over her so that the sound of the party faded around the two of them to leave just the ring and Amanda's pride in it.

'Want to wear it?' asked Amanda.

Esther nodded and it was slipped over her forefinger. Her fist clenched to keep it in place and she raised it up to the light. The ring's gold was deep and dull and it had minute scratches and wear marks on it.

'Oh!' said Esther, for it was indeed a thing to be proud of.

'Here's Jimmy,' said Amanda.

He was tall and much better looking than Esther had expected. His hair fair and neat, and his clothes sober. He kissed Amanda in an old-fashioned way on the cheek and said, 'Sorry I was long. Is this Esther?' It was only in his slowness of speech and in the time he took to look at her that Esther guessed he might be a little simple.

'Hello, Esther, pleased to meet you. She's showing you the ring.' He grinned. 'It was my mum's and now it's Mandy's.'

'Skyagree,' said Esther.

'Skallagrigg,' said Amanda, interpreting.

'Yeh,' said Jimmy, 'but it's sposed to be a secret. You!' He thumped Amanda affectionately on the arm.

'Tell her,' said Amanda.

'I will then, now. Right.' And he launched straight into one of the key Skallagrigg stories.

One day Frank took ill, well not really ill. More sad like, depressed. So people said, 'What's wrong?' But he wouldn't say.

One day he got a message to go to see Father James. 'You're not your normal self, Frank, what is it?'

Frank always told the truth to the Father.

'I'm ill for Arthur. He's unhappy again. He hasn't been unhappy for a long time but he is now.'

'What's he unhappy about?'

'Linnie,' says Frank.

'Linnie?' says the Father not knowing that was the name of the girl that Arthur's fallen for, and wants as his girlfriend.

'It's wrong is that,' says Frank who thinks girls is wrong for boys and boys for girls, unless it is in sight of the cross. 'We had an argument when he says for me to get her to talk to him and I says no because in the Bible you said it was wrong and the nurses say it's wrong.'

'What's wrong?'

'Sex,' says Frank eventually.

So that's the truth of it: Arthur wants sex with Linnie and Frank won't help him even talk to her.

'Sex?' says the Father.

'Touching,' says Frank. 'You know like they do at Christmas after church. Hands and that. Mouths all wet. Cock and cunt they call it. I says to Arthur I don't agree with that and Arthur says nature's nature and love has not come his way before and I said *it's* filthy dirty and Linnie's wrong to make him feel that and Arthur shouts at me that Linnie doesn't even know and I says, best that way and *I'm* not going to tell her. Not so long as Arthur does not believe in the cross, and the bread and wine. It wouldn't be wrong if Arthur believed in God and asked forgiveness, or got His permission, I said that wouldn't be wrong Arthur to have cock and cunt after you're blessed by the cross the Bible says so. You could then.'

'Would you like me to talk to him?' said the Father.

'No,' said Frank. 'It's between us two.'

Then the Father said, 'Can you be sure Arthur doesn't believe?'

'Yes,' said Frank. 'Don't I ring the church bell? Don't I hold the brass dish? Don't I pour out the wine into the big grey jug and get the bread from Mrs Rosy? Well don't I do that and don't I know who believes?'

The Father had to agree, discovering later that Linnie was one of the girls who came in because she got a baby when she shouldn't.

A few days later on a cold sunny afternoon the ward door opened and who should come in but Linnie. She was not carrying a bucket and broom or any clobber at all.

'I've come to take Arthur for surgery at three,' says she.

Frank says, 'Why, where's Dilke?'

'Sick,' says Linnie grinning.

Staff nurse got Arthur into his chair. The other boys fell silent. No boy had ever been taken out of the ward by a girl before. It was historic.

Some of the boys started giggling, others started frigging about and Staff had to stop them. Maybe it wasn't such a good idea.

'Go on, scarper,' says Staff once he's got Arthur ready. The boys started chattering with excitement. Not often did one of them go off with a girl like that.

Frank stood up and he said to the lads, 'Arthur says, "Belt up or he won't be pleased." Belt up!' The boys fell silent.

In the silence Linnie, who should have scarpered off with Arthur long before, says 'Does Arthur speak, then?'

'Yes,' said Frank, 'I say he does.'

'Like shit speaks,' says Staff, laughing.

Then Frank looks at Arthur and Arthur looks at him saying nothing but in his eyes was more words than in the Bible and they said, 'I want Linnie to know I love her.'

So Frank goes over to the door and he says to Linnie, 'Arthur speaks special and he talks about you. Arthur thinks the world of you, Linnie, so you take good care of him else you'll answer to me. And all the boys.' And the boys stood silent, staring, and Staff was silent too.

'Come on then, Arthur,' says Linnie softly, and she took him off to the doctor.

That was the beginning of how the Skallagrigg arranged for Arthur to have a girlfriend and after that more women came to help out with the cot and chair boys. Not on the wards mind, which wouldn't be right. But ferrying to and fro. And Linnie took to taking Arthur for walks down by the glen where the ambulant patients had always been allowed alone but not the cot and chairs. They had to be supervised down there. But after the war and the hospital came back there wasn't the staff no more so that's why it was easier.

One day months later there was a knock on the Father's big oak door, Frank's knock. A sliding down the wooden carvings and a thump.

'Erro!' says Frank from outside.

'Come in, Frank,' says the Father.

Frank says, 'Arthur wants to kiss his Linnie now and that but he won't if I don't approve because he says I'm his best friend apart from one other but it's wrong if they're not under the cross first. So Arthur's been ill again worrying. So I thought, "I don't think Christ Jesus would do this to Arthur even if he didn't believe, I don't believe that." Then I remembered about blest are the merciful and decided what to do.'

The Father said, 'What *are* you going to do?'

'That's why I come. Is the church door open in the afternoon?' Frank had never been there in the afternoon as they always had patient activity.

'Yes, Frank.'

'O K then, I said Linnie could meet Arthur under the eyes of the cross and then there will be no wrong.'

'How can you arrange that?'

'We got ways. You're to give a Bible class. That's what we told Dilke and his sort. They're afraid of God.'

'Does Linnie want to?'

Frank's voice changed.

'Yes,' he said. 'But you're not to tell.'

'I never tell, you know that.'

'They're getting wed this afternoon under the cross,' says Frank.

'Wed?' says the Father.

'Where the cross will see,' says Frank.

So the Father went to the church that afternoon to see things were all right and sure enough there was Arthur and Linnie up by the shiny brass rails with Frank. Arthur was in his chair and Linnie in the superintendent's pew. None of them saw the Father.

'So you want to get blest in the sight of God?' shouts Frank like a minister.

'Yes,' says Linnie.

Arthur spoke.

'Yes, Arthur says,' said Frank. Then he was silent.

'Don't know no words,' says Frank, eventually.

'I do,' says Linnie.

'Go on then,' says Frank.

'To love and to hold till ashes to dust, to love my Arthur I will. He's my man.'

Arthur spoke.

'Why?' says Frank.

Arthur spoke again.

'Arthur says he knows the words, he's heard them on the wireless.'

'He can say them then, I said mine,' said Linnie.

'My name is Arthur and I take you Linnie,' says Frank speaking the words after Arthur so Linnie and the cross could hear them, 'to be my girl to have and to hold for better for worse and to look after as best I can and to love always for ever and ever.'

Then Arthur says something and Frank looked a bit shocked. But Arthur insisted.

'You got to kiss him Linnie.'

'I know that,' says Linnie. But she didn't, not for a while.

She just held his hand like it was the best thing in the world.

'You push off for this,' says Linnie.

So Frank said, 'All right,' and went up by the altar and pretended to straighten the golden cloths.

'I love you, Arthur,' says Linnie softly, bending down to him. Then she kissed him. That was the first kiss he ever had from a girl. He waited years for that kiss and it was worth waiting for. Just on the cheek that one was. And Arthur's hands and his legs stopped fretting, and his head went high and proud and he spoke.

'What is it?' asked Linnie lovingly.

Frank came to them.

'Arthur says the Skallagrigg knows. Arthur says the Skallagrigg is pleased. Arthur says . . .' and then Frank stopped and stood up. 'Arthur says the Skallagrigg is here now and the Skallagrigg believes in the bread and the wine, and the cross.'

Then Frank says, 'Now I'm going to say my piece. Arthur's my friend and now you're my friend, Linnie, for always and ever and though it was hard coming here I'm glad I did 'cos now Arthur'll always be happy. You got to learn how he talks, Linnie, and got to learn how she thinks, Arthur, like how we learned each other years ago. And, Arthur, when the Skallagrigg comes for you you're to take Linnie with you now and not go alone because she's with you now and yours to look after like I look after you. And if you don't believe in the cross it don't matter because God's mercy is big and you're forgiven. So now that's everything.'

Then Arthur speaks and Linnie says, 'What's he say?'

Frank says, 'Arthur says thank you to me and and . . . and no, Arthur.'

Linnie giggles and gets up. 'I know what he says really,' and there's a smile on Arthur's face big as Christmas. And Linnie goes up to thin Frank and she puts her arms right round him and kisses him on the cheek.

'That's from Arthur and me,' says she. Thin Frank blushes like a red omnibus and can't think of one word to say, so he takes Arthur's hand and says to Linnie, 'You're to push his chair up the aisle.' So she does, pushing it back up the long aisle while Frank holds Arthur's hand all the way to the porch door. When they get there Linnie says, 'There's one thing and that is we haven't got rings all gold and shining

like real people.' For a moment there's silence but then
Arthur speaks, his voice strong and his hands waving.

'You angry or something Arthur? Did I say wrong?'

Frank listens more and then says, 'Arthur says never you
ever forget not once not never again not in his hearing that
you are a person like any other and better than most and his
only ever girl. Arthur says you don't need no ring to remember that always. You just look where the sun shines
golden and where that is Arthur says that's your ring. Arthur
says whatever comes in the future you will be in his heart
until he dies.'

Amanda and Jimmy grinned at Esther.

'Yer?' said Esther, raising her hand on one finger of which their
ring was still attached.

'She wants to know about us,' said Amanda.

Jimmy said: 'We went to chapel at lunchtime. Mandy had her
white shoes on, these ones. I got my suit. We said to the Skallagrigg
in the silence, "Can we wed?" Mandy said she heard his voice.
Says she saw him, says he was there.'

'He was,' said Amanda, 'I saw him.'

'I think I saw him,' said Jimmy. 'So anyway we got wed. We had
biscuits and coke for the bread and wine and I gave Mandy the
ring.'

A dark shadow fell across them and the music seemed suddenly
intrusive. Amanda and Jimmy grinned nervously.

Andy Moore had come.

'I told her,' said Jimmy.

'Wh . . .?' said Esther. ASK THEM WHERE THE STORY COMES
FROM.

Suddenly it was important for her to know because in knowing
was the resolution of that pattern she detected but could not yet
fully see.

WHERE?

'Esther wants to know where you got the story from.'

'Told me,' said Jimmy, suddenly defensive. 'Didn't steal it.'

'It's all right Jimmy, she's one of us. Where did you hear it?
Sturrick Royal?'

Jimmy nodded.

'That was the long-stay hospital he was in.'

'Wh . . . oo?' said Esther.

Jimmy understood this.

'The boys told me. All the boys knew them. They said lots of stories. First day I was there they played a joke. Said Dilke would get me. Said Dilke lived in electric plugs. Said Rendel was down the boghole and put his hand up for you if you weren't quick.'

Mandy said, 'Dirty.'

'Let's dance,' said Jimmy suddenly amorous.

'Bye, Esther, bye-bye. Pleased to have met you.'

Jimmy formally took her hand and tried to shake it.

'They'll never have a house,' said Andy Moore when they were gone, 'and they'll probably never get married. Did she show you her ring?' He laughed. 'The worst kept secret in Manchester. I've been talking to your grandmother who doesn't like me. She's got a lot to learn.' His mouth was a sneer and yet Esther was glad she was alone with him. She felt excited with him, important and she was fascinated by his hands and his mouth.

He had on a bright red silk shirt and a yellow neckerchief. His hair was brushed, but Esther saw his nails were dirty. He came nearer.

'I want you to help out with HLF,' he said, 'that's what I said to your grandmother. You can form a cell at your school and raise money. We're saving to buy a videocamera so we can make our own films. We're . . .'

But Esther did not take in much more. Time had passed and she was tired. She sensed that her grandmother, who was across the room talking to a woman in grey, was tired too.

'There's other people can tell you stories, but all in good time. You get HLF going first . . .' He grinned maliciously.

Then he came nearer and his hand was on her arm. His eyes were strange and flicked over her body and her dress. She felt exposed, but it was not unpleasant.

'Peace,' he said, and he leaned forward so that his male smell overwhelmed her and she felt the rough touch of his cheek on hers and then his mouth on hers. And his hand, between them, hidden from sight, tightening on her thigh and slid in the darkness between them and touched her pants through her skirt, as if by mistake. Just for an instant.

'Peace!' he said pulling back with an innocent smile.

Margaret came quickly.

'I think it's time we went now, Esther, the car will soon be here.'

'Yeh,' said Esther. 'Yeh, Nana.' And Nana saw that Andy Moore's kiss was fire on Esther's face; but she could not know that his touch was strange fire on her body too.

THIRTY-EIGHT

The Sturrick Fest, at the beginning of 1982, was a unique celebration by patients of the closing down and demolition of one of the largest of the British Victorian sub-normality hospitals whose creation had done so much to isolate the mentally ill, the physically handicapped and sometimes the merely socially deviant from the community which, as a result, was made to misunderstand and fear them.

Its special interest for us is that it gave Esther Marquand an opportunity to collect Skallagrigg stories from a key source-hospital, and the experience of touring the site before its demolition gave her an insight into what such a hospital could be like. Sturrick was to be the basis for Esther's creation of the Level One maze in 'Skallagrigg'.

The Sturrick Royal Hospital, which in the 1970s came under the control of the North Central Regional Health Authority, was progressively phased out between 1971 and 1982. No new patients were accepted, younger ones were put back into the community or into smaller hospitals, while the older ones, the institutionalized, the ones to whom Sturrick's grim walls and cavernous damp corridors had become their only home, waited. Some died in those years of decline, some survived, feeling the dereliction close in on them. For even the most hopeless feel the decay of their home, however tragic that home may be; even the dumbest begin to despair; even the humblest and most meek can weep.

But the decline had begun decades earlier with the nursery and kitchen gardens, which in the early part of the century were fully working using patient-labour effectively. These began to die in the 1940s, and by 1980 were overgrown and broken down, the yellow walls rotten with ragwort and valerian.

Then the great laundry rooms, once one of the hubs of the place, where ambulant patients had had jobs to do in conditions of cold

and damp and heat and steam beyond belief; but where they had
had some kind of life and sometimes found a moment's love in
among the harsh towels and sheets which had seen God knows
what horrors of human pain and suffering. All washed, steamed,
starched, dried, ironed and put away, once a week. Yes, sometimes
in the great laundry cupboards where those same sheets were
stacked neat and dry (for the time being), patients saw gentler
things, and more violently loving things on the floor among the
calender machines. One dilke and one patient, Miranda, lived their
whole love by that great machine on which, even at the end, their
names were still scratched: 'Miranda loves Ted.' In 1968 the
laundry washed, ironed and sent out its last sheets and pillow
cases and was closed for ever. It had been a hell and yet Miranda
still sometimes came to stare through its grimy windows at the
floor where she had lain and he had taken her and given her
ecstasy. Then one day an old bus came and she was driven away
for ever.

Soon after that the boiler, which had been the functional heart
of the hospital since its creation – the boiler that had once exploded
and killed two patients; the boiler whose deep sound was all the
children heard outside for decades; the boiler against which the
dilkes had been known to push a patient to torture him and to tell
him he would be thrust inside – the boiler failed.

It was replaced by a smaller, new one, white-sided and without
character, which was inadequate for the whole hospital, but no
one cared any more since the place was being phased out. That
was the moment that whole sections of the place were emptied of
furniture and people and sealed off with galvanized locks, leaving
their wards and corridors to the cold and damp: the western corridors, whose brickwork had not been decorated since 1937; the
old gym where there were dances before the war (the First World
War), the upper two floors of the north wing, from whose windows
once upon a time young girls looked – their crime their mar-
riageless pregnancy, their fate sometimes to stay for ever, their
child never theirs, their shame and their loss their madness, their
condition. Those floors were closed, and the light faded on the
names those girls, clinging on to the little they had to call their
own, had written on the walls: Beth, Elizabeth, Margret, F. Horton,
Linnie, Maud; and the names of the children they never knew,

taken from them in the infirmary and passed to other better, cleaner, different arms: Bessie, Jimmy, Baby, Joy.

The infirmary, the glory of the hospital at its opening in 1863, which had even had its own operating theatre for a time, closed but for one single room in which, after 1958, the nurse sat, and after 1967 sat only sometimes. All gone, the valuable things stripped, the individual injuries long forgotten, the fear and the deaths unrecorded, but the grim feel and sense of them still present in the walls.

By 1976 the number of patients had dropped from the 1,784 the Royal had had at its peak at the turn of the century, to 232, of whom two-thirds were female.

But one of those males was Harry Barr, the man whose film, scripted by Andy Moore, Esther Marquand had seen. Harry had written a book, twenty pages long, and it took him seven years. He typed it with his foot and a Staff, white-coated and gentle-faced, watched over him and encouraged him.

The book was Harry's life.

When it was done Harry's friend, who taught him all he knew, sent it to a charity for spastics and they published it at two shillings and sixpence. It was that book that Andy Moore came across and wanted to film. That project brought him to Sturrick, and to the realization that this great and terrible place still contained within its walls much, if not all, that was worst and most terrible of the great sub-normality hospitals. Decayed now, locked away, almost forgotten except in the memories of a few patients who would never forget.

Andy Moore, on the pretext of looking for the right places in the hospital to film Harry's life, had persuaded the authorities to let him explore the buildings from cellar to attic, from west wing to northern stairs. They did not go with him, they had other things to do. They themselves had never been. It was past, they were new and young, they had better things to do.

So he went with Mr Thomas Young, who had started at Sturrick after the First World War as a gardener and had finished fifty-four years later as a handyman and the only person who knew the whole hospital.

He took Andy Moore all over, with a young girl helper who did not say much but insisted on pulling the wheelchair up stairs and down stairs which had not been passed by in years. Mr Moore had a camera and no one said he wasn't to take photographs. No one *said*.

Andy Moore recorded Tom Young as he spoke in his slow way of men, urinals with no walls: 'You did it in public and got hosed up the arse.'

Of the thin rope still tied to a metal bedstead in B4 which had been used to tie down a patient whose name and life was long forgotten.

Of the iron balustrade on the top of the south block where the dilkes had chased a man and he had jumped and he, Tom Young, had covered the head but couldn't stop the blood running out red on the concrete. 'Their blood was red like mine, and that shook me, I can tell you.' Andy Moore took a photograph of that balustrade.

Of the airing courts with the bars, which was all the outside some of those 'poor souls' ever saw.

Of the archive book in the cellar lying in dust, gnawed by rats, beneath shelves, racks, rows, of rooms and corridors, lightless now, where the files were. Files of lives most of which had been quite wasted. Of Punishment Books, a legal necessity, which showed that on 8 June 1926, Tommy Chakin was stopped cigarettes for a month for going out of grounds; and that on 12 January 1929 Emily Pruly of W2 was confined to bed for eight days for swearing and striking a dilke, after persistent warnings over disobedience. Emily Pruly who in 1908, then fourteen and looking it perhaps, had given herself not knowing what she did to a builder's man in Agate Street, Manchester, and by that deed, her parents being shocked, confined herself to hell. She died of tuberculosis in 1937, aged forty-three, and her child then aged twenty-nine never knew. Of those forgotten entries Andy Moore took photographs.

Of the name of girls like Emily Pruly scratched on the walls. Of the girls themselves. The dilkes had had favours for favours, favours for nowt. And Mr Young wasn't saying he was perfect where that was concerned, with a male laugh, but now he regretted it and saw it was wrong.

As Andy took these photographs he had an idea beyond just exhibiting them. It was this: to celebrate the closing of this place and all it stood for when the last patients left. Andy Moore would have a fest, and he would ask as many people as possible, and he would show them what their fathers and grandfathers had done; and he would film that celebration and hope what he filmed would be seen.

That was his dream and that is what he persuaded the new socialist authorities responsible for Sturrick to let him do, not telling them, or anyone, his real intent, which was to make a brief anarchy of Sturrick as it had made an anarchy for so long in so many lives. And to film the result.

The authorities, who were even persuaded by Andy Moore into giving a grant towards this 'fest', naturally assumed that just a few of the better-behaved token patients would come, and some of the old staff and nothing much would happen except a few drinks and valedictory speeches.

But Mr Moore's guest list was not sanitized.

He sent the specially printed embossed and official-looking invitation card, based on one printed for the Medical Superintendent of Sturrick Royal Hospital's Coronation Ball, 1907 (found lying in the dampness of the cellars), to the strangest of people.

To Jane Pruly, seventy-two, sister of ex-patient Emily, living in a council-run home in Manchester.

To Richard Strachen, sixty-six, crippled street melodeon player, once resident at Sturrick.

To Jeremy Stone, former nurse at the hospital, author of an internal report condemning violence by older dilkes in wards B2, B4, and W and itemizing violent incidents, sacked by the hospital in 1961.

To Edward Hayes and Elizabeth Hayes née Marker, both named in the Stone report as guilty of wet towelling patients (nearly strangling them without making a mark) and now married and working together in Liverpool in charge of a council-run home for young offenders.

He sent ten to Harry Barr with the suggestion that he send nine of them on to friends.

To Chrissie Lawrence, mental age three, aged forty-seven, blind, whose first memories were of a boiler's roar and the clink of coal on metal, who screamed for ten years until someone discovered she was only comfortable on her right side and horizontal, marked 'Personal'.

To Miranda Smith, seventy-eight.

To Ted James who was once in charge of the hospital laundry.

To one after another he sent them.

And to some who had no connection with the hospital at all but who he felt should come: to Lorna Darrell, social services correspondent of the *Guardian*, to John Snow, deputy director of the Spastics Society; to Richard Wainwright, controller of Mencap. And others like them.

And to certain young people who might once have been committed for life to a Sturrick, but who now, in marginally better times, would not unless they were unlucky enough to be born in one of the few remaining backward area health authorities . . . to them he sent invitations. For he believed that these handicapped youngsters should be shown the past for one day since they or their children would have finally to raise the battle flag of their own handicap and wrest power from the able-bodied, as through the ages the weak have always had to wrest power from the strong.

It was in this spirit that he sent an invitation to Esther, enclosing with it another for a 'friend' to come, of her own choosing, a power for action from which the lives of others in the future might benefit.

So Esther, Tom and Marion came to Sturrick that weekend with the special instructions that all visitors received; accommodation would be provided at the hospital so that guests would witness the first bulldozer move in on the hospital buildings to begin its final destruction.

Esther toured the old hospital and saw its horrors – things she had seen before in the black and white pictures that formed the exhibition Andy Moore had mounted at Netherton School. She saw them in silence with Marion and Tom, and afterwards joined the many people who had come to see that film Andy had made about Harry Barr.

Just before its showing, when only a spotlight remained on the screen of the great dance room in which the film was shown, a side door opened and a man in an old-fashioned canvas and spoke-wheeled wheelchair was pushed in: Harry Barr.

He was pushed to the front and turned full into the light to face the audience.

'Mahgg narrghm ssssh Haghhbrh,' he said incomprehensibly.
'Nnn ahhm ggoo . . .' he continued, gulping as if he was swallowing
himself, his head thrust forward and sideways, spittle on his chin.
His arm waved up, his hand catching the light and forming a
grotesque and mutant form of life in shadow on the screen. He
laughed. And in the silence that followed all of them there, perhaps
one hundred and twenty people, heard Tom say to Esther Marquand, 'He's showing a film, Amh. He is. He says.'

Harry's head turned jerkily round towards where Tom was,
somewhere halfway back.

'Yeahhh!' he said. 'Wazhyrnamh?'

'Toh,' said Esther who didn't care that people were there,
'*Toh!*'

'Tom,' said Marion.

'Yes,' said Tom. 'My name's Tom.'

Harry Barr grinned, and the warmth of it cut through the nervous atmosphere of that room.

Harry Barr shouted loudly, his whole body lifting from the chair
and the light went out. The projector whirred and the film of
Harry's life, the one Esther had already seen, and filmed in Sturrick
in those very places that Andy Moore's exhibition had taken the
audience to earlier in the evening, began. The audience was silent
as the dead.

When the film was over the french windows were opened up
and they all trooped out on to the terrace, and from there down
on to the lawn, the wheelchairs pushed down the ramps already
in place. A table lit by candles in jars had wine and beer upon
it.

A spotlight shone suddenly on the terrace and they saw that
Andy Moore in his wheelchair had come out. He held a piece of
paper in his hands, and made a brief speech into a microphone.
Above and behind him the dark buildings of the dead hospital
were ranked. He waved briefly back at them and then said, 'You
have come to witness the end of an institution which has been
home to five generations of the mentally ill, the handicapped, and
the socially deviant. For them, most innocent, most quite defenceless, it has been both home and place of punishment.

'For some it was a hell, for some it was the cause of their illness;
for only a very, very few was it ever a place of sanctuary.

'Within this place, whose corridors you have walked and some of whose sights you have seen, lives of crushing impoverishment have been led by both residents and staff.

'I want now to read out the names of some of the former residents and staff, now dead, who for one reason or another are remembered. I am grateful to Harry Barr for most of these names.'

He spoke them slowly, with a pause between each one as if they were the roll-call of a village's lost men in one of the world wars. Their names, his voice seemed to say, liveth for ever more:

> Alda Tichener, resident 1883–1944, loved.
> Herbert Shedder, resident 1901–1942, a kind man.
> Catharine Dray, laundress in the twenties, much loved.
> Peter Goodrum, resident, 1928–1933, died of dilke violence.
> Stephen Juxon, resident, died 1957.
> Francis Cabourne, staff nurse, loved.
> Archy Munday, Harry's helper and friend. Died 1961.
> Diana Church, matron, feared.
> Joseph Paton, chief staff nurse in twenties, hated.

When the brief list was complete Andy Moore paused for a long time. The crowd stared at the former inmates, patient and dilke alike, and the inmates stared back. It was an ending, and finally there was nothing to say.

Esther could hardly bear the intensity of the silence and eventually stared above Andy at the black angled silhouettes of the massive buildings set now against a night sky in which stars were beginning to appear.

Eventually Marion leaned down and gave Esther a sip of wine. 'To warm you up,' she whispered. The red wine seemed like fire on her lips and down her throat as she stared, the sound of those few names of men and women loved and feared now seeming to die away only slowly around this place where they had lived and mostly died.

Then Andy Moore continued: 'I do not think it is enough for us today to explain the past in terms of society's ignorance then, and to be kind about what they did. Nor is it enough to vent our anger on the administrators and staff at places like this now. They too were victims of a system our society created and imposed in the past and which, through continuing ignorance, fear and wrong priority, we – *we* – still maintain today.

'But the old attitudes are weakening before a force which will ultimately be as strong as any just revolution of the past. That force is the collective might of those very same outsiders who once so meekly allowed themselves to be locked in. Theirs is a faltering voice, uncertain and often weak; vulnerable and slurred, but still a voice that says "Listen, for we will be heard."

'It is an angry voice, angry with you who are not outsiders, you who are able-bodied, you who are mentally "normal", whatever *that* may mean . . .' Andy Moore's voice was getting stronger and more passionate, and Esther felt stirred and excited. He was speaking for her, for people like *her* and she wanted to shout out, YES YES.

'That voice has only just found itself, and like a child it shouts abuse at its parents and its parents respond with abuse, or with weakness. That voice will deepen, that voice will mature and finally that voice will be an adult's, and expect an adult's in reply.

'But for tonight and tomorrow, here, that voice can be the child's. For we are celebrating the end of Sturrick, and our shouts of joy are loud because they are not just for ourselves, but for those thousands who were once here and whose voices are now gone, whose shouts died in despair within Sturrick's harsh walls. Some, just a few – Harry Barr, Chrissie Lawrence, Dudley Stocks – survived and are here with us. Honour them. Others are here too who, had they been born earlier, in the decades soon after Sturrick was built, might easily have found themselves here, locked away for the full course of their unnatural lives: Ruan Jones, Lesley Daize, Esther Marquand . . .'

Esther lowered her head in the darkness imagining that everybody was looking at her. She, here! Oh, please God, she had not thought of that.

Andy Moore jutted his head forward so that as it lowered it seemed almost as if all his wheelchair held was a wild dark head with eyes that stared. In that long pause she saw a small light on the roof of the distant north block, a stuttering, moving light which bobbed up and down, disappearing and then reappearing; then a man's silhouette.

Andy Moore continued, his voice weary: 'We will shout out now

and we will celebrate the end of this place.' He paused again and
Esther's gaze, tired from the strain of trying to catch that light high
up on the distant roof, turned back to him. He stared and then
slowly began to raise his arms as he shouted, 'We must celebrate!'

And as he shouted it out there was a sudden flare of yellow
light, a whoosh of distant sound, as a rocket rose from the roof and
with a thunderous bang burst out into a bright white expanding
ball of stars, hanging in the sky and enhancing the silhouette of
the building.

Then Esther felt the strangest of excitements, the sense that she
was seeing a light towards her future, and that future lay in some
way with the Skallagrigg, whose name formed upon her lips.
Another rocket and another, and then yet one more roared up
massively into the sky and broke into a hundred thousand cas-
cading stars of coloured light, the bangs of their explosions echoing
and re-echoing in the buildings.

High high upon the roof of the north block the figures of the two
men setting off these pyrotechnics darted back and forth with
tapers of light on rods in their hands.

'OOO!' said the crowd and then a long 'AAAH!' as another
rocket exploded into light.

To Esther it was the most dramatically beautiful thing she had
ever seen, enhanced by a gentle breeze which wafted the acrid
smell of smoke to them all. The shivery cold seemed only to en-
hance the experience, with Tom standing by her side, head
upturned, and whispering his own Ooohs! and Aaahs! though not
quite in time with the rest of the crowd.

The display was followed by the lighting of the huge bonfire
built by the men who had already begun the demolition and who
stood around carefully tending it, their faces screwed up against
the heat as, with long metal poles, they pushed back pieces of
timber and old rolls of linoleum into the flames. Doors of oak, brass
fitments, a wooden fireplace, chairs and tables . . . the unwanted
furniture of a dead institution.

The guests gathered in a crowd around the fire, someone dis-
tributed sparklers and Tom took two for Esther, holding one to her
fingers as he lit it from Marion's and then, ever careful of her
safety, clasping his hand to hers and hers to it as he waved it
around her head and the sparkler burnt down its bright length.

Music from somewhere then, and wine, more wine, and the heat from the fire glowing in the benighted cheeks of the visitors, making them relaxed and jovial, jovial and laughing, laughing and joking, joking and shouting, 'Down with Sturrick! Down with Sturrick!' as a band struck up with melodeons and a recorder, and an impromptu dance began round the fire.

Esther was whirled and twirled, and Tom whirled from her and her head was wild in the night, the hands at her chair unknown and she was laughing and in her own way shouting out the celebration that this place was dead. Long live the bonfire! Another rocket shot high, high above them, and another and a series of sharp cracks one after another, quick as a flash in the night. And Esther had more wine to drink, then more.

Faces, hands, legs dancing. Val Dove grinning nearby, then gone into the flames and shadows and flaming light. Smoke and burning ash powered up into the darkness of the sky. Faces. A face was near her, male and grinning, the fire sending orange shoots high either side of it.

'Hello!' and someone was kissing her suddenly out of the fiery darkness. Shaken, the wet of his mouth on her chin, she was alone for a moment, though not isolated. Music, people, dancers, wine, the rising shoots of flame gyring high above with sparks and ash. Esther looked around her. There was Andy Moore, the wheel spokes of his chair wildly reflecting firelight, his eyes dark on her and his wide mouth smiling. It was carnival.

'Miss Marquand!' he said. He brought his chair alongside hers, facing her. His hands were on her legs, against her thin girlish thigh and then rasping on her cheek.

He kissed her slowly on the mouth, and she did not care, her mouth slow and comfortable to his before it felt to her that she was being overwhelmed. She could smell him, a smell just as she remembered: powerful and male. His hand was over her lap.

'It's a night to remember,' he said.

She pulled away, his caress and his kiss too suddenly over for her to react fully to them with anything but retreat. Yet she liked the feel of his touch, and she did not know why.

'Yeh!' she said and then, uncertain what else to do and suddenly embarrassed, she looked to the night sky as yet another rocket zoomed upwards.

'You've got good skin, soft as a baby's,' he said to her.

She felt the heat of his breath, and his hand lingering between her thighs in the darkness, as if accidentally. She was suddenly afraid, yet when his hand left her she felt deserted. She saw Tom standing still in the mêlée, watching. Then with a laugh Andy was turning away towards another group and Marion was coming over to her.

'Did he kiss you!?' she exclaimed. 'Someone kissed *me*. Men!'

Esther nodded and giggled, her eyes shining in the dark.

'I won't leave you again. Where's Tom?'

Esther said nothing. Tom made her feel guilty. But she did not want to. She wanted to go on feeling wild. She raised her hand to her mouth. She wanted more wine.

'No, Esther, you've had enough!'

'Nah!'

'Yes you have!' laughed Marion.

Now Esther was miserable, thwarted. She *wanted* more wine.

Tom was suddenly there, taking the handles of Esther's chair.

'Going now,' he said to Marion. It was an order.

'Nah,' said Esther, but weakly.

'C'mon,' said Tom. 'Going to bed.' He did not look at the bonfire or the people or the buildings, not any more; nor did he stop to watch another rocket rise into the sky. He wanted to leave, and he was taking his Esther with him. He sensed that she had had enough.

'*C'mon!*' said Tim.

And Marion followed all the way round the old buildings to the hostel dormitories and put Esther to bed.

The following morning, promptly at nine-thirty, a small group of the guests from the night before reassembled by the still smouldering bonfire to watch, from a safe distance, the beginning of the structural demolition of Sturrick Royal Hospital.

There were photographers and reporters there as well because, to make the point in the most dramatic way possible, it had been decided to start with the demolition of the chimney which for nearly a century had been a landmark to the south of Manchester.

Several of the former patients sat in chairs or stood about uneasily, staring for the most part towards the chimney to which, most seemed to understand, something was about to happen.

It stood stark against the morning sky, and men wearing blue boiler suits and protective helmets conferred beneath it. They carried walkie-talkies. Eventually only one remained at the chimney's base, the rest backing away to a point out of sight of the watchers.

The last one disappeared inside the old boiler room. A silence fell. He came out, looked briefly up at the chimney and then walked away from it.

All was silent then but for the light patter of rain on the cagoules worn by the wheelchair watchers. Then there was a muffled explosion, and a puff of brick dust came out from the base of the chimney, which rocked for a moment, and then slowly, so slowly, toppled to the left, collapsing in on itself as it did so, down, down and down with a roar, its final crash lost in a cloud of brick dust.

There was a sporadic round of applause and somewhere near a bulldozer's engine started up as, from out of their safe lair, the demolition men emerged and approached the remains of the fallen chimney whose collapse had left the remaining buildings stark and bereft.

One of the old patients started to cry. This former hell had been his home. Another cuddled him.

Esther stared at them, and then back at the buildings, and then round about her. There was rain on her face and she seemed older. An innocence had gone for ever from her grey eyes.

THIRTY-NINE

Now Esther's great work began as she collected more stories in Manchester, and began to see their interconnections and their variations. Many were in the voice of Frank, some of James Freeman, the Father, and a few of Arthur. None was in the voice of the Skallagrigg, for he was mighty in the minds of the handicapped who knew of him and his comings, and his voice was not to be ordained by men.

The stories or fragments she heard she entered into her book, careful to list where she had heard them, and to whom they should be attributed. Where she could she listed the institutions or towns where her informant had been, suspecting that the answer to the pattern she sought might be linked with places where the stories were most told.

In later editions of *Stories* the various versions were often amalgamated into one. The following comes principally from a version by John Madgett, formerly of Sturrick Royal, which she heard in Manchester during the Sturrick Fest . . .

One day in the glen, Linnie says to Arthur, 'These walks you take me on is good, the best thing I ever had.'

Arthur says, 'Look up. Look up, Linnie, not at the ground.'

Linnie's getting to know her Arthur and that had to be done quick 'cos they didn't have much time for their love. Spastics are given plenty of time for nothing, but no time for the things they care about.

Linnie looked up where Arthur looked and pointed, his head stretched right back and his hands jerking and his mouth all about. She could tell he was happy from his eyes. She could tell where he was looking: right into the green leaves of the tree glimmering against the sky singing with colour.

'Look!' shouts Arthur at his girl.

Linnie stops the chair, puts the brakes on, goes on ahead and does what her man says, she looks. Up and up she looks so she totters about and nearly falls over! But she don't care does Linnie because she's seeing something for the first time. It's the great world up in the tree, which she'd never seen before. If that was all Arthur ever done for her it was enough to make her love him.

Linnie, says Arthur in a noise that isn't 'Linnie'. But since they got wed by the cross she's getting to know the meanings of his voice. So she looks up again.

He doesn't though! He's looking at her looking up and thinking to himself that she's a different beauty than the sky caught in a tree but just as good. He wants to touch her and nobody to see, and no Staff watching, not just here. Staff's having a ciggy and a screw with Wim.

So Linnie comes to him and says, 'Yes, Arthur?' and she's not shy, not Linnie, not with Arthur. Her face is smiling with the world she's seen and Arthur can almost smell the goodness of her body. She took his hand and held it to her sex parts.

'You can, Arthur, only you now.' And she kisses him, doesn't she. She doesn't mind his cuts from the Staff shaving. She knows if he could shave himself there never would be cuts, not one. He's that good in his heart where the real him is. She runs her hand on his face where she's kissed him and that is more beautiful to him than anything he knows. Arthur speaks. He's trying to say he loves her, and that he's happy as he's ever been.

'I know you do,' says Linnie, 'I know you are. You're my beau.'

'Skyagree,' says Arthur.

'Why do you always say him?' says Linnie grinning.

'Me,' says Arthur in his way.

'You?' says Linnie cuddling his face to her breasts.

'Skyagree,' says Arthur breathlessly, and grinning.

'I'll love both of you then,' says Linnie, the world in the tree above (where the leaves is green against a sky as blue as all the colours in the rainbow) looking down on them.

Arthur's suddenly still, deathly still, and he's staring at her, through her, as if there's a ghost up there in that world he's made her see.

Arthur's gentle eyes are full of tears. Arthur's cheek is wet as he speaks beyond her, to the Skallagrigg, and Linnie

knows he speaks with love. Love beyond even their new
love. Arthur wants the Skallagrigg to see his Linnie. Arthur's
proud of her and wants to share. Arthur's tears are clear,
clear as he says, 'Look!' and up there, if only she knew how
to see, is the Skallagrigg.

Linnie says, 'Arthur, you're the best there is and you will
always be my beau.'

Arthur grins like the boy he once was, proud to have a girl
to call his own.

They're in the glen and everybody knows what happens
there. Dilke does it there regular, more than anyone else.
Only he takes them and gives them bruises and favours for
favours. Linnie leaves Arthur and looks out for Staff. Staff's
buggered off proper hasn't he with that Wim who does it
with anyone. Cock and cunt down in the grass.

The sun is hot on Arthur's face and he's getting hard just
remembering Linnie's breasts soft in his face, let alone seeing
her looking out for Staff up there by the tree.

'You're my man,' says Linnie coming back and calm as
anything she pushes Arthur's wheelchair down down into
the long grass and bushes of the glen where nobody sees
'cos nobody is going to look, not for a while. And she's got
a look in her eyes and her hands are at Arthur's flies and
then at the canvas straps that hold him in the chair.

Arthur's body's all over the place and his breathing's gasps
as she lays him gently on the grass and stares down at him
and he up her frock to her legs and her brown stocking tops
and her flesh he wants and at the elastic of her knickers
where he wants the whole of him to be.

She pulls her dress up does his Linnie and lies down with
her legs on his weak ones and her thigh against his hard
cock.

She says, 'Arthur, you're my beau aren't you?' and he
feels pride like never before, and wants her. She touches
him long and gentle like the swaying grass above them and
his desire is a pain in his cock.

'Arthur, is this your first time?'

Arthur isn't sure of that. He thinks so. 'Yeh,' he says.
Linnie. He's filled with love and desire, like it should be.
Arthur's blest with good things.

Linnie wraps him in her arms and then undoes his trousers
more.

She pulls his hand to her sex parts but like that his arm

isn't straight enough. She takes her arms from him and she pulls her knickers off, her thighs coming up so he sees them.

'Do you want to see?' she asks. Linnie knows what he wants. She pulls away and turns to him so he can see his first and only ever woman so he never forgets. Soft, dark, a dream place and she comes up so his hand's on her and she says, 'You're a big man, Arthur, and you're mine.'

Then she takes him in her arms and rolls him on to her and she helps him until he's there where he's been allowed to look, only now he can feel it, that dark softness, and his hand's caught against her suspender and she has to free him so that at last he goes into her and she slides under him and closer and she says, 'Arthur, you're a man,' and he is a man, because her eyes are closed and she feels his love inside her deep and deep and he's more man, more loving man, than all the men she's ever known. The power of her Arthur's love makes them others seem like boys. And Arthur's sounds now are pure joy, innocent and strong, as her legs open and her thighs come up and they deepen into each other for the end that never ends if it's done in love.

'I love you,' says Linnie then, as Arthur is all inside her and she is overwhelmed and holding him in her and over her.

All that year they went to the glen and Linnie helped Arthur be a man and Arthur showed Linnie she could be loved as a woman; and above them in the trees was the big world beyond the hospital where (Arthur made Linnie slowly understand) the Skallagrigg his friend, more than his friend, was, and one day that Skallagrigg would come for him at last and take him back where he belonged.

Says Linnie one day after lying in the grass, 'I know letters A B C D E,' and Arthur whispers, 'Skyagree,' and Linnie has her hand on him gentle like they do after and says, 'An S and a K and a and a and a . . .' 'cos she can't spell that.

Then Arthur teaches her and she does learn slowly to spell that long word with an S and a K and an A and an L and an L and an A and a G and an R and an I and a G. Linnie learns that good.

'I'll remember that till I die,' says she, 'as it's what you always say. What is it, Arthur? Skallagrigg?'

Then Arthur opens his mouth and looks at her, deep in her eyes, and she knows whatever it is he's lost it and wants it back. He starts crying, and Linnie holds him close in her arms like a baby.

'There now, Arthur, I got you crying. If I could I would get it back for you.'

Arthur shakes his head. 'Nah!' he says.

'But Frank says the Skallagrigg is coming.'

'Yeh!' says Arthur.

Linnie's silent at that since it don't make sense.

'Know what?' says Linnie after a bit. 'One fine day I'll give you a ring to wear all gold like the sun 'cos I love you, I do.'

This story, first told to Esther in Manchester in a much more innocent version (the lovers held hands and had no more than a kiss), was one of the most recurring of the Skallagrigg myths: that he was there, watching, guarding, and that Arthur desired to share with his god the Skallagrigg the good things that happened.

Sometimes the Skallagrigg miraculously intervenes and helps Arthur to achieve something he desires. As in the story Esther heard from another long-term Sturrick patient:

The trips came with Mrs — don't know. She brought them. Those two coaches came up the road and you could see them shiny red and white and polished. What a palaver getting the boys all on!

But first year Arthur couldn't go 'cos of Dilke. So Frank wasn't going but Arthur says you go for me, and Frank says, 'Yes, Arthur,' and got him some rock. Next year Dilke says Arthur's been misbehaving and boys who do that don't go. Five of them weren't allowed and they been looking forward to it all year. Dilke said, 'Your fault and you can come and watch and see what you're missing.' Dilke stayed behind, didn't he, and said he'd give them what for for ruining his day.

Third year Arthur got a cold. He was nervous and Doctor said it was all right but Dilke said best not. He didn't go.

Fourth year Arthur says 'Skallagrigg, I want to go this year and you make it right.'

So Dilke got ill and the boys knew the Skallagrigg did that. So this time Arthur was put on the bus.

He sits there, the plastic and leather all smelling new and Frank watching over him and Norman behind and a Staff making them sing. They was happy, though, so that was all right.

Then Arthur stares and stares out and Frank says, 'What's wrong Arthur, don't fret.'

Arthur spoke and he was nervous.

Frank says, 'Arthur's to move to the other side of the coach.'

'Why?' says the boy sitting there.

'Don't know,' says Frank. 'But Arthur says.'

The boys always did as Arthur asked. He was their boss. So Norman moved him.

Arthur stares out of the window and Frank holds his hand.

'Don't fret,' says Frank.

Arthur's staring at the fields and watching the wooden fences go by. One hour, one hour and a half. Suddenly Arthur shouts out and is excited and Frank stands up and says, 'Stop this bloody coach, Arthur is sick.'

Staff tells him to fuck off.

Arthur shouts more as he stares out at the big fields beyond the wooden fence with the long grass and the poppies he likes and he's crying. Then he says, 'Skyagree'. That's Skallagrigg of course.

Frank relaxes.

'Arthur's telling the Skallagrigg to stop the coach,' says Frank to the boys. They grin.

And the coach stops there and then, dead. By a field by a wood with a wooden fence.

Staff says to the driver, 'What's wrong?' and the driver says, 'Don't know.'

So while he's seeing to it Frank says, 'Can Arthur come out he's sick.'

'Oh all right,' says Staff.

So Norman carries Arthur out and takes him over the grass to the wooden fence and Frank goes along and Arthur speaks.

'Put him on the grass,' says Frank.

Arthur is on the grass and he stares through that fence. He speaks again.

'OK,' says Frank. 'He's seen what he wanted. He'll be all right.' Arthur grins.

Norman carries Arthur back to the coach and they get in.

'We're going to be here all day,' says Staff.

Driver says, 'I don't know I'm sure.' He sits back in his seat and tries the key. That gleaming coach came to life once more and the boys gave a cheer.

'Skallagrigg did that,' said one or two.

'Bloody mystery,' says the driver.

'Get on with it then,' says Staff.

'Skyagree,' whispers Arthur to Frank, looking out over the field, over the top of the wooden fence to where the grass was long and swayed in the wind and there were poppies red and bent,

'Will he come then, the Skalg?' asks Frank. 'One day?'

Arthur looks at him and the coach starts off down that road, past the field and into the shade of the wood.

Arthur looks across the coach and out of the far window and says nothing.

While Frank thinks, his hand holds Arthur's. 'He *will* come one day, Arthur, don't fret.'

Arthur stares and eventually he speaks.

'Arthur says,' says Frank, 'that the Skalg will come and he go over the fence into the grass.'

Frank thinks about that and then asks, 'Did you ever walk, Arthur? Properly like Dilke?'

Arthur's head turns to his friend Frank and his eyes looked at Frank and then away like he wasn't there. There was that silence around Arthur which always scared Frank. Even Norman turned to look.

'Yeh,' replied Arthur. YEH YEH YEH and he suddenly giggled; like a boy he sounded. Like a young boy he looked. For that moment all the long years in cot and chair was gone right off his face.

Esther Marquand came back from Manchester with several stories like this to write up and other shorter ones, as well as an account of the closing of the Sturrick Royal.

Andy Moore said she could have others but she would have to agree to start a cell of the Handicapped Liberation Front at Netherton.

'Do you understand?' said Andy at the goodbye. His voice was harsh and direct and she was in awe of it, and of him.

She nodded.

He brought his chair round beside hers and, with a quick look first towards Marion, he gave Esther a peace hug which ended with a rasping kiss, and that hand, firm and sure, on her shoulder, sliding down to her small breast where it lingered for a moment.

She blushed with slight embarrassment, but smiled with guilty pleasure.

'Peace,' he said.

'Pah!' she managed, looking round immediately towards Marion. She felt proud that he paid attention to her and saw nothing of his deformity, his grotesqueness or the calculated sensuality behind the kisses.

He turned, and went to say goodbye to others, before she had left.

Netherton's HLF cell was formed at a meeting convened by Esther two weeks later at the start of the new term. Esther asked permission of the headmaster who, though marginally concerned by the aggressiveness of the name 'Handicapped Liberation Front', gave it his blessing and a grant of ten pounds for stationery from a special activity fund the school governors had.

The first meeting was announced on the school's club notice-board and Esther made sure that Graham Downer, Betty Shaw and a couple of other friends attended, with Graham agreeing to take the chair at the meeting. She wrote out HLF's 'Aims and Objectives', borrowed largely from material Andy Moore had sent her, and told Graham that although no officers were to be elected, a 'People's Secretary' would be appointed and a 'People's Chair-person', subject to a small yellow HLF cell rule book with 39 Articles. Andy Moore's revolution was derivative not only of communism, but of protestantism as well.

In the event eight people attended the meeting, one of whom was Ronnie Warburton. His presence was the main issue at the meeting since Tony Essel, a hydrocephalus patient in Graham's form and, lately, increasingly aggressive, proposed that Warble be dismissed from the meeting because he was able-bodied: the 'Aims and Objectives' were clearly directed at handicapped people so it would be 'ridiculous and wrong whatever we may think personally of him' for Warble to be involved.

Warble took this with good grace, and though he said nothing in his own defence he did say that if the group needed his help at any time they could have it. Then he left.

Esther watched all this helplessly and with a cross expression on her face because she felt that Graham should have been more forceful. She never had liked Tony Essel, especially in these last two terms when he had started to shave. Some of the boys were getting obnoxious. She was surprised to see Betty Shaw vote in favour of Warble's dismissal and noted that Betty's eyes did not meet hers again during the meeting.

But she was placated when the small group elected her 'Honorary People's President', in which role she could be fully involved without having to run meetings. It was the beginnings at Netherton of a revolution that had started among the handicapped in Britain some fifteen years before and which would, though haltingly, take up the right of self-determination for the handicapped.

It was a mainly unsung revolution often of greater courage than the one which had overtaken school and university student bodies. A revolution in which humble, modest and disadvantaged people, the physical and mental dregs of a society geared almost exclusively to success linked to physical attractiveness, would one by one stand up and speak their minds; though their legs might be stunted, their speech distorted, and their minds blocked and awkward of thought.

'We got feelings like anyone,' said Tony Essel at that meeting, 'and we're the ones to say them.'

In Spring 1982 Esther was chosen, along with Graham Downer, to go for two days to Torquay to demonstrate the use of computers at a holiday camp which had been taken over for a week by a cerebral palsy organization who had brought together groups of spastics and their helpers from institutions and private homes all over Britain.

The experience gave Esther further opportunity to collect stories about the Skallagrigg.

From the Marquand Collection: Disk 3, File 'MARQ06'

I don't know if you have holiday camps in America but I bet you don't have them like us. Only the British could do it: rows and rows of horrible wooden huts with a view, not of the sea, but of a badly built canteen with enormous black metal chimneys.

The reason they chose the place was (a) because it was tarmacked all over and good for wheelchairs and (b) it was cheap.

When Graham and I arrived the rain was sleeting down out of a grey sky (just like here sometimes, Daniel!) and across the 'parade ground' as the older men called it we could see a pathetic huddle of wheelchaired men waiting to be boarded into a coach. Several of them had bright yellow sou'westers on and the rain was dripping off the rims. In fact it was so bad that our helpers decided we should stay in our minibus for a time.

We were going to stay two nights but the place was so badly organized that there was trouble with electricity in the room where we had the computers and so we had to stay an extra day. I'm glad we did because it meant I met some of the people at a party. It was in a big old-fashioned dance hall and in all that crowd who should I meet but Eric, the man I met in the Spastics Society HQ who told me the Skallagrigg story about The Racks.

'Hello, hello!' he said. 'It's Miss S!'

At first I didn't understand but then I remembered that's what he and his friend called me when I had tried to tell them my name. This time I had a lapel badge on.

He read it and smiled, but that same sadness was in his eyes as he had had when I caught a glimpse of him at the Brighton conference. I think I mentioned that before.

'Ch . . . cha . . .' I said. '. . . ck!'

'Jack,' he said. 'You remember?'

I nodded.

'Spastics need memories like elephants,' he said. 'My friend Jack got killed. He got crushed by a car right in front of me. I couldn't even get down to him and people came in front of me to tend to him so I couldn't even see him. He was calling my name and no one knew it. They tried to wheel me away but I stopped that. The blue men came and took him away in an ambulance. He saw me and I saw him and I knew he didn't want to go, not Jack. He was my best friend. The last thing he did before they closed the doors on him was say goodbye to me. I saw it on his mouth.'

The terrible room with its strip lighting, the jollied crowd, the music, the great red crushed velvet curtains on the stage, the people close

by . . . I forgot that and wanted to cry. I remembered Jack so well.
Eric came closer and put a hand out and touched my arm.

'I shouldn't have spoken but it's the truth,' he said. 'Funny thing
meeting you because he remembered you. He said if he had been
twenty years younger he would have fancied you! Liked the ladies did
Jack.'

You couldn't help smiling with Eric and he wanted to talk about
Jack. I spent most of that party talking to him, and Graham got quite
annoyed with me, but I didn't care because by then I was into collecting
Skallagrigg stories. I told Eric about my self-imposed task and he said,
'Why?' and I sighed, 'I don't know.'

Eric said, 'We all need something to live for, don't we? Maybe for you
it's writing down about the Skallagrigg. Can I help you?' He fixed his
eyes on mine and I knew that what he had lived for was his friend. I
thought of Frank and Arthur. Graham came by again at that moment,
looking sulky, and for the first time I saw he looked like a boy. Eric
grinned at him in a friendly way but Graham got annoyed and looked
even younger. Then he went off and I sighed inside.

'Jack knew a lot of the Skallagrigg stories and used to tell
them.'

What was his favourite? I wanted to know. Eric eventually understood.

'He sometimes told the one about The Racks because he liked the
sea. Jack could watch the sea with pleasure until the world died. He
liked the one when the Skallagrigg came to Arthur in the cell where
Dilke put him. Jack was once in a cell like that when he was a boy so
he understood it.

> In those days Dilke was young, same age as Arthur then. He
> wasn't big like some Staff but his anger made him strong and
> all feared him. He already had his window stick with the
> hook and used it often enough so the boys were scared.
>
> Dilke would tie the legs of wanderers to chairs, or take
> their pyjama bottoms. He did both to Arthur, and put his cot
> in the middle of the corridor where everybody passing could
> see. He knew Arthur didn't like having no privacy; who
> would?
>
> 'Messed his sheets didn't he, so let people see what a filthy
> bugger he is,' Dilke said.
>
> Dilke could be sweet as pie showing folk round and 'course
> Staff moved Arthur then, and untied some. But you can't
> hide the smell of shit or tidy away the sense of fear. So the
> best thing was not to have visitors at all. As Dilke got power

he saw to that and no relatives ever came on the wards, the boys being got up and taken to them down past the wire baskets to the visitors' room where there were flowers.

One day one of the boys said, 'Arthur doesn't like it there in the corridor,' and Dilke flew into a rage. He raised his stick and brought blood to several legs. Young Staff heard and came to look. They liked that sport.

'How do you know what this bugger wants,' says Dilke putting his hand on the sides of Arthur's cot and looking down at him and shouting. You could see the yellow of his teeth and drips on his mouth, and his hands were shaking with rage.

'You don't like being here, eh?' shouts Dilke. 'I don't think you've got any bloody idea where you are and I'm going to prove it.'

And he lets the cot side down and gets Arthur's leg and drags him out of that cot thump thump and down the corridor. Arthur cries out and starts to pee with fear and the pee on the polished floor makes Dilke even more enraged. He grabs Arthur's head and rubs his nose on the floor where the pee is.

'Don't you fucking mess my wards,' says Dilke. 'You pissing wanking useless fucking bugger. Don't you do that.' And Dilke hits him so hard that for a moment Arthur lies still. Then he tries his best to get away and he's crying. Dilke cruelly watches Arthur for a bit crawling desperately through the muck of that floor. Arthur's so twisted he can't crawl two inches. Then smiling Dilke drags him through the lavatories to the cell by the old Back Ward.

He has keys has Dilke, keys all jangling. Keys to hit and poke with if he's a mind. He gets a big old key out and opens that cell door and pushes Arthur in.

'You're an animal and I don't think you know where you are at all. You'll stay here till I say you can come out and I'll send Rendel to feed you.'

'Nah!'

The boys hear poor Arthur cry, and that one noise, 'Nah!' It's better not to be alone with Rendel.

Three minutes later Dilke's back with a bucket of water and Dettol and throws it over Arthur and scrubs him up with a bristling broom.

After Dilke goes Arthur cries and shivers in the cold, and then lies still.

'Skallagrigg,' he says, 'please help me.'

But nothing happens, he only gets colder.

The door opens and Rendel comes in with food. Rendel kneels by him smiling. Then Rendel hits him. Then Rendel does terrible things hurting Arthur. Rendel kneels over poor Arthur and touches him hard and Rendel unbuttons him and unbuttons himself and Arthur feels pain where Rendel sexes him, and he smells Rendel's breath and can't get away. They hear Arthur's screams. That was before Frank because if he had heard it would have driven him mad.

After, when Rendel's dirty work is done, Arthur is ashamed. Arthur thinks he's done wrong. Arthur is so ashamed and he cries. Satisfied with himself, Rendel goes and Arthur wants to die. He hurts in his face and in his bum. Arthur never was so low as that, not never, not ever.

Lying on the wet mattress, not even able to wipe Rendel's filth off himself, Arthur watches the night fall over the floor. Arthur says, 'I got to live. I got to live. I got to live. I got to live.' Over and over he said it.

Then he spoke saying, 'I live for the Skallagrigg. I live for you. I live for you because if you knew you wouldn't let this happen but you don't. One day you'll be strong enough to come. Till then I got to be the life for both of us.'

But then Arthur cries because if the Skallagrigg came he would be too ashamed now to receive his love. He felt Rendel had made him dirty inside for ever.

Night fell and Arthur slept a bit. When he woke there was a silvery light and black lines on the floor. It was the moon. The lines was the shadow of the window bars. Arthur turned and looked up. The big silver moon was there and across it was clouds moving like ships.

Arthur says, 'That's good to see that and I'm hungry.' Arthur turns to the food and he knocks the tray over even though he knows Dilke will punish him. Arthur eats the food and cold greasy soup off the floor, careful not to bang his teeth. He's got good teeth has Arthur, that's one thing he has got.

Then he looks at the moon and he thinks about his hurts and they're going. His head doesn't hurt and his bum is all right now. The moon shifts and then dawn comes and suddenly that cell is full of bird sound like you never get in the ward. And there's a touch of sun on the window and up its side there's ivy.

Arthur hears the voice of the Skallagrigg then, 'That's a

blackbird, that's a thrush, that's a robin, and that's a pigeon in the tree.' And Arthur hears their sounds and listens as the Skallagrigg talks to him: 'That's the sun and that's the road, and that's the wood and that's the wooden fence and that's . . .'

But the door crashes open and it's Dilke and Arthur hears the voice saying, 'Fucking messed the food again,' and feels the stick hitting him on his legs and rapping on his fingers, but Arthur doesn't hear that much because the voice of the Skallagrigg is louder in that cell and it's lifting him, 'and that's the fence and we can go over if we try because you want to Arthur,' and Arthur doesn't hear or feel or see Dilke any more, or Rendel standing behind, but only sees right out of that high window and beyond the walls and beyond the grounds and far far far far on where the Skallagrigg smiles to him and says, 'Lead me, Arthur, you go first, you're better than me at it,' and Arthur's legs are sure as they climb that wooden fence on the warm day, and the grass is swaying in the wind and the Skallagrigg who was with him is now beyond him calling him to wait. He's so happy is Arthur and he can forget Dilke because he sees that Dilke is nothing to do such things, nothing. Dilke is the handicapped, Dilke is the afraid. Dilke is the one to pity.

Then he turns over and faces Dilke and looks at him with his grey eyes and Dilke sees forgiveness and pity in Arthur's eyes and no fear. Dilke can't take that. Dilke crashes his window stick down on his face but Arthur knows who's won even as the cracking darkness comes.

When they took Arthur out of that cell and the doctor came, there was whispers and Dilke was hauled up and warned and nothing happened. His defence was he had to isolate Arthur for his own protection 'cos he's queer. The medic super believed that because he had it in for queers. But afterwards the boys saw Arthur was changed and stronger. They heard that the Skallagrigg had come to him and taken him to safety for a time where Dilke and Rendel could not hurt him whatever they did to his poor body. They saw that Arthur was no longer afraid. And they saw that Arthur could laugh and make them laugh and from that time Arthur began to be their boss because he had suffered the worst of them and come through and found a way to beat Dilke and make him nothing.

Eric said, 'You asked and I told you: that was Jack's favourite, because Jack knew about the cell. You asked for the truth so you must be ready for it. Jack was somewhere like that once. Jack knew about Staff like Dilke. My friend Jack said to me that he got through without going mad because he had something to live for, and that was me. He said, "I thought of protecting my friend Eric when I was low, I thought only of that, until in the end there was only that name Eric Eric Eric Eric as the last thing to think. Like Arthur and the Skallagrigg."'

Eric continued: 'Jack said, "You've got to have something to live for because that's what keeps you alive. People who have nothing to live for die before their bodies. I've got you and you've got me." So that was Jack's favourite.'

I wanted to know where Eric came from and they had to find a signing board for that. Someone had a Bliss board on their chair and so I used that, with me on one side and Eric on the other and the girl whose board it was right there in the middle, happy to be useful.

I raised my fingers to the Bliss symbol for home, a picture of a house.

Eric said, 'I come from Merseyside but I don't remember my home.'

'Where are you from?' Eric asked the girl whose Bliss board we were using.

The girl, who was about twenty, indicated the top of the board. In felt-tip pen, covered with plastic, it read, 'My name is Rachel, I come from Tunbridge Wells, Kent.'

'Having a good time here then?' asked Eric.

'Ooo yeh!' said Rachel.

Eric said, 'We've been telling stories about the Skallagrigg.'

The girl began to speak.

'Not so fast! Start again! Oh *you know* one, you want to tell one.' Rachel's hands travelled over the Bliss board and bit by bit they unravelled the story she told.

Did you know Arthur escaped once? It's true, and no one ever knew! That was after his friend Frank found out Arthur liked music . . .

Eric nodded and muttered, 'I thought I knew this one. No, go on, you tell us your story. Esther here's going to write it in a book, aren't you Esther?'

I nodded. Rachel looked worried. 'Skallagrigg secret,' she signed. 'Not any more he's not,' said Eric.

So anyway [continued Rachel], there was a new medical super and he liked music and he said the patients should have music. Staff didn't want to because of the problems of control and how could patients play music? If they buggered up the gramophones what would they do to an instrument?

There was an old piano in the recreation hall which hadn't been tuned in years. The medical super said, 'We'll have that tuned and see if it works.' They had to break it open because the key was long lost.

One day Arthur, Frank and Norman are on the way to occupational therapy and suddenly the air is filled with real piano notes. Ding ding ding dong. Ding ding deeng deng!

Arthur looks like he's had the fright of his life doesn't he?

Frank says, 'That's only a pianer like in the church.' But Arthur doesn't seem to see it that way. To him it sounds different.

So Arthur got Frank to take him into the hall and they see a man tuning the piano.

'Hello,' says he, 'you the concert pianists then?' They all think that's a good laugh. 'Want a go?' says he.

Arthur says no and wants to watch, so Frank and Norman go across that big wooden floor echoing and they are allowed to play some notes. Frank sits there and the tuner stands by him and Frank plays. Arthur just stares across the floor, the air dusty and the sounds hollow.

After that Arthur was thoughtful for weeks. Very thoughtful. Eventually he speaks to Frank and Frank says to the boys, 'Arthur says he's fed up with that music you play on the radio in the courts all day in all day out and he wants to listen to something else.'

The boys didn't know what he was on about.

Then one day Frank fiddles with the radio for Arthur and they get on to some classical. The moment the announcer comes on Staff says, 'Get some decent music on.'

Norman stood up and went to the radio looking at Arthur.

'No,' he says.

'Suit yourself,' says Staff intimidated. Just as well it wasn't Dilke because he would have told Norman, Frank and Arthur to sod off, and bashed them.

The announcer says something and Arthur listens. The man's saying what the music is. Then the music plays and Arthur listens right through. Frank didn't like the music 'cos he liked pop but he was content because Arthur seemed happy.

'O K?' he says to Arthur when it's over.

Arthur nods and Frank turns the radio back to 'decent' music.

After that the boys got used to Arthur's liking classical music provided he didn't listen too long.

Sometimes one would say, 'It's Arthur's turn now,' and they would fiddle till they found where the classical music usually was. Sometimes that music was the best bit of Arthur's day, and that made it the best bit for Frank 'cos he could see Arthur's body stilling under the music like the music was a physio for Arthur.

Meanwhile the piano got tuned and the medical super used to play on it. One day one of the boys went into the big room and sat at the piano and knocked out a few notes.

Dilke found him.

'Enjoying yourself?' says Dilke. The boy wasn't clever enough to know that Dilke wasn't being nice.

'Yes,' says that boy.

'You're not bloody allowed to play the piano!' says Dilke, slamming the cover on the boy's fingers.

'Wasn't playing, Mr Dilke,' says the boy adding 'sorry' in a whine and crying 'cos his fingers hurt.

The medical super gets to hear and says, 'I really think that on the whole and if you don't mind and I know it's a nuisance, Mr wonderful Dilke, who knows better than me, that there's no *harm* in the boys playing the piano.'

'They'll knock it out of tune,' says Dilke.

'So?' says the medic, finding his courage against Dilke.

'If you insist,' says Dilke, his eyes dark.

Afterwards Dilke gets that boy whose name is Joseph and drags him to the piano and says, 'Medic super says you got to play, you bastard.' So then he gets other boys and makes them sit in a row watching the boy who tried to play which of course he couldn't. The boy couldn't touch a note and sits there miserable. He's a quiet boy who never does no harm. So the boys sit there feeling bad and Joseph sits there his head low 'cos he can't play and Dilke and another Staff are grinning all smug and then laughing 'cos they think it's funny doing that to the harmless boys don't they?

Arthur speaks and Frank stands up.

'Yes?' says Dilke enjoying himself, everyone waiting to see what'll happen next.

'Arthur knows a tune,' says Frank.

'Oh yeh!' says Dilke. 'Come on then!'

He's enjoying the sport and other Staff come in to watch. It's hard to say if it's a joke or not but at least Arthur's got that poor boy off the hook.

So Frank wheels Arthur up to the piano.

Arthur speaks and Frank sits down.

Arthur speaks and Frank puts a finger on a note. He plays the note. Then Arthur thinks a bit and tells Frank to try another. The first was wrong. Arthur nods with satisfaction at the second note.

Dilke says, 'Good tune that, Arthur, good as a fart in church.'

Arthur speaks and Frank plays another note. Then one more.

Arthur speaks and Frank plays all three notes together and it makes a chord, the chord of middle C. Arthur makes Frank play that several times.

Even the dimmest boys recognized that that was the beginnings of music and some of them clap.

Frank does it again and Joseph's forgotten Dilke and comes forward and Frank shows him.

Then the boys get round the piano and they learn that chord, those that want to, and that boy who first tried to play discovers that if he plays another note up the piano with the other hand he can play a bigger chord, and if he plays one after another he's got the beginnings of a tune. Dilke gets angry and takes the boys back to their courts.

Joseph says, 'How did you know that, Arthur?'

And Arthur says, 'Skyagree.'

Then the boys all know that the Skallagrigg came that day to help and from then on for ever more the boys know that Arthur is the one who knows about music. Once again the Skallagrigg's coming made a new friend for Arthur.

One day the boys were surprised to see new people in the church waiting, about twenty of them, maybe more. It was a choir the medical super had brought in for a special anniversary. The choir sang classical music and halfway through Frank had to put his hands on Arthur's shoulder because Arthur was crying. It was so beautiful to him, you see. After that if there was choral music on the radio Arthur was especially happy and Frank would turn it up for him and the boys had to put up with it. Usually they did.

One day the medical super said that twenty of the boys could visit the big church outside the grounds because there was to be a concert. Dilke said this to some of the boys but then his eyes turned dark and he said to his enemy of old, 'You're not going, Arthur and you're not going neither, boy.' That was to Joseph whose fingers he hurt, who learnt a tune from Arthur. He knew that of all the patients these two would most like to have gone. Maybe if the medical super had known it would have made a difference but to him Arthur was down as a congenital idiot. You had to know Arthur a long time to know he had brains.

'You're going,' says Dilke to Frank knowing he would not like going without Arthur.

'No,' says Frank.

'Shall I get my window stick?' says Dilke.

Arthur spoke.

'Arthur says I'm to go.'

'Well, fuck you, Arthur,' says Dilke his face red round the eyes, 'fuck you always.'

'Yeh,' said Arthur. Arthur pitied Dilke and was no longer afraid of him. Dilke didn't have the Skallagrigg, so he had nothing. He had nothing to live for but hurting, and that's not much.

But when the evening of the concert came and Frank was gone with the other boys Arthur was alone. Arthur was sad. He was thinking of the music he could have heard in a new place. As he was sitting there he thinks of the Skallagrigg and he says to him, wherever he was, 'I would have liked to have gone. I know Frank won't be happy. He only hears music through me. It's almost the only thing I can do like an able-bodied person, is listen. I would have liked to have gone.'

Then he sat silent.

Then Joseph comes and says to Staff, 'Can I take Arthur to the big room and the pianer?'

Staff says yes, letting them go because he doesn't like what Dilke's done.

And Joseph pushes Arthur's chair slowly, slower than Frank. And he pushes it where he shouldn't, down the corridor by the baskets and past the big oak doors and out past the back kitchens and then to the laundry. And who should be there but Frank.

'Come on then, Arthur, you're coming to the concert. Joseph will push you back so you must remember the way for him.'

So this is an escape. Frank has slipped out of the chapel, clever Frank. Frank's that clever when he's thinking of his friend.

They come to the church which was by the village and the lights were all on.

'You stay here,' says Frank, leaving them by the back of the church and three big windows rising to points all coloured with glass and lights. Jesus windows.

Then Frank goes back into shadows and is gone.

Arthur thinks, 'That was a brave thing. No man is alone who has a friend and I have two. I have Frank and the Skallagrigg; one here and one beyond the wooden fence.'

Then his thinking stops because out of that window comes the sound of God as the choir begins to sing. And listening, out there in the cold and dark, unseen by Dilke, among the gravestones and the old yew trees, Arthur feels a pain in his heart for the Skallagrigg is near and he wants to reach out to him. He's near there with him, listening to that great music which is mountains above him, and hanging like stars in the green trees all around.

'If I had been normal,' thinks Arthur, 'I would have played music.' And he's happy because Joseph is standing there by him, his hands on the handles of his chair, and he's listening too, and hearing as well. One's all right but both is best. The Skallagrigg is there with Arthur, sharing that lovely sound. After an hour or so and it's got dark Joseph says, 'Got to go now, Arthur,' but Arthur doesn't want to because he's near the Skallagrigg and doesn't want to leave. But he knows he must.

'Yeh,' ne says.

Joseph can't remember the way back but Arthur can, all

the rights and lefts. And as they go they hear that music fade behind them until by the time they're by the greenhouses it's gone. And they're back to normality.

Staff says, 'Where you two been?' He wasn't angry.

'Round,' says Joseph.

'You got mud on your boots,' says Staff. 'You been out.'

Joseph does a bad job looking innocent, and Arthur grins and winks. He knows *that* Staff likes him.

'I ought to clobber you,' says Staff.

'Yeh,' says Arthur his grey eyes happier than for years.

'Go on, off you go,' says Staff, and he looks after them. Maybe he's thinking Arthur should not be there at all. Maybe he's thinking the patients know more than they let on.

It's a funny thing, but Joseph starts at the piano after that whenever he can, and Arthur likes to help him. Nobody knows that's what he's doing.

One day the medical super comes in the big room and can't seem to believe his ears. Joseph is playing a real tune, a classical tune, with two fingers and a chord.

'Now where did you learn that?' says the medical super.

Joseph says nothing and Arthur watches.

'It's . . .' and the medical super gives it a name.

'Yeh,' says Arthur who knows its name as well because he heard it on the radio and he also heard it in a churchyard where no one knew they were.

The medical super says, 'Well I never,' but he never stopped to really think about it. If he had he might have found the answers disturbing. Not for the first time and not for the last, those that looked after Arthur didn't ask no questions about his brains. It was easier for them to think he had none and was the idiot the yellow card files said, than to think he might not be and have to answer for the consequences.

When Rachel finished Eric asked her, 'Do you play music?'

She nodded.

'Piano?'

No, not that.

'Violin?' She giggled at Eric's joke.

'Percussion?' says Eric.

Rachel nodded, eyes alight.

'I bet . . . I bet it's . . . it's cymbals!'

'Nah!' screamed Rachel excited and laughing.

'Drums?' said Eric.

'*Yeh!*' says Rachel, banging her fists as fast as she could, which was not fast, upon her Bliss board.

'Is that why you like that Skallagrigg story?'

She nodded. Yes, that was why.

So, little by little, I collected the Skallagrigg stories, writing them down one by one.

FORTY

But Sturrick was not the only world that was breaking up. So was Esther's. There seemed now a constant stream of reminders that the world she had known before her grandfather's death was vulnerable, and she vulnerable with it.

After Sturrick she had been due to stay a few days in Charlbury with Margaret but that was cancelled. Margaret had had to go into hospital for a small operation. Nothing serious. Just a few days. Just a check-up. Richard Marquand seemed unable to find an easy way of expressing the truth to his daughter.

The trouble was that he had promised Margaret not to tell the truth which, left unspoken, assumed such significance that it quite blocked out the excitements of Sturrick.

WHERE IS GRANDMA? Esther asked on her Possum.

'In a hospital in Oxford.'

CAN I VISIT HER? She looked at him with angry appeal in her eyes.

Maybe. Perhaps. Possibly. He would phone the hospital.

WHAT'S WRONG WITH HER? she asked again.

'It's probably nothing. Just a routine check-up. Grandma's getting on and . . .' Her father did not look her in the eye and Esther lapsed into anxious silence.

But three days later, after a phone call to the hospital, her father seemed relieved – which suggested that there had been something to fear. Marion was allowed to take Esther to Oxford's Radcliffe Infirmary.

Margaret lay in bed in a ward on the first floor, quite visible from the corridor, propped up and looking a little shrunken. As Marion wheeled Esther in, Margaret turned and saw them, and said, 'Oh, Esther!'

Esther began to cry, and Marion brought her nearer so that

Margaret could reach out to her. She understood immediately what was wrong.

'It's all right, my dear, I'm quite all right. You see I had a little scare, a growth. The doctor wasn't sure and so they do what's called a biopsy to check that it is not . . . that it is benign. That means . . .'

Esther nodded, sniffing. She knew what benign meant. It meant non-malignant. It meant it had been about cancer. It meant Margaret was all right . . . for the time being. But it meant that things *had* changed and Margaret, who had been such a source of constant strength to her, was now beginning to weaken and that the world of her adulthood was coming faster and faster towards her, and in it she was going to be alone.

Yet, somehow, Esther managed a reassuring smile, for she saw in Margaret's eyes a fear that mirrored her own. Margaret's faith in herself and her body had been shaken and, feeling vulnerable, she looked older.

'Did you have a nice time in Manchester?'

So they talked about Sturrick, and Margaret did her very best to be interested, though it was difficult because since her operation all that seemed less important. Helen would be interested, yes: she would be interested for her.

Esther Marquand's sense of vulnerability, increased by exposure to Sturrick, and to Margaret's sudden scare, deepened the moment she got back to Netherton.

A careers officer from Hampshire Education Authority came on the second day of term and spoke to everybody in the sixth form. Prospects, he said frankly, were not good and he painted a bleak picture of life after school. Qualifications would help, but not necessarily. Unemployment levels among school-leavers were alarmingly high, and among handicapped school-leavers even higher.

'Some students here, more than in most schools, have real knowledge of and experience with computers. This will help. Our department will monitor school-leavers' jobs in this area especially.'

Esther and Graham looked at each other. And Betty Shaw, she exchanged looks as well. School-leavers. Panic! Despite all the

words of reassurance that followed they were left with an aching
sense that soon they might have nowhere to go and that this place
might be a memory more precious than they could ever have
imagined.

Disturbed now, pressed by looming examinations, worried by
the seemingly purposeless future, Esther pressed on through the
long days that followed, innocence and confidence for ever gone
from those final terms.

She wrote in her diary (13 May 1982): 'Long exeat coming up,
thank God. Everything's so gloomy here, made worse by the weather which has been terrible. Snow fell two days ago in the Mid-
lands and it's May! Going to stay with Helen Perry-Wilcox in
Woodstock Road Oxford where Grandma is convalescing. Would
have preferred Harefield but Daddy's away again. Helen's asked
Tom as well, probably because she knows he's good with me.
Helen says all the blossom's late with the bad weather this year
but might be out in time to celebrate my arrival!! Betty's going up
north and has an extra day granted from Mr Imray because of the
distance. Betty says maybe I'll find a boyfriend among all those
attractive students. She says there are 12,000 sex-mad males in
Oxford during term and that even I ought to be able to attract at
least one of them! If not I might as well cut my throat. Doubt if I'd
have the strength or the agility! Well, at least I can look at them.
Betty had the curse again this week and says she can't understand
why I worry about it. She says, 'You're lucky not to have it.' I
don't think so.

Helen Perry-Wilcox's home was a large detached nineteenth-
century house on Oxford's tree-lined Woodstock Road. Its front
garden was severe English: a prunus hedge with standard roses
beyond, regimented to rectangular beds by grey paving stones,
leading to a nondescript green front door.

The windows were lace-curtained, the curtains themselves lined,
the walls hung with old oil paintings, and the furniture for the
most part antique.

But these were the formal front rooms which faced north-east
and got comparatively little sun. The back rooms, like the back
gardens, were Helen Perry-Wilcox without the severe middle-class

mask. Greenery dominated: mock orange shrubs formed a hedge outside the kitchen windows, there were several apple trees with unpruned ancient branches which seemed to wish to grow in at every window, and forsythia which, its yellow flowers now quite gone, formed a hedge ten feet high.

All this was visible from each of the three rooms backing on to the garden, the most lovely of which was the kitchen, a huge and ordered space with new beech units and a cork floor, and comfortable chairs round the small range.

Her sense of colour was warm, and despite the shaking of the greenery outside from the fractious wind of that wet and bitter early summer, there was a sense of glowing pinks and reds, soft greens and good light which invested everything with cheer and a colourful harmony.

She had that sense of home that Margaret did not, and visitors, of whom she seemed to have many, soon relaxed in her house.

And there were books. On the mantelpiece above the range there were always three or four library books with leather markers in, for she liked to have several on the go at once; on a shelf by the kitchen units, next to shelves of spices, were cookery books, a lot of them; and in polished mahogany bookcases on either side of the chimney breast in what she called her garden room were yet more books, poetry on one side, religious and travel books on the other. While on top were framed black and white photographs of her father, her mother (in separate frames), a group of three small children (her cousins), and a man with a pipe and kind eyes.

There were red rugs over the fitted carpet and an air of organized comfort. It was, in fact, precisely the kind of home that Margaret Ogilvie had always wanted but somehow never quite had the eye, the heart or the energy to create.

The house was larger than it looked. Upstairs there were three bedrooms and a substantial bathroom, and on the attic floor above that a small bedsit flat. Helen had only been able to afford to run the house by supplementing her salary as librarian at the university's Bodleian Library by taking in lodgers, usually post-graduate couples.

The last ones had left the previous term and so, for the summer months at least, the house was entirely her own.

Margaret had already been staying for two weeks when Esther

arrived, dropped off by Betty Shaw's father on his way north. Tom had made his own way to Oxford by train to join them, and was safe, sound and pleased with himself.

There was tea in the kitchen with a bright checked table-cloth and matching napkins. Tom tucked his carefully under his chin.

'Well, my dears, I wish the weather was better for you,' said Helen. 'I was hoping to take you all to Blenheim this afternoon but it hardly seems worth it.'

Rain was lashing against the french windows that led from the kitchen to the garden, while the wind made the mock orange, its buds still tightly closed, tap fretfully against the window over the sink.

Tom had eyes only for the cake which sat in the middle of the table, round and moist and gingery, with powdered sugar on the top, set neatly on a special plate. There was a wedge-shaped cake knife ready.

Margaret sat relaxed, looking better than when Esther had seen her in the hospital. She was always at her ease with Helen Perry-Wilcox, the friendship between the two women having deepened rapidly since their first meeting the previous summer, and naturally expressed by Margaret's convalescing here.

But Esther, like the weather, was out of sorts. She looked pale and her hair, normally soft and glowing, was lank, as if she was ill. Her eyes, which would normally have been looking about her curiously since she looked forward to this visit, were staring uneasily out of the window into the garden as if she had no interest in any of them, or tea.

'Are you all right, Esther?' Margaret had asked more than once.

Esther had nodded and then looked quickly away, bored, indifferent, restless, and uncommunicative.

'Darling, what's wrong?' Margaret had tried again.

'Nana!' said Esther irritably. She had no wish to respond to anything. Nothing was wrong, wasn't that obvious?

Helen and Margaret exchanged glances and pressed on through tea, talking of things they would do during Esther's brief exeat and resolutely ignoring Esther's behaviour which they put down to adolescence.

Yet it was more than that. Much more.

From the Marquand Collection: Disk 17, File 'MARQO9'

I knew I was behaving badly and I wanted to say, 'I'm sorry I'm sorry I am glad to be here I am I am I am. But I feel ill and my head's going round and round that problem: something in the stories, there's something wrong with them. And I had an image of Arthur in my mind and I couldn't get it out of my head. He was in a cot just like some of the children in the Harry Barr film had been at Sturrick and his hands were coming up as if they were on slow jerking wires. I was there and his head, hidden at first, turned suddenly towards me and I could see his eyes through the cot sides, which was like a wooden fence. It was the first time I had created an Arthur story of my own, and I was in it. This was not something anybody had told me. His mouth was opening and he was trying to speak and he was saying over and over again to me GET THE SKALLAGRIGG YOU GET THE SKALLAGRIGG and I couldn't move towards him. And I felt ill and headachey and I was bursting with this Arthur cry inside my head and his eyes and his helplessness which was my own. And he kept trying to say GET HIM GET HIM GET THE SKALLAGRIGG and I started to try to say STOP STOP STOP I CAN'T I CAN'T I CAN'T and I felt ill and suddenly

Suddenly Esther burst into terrible sobs. And since she could not do what she wanted, which was to run out of the room and collapse upon her bed behind a shut door, she could only bend her head and try to bring her hands to her face as she wept uncontrollably.

'Oh, my dear, my dear, what is it?' said Margaret going to her. While Helen got up as well and said, 'Perhaps she wants to be quiet for a little while,' which suggestion brought yet more tears.

Outside the trees bent and the rain continued, blown in spattering patters across the window.

Only Tom stayed calm. He finished some cake, drank all his tea and carefully put the cup down. Then he got up, went round to Esther and said in a voice that gently cut through both her tears and Margaret's comfortings, 'Amh? Amh? Let's go out.' And he waited.

There was a waver in Esther's cries, a momentary lull.

'For a walk. Like at home.'

Like at home. At home. Home. Arthur. Home. ARTHUR WANTS

TO GO HOME. HE'S CALLING TO THE SKALLAGRIGG TO TAKE
HIM HOME.

'Like at home,' repeated Tom.

'Yeh. *Yeh*!' said Esther her eyes suddenly clearer than they had
been for days. '*Yeh*, Toh!'

Margaret agreed. The two women wrapped her up in a blue
cagoule, and Tom in his new yellow one, Margaret brushing aside
Helen's concern.

'They often go for walks at home, you see. Don't you?'

'Yes,' said Tom.

'But they don't know the Woodstock Road.'

A look from Esther reassured her. Esther would not allow them
to get lost, and Tom was more careful of his charge than anyone
else could ever be. He would rather die than let her suffer harm.

So out into the rain and wind they went, the tea only half
consumed, and the two women worried but relieved. That crying
had been most odd, its cause a mystery. Better a walk in the rain
than inexplicable crying in the house.

'Oh it's just a phase, probably,' said Margaret. 'She is beginning
to grow up. Though. . .'

Yes? said Helen without saying anything, using a non-verbal
interrogative which is one of friendship's shorthands.

'She's not normally moody.'

'No?' said Helen. And she poured another cup of tea for them
both and smiled. Perhaps Esther was growing up faster than her
grandmother realized.

'I hope they don't get too wet!' said Helen.

'I have every faith in Tom,' declared Margaret.

But Tom did not have every faith in himself, for the wind was
stronger than he had expected. A walk might be what his Esther
needed, but achieving it in freak weather was proving difficult.
Above them the stiff urban trees that lined the road bent with the
wind, and twigs fell, or had fallen, across the path, making it
difficult to push the wheelchair.

So there was a look of intense concentration on his face as he
pushed her chair along the pavement past house after house like
Helen's, and a rush of traffic close by coming in the opposite
direction. Several times he came to a halt as the wind combined
with the uneven paving slabs to stop his progress, and once the

wind gusted so strongly that he had to hold the handles of the chair down to stop it tilting.

'Amh. . .' he began.

GO ON TOM IT'S ALL RIGHT.

Then a few moments later, the chair shaken by the passing of a lorry and a scatter of wind in all directions: 'Amh . . .'

GO ON, TOM.

'Yes, Amh.'

Esther's face was wet, not with tears now but with driven rain. Her cheeks were red and her eyes alight. She was thinking of the Skallagrigg, she was excited with the proximity of a solution to the problem of what was wrong with the stories and she did not want to stop thinking about it.

Turn right, Tom.

TOM. TURN RIGHT.

'No, Amh.'

They had come to the entrance to some school grounds, and a sports centre. It was wide and gateless, between two houses, and a neat tarmac road led a little downhill to modern buildings and playing fields. A notice read, 'St Edward's School'. The traffic was getting on Esther's nerves and it looked quieter down there. But Tom only liked going places where he knew they had permission. Tom did not like breaking rules. He would gainsay even Esther if he felt that what she wanted to do was dangerous.

'Not allowed,' he added.

IT WILL BE ALL RIGHT, said Esther's garbled voice.

'No, *can't*,' said Tom, getting hysterical. He could sense there was going to be a real battle.

'*Yeh*,' said Esther aggressively.

'Naughty,' said Tom.

'*Nah!!*' said Esther angrily. Who would mind? A couple of handicapped people out for a walk. Nobody *minded*, a quick stare, and instant forgetting. Nobody would care.

Tom looked at the driveway and then up at the notice. PRIVATE GROUNDS. He could not read 'private' but he knew a threatening word when he saw one. He began to push her on.

But Esther did something unusual. She turned round a little in her chair, looked up at him as best she could, bending her head right back and said, 'Skyagree.'

TOM, IT'S FOR THE SKALLAGRIGG.

'Is it, Amh?' His voice was hushed and he brought the chair to a halt.

YES, TOM. PLEASE DO IT. PLEASE.

'Okay, Amh. For Skalg.'

And he turned the chair back, and resolutely swung it past the notice into the school grounds.

Across the wet black pathway down which he pushed her were scattered the pathetic fresh green leaves of the trees. A small branch had even broken off at one point, and somewhere else a marking flag had been blown across the turf until its passage was halted by the base of a tree against which, forlorn and redundant, it now rested.

Esther felt a growing wildness and excitement and was glad to see the place quite deserted.

Then Tom hesitated, for the road suddenly dipped down a few feet to bring them on a level with lower fields. She shouted at him to continue. So down they went and saw, across the field, the straight line of a canal, and at one end of it, in the distant corner of the playing field area, a small cantilever bridge. Rising above it was an enormous towering tree in whose side, white and yellow red, was a gash, a wound, and at whose base was the cause of that wound: an enormous broken branch.

They made their way towards it along the private road, which turned sharp left to run along the side of the field, and then sharp right at its end down towards the bridge.

It was a small canal bridge constructed so that when it lay flat over the canal for someone to cross, two thick weighted struts rose from the end hinged to the bank. Their weight was equal to that of the treads of the bridge, and a light touch brought them down, raising the bridge to allow canal boats to pass. There was a chain which hung free when the bridge was raised so that people on the far side of the canal could reach up and pull the structure down, if they wanted to cross.

The boards of the bridge tilted up like a wall across the path; moving, creaking, rising and falling as the strong wind first lifted it, and then pushed it part down again.

STOP HERE, Esther called out some ten yards from the bridge. She wanted to be near the great tree.

Tom turned the chair to face the tree. It strained wildly above them, bending and twisting in the air, the enormous branch fallen on the ground with the white raw wood at one end an open wound.

I WANT TO STAY HERE.

'But, Ahm . . .' Worriedly, Tom looked up at the tree's branches above them, and then at the bridge, caught now and again by a gust so that the weight knocked against the ground. The leaves of the branches of the fallen branch whipped and pulled in the wind. Squalls of wind travelled the narrow canal, dark moving ruffles on the grey surface.

Tom stood uneasily, his hands as ever on the handles of Esther's chair.

SET THE BRAKES. GO AND PLAY. I WANT TO THINK.

As he bent to the wheels the bridge suddenly began to lower itself and then, caught once again, rose up so that its weighted arms thumped the ground. Esther could see that a chain that held it in place had broken.

Tom pushed Esther on to a drier part of the grass, made her chair safe, and then impulsively set off the few yards towards the fascinating bridge. The rusty broken chain, clattering against the metal weights, pleased him. The bridge lowered and he dared put his hand on the rail. He pressed and it lowered further, the whole structure thumping as it made juddering contact and stayed in place. The path suddenly was complete, the gap gone and the bridge's planks invited feet to travel them. On the far side was a towpath, and beyond that a wooden fence, old and worn, the kind boys remember from childhood if they were reared in the country; the kind boys want to climb to see what's on the other side.

'Amh?'

YES, TOM. GO ON. GO AND LOOK.

She felt wild with the wind, excited and bursting with discovery and she looked up, up above her, at the tree that threshed and threatened her, at the red tear in its side where, so recently, the great branch had been.

GO ON, TOM, GO ON! she screamed. Her eyes were alight and her cheeks red with wind and wet, and her cagoule buffeted by the gale.

'*Yes*, Amh!' and he did, first one foot and then the other on to

the strange bridge which rose and fell so magically, and had
become a road over towards a fence on the other side. Yes, *yes*, and
he leaned over to look into the water and then went on the few
feet to the other side of the canal. He stared down into the water,
and then wandered a few feet away beyond the bridge to look over
the fence.

So he did not see the wheels of Esther's chair begin to slide in the
mud down the little slope towards the tree, faster as the wind
caught at her; nor hear in her cries the excitement changing to
alarm.

Only as he slowly looked up, aware that Esther's cries were
changing, did he see the chair slew sideways as one of the front
wheels sank into mud, and Esther falling, her hands trying to raise
themselves to protect her, as slow slow slow slow on the far side of
the canal from him she fell with her chair beneath the great stressed
tree.

'*Amh!*' he shouted raising his hands to his face in alarm. '*Amh!*'
The wind snatched her name from his mouth, and, even as he
stepped forward to cross over again, it buffeted the raised weights
on the bridge which sank to the far side, raising the bridge with a
creak up up in the air, out of Tom's reach and the canal open and
cold-grey beneath him. He tried to snatch the chain that would
have allowed him to pull the bridge down again, but it was rusty
and broken and too short for him to reach.

He looked wildly across to Esther and saw her legs and feet and
then her arm as the straps tying her to the chair gave way and she
rolled clear and lay still, face in the mud, one hand caught under
her, her blue cagoule twisted and muddy.

Esther, whom he loved and would always protect, did not move.
Esther was in danger. Then for a dreadful moment she raised her
head and screamed out, 'TOHOOHOH! TOH!'

'*Amh!*' he shouted, his feet jumping from the ground in his
anguish, and his hands reaching across the fearful water, and
then up to the out-of-reach chain swaying and dangling above
him.

'*Amh!*' And he began to cry terribly for he had hurt Esther and
she needed him.

'Toh, Toh, Tttt!' Her cries now were whimpers into mud from a
face whose whitened frightened eyes could only peer round on the

ground to see ... to see Tom, standing staring from across the canal. To see the suffering tree above and hear the wind rising and falling in awesome destructiveness.

'*Amh!*' he cried helplessly.

She felt a sudden calm. Then she shouted to him her head rising and falling with the effort in the muddy grass.

RUN ALONG THE BANK, TOM. DOWN THERE. RUN. Think, Tom. There's another bridge. Canals have lots of bridges.

The tree groaned. The bridge creaked and seemed to try for a moment to lower itself back down, but it could not and Tom reached up precariously towards its edge, teetering over the dangerous water.

NO, TOM, NO!

Weakened by the strain of the fall and her effort to right herself she watched Tom dither, his hand and fingers going up to his mouth, staring around with the wind at his short hair and round eyes and glasses as if he thought someone would come to help.

But there was no one except Amh and she was on the ground in the mud beneath the tree and the wheelchair was on its side, one wheel still spinning in the wind. He was going to get blamed. He stared at the narrow canal but it did not occur to him to try to wade or swim across it. He knew water was death and that took him beyond helping Amh. He stared along the path. Perhaps if he went down there he would find someone who would know what to do. They were going to blame him and they wouldn't be able to come to the canal again. Tom started to cry, and turned away along the canal. Some way off he turned back for a moment and shouted '*Amh!*' with such effort that his body seemed almost to lift off the ground. The cry was torn from his mouth by the wind.

Esther heard his shout and watched him go.

FIND THE NEXT BRIDGE, TOM, AND COME OVER IT TO ME. YOU CAN PICK ME UP AND PUT ME IN THE CHAIR. IT'LL BE ALL RIGHT. THEY'LL UNDERSTAND.

The wind raced over her, cold, bitter and indifferent, and as Tom disappeared from view her gaze travelled up into the threshing branches. She struggled to pull her pinned arm free, heaving her body up and pushing with her arm, the free arm wandering and jerking here and there, its movements wilder than normal because of the wind that tore at it. Its fingers ran through mud and then, slowly, pushed into it. Her side rolled, her arm was free. Her head ached from the fall and the mud was thick in her hair and on her ear. Some had caked on her mouth. She lay still on her side, staring up at the tree.

She was angry, bitterly angry. Not with Tom, nor herself, nor the people in her life. She was angry with whatever chain of events had led her from before her birth to be what she was and where she was, now, hurt and helpless on the ground, undignified and vulnerable, unloved and alone. The wind drove sudden hail into her face and it hurt and she heard her voice cry out. Her anger turned on the wind and in doing so the tree above her seemed a friend. For a moment she let her eyes close and she listened to the roar of the wind, and the voices of the trees roaring out in it. Voices crying out, her voice joining them, shouting and screaming, not in semblance of able-bodied sound but wild and sibilant, her own sound, her own cry which came from all of her and expressed her helplessness and, strangely, in doing so, expressed her strength; herself. And to whom did she shout and shout, her voice forming and re-forming like the wind. To whom did she scream?

SCREAGH

SCRAHGE

SKRAGEHH

SKAGGRAH

SKALAGGR

SKYAGGAH

SKYAGRH

SKYAGREE.

'Skyagree.'

She finally whispered it, her cry to him who would come, her voice at one with the wind about her now, her cry softening to nothing as she listened and she heard the wind, a friend now, a lover of the tree that thrust up above her, beyond her open legs, louder and louder in it, and then stretching back from it, back over the canal, back among the rails and weights of the bridge, back and back to the struts and the horizontals of the wooden fence and back beyond even that the sound of her own voice calling down the years, calling and calling on the winds of time, shouting a name, the name *she* spoke, the name of the Skallagrigg. Which in her dialect was Skyagree.

Then there seemed to be one voice that cried out as hers did. Her eyes opened and the voice she heard was louder, and louder though the wind was no stronger. Louder in the tree above her, ever louder, calling out to be heard, calling out to her. It was the voice of insight.

'You can understand. You know. You can hear me now. For I am the Skallagrigg and I have waited to be heard. Can you hear me, Esther? Can you hear? Can you see the pattern behind Arthur's cries? Can't you see the pattern now?'

Suddenly all fell silent, her mind cleared of doubt, the pattern falling into place inside her before the anarchy of the wind about her and of her twisted strange position in the mud on some deserted playing fields. The pattern clear, the doubt about the stories answered, the wrong righted at last.

THEY ARE TRUE. THEY ARE NOT STORIES. THEY ARE TRUE.

And she began to cry with that truth for it was certainty in her telling her: THE STORIES ARE TRUE. ARTHUR IS REAL. THE SKALLAGRIGG IS REAL. FRANK IS REAL. DILKE IS REAL.

Then Esther began to scream out into the wind, her head rising a little off the mud and grass with the effort: 'Yes I can hear. You are real. You are *real*!' and her tears were for Arthur for it seemed to her that all these years he had been calling and no one had heard, not until now in this place distant from where he was, years and years too late probably.

The mud, the cold, the wind, the wet, the discomfort, the looming wind-thrashed tree; all was forgotten. Her mind raced round the idea of Arthur being real, and the Skallagrigg existing. How, where, when, why she did not know. But they *were*, as she was, as the mud was, and the cold, and the wind and the wet. REAL! She wanted to scream and perhaps did scream, for her legs, bare to the wind, raised and kicked in the mud and wet of the wind and her clenched fists full of mud and grass raised and dashing slowly on her chest and only the word REAL was real any more for a time.

So in the end the stories are true.

Then she relaxed back and looked no more against the wind over the canal, allowing the excitement of discovery to suffuse her mind and her body as first she grinned and then she laughed a laugh that anyone could have interpreted, able-bodied or not: it was a laugh of relief and delight. And she no longer felt cold, or ill, only exhilarated.

Then Tom came running, having found the other bridge and worked out how to get back all by himself.

'*Amh!*'

IT'S ALL RIGHT, TOM, I'M ALL RIGHT.

But looking down at her his eyes were wild with fear.

IT'S ALL RIGHT, TOM, REALLY IT'S ...

He touched her legs and her clothes and held his hands up with such fear in his eyes.

'Amh.' His hands were red with blood.

'Amh.' He was beginning to cry.

She strained to look, and saw that her legs, her dress, her cagoule, even one of her shoes, were covered in blood, red against the mud, diluted in places by the rain.

OH, TOM, OH! and then she began to smile, began to laugh so freely, so fully, that Tom's eyes lost their fear as he looked at the blood on his hand.

IT'S ALL RIGHT, TOM. IT'S GOOD, TOM. IT DOESN'T HURT, TOM. I CAN'T FEEL IT. IT'S JUST ME, TOM, IT'S ME.

THE BLOOD'S ME.

Tom looked doubtful.

ME, TOM, ME. NOW OH IT'S ALL RIGHT, TOM.

'Not hurt, Amh?' he said, wondering.

'Nah,' she said.

Then Tom grinned. 'OK,' he said.

He righted her chair, straightened her dress, and he bent down and put his arms around her, one round her legs and one round her back.

'C'mon, Amh.' And gently, for she was his most precious thing in the world and she had survived, he picked her up and put her in her chair.

'I was silly,' he said, doing up her straps and taking off his jacket to cover her blood-soaked dress and legs. The blood made smears on her legs. Better for no one to see until they got home.

NO, TOM, YOU WEREN'T. YOU KNEW WHAT TO DO. YOU FOUND
ANOTHER BRIDGE AND YOU CAME BACK. OH, TOM, I LOVE YOU I
DO!

'I know, Amh,' he said, pulling her chair back up on to the hard
surface of the path, and then, after casting one reproachful glance
towards the bridge, turning her towards home again.

'C'mon, Amh.'

'Yeh,' she said softly. Happy, protected and her mind full of love
and certainty for Tom, and for a future in which she would set out
to find the real Arthur and the real Skallagrigg.

As they approached the houses on Woodstock Road Tom turned
her chair to look back at the fields. The wind was dying now and
the air dry, even warm.

'Where's Skalg?' he asked. For that was why they had come in
the first place and he had just remembered.

She waved a hand happily across the battered fields and trees,
and on down over the canal.

YOU'LL HELP ME FIND HIM, TOM.

'Down there?' he said.

'Nah.'

'More?'

'Yeh.'

'Over the fence?'

She nodded.

'Can I come, Amh?'

She looked up at him and said, 'Yeh, Toh.'

'Amh?'

She nodded.

'Can you walk. There?' He pointed to the distant fields beyond
the wooden fence by the canal.

'Yeh.'

'Can you run. There?'

'Yeh.'

'Amh? Like this?' And Tom ran a few steps back down the
private road, his clumsy run, and then grinning back to her.

'Yeh.'

'When?' He bent to look in her eyes, his face inches from hers.
His glasses still spotted with rain.

SOON, TOM, SOON.

'C'mon then, Amh. Take you back to Helen's now.'
YES TOM.

'Nana! Nana!'

Esther's cry at the front door brought both Margaret and Helen running, but their shock at seeing the blood of her first period all over her legs and clothes was quelled, as Tom's fear had been, by the power of Esther's delight, and purpose.

'Nah, nah, nah,' she shouted when first Margaret and then Helen tried to take her away to be cleaned up. She wanted to tell them her discovery.

'What is it, Esther?' Margaret was eventually forced to ask, kneeling at her side.

'Nana,' said Esther more quietly, 'ssst Skagree!'

'Skalg,' explained Tom who, like Esther, had refused to be moved from the front hall, or even to take his cagoule off until Esther had been heard. The two of them stared at the adults, their faces so obviously full of light and excitement that Esther's condition was forgotten for a time.

Margaret got Esther's simple alpha-numeric board.

Esther spelt out SKALLAGRIGG.

'What is that?'

Esther looked blank.

'Tom, what is it?'

He looked away to avoid the question for he remembered being admonished by Esther for mentioning it in front of Richard Marquand. Slowly she signed out: HE'S A REAL PERSON. HE EXISTS. OR DID ONCE. I WANT TO FIND HIM.

'Who is "Skallagrigg", Esther?' asked Margaret again. And then, seeing her face blank and waiting for another question, Helen Perry-Wilcox said, 'Who is it?'

Esther giggled and shrugged. DON'T KNOW. HELP ME FIND HIM? she signed.

'Of course I will,' said Margaret, 'if you tell me who he is.'

Esther signed, ARTHUR'S FRIEND.

Margaret waited.

AT A HOSPITAL LIKE STURRICK.

'Darling,' said Margaret eventually, 'if I say I will help you find these people once you explain who they are will you please let me

take you off to the bathroom and be cleaned up. I mean . . .'
Margaret couldn't help smiling at Esther's pleasure. And why,
after all, should a girl who had been toileted by others all her life,
and who still ate food messily and always would, and who could
not always control the spittle in her mouth, feel the slightest
embarrassment about a period she had wanted to have for so long.

Esther signed a name: BETTY.

'Yes, my love, you can phone Betty this evening.'

These promises made, Esther yielded herself to Margaret and
Tom agreed to go with Helen into the kitchen and help lay the
table for supper, and tell of his adventures by the canal where he
found Esther again all by himself.

'Do you know who Skalla . . . um is, Tom?'

Tom stared at Helen uneasily. He was not ready to admit that he
knew. Eventually he said cryptically, 'Amh's going to go and find
him. Over the fence. Me too.'

'What fence?'

'Amh'll find it and take me,' explained Tom.

'Where?'

'Over the fence,' said Tom.

And how strange then that Helen too felt excitement, as if the
Skallagrigg was hers to find as well.

PART III

THE
SEARCH FOR
ARTHUR

FORTY-ONE

Esther Marquand now had a dream: to find the source of the Skallagrigg stories. It was a dream that became a driving force, consuming and powerful, and gave her confidence and purpose.

She sat at her Possum with Margaret and Helen Perry-Wilcox and outlined the nature of her belief that Arthur was real and might still be alive, and the Skallagrigg was a 'god' based on someone who had once lived.

Esther typed in speedwords, Margaret translating for Helen.

'If you're right about the stories coming from real people the key question is "When were the stories first told?"' said Helen, intrigued by the whole issue. 'If you knew that then you could put an age to Arthur.'

Esther nodded seriously.

YE. L'SUE IND E L ABI.

She typed with Margaret repeating it in English. 'The best clue is the reference in one of the stories to the "war", which could only be the First or Second World War. I'm sure it was the second and if so then it works out that Arthur would have been born in about 1918, have gone into hospital in about 1925, and would be over sixty today. If you assume that the Skallagrigg was a real person then he would have probably been a good bit older, like a teacher, and so would be say eighty today.'

Helen nodded and said, 'So they could both be alive.'

'Yeh,' said Esther.

'I wonder what the life expectancy in a long-stay hospital is?' said Helen.

Esther looked blank. It was not something she had thought of.

'Lower than in normal life I would have thought,' said Margaret.

Esther went into action again: E U D O T I N D Z A B L H O S P I T A L U L E R Z.

'There are many . . . no . . . a lot of other clues about the hospital and the people there,' continued Margaret for Esther, 'like it is a traditional Victorian hospital and the grounds are very big and that it is set on a hill overlooking a hollow or glen where ambulant patients go walking. There is a chapel or church with brass altar rails which is separate from the main building or buildings. Arthur's best friend is called Frank and he can walk. He also works in the chapel. There's a male nurse called Dilke who will be a little older than Arthur, and a patient called Rendel. Other patients' names are Jerry Baxter (whose cot Arthur took over, so he died in about 1925) and also Joseph Ryman who nearly died in one of the stories. There's . . . a Norman, a priest attached to the hospital called Father James Freeman.'

'Have you got the stories written down, Esther?' asked Helen.

Later, over tea, Esther suddenly began to type again: J R F A U . . .

'We could make a list of all the things we can do to follow up the clues, like writing to hospitals, find out which ones have chapels.'

Then she stopped. She was thinking. She began to type again, J Y PU K . . . 'I was thinking there must be a short cut, one clue that will lead us straight to the hospital. That's the main thing: to find the hospital.'

'Yes, yes, I was just going to say,' began Helen, putting down her cup and leaning forward very seriously. 'You seem sure of the name of Dilke for the nurse. Now I don't believe that's a very common name, in fact,' she said, getting up and going over to the telephone and rapidly flipping through the directory, 'in fact, there is not one single Dilke in the Oxford book! Not one. Now there must be a professional body for nurses which we could write to . . .'

'*Me!*' said Esther, potentially upset.

'Yes, you,' repeated Margaret. 'Helen's just throwing out an idea.' Esther subsided into her chair, her head lolling to one side as she listened to Helen's idea.

'. . . and ask if they can trace the name. Hopefully, there'll only be two or three and we can contact them and . . . and see . . . and see what . . .'

'See what they have to say for themselves!' said Margaret. 'Dilke was not a nice person from what Esther says.'

'Nah!' said Esther.

That evening Esther wrote the first letter of many in her Skallagrigg research, a simple request to the Royal College of Nurses in London concerning Dilke. So excited was she to have done this and anxious to get it off that the following morning, before Helen drove her back to Netherton, Tom wheeled her down the road to a postbox where, at her insistence, he hoisted her up and helped her post the letter herself.

'Who to?' asked Tom.

'Skyagree.'

Tom stared at the black slit in the postbox and put his ear to it. He tapped the red painted cast iron. He put his fingers in the slit and peered in. Postboxes were always things of awe and of mystery to him.

'*Skalg!*' shouted Tom into the postbox's depths.

'Yeh.'

'Coming in to us,' said Tom.

Esther was silent. She wrote in her diary that day: 'Tom said, "Coming in to us," and I thought how like "Coming home to us," that was. Coming home. Home. Arthur and the Skallagrigg was about coming home. I could not get that out of my mind.'

After two weeks Esther received a typed letter in a nice white envelope. It was from an officer of the Royal College of Nursing in answer to her query and explained that the RCN did not admit male members until 1960 and so would have no record of a pre-war male nurse. However a male nurse working in psychiatric and mental handicap hospitals (Esther had mentioned Dilke's field of work) would probably have been a member of the Royal Medico-Psychiatric Association but, explained the RCN information officer, 'our inquiries suggest that their records going back that far do not exist.'

Esther discussed the letter with Margaret who came down to Netherton with Marion one weekend. 'I think Helen's got some ideas on how to go further,' said Margaret, 'so next time you come for the weekend you can work something out with her. She's much better than me at that sort of thing, with her library training and so on. I'm sure she's very good at finding out information but she is a bit worried about taking it over from you.'

'Nah!' said Esther vehemently, looking quite upset. *'Yeh!'* I WANT HER TO HELP NOW, YOU AND HER, she typed.

Margaret was touched. 'She's becoming such a good friend, Esther,' she said, 'and I wouldn't have met her but for you.' She was silent for a time before adding, 'It's strange how things happen isn't it? I mean . . .' She stopped, having no need to go further. Fate, or whatever it was, seemed to provide the very people, weapons and compensations needed to combat the adversities it also created.

The two of them pondered this paradox without saying another word about it. What else could they say?

'I'll be seeing Helen later this week so I shall tell her you don't mind if she helps. I'll write, my dear, and see you at Harefield when the holidays start. Your father may have to come and fetch me. Or send me one of the company cars with a chauffeur! You see I got rather tired driving today.'

'Mah . . . Mah . . . ,' said Esther: Marion. She could drive.

'I'm still taking lessons, Esther, and your Dad said I could drive one of the cars when I've passed,' said Marion, who on these occasions kept in the background. 'Then I can drive Margaret when necessary.'

'Well, yes, that would be nice,' said Margaret carefully. 'Meanwhile your father did promise me a company car on occasion and I would rather enjoy that!' She smoothed her dress and sat up a little straighter. Esther and Marion exchanged grins.

It was nice to see Margaret enjoying life once more. Brian's estate and Richard's success meant that money at least was not a problem.

'Now I had better go, dear, because I'm feeling tired. The excitement of this visit, I expect . . .'

Later, when they had gone, thinking about the letter from the Royal College of Nursing, Esther did not believe it possible that there was no record of male nurse Dilke anywhere. Could his existence really now only be in the memory of his victims?

Esther responded to this first setback with typical energy by writing to Helen Perry-Wilcox asking her advice. Helen phoned the school one evening, and suggested that Esther wrote to the

Department of Health and Social Security, asking if there was anywhere where she could get a list of hospitals for the mentally handicapped and ill in Great Britain. Then letters to some of the hospitals would enable them to track down Dilke.

Esther herself decided to write to her old social worker Eileen Coppock, now in America, asking if she remembered where Peter Rowne had been before he had come to the Dale Centre. All she could remember was him telling her that he had heard the Skallagrigg story from someone 'where he was before'. Yes, agreed Helen, there would be a record of that somewhere.

At the same time Esther began to reformulate the information in the stories and, in return for helping him with some of his programming, got Graham to mark up a map for her with the locations mentioned in the stories: London (where Father Freeman had come from), The Racks down in Cornwall somewhere, and Blackpool where the boys had gone on an outing, and Arthur had gone at some other time. Graham made red dots on the map at these locations and marked each with a number to indicate the story it came from.

There was one other location, a name that recurred in two of the versions of the younger stories: Apsham Wood. She had, naturally, looked this up in a gazetteer of the British Isles but it was not in there. She got Graham to write the word 'Apsham' above the map of the British Isles. Maybe it existed somewhere and there would be a way to find it.

She also began a file on Arthur's hospital, detailing all the points that the stories brought out, so that she could build up a picture of what it would be like: the glen, the chapel, the brass rails, the pews, the wire baskets in one of the hospital corridors (mentioned in three stories) and the airing courts.

'I'm going to find you, Arthur,' she would whisper to herself sometimes, looking out of the school windows across the lawns to the farmland beyond. 'I know you are still alive . . . I know it.' But she said it to reassure herself, for if her calculations were correct Arthur would be over sixty and that, as Helen had hinted, might be a great age to survive in the kind of grim hospital Arthur had been put into as a boy.

'Please be alive,' she would plead in the night, lying in her bed, listening to the sounds in the dark outside.

FORTY-TWO

By 1982, Richard was forty-one and rich. Valuations at that time
of his share-holding in ComputaBase alone put his worth, at
prevailing prices, at about 11.6 million dollars; with his stock-
holding in Fountain Systems his total worth was about 15 million
dollars.

But there was more. He had begun, in a quiet way, to invest in
real estate in the High Wycombe area through his own company,
Corsant Ltd, whose other director was his solicitor. But this venture
(which by 1982 was worth about 1.1 million dollars and held one
small office building in Wycombe and several residential properties)
began with a most significant purchase – the property next door to
Harefield, discreetly acquired in 1980. He already had in mind the
possibility of dealing with Esther's future in a very effective way:
by setting up a residential home for the handicapped that would,
naturally, give her a permanent place for life should the need arise.

Like many of the successful new technology businessmen who
emerged in the 1970s and '80s in North America and Europe,
Richard wore his wealth quietly, almost with embarrassment. Like
them he preferred to keep a low profile, directing his growing
business behind two or three deputies who deflected any media
attention.

A chauffeured car now picked him up every morning at seven-
fifteen when Esther was not at home, and at eight-thirty when she
was. His return time was less predictable. He had made a rule
never to bring work home, or to have business meetings at Harefield, though this may have been simply because he did not have a
wife to handle the social side. He rarely drank, and he stayed slim,
swimming three times a week at the Wycombe pool en route to the
office, and exercising at home before bed (10.15, sharp). His
holidays were infrequent (being tied mainly to Esther's) and his
friends very few. His interests were mainly business or the garden

of Harefield. It seems, in retrospect, a curiously dull life, one still benumbed perhaps by the Sheila/Esther tragedy.

For two weeks in August Marion had asked if she might take a vacation, though it was hardly to be a holiday. She had been selected for an exchange programme involving a stay with a young Christian community in Lyon engaged in local social work.

An agency found another girl to take Marion's place and Esther's own account records bleakly: 'She told him [Richard] that she had experience with handicapped people but it must have been young children as she was tiny, smaller even than me, and could hardly push the chair along the road or get it up kerbs. I took an instant dislike to her because she spoke to me as if I was a child, and she had pointed fingers that hurt when she dressed you, sort of pinched. Also she was obsessively tidy and accused me with her eyes if I spilt food or anything. She had a thing about time and got uptight if things did not happen punctually! Daddy was run-down from work and missing Marion who made the house run smoothly. It was the first time she had really been away when he needed her and made him realize how much he relied on her. But Marion had to make her own life too. Also, I was only just recovering from a cold.'

On the morning of 19 August the helper had taken Esther by bus into High Wycombe – Esther liked this journey and in mid-morning the conductors had time to be helpful with her chair. They were to do some shopping, have lunch, go to a film and come back for tea. At about midday Richard was summoned from the garden by the telephone. It was the helper in a call box, hysterical, the sound of traffic and people around her, and another sound, one that Richard had not heard for a long time: Esther crying.

'Mr Marquand. Mr Marquand, I've tried everything. I've asked her everything it might be. I . . .' She sounded a little angry, as if whatever it was it was Esther's fault. Richard, angry in return, said icily, 'Put the receiver to Esther's ear please and have more money ready, this may take a little time.'

'I haven't any more change, Mr Marquand, not 10p pieces, I don't think . . .'

'What number is on that phone?'

'There isn't one, it's . . . been ripped off. They must have . . .'

'Where are you?' said Richard calmly.

'In the market square, opposite Boots.'

'Tell Esther I shall come immediately. Tell her I'm coming and please, *please* stay where you are.'

'He's coming all this way, he's having to come . . .' he heard her say accusingly to Esther before she replaced the receiver; and hearing it he knew she would have to go, and go that day.

He put down the phone and thought for a moment, breathing heavily. He phoned the home help agency. He spoke briefly and they did not argue. There were times when Richard Marquand could convey passion, and on that occasion it was passionate anger. They were to find a replacement, today. Yes, that day.

'Yes, Mr Marquand.'

Richard drove straight to Wycombe and soon found them. They were sitting on a bench near the public phone, the picture of non-communication. The helper, looking irritated and angry, was watching out for him one way, and Esther was facing the other: pale-faced, puffy-eyed and sniffing miserably to herself.

'I'm sorry, Mr Marquand, but she . . .'

Richard knelt down by her chair.

'Right now,' said Richard, ignoring the helper and going straight to Esther, 'is it something hurting?'

'I've asked that, Mr Marquand. I've tried everything.'

With a look he shut her up.

'Nah,' said Esther.

'Is it . . .'

Esther looked from under her angry brows at the thin legs of the helper standing by their side.

Richard paused and smiled slightly.

'. . . anything serious?'

'*Yeh,*' shouted Esther. And from the tone of her voice she might have added 'For God's sake', had she been able.

'To do with your safety or health?' he finished.

'Nah,' confessed Esther more quietly. 'Nah.'

'Oh, Esther!'

They stared at each other, father and daughter.

'She started quite suddenly but wouldn't tell me what it was,' said the helper. 'I asked you, didn't I?' she added, speaking slowly and loudly as if she felt Esther was of below average intelligence.

'When and where?' asked Richard.

It had been at the far end of the High Street, just past Marks and Spencers. Esther had suddenly shouted, 'Me, me,' and the helper had asked, 'Me what?' and got no further, pushing the chair on and distressing Esther the further she got from something she had seen.

'Nah.'

'Heard?'

'Yeh!'

'Heard. A car?'

'Nah.'

'A person? A conversation?'

'*Yeh!*'

'In the street?'

'Nah!'

'In a shop?'

'Yeh.'

Richard thought of the shops. Butcher, estate agent, the boutique, the music shop.

'*Yeh!!*'

'The music shop. The record shop?'

'Yeh.'

'They were playing a record you liked?'

'Yeh.'

'She didn't *say*,' said the helper.

'Well, Esther, you could surely have waited until you got home and told me on the Possum.'

'Nah,' said Esther coldly.

'Well, come on, let's go and find out what it was. Were they playing it on the public system? Yes, that was it,' Richard sighed. They set off back down the High Street, more colour coming back into Esther's cheeks with each step. Richard got rid of the helper, telling her to make her own way home and he would look after Esther. He would save the dismissal until later.

The shop had two counters, one at the front for pop and the other at the back for classical. Esther seemed to think it was probably classical.

The girl – the woman – behind the counter was tall, with brown eyes and a thick wool pullover whose design had a large sheep grazing in woolly green grass right across the front. On the back, revealed when she turned around, were more sheep and a wooden fence.

Richard explained the problem. His daughter had been passing by and heard a record she wanted playing, was there any way of knowing what it might have been?

'You sure it wasn't one of theirs?' said the assistant, indicating the pop counter. She spoke directly to Esther.

'Nah,' said Esther, suddenly rather shy.

'You'll have to speak up,' said the girl, coming round the counter and kneeling by Esther's chair, 'can't hear a damn thing in here.' She spoke with an Australian accent.

'Nah!' said Esther more loudly.

'Well, let's see, what have we had on, wait a jiffy, when was it? Any idea?'

'About three-quarters of an hour ago,' said Richard.

'Well now we've had a bit of Mozart, Bach . . .'

'Nah,' said Esther.

'Hang on. I'll have a look at what I've played.' She went back behind the counter and disappeared from view.

'Janacek, another Mozart, it's his anniversary week, wait a moment. Wait . . . a . . . moment.'

The girl stood up again, holding a record with a green cover to her sheep.

'Da . . . dum!' she announced with a grin and revealed before Esther's gaze a record with a young girl's face on it in a rural bonnet.

'English country dances!' said the assistant. 'Got to be!'

'Yeh,' said Esther.

'Hey, have you been dancing?' She looked at them both.

'Yeh,' said Esther.

'With her grandfather.'

'Me!' said Esther.

'What?' said the assistant, coming back to Esther and holding the record sleeve before her. 'Do you want to tell me something? Something you've done?'

'Yeh.'

'My, well. I'll have to guess.' She looked up at Richard for a moment. Esther noticed that her eyes were warm and sparkling. And Esther noticed that her father was smiling, and looked suddenly younger, much younger, not like her father at all.

Richard liked the way she addressed Esther directly and left her to make her own reply, which was a nod of the head and an excited stretching of the legs and flexing of the hands.

It was immediately put on, and headphones carefully set by the assistant on Esther's head, the volume adjusted upwards from silence until Esther indicated that it was at the right level.

'Well, we can hear it as well,' she said to Richard, flicking a switch so that it came over the shop's main hi-fi system.

'Not again, Kate!' someone shouted from the pop counter.

'I like it,' she shouted back. 'Better than the rubbish you're playing most of the day!' She turned to Richard. 'Did you take your daughter to the show?'

Richard shook his head, not speaking, because he rather liked the music, melodeons and trumpets playing the kind of tune he remembered Brian Ogilvie dancing to on the single occasion he had been to one of the Charlbury Men's dances.

Esther seemed lost in a world of her own, her head now bent down as she listened looking small and waif-like under the black padded headphones.

'She's athetoid isn't she?' asked the assistant when Esther was settled.

'Partial,' said Richard.

There seemed nothing remarkable in the fact that she should know or that she should ask. There seemed nothing remarkable in any of it, as, after a very long journey, two people who have gone separate ways find themselves coming together on the same road, at its final turn to home.

'Have you worked with spastics?'

'In Melbourne. Did a stint in a home for handicapped children. Terrible place.'

'Touring Europe?'

'Earning money at the moment to continue my Grand Tour,' she said. 'Rather late in life maybe!' She looked in her late twenties.

'I . . . I . . .'

'Yes?' she said.

Their eyes met for a long moment, the music of country and dance and rural love about them and Richard had never felt so calm before a woman before, nor so inwardly certain.

Skallagrigg

Esther looked up and said, 'Dada!' She wanted the headphones taken off, but the interruption did not disturb their sudden communion.

'I should like to take you out for a drink,' said Richard evenly.

'Yes, I'd like that!' she said laughing a little. 'And *did* you like it enough to want to buy it?' she asked Esther, turning the music off and taking the headphones back.

'Yeh!' said Esther.

'Do you, Esther?' Esther nodded.

Richard paid the bill and on the receipt she calmly wrote her name: Kate Munro and a High Wycombe telephone number.

They met a day or two later, and within a month Richard Marquand brought Kate home and introduced her to Margaret. She had already met Esther again.

Tom was also there and he shook her hand formally, said hello, and went off to the vegetable garden. He sensed when trouble might be afoot.

Margaret was out in the garden, sitting by the wooden table on the lawn, her face shielded by the green umbrella. She wore a white summer jacket and grey slacks, and round her neck was a thick gold chain with a pendant on it. She wore old-fashioned sunglasses and her face was shiny with sun oil, as was Esther's, who sat near her.

Kate, ushered forward by Richard, approached them and Margaret affected at first not to see her, though Esther let out a cry of recognition. Then Margaret looked around, took off her sunglasses, wiped her hands with a tissue, and said something about 'Esther and I are covered in sun oil, aren't we, darling?' which established her involvement with Esther. Finally she put out an unenthusiastic hand.

Kate responded, a little too loudly, sat down a little too quickly in one of the wicker chairs, and looked around a little too soon for Richard's support. He had retreated, ostensibly to bring out tea for everybody but really because he felt that his absence might be the easiest way for them to get to know each other.

'You're from Australia I understand?' said Margaret. Her old iciness was there, and she gave a chilling inflexion to the word 'Australia' which seemed to cast that country and all its people out into some global waste-tip of inferior places.

'Yep, that's right,' replied Kate, finding to her alarm that as if by some patriotic response her voice and accent had, against her wishes, become at once louder and more pronounced. 'Yes,' she added more softly.

Margaret raised an eyebrow and waited for more information while Esther, sensing immediately that her grandmother was treating Kate as if she was a dangerous interloper, herself assumed a hostile attitude, her smile gone as she waited for Kate's response.

'I'm from Melbourne,' added Kate finally. She shifted uneasily in her chair while Margaret put her sunglasses on again, turned to Esther, smiling with an exclusive affection. 'Daddy will be out with tea soon I expect. I hope he remembers the Battenberg cake we bought,' and turned back to Kate, the affection disappearing from her eyes.

'What do you do ... er ... Kate?'

Kate forced herself to say softly, 'I am assistant manager of the classical department of a record store in High Wycombe.'

'But that's just temporary, I presume. Aren't you on this tour Australians and New Zealanders do round Europe and the world?'

'Yes, sort of.'

'So what do you plan to do? Eventually.'

'Eventually? Eventually I plan to do what most women plan to do I guess: find the right man, make a home and have some children.'

'I thought your generation were liberated from that,' said Margaret coldly.

Kate smiled. 'So did I!' she said laughing. But the laugh faded before Margaret's seeming indifference.

'What did you do, in Australia?' asked Margaret.

The question released a sudden flood of home feeling in Kate who got up restlessly and peered up at the house, and then round about the garden.

'I worked as a secretary for a time, then for a long period in a children's home, doing a second job in the evenings in a sports centre to raise funds for this trip. I've got a teacher's training qualification but I never used it.'

As Margaret raised her hand against the sun to continue her interrogation, Richard appeared on the patio by the house carrying a tray and Kate turned, went to him, said immediately, 'I'll take

that!' and removed the teapot from the tray for fear it might slide
to one side. They exchanged a look. Richard said something softly.
Kate laughed easily.

Margaret saw it all with a half-smile, for it was good to see
Richard with a woman at his side carrying a teapot and the lovely
house rising behind them both. Margaret glanced round at Esther
thinking that the problem – and there was going to be one – would
be with Esther and not herself.

She felt she had not handled this first meeting well, but then she
had never been good at meeting people. But these last few years
with Esther, and more recently through knowing Helen, had been
easier, and she liked what she had seen of Kate. And anyway . . .
anyway, during her illness and convalescence she had lain in bed
or sat in seats like this one and had time to think that life is too
short to spend it worrying. Be grateful for what good things you
have.

'Oh dear,' thought Margaret, 'I wish I knew what to *say*.'

'Where's Tom?' she said.

'I'll go and get him,' said Kate, glad to get away from the
awkwardness that seemed hovering around the table. Richard
wasn't the same here with his daughter and . . . mother-in-law, he
was all stiff.

Kate went off and when she had gone Margaret found what to
say without looking for it. She watched Kate's tall and rangy
figure disappear behind the hedge and she said, almost involuntarily, 'She's nice, she's very nice, Richard,' and she was rewarded
by Richard smiling, almost shyly, and looking for a moment quite
boyish, a look she had not seen on his face for so very many years.

Kate reappeared with Tom's hand in her own, laughing and in
conversation with him.

'Tomatoes? How many?'

'Don't know.'

'But what are you going to do with them all?'

'Going to make chutney with Helen,' said Tom.

'Who's Helen?' asked Kate, and they all explained, glad to have
something neutral to talk about.

As they came to the table, Richard explained that Margaret's
chutney was a new idea, Margaret explained that it was really
Brian's chutney since it had been his mother's recipe and they had

always meant to make some. Kate said, 'Look, Richard did re-member that Battenberg cake. Didn't you buy that with your grand-mother, Esther?'

Esther. A cloud had come over her face, over her life.

'Yeh,' she said coldly, begrudging the fact that Kate had found a question that forced a positive response from her. She had seen the little exchange between her father and Kate up by the patio, and been jealous. She had seen Margaret quickly, too quickly, won round, and been angry, felt betrayed. She had seen Kate eager to please Tom and make up to him and felt sick. And here she was now, cutting the cake as if she was one of the family.

'Esther, that's your piece,' said Margaret, passing it on to her.

'Nah!' said Esther nastily, with a look of dislike at Kate, and the chill wind of adolescent insecurity blew over the tea party, the first small signals of the gale that was to come.

FORTY-THREE

Esther quickly adopted a coolly polite attitude to Kate, accepting her help when it was needed and, by reserving her smiles and charms for Margaret, Marion and her father, making her non-acceptance the more obvious. She was soon expressing her dislike – or fear – in letters to her close friends, writing to Betty Shaw in early September that her father's 'new girlfriend is tall, comes from "Orstaahlia" and speaks with an accent. She takes up a lot of his time in the evenings and he has failed twice now to come and help me with things when he said he would because of *her*.'

Just before the start of the new term that same month she wrote also to Graham Downer: 'And anyway I'll be glad to get away from here not just because it'll be good to see you but also because of the latest "affaire" at Harefield – my father's picked up some girl in a shop and she comes here more and more. Yesterday she tried to get a barbecue going but got it all wrong. I could have told her the wind was in the wrong direction. Well, I couldn't, but if I had been able I wouldn't!! Some people I can't stand.'

Whether or not Esther knew what she meant by 'affaire' we cannot now say, but in fact Richard and Kate were not then, nor for some weeks, lovers. It seems they had discussed it but there was a feeling between them that their relationship – their friendship – was in some essential way more important than either had experienced before and that this seemed to have lifted from them both the pressure of being too quickly physical. Kate appreciated the fact that Richard was in no hurry, while Richard understood and sympathized with Kate's wish to be friends before being lovers.

TOM, I'LL MAKE YOU A GAME WHILE I'M GONE. ONE YOU CAN PLAY I WILL I WILL!! ONE ESPECIALLY FOR YOU.

'Will you, Amh?'

'Yeh, Toh.'

'For me?'

Tom raised his two hands, cocked each set of fingers into pistol shapes, and fired them at the front door.

WHEN I NEXT COME BACK.

'OK, Amh.'

The two talked incomprehensibly to each other while Richard and Tony, Graham Downer's father, helped Marion pack the van with the paraphernalia needed for Esther's return to Netherton.

Graham was inside the house, dismantling the computer which he had brought down for the day and whose game, 'Space Battalion', had inspired Esther's sudden promise to Tom. Because, as always, he had stood watching them play – Esther now able to use an adapted joystick – helpless before the machine's speed. His fingers and his mind did not work that fast. But he liked the colours on the screen, and grew frustrated. It had always been a problem for him.

WE COULD SLOW IT DOWN FOR TOM, Esther had told Graham on her Possum.

'We could,' said Graham doubtfully, 'or make up something like it, which would be easier.'

WE WILL, typed Esther.

Graham looked uninterested, but Esther's interest in the problem was aroused and so her promise was made.

Then she turned to her father: 'Dada!'

'Yes?'

'Dada eyer amg me! Meah!'

Richard understood: 'You want me to let you know if you get any replies to your letters. All right, all right, I will, I *will*!'

Esther and Margaret had prepared several more letters in pursuit of the Skallagrigg. One was to the organizer of the section at the Royal College of Nursing that dealt with psychiatric nursing, asking if he knew of any way to reach older nurses who might know pre-war colleagues named Dilke; a second was to the Institute of Health Service Administrators asking for a copy of the *Hospitals and Health Services Handbook* which was the best source for information about British hospitals; a third was to Harry Barr, asking if he knew any Skallagrigg stories; and the fourth was at the suggestion of Richard who had asked if there was a magazine spastic people read and, if so, why not put an advertisement in it. Esther had looked doubtful,

but the magazine had been found – a monthly published by the
Spastics Society – and the letter containing the copy for the small
classified ads sent: 'SKALLAGRIGG, DILKE, FRANK. Information
on any or all of these, however "unimportant", will be gratefully
received by research student.' Followed by a box number. The
'research student' was Esther's idea, the obscure wording of the ad
Richard's, since, he argued, only people who knew what the words
meant would reply anyway.

'Yes, I'll let you know if there are any letters,' he said again,
pushing Esther's chair on to the lift at the rear of Tony Downer's
van and seeing her safely up into it.

Margaret had already returned to Charlbury so Richard now
stood alone with Marion and Tom to say the final goodbyes. Quick
waves, some last kisses, as Tony started the engine.

'Good luck, Graham. Thanks, Tony,' said Richard.

'Bye, Amh,' said Tom.

Richard smiled, a little tired and anticlimactic now the school
holiday was over. Esther would not be back for a weekend for six
weeks.

'Bye, darling. Have a nice time,' he called out as the van U-
turned and scrunched off slowly down the drive into Abbey Road.
Marion left later that morning for a Christian weekend so that
with everybody but Tom gone Harefield seemed almost deserted
and derelict in the grey blustery September afternoon.

'Kate's come,' announced Tom the following morning in the
kitchen as Richard prepared a salad lunch for three. Tom had
heard her car.

And she had, parking her Mini by the garage, slowly getting out
to place her bag on the gravel. Tom opened the front door, Richard
behind him, and Kate turned towards them and waved, smiling.
She wore white shorts, pink trainers and a classy looking T-shirt,
with 'Le Club' woven in white over the right breast.

'What are you looking at?' called Richard, stepping out on to
the driveway and looking up at the sky.

'The swifts,' she said, pointing. For there were dozens of them,
high high above Harefield and its grounds, darting back and forth
as they turned and turned again to feed.

'Lo,' said Tom going straight up to her and putting his arms round her waist and bending his head low to her side. He had grown these last two years, and he was thick-set, but Kate was still three or four inches taller.

'Come on,' said Tom.

He took her hand and led her laughing round the back of the garages and she waved again at Richard as she disappeared towards Tom's vegetable garden.

Richard laughed, his face quite changed from the evening before: young now with the sun shining on it just as it shone on Kate where she stood upon the path. He went to pick it up, turned and then stopped after a few steps, as she had done, to stare up over the house to the sky, where the swifts flew back and forth and back again. He felt his heart begin to soar, but controlled it with a shake of his head, and went back into the house.

Tom was their chaperone, sleeping in his normal room upstairs which lay between the biggest, Richard's, and Kate's, the guestroom, which lay at the north end of the house and had been decorated with a heavy Morris wallpaper of rich colour and design, and furnished with Victorian antiques.

So Tom was between them, and shared those days of growing intimacy which made up their holiday, inveigling them both to spend time on his tomatoes and to watch the wasps' nest he found under the roof of one of the sheds, whose workers commuted back and forth between the ripening apple trees in the orchard and their nest.

'Bzzz. Bzzz. Bzzz,' he would say, his eyes white with pretended fear as he danced his fingers about like wasps and then pointed and darted them in symbolic stings.

Other times he preferred to be alone, and Richard and Kate worked at a bit of weeding, or pruning, or started up the petrol-driven mower and cut the grass roughly under the trees.

One day they went to a garden centre and bought some hawthorn bushes to plant along the east boundary where, two years before, a wall had partially fallen down and the neighbour, whose responsibility it then was, had put up a length of high fencing. Richard wanted a hawthorn hedge and some field maple because, he had read, it made a good habitat for birds.

'Not there,' said Tom pointing away down towards the orchard and past it to where, out of sight, the old wooden fence, ever moist and ivy clad, still defined their land.

'No, here,' repeated Richard.

'Why not?' Kate asked Tom.

'Because of Amh,' said Tom, digging another hole for a hawthorn bush.

Another afternoon Tom suddenly took Kate and led her into the shrubbery and on to the wooden fence.

He stood her there and said, 'When's Amh coming back?' as if, suddenly, he had missed her.

'When her next long weekend comes,' said Kate. 'Not for a bit.'

'When's Marion coming back?' Marion was away again, her final week's holiday that year.

'Next week,' said Kate. 'What's special about this place?'

Tom did not reply. He was looking over the wooden fence.

'What are you looking for, Tom?' Kate asked.

'Skalg,' he said.

'What's Skalg?'

'Skalg's coming for Amh.'

'When, Tom?'

'Don't know.'

'What's Skalg, Tom?'

Tom raised his hands as if in supplication to the copper beeches which rose above them beyond the fence and filtered the light into shadows. He puffed out his cheeks and thrust out his chest.

'Skalg is . . . is,' he faltered, deflating. He stared over the fence, his head a little bowed. 'Skalg will help Amh,' he said.

'How, Tom?'

'Skalg will make her run.' And he ran a few faltering steps and rested his hands on the fence, which shuddered under his weight.

'Is Skalg Skallagrigg?' asked Kate. She knew about Esther's researches.

'Yes. But I'm naughty.'

Kate smiled and hugged him.

'Shouldn't you have mentioned it?'

'No,' grinned Tom wickedly, adding: 'Not never.'

'*She* has!' said Kate.

'Yes,' said Tom, dubiously, furrowing his brow. 'Kate?'

'Mmm?'

He bent his head shyly. 'Do you like Richard?'

'Very much.'

'Good,' said Tom with evident relief. He took her hand and led her out of the shade into the light, to Richard.

Later Kate told Richard of this last part of the conversation – she had the feeling that the Skalg part was meant to stay private – and of how Tom had said of them 'good'. Richard smiled easily, his shoulder comfortably against hers as they did a joint task in the kitchen. 'Good,' he repeated. It seemed that Tom had blessed them and there was something in that blessing that freed them now to be finally themselves. Richard turned to kiss her and she knew they were ready to love and give with all they had.

That same evening Richard and Kate went to London to see a show. Until that year Richard had always made sure someone was in the house if Tom was alone, but Tom was nineteen now and said he did not want a babysitter. He took pride in doing things for himself, and was more careful about electricity, running water, fires and leaving the place secured than the average normal adult.

So they came back and found he had gone to bed, and was asleep. He had left a tray of tea things for them as he knew this was something Richard liked.

It was a warm evening, so they made the tea and took it outside into the darkened garden. Richard brought out a liqueur for each of them and they sat quietly, the rustles of a nocturnal garden about them, the light from the kitchen softly yellow on the patio up by the house, and they beyond its reach. The tea was refreshing, the liqueur sweet and fiery. It lingered on their lips. Kate reached out a hand for Richard who took hers and held it. She could feel his tension and her own desire which had grown for days, for weeks perhaps, which held her now, as it seemed to hold him, waiting and breathless. He stood up, let go of her hand, and bent down to kiss her. When they had kissed before it had always been a little circumspect: tender, gentle, but wary. Now their lips met freely, lingering and long and then more urgent, tongue to tongue, as he pulled her up and they stood pressing ever closer together, her breasts and soft dress to his chest and shirt.

They broke from their embrace and walked arm in arm further into the darkness under the apple trees, and there, free of all light from the house, barely able to see each other, their bodies became

even freer as she leaned against the rough warm bark of an old
Bramley apple tree. His hand slipped down to her hips, and
pulled them to his mouth and his lips were at her thighs then,
as he knelt before her, her back arched out from the trunk
against which her shoulders rested, her head back, her mouth
sighing and open, as she looked up on to the deep silhouettes
and darkness of the apple tree and her hands played in his hair.
She stood up before him, kicked off her shoes, raised her skirt to
step out of her pants. She knelt before him, caressed his thighs
and then lay beside him, her hands and fingers playing over his
chest and his stomach. Then she undid his trousers and felt him
as he turned to her, kissed her, rode his hands over her blouse,
undid the buttons, found her nipples, slid his hands to her thighs
to raise her skirt as he came over on to her, and harder and
deeper and surer they were with each other, Kate sighing his
name and he, the scent of her body and the scent of her hair
mingling with the raw scent of grass and earth below and ripening fruit above . . . he drove into her, again and again in violent
release, and they shuddered holding each other tight, as if the
other was all the world, the only world of light in the deep
night-time darkness in which they lay.

They lay quiet after that until Kate began to grow cold, and then
they gathered themselves and their things, dressed themselves,
kissed again, and slipped back to the house silently, turning off the
lights, and Kate saying, 'My love, I'll sleep with you now,' firmly,
for she knew there was a time when she must claim her own and
instinct told her not to acquiesce in a scurrying affair to save the
feelings – always unknown – of children. Children would know
anyway.

Next morning Tom knew. That was sure. He did not knock on
Richard's door next morning as he usually did, getting himself up
instead, going down to the kitchen and fixing himself some
breakfast, and finally going out into the garden to collect and
wash up the tea things they had left out the night before in the
darkness on the garden table.

Then he gathered the mail, and put it out on the kitchen table,
in a neat row, one letter after another, not realizing that one of the
letters was for him.

'Lo!' he said when Richard came down. 'Nice day!' And it was, a day when Kate and Richard could not but touch each other, and Tom could not but join in their happiness.

The letters included two from Esther – to Tom and Richard – and two for her. One was an acknowledgement for her advertisement, which would be going in the October issue of the spastics' magazine, the other was a holding letter from the psychiatric nurses' representative's secretary saying that Mr Nubekian was on holiday but would be in touch when he was back, meanwhile she had 'taken the initiative' of passing a copy on to Miss Margaret Monell who was the oldest-serving member on the committee and might also have some suggestions to make.

It was at least not negative, and Richard, as he had promised, phoned Esther about it. She sounded pleased, even excited. Graham came on. Yes she was having a good time, she and Graham had spent a lot of time programming some computer games. They had done one for Tom. Now Esther wanted to speak to Tom. Tom listened, and said, 'Yes, Amh, *yes, yes!*' seeming pleased.

Richard spoke again finally, and, with Kate in the room along with the wonder and beauty of her (as it seemed to him), the obvious fact that she was Good News blinded him to the memory of Esther's hostility.

'Would you like to speak to Kate?' he said, regretting it on the instant as Kate shook her head and groaned and Esther fell silent before saying a spiteful 'Nah!' End of conversation. Their honeymoon period, he and Kate realized, might soon be over but not – and a twinge of guilt passed over Richard's soul as he thought this – until Christmas perhaps, before which Esther would not be back for more than the odd weekend.

FORTY-FOUR

Three days before Esther's October half-term, Richard had a letter from her. Could she spend the first few days of the holiday with Graham as they were 'into some computer programming and want to finish it while we can'?

Richard gave his consent knowing that there was more to this than met the eye. Kate was frequently at the house now and when Esther had come for a brief exeat, on the one occasion Kate and she coincided there had been trouble: Esther sulked and was rude. The more so because it was obvious that Marion and Kate respected each other and there was no friction between them, leaving Esther feeling isolated. So now she had found a good reason not to come home, and Richard was as happy as she was to avoid confrontation.

Yet perhaps after all it *was* just the craze for computing. Two days into half-term Tony Downer called: 'It's extraordinary, Richard, they do nothing all day but sit at their computers in Graham's room and work away at the games they're designing,' he explained, baffled. 'I've had to make rules about going out for fresh air in the morning and afternoon but they go on about their programs even then, and over meals. Anne and I have banned them talking about it over the evening meal but then an awful accusatory silence reigns and they look at each other in a resigned kind of way. As for the beach ... they never see it!'

Richard laughed – he laughed a lot these days.

'I see that kind of tunnel vision among a lot of the programmers I have in ComputaBase. Be thankful they're not losing sleep.'

'Oh but they are. Well, I mean, they only go to bed when Anne insists. But don't worry, Esther's happy enough. And she really isn't any bother. We like having her because she makes Graham more sociable, if you call what they're doing sociable.'

Esther and Richard talked, and Richard gave his permission that

she should stay three days longer. She herself said she must come
back then because of Tom. She knew he would be missing her, and
she had made a game for him.

'I'll come and pick you up on the Thursday, darling,' said Richard. 'Tom's coming down so I'll bring him with me. We'll all
come.'

'Yeh!' said Esther enthusiastically.

Richard's 'all' meant Tom, himself and Kate. Esther's 'all' evidently substituted Marion for Kate. Richard opened his mouth to
make sure she understood but his courage failed him. 'See you in a
few days then,' he said.

'Yeh,' whispered Esther, troubled. She could tell when her
father's voice tightened. He wasn't going to bring Kate down, no
that wouldn't be fair. He *couldn't* do that. Surely . . .

But, perhaps insensitively, he did and Esther was not pleased to
see Kate in the car when they arrived in Weston-super-Mare to
pick her up. She grew positively hostile when she discovered they
had come not down from boring old High Wycombe but up from
an exciting few days in the West Country and had taken Tom with
them.

'It was good, Amh,' said Tom naively, oblivious to the daggers
in Esther's eyes and the set tightness about her mouth, or the
gloom that furrowed Richard's face and troubled Kate's.

The hostility degenerated to rudeness in the first service station
they stopped at: Esther spat *'Nah!'* at Kate when she tried to help
her out of the seat in the car. 'Dada. Toh.' Her father or Tom. And
later when Kate knocked over a cup of coffee as she was unloading
the tray of food and drinks Richard had brought, and it spilt over
her own dress, a look of smirking triumph went over Esther's face.
And she laughed, willing Tom to laugh as well.

'Esther! Stop that!' said Richard sharply, over-reacting perhaps
because there was now so obviously a pall over what had been a
lovely break. Esther stared defiantly at him and then sank into a
rebellious uncooperative silence before turning to Tom and
somehow, in that language of theirs, making him giggle and say
'Yes, Amh,' in a way that managed to exclude Kate.

Kate made herself scarce for the two remaining days of Esther's
holiday, returning to her flat in Wycombe in preparation for
starting her job again after the weekend.

So long as she was there Esther was rude and tense, and able to make the rest of them miserable, especially Richard who in less than twenty-four hours lost the buoyancy and spontaneity that had been with him over the past weeks.

With Kate gone Esther seemed her old self again for the weekend – active, cheerful, especially nice to Richard.

There were more replies to her letters about the Skallagrigg, and a big fat *Hospital and Health Services Handbook* had come. At the back it listed every hospital in Britain under different categories.

She spent a morning going through the book, and counted the different kinds of hospital: mental handicap hospitals (adults), 211; mental handicap hospitals (adults and children), 108; mental handicap hospitals (children), 31; mental illness hospitals, 310.

She did a quick mental calculation: 660 hospitals with, say, one hundred patients in each – 66,000 altogether. How was she going to find Arthur among all those hospitals with all those patients?

She remembered Sturrick; she remembered some of those patients whose records she had seen burnt on the bonfire. The page-turner turned through page after page of hospitals: Abbeyfields, Admiral's Court, Aldingbourne Court, Aldingham Hall, Allt-y-Mynydd Hospital, Amberley House, Anchor Lodge Hostel . . . page after page . . . Lawn Hospital, Leigh House, Leverndale Hospital, Littlemore Hospital, Lochmaddy Hospital, Long Grove Hospital . . . Storthes Hall, Stratheden Hospital, Sturrick Royal Hospital . . . Sturrick! Still listed; the book must have been prepared before they knew it was closing.

The task of finding Arthur, even if he was still alive, seemed impossible. But she set to it with determination, ordering what material and data she had from the stories, and when Margaret called to say that Helen was driving her over the next day Esther asked Helen, through Richard, to pick up some books in Oxford mentioned in the *Handbook* which introduced her to the full horrors of institutions for the mentally and physically handicapped.

Esther herself later left the following account of the impact the first reading of this material made upon her in her notes for Daniel Schuster:

There was a caption in one of the books: 'These institutions were designed to cram as many patients as possible into the available space.

The dormitories also served as dayrooms. The inmates' entire existence, with the exception of meals taken in the dining hall and occasional excursions to the exercise yard, was spent contemplating these four walls.' And I knew Arthur had been confined in such a place. That much was clear from the stories.

God knows what happened to spastics in places like this in the nineteenth century when some people believed such conditions were a punishment from God for sins committed! What terrible lives did they live? I started having nightmares and once Marion found me hysterical, panting and gasping as I had sometimes as a child and able only to shake and say 'Dada Dada Dada Toh Toh Nana Nana!' I think Daddy must have mentioned it to Helen because she apologized for bringing the books. But I explained it wasn't anyone's *fault*. You can't stop people getting hurt by trying to keep the truth from them.

I always considered this period of reading a time when I became committed to making a noise on behalf of all handicapped people who, against their will, were limited in life. Initially I saw it purely in terms of the spastic handicapped and their physical restraint, but as time went by I widened my definition of handicap until it included almost everybody. I came to realize, principally through my final understanding of Dilke, that the greatest restraints are self-created, and are essentially of the mind. That is what the wooden fence and the struggle to get over it symbolized; that is what the game of 'Skallagrigg' made players experience. My reading made real the suffering I had instinctively sensed it was Arthur's task to face and conquer.

A few days after her return to Netherton, Esther received the first of two lots of replies to her advertisement for information about the Skallagrigg.

One, postmarked Chester, was in a stiff white envelope, neatly typed and looked official. The others were handwritten and less substantial looking, and these she decided to have opened first.

Graham did this for her, careful not to look at the contents before she did as he laid out the letters on her tray.

The first was poorly written in blue felt tip pen and said, simply:

Dear Advertiser,

I saw your ad and could make no sense to it. Are you some kind of nut putting in ads like that and cluttering up the pages for what might be useful things. If your word means anything you might tell me and I will tell you what I know.

Signed,
E. M. Bird.

There was no address but the postmark on the envelope was Northampton.

The second, written in pen, was more interesting:

Dear Sir/Madam,

I am very intrigued by your advertisement in the September issue of 'Spastic News' and would like to know more about the nature of your inquiry. In 1964, I was working as a probationary nurse in Hollitcray House, which was then a long-stay hospital for mentally handicapped children in Huddersfield. I believe its patients have now been absorbed into the Psychiatric Unit of the Huddersfield Health Authority and Hollitcray itself put to other uses. The reason I am writing is that I remember very well – and have often wondered about – that one group of the children, more advanced and several of them cerebral palsied and probably wrongly placed, played various 'skallagrigg' games, and made up stories using that name. I often wondered about it and might have forgotten about it but that in my later work in quite different places – I moved into paediatrics and qualified as a doctor – I heard that same name mentioned more than once. I doubt if I can help you, but I would be most interested to know what the name means. I enclose a stamped addressed envelope.

The letter was signed Raymond Innes and had a Derbyshire address.

Esther re-read this with some excitement. Huddersfield. North again. Always north. A tendency confirmed by the remaining two letters.

The next was from Edinburgh and the paper it was typed on was familiar: it was the white roll paper used with Possum machines, and the type was capitals, blurred because of an old ribbon. A spastic had sent it.

> Dear Advertiser,
>
> Am astonished to see your notice in the news because I was that morning making one of my Skallagrigg paintings, see enclosed sketch. I draw with my feet. I am CP. The Skallagrigg and Arthur were my favourite at Tilworth. Now I'm married and painting is my hobby. I was astonished because we used to say SK————G was a secret so when I exhibit I never put a title, except I have used Arthur's name. Maybe you'll write and say what you're about? If I can help I will depending on what you're doing. I'm 56 and have been married three years to my husband. He is able-bodied and works packing for Boots. I'll be interested in your reply.
>
> Yours very sincerely May Adcock.

Esther's final letter, the official-looking one, was on the headed notepaper of the Chester Health Authority and came from an assistant nursing officer, E. Gunnarson, SRN, RMN:

> Dear Box H1131,
>
> A colleague has drawn my attention to your advertisement because she is aware of my interest in linguistics and etymology and some research I have done into sub-languages and dialect used among patients in long-stay hospitals where I have worked. 'Skallagrigg' is a name used widely in the Midlands and north of England by many patients for a character who appears to have some sort of mythical status among them. My researches have not been exhaustive but I have reason to believe that it derives from a very well known Icelandic saga character, Egil Skallagrimmson, familiar to English readers from 'Egil's Saga'. How this filtered into hospital dialect is hard to say and I have no information on that, but I rather think it would have come from someone familiar with the Icelandic sagas who worked in a hospital and perhaps told the story to patients, or referred to it.

The printing of the word 'Dilke' with a capital in your
ad is presumably a mistake as it is not a name but rather
a very common abusive slang-word used widely in
hospitals. It means 'male nurse' and is usually applied
negatively.

If you would like more information please get in touch
on the number at the head of this paper. My extension is
237.

Initially, a wave of disappointment came over Esther as she read
this, casting cold water as it did on any notion that the Skallagrigg
was real and alive. But then she relaxed. This linguistic
explanation, assuming it was correct, did not preclude the
possibility that Arthur had adopted the idea of Egil Skallagrimmson
to create a name for someone he knew and loved, whom he called
the Skallagrigg. Yes! Yes, thought Esther, the search is still on.
Anyway there's still Arthur, and he must be the key to it.

Esther was now faced with the problem of how to follow up
these letters. It was one thing to invite interest, another to respond
to it, but after a day's thought she decided the best thing was a
holding operation, writing the same letter to all of them thanking
them for their replies and saying she would be in touch more fully
very soon.

But she impulsively decided to write more personally to May
Adcock, who sounded nice and had sent her drawing of . . . well
. . . it was hard to say of what: a futuristic landscape with a being
surrounded by radiating coloured lines.

Dear Mrs Adcock,

Thank you for your reply to my advertisement. My name
is Esther (Marquand) and I am a student at the
Netherton Manor School for Special Needs in Hampshire.
I am CP like yourself. The reason I advertised was
because I am doing a project on the Skallagrigg stories
and am interested to trace their origin if possible. I
thought the ad would put me in touch with some
people who might help and I got four replies one of
which is yours. The trouble is I'm not sure what I'm
looking for unless of course *you* know where the stories

come from?! But what I've done is to compile all the
stories I could find and put them in a file and now I'm
trying to sort out the information in them in the hope it
will lead me to the hospital where they started. Ideally
I'd like to talk to you if you would allow it, but we might
have communication problems. I'm not sure how good
your speech is – mine isn't very good but I have a
portable computerized screen and I can type up what I
want to say.

Anyway it wouldn't be easy to come to Edinburgh at
the moment as I'm in the middle of studying for 'A'
levels. You mention 'Tilworth' and I believe there is a
Tilworth Grange Hospital near Hull. Is that where you
are from? A lot of the Skallagrigg stories seem to come
from the north of England so that fits. It's a lot to ask but
if you could write down any of the stories you know on
your Possum including as many details as you can remember of the story as told to you that would be helpful.
But if that's not possible let me know and I'll think of
something else. Thank you for the sketch which a friend
has put on my study wall for me. I enclose a stamped
addressed envelope for your reply.

Esther was now less than eight months from her 'A' levels and
very near the time when she and Richard would have to plan her
next move. For the time being the family was waiting to see if she
could get a college place, preferably at Reading or Oxford because
of their closeness to Wycombe or, failing those, at the Buck-
inghamshire College of Further Education which occupied a
number of sites very near Wycombe.

The school believed that Esther, like Graham Downer and one or
two other students of her outstanding year, ought to be able to
gain places at a major university, and facilities for the handicapped
were better than they had ever been. The advice was to apply for
university entrance in the usual way, and then wait and see what
she was offered and how she did in her examinations.

Esther had her academic work easily under control, and time to
pursue her other activities, which were now principally the continuing research into the origin of the Skallagrigg stories, and

creating computer games. There were, too, occasional forays out
of the school for its chess team for which Esther played second
board, and work on the editorial board of the school magazine.

Meanwhile she had worked with Graham on a special computer
game for Tom which marks the beginning of her more creative
involvement with computer games programming and came at a
time when new computer games, written mainly by young
amateurs, were beginning to find a commercial market.

Like many others, Esther and Graham started by simply using
reprints of games programs from specialist American magazines.
But perhaps because Esther was designing a game disciplined
enough to work for a specific purpose – to appeal to Tom – she
managed to create one that worked for a much wider audience.

Previously Esther had been held back because she had no easy
inputting method for anything except her Possum and the Rank
Xerox hardware her father had at home. But Leon Sadler's new
keyboard meant that inputting was no problem; and the Sadler
screen had made a significant difference to her ability to express
problems to others, and think them through for herself.

The game she finally came up with for Tom was called simply
'Tom's Game', the title being a play on both his name and his
passion for growing tomatoes. The game involved 'growing'
tomatoes by manipulating a cursor and then 'harvesting' them
against a time limit. The scores got higher as the time got less.

When Esther tried it out on Tom it worked very well and held
his interest for a time. At last he had something he could do on the
computer. But she had it at school and the unexpected spin-off was
that a lot of younger children with poor dexterity tried out the
game and enjoyed it, and from there, as the possibilities began to
widen, she rapidly improved it, adapting it for use by students with
normal motor control by a clever grading of dexterity levels based
on the skill levels then commonly used for computer chess games.
Neither she nor the school seem to have been aware of the
educational value of this approach for it created a series of
successive standards which students with severe handicap could
aim to beat; this encouraged a real concentration on dexterity
skills among players, while enabling them to play others with
greater mobility on a conventional sports handicap basis. But for
the time being the game was quite unknown outside the school.

Her interest in computing science was deepening, and Graham Downer* later wrote that in effect she did the additional 'A' level computing science course he was following by correspondence with him. 'By then her real interest was gaming, because she could see the fun it gave her fellow students, and almost as an ancillary to this, she created her own programs for speeding up the ways in which she could interact with computers, particularly for word-processing and programming enhancement – using, and frequently developing, techniques which saved inputting time. Neither of us realized how advanced some of the work we were beginning to do was, or that it might have commercial value.

'I believe now that if her relationship with her father had been closer then he or one of his experts like Leon Sadler would have spotted the significance of what we were doing. As it was we worked very much alone and, to be honest, did not encourage others to be interested in what we were doing. Typical teenagers, in fact.

'By then – it was 1981 or '82 – graphics was just developing, inspired mainly by work in America which was well ahead of us in Europe. Obviously I was aware of her interest in Skallagrigg, though I don't think she had yet perceived that she could make a "game" of it. That research, and her computing, were separate, but they were drawing inexorably closer. I think her first real exposure to the potential for computer graphics was a school visit we made to the 3rd Micro-computer Show in London. We bought several of the new games on show there and broke into their programs and saw what they were doing. You could do that kind of thing in those days! Well, you still can I suppose. We were also into databasing by then and programs like dBaseII were just out and really revolutionizing the way ordinary computer-users could manipulate data.

'In other words, all the elements – gaming, Skallagrigg, graphics, database techniques – were coming together in Esther Marquand's interests and work. It just needed something or someone to focus them for her. It turned out to be "someone", didn't it! And who better than Daniel Schuster!'

In November she had a second letter from May Adcock in

* G. Downer was later to pursue a successful career with Digital Computers (UK) Ltd, and served in 2010–11 as a vice-president of the British Computer Society.

Edinburgh enclosing a copy of a tape she had recorded of herself
telling two Skallagrigg stories.

> It was quicker to speak them than to write them, and I
> don't think my speech is too bad. Sometimes I repeat
> words I have trouble with. Maybe you know the stories
> but they are ones I like. I know more, so write and say
> what you think. My husband (Alastair) was interested in
> your letter and said that if you are ever this way you
> should visit.

Esther wasted no time listening to the tape. May's voice was
typical cerebral palsied, long in some vowels, sibilant and oddly
extenuated in places. A warm woman's voice recorded in a normal
world of domestic sounds – someone moved in the background, a
car started in a street, and the quick sudden sound of a hammer in
the distance.

One day Arthur thinks, 'I'm bored with these four walls I am
and the same people all year long,' so he tells Frank to ask a
good dilke a question.
  'Arthur wants to know something,' says Frank.
  'Does he now? What's that?' says the dilke who was
friendly.
  'Arthur wants to know what goes on in the old annexe.
No one goes there, no one come from there. Are they still
wards or what?'
  The dilke says, 'That's under review.'
  After a time Arthur speaks to Frank. Frank goes back to
the dilke: 'Arthur says, does that mean nothing's there and
nobody?'
  'Yes.'
  Arthur thought about that for months, thinking, 'That's
strange, our ward's crowded out with beds and they're
always squeezing more in and the same's true in every other
ward. So why is the old annexe empty?' He knew it had
been like that years.
  Eppie says, ''Cos there's ghosts there that's why.' Ha ha
ha ha.
  Frank says, 'Arthur says the only ghosts are in your head
and that's not the reason.'

Then Frank adds, 'Arthur says, if you went to the old annexe do you know what you'd find, Eppie?'

Eppie looks to Frank for an explanation.

'Arthur says Skallagrigg's in the old annexe.'

'Stupid,' says Eppie, laughing so people want to smash him.

Summer came and there was a fête, and that was the day Arthur decided to prove his point to Eppie. The dilkes can't watch everything at once though Dilke himself comes near to it. But Arthur tells Frank to take him to the old annexe and they set off when they think Dilke's watching the sports. But Dilke's that cunning and Arthur's fooled for once.

When they get inside the annexe they're in a corridor leading to a big room that looks like a ward with the beds taken out, and sure enough Eppie's followed them.

'What now?' thinks Frank.

'Explore while we can,' Arthur tells him. The corridors are cold and filthy like no one's been there for years and there's stairs up to floors above. When they move there's echoes in the cold high places behind them, and they start in fear at the sound of themselves. They can see the sun outside, and sometimes hear clapping from the sports through a broken window.

'I want to go out again now. There's no ghosts, no Skallagrigg,' says Eppie but Frank pushes on ward after ward. Arthur's silent, his head down, staring ahead.

Eppie says, 'We're lost. Stupid. We got ourselves lost.'

Frank says, 'Arthur knows. Arthur's got a brain and can remember.'

Frank stops. Eppie says, 'What we stopping for?'

Frank says, 'Arthur's going back in his brain to when he was a lad. Arthur was in a ward here once.'

After a time Arthur speaks. Frank says, 'Arthur says this place has seen dreadful life.'

They move on. The corridors are dark and heavy on them. There are padlocks still on the open doors. Is it just the echo of their own steps they hear? A place like that can smell of ghosts.

They came to a ward like no other. It was a children's ward 'cos you can tell by the size of the cots and they're wooden not metal. They stop by the door looking in. Arthur, his head down, Frank behind him, Eppie grinning with fear, all close together for comfort. Not one of them speaks.

They're looking at where their childhood was, a ward like
that. At one end there's a clearing, and a pole from floor to
ceiling. There's restraining rope round it, frayed, dry-old,
coiled on the floor and knotted. They know what that was
for. For punishment. Eppie's white with fear. Frank pushes
Arthur in a little and one of his hands reaches out to touch
the bars of a cot.

'Don't,' says Frank. 'Don't please.' He says that because
now Arthur's crying and Frank can't take that.

'Come back,' says Frank.

Arthur's gone, his head slumped forward and tears on his
creased cheeks. He can hear what once this ward sounded
like and he's back where he once was.

'Skyagree,' he says.

Eppie starts to laugh.

'Shut up,' says Frank. '*Shut up shut up, Eppie.*' Then he
says gently to his friend, 'Come back, Arthur, please come
back.'

Arthur looks up at him and reaches a hand up as best he
can and Frank comforts him.

Arthur speaks.

'What's he saying?' asks Eppie. 'What's he say?'

Frank listens and then says, 'Arthur says the Skallagrigg is
near us now. He knows Arthur's here again. Skallagrigg
knows.'

Eppie's silent.

Arthur speaks and Frank says, 'No I won't.'

'You won't what?' says Eppie. 'What won't he, Arthur old
pal?'

Arthur speaks and Frank says, 'He wants me to lift him
into that cot. He wants to be put in one of the old wooden
cots, just like he used to be when he was a boy.'

Arthur says, 'Yeh.'

Frank says, '*No!*'

'Yeh,' says Arthur looking at him. It's a command.

'You'll do it now,' says Eppie. Grinning, ha ha ha.

Frank leans down, undoes Arthur's canvas straps and
gently puts him in the cot.

Arthur speaks. Frank obediently puts the side up.

Outside there's a cheer and clapping, carried on warm
sunlit air. The warmth stops at the cracked panes in the high
barred windows above them.

Arthur lies back and strains his head round to look out of

those windows, as he did when he was a lad. He's crying and his mouth's moving. He's saying, 'Skyagree, Skyagree' and Frank is looking at him and mouthing the word after him: Skallagrigg, Skallagrigg.

Then Arthur turns his head away and looks at Frank, and he speaks like something in him is dying.

'What's wrong with him?' says Eppie.

Frank goes down on his knees by his friend and he says, 'He will he will he will he will you said he will he will, Arthur.'

'What's he saying?' repeats Eppie.

'Arthur says the Skallagrigg won't ever come, not never. But that's because he's here and can't think right. I told him he's wrong.'

Eppie says, 'Frank's right, Arthur. I shouldn't have said what I said before. He'll come for you one day. If he didn't where would you be?'

Arthur's eyes fill with tears and Frank reaches down to him and puts his arms round him and holds him while he cries. He's crying for the Skallagrigg. He is afflicted with despair.

Then they hear steps, heavy steps, quick; steps somewhere down the corridors and they're scared.

Eppie's eyes are as wide as saucers.

Then they hear the harsh sound of a window stick being knocked on metal bedsteads rat-tat-tat, rat-tat-tat, rat-tat-tat. It's being deliberately tapped to scare them.

'Who the hell's in there?' says a voice they know and hate.

Dilke's followed them in. Dilke's got them where he wants them. Dilke's got his window stick and nothing will stop him. Eppie and his friend start making frightened noises and Frank lifts Arthur back into his chair, does up his straps and stands in front of him to protect him.

They wait as the sound of angry Dilke approaches through the old corridors. Then Arthur shouts: 'Skyagree!' and his voice is like a boy's, but loud loud and it echoes all round the old ward, along the dusty floor, between the cots, up the restraining pole, over the ceiling and down to a window barred and broken, and it escapes like a bird into the sky just before Dilke's shadow comes to the door and spreads over the ward's floor. He's standing there with an evil smile on his face.

'Well well well,' he says tap-tap-tapping his window stick

on the palm of his left hand and looking first at one and
then another.

'What are you snivelling for, Eppie?' he says with cruelty
in his eyes. Eppie's crying now. Frank says, 'Arthur says it's
all right, Eppie, he's called the Skallagrigg and he's heard.'

'What?' says Dilke. 'Speaking fucking nonsense again are
you, Arthur? Going to tell us what he says before . . .?' and
then he raised his stick to hit Frank out of the way when
there's a cough, a woman's cough and they were all of them
struck dumb and still. A lady's cough!

That stopped Dilke short all right. Frank slowly lowered
his arm which he had raised to defend himself and they all
looked round to where the cough came from: the doorway
into the old washrooms and all that bit beyond.

A woman stood there dressed up to the nines and with
pretty shoes and elegance from her ankles upwards. She
had on a summer hat with a feather in it. She stood staring
with an alarmed smile on her face.

'Oh,' she said, 'I didn't expect anyone to be here.' She had
a nob's voice, quite loud, and she changed from surprise to
annoyance. She looked like one of the ladies who was
allowed on the right side of the rope on the cricket field.

Dilke recovered himself in a flash. He lowered his stick,
fiddled with the hook on its end like he had been looking at
it, stared up at the broken window, and then put that smile
he wore with visitors on his cheeks.

'Can I help, madam?' he said.

The lads looked at each other, their eyes popping out of
their heads, except for Arthur. Arthur looked tired.

'Isn't this the old annexe which is being done up?' she said.

'Yes, madam,' said Dilke, his face falling over itself to look
nice.

'My husband mentioned it. I felt I should take a look, I got
rather hot out there you know.'

'Your husband?' said Dilke, insinuating, wanting
information.

'Yes,' said the woman as if everybody should know who
her husband was.

'What were you doing with these patients?' She sounded
a little angry. She sounded like she knew what Dilke was
about to do.

Eppie saved Dilke's skin. 'Nothing,' says Eppie. 'Mr Dilke
is doing us a favour, that's what.'

'Really?' said the woman.

Frank and Arthur stared.

Eppie said, 'Come to explore haven't we, and Mr Dilke takes care of us. He's our favourite.' Then Eppie laughed like he was going to be sick and put his arms into Dilke's and pulled so hard that he nearly fell over.

'Oh, well! That's good, Mr Dilke. My husband has mentioned you.' She looked doubtful, which isn't surprising.

Then she said, 'Well, I've seen enough,' and started walking past them without another word.

Arthur speaks and Frank says, 'Missus, Arthur says thank you.'

The woman stopped and looked round at Frank.

'Arthur says thank you very much,' he repeated.

The woman looked down at Arthur. Arthur stares back. Only his blue eyes were still, the rest of him was all ugly stress and movement.

'You're named Arthur are you?' says the woman.

Arthur's head jerked, his legs slewed sideways, his long hooked hands entwined, his mouth opened and closed and his nose snorted as he spoke, finally.

Frank said, 'Arthur says yes.'

The woman looked a bit afraid.

Dilke said, 'That's enough now, lads!' jocular-like, as if he was their friend.

The woman said, 'For what? Thank you for what?'

Frank looked at Arthur and Arthur moved terribly, straining to speak, his mouth and throat terrible to see in its effort.

Frank said, 'What, Arthur?' Then he knelt by Arthur and put his hands on Arthur's and stared into his eyes and said, 'What?' The woman watched this. Her eyes were softer now. Arthur calmed down and managed to speak.

Frank stood upright and turned and looked at her. Frank said, 'Arthur says for thinking of us.' The woman stared for a bit and then turned quickly away. She had tears in her eyes.

Dilke said, 'Well, of course these boys shouldn't really be in here!'

Frank said, 'Arthur says it's Open Day!' and Arthur grinned.

The woman said, 'Well, Mr Dilke, I daresay they got rather hot as I did and wanted to be in the cool! They seem to have come to no harm, though I feel the door should not have been left unlocked.'

'Builders most likely,' said Dilke who knew how to shift
the blame.

'Yes, probably so,' says the woman. Then she turned and
said, 'Goodbye, then. I'm glad I visited. I hope the old annexe
will be new again soon.' She went down the long corridor
back through those old wards which in all their long days
never saw a woman as pretty as her.

Frank pushed Arthur after her and Dilke followed, silent for
once.

Then he said, 'You said the right thing there, Eppie.' Eppie
looked at Dilke's window stick.

'It's all right,' said Dilke looking pleased with himself,
'that's all right Eppie. All's well that ends well, but get out of
here before I change my mind, if you can find the way.'

But that wasn't hard. The woman had gone before them,
and the air carried a lovely scent where she had been. So
they followed that.

Esther's response to this story was significant. She wrote in her
diary: 'Arthur is in a maze like Hammerhead. Like Graham now.
Like everyone. Skallagrigg is outside it and that's where Arthur's
calling. To get to Skallagrigg I must get to Arthur. I feel I must do
it soon. I feel it is more urgent than anything in the world. More
important than my examinations. With my whole body I can feel
Arthur calling. I cannot tell Graham, or Betty, or Daddy. Can I tell
Nana? I can only tell Helen because I reached her through the past
and she understands. I cried for Arthur last night. He is calling and
no one hears. *But I have heard.* I have, Arthur. But I don't know
where you are and that's why I cried. I don't know where you are
and I'm trying so hard to find you. Please wait for me.'

The significance of this note is Esther's association of Arthur's
predicament with that of a player in a computer adventure game.
The game Esther was thinking of was Temple of Apshai, one of the
games she and Graham Downer bought at the Micro-computer
Show they had visited. Hammerhead is the fictional character its
creators use in the manual to demonstrate the game. Esther
Marquand is already beginning to conceive of the institution where
Arthur is trapped as a role-play dungeon, with many chambers,
like the labyrinths of Apshai. She is perceiving herself as the player
on a journey, first to track down Arthur in the dungeon, and then,

with his help, to move on to a different level to find the Skallagrigg.
She is beginning consciously to experience the material that she
will later, with so little time left, make into the game that was her
testament to life.

FORTY-FIVE

'Kate will be there.'

Richard had finally confessed. 'I mean, not just tonight but for the whole Christmas week,' and Esther had fallen into a grim, malevolent silence.

They were in Richard's new black Mercedes 500SE travelling smoothly back home from the last day of the December term. Christmas was six days off, and the villages and towns they passed through were bright with Christmas lights and decorations and busy with evening shoppers muffled against the cold.

But this good cheer stopped at the polished side-window out of which Esther bleakly gazed; and if her eyes were the mirror of her soul, her soul was oppressed by anger, hurt, disappointment, and trepidation, all born of insecurity. Somewhere too was guilt: for being jealous of her father's legitimate happiness, for being selfish, for simply being alive and as she was.

Richard had known Kate's presence for the holiday would be ill-received by his daughter but he had dithered about how to announce it, leaving it to this awkward moment in the car when he was not looking at Esther, and had the excuse of driving to avoid real confrontation. Richard Marquand's successful management skills and decision theory failed with his daughter Esther.

He tried light-hearted conversation, he tried reason, he tried anger, but Esther stayed silent and withdrawn. The more so because, unknown to Richard, the first thing she had noticed when she got into the car was Kate's scent. She had noticed it when she first met Kate, and it did not help that she liked it herself. It hung subtly in the car, enveloping her with its pleasing freshness, but she felt attacked by it.

Finally exasperated, Richard put on a cassette of the choir of King's College, Cambridge, in the hope that it might change Esther's mood.

'Do you remember how we used to listen to this at Christmas when you were younger?' he said as the first track came on. Esther stared bitterly out of the window, ignoring him.

Their silence was overtaken successively by the vigour of 'God Rest You Merry Gentlemen', the sweetness of 'Quem Pastore', the breath-holding serenity of 'Silent Night', as passing Christmas lights crossed and re-crossed Esther's stolid face. But when the tape ended, the angry silence had not gone away and Richard's fingers drummed on the steering wheel as he drove on silently, not putting on another tape.

He remembered another Christmas, the first one in Charlbury, which had started badly, and he could only hope this one would improve as that one had.

But there was another cloud, darker and more thunderous than the temporary one of Christmas that now enshadowed them.

Kate's decision to stay in England for Christmas had meant deferring until the end of January the trip home to Australia she would otherwise have made. And then – and this was the cloud – Richard intended to accompany her. It was a trip he had long planned for business purposes, for there was enormous potential for his kind of computer consultancy/retail operation in South-East Asia to where they had been making increasing exports, and from where they had gained a number of lucrative agencies for the European markets.

To go with Kate, to see her home, to meet her parents, was now as attractive to him as it was to her. For Kate and Richard were in love, a love that had taken each of them by surprise. It was quiet, simple and deep, a thing less of words than of touching and silence.

It was fortunate that Marion, now more involved with her boyfriend Jeremy, accepted their relationship with good grace, even pleasure. Kate's increasing presence changed the routine at Harefield, for though Kate had never meant to take over Marion's role, inevitably she began to do so, mainly over meals which Richard now took more at home than before. In any case, Marion was spending many more evenings out than she had when she first began to live at Harefield.

So she welcomed Kate, and it was tacitly recognized that Marion would leave soon, or at least that the nature of her role would

change as Kate fulfilled more and more the role of Richard's partner
and wife.

All of them knew that a key problem would be Esther, for she
would always need help, day in and day out, and this might not be
a role that Kate could, or should, accept. There was another uncertainty too, for Marion had grown to love Harefield, and her work
with Esther had given her an interest in and vocation for working
with the handicapped which, when Esther was away at Netherton,
she fulfilled by doing voluntary work.

Jeremy did similar work and Richard was beginning to realize –
from telephone calls for her at Harefield, from letters, from people
who talked to them in the street when they were out together –
that his modest 'housekeeper' and her man were, almost, a private
help organization all on their own. He could see – or perhaps Kate
had made him see – that soon they would want to marry and take
a job that brought them together.

Now, with these changes in the air and term ended, Esther sat in
the back of the car, coldly alert as her father turned into the drive
of Harefield.

Kate had put the outside light on, and over the door she and
Marion had put a Christmas wreath with some spray-on snow in
the corners of the door's windowlights.

Hearing the car, Kate came out to meet them. She said hello to
Esther through the window as Richard got her chair out. Together
then the two of them lifted her into it.

For a brief moment there was an awkwardness as Richard got
more things from the boot of the car and Esther looked away from
Kate, feeling lonely and upset.

Suddenly and spontaneously Kate bent down and kissed her on
the cheek. Her thick hair brushed Esther's face, her lips were soft
and warm, her scent good, always good.

Oh oh oh, and Esther wanted to be enfolded, enveloped.

'Nah!' said Esther rudely.

Kate smiled, pretending she had not heard, glad that Richard
hadn't.

'Come on, let's get in out of the cold. There's supper ready for
you both.'

'Dada,' said Esther, meaning that her father should push the
chair.

'No, Esther,' said Richard firmly. 'I'm carrying the bags, Kate will push you in.' Esther recognized a new confidence in her father's voice and she knew instinctively it had to do with Kate. Her fears deepened.

FORTY-SIX

Two days later, Margaret came for Christmas. She had grown thinner in the year since her operation, and her hair was whiter than before. But she arrived determined to take Esther over as she had in the old days and announced soon after her arrival that she and Esther were going into Wycombe to do some Christmas shopping that very afternoon.

They were having lunch and Esther, who had stolidly maintained her disagreeable front of the past forty-eight hours and was at that very moment eating with distaste the exotic Lamb Tenajelle that Kate had made, smiled and nodded, positive for the first time that day.

'Yeh!' she said. She was always sweet for Margaret, and her prejudice against Kate was so studied that it would have been comic but for the evident gloom it cast over Richard.

Richard withdrew into himself, not responding so naturally now to Kate's public affection, sinking wearily into her arms at night. On Boxing Day he spent much of the morning alone with Tom in the garden, turning over frosty soil and lighting a bonfire of the last garden rubbish. Its smoke hung silently in the fruit trees and filled the house with scent, but Esther, who had always loved bonfires, would not go out to enjoy it.

Instead she watched from her bedroom as Kate took a mug of tea out to Richard, and stood with him for a moment, looking into the flames and smoke. Esther's eyes fell when she saw Kate's hand rest for a moment on Richard's hip and then slide across his back. But she looked up again, white-faced, in time to see her father turn, lean over, and kiss Kate, his eyes smiling with what, Esther supposed, *they* called love. She turned her chair from the window and did not look out again.

She made arguments, created unpleasantness. She sulked all through one meal and Richard scolded her. She refused point-blank to let Kate help her wash. She turned her chair out of the lounge during the last ten minutes of a family film they were enjoying on television with such ill grace that it spoiled the film even for Margaret.

Then she adamantly refused to go swimming in Wycombe with them all.

'We can't leave you here alone,' said Richard.

'Nah, nah!' said Esther.

'Come on, Amh,' said Tom, who liked swimming in the children's pool which was specially heated. 'With me.'

Esther looked savagely at him.

DON'T INTERFERE, TOM.

Tom dropped his head, toying uncomfortably with the cord of his bathing costume which was hanging out of the towel he had rolled round it in readiness.

'Oh Esther, why not?' asked Richard.

Esther's eyes told the truth. Because Kate was going. I hate Kate. I don't want Kate coming. Not Kate. She looked at Kate with intense dislike.

'Esther!' Richard, unusually, began to sound annoyed. 'You can work on Skallagrigg this evening,' he added, to change the subject.

'*Nah!*' screamed Esther suddenly, swinging her chair violently out of the room. '*Nah!*'

Margaret went to her, her voice soft in the distance against Esther's crying. When she came back she said, 'Perhaps it is rather cold for swimming, so you had better go by yourselves, Richard. I'll take Esther for a walk.'

'You can't manage the chair any more.'

'I'll push it,' said Tom, putting down his swimming things. 'I'll take Amh for a walk.'

Richard stood uncertain, caught between his daughter and Kate.

'It's best, my dear. She'll come to understand I daresay. You two go and swim.' There was something disapproving in Margaret's offer of help which sent a shiver through Kate. But at least it gave them a chance to escape the house and be alone together for an hour or two.

But before they left Esther re-appeared with a printed note for Richard.

YOU DON'T KNOW ANYTHING ABOUT SKALLAGRIGG, it read.
'Then you'd better start communicating, hadn't you?' he said
shortly.

When they returned from swimming, Richard found one of Esther's
notes on Skallagrigg on the kitchen table. It said: THIS IS
COMMUNICATION.

That night Kate went to bed but Richard did not immediately
join her. He stayed downstairs and read Esther's notes. Night
deepened around him as, for the first time, he began to understand
the work she was doing. Much later he went outside into the
garden, through the damp cold undergrowth, and stood in the
dark by the wooden fence Esther and Tom loved.

He stared over the fence into the night and felt a stranger in his
own land, as if, spiritually, he had left it behind him and climbed
the wooden fence. On the other side lay Australia. On the other
side, the children said, was the Skallagrigg. Helen and Margaret
had told him everything; Esther was looking for someone called
Arthur and the Skallagrigg. Dead probably, if they were ever alive.
Brian dead now, gone. Sheila gone and no hold over him now,
none. Margaret's been so ill, looks ill. Esther whose weight he
could not bear, whose shadow he desired to escape. The top of the
fence paling was moist and cold to his touch but he knew now
how to climb it and leave it behind, and he would.

He turned back to the house, touching for a moment the apple
tree under which he and Kate had first made love. He looked up at
the house and saw the light in their bedroom had been turned off.

Richard had a sudden sense of overwhelming purpose. Skallagrigg: he would help Esther find him, or it, whatever it was
before he left and then he would be free to be the stranger that he
was and leave all this behind. He wanted to be free.

He felt relieved and full of love. For Kate. Who lay upstairs,
asleep probably, and was his to hold on to through the dark nights.
He went upstairs to bed, shivering with cold. He took his clothes
off and, naked, lay beside her and she, more sleeping than awake,
and warm and soft and seeming all his world, took him in her
arms, her breath warm on his cheek.

She said, 'What is it?'

He said, 'Nothing.' And even as their lips met, his body softened into sleep with hers and they drifted towards a continent of dreams.

The next day Richard talked with Esther, and told her he was going to visit Australia with Kate, some time at the end of January. He talked with her alone, and found himself saying he loved Kate, that he had been lonely, that he understood Esther's fears about Kate and the future.

Esther sat in her chair looking at him occasionally. Most of the time she stared at her hands. Margaret and Marion had dressed her that day in a red skirt and blouse which revealed the clean white lines of her bra. She wore pale tights, and red shoes. Her hair was washed and nicely brushed, but her face was pale. Puffy. She had a spot below her bottom lip. She was lightly made-up.

'Kate's really very nice,' he said. 'Couldn't you be nice to her?'

Her head lowered and her mouth turned down. She shook her head.

'You may *have* to become friends with her,' he said.

So now the threat of permanence hung over Esther, the permanence of Kate.

'Nah,' said Esther. She refused to use the screen to communicate.

'Darling,' said Richard, 'we'll have to talk about this again, but meanwhile there's another thing: I'd like to help you with Skallagrigg. I'd like . . .'

'*Nah!!*' said Esther, the violence of her shout surprising him. 'Ohhar me. *Me.*'

'All right, all right, I just thought, I mean I wanted . . .'

'*Nah!*' said Esther. Then she typed up on the screen: I WANT TO FIND THE SKALLAGRIGG ALONE. I DON'T NEED YOUR HELP. HELEN'S HELPING ME.

Richard felt hurt and rejected. His impulse of the previous night had been thwarted.

'Well, if you ever need any help, darling . . .'

'Yeh,' said Esther with a sneer.

ENJOY YOUR NEW YEAR WITHOUT ME. WITH YOUR GIRLFRIEND, she typed up. The sentiment was hard in its impact as it appeared letter by letter, word by word, slowly. She stared at him, defiant in her unfair rudeness.

'Oh, Esther.'

She turned her chair from him. She had ended Richard's attempt at reasonableness.

All of them were relieved when New Year's Eve came and Margaret drove Esther and Tom over to Oxford to stay with Helen Perry-Wilcox for a few days.

With Tom there, Marion was not needed because he could lift Esther, and since his witnessing of her first period in the storm in St Edward's playing fields, she accepted his care.

He could lift her on to toilet seats or into and out of baths more easily than anyone else except Marion, and wiped her dry or clean as was needed, tenderly and without embarrassment.

'Amh's not finished yet,' he would say, standing outside the toilet patiently. For she liked privacy for that part. Then she would call and he would go to her, wiping her, pulling up her knickers, adjusting her dress.

It was not that he was unconscious of sexuality or sexual differences, but, rather, that Esther was like a sister to him, a dear charge whose duty he honoured, and for which he would lay down his life. But he could be jealous. Margaret, Helen, Richard . . . they were all right. Kate . . . well, he knew that Esther did not like her and, not wishing to face a conflict of loyalties (for he liked Kate), he avoided it by making himself scarce when they were together.

Esther took all the Skallagrigg material with her to Oxford and that week began her researches again in earnest, planning out a scheme of library research with Helen who had arranged for her to visit Oxford University's prestigious Bodleian Library and get a reader's ticket once it re-opened in the new year.

Meanwhile she and Helen began systematically recording all the Skallagrigg stories on to filing cards, a method suggested by Helen, so that each character and location was given its own card, with all details recorded and cross-indexed with the number of the relevant story.

They installed themselves in the little-used dining-room of Helen's house, setting up Esther's word processor and printer there and those few books she had so far accumulated for her research. Tom had got used to her computer, and though he could not set it up he did take upon himself the role of feeding

paper or filing cards into her printer, and removing them when
they were ready.

It was some time during these few days that Esther typed up the
second May Adcock story, which was a longer variation of one
Esther had collected in Manchester and takes the relationship
between Arthur and Linnie further than before.

One hot afternoon Dilke was supervising a walk in his usual
charming way. But then comes Frank: 'Arthur says he doesn't
want to go, he's ill.'

Dilke leans down and looks at Arthur, Arthur stares back.
Dilke taps his window stick on his palm.

'Ill my arse. Malingering. He's going.'

But in the bright sunlight of the glen Arthur goes pale. He
can't seem to stand the sun. His eyes hurt and he's beginning
to moan. Arthur never ever moaned, not like an animal in
pain. Except when Dilke beat him up. Even now he tries to
stop Frank complaining on his behalf, but Frank won't
listen.

'My friend Arthur's ill. He should go inside.'

'He'll be inside soon.'

Arthur stares up into the trees and starts crying silently.
Frank is troubled for him.

'What is it, Arthur. Can't Skalg help?'

Arthur looks at the trees and he's moaning and even Frank
can't understand. Maybe he's saying 'Look, look, look,' like
once he said to his Linnie, his girl in good days gone by.
Maybe he's crying 'cos he remembers her unstrapping him
and taking him down into the long grass and giving him her
sex. Maybe he's remembering the best days of his life.

All good things end and Linnie had long gone, out beyond
the high yellow-brick walls. Arthur had said she was to and
to never come except just to say she was all right. Her
freedom was his happiness, so she did what her man bid.

'You'll be in soon,' whispers Frank again.

Arthur closes his eyes, but tears squeeze out from them
and Frank isn't quick enough to wipe them all away.

Arthur's got blood poisoning, poor devil. Nobody knew
he was that ill except maybe the Skallagrigg. They take
Arthur off to the infirmary where he hasn't been to stay
since he was a young lad.

For a week Dilke won't allow Frank to visit, saying, 'Super says it's dangerous.' That's a lie for one thing. All Arthur wants is for his friend to come but Dilke tells super, 'No one has expressed a wish to visit him.' Lies, wicked lies.

But when a week is up Frank is allowed to see his friend after chapel. It's on a Sunday when the Father seems to have more power to arrange good things and Dilke's off.

So Frank is taken to the infirmary, which he remembers from old. That's where he had his TB; that's where he made proper friends with Arthur; that's where he found purpose to his life in helping another.

'Hello, Arthur,' says Frank.

'Ehro,' says Arthur weakly. Then says some more. He looks fed up.

'Dilke wouldn't let me before now. Are you better?'

Arthur lies in bed his head on a health authority pillow case and he looks ill as death.

'I said a prayer for you,' says Frank.

Arthur grins. 'Maybe the Skallagrigg will answer it then,' says he.

'It's to God,' says Frank.

'There is no God,' says Arthur.

Frank sighs. His Arthur's a lost cause as far as believing in God is concerned, but Frank loves him all the same.

Arthur speaks a long time. Then Frank goes. He goes back to the chapel. He kneels by the brass rail alone but for the Father watching from a distance and he says, 'Lord, Arthur says Skalg's ill. That's why he's ill. So Skalg can't help him. So I pray for you to help him even if he doesn't believe. He's the best there is, is Arthur and he's ill and might depart. If that's your will so be it. But if it isn't, you help him please because Skalg can't for now. He won't be better till you make Skalg better.'

Next day Frank is allowed to see Arthur again. He's no better. Frank goes to the Father and says, 'Arthur says Skalg's very ill so he's ill. Arthur says he's giving his strength to Skalg to help him. Arthur says he has no more strength to give and needs a miracle like Jesus did. Arthur says he wants you.' Frank is so worried he's forgotten he's not to mention the Skallagrigg. But with the Father mum's the word.

The Father comes and asks Arthur, 'What can I do, Arthur? Do you want a prayer?'

Arthur speaks and the Father asks Frank what he's saying.

Says Frank after listening some more, 'You're to say a prayer for the Skalg through Arthur, it's the only way. You're to ask God to make a miracle like he did through Christ Jesus.'

And Frank takes the Father's hand and puts it in Arthur's. Then the Father says a prayer.

The days pass. Arthur's never been so ill. Those days are an agony like the cross for Arthur and no miracle seems to come. Days seems like years, and he forgets time until one day out of the blue there's a nurse's face right over his and speaking, and someone standing there.

'Someone to see you, Arthur,' says the nurse.

And Arthur raises his eyes and Linnie's there like she always was, looking down at him, there in the ward, come avisiting.

'I bet I'm a surprise,' says she.

Arthur stares up at her. He can't speak. He tries to reach up to her to see if she's a dream. She's beautiful to him like she always was and he feels her hand taking his and he knows she's real. Older now, a bit of grey hair, plumper too, but eyes don't change, not never; not if they still love.

'I just came,' says Linnie. ''Cos I been thinking of you, worrying about you. So I just came. It's a long way, but I wanted to come, just once. I never forgot you and you made me say I would when I was all right, and I have and I am. I'm going to hold your hand till you tell me you're going to get better.'

She held his hand. A long time. Long long long, in and out of sleep, and she didn't go away. She was better now and free, and so she could do as she pleased. She was a normal was Linnie by then: never been anything else! Her hand was pulling him into shore. Nearer and nearer to safety. Then he felt a ring on it. He opened his eyes and there was a gold wedding ring.

'I'm not married,' says she, 'but it's easier with that. I saved for it and it took time. Eighteen pounds, nine carat. But men don't pester so much with a ring. When I put it on I did it in church all alone and said, "Arthur's my beau and always will be, always always and one day I'll see him so he knows I'm all right."

'I promised you something, Arthur, and I keep my promise. When we wed under the cross with Frank I decided you needed a ring. Now I'm going to give you this one. That's why I saved up for it all that time. For the day when I would come and visit you again. For today.'

Linnie took it off and held it up for him to see. 'It's helped me get all right, now it will help you get all right.'

Then she put that ring on Arthur's finger and left it there for keeps. That was the miracle a prayer could make.

Linnie stays with the Father so she can visit next day by special permission of the medical super and she sees at once Arthur's better. He's got his old grin back in his eyes. And one hand touches the other where the ring is, and won't stop.

'Nurse says I can get up for a walk, just for ten minutes.'

Linnie gently gets him up and puts him in a chair. He's lighter than a baby.

'Just to the veranda and back,' says the nurse.

At the veranda they look down towards the glen. Frank's there with Norman and a boy. They wave and the boy stares up at his Mum standing on the veranda with the funny man Arthur in the chair.

'I've had a boy and he's all right,' says Linnie. 'He's getting on with Frank isn't he? But you're my beau, Arthur, only you, whatever else.'

Arthur looks long at the boy with Frank. He's looking at a world he can never ever go to. How old's the boy? He can't judge. No boys here. Nothing normal. So Arthur can't guess the age of a boy, not really. All boys stay seven to him. That's an age he remembers. Before that Arthur was not.

Arthur wants to say: 'Is he seven?'

Linnie leans down close. Her hands feel like love upon his shoulders.

'He's a good boy, Arthur, and we're all right. I know you don't want me never to come back again, not never. But I know you wanted to see everything was all right with me this once.'

Arthur nods his head as his love Linnie stands behind him, her hands on him, and together that once they stare out at her boy, dark-haired and strong. He knows his time with Linnie is coming to an end now but he's not sad. He's had more love than most get in a whole lifetime. Arthur's not one to spoil the good things of life by thinking of the bad.

She can't come back because it wouldn't be right. Not ever. He's the one decides. Linnie would come back

otherwise. But not here in this hellhole place; she and her
lad had better not come here.

'I remembered what you taught me,' says she.

'Skayagree,' says Arthur almost managing his old smile.

'That's an S and a K and an A and an L and an L and an A
and a G and an R and an I and a G two of them: S–K–A–L–
L–A–G–R–I–G–G. I don't forget the most important thing
about you.'

Frank comes up leaving the boy with Norman. The boy
stares at the veranda where the funny men in chairs are and
won't come near.

Frank says, 'You seen Linnie then?' He looks pleased. He
believes Christ Jesus has answered the Father's special
prayer by bringing her here after so long.

Arthur speaks. Frank says, 'Arthur says he's glad you come
because you're his best love. He's proud he says. He'll get
better because otherwise you'd fret. He'll never have the
ring off, not never. You're not to come again because he
loves you too much. Better not, and now he can rest easy.
He says the Skalg knows you've come so he'll get better
too. He says you're the miracle, Linnie.'

Arthur speaks again.

Frank nods and says, 'Arthur wants to know if you remember the glen?'

'Yes I do,' says Linnie, the light of the sun in her eyes.

'Arthur says, "Always?"'

'It was the best in my life,' says Linnie.

Her hands tighten on Arthur's shoulders and she looks
down at him, at his crooked hands, at his thin twisted legs,
at his jerking head, at his mouth that dribbles, at his pyjama
jacket where it was open on his thin chest all white, at his
toes turned crooked and calloused with time. She comes
round to the front of him and kneels down and looks into
his eyes, still grey and weak with illness.

'My Arthur is the only real man I ever knew,' says Linnie
truthfully, and she kisses his weak mouth for all the nurses
and the boys to see and bugger the lot of them.

Then she goes for ever, out down the steps of the infirmary
veranda to her boy and she kisses Norman bye-bye, and
takes her boy's hand and she walks away with him, the sun
on them, and Frank and Arthur watch until they can see
them no more.

FORTY-SEVEN

'I hereby undertake not to remove from the Library, or to mark, deface or injure in any way, any volume, document or other object belonging to it or in its custody, not to bring into the Library or kindle therein any fire or flame, and not to smoke in the Library, and I promise to obey all the rules of the Library,' Esther did not say.

Instead Helen Perry-Wilcox said it for her while Esther sat listening, staring at the Reader's form for a ticket to the Bodleian Library, as the light from the transomed windows of the Schola Musicae was cast down upon her.

The admissions officer, a kindly man with gold-rimmed spectacles and a thin face, looked apologetic as he went through this procedure which was so clearly irrelevant to the young woman before him, whose head was tilted to one side, and who had a mouth that seemed to move uncontrollably and spoke strange words which the youth who pushed her chair attended to as if they made sense.

The formal words delivered, the officer held up a little ticket with a black and white photo of Esther laminated into it, uncertain quite who to give it to.

'Me,' said Esther, the mouth suddenly commanding.

Tom leaned forward and guided Esther's pointing, struggling hand to the officer's, and she took the ticket.

Esther grinned, held it up and inspected it, uttered a small cry of pleasure, and nodded her thanks.

'Amh says thanks,' said Tom.

'Ah, good. Yes. Well,' said the officer.

The brief ceremony over Tom pushed Esther, still clutching the precious ticket, across the Old School Quad quadrangle beneath an arch and into the cobbled grandeur of Radcliffe Square itself where, awed by the rising heights of James Gibbs' eighteenth-century

Radcliffe Camera, he brought Esther's chair to a halt and refused for the moment to go on.

The sky was solid grey above them and the domed shape of the Camera rose into it as if each was a piece in a perfectly cut jigsaw puzzle. Beyond the Camera were the castellations of the university church of St Mary and to their left the imposing frontage of All Souls College. To their right, across the cobbles so hard on a wheelchair, was narrow Brasenose Lane, with its medieval central gutter and high walls behind which rose ancient horse chestnuts from Exeter College's private gardens.

There was a distant subterranean clatter of aluminium tureens, and a radio playing: it was eleven in the morning and the chefs in Brasenose were preparing luncheon for those few senior members who had stayed up for the vacation.

Walls, doors through which they might not pass, inaccessible towers, the looming sky itself, all seemed to conspire to hem them in. Esther stared about her, paralysed as Tom was, unsure that they dared go any way at all. Then she looked at her ticket, and looked over the cobbles to the Camera whose doors at the top of some awkward balustraded steps were closed against the cold.

'Yeh!' she said as if finding her strength to press on again. 'Yeh!'

It might have been the cry of Boadicea as she led her stalwart troops to do battle against the might of Rome.

Tom heaved her carefully up the steps, and then equally carefully down a few steps inside to a reading room which was huge, round and shelved, students looking up and staring in dusty silence when the three of them came in.

They did not look like normal scholars: a mongol, a severely spastic young woman in a battered grey wheelchair, and a woman grey-haired and neat, not a fool at least. She it was who went forward to the inquiry desk. She seemed to be known by the assistant, who smiled; for once.

The woman spoke but it was hard to hear what she said; Select Committee Reports by the sound of it, down below in the stacks.

Down below? But we're in the lower reading room already. The librarian pointed to the stairs behind her, and then looked questioningly at Tom and at Esther's wheelchair.

'They can use the lift,' she said to Helen. 'Do you know the stacks?'

Helen shook her head. 'It's not for me, it's for Miss Marquand,' she said.

'Ah,' said the librarian, her head jerking nervously. 'I had better show you then. If you . . .' her voice trailed away as she realized she had to address the mongol youth who stared grinning at her, his thick glasses smudged.

'Can he go down in the lift with the chair?' she asked Helen, giving Tom up.

'Tom, you'll have to take Esther down in the lift. We'll meet you down there. It's downstairs. Under there.' She pointed to the floor.

'Ten four A O K,' said Tom loudly, his slow voice rolling around the ancient books in the towering shelves above.

Scholars and students watched as the mongol youth, deliberately as if he had to think out each lumbering movement, reversed Esther's chair and pulled her into the lift behind the inquiry area. He had, somehow, the huge grace of an elephant tending its young. They went through the dark doors, closed them, and disappeared.

Down below were the stacks: down, down and along, stack after stack of books which waited, perhaps more than one lifetime, perhaps more than two or three lifetimes, for someone to need them; to seek them out, stack after stack, to search in the gloom and dust of shelf on shelf, and to find what otherwise might be for ever hidden.

'It's scaredy,' said Tom, as the old, gold-painted lift clunked down clumsily to a halt and he pulled the rickety metal doors open and pushed Esther out.

They were in a labyrinth of seven-foot-high metal shelving corridors, dark green and dusty, stretching into gloomy distances, miserably neon-lit.

The air was cool and still, heavy with the smell of administrative paper and books. It hummed too, with those unidentifiable below-ground sounds which inhabit the basements, cellars and crypts of extensive old buildings. The rush-hish of air-extractor fans, the rumblings of cast-iron pipes, the muted clatter of feet above in the lost windowed world of light.

Somewhere not too far away and approaching, maybe down that corridor of books, or past the single human being they could see (a little man with glasses, his face pale in the poor light, and reading a volume big and thick as an encyclopaedia), or from somewhere behind the lift, they heard voices, and the harsh clatter of feet on cast-iron floorgrids. One of the voices escaped its own echoes and reverberations and became Helen's.

The other said, 'Round here,' or perhaps, 'Down here,' – the echoes of the place muffled exact sound.

Esther eyed the shelves. Book after book after book, old books with titles faded and obscure, shelf labels printed white on black.

'It's very scaredy, Amh,' repeated Tom, uneasily.

'Nah,' said Esther, IT'S NOT, TOM. IT'S EXCITING. WE'LL FIND THE WAY TO THE SKALLAGRIGG HERE. And this, and his hand holding on to the familiar security of her chair handle, seemed to satisfy him.

The librarian appeared and rapidly outlined the system by which the shelves were numbered and ordered.

'Now your reference is . . .' She held a slip of paper up, the better to see it in the obscure light. 'Pp Engl 1814–15/4. That'll be down here.'

She led the way down a narrow corridor between the stacks followed by Helen and Tom pushing Esther. They turned left and then right and then right again straight into a narrow cul de sac. The librarian reached forward to the great seven-foot shelves that blocked their way, leaned into them, and astonishingly they slid to the left into line with the others, and their way was clear.

'They are sometimes a little heavy and stiff but don't pull them too hard as once they start moving they come very easily,' said the librarian. 'Actually, they sometimes come out of their own accord.' Adding wearily, 'Especially on stormy days.'

Straight ahead, right, quite lost, Tom stopped the chair which had caught on a protruding, sliding shelf. To her right there was a gap between books and Esther saw a man sitting at a table with yellow light on his pale face. He was staring straight at her like a disembodied face set upon the top of a row of volumes. Staring in a way she did not like. Tom got the chair going again. They crossed a corridor and someone was standing in the distance stock still like a dummy staring down. It was a strange place.

Tom pushed on, catching up with Helen and the librarian as they turned left again.

'Here we are,' said the librarian.

The place looked like all the rest, but the shelf references were earlier and the volumes more tatty: '1814–15' Esther read, and she knew that the committee report they wanted to see, which had exposed the Norris scandal, was dated 1815. Tremendous excitement came over her, the excitement of reaching a source of real fact. Not a copy, not a synopsis, not a précis, not a quotation, not a commentary, not even a facsimile: but the very source itself on which one hundred and seventy years of those copies, synopses, commentaries and opinions had been based.

'This is it, I think,' said the librarian taking down a huge volume with some difficulty. It was the Report from the Committee on Madhouses in England ordered to be printed by the House of Commons, 11 July 1815.

'All right?' said the librarian. 'Good, then I'll leave you, Miss Perry-Wilcox and . . . er . . . ah . . . Miss . . . ah . . .' and she nodded uneasily down at Esther and turned away, in a quite different direction from the one in which they had come. She was some distance away before she stopped, looked back, and said, 'You will find a number of work places about. Er . . . I'm sure that you will manage to accommodate the wheelchair.' Her voice seemed caught up in the labyrinth, disembodied, as if it was not coming from her at all. Then she turned and was lost among volumes of Pp Engl 1847.

Helen picked up the 1815 Report, which had worn beige cardboard covers, and showed it to Esther.

'Me,' she said. She wanted to be the one to open it, if only symbolically and with Tom's help, for so heavy a book would always be beyond her. The pages smelt musty, and the print on the off-white rough paper was pressed through from the other side and felt semi-embossed. Nice to the touch.

'What are we looking for, my dear, do we know?'

Esther shook her head, eyes bright in the gloom.

'No? Not sure? Well, that's part of the fun of research. It is fun isn't it?' said Helen breathing in the air as if it was bracing sea air. 'I used to love the stacks in the main library you know, I found such peace there. And sometimes, coming across obscure forgotten works, or working out a reference for one of the Readers, I felt such achievement. I think archaeologists must feel the same: seeking and finding forgotten facts and truths. It is strange to think, isn't it, that each one of these books was written by someone, a real person, even these government reports. Now, then, let's get going on *this* report.'

They found a work desk nearby and Helen sat down by Esther's chair. Tom seemed happy to hang about behind them. But he stayed close, looking over his shoulder sometimes as if afraid of the endless stacked corridors whose sides were made of huge metal shelves that moved, and whose turnings were dark, and which creaked.

Helen had helped Esther read books before, and knew that her method was to study the contents page for some minutes, indicate which section she was interested in, and then have her helper skip very rapidly through it. If she saw something she wanted to read she indicated with a nod of her head. Esther did not like helpers who said anything about what she was reading, or tried in any way to talk; nor did she appreciate those who failed to notice when she wanted to stop or move on, or the ones who found it difficult to locate cross-references . . . in short, she had difficulty with almost every helper she was likely to come across since what she demanded was patience, intelligence and a passive interest in what she was doing.

In practice, the electric page-turner had made it possible for her to work without helpers, though she needed someone to set up the book and machine in the first place. But it did not function with newspapers or in public places or, as now, in a library.

So far Esther had found only two really good helpers for reading apart from Margaret: Marion (who was good with fiction) and latterly Helen, who understood books and the nature of research. Tom was a useful stand-in, but his concentration lapsed easily and sometimes the interruptions implicit in reminding him to turn the page were enough to break her flow of thought and association, so fundamental to original thinking. Nor was Tom capable of finding places in books without Esther's indicating the page number on her board and counting him through it.

At one time note-taking had been a problem, but Leon Sadler had further developed her keyboard and screen with word processing software which made her able to write as fast as able-bodied people. Its keyboard was the same as her normal one but with an enhanced memory which held more than she could type up in a few hours, the most she was likely ever to work away from her computer. It had batteries as well as a mains adaptor and so was quite portable.

They managed nearly two hours on that first visit to the Radcliffe Library before the cold and fatigue overcame them. They had spent most of the time working their way through the 1815 Report whose detail shocked them both:

> When taken from their cells in the day time they were
> chained to the wall in rooms appropriated for that
> purpose five or six in each. These persons presented a
> horrid spectacle; and the rooms in which the dirty
> patients were appeared to me to be in a more filthy and
> offensive state than was necessary.

But by the end of two hours they had read through only a few dozen pages out of hundreds, and checked over some of the appendices at the back. The research, Esther was beginning to realize, would take time. Before they left Esther got Tom to push her wheelchair up and down some of the stack aisles to see what else might be there, and she saw that there were other reports worth looking at.

She felt tired but excited. Here she could seek and delve, a journeyer back in time to places where, with the present help of Helen and Tom, she was not at an especial disadvantage. Here she was an adventurer making her own adventure, and the sense of tunnels and mazes which had already come to her with this work was enhanced by the strange subterranean environment of the stacks whose passages were for the most part empty, but whose monsters, as in a good fantasy game, had not yet shown themselves.

They finally stopped when Tom, who had been patient all afternoon, suddenly said, 'Amh, are we going yet?' Helen, who had been as absorbed in this grim past as Esther, saw that his face was pale and he was cold, and they decided to go.

At the lift he turned and looked about the receding gloomy place and said, 'Are we coming back?'

Esther nodded.

'OK, Amh.'

DO YOU MIND?

'Don't mind coming, Amh, with you. I help.'

He stared around again, his face pinched with cold, at the shadowy recesses and endless reports and books that stretched into unexplored distances, and asked, 'Was Skalg here?'

'Yeh,' said Esther. She felt suddenly confident, as she always did when Tom forced her to be positive. YEH, SKALG WAS HERE AND WE'RE LOOKING FOR CLUES AS TO WHERE HE WENT.

'Yes, Amh,' said Tom, awed. Then he opened the lift door, pushed her carefully in, and closed it, and they rose up into the real world, as Helen went back up the stairs.

That was the first of what became almost daily visits to the Radcliffe stacks. It was the beginning, too, of Esther Marquand's methodical note-taking which chronicled her research and which, since they were all word processed and filed on disk, now form part of the Berkeley University Marquand Collection. The notes probably owe something to Helen Perry-Wilcox since they are impeccably referenced, starting with author and title, and giving the Bodleian Library catalogue reference where she used their material.

It is clear that this period of search – a search which was indeed to culminate in a discovery that justified the trouble and time it took – helped create Esther's idea that the search for the Skallagrigg in the game she made should be labyrinthine in its mood. She later wrote for Daniel Schuster that:

The weather during that fortnight seemed permanently black and cloudy and, because of the difficulty of parking in Oxford, we always had to leave the car some way from the Library, necessitating a walk through the old streets. I remember the windows of the houses and colleges seemed dark, the streets like tunnels beneath the sky. Dark dark, and Tom muttering behind me about the 'Skalg' and us blown about by the wind, and made to huddle in doorways because of the rain. It seemed we were in tunnels and unsure which way to go.

Then into the Library and down down down in that ricketing old lift, to the silence of the stacks, like a deeper level in a fantasy game, where we suspected there was a clue, but we did not know where or what it was. And setting the mood was the material we were going through, the story of the 'madhouses' in Britain in one of which Arthur must later have been incarcerated.

I really did not know what I was looking for, but instinct told me to

carry on. I guessed that when I found it I would never need to go down
into the Radcliffe stacks again . . . an idea which I'm using in the design
of 'Skallagrigg' the game.

They continued their daily visits to the Bodleian, working their
way through the Minutes of Evidence and findings of Selected
Committee Reports on lunacy and madhouses from the beginning
of the nineteenth century onwards.

Hereford, York, Bethlem . . . the names of the grimmer and more
notorious establishments became familiar to Esther, and the true
horror of conditions began to penetrate her imagination as, bit by
bit, she began to see beyond the neat, old-fashioned print to the
real events that had given rise to it. Evidence of rape, of murder, of
ill-treatment beyond belief, of places so heavy with the smell of
faeces and physical decay that contemporary investigators reported
vomiting at what they saw and smelt.

There is no doubt that those days' researches deep under the
Radcliffe Camera, in winter, in 'corridors' that could arbitrarily be
sealed off by pulling a dull green, cast-iron stack on rollers, made
a profound impression on Esther Marquand, aggravated by the
tragic and often unpleasant nature of the material she was reading.

That the stacks became for her a paradigm of the very maze she
believed Arthur himself to be in, and herself, is obvious enough
from the game she eventually created. Level Four of 'Skallagrigg' is
called 'The Stacks', and there seems no doubt that the idea for the
sudden random blocking off of its corridors came directly from the
quirky way some of the shelves, less absolutely level than others,
slid, unaided and without warning, to block off a route that had
been open before. Worse, such blockings served to disorientate the
Readers who, turning back the way they had just come, would
find it no longer existed, and would turn yet again and lose their
sense of direction.

Then, too, there is the appearance in Level Four of the Lost
Helper, whose cries can be heard but whose position is not known
and must be found.

On the afternoon of 12 January, nearly two weeks after their
researches began, Helen was forced to leave Esther and Tom alone
in the stacks while she kept an appointment in nearby Beaumont

Street. She left Esther with several of the volumes out and Tom at her side.

Some time after Helen left, Tom became separated from Esther among the stacks. Perhaps he simply grew bored and wandered off, perhaps she was attempting to get him to find another volume; or perhaps someone who seemed familiar called to him and he responded. Someone in the shadows, someone there among the stacks, wandering, another never identified Reader.

Tom turned and turned again, as a stack slid open of its own accord, blocking a shelf corridor, and Tom, disorientated, wandered among the stacks turning right and left and left and then into the labyrinth of Reports, past forgotten paragraphs, puzzled by forgotten years, the lights above casting strange shadows on his frightened face as, afraid, he whispered, 'Amh? *Amh?*' and lolloped into a panic run, turning right and right and right and right, or maybe left, and seeing only those hanging dusty iron shelves with faded titles and numbers which did not make sense to him all blocking his way back to his charge.

'Amh?'

Then footsteps, surer, leather shoes upon a floor, and a face, with malevolent voyeuristic eyes, dark and dead, staring from beyond a shelf, through gaps between great books, eyes staring, unseen but frighteningly sensed by Esther who could not turn, staring at her as she heard from somewhere the echoing confusing gallumphing of Tom's feet, and his desperate whispering of her name.

Then a shelf was pushed suddenly across the way he might come back and the diffident man diffident no more; male, black eyes, standing staring at her with a strange and frightening look on his face; in one hand an irrelevant pink slip of paper which fluttered to the floor, the other hand playing at himself while she, helpless, watched him approach.

That other hand came towards her, where she sat staring, her body still with surprise, and touched her leg and then her breast as if the very shelves themselves had come to life and, disliking her intrusion, had personified themselves to molest her helplessness.

'*Toh!*' she shouted, suddenly, but weak, so weak, no more than whispering, so stressed was her neck and throat with shock. The hand settled, touched, horribly caressed and moved down then between her legs and touched her there where her knickers were, then soft like slime against her inmost thigh inside. Hurting not much, pulsating those eyes that hand quicker and quicker those eyes popping and strange and that breathing.

Tom running and panting, 'Amh, Amh, Amh, Amh, Amh,' approaching as the hand was whipped away, the man's lips twisting into a weak pathetic smile and muttered 'Sorry' as if it was an accident, a slip, and then the shelf moved back and he slipped away, knocking the volumes she had been reading off the table, the books fallfallfalling down. Seeing the open cartwheeling pages she cried out two words in one 'Nah' and 'Yeh' ... NEH!

Because the books fell down.

Fell down and then.

And then she cried out YEH for sure.

'Sorry, Amh,' said Tom, back from his nightmare of being lost and separated from her.

Esther was white-faced, but her eyes were on the volumes slewed now upon the floor. She had seen something. But in which one, which open falling pages? And what? What had she seen?

PICK IT UP.

'Yes, Amh. Sorry.'

OPEN IT THERE, NO THERE. NO NO NO, THERE.

'Where, Amh?'

She could not tell where what she had so briefly seen in the book's flight down might be.

She said, so much later, to Daniel Schuster: 'As the book fell down I saw something, a word, a phrase, I did not know: *something*. I saw what we had been looking for, but only vaguely, in the distance. Enough to know that it was there. But when we looked again, Tom leafing through the pages for me, I could not see it or tell which volume it had been.'

But what of the sexual molestation? Why did Esther never mention it to Helen? Her reasons are most odd.

Isn't that strange! [she wrote for Daniel], I never said a word to anyone, and I don't think Tom saw. For one thing I thought that if I did Helen might not allow me into the library again. Then there was the feeling that it was my fault!! I had provoked the man in some way. But more than all that, and you may find this difficult to understand, I felt grateful to him because his action gave me an insight into Arthur and Dilke. You see, at the moment he 'attacked me' I was immersed in those volumes and when he suddenly appeared I was locked up in that institutional world where Arthur was. In fact I felt as if I *was* Arthur and the moment his hand touched my breast I felt it was Dilke's hand and I understood something very important about Arthur and Dilke: Arthur was strong and Dilke was weak. In touching me that man made me understand Dilke for ever. He was weak and pathetic and had to abuse Arthur to give himself a sense of power. So, feeling as if I was Arthur I did not really feel scared about the assault as in effect it was happening to someone else. I bet you think I'm mad, but that's what it was like.

And then the falling book, and a word glimpsed inside it too quickly to read and take in consciously, but slow enough to know that it was crucial. And yet, when Tom and I looked for it I could not see it, however hard I tried. We couldn't find it the next day either, nor the next and I began to doubt myself that I had the right three volumes although I was sure, I was sure ... 1847, 1867, 1882: one of those. That much I did tell Helen.

As the last days of the holiday approached I began to doubt even that that man had ever been there, or the strange assault had ever taken place. Down there, among the moving stacks, where a corridor was not a corridor and where massive shelves moved for no reason at all, everything was unreal.

But in those last few days I had this strong feeling I was getting nearer to Arthur. That was a greater reality than the assault on a girl of such innocence, as I had then meant almost nothing. I had been so protected from all that you see. Just a few kisses with Graham and at the wheelchair dances, and the gropings of Andy Moore which I hadn't really minded. In fact I often thought of them ...

The last morning they had free for research they made an early start.

'You've been through this 1867 Report before, my dear,' said Helen.

'Yeh,' said Esther stubbornly. She had, and might again; she insisted there was something she had missed, something still to find, not having yet explained about the incident when the books fell down.

But as the two hours passed and it got to near lunchtime and Tom said he wanted to pee upstairs, they all felt an end had come. No more research now. Start again at half-term or something.

Outside a clear winter sun was shining and the air among the buildings seemed crystalline and pure and the bells of St Mary's rang out, peal after peal, as if for them, as if for Esther. Impulsively they went to the service, and during it Esther found a peace and blessing upon her, and in that state, with Tom holding her hand, every word sung or spoken in the service had special meaning and seemed, rightly or wrongly, a sign from God. The psalm was for her, and her slow mouth assayed its words with as much conviction as if she could sing them out clearly for all to hear:

> Oh God you are my God:
>   eagerly will I seek you.
>
> My soul thirsts for you my flesh longs for you
>   as a dry and thirsty land where no water is.

She was aware of her stricken limbs and her weak back, and her head that jerked as its mouth tried to sing the unsingable. And every word had meaning to her, and her God was a jealous God, an avenging angry God, as she was angry, with an anger that she wished now to turn outwards and visit upon the dilkes of the world, who were not just her enemies but Arthur's as well.

At the end of the service coffee and biscuits were served on a trestle table at the back of the church. She indicated to Helen that she wanted some, and was pleased that one of the priests came up and said a few words. There was a young man in a suit talking to a girl; the girl smiled at her, but Esther wished it had been the man. She felt she had something to offer. But . . . not just any man! No, he would have to be worthy! He would have to believe in God, like her. Now.

As Tom pushed her chair round to leave she caught a brief glimpse right down the aisle to the golden cross that stood on the altar. The cross alone.

Arthur.

Dilke alone as well. Like that man who touched her among the stacks and whom she now forgave.

GOD FORGIVE HIM, she said at the cross.

Then, GOD SEND ME A LOVING BOYFRIEND. A fierce prayer for now she did not want to be alone as she knew so many were; if she was going to be crucified she wanted it to happen with a boyfriend at her side.

GOD LET ME LOVE ANOTHER.

GOD IT IS NOT WRONG TO WANT A BOYFRIEND.

And then, as if reversion to being a good Christian and thinking of others might somehow make God look more kindly on her desire for a soulmate, she said again:

GOD FORGIVE THAT MAN.

GOD I BEAR NO GRUDGE.

OH GOD OH OH OH GOD.

And as Tom pushed her out into the clear winter sunlight she found herself understanding Arthur and Dilke even more deeply for she shouted out from her silence as she knew suddenly Arthur must have done, as he had done in one of the stories.

OH GOD FORGIVE DILKE FOR HE KNOWS NOT WHAT HE DOES.

Then, ever analytic, Esther Marquand asked herself why she made such a prayer but could find no ready answer. Just the name DILKE DILKE DILKE drumming in her brain.

FORTY-EIGHT

Richard and Kate left quietly for Australia at the end of January 1983, a week or two after Esther's return to Netherton. She herself said nothing about their trip and had not conceded a single smile to Kate throughout the holidays, not even a bleak one. On the last morning she had simply stared blankly out of the car window, closed against January rain, as Richard drove out of Harefield into Abbey Road for the trip back to school. To the last Kate smiled and waved her farewell, but she felt inexpressibly sad when they had gone.

A chilling rain had been settled for weeks over Netherton, and whenever Esther looked out of the window it seemed that the weather was worse than before. Trees stood wet and bleak in a grey landscape, bent and battered by north-east winds, and people came in from outside cold and dripping, the wheels of the chairs muddy, and water caught in their shoes.

'A' levels were beginning to loom and though few had doubts that Esther and Graham would pass, yet both were tense and working hard; Graham the more so because the school had agreed to let him sit his computer science 'A' level, even though he was doing it separately from the normal curriculum. But Warble was supporting him and pushing him on, admitting that both Graham and Esther were stronger at computing than he was.

A card from Singapore all blue and sunshiney came for her at the beginning of February. 'Having a lovely time and we're glad you're not here' was how she imagined the message should have read when she wrote about it in her diary. In fact it simply recorded a safe arrival, said inconsequentially that they were flying to Sydney on Wednesday; much love Daddy. Kate had written a brief note under his: 'Wish we could send you the warmth and sunshine, love Kate.'

Esther did not want the card put up over her bed, which was where she put most postcards she received, but had it tucked out of sight in a drawer. Her jealous anger had given way to a cold indifference and her diary for 6 February 1983 reads: 'I try to imagine them there but I can't. I feel utterly uninterested. Their life is nothing to do with me any more and I won't be surprised or care if he marries her. Betty says Singapore's a good place to get wed and if they do it out there it will save us all the embarrassment of having to ask me to attend.'

Esther's work on the Skallagrigg now proceeded by letter and she had written several more just before she left Helen's house for Harefield in the new year. There was a brief, efficient reply from Einar Gunnarson, the nursing officer in Chester who had offered a derivation for Skallagrigg. Esther had asked him if he had any records of where he had heard the word used and his reply was surprisingly detailed:

I have such a record because naturally I crossfile by
source words that interest me (and many that don't) but
the results may not be of much significance. The word is
ubiquitous – I do not know an institution I have visited
where I have not heard it used. Of course, since the in-
hospital tradition is an oral one there are very few
written spellings of it. Indeed it is an odd fact which
you may be able to enlighten me about that in those
hospitals that have patient-media the word has never
to my knowledge appeared, as if its public usage is
proscribed. My impression had always been that it is,
as you suggest, a northern usage and what I have done
is simply to note down certain weightings for population
and so on. This is really very rough and ready and in
no circumstances to be quoted academically, but it
confirms your impression that usage concentrates in
the North West, in the area between Manchester and
Carlisle with a second concentration in the North East
around Newcastle.

The word 'dilke' remains a puzzle, but for your interest
I have checked its distribution and interestingly it
roughly parallels that for Skallagrigg, though it is found

over a wider area. Incidentally the first record I have
for it is 1897, in minutes of evidence given by an
inmate to an inquiry into a fire that caused twenty
deaths in a hospital in Birmingham. I will send you a
photostat of this as it may interest you. Finally:
'Arthur'. A difficult one, because of the obvious scope
for confusion with the legends. But I have occasionally
heard it used in connection with Skallagrigg and have
a verbatim 'story' recorded in a Huddersfield hospital.
I'll send it with the other photocopy. I would be *most*
interested to see copies of the stories you have collected
if that is possible. I would not of course use them or
quote them without your permission and a full
acknowledgement.

Esther also had another letter from Dr Innes in Derbyshire, who
had replied to her advertisement saying he remembered spastic
children telling each other Skallagrigg stories at Hollitcray House
in Huddersfield:

Dear Miss Marquand,

Your project sounds fascinating but I doubt if I can help
further myself. Your best bet may be to see if you can
trace any staff who were at HH when I was. I attach
a list of names I remember, and some I don't (it's from
a sports day programme I have in which participating
staff are listed) and some should still be there. If you
have time let me know the results of your inquiry.
Please don't hesitate to quote my name and hospital if
you feel that will help.

Esther immediately checked the names against those few that
appeared in the *Hospital and Health Services Handbook* for the
Huddersfield area but none coincided. Instead, she wrote to the
authority about her 'project' asking for their help in tracing old
staff of Hollitcray.
Meanwhile Helen Perry-Wilcox was helping in the way she was
most skilled at, by following up references to mental hospitals and
their archives through library research. She was sensitive to the

fact that Esther wanted to do the actual reading of material herself, and wrote to Netherton in mid-February saying:

> I have checked out most of the references in Scull's
> book and they are in the stacks of the Bodleian for you
> to go through when you come in March. Also, I've
> come across other mid-nineteenth-century material
> which will interest you. The reference your
> correspondent Mr Gunnarson gave you is definitely
> here. Finally, one of my friends in the university has
> suggested we contact something called the King's Fund
> Library in London which specializes in this field. I
> expect you'll prefer to write to them so I'll include the
> address as a P S to this. I wish we knew what you were
> looking for . . .!
>
> Much love (and to Graham) Helen.

But as more and more leads for her to follow appeared Esther was beginning to find the correspondence took too much time when she was working hard for public examinations. She was also worried by the fact that she would have to visit some people for interviews, notably May Adcock in Edinburgh and perhaps any staff who turned up from the Huddersfield lead.

She wrote to her father before his return from his Far Eastern trip saying that she wished to stay with Helen in Oxford over the first part of the Easter holiday so that she could visit the Bodleian, and asking if he could arrange for Tom or Marion to come to Oxford and help out 'as Nana can't do it any more and it's unfair on Helen'.

The Bodleian was beginning to be a preoccupation of hers – she had asked her grandmother to send her postcards of Oxford and especially of the Radcliffe Camera: 'I'd love a photograph of the underground stacks themselves as they're so interesting,' she wrote, 'but I don't suppose that's possible!? Or is it?'

It was not. Esther never got a photograph of the stacks. But the image, or her idea of it, became an obsession. In retrospect it seems that her visits there were as much for their own sake as to find clues to the origin of Skallagrigg and especially Dilke, by whom she had been obsessed since the strange assault on her in the stacks the previous holiday. She was beginning to realize that the journey might be as important as the goal itself – a notion that is fundamental to her conception of 'Skallagrigg' the game.

But: 'I am scared of the stacks,' she confided to her diary in March, 'because they're big and they move and because of what happened. But I'm not scaredy scared as Tom would say. I know I must go back. It's irrational, but I know Dilke is there and that among all those hospital names that recur in the committee reports year by year must be the name of the one where Arthur has been confined. I *must* find it and so I must keep going back until I do.'

FORTY-NINE

IS SHE GOING TO BE THERE OVER EASTER?

'She' was Kate, but Esther avoided using her name as she asked her father the vital question about the coming holidays. It was March and he was on his first visit to Netherton since his return from Australia.

He had a suntan and looked younger; even (she thought) attractive. 'Dishy' was the word Betty Shaw used.

Richard gazed at Esther steadily and smiled with the indifference of someone whose mind has stopped wavering and is now comfortably made up.

'Darling, Kate is going to be living in Harefield now. I know you think you don't like her but you'll just have to face the fact that things have changed. We love each other as I love you, and we don't like being apart. Anyway, she lives in a small flat in Wycombe and it's just silly . . .' He stopped, realizing he was beginning to justify something he had no need to.

Esther's gaze did not waver, but it was wary and vulnerable.

ARE YOU GOING TO GET MARRIED? she typed up on the screen. The words came up instantly, quicker than ever before and Richard was surprised. He hesitated and then played for time.

'Have you got a new word processing program?' She nodded and looked around, hoping Graham was nearby to explain. They were in one of the common rooms, but he had made himself scarce. They all knew the situation between Esther and her father was sensitive.

She nodded briefly and then worked the keys again.

ARE YOU?

'I don't know . . . it's a bit early for that. I think that's something to talk about later . . .'

There was an uncomfortable silence.

'I brought some photographs of Kate's home and her family. I thought you might like to see them . . .'

CAN I GO TO HELEN'S AT THE END OF TERM? AND COME
HOME AFTER EASTER

'Yes, of course, though I would have liked . . . we would have
liked . . .'

THANK YOU.

Esther was becoming expert at using the screen just as able-
bodied people use conversation, to parry and thrust through things
that were uncomfortable to talk about.

She had filled out a little and, except for her expression, she
looked almost pretty. Certainly intelligent. Yet Richard felt he was
with a stranger and that the warmth of their relationship over the
past years might almost never have been.

ARE YOU GOING TO SHOW ME THE PHOTOS OR NOT?

He did his best to grin at her cheekiness, at least pleased that she
had asked, though just a little chilled that she looked indifferent as
he opened the packet and took out the first one.

She saw a family group on a large, elegant patio with a brick
barbecue to one side and all of them smile smile smiling with sun
on their faces as someone (her father who once upon a time had
been her own Daddy, mysterious and loved, only hers then) took
the aliens' photographs . . . She hated Kate.

A grey British sky loomed outside the windows as Richard set
down the last of the photographs in front of Esther saying, 'This
one's a bit dark because the sun was setting . . . we were on a trip
into the Northern Territories with horses,' and as he said it he
could feel the sun on his face and arms, and his hands on the
warm rock of a country he knew deep down might become his
own. Free there of the darkness that was Europe. Free there of
everything.

Esther said nothing to her father but stared at the photograph
which seemed to be of people and a place she could never know.
This man this face, smiling with the sun, utterly relaxed, happy, so
happy.

'Dada,' she began, 'Dada?'

'Yes, darling?' he dared whisper, as in the old days, because for a
moment she was like she had once been, trusting and loving.
'What is it?'

Dada I feel so frightened.

He saw her eyes wander, her mouth try to form words it could never say, and a despair he did not understand, of a woman, young and too vulnerable, beginning to sense she was fighting a battle for his love. It was a struggle between his love for her as a parent, and his love for Kate as a woman; two needs in conflict. But she was no longer a child, though she had a child's needs, and already she sensed it was a battle she could never win and whose outcome would be, in one way or another, that she was alone.

Then the look was gone and Esther was her rude self again.

THEY'RE A BIT FUZZY I THINK, the screen said.

'Well, they're a good memory,' said Richard, retreating. Then, changing the subject, 'So you'll go to Helen's for a week or two? To do some more of that research?'

Esther nodded briefly. Then, 'Dada,' she said again, wanting so much to ask about Kate and more about their holiday, and to share at last and not be so alone. But she shook her head, and turned away. Not Kate. A terrible instinct told her not to get involved.

Easter came. Down, down, clankety down, went Esther, out of the spring light that had come to the high walls and turrets of Radcliffe Square, into the darkness of the Bodleian stacks once more, and into the subterranean mazes of heavy sliding iron bookshelves and narrow corridors. Into the world she had become obsessed by, where she believed Dilke would be, and a lost hospital's name be found.

She and Tom became familiar figures to the pasty-faced librarians in those two Easter weeks: the ugly young man with glasses pushing the chair of the young woman with the nice clear grey-blue eyes who was working her way through successive nineteenth-century Select Committee Reports. Both wrapped up well against the chill down there.

'Toh!'

'Yes, Amh?'

'Th . . . a . . . wohh!'

'This one?'

'*Nah!*'

'That one!'

'Yeh, Toh. Thaaah . . .'

'OK, Amh.'
And he would reach up to replace one volume and take down another, his grinning grunts audible to the hunched scholars at the little desks provided for stack researchers.

'Big one, Amh. Big as me.'

'Ssh! Toh . . .'

Then Tom would stand quiet, or sit if he could find a seat, watching out for Amh, never out of sight and call of her since the scare in January when he had lost himself among the scaredy hanging green shelves and that man. But often she needed him next to her because the reports were too big for a page-turner.

She read the pages rapidly, frustrated if Tom did not turn fast enough when she needed him to, obsessively working her way through Minutes of Evidence of conditions in madhouses, attitudes of the Commissioners in Lunacy, schemes for building new hospitals for pauper lunatics, and architects' plans; immersing herself in the world that she believed Arthur must have inherited. Here were the airing courts, the 'rooms for noisy patients', the punishments by deprivation of privileges, by ice-cold shower baths, by sub-starvation diets that masqueraded in the reports as 'medical treatment'; conditions which Arthur knew and which must have formed his life.

But even skimming through the reports as she was, stopping only for those passages which seemed interesting or helpful, took time, and she grew tired. Her mind wandered, her note-taking with the computerized mini-writer designed by Leon Sadler became slower and slower.

Meanwhile, in another part of the library, Helen Perry-Wilcox was pursuing research into the literature of mental asylums in the nineteenth and early twentieth centuries. Books she thought were interesting she made detailed notes of, and in some cases took down to Esther in the stacks. In the evenings the two of them compared notes and steadily built up Esther's files on disk.

'Do you have to continue working down in that place?' Helen asked more than once. 'It's dreadfully cold. You could have the Select Committee material brought up to a warmer reading room.'

'Nah,' said Esther.

'Why not?'

I LIKE IT DOWN THERE. IT KEEPS ME GOING.

'Well, I think you're strange.'

CORRECT.

'I mean in the head, my dear.'

BLAME THE MATERIAL, typed Esther with a grin. BUT IT IS
EXCITING! I'M SURE WE'LL FIND SOMETHING.

'Well, I agree. It is exciting. Poor Margaret can't understand it.
But she said today, I spoke to her on the phone, that if it's what
you feel you should do you should do it.' Then she added rather
too casually: 'Oh, Esther, I meant to say . . .'

Esther's grin faded. She could read Helen's voice like a book –
like a confessional perhaps – and she knew something was
worrying her, something had happened, something about her grandmother. Her eyes were alert.

'Margaret's coming over this evening.'

WHY? typed Esther immediately. SHE WASN'T COMING UNTIL
TOMORROW. WHERE DID SHE GO TODAY? WHY?

'She'll tell you herself, it's not for me . . .'

DID SHE GO TO THE SPECIALIST AGAIN TODAY? WAS THAT
IT?

'Yes,' said Helen. 'Yes, I'm afraid she did.' Margaret had not
been due to go until June and an early visit meant she was worried
about something.

'Ooh,' said Esther quietly. She was silent, staring here and there
for a moment, her head movements stressed.

I'M GOING TO FINISH TYPING UP THE GUNNARSON
STORY, she typed, blocking out the unpleasantness, turning
from Helen.

'All right, my dear,' said Helen.

Then Esther entered the world of the Skallagrigg, to escape her
own world of pain.

One day the Father went on holiday and when he came back
the boys saw he was different. There's no secrets in a hospital,
so even in the cot and chair wards they soon heard he was to
get wed.

Arthur spoke and Frank says, 'Arthur's decided we're going
to give the Father and his sweetheart a present all together.
He's been good to us and we must be good to him on his
happy day. It only comes once.'

Eppie was still with them in them days and says, 'What'll we give?'

Frank says, 'Arthur hasn't decided.'

Arthur thinks for days and then tells Frank who says to the boys, 'We'll give him what we can all do together. Arthur says a picture with a frame like the one in the Super's office you see through the window. Father'll like that. The wood bit can be made in O T and the colours in Art.' Then Frank told them who would make what 'cos only a few could make anything useful. The rest were daubers.

Eppie says, 'Why that? What's a picture?'

Frank says, 'Shut up, Eppie,' but Arthur speaks.

Says good Frank, 'Arthur says you give what you most want yourself.'

'Who wants a picture?' says Eppie, quick as a flash.

Arthur's grey eyes look round the walls of the ward they've looked at twenty years. There's nothing on them walls. Dilke says it's a danger. Could fall. Could break. Could be used to bash others. Loose things is dangerous things.

Arthur says, 'Me.'

That's good enough for the boys. So the O T man's asked and he winks and says, 'Mum's the word, lads.'

Norrie marked the wood.

Eppie got the saw.

Norman held the wood in the vice.

Jim sawed.

Henry caught the bits and swept.

Alec screwed.

Norrie put a nail in.

Frank cut the cardboard.

Arthur held the poster paints.

Eppie said, 'What'll we paint?'

Arthur speaks. Frank says, 'There'll be a cross for God and Christ Jesus 'cos of what Father James is and white for wedding's peace.'

So it was to be. One by one the lads made it, over weeks, with Arthur guiding 'cos he had the brains.

And mum was the word because no one let on, except Norman grinning at the Father and said 'You,' 'cos he couldn't keep it back. But Father couldn't make sense of that so it was all right.

When the picture was done all the boys gathered and looked at it. There was beauty in that little picture and the cross was red and blue and behind was white for the wedding. It was a happy day they finished it.

Where does happiness go? No one knows that right. The word went round the wedding was off. The Father became ill. He had to stop in a service and go out and another finish. He wasn't feeling well said the dilkes. But the boys knew he had a broken heart. And maybe some of them knew that the Father was lonely and in the darkness where God and comfort is absent.

Then one Sunday Arthur says for the boys to have the picture among them. The Father's come back all right, but he was thin and ill and his voice not its normal self. That's what loss of love can do. Some of the boys know that. Arthur for one.

At the end when Dilke says, 'All right out row by row no talking shut up quick quick *quick* you there,' like usual, Frank stands up like he did once long before for his first communion.

All the nobs and the Super and everyone there waiting to get out but Arthur speaks and Frank stands up.

'No,' says he. 'We got a pressie for the Father first.'

'Shut up,' says Dilke. Then Dilke sees he's got the little picture the boys made in his hand and he grabs it thinking it's off the wall of the church. It pulls apart and the cross and the white wedding falls on the aisle floor out of the frame. Norman looms.

'No,' he says and he would have killed Dilke but Frank said, 'No, Norman.'

You should have seen the boys' faces seeing all their work broken. They were like to cry. No one moved in the silence.

Arthur speaks, his voice funny all loud in the church and everyone hearing.

And Franks says, 'Yes Arthur.'

He bends down and gets that picture and he holds it together precious as a baby new and he says, 'Father!' And Father James comes through the worried dilkes to where the trouble is.

Arthur speaks and Frank says, 'Arthur says we made this for you when you get wed and now you're not so Arthur says you're to have it all the same because the boys love you and made it for you for all you've done. It's a cross and white for your wedding which will not be now but Arthur says one day maybe.'

The Father stands in silence and even Dilke shuts up. Dilke was always silent in the face of love. The Father is without words.

Arthur speaks and Frank says, 'Arthur says God is mystery and white is goodness and that never changes so it's for you 'cos you're always good even now bad's come your way. Arthur says the boys understand better than most and are glad that you come back to us today.'

Then the Father took that little picture and looked at it and he smiled. His eyes had aged in the weeks past; now they filled with tears.

The Father says, 'Thank you. The picture is broken like my spirit was broken but as my spirit was mended so will this picture be.'

Late that night Arthur's grey eyes are open, and they stare at the high windows where the bars on his darkness are; but his eyes don't see the bars, they see the bright stars beyond.

FIFTY

The stay with Helen in Oxford over Easter suited Esther and Richard equally as it allowed them to delay facing the emotional consequences of the fact that Kate had moved into Harefield.

But with examinations looming Esther could not continue to stay away indefinitely and in mid-April, with a fortnight of the holidays remaining, she returned to a house – her home – that had changed.

Kate's things were now in evidence – her coats and her boots in the hall cupboard, a red apron in the kitchen, a calendar and a clock on the kitchen wall, neither of which had been there before. In the sitting-room pictures of the recent Australian trip and Kate's parents had displaced several of the family photographs of Esther, and of Tom and Marion.

While Esther had been away Marion had got engaged to Jeremy, a quiet boy from the church whom they had seen so rarely. She had a pretty diamond engagement ring and the first thing she did when Esther was settled was to say, 'I was going to write but it only happened a fortnight ago and I thought I'd save up the surprise to tell you myself.'

'Whe . . .?' asked Esther.

'Autumn,' said Marion. 'We've not fixed a date yet, but you'll be coming. Jeremy asked especially.'

She looks so happy, she is so happy, thought Esther, fighting the uncharitable jealousy she felt, and suppressing the fear other people's good news for the future always roused in her.

'Wha . . .?' asked Esther. What's going to happen now?

'Well; Richard's got plans for us, we're so excited.'

So that's why she didn't tell me before. Daddy's involved. And Kate. Probably.

'But I'll leave it to your father to tell you.' Esther hated that, she had to wait and could not ask and badger like an ordinary person.

If she had been able to speak properly she could have got the information out of Marion in minutes.

Kate and Richard had been out when Esther arrived, both working. Kate, it seemed, was continuing her job for the time being. Daddy was as busy as ever. Esther drove her wheelchair around the ground floor, looking at the photos. She was pleased to have the privacy to do it, angry they were not there to meet her.

'There's no pleasing me,' she thought ruefully, able to laugh at herself. 'I'll be nice to Kate when they come back, I'll smile,' she promised.

'Don't make a scene, Esther! You know it's not Christian,' said Marion, echoing her thoughts. They grinned at each other.

'Oooh . . . achk,' said Esther. OK!

But when Kate's car crunched into the drive and Kate's steps came to the front door, Esther felt a terrible tightening in her chest, and her face froze into coldness.

'Hello, Esther,' said Kate, coming straight to her room where she pretended to be reading with the door open. 'Can I come in?' The same fresh scent, the same warmth, the same niceness she had shown when Esther arrived at Christmas.

'Ehro,' Esther managed.

The two looked at each other and Esther saw that Kate was concerned and perhaps not yet secure. She felt guiltily pleased in that secret place where people enjoy their power over others even though they feel it to be wrong. While to Kate Esther's grey-blue eyes seemed cold as Margaret's did sometimes and she wished she could make her know she wished her no harm.

They talked a little, Esther willing to use the screen and astonishing Kate with her speed.

IT'S A NEW PROGRAM DADDY'S FRIEND LEON DID. IT'S GOT A MEMORY BIGGER THAN MY HEAD!

Kate laughed and for a moment so did Esther. Then back she went to being distant.

WHEN'S DADDY COMING HOME?

'He said between six and seven.'

'He said.' This morning when he left and you were together, that's when 'he said'. Esther hated the intimacy this woman had with her father. And she hated hating it, and her mind was in circles of despair.

'Do you want some tea? Come and talk to me while I make some supper.' Esther nodded. At that level at least she could be civil.

When Richard came home he went all formal, summoning Esther, Kate and Marion into the sitting-room. He made a point of pouring a Perrier for Marion (she did not drink alcohol), a sherry for Esther, and gin-and-tonics for himself and Kate. There was the civilized smell of good French cooking from the kitchen.

'To the future!' said Richard smiling at them all. Marion helped Esther sip her sherry to toast the frightening unknown. They all looked at her expectantly with smiles and she realized with a shrinking feeling that they knew something she did not, and that her father was about to say what it was: it was the thing Marion would not talk about.

'We've something to tell you, Esther, some really good news. As you know Marion's got engaged to Jeremy and while this is very good news it does rather pose me a problem ... ("It poses *us* a problem," thought Esther) because frankly it would be hard to find someone as good as Marion to look after you when you're here.'

Marion looked down at her engagement ring. Esther avoided looking at Kate.

'Frankly, I did not feel it fair to ask Kate to do it even if she had been willing because she has her own life to run now in relation to ComputaBase and all the commitments that will bring her as my partner ...' Richard was sounding too formal and was already regretting this whole scene. He wished he had talked to Esther by himself, not here where she was exposed, but he pressed on.

'Well, anyway, there is a solution. It's to make Hill House next door into a home for handicapped children which Marion and Jeremy will run with some outside guidance at first – we have a board of trustees – and eventually I'm sure very much by themselves. There are a number of details I want to talk to you privately about because I think that's fairest on you ...' (Esther relaxed at this, at least she could save her more personal questions until later) 'but the main point is that whenever you are at Harefield there will be helpers for you at Hill House. In fact, one of the key points for us all, Esther, is that Hill House will provide you with the help and security you will need if the situation arises that we are not here any more. One must be quite realistic: I'm not immortal, nor is any of the family, and the chances are that you are going to outlive us and I want you to have complete security.

'I have put the house in your name and when you are twenty-one you will become the principal trustee along with myself, and although you won't be able to change the usage of the place you will always have the right to be cared for there, and to use the facilities and staff.

'We think it is going to take a year or so to set up – there are a lot of alterations to do, and I'm anxious that Marion and Jeremy go on certain training courses as well. It's an unusual opportunity for them. Of course, the place will not be run at a loss though it may have to be subsidized at first. We'll be looking at ways to make it profitable, perhaps with residential holiday stays and so on.'

Esther stared at them all expressionlessly, but she smiled when Marion went to her, cuddled her for a moment, and said, 'It's very exciting and it is the best way. Kate's here now and things have changed. I can't do the same thing for ever. It means so much to Jeremy and me to be offered this kind of chance. Do you under-stand?'

Esther nodded bleakly.

'Dada,' she began, and her voice sounded so lost for a moment that Kate instinctively pushed Richard forward and with a nod to Marion indicated that they should leave Esther alone with him.

'Dada . . .' WILL I HAVE TO LEAVE HERE?

'No, darling, of course not. This is your home. Hill House is the future in case anything happens and I have to make plans.'

But she looked worried and lost and was beginning to breathe faster as if trying to control the tears that wanted to come.

I DON'T WANT TO LEAVE HERE.

'Oh, darling, I know, and I don't want . . .'

Then she started to cry, her hand fretting at the mini-writer unable for a moment to type up words. Then:

WHAT'S GOING TO HAPPEN TO TOM?

'When?'

IN THE FUTURE. WHEN YOU'RE GONE? WHEN I'M GONE?

Richard looked at the words on the screen and perhaps for a moment saw and felt the terrible vulnerability which she masked as so many adolescents do. Then all the difficulty and stress of these past few weeks – when in truth he had been thinking about living away from Esther, and harbouring the guilt-inducing fantasies of her death that trouble such parents – welled up in him.

'Oh, dear,' he said. He sat down and his face creased and he began to cry. 'Oh dear, I'm sorry, I just can't stop thinking, because I love you and I can't, I'm sorry, I don't know, it's so terrible because I can't help you, only make plans that no normal parent ever has to make . . . I need Kate, you see. She loves me. I wish you could see what that means.' And he sat before her weeping, his hands to his face, rocking side to side. He found nothing more to say, and Esther, try though she might, could not find the will to reach forward and touch him. She felt unmoved by his tears.

'I'm sorry,' he said at last. And that was all, finally, he could say. While Esther, seeing her father break down for a few minutes and not yet old or wise enough to understand quite why, felt only more uncertainty about what, in this house that had once been her home, her role might now be. To her the Hill House idea seemed no more than a way of getting rid of her.

Esther spent the rest of the vacation working hard towards the summer examinations, maintaining her cool attitude to Kate, accepting with ill grace the help she needed from time to time. While Kate, for her part, refused to react to Esther's coldness and remained, on the whole, kind and good-humoured about it, believing that one day Esther would give up and start smiling at her, as she did with everyone else.

Towards the end of the holiday she heard from Graham that he had won a sponsored scholarship to Cambridge University from a successful computer software group. It guaranteed him a better income at college than he would get from a grant, though it tied him to a job with them for five years. Esther was pleased for him, and wrote to say so, but it undermined yet further her trust in the usefulness of her own future.

'Why don't you contact some of the firms as well? I bet Richard would help, he must have lots of friends in the right places,' Graham suggested during a telephone conversation. In fact that is precisely what Richard had wanted to do but she was determined not to take his help and Kate, who understood Esther's desire for independence, had dissuaded him. 'There's plenty of time,' she had said. 'She'll come round, just let her do it at her own pace.'

Now, to Graham, Esther simply whispered, 'Nah.'

'You can't go it alone, Ess, you've got to accept help. You're too proud that's your trouble.' He spoke with the confidence of one who has successfully found his own way, and before it Esther fell silent.

'Well, see you in a week or so,' said Graham. 'And cheer up for God's sake, you've got more going for you than most of us. Sorry! Didn't mean it. You just aggravate me sometimes.'

'Yoooahh!' shouted Esther down the phone.

'I know *I* annoy *you*,' said Graham. They laughed together. 'So how's the Skallagrigg research going?' he asked finally, to end on a cheerful note.

On a blank piece of wall in her room Esther had Tom stick up a piece of paper on which she had printed out some key Skallagrigg propositions and questions:

1. ARTHUR IS REAL.
2. I believe Arthur is still alive because otherwise there would be a story about his death.
3. The Skallagrigg was a person who was once alive and might still be.
4. WHO IS DILKE?
5. There is a hospital where Arthur is. I WILL FIND ITS NAME.
6. The most elegant way of finding Arthur is through Dilke who doesn't want him found. THAT IS JUSTICE.

FIFTY-ONE

On the eve of her first 'A'-level examination in early June Esther received one of the few letters she ever had from Tom: 'GOOD LUCK LOVE TOM!!' it read. The letters were written with a black felt-tip pen.

The envelope was postmarked Wycombe and addressed in Kate's strong, clear hand. Esther had to admit that she was glad to have the letter and she deduced from the fact that Kate had done the envelope that Tom had got bored. The letter had probably taken him a day to write anyway. She smiled to think of Kate bullying Tom into it and, away from Harefield, allowed herself to feel secretly pleased that she had bothered.

She had the card stuck on the side of her chair where everybody could see it and then she pressed on with what she was doing that final day: programming a new version of 'Tom's Game', by now the school's favourite computer game.

It had been selected by Warble to go on display to parents and visitors on the coming Open Day on the last day of term, and Esther was doing a version for the Commodore computers, three of which the school had recently acquired.

That she was doing it on a day when everyone else was doing last-minute revision was typical of her, and perhaps a little smug. But they had had a talk on how to pass examinations and she had taken seriously the advice that candidates should relax on the last day. And anyway, there was nothing much more she could do – she did not really doubt that she would pass, the question was at what grades: Reading University wanted two A's and a B, and while History presented no real problem English Literature was less predictable.

That same day she wrote a letter to Margaret, who herself had written one of her brief untidy letters to wish Esther luck. Margaret's letter did not tell the full truth. She had another growth operated on at the Radcliffe Infirmary the week Esther's examinations began but insisted that this was kept from Esther until after the exams.

The operation appeared to be successful, and Helen came in to see her every day, popping in after sessions at the Bodleian doing bibliographical research for Esther.

'Is it going to get anywhere, Helen?' Margaret asked one day, sipping tea and fluffed up neatly in bed.

'Well, I don't know. It's fascinating, that's certain. The conditions in those big mental hospitals were just awful and probably still are.'

'What are you both hoping to find out from all the research?'

'We don't know. Esther is looking for clues to a hospital where she thinks Arthur is. We don't think there'll be much trouble identifying the hospital once we're there because we've got a lot of information about it. For example, it's got a building called the "Old Annexe". There is or was a pavilion in a sports field opposite the main building. There's a chapel, big by the sound of it, with a brass communion rail and it forms a separate building. And so on.'

'Surely, that'll be easy to find.'

Helen laughed. 'My dear, there are over six hundred hospitals in Britain, all of them are subject to changes and rebuilding, and most of them have chapels, fields and annexes! No, Esther thinks that by reading about it she'll see some kind of pattern . . . and she has already. For example, it seems likely that Arthur's hospital is in the north, and is almost certainly one of the big mid-nineteenth-century ones, so that limits the field.'

Helen had decided to suggest that Margaret, Esther and she should drive north in the summer holidays to look at the area where the Skallagrigg stories seemed to come from, and perhaps to talk with some of the contacts Esther had made through her advertisement and letters.

'What *is* the Skallagrigg?'

'I think it must mean "God" to handicapped people in institutions. A kind of deity. Every society needs a god.'

'Yes,' said Margaret doubtfully. 'God. Brian believed, I do not. Especially since . . .' she waved her hand over her sick body to suggest illness. 'And Esther,' she added heavily. 'There is really a God? I think there's nothing after death. Just nothing.'

The two women were silent. It was a subject they disagreed on. Then Margaret said, 'I hope she is not disappointed. I am so grateful to you for helping her, I can't seem to find the energy for that kind of thing, you know. You're more used to it.'

Helen smiled. 'You have no need to thank me. You and Esther have given me so much. You're like a family. Well, you *are* a family.'

'I shouldn't but . . .' Margaret smiled weakly and a little weepily. 'If I should . . . if anything, if I should die you will keep an eye on Esther, won't you? I know there's Richard but he has his own life to lead and he won't understand some of Esther's needs. Esther never had a mother and I've been the only one she's had. Not much good at that I'm afraid. Brian was better than me. But if . . . I would like to know you'll keep on eye open.'

Helen nodded, not trusting herself to speak.

'The future's such a worry with a child like Esther. It's such a burden that it's not fair to expect Kate to take it on. I'm so relieved about Hill House. I think Richard has done a good thing there. He's always surprised me you know. I was unkind to him after our daughter died.'

Helen said, 'There's no need to talk about it to me. Really.'

'I want to. I've got to face the future and do what I can for it. Esther will get all I have which doesn't seem much these days, but Richard's there so that's all right and I'd like you to be an executor as well as Richard. The other one is my solicitor in Charlbury but you'd be better, you have a sense of humour!'

'This is a bit premature, Margaret. We're all about to go on holiday, if only to meet handicapped people and look at mental asylums! You're coming with us. You're not going to die quite yet.'

'But . . .'

'But, of course I'll be your executor and you can spend the next ten years telling me how you are going to change your will yet again. It will give me something to do in my old age.' They grinned at each other and had more tea.

'You're staying with me again when you come out of here at the weekend.'

'Am I?' said Margaret weakly.

'Yes, you are. And now you're going to sleep.'

Helen got up, bent down and kissed Margaret. 'I'm glad you're so much more rested.'

'Yes,' whispered Margaret, her eyes closing.

Helen stood looking down at her. Then she looked up for a moment at the high window in the little room, through which she could just see sky. From somewhere came shouts, indefinable, and a curious scream or call, hard to say which. The echoing sounds of a hospital. 'Such a window as this,' she thought, 'Arthur once looked out of.'

Patterns. Arthur would have been in a cot. The walls would not have had pictures on them. There would never once, in fifty years, have been a tray with pretty tea things on.

Helen tiptoed out into the corridor and closed the door behind her. Family and friend: she had never expressed the thought before that Margaret and Esther were like family, and it moved her to think that Margaret should trust her enough to ask her to watch out for Esther. Well, of course she would, she always would.

But Arthur, who had kept a look out out for him? Only Frank and Norman. The names came to her as she wound her way through the confusing corridors and turns of the hospital. Family. Had Esther ever noticed that in the Arthur stories there was never mention of his family? Perhaps he had been there since birth, the illegitimate child of a naive or stupid village girl forced into the local mental hospital to have the baby. Her researches showed there were plenty like that years ago.

Her imagination tried to take her into the maze around her: above, left, right, up again, forward, left by the lifts, right again on to another level and then second left, no right, far away from her in this same building, Margaret slept. A window like Arthur's above her on the sky. Then, much much further away, was Esther, sitting her exams. Yet further away, goodness knows where, was Arthur, she hoped. A child no more.

Helen Perry-Wilcox stepped out into St Giles and turned in the June sunshine under the plane trees that lined the wide old street. She was glad she could walk. Glad she had health. Glad she had purpose and the trust of people she respected.

'We're going to find you,' she whispered, as if Arthur could hear her.

No . . . as if *she* could hear Arthur.

She paused under the trees as shoppers and students hurried past her. She was thinking that, though she had intended to go to the covered market, she felt so positive that she would go back to the library and do just a little more reading. On the way she would buy a card to send to Esther because people sent cards at the beginning of exams but never in the middle when you most needed them.

Spurred on by an indefinable sense of urgency, she pressed on to Radcliffe Square and into the Camera as if drawn. She went down into the stacks where Esther liked to work. It was cold and gloomy even on a day like this and she wished she was wearing more than a cotton dress and cardigan.

But now she was here, and she wandered among the shelves, starting as Esther had at 1815 and the key initial report. She stared at its spine but did not take it down. The next key date was 1832 and then 1847. Then 1867. Someone coughed and pulled a sliding metal shelf.

Esther had seen most of these already and in her methodical way kept notes. Helen reached up and took down the 1867 volume. The Report was mainly the usual Minutes of Evidence, page after page of verbatim accounts by witnesses cross-examined by Commissioners, telling of conditions they had seen:

> This ward was evidently overcrowded and the air at
> night must consequently be rendered foul and highly in-
> jurious to the patients; and to add to the evil we find that
> from want of an infirmary the sick and healthy cases are
> obliged to be accommodated in the same apartment.
> There are cells leading off from two of the airing-yards,
> quite detached from the wards, consisting of five or six in
> each range . . . The cells are damp, dark and dungeon-
> like, badly ventilated and the mode of heating is rendered
> totally inoperative owing to the stoves being too small
> and partly out of order.
> . . . there was an epileptic patient confined to his bed in
> one of these cells labouring under a bowel complaint: his
> legs were oedematous and had every appearance of
> running rapidly to gangrene. I found another patient
> who was greatly emaciated with contracted limbs in a
> most wretched and feeble state . . .

It did not sound to Helen as if much had changed from the conditions she had read of in the 1815 Report, and she thought wearily that the wheels of bureaucracy turned as slowly then as they do now. She shivered a little at the unaccustomed cold.

But this was all one hundred and twenty five years ago, so surely conditions had improved? Not according to some of the recent Royal Commission reports she had read for Esther.

Would Esther and she ever actually *visit* such hospitals? And how did one get inside? Helen Perry-Wilcox, sixty-four, former librarian, contemplating a visit north with an eighteen-year-old spastic girl, continued to read about hell.

'Did you at any time have occasion to examine Gillie?' 'No, he had died three months before I first attended the hospital.' 'But to your knowledge the treatments which had led to his death were still being applied to existing patients?' 'Yes the court wash was still being prescribed.' 'Can you explain the term "court wash"?' 'Dr Craigie had recommended this procedure to pacify noisy patients and in time it was found remedial on excited patients as well. The procedure was to take them into Back Court and divest them.' 'Completely?' 'Yes, they were naked. They then stood or were laid in a restraining jacket on the ground and successive douches of water were played on them. My part was to judge medically when the treatment might be deemed to have reached a traumatic point.' 'How did you do that?' 'I was uncertain concerning the matter but was told that Dr Craigie had done it aurally from a window, entrance to the court being barred and the douches being applied from a window above. This isolation of the patient was regarded as essential for the full benefit of the treatment.' 'Did you agree with that?' 'I did not. I regarded the treatment as not efficacious and as barbaric.' 'What happened on the occasion you first witnessed it and before you attempted to put a stop to it?' 'I judged within minutes that the patient had suffered sufficient and had need of no more.' 'What was his condition?' 'He had been standing at the beginning but the force of the water was such

that he fell over and could not rise against it. He began
by calling for the treatment to be stopped.' 'Calling?' 'He
could not speak. He was shouting incomprehensibly. He
was an idiot.' 'What then?' 'The patient collapsed and
the douche was continued. I judged the treatment was
sufficient and ordered that it be stopped. After an
altercation the treatment was stopped.' 'An altercation?'
'The assistants said that I was ending it too soon. In
their experience a longer time was necessary. I was told
that a court wash was never under a duration of half
an hour. In winter longer.' 'Longer?' 'The cold was
adjudged to be beneficial. A senior man was applying
the douche and would not at first desist even under my
direct order. We argued about it.' 'What were the staff
involved?' 'There were three and they were all
experienced. They were Johnson, Wate and Dilke. Dilke
was the senior man and much respected by staff and
patients alike.' 'Respected?' 'Feared would be the better
word.' 'Was this the same Dilke indicted in the Gillie
case?' 'I was told he was the same.' 'It was not proven.'
'I believe that was the finding.'

Dilke.

The stacks were deathly silent about Helen Perry-Wilcox as she
sat staring at the name on the printed page. She repeated the
name to herself, *Dilke Dilke Dilke Dilke*, and urgent questions came
to her one after another: Is this where he started? Does this mean
Arthur goes back further than we thought? Does it mean that he
cannot now be alive? Is this name here just a coincidence?

Dilke. The name thundered inside her head as before her she
seemed to see not pages of an old forgotten report but the sunless,
brick court of a mid-nineteenth-century mental hospital, a naked
man out of his mind with cold and fear as water was hosed upon
him from a window, powerfully, cruelly as he 'called' out that they
might stop. She saw how a young doctor had heard a cry for
mercy, and how this Mr Dilke had not.

She quickly leafed back through the Report to find further
reference to the Gillie case which might give her a clue about
Dilke. She could find none, but in the appendix she found a list of

witnesses who had given evidence for this Report and among them, listed as giving evidence on the 16 February 1867, was the following: John Dilke Esq., nurse, Meern Moor Hospital, Lancashire.

She stayed calm; the frantic, artificial calm of the discoverer who does not want to believe the marvel he has discovered for fear it is a mistake and seeks ways desperately to confirm his discovery.

'I must check. I must *think*.' Helen read the entry again. And again. Yes, the name was correct. But Meern Moor Hospital? It rang no bells. But again it was a northern location which fitted Esther's theory.

Unable to contain her excitement further, and wanting some kind of action, she made a note of the reference, checked a final time for other mentions of the Gillie case, put the volume on one side with a Reader's Ticket inside to indicate that she was coming back to it, and went off to the main library to see what she could find about Meern Moor Hospital. Once she was in daylight again, Helen had a powerful urge to telephone Netherton and tell Esther the news, but she resisted it; Esther was sitting exams. It could wait. Just two weeks. Esther would want to do the follow-ups herself. It must be Esther's moment not hers.

But she could not resist looking up the listings in the library's copy of the *Hospital and Health Services Handbook* to see what it said for Meern Moor: Meadowslea Hpl, Meanwood Park Hpl, Meare Manor, Mearnskirk Hpl, Meathop Hpl. The nearest, Mearnskirk, sounded Scottish and sure enough turned out to be on the outskirts of the Glasgow.

Meern Moor? She found the north-western region section of the *Handbook* where the hospitals were listed in more detail. She carefully noted the twelve mental handicap or long-stay units mentioned for the region:

> Brockhall Hospital (Blackburn)
> Hulton Hospital (Birmingham)
> Calderstones Hospital (Blackburn)
> Florence Nightingale's Hospital (Bury)
> Eaves Lane Hospital and Heath Charnock Hospital (Chorley)
> Royal Albert Hospital (Lancaster)

Herstorne (Grisedale)
Westhulme Hospital (Oldham)
Scott House (Rochdale)
Sturrick Royal (Manchester)
Swinton Hospital (nr Manchester)
Offerton House Hospital (Stockport)

She tried another approach: *The Concise Oxford Dictionary of English Place Names.* They had already tried this for Apsham Wood, the name that appeared in several of the stories, and not found what they wanted. Now she went through the pages again and found what she was looking for without difficulty: Meern Moor, Lancashire. The source references, apart from that to the Domesday Book, meant nothing to her, but in a gazetteer of the British Isles she traced the location more precisely: Meern Moor was a few miles east of Lancaster, and clearly marked on the map.

For the time being, Helen decided, that was as far as she would go with the research, but now, clearly, they had reason enough to make their trip north.

On the morning after Esther's final 'A'-level History paper when she was feeling anti-climactic and thinking of home, a postcard of a misty Oxford college scene arrived for her. It read: 'I think I have traced the origin of Dilke. Please phone and I'll tell you everything. Much love, Helen.'

Esther phoned from the school office at lunchtime, the phone held for her by a jubilant Graham who had that same morning taken his last computer science paper.

Helen rapidly explained what she had discovered, omitting nothing. Esther listened in absolute silence. Only when Helen had finished, stressing the fact that Meern Moor Hospital no longer existed, did Esther speak.

'Graaah!' she said waving towards her mini-writer. Graham took the phone.

'Essie's going to key up a couple of questions. Right. Now. Can we visit Meern Moor even if there's no hospital there now?'

'Well I think we should,' said Helen. 'It'll be quite interesting. Quite how the authorities get rid of a hospital I don't know. I expect the building's being used for something else.'

'What's the nearest existing hospital to that site?' read out Graham.

'I think it must be one of the Blackburn ones.'

'Blackpool's in the stories. Is there one there?'

'No, but it's only a matter of miles. We're getting warm, Esther.'

'You said the date of the reference was 1867. That means there's no chance of Arthur being alive. But that doesn't fit with the other facts.'

'I agree, it's odd. It could be there's another, later Dilke, but the location and everything else points to this one being the original. It's just too much of a coincidence otherwise.'

'Son of Dilke!!!'

'What?'

'Nothing, Helen, just one of Esther's macabre jokes,' said Graham.

There was silence as they all thought about the Dilke discovery, and the school secretary looked up askance, worrying about telephone bills. But Graham winked: there was a festive air around the school with the exams over. Summer was in the air, and Open Day to look forward to.

'Have you checked out any more of the 1867 Report?' repeated Graham for Esther.

'I thought *you'd* want to. It's your project! But there are some things. I don't think I mentioned, there's reference to a "Gillie Case".'

'Yeh!' said Esther immediately. YES!

'Does it mean something?'

'I read about it. There's something in one of the Annual Reports. Gillie. There's something there,' Graham read.

'Well, this Dilke was involved.'

'I would have remembered that. Maybe I just missed it. Maybe that's what I saw the day the books fell down.'

'You're going to have to come to Oxford.'

'I'm meant to be going to Harefield this weekend. It's an exeat. But could you fix with Daddy for me to stay with you instead?'

'I'm not sure . . .'

Graham laughed. 'Esther is about to key in "Oh go on" and I'm saving her the bother: Oh go on, Helen.'

'Well, I'll try. I'll talk to Margaret first. She does want to see you,
I know that.'

But the Oxford visit was not made, because that weekend was
the last before Richard Marquand made his second visit to Aus-
tralasia and he wanted to see Esther before he went.

So she had to wait until the end of term, doing what research
she could from the school library, and checking and rechecking
the stories for any reference that might shed further light on Dilke
or Meern Moor.

In fact, the delay may have been a good thing. Esther, like
others in her year, was tired and needed the winding down that
the final weeks of term offered. It was a period in which the older
students enjoyed themselves, and made preparations for Open Day,
which in Esther's case meant typing up a report on 'Tom's Game'.

She was in the middle of doing this one lazy afternoon when
Graham appeared by her side and put a copy of a magazine on her
tray.

'There's something in there for you,' he said. 'Page 126. Your
chance of a lifetime.'

The magazine was the current number of *CODA*, the specialist
small systems journal from America. Graham always got his hands
on the school copy first. The cover headline was 'Computers and
Learning'.

'It's got a whole section on the way computers are being used
for the handicapped.'

He turned to the page for her.

'Wha . . .?' she said, looking at the close print of the articles
among the advertisements.

'They're offering a prize for the best computer game for special
needs learners. You could send them "Tom's Game". You never
know . . .'

Esther looked at him doubtfully.

'I agree,' he said, 'I wouldn't normally recommend it. These
kind of so called competitions are just cheap ways of getting their
hands on a lot of programs they can exploit. But *CODA* is a re-
spectable magazine, and the offer's from them and not a manu-
facturer. Why not try it, Ess? It's a good game.'

MY GAME'S TOO SIMPLE, she typed.

'That's what you think. It's not simple at all in programming terms. The graphics could be better maybe, but show me a game where they're good enough. There isn't one. Graphics are lagging behind. The beauty of "Tom's Game" is that the skill levels make it playable by virtually anyone who can input, however crudely, and the way you've scored it so that different level players can play fairly against each other. There's 2,500 dollars in prize money, with a 1,000 dollars first prize. If you don't send it up I will.'

'Nah!' said Esther.

'How are you going to stop me? I'm bigger than you.'

NOT BY MUCH.

'Enough.'

I'LL THINK ABOUT IT.

'You make sure you do.'

On the day before Open Day, the last day of term, Esther Marquand had Graham cut out the entry form for the *CODA* competition, and typed up a covering letter which she finished off 'E. Marquand'. Graham wrote in a signature for her.

'Shall I put it in the out-tray?' Graham asked.

NO, she typed. TOM CAN POST IT FOR LUCK. HE ALWAYS POSTS MY LETTERS IF HE'S AROUND. HE'S COMING TOMORROW FOR OPEN DAY SPORTS.

Some time on the way back to Harefield after Open Day, Esther asked Richard to stop the car by a red postbox by the roadside. Tom knew what he had to do.

'What is it you're posting?' asked Richard.

'Sshh!' hished Tom. 'Secret.'

'Go on then.'

He hurried over to the box, peered inside as usual, whispered his invocations to the Skallagrigg who he believed was down there somewhere, and posted the letter to *CODA*'s editorial office in Peterborough, New Hampshire.

'At least you can tell me who it's to,' said Richard teasingly.

'Skalg in Amercky,' said Tom. Esther had told him it was going to America and she didn't look as if she would mind him saying.

'Nah!' smiled Esther. Not Skallagrigg.

'Yes,' he whispered to himself, his breath steaming the car window glass for a brief brief moment. 'Yes! Skalg in Amercky.'

FIFTY-TWO

Helen's discovery of the Dilke link with the north-west was well timed. It gave Esther the excuse she needed to plunge herself into Skallagrigg research and so block out unpleasantnesses like Margaret's recent illness, the threat that Kate seemed to pose to her future, and the long wait for her exam results.

Esther quickly decided that she should make a trip to Meern Moor in Lancashire, and she was impressively thorough in planning it. Not only did she arrange to visit her correspondents in Huddersfield and Edinburgh, but in the idle last few weeks of term she had word-processed a letter to all the pre-1900 mental handicap hospitals in the north-west to ask what records they had concerning 'John Dilke', and for information on the history of Meern Moor Hospital.

Nine of the eleven hospitals replied. Five were helpful, sending material about their history and existing services and regretting that they had no record of a 'Dilke'; four more answered briefly with polite negatives; two did not reply.

But Esther did succeed in tracking down an account of the 'Gillie Case' – it was another case of a court wash in Meern Moor Hospital administered by Dilke. Gillie, an 'idiot cripple', had died of a sudden 'congestion' some days after the treatment, and relatives had raised questions. There was the suggestion of violence and medical indifference and though the inquiry yielded no conclusive results it was clear that the name of John Dilke was associated in some minds at least with an unacceptable level of violence in 'medical treatment'.

Then, a mystery. In the 1883 National Hospitals Report, Meern Moor Hospital was omitted from the annual statistical tables of lunatic admissions, discharges and deaths, with no reason given. The hospital might never have been.

The trip finally started in the first week of August after two delays because of Margaret's health. Finally, reluctantly, she decided not to go and, feeling they could delay no longer, Helen offered to do all the driving. Reluctantly it seemed, Richard allowed himself to be persuaded they could go. They were allowed to use one of the special transporter vans planned for Hill House. It had a lift which solved Helen's problem of getting Esther and her wheelchair in and out by herself.

Esther's first trip north made a considerable impact on her. As a southerner, living an unusually sheltered life both at school and home, she had not been exposed before to the stark contrast the industrial north then presented.

In the 1980s its decline from the glories of the late nineteenth century was almost complete. Unemployment was high, factories shut down, and the clothes, the shops, the cars, the very faces of the people living there seemed impoverished.

Esther saw it from the transporter van while Helen drove, staring out at a world that seemed to grow darker, more ruined, more miserable, the further north they travelled. Afterwards she remembered how the houses seemed sombre and vulgar, streets of post-industrial depression; and how Edinburgh, prosperous then from Britain's North Sea oil, seemed the only bright place they visited. And yet she found the people she met in Birmingham and Huddersfield friendly and direct, more than in the relatively prosperous south-east.

All this found its expression in the game 'Skallagrigg' when she finally came to create it, and it accounts for the progression of the game's graphics into an environment of dark and ruined despair the nearer the journeyer comes to Arthur and the Skallagrigg, yet peopled with cruder, more direct characters.

The trip brought Helen and Esther together, and Esther came to understand that Helen was not quite the spinster she had seemed. She had had men in her life, lovers indeed, and had even lived with one for a time in London. One of the rings she wore came from him.

'He was good to me,' said Helen one warm August night when they sat out beside the moor above one of the Yorkshire Dales, 'and kind. I really was not used to men, you see. I didn't know how to run a home. He showed me things.'

Esther saw Helen's face soften in the starlight.

'Wh . . .?' she began. Why did it finish?

'I had to bring it to an end. It isn't fair keeping a man hanging on when you can't deliver the goods! I felt he was giving everything and I was giving nothing. And . . . well, there was a spiritual difference between us. I do believe, you see. He did not. I came to feel I did not love him. Perhaps I was rather a fool and should just have taken a risk. He wanted to be married and could not understand.' Helen sighed: 'It's probably too late now though!'

'Nah!' said Esther. *'Nah!'*

Helen laughed. 'You're a romantic and only just eighteen. But I'm sixty-four and I know better. However, I did make a promise to myself years ago. If ever I meet someone who makes my heart sing I'm going to hang convention and ask him to marry me! Life's too short to wait for men to ask. One advantage of growing old is you don't care so much what people think and so you do more. When I retired I would never have dreamed I would be sitting here like this looking at the stars and talking about men. You're a good influence on me, Esther.'

She reached out and squeezed Esther's hand. 'And you? What'll happen to you?'

Together they sought the answer in the deep, dark and endless mystery of the stars above them.

'Shall we each make a wish?' suggested Helen.

Esther nodded.

Silently they did so, though whether each guessed that the wish they made was for the other, and was romantic, and spoke of love and partnership, only the stars could tell. Winking, twinkling, turning through the heavens, shining down their promises upon two women whom life seemed to have passed by.

'Life's strange,' mused Helen Perry-Wilcox.

'Yeh!' whispered Esther, loving the dark night.

But how strange, and how promising, neither could have guessed.

They finally met May Adcock and her husband in Edinburgh, being entertained to tea in their house two afternoons running. Mrs Adcock told Esther several Skallagrigg stories but they added little new to what she had already collected. She found she was beginning to tire of the stories now, sensing they had served their purpose and that the real way forward was through the research into Dilke and Meern Moor. She felt guiltily pleased when her interviews with Mrs Adcock were done, and she and Helen were free to sightsee in Edinburgh for half a day.

Then, at last, they drove west to Glasgow and southwards on to the M6 to Lancaster. Holiday traffic was streaming south, heavy lorries flowing north. The skies were blue, the cumulus clouds high and white. They were excited. And at ease with each other, as Esther was with Margaret. They felt cheerful and light-headed, footloose and free.

But the moment they took the roundabout off the M6 into the uplands of Bowland Forest their mood changed. Esther fell silent, staring at the grim blackstone walls that lined the roads, higher than the light limestone walls they had seen in Yorkshire, and more forbidding.

In the distance too they caught glimpses of high lonely moors whose heather was turning purple and whose edges were scarred with gritstone scarps to the sides of which, even on an August day, dark shadows seemed to cling.

Their plan was to drive to Meern Moor, which was marked clearly on the map, and see if they could find any clues to where a hospital had been from someone in Helkskill, the nearest village. Then they planned to drive back to Lancaster, where they had booked into a motel, to visit the local reference library and newspaper offices looking for past records of a hospital.

They came upon the moor before the village, for the narrow road rose up before them on to its boggy flanks, which even in summer seemed bleak. The sheep there were of a darker stock, the road barren and carless. They reached a point where they could see below them in the distance to the north a great tarn, the biggest on the map. There was nothing else there to speak of, certainly no great nineteenth-century asylum buildings. No buildings at all, just moorland and the road across it.

They drove on for three miles until the road dropped down by a farm, then past a sign for 'Meern Moor Pottery' pointing down a track, a row of nineteenth-century farm cottages, and finally a school. They had arrived. A small high street, an uninspiring little square-towered church built of the ubiquitous black gritstone rock, a few shops and a garage-cum-petrol station on whose forecourt stood three second-hand tractors for sale.

'Somebody must know something about where the hospital once was,' said Helen, 'so we'll ask.' Somebody did: the bookshop owner. His shop was small but bright and had local history books and tourist guides displayed in the window. Helen went in to inquire.

The owner came out to the van with Helen and said, 'You passed it if you came down from the moor. That's Meern Moor Road and the hospital used to be where the pottery is now. As I was saying to the lady, I believe they closed the place down in the 1880s.' He had a little book in his hand called *Helkskill Walks* and he opened it: '"The bridleway takes you along the edge of what was once the estate of Meern Moor Hall which, for a short period last century, was an asylum for lunatics. It was closed in 1882 after a fire which destroyed much of the building and the patients dispersed to other asylums in the area, principally Laydale Asylum, south of Newton. The remaining Hall buildings now house a pottery which makes fine examples of local ware which may be purchased." That's the best I can do.'

'Yeh,' said Esther excited.

Helen laughed. 'Does that mean you want to buy a copy?'

She nodded, and Helen bought it, thanking the man and then driving them back up Meern Moor Road and turning down the lane to Helkskill's pottery. They were greeted by the potter himself, a stocky-looking bearded man in his forties wearing a checked shirt with the sleeves rolled up and a stripy blue clay-covered apron.

The place was wild, the old raggle-taggle buildings dominated by a stand of oak and ash trees in which rooks had established themselves, whose rough deep calls were carried by the wind that seemed to sweep off the moor. Helen explained their search and he showed them round.

It was not hard to see which part of the buildings was the original Hall, or asylum. It was now merely the outhouse to a more modern brick-built building, the windows square and faced with gritstone. The potter knew little of the history except that it had been an asylum. 'They virtually demolished the place, I think, and reused the stone and hardcore for building the cottages further down the road. It must have been quite extensive. You can see the foundations in one or two places but that's about all. As for this

section, I don't know why it was left – maybe just as a cattle
shelter or something. We came here in the sixties when the place
was a small-holding. It was all we could afford. I did up this
outbuilding for my workshop but we sell mainly in the Bowland
markets and in shops in all the local centres. There's not enough
passing trade to make the pottery viable as a selling centre itself.'
He smiled and added, 'Anyway, we like our peace.' Somewhere a
child cried and then started to laugh and a woman called out,
'Henry!' and he left them alone.

They looked around for a little longer, declined a cup of tea from
Henry's pleasant wife but bought a mug for Margaret, and left
after a final stare at the surviving building. Esther tried hard to
imagine pauper lunatics lined up and miserable where stacks of
unfired pottery now stood on shelves, an electric kiln hummed,
and a friendly man stood wiping his clay-red hands on a cloth; but
she could not. The place and the people were too cheerful despite
the house and the rookery.

Life had moved on from the days of the Gillie case at Meern
Moor Hospital. That tragedy was done, Dilke must have left with
the other staff and there was nothing here for them now except
the sense that some people, like this potter, seemed to know how to
order their lives.

Their brief overnight stay in Lancaster was uneventful, the local
library producing nothing of interest, and by mid-morning of the
following day they had driven thirty-five miles and were approaching the ivy-clad yellow-brick walls of Laydale Community
Hospital, the former workhouse asylum beyond Newton. The
refugees from the Meern Moor fire had come there and perhaps
there would be a clue to Dilke and the hospital where Arthur had
been confined. It had been one of the hospitals Esther had written
to.

Laydale's wide entrance into a tree-lined drive was attractive,
and the drive past a neat sign which read 'North Central Regional
Health Authority' by new one-storey buildings gave the impression
of order and safety.

The main building itself looked much as it must have done
when it was built in the 1860s but, as such hospitals went, was
not unattractive. It was tall and solid, with wings either side of its
porticoed main entrance.

By the main entrance itself a man stood still and staring; he had Down's syndrome and wore brown trousers and a T-shirt. He grinned and said hello to them and shook their hands. 'Herroherro herroherro,' he kept saying.

Inside they got nowhere slowly. The administrator was a Miss Roskill and when Helen finally managed to speak with her secretary it turned out that she was away in Bristol for two days. They should have arranged an appointment, and unfortunately nobody else could help. In the echoing foyer people came and went, women in blue overalls and patients in chairs or wandering slowly. No one paid any attention to them except for the man at the reception desk whose phone Helen had used to call through to the administrator's office.

'No joy?' he said sympathetically. 'Well, that's no surprise. All change here, you know. Miss Roskill's new, and very nice too. Bit busy, but if you write . . .'

'We did write,' said Helen.

'Oh,' said the man. 'What's it you're here for then?'

'To do some research for a school project,' lied Helen expertly. 'Trying to trace a former member of staff named John Dilke, and patients from a former hospital in Bowland called Meern Moor.'

'Plenty of dilkes, but can't say I've ever heard of one called by that name. Bit of a long shot that! Meern Moor's a different proposition. We've got a ward named that . . .'

Esther looked up with sudden interest.

'It's on the map, on the board down the corridor.' The man winked. 'Nobody'll mind if you have a look at the map and don't come back so quickly. Know what I mean? My kid at school's always doing projects.'

The map showed Meern Moor Ward quite clearly, but it was not what finally caught Esther's attention. Adjacent to the board was a display entitled: 'Know the North Central Region Hospitals.' It was a map, with photographs of the different hospitals and an arrow pointing to their precise location. Some were in colour, some black and white.

She looked to where Meern Moor was and saw that the nearest hospital was to the north of it. Its photograph, in black and white, showed a stark and grim building on one side of which was a veranda. Beyond the veranda were lawns. Beyond that trees. All strangely stark, and the photograph rather old and grainy.

Esther felt a strange shiver looking at it, and she knew, she knew that it must have taken some of the Meern Moor patients and staff after the 1882 fire.

She read the name: Herstorne.

One of the two that had not replied to her letters.

'Heh . . .' she called. Helen.

'Yes, my dear,' said Helen turning from the map to her.

Esther pointed excitedly. Helen looked, first at the photograph and then at the location. Then she looked at Esther.

'Yeh,' said Esther.

'Wishful thinking?' said Helen doubtfully.

'Nah,' said Esther firmly.

'No,' agreed Helen. But she said no more. For the feeling she got from the photograph and the name on the map was not the dark grim certainty Esther had that Arthur and Dilke were there, or once had been, but a light and warm sense of hope as if, suddenly, she had found the place she had come on this odyssey to discover, but did not yet know why.

'We must go there,' she said softly.

Esther nodded.

'Another trip, so . . .'

Esther nodded again. So they could prepare the ground better, write letters, get an invitation; and arrange to visit Laydale and meet Miss Roskill and ask about the naming of a ward after Meern Moor.

This trip had suddenly proved successful: they had the leads they wanted and now knew what was possible.

'It's time we went home,' said Helen.

And they did; not even bothering to visit Meern Moor Ward, for that could wait now. They knew where they must go.

At Harefield several letters were waiting for Esther but, disappointingly, not one from Herstorne Hospital. But there was a letter giving Esther her exam results. As everyone had expected she had passed easily, with an 'A' for English and a 'B' for history. Added to the maths result of the previous year that gave her two 'A's and a 'B' and guaranteed her place at Reading University.

Yet the trip north had changed her. She felt dispirited and tired of academic work. In only two months she would be starting again: a new place, new adjustments, new people, new helpers helping and the struggle forward, to what? To uselessness.

'You're just tired, Esther,' said Richard one evening. 'We should have planned a proper holiday and perhaps we still should,' but he sounded uncertain about it. If Kate was not there he would not be.

'She's tired,' she heard him say later to Kate in the garden. 'Maybe . . .' but his voice trailed away. Maybe a holiday. Maybe a break. But breaks and holidays only mask realities, thought Esther, and the reality is me. Useless me.

She stared round the garden and listened. The builders were at work in Hill House, thump thump thump. Tom was coming at the weekend. She could go and stay with Betty or Graham, that had been half planned for these weeks. They were through as well, and Graham had an 'A' for computer science.

'You should have done it, Esther, you know as much as I do.'

She could do it in December if they did one then. But her mind retreated from the thought of more exams. What could she do? She sat staring at the garden and listened to the murmur of her father's voice with Kate's, like the song of the birds and the buzz of the bees among the rhododendrons. She could read a book. She could deal with some of the Skallagrigg mail. And there were more stories to type up. But she was tired, and did nothing for a day or two, except write a letter to Margaret promising a visit and beginning, rather half-heartedly, to arrange the second trip north to visit Herstorne and Laydale.

Then one morning a letter from America arrived for her. Printed elegantly along the top of the back of the envelope she read '*C O D A*, Editorial Offices, 70 Main Street, Peterborough, New Hampshire 034585'.

'Shall I open it?' offered Marion who had brought the mail in.

Esther nodded. The paper was expensive white, good rag paper, all crinkly.

It opened out crisply and was word-processed.

·'Dear Ms Marquand,' she read, her eyes racing along the type, 'I have pleasure to inform you that your game "Tom's Game" is the outright winner of . . .'

Winner of, *winner* of . . .

502   Skallagrigg

And the rest was a jumble before her eyes: 'The 1983 *CODA*
Games Programming Award . . . Best Game in its category . . . Best
Game overall . . . voted an original piece of professional pro-
gramming . . . winner of, winner of . . . we shall be sending you
$1000.00.'

Then more, which she did not read because she was too excited.
At the end was a signature, quite illegible. But typed neatly under
it was the name of the signatory, in capital letters: D A N I E L M.
S C H U S T E R (Contributing Editor – Games Software).

'*Emm!*'

'What is it, Esther?'

'*Emm*, fff-Dada!' Phone Daddy.

'What is it!' said Marion laughing and putting down a cloth. She
took up the letter.

'Esther!' she said. 'You've won a prize. But what's it for?'

'Dada, Dada, Dada.' She wanted to tell him.

He was tied up until two. His secretary would have him call.

'Shall I tell Kate?'

'Graaah . . .'

'You want me to phone Graham?'

She nodded. 'Yerhh.'

'Yes, I'll tell him.'

Graham was not there.

'Shall I tell Ka . . .?'

'Nah!'

Marion laughed. 'You'll just have to wait!'

They read the letter again. Esther was to send a few biographical
details by return of post and answer a few questions. How did she
come to create the game? Did she have direct experience of special
needs education? What was her employment, or was she still at
college? What other games had she programmed?

Esther took the letter to her room and Marion set her up with
the word-processor. Esther sat in her room reading and re-reading
the letter.

One thousand dollars. But it wasn't the amount of money, it
was the fact of it. It was the first money Esther Marquand had ever
earned in her own right and in competition with ordinary people.

She looked out of her window at the garden and she felt full of
hope. She looked again at the letter and slowly moved her hand to

her Sadler keyboard and began 'Dear Mr Schuster', and her mind wandered excitedly into daydreams and thoughts of success, and how she would write other games programs.

'Dear Mr Schuster.'

But even before she began the first sentence of the letter Esther Marquand resolved there was one thing this Mr Schuster need never know. She had won the competition against ordinary, able-bodied people, and she had no desire or obvious reason to inform anyone across the Atlantic that she was handicapped.

Dear Mr Schuster . . . and she rehearsed the letter in her mind: Thank you. I am pleased to win the prize. I am eighteen years old. I have just passed my 'A' levels and am going to Reading University. I . . .

Eventually she wrote it, telling *CODA* magazine the few facts about herself she could muster, leaving out the most important one.

She re-read the letter they had sent her. She had failed to answer the question about what other games she was writing.

Dear Mr Schuster . . .

. . . I am writing a game called 'Skallagrigg', she wrote. And if it was not quite true, neither was it quite a lie because a long time ago she had started a search, and she was near the end of it now, and when she was successful she could make a game of it, and into it she was beginning to see she could put her life.

Dear Mr Schuster . . .

Writing to you was one of the best things I've done for a long time, even if most of what I wrote I had to take out again and I haven't told the whole truth about myself because I don't see that it matters. I wish I wasn't handicapped, then I would not have to not tell you!

Esther grinned to herself at this absurdity, and felt light-hearted for the first time in weeks.

FIFTY-THREE

But there was an argument about the competition between Esther and her father, who believed she had made a mistake accepting the prize since acceptance appeared to give *CODA* magazine a global licence to market the game.

Richard wanted to call Daniel Schuster on her behalf; but Esther did not want her independence undermined, and anyway, was terrified that the fact of her handicap would come out. A compromise was reached: Leon Sadler phoned on her behalf and checked *CODA*'s intentions. But after all the fuss, they seemed honourable.

A week later she heard again from Daniel Schuster. He had her letter and had spoken with her 'partner' Mr Sadler. There was no objection to her retaining rights though *CODA* had set up a subsidiary organization to handle computer games and give young program writers full commercial protection. He was sending a catalogue of the existing games. The letter was signed 'Best wishes, Daniel M. Schuster', and he had added a postscript:

> Glad to hear you're working on another game. Maybe you've got some others?? I enjoyed your letter but you didn't send a photo so you missed your chance of national fame in North America! Mr Sadler said you're just starting college. Are you majoring in computer science? PPS: If you write again address it to me at Hanniman Beach, California. 'Contributing editor' means I work from home. I'm a graphics programmer now.

Esther must have read this letter ten times looking for clues to the man behind the name. He sounded nice, and the 'now' following on from the reference to her just starting at college suggested he might have only just graduated himself. So he would be about twenty-one or two. She looked at his name again and again and liked it. What, she wondered, was he like? Esther Marquand began to slide down the slippery slope of transatlantic fantasy.

A few days later, on an impulse born of the fact that Richard and Kate had gone away for the weekend and she was lonely, Esther replied to his letter.

Dear Mr Schuster,

No I'm 'majoring' (we say 'reading' but I won't hold it against you) in English Literature. My computer programming is a hobby and I only entered the competition because a friend made me. But I'm glad I did. Leon Sadler works in my father's company – he's involved with computer systems – and is also a programmer, quite a well-known one. He lives in London and is at least thirty-five. Are all professional programmers as old as that, like you for example?

I'm still researching the 'Skallagrigg' game I mentioned and it's not easy. Too difficult to explain briefly but it involves trying to find someone 'lost' in an asylum. If you're ever interested I might try to explain.

I looked at the catalogue you sent and see you have three games in it. They look more graphics-orientated than mine. I was thinking of a text-only game for 'Skallagrigg' like Avalon's 'Empire of the Overmind' which I think is very good. Too easy though. Do you know it? I would love to see one of your games. Sorry, I shouldn't just ask like that should I!?

I'm not doing much today which is why I'm writing to you. My father's away with his fiancée so I'm alone in the house except for the housekeeper.

Your address sounds like you live near the sea. Do you mind my asking if you do? I must close now because we want to catch the post. 'We' being myself and my friend Tom, a boy with 'Down's syndrome' who is a friend of the family and for whom I wrote 'TOM'S GAME' (needless to say!!!). He likes posting letters so he can post this one for me!

Best wishes, Esther Marquand.

Tom and Esther took the letter to the postbox at the end of Abbey Road.

'Where to Amh?'

AMERICA.

'Amercky! Skalg!?'

'Nah, Skyagree!'

'Ssshhhh,' hissed Tom, extending his arms and rocking them gently in semblance of waves. He had seen a film about the Pilgrim Fathers and knew that America was across the sea; and a rough sea too.

PUT IT IN, TOM.

'Yes, Amh,' said Tom, putting the letter into the postbox.

The reply came quickly:

Dear Esther Marquand,

Great to hear from you. I have sent the Sinclair version of two of my games and another one called 'Sword of Golgotha' not in our catalog. Hope you enjoy them.

You're pretty cute aren't you? How did you guess Hanniman Beach is by the sea? You might not have heard of it. It's called the Pacific. I was reared here by my aunt as my parents split up in 1966 when I was five years (a numerate lady like you can work out my age from that). She's a character and took me on board. I don't live with her now but my Dad gave me the money for a place on Beach Drive. Famous for windsurfing but since last year I quit. Too involved in my work I suppose.

I've been a contributing editor for *CODA* for just a year, and started writing for them when I was at Berkeley. I'm surprised you're not 'reading' for computer science, seems a waste of talent. I'm impressed too as some of the routines you use are very advanced, even original. Yes I'd be interested in the new game and you can trust me (which is what I told your friend Sadler). There's a lot of shysters in this business now. I'm not one of them: put it down to my Baptist upbringing. Aunt Rhona's a believer with a capital 'B' but I guess I'm on

her side. Do you have a religion or maybe it's not important for you? It matters to me. But I guess if you work
with handicapped people like Tom you must have faith.

    I know the Avalon game 'Empire' and it's OK except
for the graphics! (There aren't any) . . .

Perhaps Esther would have replied to this letter sooner but a few
days after she received it Margaret Ogilvie was admitted once more
to the Radcliffe Infirmary in Oxford and now cancer of the stomach
was confirmed. For two days Esther was prevented from visiting
her while doctors attempted to make a prognosis of what was, in
fact, a sudden escalation of the disease.

Then, at the end of August, Esther visited her in hospital with
her father, and it was clear there had been a rapid deterioration.
Esther had been warned by Helen that Margaret was likely to be
drugged, but she was not prepared for the gaunt and thin old lady
who now lay half-awake in bed.

Margaret's face lightened into a smile when she saw Esther and
she reached out a hand with some difficulty and placed it on
Esther's. Her eyes focused on Esther for a little and then closed as
she whispered, 'I'm sorry, my dear, don't go.' For the next three-
quarters of an hour Margaret lay there, her mouth opening
sometimes as if trying to speak.

'Esther. Esther?'

Margaret was more awake.

'My dear, thank you for coming. Listen, can you hear me?'

Esther nodded. She had cried earlier and her eyes were still red.

'You shouldn't cry.' Margaret smiled wearily. 'I was never much
good at it. Brian cried you know.'

'Nana.'

'Yes dear?'

WILL YOU COME TO HAREFIELD AGAIN WHEN YOU'RE
OUT?

'I'm sorry I can't . . . Richard?'

Richard read the words out.

'Yes.'

TO RECOVER.

'Esther, I'm not very well. Feel awful. They say it's the drugs but
I'm not well.'

'Nah,' said Esther softly. Their hands were intertwined and Esther felt that Margaret's were thin and cold.

'Helen's a good friend, and you're a good granddaughter.' She seemed unable quite to say the last word and her voice slurred a little, and her eyes lost focus. 'She says you always work so hard and that you're clever but I know that. Listen to me. You're very special and we are proud of you. I have arranged things so you'll be . . . as best as I can. Helen and Richard know.'

'Nah, Nana.' Esther was leaning forward, her eyes on her grand-mother's and her mouth trying to speak.

'It's no good saying "no". I am not well. They say they will operate on me but it probably won't do any good and I feel so awful. Sometimes . . .' And Esther saw her grandmother weep, and that the tears came from frightened eyes. Then Margaret's old spirit returned as she said, 'I'm so worried for you, my dear, but I probably don't need to be. Richard is so good.' She smiled over at him, but her eyes and attention were all for Esther. Then, still holding tight to Esther's hand, she fell into restless sleep.

Two days later Esther visited again with Helen, buying some sweet-smelling freesias from a stall outside the hospital. Margaret was better and colour had returned to her cheeks. Helen sat on the edge of her bed and Esther was close enough to put her right hand on the counterpane. A nurse brought them tea, but Margaret was not allowed to drink it. The windows in the room were open on a late summer's day and the busy street sounds of Oxford came into the room.

Esther was taking the opportunity of the visit to do some more library research and they were going clothes shopping for her first term at college. They told Margaret about the special arrangements that were being made for her accommodation and welfare, and the help she was going to get with studying. Graham Downer had agreed to come over with his father to oversee the installation of her computer aids.

'It sounds very sensible,' said Margaret safely, uncertain quite what they were talking about. 'You seem to understand computers very well, Helen,' she added.

'Not "very well" – just enough to be able to keep up with Esther's needs. You just have to be careful about which button to press or you can lose files.'

'Ah,' said Margaret. 'It sounds very complicated.'

'Nah, Nana,' said Esther affectionately.

'Now,' said Margaret, changing the subject and looking fierce, 'I want to talk about Kate and your father.'

'Oh,' said Esther.

'Kate is a very nice woman and your father loves her and I think it is time, my dear, that this nonsense of yours stopped.'

'Wha . . .?' said Esther innocently, her eyes wary.

'You know perfectly what I'm talking about, and so does Helen although she's too polite to say anything. I want you to start being nice to Kate, and thinking about your father's feelings. Has he said anything?'

'Nah . . .' said Esther immediately: HONESTLY, HE HAS NEVER SAID A THING!

'Exactly,' said Margaret icily. 'He has not said anything and I'm sure that's because he feels if he does it will make matters worse. Brian would not have said anything either. I am not as nice as them, my dear. I am saying you must forget your own selfish feelings and think of Richard who has done a lot for you, more than many fathers in his circumstances. Don't you agree?'

She fixed a firm gaze on Esther who, after a moment's pause, keyed up: I'LL THINK ABOUT IT. I PROMISE.

'Good, I hope you do. Helen, see that she does.'

Helen laughed. 'I'm not family, so I mustn't get involved.'

'Yes you are and you will. You tell Esther off when it's necessary, everyone else is too intimidated by her handicap to do it. But if she's not treated like everyone else she won't think like everyone else and see their needs. I have been thinking about a lot of things in this hospital bed.'

Esther and Helen fell silent. Then Margaret subsided, the effort of looking fearsome too much for her. 'Have some more tea or something, and tell me about how Hill House is going and about Marion's wedding plans. It should be quite soon.'

They talked some more and then, seeing that she was tired, they left. The doctors were uncertain about when she might come out, or even what her condition was. She was weak, she needed careful monitoring, and yet she had been a little better.

Four days later, just before midnight, Esther was woken by the sound of a car coming into the drive of Harefield. Her father went quietly downstairs and opened the door as if he had been expecting a caller. There was a muffled conversation in the big hall and Esther recognized Helen's voice.

She lay in the darkness filled with dread. There was a knock on her door and then it opened. It was her father. He came over to her bed and sat on it.

'Are you awake?'

She nodded in the half-light from the hall.

'I'm afraid it's about Margaret. Helen has just come. Did you hear her?' Esther nodded feeling a mounting fear.

'I'm afraid Margaret died earlier this evening,' said Richard simply.

Esther lay quite still, staring up at him.

'It was during the preparations for another operation and quite sudden.'

'Wha . . . whu . . .' Esther's eyes and mouth struggled terribly. Was she alone?

'Helen was there with her. She just didn't have the strength any more, Esther.' He took her in his arms and she later remembered thinking, 'Oh I can smell Kate's perfume on him and Nana said to be nice,' and she felt and heard his sobs. But none came from her, she just felt numb.

Then Helen came into the room and Esther reached out to her as she said, 'I'm so sorry, my dear, but it was so unexpected. But at least it was peaceful and she will have no more pain.' Esther saw in Helen's face that she had lost a friend, and then she did cry, and they sat together on the bed in the semi-darkness learning what it felt like to know that Margaret had gone. Esther felt calm again, so calm, saying to herself, 'I must be calm, I must be calm.' They got her up into a dressing-gown and her electric wheelchair and Kate poured tea for them made by Marion and which they had in the kitchen, huddled in the night like survivors. Kate, who was in a dressing-gown too, had kissed Esther and said, 'I'm sorry this has happened.'

Esther thought: She *is* nice and I've been horrible to her. She's always been nice to me. Nana said I must be nice . . . Nana said . . . and as they sat in the kitchen Esther cried silently, and accepted Kate's ministrations of tissues and comfort.

They talked into the early morning, Kate and Marion finally

going off to bed and leaving the three of them to share memories in the way the bereaved must. It had all been so unexpected but now seemed so inevitable. Helen admitted much later that Margaret had been in great pain for weeks but had not wanted Esther or Richard to know.

Afterwards Esther barely slept and when the bleak morning came she felt restless and anxious to get out of the house. At breakfast, a sorry wordless affair, she said, 'Ka . . . Kai . . .'

They all looked at her. It was the first time she had ever tried to say 'Kate'.

WILL YOU TAKE ME FOR A WALK?

Kate did so and sometime then, away from the house, Esther turned to look behind her saying again, 'Kayher . . . Ka . . .' and Kate stopped the wheelchair, came round to her, and Esther began to sob uncontrollably. Kate instinctively cuddled her which made her cry even more.

Later Esther typed up: I'M SORRY I HAVE BEEN HORRIBLE SOMETIMES. YOU'VE ALWAYS BEEN VERY NICE.

'It's all right Esther, I understand.'

DO YOU? Esther looked straight at Kate. DO YOU REALLY UNDERSTAND?

Kate was silent. For a long time.

'I try to imagine sometimes, you know, but it isn't easy. I know you must get very frustrated.'

IT'S NOT QUITE WHAT PEOPLE THINK. NOT THE PHYSICAL BIT ANYWAY. I'M USED TO IT NOW. I'VE NEVER KNOWN ANYTHING ELSE AND I KNOW I'LL ALWAYS BE LIKE THIS. ALL I'VE GOT TO OFFER IS MY MIND AND NO ONE WANTS THAT. NOT REALLY. WHAT'S FRUSTRATING IS THAT I CAN'T MAKE MYSELF UNDERSTOOD EASILY AND PEOPLE ARE SLOW. AND IT'S UNFAIR BECAUSE ABLE-BODIED PEOPLE HAVE OPPORTUNITIES I DON'T.

Esther was silent as they walked on.

KATE, Esther keyed up eventually, ARE YOU AND DADDY GETTING MARRIED?

'He hasn't asked me,' said Kate carefully.

DO YOU LOVE HIM?

'Yes I do.'

DO YOU MIND ME ASKING?!

'Nn ... no.'

YOU SOUND DOUBTFUL.

'You don't miss much.'

TRAINING FROM AN EARLY AGE! SPASTICS HAVE TO LEARN
TO READ BETWEEN THE LINES.

'What else have you "read"?'

THAT DADDY LOVES YOU. ALSO HE'S WORRIED ABOUT ME
ALWAYS AND THAT MUST BE DIFFICULT FOR YOU.

'I . . .'

I MEAN FOR BOTH OF YOU. ALSO I SUSPECT THERE'S MORE
TO OPENING AN OFFICE IN SINGAPORE, WHICH IS WHAT HE
SAID HE WAS PLANNING TO DO, THAN MEETS THE EYE.

'No comment, Esther. I'm not going to start . . .'

IT'S OBVIOUS. HE KEEPS LOOKING LONGINGLY AT THE
AUSTRALIAN PHOTOS YOU BROUGHT BACK.

Kate laughed, her eyes bright.

'Does he?'

YES HE DOES!

'Well,' said Kate, looking away; and Esther did not miss the
longing in that look nor the worry, which she guessed concerned
herself.

I'M SORRY I'VE BEEN VILE, typed Esther impulsively, looking
away in her turn.

'Oh!' said Kate, moved almost to tears. 'There's no need to be
ever,' and she cuddled her again.

WHATEVER HAPPENS IN THE FUTURE WILL YOU REMEMBER
I LIKE YOU AND LOVE DADDY, KATE?

'Esther, there's no need to say such things.'

WILL YOU?

'Yes, of course.'

WHATEVER HAPPENS?

'Yes. Whatever happens.'

On the way back home Esther was silent, thinking. The thinking
did not stop in the days that followed.

The funeral was at St Mary's, Charlbury, just as Brian's had been,
but there were fewer people. Just the family and Tom and Helen
and a brother they had never met before. The reception afterwards
at the house was quiet.

Richard made the arrangements, and Marion had come over to tidy and clean. She freshened the place, opened the french windows into the garden, and put flowers in the downstairs rooms.

'Margaret wanted you to do the garden for her, Tom,' said Richard.

'Will do,' said Tom.

'Well, it's too late now,' said Richard, not sure if Tom quite understood.

'OK. But I'll look. Shall I? Amh?'

She nodded and Tom wandered off into the garden and looked.

It was early September and the grass had not been cut for a month. The roses were scented red and pink and tumbled over themselves and their green leaves. Esther watched Tom wandering by himself, poking here and there among the undergrowth and disappearing altogether at the bottom of the garden where there was a small outbuilding of Cotswold stone, once a pigsty. Brian had turned it into a tool shed, Margaret had not been into it since his death. Tom reappeared and wandered back up to the house.

'No veg,' he announced. 'No toms.'

Esther smiled, remembering Margaret's comment about him helping her with the garden. 'Would it be wicked to ask him?' she had asked, and Esther thought now: 'No, it wouldn't have been wicked, Nana.'

Later Helen said to everybody, 'I think Margaret would have liked to think of you each taking something small from the house as a memory of her and Brian, so please do so.' Since they were all close family or friends it was an offer worth risking, and most took a little memento – a photograph, a book, or a picture. Helen had discussed this with Esther and Richard first, and those things they especially wanted had been put to one side: it was all Esther's now but she did not feel it was hers.

'Can I?' said Tom. 'Amh, can I please?'

She nodded. OF COURSE YOU CAN. THEY ALWAYS LIKED YOU AND ENJOYED YOU COMING.

Tom disappeared back into the garden, went straight down to the shed, and reappeared among the formally dressed guests carrying an old hoe with a handle polished from past use.

'For me,' he said, showing everybody by holding it up and knocking the light above. 'Sorry.'

Kate laughed, and so did Esther.

It had been Brian's. On the day Tom first visited Brian had taken Tom into the garden and got him to help hoe some beds.

'It's good this one,' said Tom. 'Better'n Harefield's. Better'n Centre's. I don't like work. I like this.'

It was the first time he had publicly said he did not enjoy the job at the Remploy Centre for handicapped workers where he was working in London; the first time he ever declared what it was he wanted most to do.

'Like this,' he said, holding the hoe's handle lovingly and looking out towards the garden as if he could see things others could not. 'Always.'

Esther's 'thinking' continued and cast a pall over Harefield. Mourning was one thing, but it soon seemed more than that. Then, a fortnight later, Esther made a preliminary visit to Reading University to see the special hostel where she would be living. She said almost nothing, and did not respond when asked questions. Richard decided to tackle her about her mood.

'I wish you'd talk about it,' he said. 'You'll be starting in less than a month and if there's anything worrying you it's best to sort it out now.'

Esther stared solidly into the middle distance. Then she moved her hand to the mini-writer and keyed up: NOTHING'S WRONG.

'Well, of course something's wrong.'

'Nah!'

'It's hardly surprising. It takes time to get over something like Margaret's death. But . . .'

IT'S NOT THAT.

'What is it then?'

Silence descended again, and she would not talk.

But the following evening with her father and Kate in the living-room, Esther suddenly said, 'Dada?'

'Yes?'

I DON'T WANT TO GO TO READING.

'What do you mean?'

I'VE DECIDED I DON'T WANT TO GO. IT'S POINTLESS.

'It's not pointless, Esther, it's essential.'

WELL I'M NOT GOING.

'Let's talk about this,' he said reasonably.

THERE'S NOTHING TO TALK ABOUT.

'I should have thought there's a great deal to talk about. Like "Why?", for example. Like all the people involved. Like how important it is for the future. Like what you'd do if you didn't go.'

I'VE THOUGHT ABOUT THAT.

Richard was not to be diverted into discussing the idea as if it might be viable.

'Look, I've done a long day's work and I'm tired and probably irritable. Could we talk about this tomorrow?'

IT WON'T MAKE ANY DIFFERENCE WHEN YOU TALK ABOUT IT. I'M NOT GOING.

'Yes you are, Esther.'

Kate tried to bring a calming influence to what might develop into one of their arguments. Richard might recognize in theory that these arguments were all part of Esther's necessary establishment of independence but when it came to it the emotions surfaced and he felt thoroughly angry. She was so damned rude; so self-centred, as if the world revolved round her.

Kate announced firmly that she would make some coffee and they would talk about it now.

An hour later Esther finally answered the question, 'Why?'

I'M SORRY BUT I WON'T BE HAPPY. NANA'S DEATH HAS MADE THINGS DIFFERENT. I WANT TO COMPLETE THE SKAL-LAGRIGG RESEARCH.

Richard exchanged a quick glance with Kate which Esther did not miss. If they thought it was a waste of time that was their business. She did not.

'You can still do that. It's not full-time is it?'

OTHER PEOPLE MISS A YEAR BETWEEN SCHOOL AND COLLEGE. WHY WASN'T THAT OPTION CONSIDERED FOR ME? READING WILL KEEP MY PLACE.

'It's just not practical.'

THAT'S NOT THE ATTITUDE YOU TAKE TO GETTING THINGS DONE IN BUSINESS I BET.

Kate smiled to herself; Richard was not amused.

WHAT HAVE I EVER DONE?

'Oh, Esther, you've done more than I ever imagined possible, I'm very proud of you. Now, please . . .'

But she was not impressed.

I'VE BEEN PROTECTED ALL THE WAY THROUGH. I'M LUCKY TO HAVE INTELLIGENCE AND OPPORTUNITY THAT'S ALL. I'M NOT SAYING I DON'T WANT TO GO TO COLLEGE, JUST NOT NOW AND MAYBE NOT TO READING. IF I MISS A YEAR I CAN TAKE OXFORD ENTRANCE FOR MATHS.

'And what will you do? Who will look after you? I told you already, I'm going to be developing the Singapore base and Kate will be with me more.'

YOU DIDN'T TELL ME IT WAS THIS COMING YEAR.

'I wanted to see you settled into college first.'

YOU MEAN YOU WANTED ME OUT OF THE WAY FIRST. WHY NOT SAY THE TRUTH?

'Oh, Esther . . .' he said wearily. Then changing the subject he said, 'Anyway what would you do, assuming the practical side could be sorted out? You're quite right; of course it could be. Money, fortunately, is not our problem, but you want to think about that some time. You're not the only handicapped person in the world.'

Kate and Esther were both surprised to hear bitterness in his voice.

'My turn to be sorry,' he said. 'I guess I'm just tired.'

I'M NOT GOING TO READING DADDY WHETHER YOU'RE TIRED OR NOT AND I KNOW I'M NOT THE ONLY HANDICAPPED PERSON IN THE WORLD. THAT'S WHY I WANT TO FIND ARTHUR. YOU WOULD NOT UNDERSTAND THAT.

Kate laughed.

'You're as bad as each other,' she said. 'Let's finish this another time.'

Father and daughter sat in brooding silence.

'We'll see,' said Richard finally.

FIFTY-FOUR

It was Helen Perry-Wilcox who provided a compromise solution to Esther's immediate future. While Richard persuaded Reading University to hold her place for a year, she made arrangements for Esther to stay with her at least until Christmas and attend courses in computer science at Oxford College of Science.

Richard Marquand arranged helpers and equipment to eliminate the danger of the physical strain on Helen – the principal problem now being lifting Esther in and out of her wheelchair, dressing morning and night, and toileting.

It was all arranged quickly, for on 7 October, a few days before the start of Esther's first term, Richard was leaving once more for Singapore. The ComputaBase operation there had been expanded into a full-time office before outlets were established in the Far East. At the same time Edward Light, now chairman and managing director of Fountain Systems, appointed Richard group director to oversee the rapidly expanding Australasian operations.

If Richard and Kate had plans to get married they were shelved – Richard still seemed to be undecided about this, not wanting to upset Esther. But, in effect, her father and Kate were living as man and wife.

Within a few weeks of starting her courses at the polytechnic, Esther must have realized that her understanding and experience of computer programming was already far in advance of what the course offered. Her correspondence with Daniel Schuster, so far simply friendly, includes this, written three weeks into her course:

> Some of the lecturing is very boring. It's all basic
> material and I can't understand why so many of the
> students seem to have trouble with it. They're at a dis-
> advantage to me because most of them don't have com-
> puters of their own and have to rely on the terminals
> here which are linked to a mainframe. There are queues

sometimes, and they have to wait for feedback and printouts for ages. And we're meant to be an age of
technology!

The data-processing work they set us is easy and I get
it done immediately and hand it in on time. Result? I've
got the reputation of knowing what I'm doing and so
quite a few ask me to explain things. It's almost like a
mini-seminar in the canteen sometimes. The lecturers
aren't very imaginative about how they explain things.

What it all means is that I can get on with other
things, like the games you sent, and 'Skallagrigg'. I've
decided not to explain it all to you – you can wait for the
results! But I have had an idea for a role-play game
which I'm calling, tentatively, 'The Weir of Dunroune'.
I'm trying to get away from the silly orc-type monsters in
the D & D-inspired games and using as my model a book
I've got on pre-Christian Gaelic magic. The black wizard
was going to be called McFeare but it sounded stupid so
I'm just calling him Feare. Wait for the next instalment. I
promise that when I have something to send you I will.
How's 'Tom's Game' doing? I expect I'll hear from Leon if
there's good news.

By now the two of them were using Christian names and the
correspondence was weekly and principally an exchange of
computer-gaming ideas. There is nothing in her letters that even
hints at Esther's handicap. Daniel was not well paid for his work
with *CODA*, and made what money he did from occasional
programming jobs. When Esther asked him in one letter why he
had no full-time job he answered:

I know I should have employment and jobs are no
problem. Not for good programmers like me! But I wasn't
so well this last year and I like working for myself. Like
you I'm from a privileged home. I'm working on certain
things I have not told you about, which may work out
big. Programming things. Games are OK, and you can
make dollars out of them, but I'm into business software,
databasing with graphics. If we ever meet I'd like to tell
you about that. Maybe you should think about it. With

contacts like Mr Sadler it would be no problem for you
researching the market.

Also I like the surf. Living here I breathe it all day
long. I don't windsurf now but I can't cut it out of my
life. Hanniman Beach is a kind of Mecca down here.
They say sailboards breed on the beach overnight but
it's a lie: I go down at nightfall and don't see any at it.

Do you like walking the shore at night? I sometimes
think of you walking here with me but maybe I
shouldn't say that . . . maybe better stick to
computing.

Esther's reply to this letter is significant; until then she had
avoided the truth, now she actively lied to conceal it, and to feed
their mutual fantasies:

Yes I love walking by the shore. The south coast is my
favourite and I have been to Cornwall and walked on the
sand there. Isn't it nice when the waves come over your
legs? I've never windsurfed and wouldn't dare but I like
swimming. I'm glad you imagine walking on the beach
with me and I don't see why you shouldn't say it. Surely
two people can imagine what they like and even do it:
provided no one else is involved to get hurt . . . Talking of
two people, my friend Marion who is my father's
housekeeper has just got married. I went to the wedding
as a maid of honour. It was white (genuine as well as I'm
sure Marion who is a born-again Christian was 'pure')
and good weather for them. They are really happy and I
hope they stay that way. I was quite envious and wished
I had a boyfriend who might love me enough to want to
marry me. I don't suppose that will ever happen!

While Daniel was tentatively considering what response to make
to these safely transatlantic suggestions, Esther was continuing
the Skallagrigg research. By November 1983 most of the key
Arthur stories had been collected and she and Helen were
arranging a visit to Laydale Hospital with Andy Moore's help at
the start of the Christmas vacation. This had proved more difficult
than they had expected, and an exchange of letters about the

nature of Esther's project had had to be made with the North
Central Regional Health Authority's headquarters to establish her
bona fides.

At the beginning of December, three weeks before the proposed
trip, Esther received a tape from May Adcock, her Edinburgh
correspondent. It had been recorded by May at a conference she
had attended with her husband. Most of the stories were familiar,
but one was different, and alarming:

> One time there was a bad time and that was when Frank
> went away. It was when the cold was and Henry was lost out
> on the snow 'cos he thought he was a POW escaping like
> the film. Henry nearly died out there but that Dilke got him,
> Dilke nearly dying himself getting Henry back.
>
> That was when the new medic came and there was
> reassessments.
>
> Eppie got three minutes, no change. Arthur got four
> minutes, no change. Henry got three minutes, no change.
> Vernon got four minutes, no change. Fucking farce those
> assessments. But Frank got forty-five minutes and the Super
> took it into his head he could be improved.
>
> 'Who's a clever lad, then?' says Dilke with a sneer. 'Frank,
> that's who. Super says he's got brains and should be
> moved.'
>
> 'Is Arthur coming?' asks Frank, worried.
>
> 'Fuck Arthur,' says Dilke, suddenly red in the face, fingers
> itching for the window stick. Then Dilke goes to Arthur's cot
> and put his face down where Arthur's is and Dilke shouts so
> his eyes are fat and red *'Fuck Arthur, fuck Arthur, fuck you,
> cunt, fuck you'* but Arthur's grey eyes did not flicker not
> once. Dilke was in a rage. Happened once in a while.
>
> 'Not going nowhere without Arthur,' says Frank.
>
> 'You'll go where's decided best for you, my lad.'
>
> Eight weeks later Frank's told to go to see the Super again.
> Three men and a woman there and a polished table with
> round legs. Dilke's there as well in a posh suit. Their eyes all
> look at Frank at once. The Super opens his mouth but Frank
> speaks first.
>
> 'Arthur says I got to do my very best,' says he.
>
> 'Who's Arthur?' says a man. Frank can't speak, too ner-
> vous. He looks at his knees and then at the floor.
>
> Dilke says in a special voice, 'Arthur is a friend who Frank

takes responsibility for. Very responsible is Frank. His friend's
a cot and chair low grade and he's good with him.'

'You can speak for yourself,' says the woman.

But Frank's too shy. Frank's thinking, 'Wish my Arthur
was here to tell me what to say. Don't like Dilke. He's saying
wrong things.'

Another man says words with a smile attached to them
that doesn't belong: 'You help out in chapel?'

Frank says, 'Father's good and I sup the bread and wine at
the shiny brass rails. Arthur doesn't never but he comes. I
hold his chair and then I can talk to God.'

The new Super says, 'Is Arthur your special charge?'

That's a word Frank doesn't know. Frank says, 'I love
Arthur next to God and Christ Jesus.'

They ask some more but Frank doesn't say much.

After a long time the man says, 'Well, thank you for coming
to talk to us, Frank. Most impressive.' Then Dilke nods and
Frank knows he can go. But he doesn't move.

'Arthur's my friend,' he says.

'Yes,' says the man.

'Yes,' says the next man.

'Yes,' says the woman.

But Frank knows they don't know what he means. Doesn't
know himself.

'Is Arthur coming?' says Frank. 'I want him to.'

'Well, well, we'll see shall we?' says the Super.

When Frank goes Super says, 'The staff can rely too much
on this kind of friendship between patients. But it leads to
bad behaviour. Best to split such relationships up I feel.'

Super's got a bee in his bonnet about bumfucks. Thinks
they're all at it. Thinks the worst of good Frank. Later that
black day Frank sees the men by themselves one by one.
They give him tests.

Final verdict? Fit to move. Unfit to stay.

Two weeks later Frank's moved.

'Is Arthur coming?'

'No,' says the dilke collecting him. 'Get moving.'

'Not going, *not going, no no no no!*' Quiet Frank's screams
are worse than Henry when Rendel bumfucked him in the
washroom. He lay on the floor and he wrapped his arms and
legs round Arthur's cot. *'No no no no no!'* he shouts.

'Get Mr Dilke,' says the dilke. 'It's window stick time.'

Then Arthur speaks, he speaks to his friend like no one

else is in the world. He speaks special. His voice shushes the whole ward, shushes the dilke. It's the voice of love.

'No I won't,' says Frank.

'Skyagree,' says Arthur. 'Skyagree.'

Frank gets up. Says Frank, 'I'll go now, Arthur says I'm to. Arthur says it's my chance. First Linnie went, now I'm going. Arthur says he don't mind being on his own if I do my best. Arthur says Henry is to do my job with Arthur till I come back.'

'You're not coming back, boy,' says Dilke coming in. 'Not ever.'

Frank says, 'Christ Jesus will send me back 'cos he will.'

Then Arthur speaks and he speaks long and his voice is like history being said.

Frank says: 'Arthur says if Skalg sends me back he will not ask Skalg to come any more.'

'Not even to leave?' says Eppie, quick.

'Not nothing,' says Frank. 'Arthur will make a silence to Skalg if I come back and Skalg will be no more and will stay with me always.'

So then Frank left to go to his new home all spick and span where others like him were and Henry did his best for Arthur.

He washed him.

He shaved him.

He fed him.

He wiped his mouth.

He wiped his nose.

He wiped his bum.

He dressed him.

And Arthur never complained even when Henry could not do it like Frank did, which was never.

'What's Arthur say?' asked the boys.

But Henry shook his head and grinned without his teeth. He didn't know Arthur's words. No one did but Frank. So the boys missed Arthur's words.

'Say what Arthur says,' said the boys again and again and again. Then Henry hit Arthur 'cos poor Henry could not understand. Arthur cried but in his eyes he forgave Henry. It wasn't Henry's fault.

'Sorry,' says Henry.

'Awhryah,' says Arthur.

Those were black months. The ice and snow were long on the ground and turned grey. Then spring came.

One day after church the Father comes to Arthur to have a word. He takes Arthur's chair from Henry and tells him he'll bring him to the ward himself.

When the chapel is empty Father sits down with Arthur and says, 'I been to Frank's new home. Frank is unwell. He won't eat, won't talk, he has deteriorated. He hardly recognized me. I don't think the move has been a success. You must have missed him, Arthur, he's missing you.'

Arthur's head is everywhere, and his body and his mouth and his lips.

'Yeh,' he says eventually.

'It's been five months,' says the Father.

'Nah,' says Arthur pointing his foot to the windows above the altar. 'Nah.'

Arthur's saying, 'Five months and twelve days.' Twelve apostles, twelve windows, twelve days. Arthur's counted every single day but Father Freeman doesn't understand.

'There's changes coming,' says the Father. 'The end of this place is coming. I will try and get it right for you and Frank again.'

The summer comes and with the sun comes change. No new boys now. Boys and dilkes getting older together. The north wards are closed. All change. Men come with machines to fell the trees in the glen and the trees fall like the world has ended.

One afternoon the old boys are on the grass and there's a tall thin figure coming right over the grass accompanied by a dilke. His face is pale and he walks slow.

Arthur sees him first and he calls out so all the boys look. That voice of Arthur's cracked with joy. It's his Frank come home.

'I'm back,' says Frank and he goes up to Arthur in his chair and looks at him and Arthur looks at him. Their faces are joy. Arthur speaks.

The boys say, 'What's he say, Frank?'

'Arthur says I'm clever to have come back.'

Arthur speaks and Frank says, 'I didn't eat no food and I didn't speak no words and I was ill. I prayed to Christ Jesus and said "Look after Arthur and send me back to him soon. Stop my sins so I don't get punished like this again." He heard me, Arthur.'

Arthur spoke.

'What's he say Frank?'

Frank looked annoyed. 'Arthur says the Skalg got me back,
but Arthur's not always right.'

'Skalg's clever,' says one boy.

'Skalg's waiting,' says another.

'Skalg's not Christ Jesus sitting in the light next to God,'
says Frank.

Then Arthur speaks low.

'What's he say?' ask the boys.

But Frank says, 'No, Arthur, you can't.'

Arthur speaks again. Arthur's crying.

'What's he's saying, Frank?'

Says Frank, 'Arthur says he won't speak of Skalg no more.
He says he promised if I came back he wouldn't speak no
more of Skalg.'

'Not never?' says Henry.

'Not ever?' says Eppie.

'Not never,' says troubled Frank. 'He promised. He sticks
with what he says. Arthur says it's silence now. Arthur says
maybe Skalg will be happier in silence. Been long, too long.
Finished now.'

But later, in the chapel, good Frank says a prayer of his
very own for Arthur and his Skallagrigg.

'Help them,' he says, 'they have been lost and now must
be found again.'

The significance of this story was immediately apparent to
Esther. It marked the end of the Skallagrigg stories: Arthur was
'silent to the Skalg' for the promise concerning Frank, the kind of
promise we have all made in bargains with God when we seek the
granting of a fervent prayer. It was a silence he would not break.
Esther believed that; everything about Arthur in the stories described a man of purpose and principle. And she shared Frank's
fear that from that day Arthur would begin to die.

It was possible from the reference to the 'cold' and 'black months
. . . ice and snow' to deduce that the incident took place during a
memorably harsh winter. The two most severe post-war winters
were 1947–8 and 1962–3, and the reference to the boys being
'old' suggested that it was the 1962 winter, though Arthur would
only have been in his mid-forties. Perhaps the other 'boys' were all
older than him. By the early 1980s, when Esther Marquand heard
this story, she deduced that if Arthur had survived his self-imposed

silence to the Skallagrigg and was still alive, he would be about sixty-five and many of his friends long dead. The story sent a chill through Esther, and the sense that she might, after all, be too late. Then, as if suddenly struck by the fact that each day might count she wrote again to Laydale Hospital inviting herself and Helen on a visit.

At the beginning of December Laydale Hospital confirmed that arrangements had been made for her to visit the hospital on 19 December, the last official college day. Helen agreed they could go.

Meanwhile, her correspondence with Daniel Schuster continued, their news trivial, their style increasingly flirtatious:

> Just to say I am going off to the north again (get out your map of England) to continue my researches. Do you find it frustrating me not telling you more about Skallagrigg?? I promise when I get back I'll write you a long letter if you can stand it. I think this is the most important thing I've ever done in my life. I'm going to buy you a Christmas card today because there are warnings about the last posting date to America in the Post Office. Also just a small gift – I hope that's not too forward of me but it's something I saw which made me think of you. Wish me luck, I'm nervous about what I'm going to find out. The game depends on it!! Warm best wishes.

Before she left Esther received a letter from Daniel which evidently crossed with hers – the coincidence of ideas was enough, perhaps, to confirm their mutual wish that their correspondence might lead to something more:

> It'd be great to have a picture of you as then I would know who I'm writing to. My aunt noticed the stamps on the letter that came yesterday so I guess the best thing was to tell the truth: I'm writing to a lady in the UK. She said, 'What's wrong with wholesome Californian girls?' so I told her they can't program and don't want to know . . .
>
> I mailed you a gift to be opened Christmas day: hope it arrives in time. Also exciting news almost: maybe an

advisory consultancy job for a company in LA. Two
days a week so I can stay here. I'm not thinking about it
until it happens. Hey, it's good to have you to write to,
Esther. Maybe we'll meet and go running through the
waves one fine day. Take care.

    Love Daniel.

Love Daniel. It had finally come. Love Daniel. Esther received that
letter the day before she set off with Helen for the trip to Laydale,
and she took it with her, her heart singing. Love has room to grow
when its reality is an unthreatening 6,000 miles away.

All the way up the M6 for mile after mile she stared out of the
car window, thinking of being loved. Fantasy. Sublimation in a
girl who looked like her, was her, except she did not have cerebral
palsy. That girl, out there, could meet Daniel Schuster at the
airport, could hold his hand, could receive his kiss and kiss back in
return. That girl, out there, could run with him over the sands and
feel the sun and the surf upon her tanned, strong legs.

Then she looked away from her dreams, up the road, mile after
mile, and sighed, as they drove nearer and nearer to where Arthur
might be.

FIFTY-FIVE

Annette Roskill, the Unit Administrator of Laydale, turned out to be a bright, attractive, talkative woman in her mid-thirties.

'The old days of autocratic medical superintendents have gone, you know,' she told Esther. 'I'm one of a team of three people who run this hospital – there's a consultant doctor, the head of the nursing staff and me for administration.'

They were sitting in her freshly painted office in the newer east wing of the hospital complex. They had been collected from reception by a young secretary whose high heels and bright clothes surprised them. They had expected dowdiness but did not find it. Even the coffee cups were cheerful and elegant.

'There was a mentality that went with the old-style managements moulded by years of putting the institution before the patients – an austere mentality that goes right back to the early punitive attitude to the mentally ill and disadvantaged, and fostered by two world wars and a depression. One of its effects was that everything had to look institutional, which meant functional sheets with local authority names on them, grim metal beds, industrial light fittings and plumbing. With no money to pay for even basic decoration, a really poor environment was created which had a negative effect on patients and staff.'

Ms Roskill sipped her coffee and smiled. 'Sorry. I'm giving you a lecture.' She held the coffee cup up before her. 'Even these. Why generations of administrators put up with cracked and stained mugs I can't think, but it's symptomatic of something more serious, isn't it?' She had an open smile and spoke fluently.

'Now, tell me what I can do for you. I know only that you're doing some kind of project and must be something of a computer expert, judging from the equipment you've got attached to that chair of yours!' She eyed Esther's screen and Sadler keyboard, adding: 'Are you?'

Esther grinned, nodded and shrugged.

I DIDN'T THINK SO UNTIL I WENT TO COLLEGE IN OXFORD.
THEY'VE SHOWN ME HOW MUCH I KNOW!!

Annette Roskill laughed.

Then Esther keyed up, HELEN WILL EXPLAIN AND I'LL IN-
TERRUPT IF I FEEL I NEED TO.

So Helen did, beginning at the beginning and describing how
Esther had become involved with the Skallagrigg stories. Soon
after she had started Ms Roskill interrupted her: 'I think this is very
fascinating and I do hope we can be of help. But I think we must
call in Ian Cutler, the deputy chief nursing officer. He knew you
were coming and is quite interested. He's been here longer than
anyone – and he's one of the new school. The hospital's very lucky
to have him. But he can tell you about the past about which he
has strong views.'

Ian Cutler was in his late fifties; short, wiry, with a lined
and healthy face and warm eyes. He spoke with a soft Scottish
accent and, having said a brief hello, settled himself down to
listen.

Helen showed them Esther's file of stories, explaining how she
had collected them and about Arthur and Frank. She described
how they had isolated as many facts as they could about Arthur's
hospital but that they had nothing to pinpoint which of the older
hospitals Arthur's might be, except that it seemed likely to be in
the north.

'Aye, they're much of a muchness right enough,' said Ian Cutler.
'Built to be self-supporting and self-contained, you see, most of
them had their farms and their laundries and their chapel. You've
not told me anything that couldn't be any hospital including this
one. Except maybe . . . you said the stories mention yellow brick?
Ah no, could be a good many places.'

'The best thing we've got to go on are the names. Arthur, Frank,
Dilke,' said Helen.

'Dilke?'

Helen explained.

Ian laughed. 'It's been a term of abuse for as long as I can
remember and I came into my first job in 1955 after the army.
That was Glasgow.'

'Was it used there?'

'Aye, it's in use everywhere. So I doubt that there's a Mr Dilke and if there ever was he's long gone.'

THERE WAS ONCE IN MEERN MOOR HOSPITAL. WHY HAVE YOU A WARD NAMED MEERN MOOR?

'Ah, now! Yes,' began Annette, 'I did a bit of looking up before your visit. Our annual report for 1883 confirms that some of the Meern Moor patients came here. About fifty of them according to the record. I imagine the ward was named after their hospital of origin.'

YOU SAID 'SOME'. DO YOU KNOW WHERE THE OTHERS WENT?

Ian Cutler replied, 'It could have been several places, depending on location, capacity at the time and the grade of patient. I have a feeling that Meern Moor was a relatively small local mixed hospital and if patients were being dispersed then they might have been directed to more specialist hospitals. The present categories of geriatric, mental handicap and so on are relatively recent, but even then the major hospitals were beginning to specialize, though crudely. Frankly, some hospitals were dumping grounds for the no-hopers. Laydale was never one of these so we might have got the better patients from Meern Moor.'

'I daresay then as now there would have been political problems between hospitals,' added Annette Roskill. 'No one wants a sudden jump in numbers unless they get the back-up of resources: the jargon has changed no doubt, but I'm sure . . .' she stopped and looked at Ian Cutler.

He smiled slightly: 'I'm sure too.'

'Where do you think they might have gone, Ian?'

'Well now . . . assuming it was within the northern area then it might have been to the west and one of the Blackburn hospitals – Brockhall and Calderstones, possibly the Royal Albert in Lancaster, or further north like Herstorne in Grisedale, across the Pennines in the north-east or maybe something as far north as Carlisle . . . och, it's hard to say. It's guesswork. Why do you need to know?'

I THINK THAT WHERE JOHN DILKE WENT WE'LL FIND ARTHUR EVEN IF THE DATES ARE WRONG. DO YOU KNOW THOSE HOSPITALS, IAN?

He read her screen and blinked in wonder.

'Marvellous really – if you don't mind me saying so. Technology. What we could have done with that years ago . . .'

Esther fixed him with her blue-grey gaze to bring him back to the question.

'Yes,' he went on. 'I've been in them all in my time. I've worked in Brockhall and Calderstones, I've been involved in patient transfers from the others.'

HAVE ANY OF THEM A PLACE CALLED THE GLEN WHERE PATIENTS WALK? AND A CHAPEL SEPARATE FROM THE MAIN BUILDING?

Ian Cutler was silent, thinking.

THERE ARE WIRE BASKETS IN THE MAIN CORRIDORS.

'And an infirmary with a wooden veranda?' continued Helen.

'Well, it's not here, that's for sure,' said Annette Roskill with mock relief. 'No yellow brick, our chapel's integral with the building, and we certainly don't have a "glen".'

'No, no I can't think of anything just now,' said Ian Cutler, 'but . . .' and he frowned and then hesitated.

YES?

'The "glen", you say. As a Scot I'd have remembered that right enough if I heard it in a hospital. And it does ring a bell . . . och, no, I can't put myself on it just now. Leave it with me awhile will you, and if I think of something I'll let you know soon enough.'

'Do hospitals of this kind keep archives?' asked Helen.

'It's a grand word for it,' said Annette. 'We certainly had a lot of material here until three or four years ago when much of it was incinerated. It was held in basement rooms which were converted to a staff launderette. We do have some of the older ledgers, and I have kept some of the things I felt might be of interest, like the punishment books and the admissions ledgers. They've been set out in the Committee Room as we felt you might like to see them. But "archives", well, I don't know. Nothing systematic.'

'Could you trace patients' dates of admission?'

'Oh yes, we could do that, and fairly easily for existing patients. Past patients, especially pre-war ones, might present problems. Have you got surnames?'

Helen shook her head.

'Difficult. But anyway, there's also the problem of confidentiality. You would not be able to work through the records yourself or see patients' files. But frankly it would be easier to ask someone like Ian who knows most of the names, especially of the older patients.'

'I know all the names.'

ARTHUR? keyed in Esther.

'I thought you might ask that,' he said.

Esther was silent. Helen waiting; Annette Roskill interested.

'We've got four Arthurs over forty but none of them is CP and none fits your description of someone who's very bright. That's the trouble, you see. By now they would have been reassessed and almost certainly be out of the institution in a special home run by the Spastics Society perhaps, or with one of the authorities. There's been a real run down over the last ten years.'

'We've got a few Franks, one very old one. I think he must have been here over forty years. But he's not your man. He's profoundly deaf. Should never have been here but it's his home now.'

'So a patient like him wouldn't go out into communal care?'

'Well, all of them will eventually. But he'd be one of the last. They like routine and familiarity you see. Change is a killer.'

Annette Roskill looked deliberately at her watch and as she did her secretary put her head round the door.

'Three minutes, Annette.'

'Well I must leave you. Ian will show you round and I'd like to see you again before you leave. About computers. Or rather, word processors.'

'Yeh,' said Esther.

'Esther knows all about them,' said Helen.

'Well, young lady, maybe you can accept a post as temporary consultant.'

But Esther did not think she was serious.

CAN WE VISIT ONE OF THE WARDS WHERE THE OLD PATIENTS ARE?

'Ian will take you everywhere. There are no locked wards these days. But we tend to call the wards villas now, sounds more appealing. We'll talk later then.'

Their tour was thorough but revealed nothing that brought them any nearer to Arthur and the Skallagrigg. Old men, strange thin youths with odd open mouths and eyes that seemed askance, a frightening group of adolescent girls, loud and aggressive, sexual and alive: ward after ward, half-open doors with people on toilets; half-closed doors with people groaning inside.

They toured in silence, patient after patient coming up to them to say a strange quick shy hello, and reaching out to be touched.

'How are you today?'

'Herro!'

'Coming coming coming coming. Morning!'

Greetings from a world they stared in at and then passed on by.

Ian Cutler seemed popular. Patients came and hugged him, and he in turn touched them, wished them well, passed a little time with them, introduced them.

'Say hello to my friends, Brenda.'

'Herrello, dear,' said Brenda, coming up to Helen and staring at her from four inches away. Then, 'Herrello, girlie,' to Esther, who was a little scared as Brenda, in a blue overall and bright pink fluffy carpet slippers, reached out a hand that had only two fingers, and those two melded together at the base.

The men they saw seemed more passive, though some grinned and rocked to see them come, staring at them in a looming way, their faces most strange. Some seemed quite normal, their eyes with laughter lines and intelligent, and Esther wondered what was wrong with them.

IT'S VERY NICE HERE IAN, Esther typed up, AND EVERYONE'S FRIENDLY.

'For the most part it's true right enough. But we've a couple of troublesome wards – the wanderers we call them – and though they're not locked they're carefully controlled. A lot depends on the staff. In the old days the numbers were too great and the drugs were less effective than they are now, though we try to minimize their use. I'm glad to have lived to see the change. But . . .'

They entered another ward and Esther guessed why he had suddenly paused. Immediately the atmosphere was different and the staff, three women dressed in blue overalls, were sitting smoking and having coffee. They did not get up or welcome them as most of the other staff had. The patients, middle-aged women, sat passive, one mumbling and another, over by a window, clutching continuously at her upper left arm with her right hand, and letting out staccato screams.

In the space of a few yards Esther felt they had gone back thirty years. At the end of the tour that was the ward she remembered most.

IAN, she typed, ARE THERE ANY HOSPITALS LIKE THAT WARD?

'Which ward?' he asked, as if he did not know.

WHERE THEY SMOKED.

He grinned and said, 'You don't miss much.'

ARE THERE?

'Things have improved radically since the reforms of 1974 and the spate of critical reports on hospitals like Napsbury, South Ockendon, Darlington, Ely and Normansfield. It's in the past.'

Esther was silent, waiting.

'Have you seen any of those reports?' he asked, her question still unanswered.

Helen nodded, Esther stared.

'Well, then, you'll appreciate that it comes down finally to management and staff training. It's management that changes attitudes.'

WHAT ATTITUDES? asked Esther.

'Protecting your ward,' said Ian Cutler shortly. 'That's where most of the problems arise. Your ward becomes your world and you may have no other standard by which to judge it. You don't realize the world outside has moved on. Teacher friends of mine report the same problem in schools.'

They were standing in the main foyer of Laydale. From somewhere they heard Christmas music and from somewhere else laughter. But Ian Cutler's kind face was serious.

'In one hospital the same sister served on the same ward for forty-seven years, treating her patients like naughty children and meting out her own often very cruel punishments. So strong was her personality and so anxious was the hospital administration not to have a fuss that no one did anything, ever. She only left when she retired, having caused untold misery to generations of poor patients. You see I think, in that isolated situation, a nurse can go mad, or at least very quirky. It's a terrible thing. Imagine the implications of one person being responsible for a long-stay ward for nearly half a century. Your "Dilke" character was one of those. It's changed now, thank goodness.'

He paused and stared out of the window to the gathering twilight of the December evening.

Esther waited.

'Some wards, some places. It's very strange. You institute changes, you have new staff, you have different patients and yet you can't make the ward better. Misery seems to be in the walls of some places and it finds weaknesses in people, and it comes out as cruelty. That ward where you saw them smoking; completely new staff there in the last two years. But it's just the same, miserable. It's always been like that, ever since I first came and before that I'm told. Some hospitals are like that and they bring out the worst in staff and patients.'

Esther thought of Arthur and Dilke. The stories presented him as powerful and cunning, but was he after all just a single incompetent male nurse who gained power over a small group of men and maintained it for decades?

WHAT HOSPITALS ARE LIKE THAT? asked Esther hoping for some names.

For a moment Ian Cutler hesitated again, as he had before, but then instead of answering the question he looked at his watch and said, 'Oh no, I can't make comments about other hospitals. Now then, look at that time. I must be leaving you now and I think Ms Roskill wants to say a few words. But I've got something you might like to read . . . I'll leave it at reception, you can pick it up on your way out.'

Annette Roskill was waiting for them and came straight to the point: 'Miss Marquand,' she said rather formally in a way that made Esther feel important, 'I am extremely interested in your views on computers. You see it's obvious that the new technology has implications for us and although we've been computerized in administration for some time – principally for accounting and finance – other uses have still to come. My worry is that there are patients who might benefit as you have, though at a lower level, who are going to miss out for years yet because of lack of advice. It's very difficult to get, you know; there are only one or two people competent to assess and advise on an individual patient's needs and they are very heavily committed into the future. But we have a need now. For example, where did you get the equipment you're using? Who advised you?'

MY FATHER RUNS A COMPUTER CONSULTANCY CALLED COMPUTABASE, typed Esther.

Annette Roskill's eyes glinted and narrowed. She leaned forward and said, 'You mean the shops I've seen that sell computers? There's one in Manchester.'

Esther nodded and looked at Helen.

'Richard Marquand really runs ComputaBase,' she explained. 'Well, he owns it, in fact. Esther's equipment was put together for her by one of his consultants. The keyboard she has is a prototype.'

'Then I wonder if you could help us?' asked Annette Roskill.

HOW?

'Would your father's company send someone to talk to us about some of the possibilities?'

I'LL TELL HIM TO!! typed Esther.

'You see, if I know what questions to ask I can probably get the funding. That's the problem in a new field: getting the right information.'

OK, keyed in Esther. BY THE WAY, COMPUTERS AREN'T AS DIFFICULT AS THEY SEEM.

'Maybe you should come and advise us. Straight from the horse's mouth so to speak!'

Esther grinned. EEOR, she typed. I'M A DONKEY REALLY.

Annette Roskill smiled briefly and then said, 'As a matter of fact I'm serious. You might be the perfect person to understand handicapped patients' needs and do something about them.'

Esther looked at her and said nothing. She was flattered at one level, but horrified at another. Her dream was to leave the world of handicap behind, not become immersed in it.

On the way out they found a big envelope from Ian Cutler waiting for them in reception. They opened it that evening.

'North Central Regional Health Authority' they read, 'Report of the Committee of Inquiry, Herstorne Hospital, Grisedale'.

It was dated March 1976, price £2.50. Attached to it on a separate piece of paper was Ian Cutler's telephone extension number and the briefest of notes: 'See par. 4.31. I hope this is what you were looking for. Herstorne fits the bill.'

It was. Section 4 of the report was the detailed evidence to the inquiry given by a former student nurse at Herstorne. Paragraph 31 read:

The ward charge nurse was notorious for his strictness

in dealing with patients. He knew the patients well, and their individual likes and dislikes, using this information against them when they offended him. The punishment for one patient, for example, who liked to watch television was the removal of his spectacles, which left him confused and insecure. Another, who was claustrophobic, would be confined in a side room. Some of the patients disliked going out, but for some the Sunday walk to the glen was a high spot. Their 'punishment' if (usually quite unwittingly) they transgressed this charge nurse's somewhat arbitrary 'rules' was, of course, not to be allowed in the glen walk with the others . . .'

The glen!

'Yeh,' said Esther, desperately pointing. THE GLEN.

'Yes, my dear,' said Helen quietly, 'I think that tomorrow we shall visit Herstorne.'

FIFTY-SIX

Herstorne is a market town in the high fells to the north of the
Bowland Forest; a dark, mean place which once, in happier times,
was peopled only by the families of sheepmen and small-holders.
Not now, not for more than a century. For where the moor rises
above the town itself, on its crest and alongside an impenetrable
black wall of Forestry Commission larches, looms Herstorne Mental
Hospital.

The grim nineteenth-century façade, high and long, its stained
yellow bricks even bleaker than that already bleak landscape, is
prison-like. The upper-floor windows are arched and barred,
identical indeed to those of the notorious west wing of Sturrick
Royal near Manchester and designed by the same architect; and to
finish it all off a squat square chimney rises menacingly behind the
main building.

In the decades after its founding, the hospital expanded rapidly
as the bad nutrition and industrial stress of the towns and cities of
the north central region spewed up physical and emotional misfits.
From where they were brought no one ever quite knew: poor men,
poor women, lying in cots sometimes, for many were idiot cripples.
Year by year they came, their eyes staring and afraid, their posture
defeated or angry or bovine, seeing only the stark walls of their
destination within which they were to be lost for ever in a complex
of wards and rooms, corridors and courts; of rules and regulations.
A labyrinth they could never comprehend; a maze of despair.

Nearly a century passed before the hospital began at last to die.
In the fifties the numbers no longer increased, in the sixties they
began to decline by natural wastage; in the seventies the decline
accelerated as health authorities were encouraged to disperse their
disturbed and handicapped patients into the community, or to
smaller, kinder units. Slowly Herstorne, like Sturrick, like all of
them, withered and its population of patients and workers began

to fade away leaving behind an architectural shell which held
memories best forgotten, and patients too old and nearly too institutionalized to move. Patients to whom, terribly, Herstorne had
become home.

'A depressing place and rather empty,' said Helen Perry-Wilcox
accurately that bright December morning when she drove Esther
up Grisedale and into Herstorne for the first time. 'What a lot of
houses for sale!' she added, as behind her Esther's eyes glinted at
the forlorn scene.

Over breakfast that morning they had had time to read more of
the Report of the Committee of Inquiry which Ian Cutler had put
their way, and which recounted certain events at Herstorne in the
early 1970s.

In 1974 a student nurse named Ruan Jones, on secondment
from Cardiff, had sent a detailed report to the local press about
what he had seen during his twelve months at the hospital. He
had published his findings reluctantly, and only after the internal
investigation had been blocked by the hospital's nursing and
administrative staff.

The regional health authority had reacted quickly to the reports
of cruelty, torture, over-medication, low standards of nursing care
and brutality that Jones's report detailed, by starting its own inquiry which reported publicly two years later.

It was willing to agree that in the four years to 1974 there was
evidence of poor nursing standards, poor leadership by the hospital
management, and some mistreatment of patients. Like other
hospitals of its age and type, Herstorne was struggling with too
few resources of money and staff, and antiquated buildings. But it
should not be forgotten that Mr Ruan Jones was only a *student*
nurse, inclined to immature over-statements of incidents and situ-
ations he had no prior experience of, though his evidence certainly
should not be entirely discounted . . .

But these reassuring findings were not what had cast Esther and
Helen into such a sombre and concerned frame of mind that lovely
December morning. It was, rather, the memory of just some of Mr
Jones's evidence, printed as an appendix at the back of the report,
which gave support to the possibility that the crueller and grimmer
aspects of the Skallagrigg stories might well be true.

Para. 38. This ward was the subject of frequent comments and reports by patients and staff concerning recurring bullying and violence. Patients were commonly poked in the testicles with window sticks. One elderly patient, small and harmless, told me he knew the SEN 'had it in' for him. His nose was broken 'accidentally' a month before this report was written.

Para. 47. Herstorne's hairdresser called his work 'sheep shearing'. Patients were unable to complain of his basin-style haircuts which made them look like convicts, and identified them as institutional.

Para. 53. A patient in this ward was locked all day, every day, in a wooden chair, being freed only to toilet and wash. The reason given was that he bit and scratched other patients. I requested permission to take him for a walk but was told there was insufficient staff.

Para. 59. One male patient was fourteen when admitted and so had matured in an all-male disturbed environment. He is placid and never causes trouble, but began occasionally wandering out of the ward to stare at the girls in the medical secretaries' office. Complaints were made and the treatment recommended was (a) heavy medication and/or (b) confinement to the ward in pyjama order. Nothing was done or is being done for the social education of this harmless individual.

Para. 64. A man complaining of pain in his pelvic area was diagnosed as 'hysteric'. ECT (electro-convulsive therapy) was prescribed but he objected (as was his right). He was taken struggling to the ECT ward and the treatment was administered. The pain persisted. Subsequent examination established that his pelvis was broken and he was taken to Grisedale Hospital. This patient was given ECT with a broken pelvis.

Para. 71. On this female geriatric ward SENs systematically pilfered patients' fruit, cigarettes and other goods. They openly ate patients' food during breaks and when challenged told me 'the bitches don't know the difference anyway'.

Para. 76. In a ward notorious for the harshness of its
regime I saw three nurses standing over a seated patient.
As a nurse offered to help him up and he started to rise
another pushed him violently down again. When he
protested and attempted to stop the 'game' he was
slapped and forced to continue. He began to weep and
they finally desisted.

'We'll be bold and resolute,' announced Helen as they drove
through the gates of the hospital, which were wide open, and past
a couple of men, probably patients, who stood bent and gawping,
staring at their car. Anger instilled by the report and a missionary
desire to find Arthur had turned Helen into a fierce companion
and a resourceful one.

Esther was surprised to see that a neat and cheerful flowerbed
ran along the base of the main building with rose bushes and
cotoneaster neatly pruned for the winter and tied back to the wall.
Pretty winter-flowering jasmine rose up the wall by the main
entrance, a solid porticoed affair with glazed oak doors and above
it, carved in stone, the words 'Herstorne County Asylum'.

A few cars were parked in spaces neatly marked out for them,
and a couple of men, one in blue overalls, were working at a
drainpipe on a far corner of the building. After looking briefly in
their direction they resumed their work.

There was an air of emptiness, of under-use, of an institution
which had had its day and was now being wound down and had
found itself at last in the hands of people who cared for it.

'I must admit it's not as bad as I expected,' said Helen rather
grudgingly, getting Esther out and into her chair, and her
equipment working.

DO YOU THINK THIS IS WHERE ARTHUR IS OR WAS?

'I hope we can find out, though I doubt if we'll get far today,'
replied Helen.

But she was mistaken if she expected stonewalling and instant
rejection. They were not challenged when they entered the doors
to the foyer, and although there were a few people about nobody
seemed interested in them, or even to notice them.

LET'S EXPLORE, typed Esther.

'Unwise, my dear, though tempting. We got our tour of Laydale

and a lot of help by doing things through the proper channels and
I think we had better do that here.'

OAK DOORS ALL THE WAY AND RECESSES WHERE THE WIRE
BASKETS REFERRED TO IN THE STORIES COULD HAVE BEEN,
typed Esther, her eyes excited.

They found a door marked 'Office' and went in. It was small and
poky, a room partitioned from a larger one with high and elegant
mouldings disappearing beyond thin partition walls.

A middle-aged secretary sat at a wooden desk in front of dark
green filing cabinets and she managed a weak, indifferent smile.
'Yes?'

She stared fleetingly at Esther and then rather blankly at Helen's
deliberately imprecise explanation of why they were there. They
were told that the administrator was a Mr Richard Vause, but that
he was at a ward party and would not be free until the afternoon.
It was a busy time. What exactly had they come for – to visit a
relative?

Perhaps, agreed Helen, it would be better to see Mr Vause.

'You'll need an appointment,' said the secretary immediately, as
if fearing that they would sit and wait for him all day. 'It's not a
relative then?'

'Well, no,' risked Helen. 'It's three patients we think may well
be here, or have been here in the past. It's rather complicated
but . . .'

'I'm sure he'll do his best to help but he is very busy with the
closing.'

'Closing?' said Helen.

'Next June. The last patients will be leaving then.'

Helen and Esther relaxed. They had had a sudden vision of their
quarries, if they still existed, being dispersed before they were able
to reach them.

'We were really hoping to contact three patients, Arthur, Frank
and Norman,' said Helen.

'What are their surnames?'

'We don't know, I'm afraid,' said Helen.

'Ah,' said the woman. 'Yes. I think this really is one for Mr
Vause. Why not write in and . . .'

'Yes, we shall,' agreed Helen immediately. That was the best
way to gain admission to the hospital and help. Getting pushy now

would get them nowhere and might lose goodwill. 'We did write before as a matter of fact, but . . .'

'Probably at the changeover was it? A few weeks ago? Well,' the secretary pursed her lips in a disapproving way, 'things were not too efficient until Mr Vause came in. There have been a lot of staff changes, you see. People leaving. Perhaps your letter got left on one side. I shall make a special note.' She took their names and promised to deal promptly with any letter they sent.

As they left Helen asked, 'By the way, have you got a chapel?'

'The chapel's by the Old Annexe.'

'The Old Annexe?' asked Helen, her voice quiet.

'Um, well yes, that's what they call it. I expect it was new once! But I'm afraid . . .' The phone rang and the woman looked relieved. She picked it up, said a brief hello, indicated again to Helen that they should write, and they were dismissed.

Outside in the corridor again Esther typed up, IT'S BEGINNING TO FIT, HELEN!!! LET'S EXPLORE, YOU CAN PRETEND I'M A NEW PATIENT.

'Not inside, Esther, it's not worth the risk. We'll be found by someone.'

WELL NO ONE WILL MIND OUTSIDE, IN THE GROUNDS.

As they turned to leave Esther saw a noticeboard and she called out to Helen to stop. There were health notices up and some postcards. But most prominent was a fluorescent orange poster:

NORTH-EASTERN ARTS TRAVELLING PLAYERS
NEW YEAR PANTOMINE
CINDERELLA
JANUARY 7th 3.00PM HERSTORNE HOSPITAL
THEATRE TICKETS FOR PUBLIC £2.00 FROM THE
RED BOOK SHOP AND AT THE DOOR
ARTS COUNCIL FUNDED

WE COULD GO TO THAT, typed Esther. GOOD WAY OF GETTING IN WHEN EVERYBODY WILL BE TOO BUSY TO NOTICE US.

'If all else fails we shall my dear,' said Helen. 'Even if it's rather a long drive to see a pantomine.'

Before they left they took the van along the roadway that ran round the grounds, as if confused about their way out. There *was* a chapel; there *was* a veranda from an infirmary ward; and there *was* beyond it, across sloping lawns, a dip in the ground where a few leafless trees and bushes stood.

They asked the man in blue overalls they had seen working when they arrived what it was called but it was the patient helping him who replied, and as he did so they seemed to know what he would say. 'That's the glen, isn't it.'

The man in charge added, 'You can't drive down there but you can walk if you want to. Bit chilly, mind.'

'Yeh!' said Esther from the back of the van.

For both of them there was an inevitability about Herstorne, a certainty that they were near to finding the truth about Arthur now, very near.

So Helen got Esther out of the van and pushed her down the wide asphalt paths, among the lopped trees where the grass was winter-short. Esther looked up at the branches and the winter sky beyond, and around at the paths and dips to the ground where once, long ago, Arthur had been with Linnie, and Dilke with Wim. Making love; no no no, thought Esther, Frank called it cocking and cunting. Looking up at the sky or down at the grass.

Helen turned her chair up the slope towards the hospital which looked small and benign from this angle, for only its upper floors and roofs could be seen. And the chimney.

THIS IS THE PLACE, HELEN.

'Yes, I believe it must be,' she whispered, halting the wheelchair and looking back at the gaunt buildings.

I THINK ARTHUR'S IN THERE.

'So do I.'

WE'VE GOT TO COME BACK AND FIND HIM.

Helen nodded.

'We'll write again to Mr Vause, and if that gets us nowhere we'll come to the pantomime in January along with other members of the public.'

YES YES YES.

As they drove back down through Herstorne's High Street they saw a sign for The Red Bookshop, and Helen stopped to buy three tickets for the pantomime.

WHY THREE?
'We might need Tom,' said Helen Perry-Wilcox, the look of the
hunter in her eye.

FIFTY-SEVEN

A parcel from America was waiting for Esther when she got back to Harefield the next day but it was not opened for her until Christmas Day.

It was a bright yellow T-shirt with the words 'Hanniman Beach Surfers' on it in chunky rounded American-style letters, orange-lined chocolate brown. The card that came with it read 'God Bless your Christmas and New Year, with love and affection, Daniel M. Schuster. To wear on those walks by the shore.'

She wore it all Christmas Day with neither thought nor desire for anything else but Daniel, whom she knew she would never meet but about whom nobody could stop her dreaming.

For a few hours at least Esther was pleasant with Kate, but when Boxing Day came the old coolness returned. A family call came through for Kate from Australia and Esther took herself to her room. When her father suggested a walk for them all in the afternoon she declined.

On New Year's Eve they were all to go to a small party at Edward Light's house in west London but Esther refused to go.

'Why not?' asked Richard. 'Because you feel in the way, is that it?'

Yes. Yes. Yes!

'Nah,' said Esther.

But it was. She felt she knew that however kind and understanding people were she would be in the way of her father's relaxation, and people would stare, always those sidelong stares, however polite they were. Her father would even have to hold the glass of champagne for her from which to drink the New Year in.

Tom wanted to stay with her, and Helen, who never did like big parties, offered to stay overnight as well.

So Richard and Kate went by themselves. Esther watched her father help Kate on with her coat. Kate was in high heels and silky stockings, and a pretty dress with wide shoulders, and her thick dark hair was glossy. Oh, she was so lovely. Esther watched them leave from the world she lived in and in which she felt stuck for ever.

Rather forlornly, Esther, Tom and Helen sat in the living-room, Tom watching television, while Esther and Helen composed the letter they would post next day, asking Mr Vause of Herstorne Hospital if he could help in their researches. The television was raucous and Esther's mind was not on the letter at all. A new year coming, and nothing nothing nothing for her. Esther did not notice that Helen was quiet as well as she got up to make them some tea and stood at the window staring out at the darkened garden.

Tom switched channels to something even more raucous.

'Toh!'

'Sorry, Amh,' and he changed it back.

Helen went out to the kitchen.

Esther stared at the Christmas tree in the far corner. It was beginning to droop and shed its needles. Then up at the ceiling and then at a clock. It was just after eleven. If she had her way she would go to bed and sleep through the silly celebrations. Perhaps she would. Yes, she would.

The phone rang.

Helen came in unhurriedly saying, 'I'll take it in here.'

She picked it up, listened, looked at Esther and said, 'Just a moment, Mr Schuster,' and stood staring at Esther speechlessly, her hand over the receiver.

Esther stared back, her eyes suddenly terrified and her hands going to her chest as to protect herself.

'It's Daniel Schuster,' said Helen eventually, 'wishing to talk to you, my dear.'

Esther shot her chair to Helen's side.

YOU MUSTN'T TELL HIM ANYTHING.

'Well, what am I going to say? He's phoning long distance.'

TELL HIM I'M OUT.

A look of disapproval went over Helen's face. She did not like deceit.

YOU KNEW WHAT TO DO AT HERSTORNE!!

Helen grinned slightly, tut-tutted, raised her eyes to the heavens, and raised the receiver.

'I'm so sorry, Mr Schuster, you've missed her. She's gone to a New Year's Eve party ... Who am I?'

HOLD THE PHONE SO I CAN HEAR.

'My name is Helen. I'm a general dogsbody.'

'Dogsbody?' The voice was pleasant, deep, youthful Californian.

'A joke, Mr Schuster. I'm a friend of the family.'

HELEN HE'S AMERICAN HE WON'T *SEE* THE JOKE,

'Why aren't *you* at the party?' he asked in a nice voice.

'Amh's here. There,' said Tom, pointing and speaking as if to the world at large.

TOM SHUT UP SHUT UP SHUT UP, hissed Esther somehow. Tom sank into submission on the carpet in front of the television and watched them uncomprehendingly.

'Could you have her call me, I have good news for her apart from wanting to give her New Year greetings.'

NO NO NO NO NO NO YOU MUST SAY NO.

'Er . . . I'm afraid I don't think Esther will be able to call. She's a very private person. She never uses the phone. Never. She will write I expect.'

There was a pause as Daniel Schuster took in this odd information. 'Well . . .' he began, sounding disappointed.

ASK HIM WHAT THE NEWS IS!!!!!!!!!!

'But perhaps I can give her a message. I mean, if you have something good to tell her.'

'Yes,' he said, 'sure.' His voice picked up again. 'Tell her "Tom's Game" is a vacation bestseller on the West Coast; and tell her we can do a major deal for her on the "Dunroune" material. But I need to work with her on it. Tell her . . .' he paused again. 'Hell, it would be a lot easier talking direct to her.'

'No way,' said Helen, the expression strange for her.

DON'T GO OVER THE TOP, HELEN, typed Esther, now rather enjoying herself.

But Helen was warming to her task.

'She was very pleased with the T-shirt you sent her.'

'Oh was she? Hey that's good, that's really good.' He sounded more cheerful again.

'I hope you're going to a party, Mr Schuster. You're behind us in time over there aren't you?'

The hesitation returned.

'Yeah,' he said, 'I'm maybe going to a party. Well I'll say goodbye now. Er, you give her my good wishes. Say God Bless for the New Year. Say that to her. And thank you, ma'am. God Bless to you too.'

'Thank you, Mr Schuster.'

'Daniel,' he said with a smile in his voice, and the phone went dead.

Helen put down the phone, stared briefly at Esther, and went into the kitchen without a word.

She came back five minutes later with a tray of tea things, a bottle of champagne, and three glasses.

'The things you make me do, Esther!' She was grinning, and so was Esther.

YOU WERE BRILLIANT, HELEN, typed Esther, eyes shining.

'I want you to know that I thoroughly disapprove,' said Helen, but her voice was cheerful, and she smiled to see Esther's pleasure.

But later, after midnight, after the toasts, after Tom had gone up to bed, Helen said more seriously, 'You're going to have to tell him, Esther, you know that don't you?'

She nodded wanly. Then her expression changed and she typed, WHEN YOU ASKED HIM ABOUT GOING TO A PARTY HE HESI-TATED. I THINK HE'S STUCK AT HOME LIKE US.

'Well, don't look so pleased about it, my dear! Really!' But Esther continued to grin, and grinned all the way to bed, the champagne and the fact that a young man had phoned her on New Year's Eve going straight to her head.

But she did not sleep. She stared at the curtained window, a grey rectangle in the dark, a gap at the bottom where Helen had left the window open just a little as Esther liked, and thought rather aimlessly about the coming year. She felt depressed. Her mind drifted to Daniel and she imagined what it would be like walking with him on Hanniman Beach wearing just that T-shirt like the girl in the shampoo ad. Did she have anything on underneath it? She imagined holding Daniel's hand. She began to feel better. She composed a letter to him in her head telling him the truth about herself. She filed that away and composed another, the one she *would* write. It did not tell the truth.

Some time after two in the morning her father's car crunched into the drive. The car door opened. Feet, her father's round the

car, to open the door for Kate. Kate's feet and then her saying
something, her father's deeper voice replying. It was one of those
still nights when sound travelled.

They came into the hall and then went into the kitchen and put
the kettle on. Esther knew that because she could hear it beginning
to bubble and steam, and then the click as it switched itself off.
Kate's heels clicked on the floor. She was making tea. Esther knew
the sounds; and anyway, they didn't drink coffee at night.

Her father said something. Kate replied. Serious. Hard to hear
the words and, in fact, at first Esther was not trying to.

The patio doors slid open and now she could not but hear.

'It's muggy, Richard. Not at all wintery.'

'Shh! Don't wake Esther.'

'I said it's close,' whispered Kate. 'Mug or cup?'

'Mug.' Richard was outside now, staring at the sky probably,
though there wasn't much to see. Esther craned to look at the sky
through the slight gap in her curtains.

Kate's heels on the patio again.

'Come here.' Kate giggled. Long pause.

'That was nice,' she said. Richard said something too softly for
Esther to make it out.

'No, the party!' said Kate. Richard laughed.

'Mmm, nice tea. Thanks.'

There was a long silence.

'Darling?'

'Mmm?'

'It's the New Year,' said Kate.

'What are your wishes?'

'Resolutions, you mean.'

'No, wishes.'

Esther heard silence. She heard kisses.

'To marry and start a family,' she heard Kate say.

It was as if her heart had stopped.

'Yes,' said her father ambiguously.

'We've got to make decisions, Richard.'

'I know.'

'I love you but I don't want to stay like this in England.'

'I know,' he said. Esther could hear the weariness in his voice. 'I
can't move to Sydney with Esther.'

Sydney? Esther lay utterly still. *Sydney?*

'Oh shit,' said Kate. 'Bloody bloody hell.'

'Darling . . .'

'We can't drift on for another year, my love.'

'I know.'

'I want children, your children.'

'Children?'

'At least ten. Maybe twenty.'

Esther envied the intimacy of their soft laughter. She hated the silence in which they must be touching.

'You looked very lovely tonight. I felt proud.'

'I always feel proud with you,' said Kate.

'I love you.'

'Mmm,' Kate sighed. 'I'm getting cold.'

They stood up, Esther could hear them, and they kissed, Esther could even hear that.

'I want you to have my children,' said Richard, 'but not in bloody Britain. In Australia where the sun shines and people aren't depressed all the time.'

'Well . . .' began Kate.

'I think the time has come for some decision, my love.'

'Yes,' said Kate. 'Yes it has.'

And they went back into the kitchen, laid the table for breakfast and went upstairs. One of them opened the window and later, in the still night, Esther heard sounds that seared her heart. The sound of Kate and her father making love. Esther lay unsleeping into the dawn of a new year.

But it was Esther not Richard who made a decision.

She wrote down her New Year resolutions the following day: 'All must now change, I have been selfish long enough. Daniel said 'God Bless your New Year', but it is up to me to behave like a Christian. So my New Year resolutions are: (a) to think of a way of freeing Daddy from me; (b) to be nice to Kate who has been nice to me; (c) to start being Christian and to read the Bible and pray for help and guidance; (d) to be grateful for the things I've got; (e) to find the truth of the Skallagrigg and reach Arthur.

'I think I've got a possible way to deal with (a) though it won't be easy; (b) is easy since I like Kate really; (c) I'm going to ask

Marion and Jeremy to take me to her church – converted me at last without even trying!!!; (d) no comment; & (e) that's up to God to work out and I'll leave Him to do it (*but please do it soon*).'

With her normal vigour, Esther Marquand began a systematic reading of the New Testament, having visited the Pentecostal Church in High Wycombe with Marion and been given a Bible study booklet for the months of January and February. She did not, in fact, stay with the church for many weeks, for it seemed to her that much of what the church said was simplistic: her faith and her reading were of a more thorough and impartial kind, and she preferred the traditional Anglican services of the kind Netherton had taken its students to, and which she had first felt so moved by in Oxford's University Church. But from that January Esther was a Christian, and Marion and Jeremy counted her as one of their Christian friends.

As for Kate, Esther chose a simple way to re-establish her friendliness: WILL YOU TAKE ME SHOPPING FOR SOME CLOTHES IN THE LONDON NEW YEAR SALES? she asked.

It was at breakfast and Kate could hardly believe her eyes. Esther had chosen a moment to ask when her father was not at the table.

'Of course I will,' said Kate with a lovely smile.

PLEASE, added Esther shyly. YOU ALWAYS DRESS SO WELL. She had only ever been shopping with old ladies – Margaret and Helen – and her father.

Kate leaned over and put her hand on Esther's.

'There's nothing I'd rather do,' she said softly.

Richard, when he found out, wisely said nothing.

Esther told Kate: I'VE GOT THE MONEY FROM THE COMPETITION AND MY ALLOWANCE MONEY IN THE BANK DEPOSIT ACCOUNT. I HARDLY SPEND ANYTHING. ALSO MY GAME IN THE STATES IS SELLING WELL SO I SHALL BE RICH!!

Kate smiled: 'You Marquands are all the same, naturally careful with money. But not mean anyway.'

CERTAINLY NOT! typed Esther. YOU CAN HAVE AN ICE CREAM IN LONDON.

They went to London twice and had a chance to talk away from the pressures of Harefield.

I THINK YOU'RE WELL SUITED AND THAT DADDY'S LUCKY TO HAVE FOUND YOU, keyed up Esther.

'Thank you! You're right! But don't tell him yet . . .'

Esther did not. She remained curiously distant when the two of them were together with her, as if uneasy about getting too closely involved with them as a couple. She had not yet resolved how to 'free' her father of her, but she sensed that it would be much less easy if she established a closer relationship with them together. But with Kate alone it was different, and from then on the atmosphere was easier at Harefield.

Esther heard from Richard Vause the Administrator of Herstorne Hospital on 4 January, and the letter was helpful. He was himself relatively new to the hospital and although he knew the names of existing patients his knowledge did not go back in time, certainly not pre-war. There was definitely no 'Arthur' at the hospital though there were a couple of 'Norman's, but there had been in the past he was told. There was a Frank and he was one of several patients who helped in the chapel. Provided they could let him have some reference from a school or university he would be happy to see them at Herstorne, and he strongly recommended that they try to visit on 7 January though it was very soon, because there was to be a pantomime and an Open Day. This would probably be the final opportunity to meet some of the old staff, who would be attending, since the hospital was being run down and converted to other uses later in the year. No doubt some of them could be persuaded to talk – it might be difficult to stop them! (he added). This was a fund-raising event and tickets cost £2.00 each. Could they let him know if they were coming so that he could arrange to see them and perhaps for one or two people to talk to them . . .

FIFTY-EIGHT

Esther, Helen and Tom set off for the north early on the morning of 7 January. Esther was feeling poorly with a slight cold, and drifted in and out of a troubled sleep on the journey from the effect of the anti-cold drugs Kate had given her. She felt detached, and when they finally turned off the motorway towards the Trough of Bowland she found herself staring at the walled fields and farm buildings of Grisedale as if she was watching a documentary, and the van windows were a television screen.

Tom spoke from a distance. 'Amh, Amh,' and she nodded with her eyes half closed, letting Helen take the questions. Tom was troubled for her.

'I had a cold,' he said.

'Yes, Esther's got a cold, let her sleep.'

'Wilco, Helen, wilco.'

They stopped at a service station to freshen up.

'The toilets smell,' said Tom. 'Yuckie yuck yuck. Didn't do it there.'

They had tea and Helen wiped Esther's face with a tissue impregnated with cologne.

'How are you feeling?'

'Yuck!' said Esther as well. But colour came to her cheeks after some tea and a doughnut. Outside the sky was a violet grey and night was falling. It was two-thirty.

Helen drove the last miles slowly, as if expecting some kind of accident along the narrow shadowy road. Turns seemed to come on them sharply, the road to split ambiguously; a man walking their way almost wandered into their path, shielding his face as if they were too hot to face. Mad? Drunk? The day was ominous and threatening.

The market square of Herstorne was deserted, with street lights unlit and nearly every house dark. They were coming to the end of the world and Tom was nervous.

But Esther seemed suddenly better now, staring expectantly at the rising road to the hospital. Only when they reached the gates themselves and saw lights and signs for cars to park, and an odd bent man dressed in a raincoat and woolly hat waved their car into a space, did they believe there might indeed be a public event on.

The hospital foyer was crowded with people, the public evidently. No one asked them for their tickets but a man came up and announced to them and anyone else who was interested that the performance was going to begin quarter of an hour late at three-fifteen; eats and cups of tea or coffee were through by the theatre and could they please move down? From somewhere came pop music, from somewhere else the dark cadences of a disturbed man's voice.

'Could you tell me where I could find Mr Vause, please?' Helen asked a middle-aged man in a brown suit.

'I am Mr Vause,' he said. Esther's legs spasmed into excitement and she grinned up at him.

Helen explained who they were. The man did not seem in the least surprised: he had the social look of someone who has been meeting people all day long, but he managed a smile and said, 'I'm glad you were able to come at such short notice; we didn't expect . . .' He did not finish the sentence. Someone came and whispered in his ear and he nodded and said, 'Quarter past, just a few minutes late.'

He turned back to them. 'I mentioned your case at a meeting of staff officers and there is no objection to your visit. We've found someone to look after you. He's one of the retired members of staff and his memory goes back a long way: he knows or knew everybody, and was here when the hospital had over fifteen hundred patients before the last war. I . . .'

Another man approached them. He was a little shorter than Mr Vause, and broader; a fit-looking seventy. His hair was grey and close-cropped and his face had that healthy baby look that some people retain throughout their lives.

'Ah . . . good,' said Mr Vause. 'These are the people, Jack.' Esther noticed that the two of them exchanged a look that suggested they had talked about the visit and prepared for it in some way. 'Mr Sprayle,' said Richard Vause by way of introduction, and then, as he hurried off, 'Perhaps I'll see you after the performance if there's anything else.'

Helen introduced them, explained briefly why they were there, while Jack Sprayle nodded to indicate he knew about their research.

'Pleased to meet you,' he said, smiling.

It was a pleasant enough smile but the eyes were dark and hard and Tom stayed firmly behind Esther's chair saying nothing. Helen explained how Esther's screen worked and that he could talk directly to her, but he seemed not quite to understand or be much interested.

'I better say straight out that I don't think I can help you very much except historically speaking,' said Mr Sprayle. 'It's not easy trying to trace patients just by their Christian name – so many you see passing through your hands. You can't remember all the boys.' The way he said 'boys' made Esther shudder. It seemed to cast them for ever into a pit out of which they could not climb to become men.

'Do you mind if we sit down somewhere . . . oh, hello, lad, hello, yes yes . . .'

The 'lad' was a man of sixty, with his hair shaved high up the back of his thin, too-long head, and a fringe cut off jaggedly at the front. He grinned at Mr Sprayle toothlessly and put his arm for a moment around his waist in a gesture of friendship.

'They don't forget, you know. Never forget. Now that one came here just after the war and his name is Dick Trabis. Harmless enough now, I daresay. We had trouble with him once. For a time.' His pink cheeks shone with pleasure at a job well done.

They walked down the corridor past the entrance into the theatre and a small barrier across the corridor which read 'No admittance to public please'.

The corridor stretched before them past shut doors. The floor was polished but the only light came from strip lighting along the ceiling. He showed them into a visitors' room whose walls were painted light hospital green. There was a fitted industrial carpet, ugly comfortable chairs, and on the walls old but colourful travel posters. The curtains on the windows were drawn, the light was flat yellow. At the far end of the room there were some people talking to a man who was evidently a patient and with his back to them.

They all sat down except for Tom who stood resolutely holding on to Esther's chair, as if ready to escape with her. He was quite silent, staring at Mr Sprayle who was smiling.

'Now then?' Mr Sprayle was a man of few words.

Helen outlined what they were interested in, some instinct making her careful not to give too much away.

'Who's the project for then?' asked Mr Sprayle without answering a question.

Helen did not hesitate: 'Oxford Polytechnic,' she said.

'Mmm. I thought she was studying computers. This sounds more like social service work.'

'It's a foundation course,' lied Helen.

'Ah. Well, I'll do what I can to help, though it won't be much I'm afraid.'

'Well, it's the names we've got. We wondered if they rang any bells: Frank, Arthur, Norman, Eppie . . .' As Helen went through them Esther noticed that Mr Sprayle was an impatient man, his eyes kept going here and there and he was tapping his fingers on his knee. He wore a neat grey suit and blue shirt, though the collar was a little big for him.

Behind him in the distance Esther saw the patient with visitors turn and stare at them, and then at Mr Sprayle. From then on the patient kept looking at him, nervously, and cutting across his relatives' conversation to do so. They were in any case having trouble keeping his attention, talking in rather loud voices, mainly among themselves, and saying 'That's nice then,' and 'Very pleased with you,' and 'You never get colds and that's a blessing at the moment,' to which he said 'Yeh, yeh,' and looked around again at Mr Sprayle.

'There's been plenty of boys with the names you mentioned, as you'd expect. Definitely not a Frank and an Arthur at the same time, though. I knew them all pretty well. Twenty-two years Senior Charge Nurse, eight years Assistant Senior before that.'

'Mr Vause wrote and said there was someone called Frank who liked the chapel.'

'Oh yes. Frank Caine. Been here almost the longest, it's his home. He's the chapel boy except there isn't any chapel now. Closed to all intents and purposes, and has been a long time. The boys go down into Herstorne for their service and communion once a month.'

'Why was it closed?'

'Two reasons. The chaplain went part-time after 1974 when things changed, and there was bad roof damage and damp. Too expensive to repair. It was built when everybody went to chapel, had to go, maybe that was best. Probably was. Gave them something to think about on Sundays even if it was a bit of a nuisance for us. But we didn't mind if the boys wanted it: we're here to look after their needs. One big family.' He smiled bleakly, and the patient behind looked around again, nervously.

'Could we meet this Frank?'

'Might not be easy. He's not that sociable, you know. In the old days they would have had to come to a theatre show but not now. Some aren't well in any case, they've had a lot of colds and bronchial troubles this winter. These boys get that sort of thing easily. The infirmary'll be the last part to close down!' He laughed, suddenly, rather oddly, and his eyes lit up briefly for the first time.

'But couldn't you ask him?'

'Well if I see him, of course, I'll try. He's not . . . you know, he's not very bright. You're not going to have a conversation with him, mind.'

'What did he do in the chapel?' It was the question Esther would have asked.

'Not a lot. You know . . . the chaplain had him there out of kindness because it gave him something to do.'

'What was the chaplain's name?'

But before Mr Sprayle could answer the question he turned sharply to Tom and in a quite different voice from the flat but pleasant one he had been using he said, 'Why don't you sit down, lad, you make us nervous standing up like that.'

Tom sat down meekly. His eyes had that same nervousness as the patient at the end of the room.

'I was asking what the chaplain's name was,' Helen tried again.

RENDEL, typed Esther. RENDEL.

For a moment, the briefest moment, Mr Sprayle paused and his body stiffened.

HAVE YOU HEARD OF RENDEL?

'Was there a patient called Rendel?' asked Helen, picking up the cue.

But it was not Mr Sprayle's response Esther noticed now but the other patient's across the room. His nervousness had been replaced by fear.

Mr Sprayle laughed, though a little too aggressively. 'Well now, you can't expect me to remember every patient, can you? Can you?' He leaned forward his eyes suddenly narrowed and his face a little flushed. Then he relaxed and smiled beatifically. 'I can't remember a Rendel, no, but that's not to say there wasn't one. Could have been. Maybe I've forgotten, maybe another part of the hospital.'

He's lying, thought Esther. He knows more than he's saying. We're close.

'What was the name of the chaplain?' The question hung between them, checkable. He could not lie on this one. Could he? But why should he want to lie anyway?

'That's an easy one. Reverend Eamonn Stanton,' said Mr Sprayle.

Helen paused. 'Not Father Freeman?'

Jack Sprayle paused again. 'Oh, yes. But that was a long time ago, years back. James Freeman.' Then, as an afterthought, he added, and it was gently done, cleverly done, 'He's still around you know, the "Father" as they called him. I can't go into why he was stopped from being official chaplain. Not right in front of . . .' he looked at Tom, and then said, 'Not in front of the lad. Don't want to dig up the past.' He said nothing, but he said everything . . .

'Oh,' said Helen rather troubled by this, 'I'm sorry, I . . .'

'Well, it's a long way from college projects, isn't it?' He laughed in a bullying way and then looked at his watch with studied impatience. 'Is that all then, because the play will soon be starting and we don't want to miss it, eh? Eh, lad?' Tom stared and said nothing.

'I wonder if it would be possible to go on a tour of the buildings before the play starts or afterwards?'

Mr Sprayle shook his head firmly. 'Just not on, I'm afraid. Too few staff on a day like this but anyway the staff don't go for tours much, never have. It's an infringement of the patients' privacy unless it's a properly instituted tour of course for medical or official purposes. I take it that's not it. Just curiosity?'

'Well . . .' began Helen, unable to say a yes or a no to this.

'No, it's not going to be on.'

'Could we see the chapel then?'

'As I say that's not so easy because it's closed most of the time.' He looked at his watch, his mouth pursing impatiently. 'If you want me to try and find Frank, and that may not be easy on an evening like this, then we'll have to stop there. The show will be starting in a few minutes. All right?'

He got up and showed them out.

'All right, Joey?' he called out to the patient who had been glancing at him.

Joey immediately got up, folded his arms across his stomach and said, 'Yes, Mr Sprayle. Yes, sir.'

Mr Sprayle nodded curtly and they went out into the corridor. 'A polite boy that, happiest that way. Like children, you see, they need to know where they are. That's the kindest way, not all this group discussion they do now. You show me they're any happier with group discussions! Don't know the time of day half of them.'

He led them into the hall, putting Tom and Esther together near the back. 'You sit there, lad, where you can help your friend,' he said to Tom, indicating an aisle seat. 'And don't you move now, don't want to lose you, do we? You come with me with the adults down here,' he said to Helen who, furious, looked back at Esther who in her turn managed an encouraging nod and a 'Yeh!' Divide and rule works both ways.

Having got Helen settled he quickly came back and sat down next to Esther, patting her knee in a way she did not like and saying, 'Just starting then!' His hand lingered rather too long and Esther could see Helen looking round nervously as the lights went down.

The audience was noisy but receptive. The able-bodied non-patients thought the references to television serials funny, while the patients chose to laugh at quite different things, mainly the wild dancing of the Pumpkin Men, the North-Eastern Arts Travelling Players' special creation. All united in a common sympathetic silence to the trials of Cinderella herself, untraditionally dressed though she was in punk gear.

There was an extended interval for orangeade, sandwiches and cakes. They were greeted briefly by Mr Vause who passed on by to talk with someone else. Mr Sprayle got up saying he would try to find Frank for them but it might be difficult in the crush . . . and Esther noticed that patient after patient looked at Mr Sprayle sideways, as if concerned he might see them, while others went up to him ingratiatingly and said a respectful hello; a few hugged him, and one might have been tempted to think he was the most loved man in the place.

But he never found Frank and they were not able to wander far in the crowds for he would not let them, keeping a beaming eye on them and introducing them to other patients who shook their hands and wasted their time.

Then the interval was over, a hush fell, there was a flurry for seats, and they found theirs were taken by other people and they had to squeeze right in at the back. Still Mr Sprayle did not desert them, squeezing in beside them by getting a patient next to Esther to move. 'Yes, Mr Sprayle. Yes, sir.'

Esther felt tired and dispirited. It was hopeless, unless Helen had found some clues, or met someone who might help. Esther had thought it significant that she had not joined them at the interval but stayed talking to some people. She would probably have more luck.

Now the pantomime seemed maddening and she felt hot and sick, as if the cold was coming back. Kate had said to take some more of the pills but she had forgotten to. She tried to concentrate on the action but it was hard, and seemed meaningless as loud, vulgar characters ran on and off the stage, laughing grotesquely, their shadows huge behind them, singing bad songs, silly songs: the spiky yellow hair of Cinderella was an obscenity; and the laughter of the audience loud about her, and she not of it or able to understand.

'Toh . . .'

'It's all right, Amh.' He hugged her, and sat close, but it didn't stop the loudness seeming to penetrate her. Oh, it was so terrible, the hopelessness, and she wanted to cry out back here where the audience was half listening, half talking, and she was surrounded by people, even Tom, laughing, ha ha ha ha ha *ha ha ha ha ha*, their laughter loud on her, maddening her and she not of it. *'Shut*

up!' A patient shouted to another whose laugh was so odd, so
loud, so terrible that again they shouted, 'Shut up, Eppie,' you
could kill from it. 'Shut up!' Ha ha ha ha ha ha ha ha ha ha ha
ha. 'Shut up . . .

. . . Eppie.'

She turned and saw him and knew it was him for certain. It was
Eppie who once shared a ward with Frank and Arthur and had a
laugh that made you want to kill him. Eppie of the stories. He was
a little man with glasses and his head was quick and nervous and
when he laughed there were no teeth and the blue green red of the
stage light caught his gums, ha ha ha ha ha ha ha, on and on, not
funny at all. The unfunniest laugh in all the world. It *was* Eppie,
she knew it.

'We may need Tom,' Helen had said and she was right.

'Toh!'

'Toh!'

'What, Amh?'

TELL HIM, TOM.

'Who, Amh? Who?' Tom's eyes wandered among the heads that
moved in the semi-darkness, laughing.

QUICK, TOM, NOW: TELL HIM ME.

'Me!' Her voice was a scream and Tom was half out of his seat
with upset.

'Who, Amh?'

She raised her left arm with a concentration of control he recognized as full of terrible effort. And he saw who she pointed at. A
small man, thin, with thinning hair. Sitting next to another man,
bigger; much bigger. Very big, scaredy big.

'What, Amh?'

But before she could think of what he might say he got up,
leaned through the seats and touched Eppie's head. Eppie turned
round and Tom pointed at Esther.

Eppie looked at her and she struggled to mouth words through
the noise and darkness. Eppie looked scared, saw Mr Sprayle sitting
next to her and then looked away.

Tom sat down again.

'No, Amh.'

TELL HIM ARTHUR, TOM.

Tom looked blank.

SAY FRANK.

Tom shook his head.

'After,' he said.

And then she cried out, *'Ehhpiahh Ehhp . . .'*

Eppie turned and looked at her and stared. Then he grinned and waved. Then he got out of his seat and came round to her. He was so small, and walked oddly, and his face seemed to have been squashed from either side. But his eyes laughed madly.

'Hello,' he said.

'You better sit down, Eppie,' a voice said at her side. Mr Sprayle. He had seen.

Eppie looked terrified and Esther knew that she had no time, for time after fifty years had almost run out.

She spoke to him as she spoke to Tom.

GET FRANK, EPPIE, GET HIM NOW PLEASE GET FRANK.

And he looked at her in that moment in the half darkness and his eyes were not laughing madly any more. He understood.

GET FRANK. CLEVER EPPIE.

Eppie looked at Mr Sprayle and said, 'Yes, sir,' and turned and sat down. Mr Sprayle patted Esther's thigh and letting his hand slide over Tom's neck he said, 'Don't you mind them, daft buggers some of them. And you stay in your seat now, boy.' Tom shrunk into his seat.

The play continued but Esther's eyes were on the back of Eppie's head, thinking, thinking. Her mind racing: that is Eppie, he knows Frank, he knows Arthur. The noise continued but now Esther did not hear it. Now, oh now was the time, now the right option must be found.

TOM, TELL MR SPRAYLE TO GET HELEN. TOM.

Tom got up and went over to Mr Sprayle. He pointed to Esther and then down the aisle towards where Helen was. He said the one word guaranteed to make Mr Sprayle leave them: 'Toilet. Amh wants to go.'

YES, TOH! YES. WELL DONE.

Mr Sprayle got up, nodding, and Esther noticed that he kept his hand firmly on Tom's shoulder and took him down the aisle as well so as not to leave them together out of his sight. Tom was Esther's mobility. And then Esther knew who Mr Sprayle was, and the world was silent in the long eternal seconds of that insight.

Eppie saw Mr Sprayle go, and he turned to his big companion and spoke to him. Ha ha ha ha, and then the laughter was gone and his friend turned and looked.

'EHHPIAHH!' Eppie. NOW NOW NOW NOW NOW NOW, Esther tried to shout.

But she had no need to: Eppie came back to her.

TAKE ME TO FRANK.

Out of the corner of her eye she could see Mr Sprayle leaning down and talking to Helen in the front. She would come immediately.

TAKE ME.

'What for?' said Eppie.

And Esther knew that whatever she said it had to be final, no argument.

She looked at him. His eyes laughed nervously. Frightened.

SKYAGREE, she said. I AM OF THE SKALLAGRIGG. I AM I AM. TAKE ME TO FRANK HE'LL KNOW WHAT TO DO. TAKE ME NOW NOW NOW NOW.

Eppie turned back to his seat.

'Eh mate, Ehey!!' The big man sitting next to Eppie got up and turned. Norman, that's Norman, thought Esther.

'Got brakes on?' asked clever Eppie.

'Yeh,' she said. He bent down beside her chair and quickly released them.

CUMMON, NORM, PUSH HER, NORM. AFTER ME, MATE. PUSH HER BEFORE DILKE COMES!

Yes yes it is Norman, Sprayle was Dilke, it is Eppie, and she was of it now, of the Skallagrigg stories, being pushed into them down the corridor, down past that notice 'No Admittance' into the maze and the labyrinth, helpless, that was how it had to be, helpless helpless, just pushed in the final stages of the quest for the Skallagrigg.

So it was that Eppie led them out of the hall and Norman lumbering and ungainly, his breath coming out in rasps, began to run Esther's chair down that long shiny corridor.

But even as they turned a corner at its bottom Esther heard a voice, a smooth voice, cruelty cloaked in velvet, come after them: 'Miss Marquand,' as ahead of them, nightmarishly, Eppie stopped, turned, gesticulated and cried, 'Cummon, cummon Norm, Dilke's coming.'

'Yeh, Skyagree,' shouted Esther, and the wheelchair gathered a careering speed and she could smell the institutional smell of Norman behind her as they turned a corner and Dilke's voice came after them again, louder and more angry, and other voices. But they were behind as ahead the corridors turned, the strip lighting changed to bare hanging bulbs and she was being rushed into a maze of shadows and darkness and feet were drumming after them on the floor behind.

On and on, turn right, turn left, on and on. 'Where are you, Miss Marquand?' and 'Amh! Amh!' That was Tom chasing after them as well.

'Don't know,' said Norman suddenly at a turn which brought them to some stairs that went up into darkness and descended into gloom. And he stopped dead, uncertain which way to go, the chasing voices and running feet behind them getting nearer. Eppie had disappeared.

Now now now now now, is the time, Norman, now Eppie, now now now now, as they ran for their old friends crying out with fear from the dilke of all dilkes. *Dilke is coming and he will punish us all,* and there was fear and evil in the air as Norman stopped by that stair, not knowing where to go and saying again, 'Don't know!'

GO UP, NORMAN THE STAIRS, GO UP NORMAN, Esther tried to order him. He did not understand.

'Miss Marquand . . .' the steps and the evil soft voice were nearer now, reaching forward to grasp them and Norman was weakening, not knowing where to turn, or what to do.

GO UP! But he stood still, uncertain.

It was from the stairs below that old Eppie reappeared saying, 'Here, Norm, down here, bring the Skalg here . . .' and Norman came to the front of her chair, leaned forward, and with one great movement picked it and her up, her head in his chest which smelt of soap, and his body screaming with effort for he was old now, though still big. And he carried her down down down into gloom.

Eppie was there.

'Good lad, Norman. Come on . . .' and the corridors seemed to divide, and turn, and split again past doors that had not been opened in decades, and filing cabinets, and a red fire hose with a brass spout.

'Stop here. *Stop* here.' Eppie laid a hand on Norman's great arm and made him lever Esther's chair into the shadow formed by a cupboard against the wall, and whispered, 'Ssh, Norm, sssshhhh. Stop here, matey. Nearly over now. I'll find Frank.' But before he left them he looked into Esther's face and said, 'You're Skalg?' and she thought it wisest to agree and he laughed silently as if that was the funniest, rummiest, oddest thing ever, *that* was.

Eppie went off into darkness as, above and around them, feet ran, down and up stairs they ran, but only looking . . . only looking over the edge, as Esther whispered: DON'T MOVE, NORMAN, JUST STAY JUST STAY, because his hands were shaking and sweating on the handles of her chair.

Steps came nearer from a different direction, creeping nearer, and Norman was shaking and sweating and groaning.

'OK, Norm, it's Eppie, just me. Sssshhhh, lad. Frank's waiting. Cummon, Norm, you done well. Eddie'll be pleased.'

Eddie? Esther said to herself. Eddie? But there was no time for thought as Norman wheeled her round, and pushed her forward again and Eppie went ahead quietly saying, 'Frank says to come. Frank's ready . . . Frank says be sharpish. *Cummon, Norm*!'

And slowly, as if there was no need to fear the echoes of the running feet and the evil whispers and cries of 'Missmarquand-marquandmarquand' and the gentler echoes that followed them of 'AmhAmhAmhAmh!' they turned another corner, came to some more stairs and Norman leaned down to pick her chair up again his chest in her face. And stopped.

'Can't, Eppie,' he said, so tired now. 'Can't.'

YES YOU CAN, said Esther, and he understood that, for she spoke with a powerful voice, like Eddie. HE GOT YOUR MUM HE GOT YOUR MUM, NOW YOU DO IT FOR THE SKALLAGRIGG, DO IT, NORMAN, DO IT.

Then Norman leaned down again, put his great hands on either side of her chair, and with a massive groaning heave picked up Esther and her chair and almost ran up the stairs. For a moment the world was a turning suffocating darkness as Esther felt the chair lift, and her face was lost in Norman's shirt and arm and she felt his muscles straining and his breath hot and groaning. And

then there was light and she was upright and safe and being
settled on the floor again as she heard Eppie announce in a loud
and proud voice, 'She said Skalg, Frank.'

Frank Caine stood in the centre of the corridor, staring at her,
utterly still. Tall, thin, with dark hair and soft eyes.

'Eddie's ill,' he said. 'You're to be quiet. Eddie's not well,'

ARTHUR, she said, desperate now for the running steps were
about them.

'Skalg for Eddie,' said Frank insistently. 'Eddie's waited, not
Arthur. OK, Norman, you push.'

Wondering, Esther was pushed down a corridor with a smell of
medicine about it. They were going to the infirmary. Eddie? The
name of Frank's friend was *Eddie*? Esther's mind raced to make
sense of it.

ARTHUR, she said.

'*No! no!*' shouted Frank, turning round suddenly. 'Eddie not
Arthur. Arthur's not now, was then. Once. Eddie . . .' and he
turned back to lead them on.

Once? The pattern of the stories was in Esther's mind turning
and turning like a chase through a maze and she trying to reach it
and make sense of it. Arthur once? EDDIE?

'*Yes!*' shouted Frank without turning round ahead of them.

Once meant before. Once before what? Arthur was before Eddie,
before the stories.

No not Eddie, the stories are about Arthur, Esther wanted to
scream, Arthur made the stories, he must have he *must* have, not
an Eddie. There is no Eddie, not really. Eddie made the stories
about Arthur; why? There was something in the pattern of all
those stories, something she had never quite understood.

Frank's friend was Eddie, Eddie was the spastic who made up a
boy called Arthur who grew as he did to be a man. The pattern
was almost complete.

Running steps turned a corner behind them. Dilke was there.

'Come on, Norman, quick,' called out Frank. They were approaching a wide ward door with glass in it.

'Right you boys, *stop right there.*' It was Dilke, she knew it was
Dilke now though his name was Sprayle.

'*I said stop.*' The voice was powerful as rock, cutting like ice.
Norman stopped, half turned the chair, and turned to face Dilke

and they stared into eyes that were red and angry, maddened eyes, and the eyes transfixed them and then travelled to the wall and the night-filled window that rose at their side; to the side of which, hanging from a hook, was a window stick. Its wooden body was thick and it was shiny with use.

'No,' whispered Norman as Dilke approached smiling on them his eyes filled with the anger of hatred and a madness that is evil. Tom stared out from behind him.

'Oh yes, Norman, because you've been a naughty boy, haven't you, doing wrong again, with Frank and Eppie.' And gently Dilke's hand reached up and took down the window stick and the other hand caressed it obscenely as the face smiled, the pink cheeks shone and Dilke raised the stick higher and higher and Norman next to Esther shook and whispered, 'No!' and Eppie said, 'Please no,' and Frank was silent, staring, one hand pushing open a door on a ward where all the beds but one were empty.

All was silent.

'Yes,' said Dilke cruelly, as he began to bring the window stick harshly down on big Norman. 'Yes, boy, yes . . .'

But even as he did so, Tom, thinking Dilke was about to strike his Esther, ran forward to shield her and the stick caught him with a vicious crack on the head and shoulder and he shuddered and staggered, but still his arms went out to protect her, and his glasses came off and shattered on the floor.

'*Get away, lad*,' said Dilke, his eyes terrible and his stick raised. MOVE, TOH!

'Mr Sprayle, stop that, stop it . . .' shouted Richard Vause who had come running, followed by Helen. 'Stop that now!'

But Dilke was back in a world of his own, the world he had once ruled, and his authority was being denied, and he had the window stick and would use it, for what else could the boys understand but that?

'Get *away*, lad,' he said again to Tom, who was one of them and must be disciplined.

'But that's Amh,' said Tom simply, as if speaking of a deity. And though blood was coming from a cut on the side of his head, and his face was pale with fear, yet even then he stood resolutely in front of Esther to defend her.

And they all saw it, what happened next. Dilke's smooth bland face contorted in rage, as hundreds of patients had seen it contort, his eyes red and his mouth stretching and his whole body spasming into anger as he brought that stick down hard, hard and *harder* on Tom: on his head, on his body, on his legs and Tom crumpled up, trying to hold on to Esther's chair to the last, before his grip gave way and he slid semi-conscious to the ground.

Helen Perry-Wilcox saw it. Mr Vause saw it. The nurse on the ward who had opened the door saw it. They saw the retired chief staff nurse against whom until then no evidence had ever stuck, beating a mongol boy with a window stick, his face covered with a rage that was a kind of madness.

But even as they shouted out Norman stepped forward, put his arms on Mr Sprayle and pushed him against the wall and then held him, powerless, the window stick falling from his grasp to the ground where Tom's broken glasses were.

Then, as other male nurses came running up and took control of Mr Sprayle and led him, still raging, away, Helen went on her knees to Tom, a nurse from the ward at her side. Esther stared down, her face white, but pride in her eyes that anyone could ever have such a friend.

Though he was badly cut and shaken, Tom was soon sitting up and his first words were for Esther: 'It's OK, Amh,' he said. But then, terribly, he began to shake and Esther cried out '*Me!*' that Helen might undo her straps and hold her so that she could put her arms to Tom. And there, slumped and crying, they stayed until more help came and Tom, able to stand again, was led away to where his cuts and bruises could be tended.

So it was some time before Frank was able to come forward, take Esther's chair, wheel it round and say simply, 'Eddie wants to see you now.' And where there had been commotion and violence before, now all was stillness as Frank was allowed to push Esther's chair quietly past the nurse into the silent ward, and down it past empty beds to one where a man lay propped up and staring at them, his eyes grey and kind, his face lined and his mouth wandering, his hands on the sheet in front of him, turned and crooked and calloused. And shaking beyond his control.

Frank pushed Esther to his side and they all saw the two of them look at each other for a long time before that old gentle man in bed began to smile and speak words that sounded like contortions and reach out his hands to try and touch her.

They saw Esther staring and then reach out in her turn, and touch him and smile, and speak words of greeting at last from the outside world.

But then when Frank said, 'This is Eddie,' they were surprised to hear Esther say a word softly, so soft it might almost have been the wind outside beyond the windows, beyond even the yellow-brick walls that surrounded the hospital, a wind from far far away in space and time: and the word was *'Nah!'*

'Yes, it's Eddie,' said Frank.

'Nah!!' said Esther with more power. THAT'S NOT EDDIE. HIS NAME CAN'T BE EDDIE.

'Yeh!' said Eddie suddenly.

'Eddie says yes he's Eddie!' said Frank.

NO NO NO NO NO NO, shouted Esther, her anger suddenly more powerful even than that they had seen from Mr Sprayle.

'NAH!!!' HIS NAME'S ARTHUR. *THIS* IS ARTHUR.

Eddie began to spasm, terribly, his face and his eyes and his mouth and his crooked legs and hands and he seemed to be fighting something that twisted his body and Frank said desperately, 'Not Arthur. That was once. Not now. Eddie now, he says Eddie now. He doesn't want Arthur now.'

HE'S ARTHUR, said Esther.

'Arhhueur!' she shouted at him, as if to make him hear what he did not wish to.

Then the man on the bed, whatever his name, turned and looked over towards the curtained windows of the ward as if beyond them he might find help to take him from the torment of two conflicting certainties: one called Frank whom he had known for so many decades and another called Esther Marquand whom he had never met until this moment. ·

'Arhheur,' she said again, simply, her confidence complete.

Then she turned and sought out Helen who had come a little way into the room and had indeed put a restraining hand on Richard Vause's arm, lest he try to break up this confrontation between Frank, Esther and ...

'Ehheurn . . .' said Esther. Helen. Then she struggled with a sentence again and again and again: 'As . . . khh . . . Ddd . . . ddd . . . khe.'

Helen came to her and said, 'I don't understand, my dear. I don't . . .' And they all waited as Esther tried again.

It was Frank who broke the impasse.

'She says, "Ask Dilke." That's what she says.'

Esther nodded.

'Mr Sprayle,' said Helen.

But it was not necessary. As if this evidence would be conclusive the old man in the bed – Eddie – turned his head to face them. His eyes were wild with a loss and grief that all there could see and feel. Esther spoke again and Frank said, 'She says his name's Arthur.'

'Is that your name?' asked Richard Vause, coming forward.

Arthur's head rolled in an agony terrible to see as he spoke a name he had not called his own for more than fifty years. His mouth turned and slewed and stumbled over that name, again and again, as Frank watched and listened in silence. Then finally Frank turned to them all and said what for both of them was the hardest thing they ever had to say.

'Eddie says his name is Arthur Edward Lane and he was born in 1920 and came here in 1927,' said Frank, and at the sound of it poor Arthur/Eddie's mouth opened again and he shouted out for the one person who could finally take him from that loss and that exile, 'Skyagree!' Then he helplessly reached for the curtained window as once, as a boy cast down into a cot, he had reached for a barred window.

As he shouted that name again and again and again he began to cry like a boy of seven and old Frank leaned down and took that boy Arthur in his arms and whispered over and over, 'Girl's come to find Skalg now, girl's come to find him. Skalg'll come now, Arthur. Long silence is over.'

Then as Arthur quietened, there came gradually into that ward a peace and a sense of love so palpable and potent that some there said afterwards that it was as if someone else had come into the ward.

While alone of them Esther Marquand knew it was not just 'someone else' who had come: that love, that presence that they sensed, *that* was the Skallagrigg.

'Skalg knows,' they heard Frank whisper finally, 'and girl'll find him.'

'Yeh!' agreed Esther. She would.

PART IV

SKALLAGRIGG

FIFTY-NINE

But promising to find the Skallagrigg was one thing, actually finding him, or even discovering who he or she was, proved more
difficult.

The one person who might immediately have told them did not,
it seemed, want to. Arthur Edward Lane – or Eddie Baker as the
hospital record had him – did not wish to talk and nothing Frank
Caine could say or do seemed to make him change his mind.

'Won't now,' said Frank. 'Wants silence always. Arthur says it's
best now.'

BUT BUT BUT BUT.

But nothing. Arthur would not talk about it.

Which left Richard Vause with a problem, since officially at least
there was nothing to find out: Eddie Baker was Eddie Baker, not
Arthur Lane. The records, as far back as they went, proved it. But
Mr Vause was not a man to follow rules in a blinkered way: if
there was a doubt, and there clearly was, it was right that the
matter should be investigated.

The second source of information, Jack Sprayle, was not talking
either, though for a rather different reason. His sudden act of
violence, witnessed by too many people to be ignored, made an
inquiry necessary, which meant solicitors and legal representation.
Richard Vause, like the North Central Regional Health Authority,
was anxious in the circumstances to avoid a public fuss – and so
was Helen Perry-Wilcox and, later, Richard Marquand, on behalf
of Tom and Esther. But in any case, Jack Sprayle was in no condition to talk, or to remember much. He appeared to be having a
nervous breakdown. He appeared, in fact, a little mad. Perhaps
completely mad.

There were two other possibilities to be pursued. One was the
records themselves – both in the hospital and in the County Record
Office. Helen Perry-Wilcox offered to do the research herself but

warned that it might take time: the pre-war hospital records were
a mess. Herstorne's 'archives', like those of so many institutions,
were simply several damp rooms in the basement where boxes,
files and cabinets of materials had been stored unsystematically
and left, literally, to rot. To find the records of an individual patient,
even assuming they existed, might, she explained, take weeks. As
for the County Record Office, this was more straightforward,
though not hopeful. The statutory recording of patient referrals,
admissions and releases was extremely limited and frequently
incomplete. Especially for so long ago. But Helen said she would
try.

The second possibility was an unknown quantity: the Reverend
James Freeman, former chaplain to Herstorne, now retired but
living in Herstorne's vicarage, but at present on retreat at a priory
outside Bristol and unavailable. Date of return uncertain but,
thought the Secretary to the Diocese, likely to be mid-February
when he had promised to cover for a local working priest at one or
two Sunday services in villages near Herstorne.

So Esther had to wait impatiently for developments, and hope
that something would emerge.

Meanwhile, Arthur was willing to talk about other things.
Indeed he was eager to do so, according to Frank, and so after
delays caused by bad weather and academic commitments, Esther
and Helen were able to visit Herstorne again at the beginning of
February.

Arthur's eyes lit up to see her, and the three of them – Frank,
Arthur and Esther – were allowed to stay alone in the ward and
'talk' if 'talk' is the right word for the odd signing, sounding,
touching conversation they had.

Esther was able to understand much of what Arthur said, usually
very quickly, but found it easier when Frank was there since at
times Arthur became so excited that he went into spasm and was
unable to communicate in any coherent way. Holding Frank's
hand, and with his old friend to soothe him, Arthur could settle
down again. But as they talked more, these incidents occurred less
frequently because for the first time in his life, it seemed, Arthur
was understood by someone as mentally able as he was.

He lay in bed in the ward, propped up with pillows, attended by
Frank, his face thin and wrinkled, and his hair cut hideously short

by Frank who had been taught by a hospital barber before the war. Arthur's eyes were a remarkable grey, and, like Esther's, intelligent, and they smiled at her, and looked with love on Frank; and on Norman and Eppie too, who came by sometimes in the relaxed way that was now possible under the enlightened regime of Mr Vause. But Arthur tired easily, and, when he chose to, would turn to gaze out of the infirmary's windows and not answer questions.

As for Frank, he was tall and thin, with his hair still dark. He wore pebble-thick glasses and rarely smiled. His life was Arthur and he would sit at his side seeming not to pay much attention as others spoke to his friend, yet making decisions on his behalf throughout the day, without, it seemed, any need for consultation.

'Lunch now, Arthur.'

'Weetime.'

'Get Staff for the medicine.'

'Arthur's tired . . .'

Even if Arthur was talking he would usually stop when Frank told him to, and lie back for sleep.

Sometimes the two men disagreed.

'Nah!' Arthur might say about his medicine: not yet.

'Got to now.'

'Ah!' concurred Arthur, Frank feeding him the medicine in a plastic teaspoon and wiping his mouth gently afterwards.

Frank was not inflexible. On the second morning of her second visit Esther came to the hospital from Lancaster at eleven o'clock and found Frank shaving Arthur, having put a bib round his chin and lathered his face with an old-fashioned brush. Arthur grinned at Esther, who watched Frank's slow and patient shaving of his friend, feeling she was privileged to share a private ritual. But why so late in the day?

'I said Arthur was to sleep and Staff said OK,' said Frank. 'All your talking!' Frank allowed himself a rare laugh, and showed his too-regular false teeth. He wore a dark jacket and tie, and looked like a former soldier fallen on hard times but still proud of his past and trying to keep up appearances. On his lapel was pinned a golden cross the Father had given him. After Arthur, it was the chapel Frank cared for most, and Esther learned that he was the only patient in the hospital with a key. The 'Father' – the Reverend James Freeman – was 'away thinking' said Frank, and until he got back Frank was not willing to show Esther and Helen the chapel. They respected his wish.

'I sweep it.' Frank told her. 'That's my job. And do the golden rails. And Arthur. I do him. Needs polishing he does!' After the chapel and Arthur there were Eppie and Norman for Frank to think about, though Esther rarely saw them on her visits. But the importance of these four men to each other was as obvious to Esther as it had become, over the years, to the hospital. She learned that it had been discouraged by Mr Sprayle for decades, and found its full expression only when he had recently left and other staff were able to move the four into one small villa by themselves, where they formed a close family unit.

'They are rather lost without Arthur,' explained Richard Vause, 'and now Frank has moved into the infirmary to be with him, the unit is split up. Let's hope it's only temporary.'

But Arthur had been ill since the previous autumn, at first with the bronchitis that recurred throughout his life, then with a viral infection which had weakened him and which he could not shake off. Since November he had lost weight and was weak, and the doctor felt it best for him to stay in the quieter and warmer infirmary ward.

The first few sessions Esther had with Arthur he listened more than he talked. Though he would say nothing about the Skallagrigg he was prepared to listen to the stories Esther had collected – Helen read some of them, and the tape made by May Adcock of Edinburgh was played.

One day he suddenly spoke at length to Frank and Frank went and talked to Eppie and Norman. Later Frank announced to Esther, 'Arthur's going to write a book and you're to do it. About what happened. Arthur says it's so there's good things not just the bad.'

'Yeh,' said Arthur, complete trust in Esther and her keyboard in his eyes. And then, without more ado, he started talking, and during the ensuing visits dictated his story to Esther and she wrote it down, never interrupting except when she needed Frank's interpretation, rarely questioning. Arthur told it his way, and in his order, and this was how it began:

I had my dreamgirl once and her name was Linnie. She was the sunshine to me and she made me a man. Before Linnie I was unhappy; after Linnie I knew my life was worth something. Many men never have a dreamgirl like I did. They have girls, maybe they have lots of girls but, if you ask me, they are not happy. There's only one girl for you in this life and I think it's luck if you find her. And when you do you better watch out because time can be short. That's why I always think I have an advantage over others: my condition made me learn to value time. Time does not return so use it right.

I was in my twenties and I had been in Herstorne a lot of years when I found Linnie, so I had had time to think about things and know what to do.

Linnie came because she was with child and her parents threw her out, which I think is a wrong thing to do. But in those days that was how it was. She was not the only one here for that. She was not all right in the head and she had no education, but her heart was strong and warm and she was lovely to see. She did not smile at everyone but she learned to smile at me. She knew I would do her no harm.

How did I meet her? One day, when I was in Back Court, I first saw her. She went past outside with another girl to the greenhouses we had then. She was in a floral dress and walked like she was proud. I could see she was with child, not much but enough. Eppie saw her and he laughed, and his laugh to me was like rudeness in the chapel. Norman shut him up and as Linnie walked by I thought: 'That's my dreamgirl, that's the one for me.'

When I next saw her, months had gone and the child been taken when she signed the paper they made her sign. Then she was lost too. The pride had gone from her. I thought, 'My dreamgirl needs me now. I will show her someone loves her.'

I knew Frank did not approve so I got Eppie to do my work for me. Eppie worked in the gardens sometimes. I told him to get flowers for Linnie like they did in romance and give them to her without laughing. His laugh would make the petals of a flower fall off! He argued as usual, but one day he did it so I could see, right by the window of Back Court. The dilkes didn't see but I did. Linnie held those flowers to her chest and looked the way Eppie pointed at the windows where the boys lived and she smiled. Eppie did that for her whenever he could so she knew she had an admirer. I thought, 'If she only knows that, it's enough to keep her content.' So that made

me happy. It was four years and thirty-six days after that that
I talked to her for the first time.

Arthur's head sank back into the pillow and his blue eyes smiled
with tears. Frank, holding his hand on the far side of the bed, was
expressionless. Then he said, 'Arthur's tired now. Go on later.'

But Esther did not want to stop. She took her chair nearer the
bed.

What happened to Linnie, Arthur?

I saw to it she got out. She should never have been here. I
arranged for her to leave for ever and told her she must not return.

How?

I used my brains and worked out a way. And Mr Sprayle never
once suspected!

But how did you do it?

You're too impatient by half. If I told you everything you'd have
nothing more to write down and then you'd never come back.
Frank wouldn't like that because he says your visits do me good.
Anyway, some things need time to tell. But now he wants . . .

Like the Skallagrigg?

I told you before, that's no more. That was once. Long ago.

How long?

You're worse than those interviewers on the telly.

Then Arthur's eyes weakened and he looked away. Frank
repeated, 'Arthur's tired now. He's to sleep.' And Frank pulled the
sheet up a bit, and took away a pillow, and gently moved Arthur's
arm under the sheet.

But Esther was not so sure that Arthur was tired, only that he
was trying to forget something that he lost a long long time ago
and which he could no longer face.

SIXTY

In March, when the weather showed signs at last of easing into spring, Esther and Helen heard that the Father had come back. But telephone calls for an appointment produced no reply, and when they went round to the vicarage one Saturday afternoon all they found was a collie dog wagging its tail at the back, and a pair of recently used black wellington boots on the kitchen step. They left a note for him asking him to call or leave a message.

They had heard a good deal about him from staff at the hospital and he seemed both lovable and eccentric. For example he had been known to stand for ten minutes, quite silent in the pulpit, after announcing the text for the day, declaring that, although he was meant to preach the gospel, he had come to the conclusion that he had, on that particular Sunday, nothing useful to say. Perhaps Christ or even God would fill the waiting silence in parishioners' hearts? His face on these occasions held an expression of cheerful optimism.

He tried a variety of schemes to raise money for the parish – keeping chickens was one of them, creating dog kennels in the vicarage garden was another. He was a great walker, a member of the Rambler's Association, and if there was a footpath to be defended, or to be walked annually to maintain a right of way, he walked it. And when the Bowland Way Footpath was established in the early seventies, it was the Father who made it possible, persuading three of the most difficult landowners to allow the Way across their land.

Yet, though he had many friends, he had a dark side.

'Troubled' was a word used of him more than once, 'troubled by doubt, troubled by the suffering of others'. It was generally known that he had been jilted in the forties, and never really recovered from it, living alone in the vicarage and resisting a succession of attempts to mother him and, later, marry him. A woman had come in for nearly thirty years to deal with washing and cleaning, but after she had died there had been no one else. Those who had been inside the vicarage reported that it was bare to the point of monasticism, the floorboards polished, the walls plain, everything simple. And clean.

The women of the parish, ever-observant, noted that when his trouser turn-ups and shirt cuffs grew frayed they were soon mended in a workmanlike way. Their vicar was an old bachelor, but one with love for others in his heart.

When he retired the diocese let him buy the vicarage, for it was old and uneconomic. And so he lived there alone, a healthy independent private man of nearly seventy; a man much loved and watched over by many in the parishes round about.

On their next visit to Herstorne Mr Vause told them that the Father had asked them especially to call on Sunday morning. There was a note waiting for them pinned to the vicarage gatepost: 'Sorry unexpected Morning Service at Bowcraile. Illness. Not returning till PM. Best to come there.'

So they did, driving the few miles across the moor to Bowcraile, and arriving at the little church a few minutes after the service had begun.

Helen eased open the ancient door quietly and pushed Esther forward past a red felt curtain hung from brass rings, into the gloom at the back of the nave. The church was large, but there were only nine in the congregation and none of them turned to look at them, for they arrived in the middle of a prayer.

Father Freeman knelt in profile to them, at the right of the chancel, leaning against the ornate structure of a dark oak chair whose carved back rose behind him. He was in a white surplice. and his head was propped up in prayer by arthritic hands. His hair was grizzled, and though he seemed small, even a little hunched, there was to his presence a sense of suffering power.

His voice was gentle and hesitant, each word, each sentence, spoken personally, almost conversationally, so that the congregation felt that they were eavesdropping on a conversation with God. For the Father's words were indubitably directed at a living Being of whom he was in awe and yet by whom he felt befriended. The sense of a troubled, searching man was increased by the fact that he paused sometimes for breath and to gather his strength to continue.

Helen knelt silently, her head bowed at first but then rising so that she might see where this extraordinary sense of strength came from: and Esther saw her stare at Father Freeman, and saw that she was herself troubled, and saw her fingers interlock tightly, and her head bend again and her lips move in prayer. Esther had never known Helen pray before and she remembered something she told her on their first trip north together: 'I am a believer, he was not.'

When the collect was over, Father Freeman read the epistle for the third Sunday in Lent. He read it as if he was thinking through the meaning of each sentence and wished his congregation to do so too, and before its end he paused, and looked up at them, and around at the old church, and at the lancet windows where soon the summer sun would come slanting in: '. . . wherefore he saith, Awake thou that sleepest and arise from the dead, and Christ shall give thee light.'

When that was done he paused for a long moment, his head a little on one side and his eyes half smiling upon them and whispered this addition to the holy scripture: 'Yes.'

The Gospel that followed, like the epistle from the St James' version of the Bible, was spoken in the old-fashioned language of Beelzebub, of paps being sucked, of the casting out of devils and of unclean spirits, and Esther did not seem really to hear it. Nor remember quite when he moved on into a brief sermon which was intensely personal, as if he was speaking to them individually or perhaps simply to himself. He spoke of the retreat he had been on and the peace he felt to be back among his own, and of a March Sunday years before when the sun had shone warmly. The bad weather was dragging on this year and they might feel that winters never stop. But they do, he said, oh yes they do, and we must be ready to greet the spring with joy.

He gave them Communion slowly, gazing at each one of them with eyes that had felt pain, and Helen noticed that the hands which held the chalice before Esther, and then herself, were gnarled and bent. Each time he spoke the ancient words he did so with meaning: 'The Body of our Lord Jesus Christ . . . the Blood of our Lord Jesus Christ.' There was about everything he did a gentle grace, the more moving because of his age and the discomforts which he bore with patience. And when, finally, he cleansed the vessels, Helen, who had never felt anything like this before, had an urge to go to him and whisper, 'You are not alone. I'm here. We're all here.' She felt so embarrassed at this sudden surge of warmth for someone she did not know that she looked down at her dress, smoothed it nervously, turned to Esther and quite unnecessarily adjusted one of her straps.

When the service was over, and the last of the old ladies of the congregation had had their hands shaken, he turned at once to where they waited, shook Helen's hand and then took up Esther's and said simply, 'I have been looking forward to meeting you. Frank Caine has told me about you both. You're the "lady with the grey hair" and you,' he looked down at Esther and then sat in a pew to be on her level, 'are "Girl helping Arthur write a book". I quote.' He laughed suddenly like a child and smoothed his cassock.

'How can I help?' He looked at them each in turn and Esther smiled but Helen looked away, oddly troubled, suddenly nervous. But she recovered herself quickly and explained the background. James Freeman nodded, said Richard Vause had explained much, and that none of it really surprised him.

'Esther believes that the Skallagrigg, whoever that is, is still alive. We would like to know what you know of him. It has proved hard finding anything out from the records though I am doing my best. Arthur himself . . .'

'Arthur?' began James Freeman. 'Sorry, I've known him as Eddie for so long.' He smiled again. 'What's in a name? In this case, I suspect, quite a lot.'

He leaned forward and said seriously, 'The heart of the matter is that the idea of the Skallagrigg is what has kept Arthur Lane alias Eddie Baker alive for over sixty years. A thing more powerful than faith in God. I know only that it is love. He loves and was loved by the Skallagrigg. You know that Frank is a Christian and Eddie is not?' They nodded.

'You know that Frank does not pray unless his hands are holding Arthur's chair? I believe he cannot pray without that. In fifty years of being a priest I have never known such loyal and trusting love as exists between those two men. But the most remarkable thing is this: Eddie's love for the Skallagrigg is greater even than that. It is greater than . . .' and he paused and turned to stare down the length of the church to where the cross stood on the altar, a little bent and scratched with time. And he fell into a long silence.

Afterwards Helen said she knew as if he had spoken the words aloud that what he meant was that the depth of Arthur's love for the Skallagrigg was a standard by which he judged his own love of God, and found himself wanting.

'Who is the Skallagrigg?' asked Helen quietly.

'I cannot presume to say, I really cannot. You must understand that the help I can give you is limited. Arthur is my parishioner even though he does not believe and has told me so many times!' He laughed briefly and rather nervously. 'I have ideas. Not important probably. What matters is that Arthur seems to want to be silent about it now. He wants it finished with. So I cannot speak without his permission and in his presence. But . . .'

He stood up and wandered away from them down the aisle of the church towards the altar and then came back.

'But that's all nonsense, you know, and of course Arthur must be helped to find his Skallagrigg.' He stared at them and scratched his cheek and said, 'Mmm,' to himself. 'He is a man with more courage than anyone I have ever known and yet in this one thing he is afraid. But is that so surprising? You hold on to a dream for half a century and it keeps you going and then you are asked to face its truth. Can *you* say you would easily or lightly do so? I know I would not.

'It's obvious that the Skallagrigg is someone he knew before he was sent to Herstorne. A family friend, a doctor, a relative, perhaps a nanny. Someone who he loved and who loved him. Now I understand that on the evening you "discovered" him something happened after he agreed that he was Arthur? Can you describe it?'

Helen and Esther looked at each other.

THE CHANGE, typed Esther. THE FEELING SOMEONE WAS THERE.

'Yes,' said Helen, for they had talked about it, and she described how the ward had seemed filled suddenly with love. 'It was most . . . striking,' said Helen. 'And moving.'

I BELIEVE IT WAS THE SKALLAGRIGG, typed Esther.

James Freeman nodded and said, 'Yes, so do I.' Then he said, 'There was an occasion many years ago, during the war, when something similar happened. It was 1942. October. The 18th.' He laughed again, delightfully. 'Just after 4 p.m. You can see it made an impression on me!

'Well, what happened is simply told. I was in chapel and Eppie came running. It was Arthur and he was ill. Then Frank came in terrible distress. Arthur was being seen by the doctor and they were to take him to the infirmary but Arthur wanted me, not the doctor. So naturally I hurried along to the ward and found they were indeed taking him away. He was pale, in appalling distress, but Frank could understand what he was saying. "Arthur says chapel, Arthur says chapel," and I had the sense as never before in my career that a profound spiritual support was needed. It is hard to describe. Jack Sprayle was in charge and being very officious. He told me to leave it to them but at such times one can be very strong. Well . . . we got him into a wheelchair and took him to the chapel with Frank.

'I took him down by the altar steps and sat with him and what happened over the next few hours was extraordinary. I can only say that Arthur became someone else. I mean, he was suffering for someone else like a shield taking blows and we sat with him and watched and there was nothing we could do but be there. He kept looking at the cross on the altar and at the windows above which have stained glass panels of the apostles. And gradually into that chapel there came the sound of war. I know this sounds extraordinary but it was so. And Arthur was suffering it and calling out that name again and again and again, "Skyagree", which I had never heard before.

'"It's Skalg," Frank kept saying, "he's with Skalg, he's there, he's with Skalg." And I had the feeling that right next to me a struggle for life was taking place and that this extraordinary handicapped man was fighting it alone for someone else. I know I prayed. I think Frank did. But the main thing was that we were there, so that he knew he was not alone. He kept talking, in a way that even Frank could not understand. Then the war-- sounds faded and there was the feeling of union and love and safety; then safety and relief. And then Arthur spoke, in his normal way, words of such endearment that they were like music. It was the voice of love. This went on for a time and then there was a sweet sadness in the chapel and I knew that he was saying goodbye and coming back to where we were, where he had to be.

'I have often thought about that experience, though never talked of it except once to my advisor who was not very helpful. It seems to me most likely that the Skallagrigg, whoever he is, and I think it is a he, was for some reason near death, and that Arthur was in some way able to give him the strength to survive. Should you ever find him ask what happened to him in the afternoon of October 18th, 1942.'

Silence descended on the little church.

'There are other things, but I do not feel free to talk about them. One day perhaps. They are private to Arthur.'

W H A T? Esther naturally wanted to know.

'Nothing that will affect you finding the Skallagrigg, I assure you.'

'Well, we are trying to trace the family but it is very difficult with no clues whatsoever,' said Helen.

I W A N T T O P U T A N A D V E R T I S E M E N T I N T H E P A P E R S, declared Esther.

'Yes, I must confess it does seem the kind of occasion when something more immediately practical than a prayer might be useful,' said James Freeman with a chuckle.

Helen laughed, rather girlishly. And Esther realized with an astonished jolt that Helen (as she put it later in her account for Daniel Schuster) 'was actually beginning to *fancy* the Father. I couldn't believe it, but it was *obvious*. I thought it was brilliant of God to think that one up!'

Certainly all that day afterwards Helen Perry-Wilcox was quiet, even rather bad-tempered. And as soon as Esther was settled with Arthur and Frank in the infirmary for another dictation session after lunch she disappeared, saying she had work to do in the basement of the hospital.

'Someone's got to do it!' she said shortly, as if she had drawn the short straw, and had to get on with the job.

Esther watched her go and then turned to Arthur, her right hand ready at her keyboard.

I want to say something now about Linnie and how she came to leave. That was the hardest decision of my life and

the best. When I think about it I see that everything that went
before – all the bad things like Dilke and Rendel, and all the
good things like Frank and the Father and Norman and our
chum Eppie, and all the things I thought and came to see –
all that came together to give me the strength to make it
possible for her to leave.

I knew I could not leave myself. I'm always going to need
help and maybe this is the best place for me with Frank and
the others. But not Linnie. I knew I had to be her courage for
her. I knew I had to be her arms and legs to go free. I knew I
had to show her what lies over the yellow-brick wall. And I
knew I had to give her a reason which was stronger than her
love for me. I thought these thoughts slowly, only after we
were wed and she made me a man down in the glen. Many's
the time after she left that I cried in my cot and my chair for
her. But then I remember it was best she had left.

I got the idea from something that happened. There was a
girl called Wim who Dilke had for two years. One day Eppie
heard from one of the girls that Wim was with child by Dilke.
We knew what that meant or thought we did! You can't have
girls in a hospital having babies. It's just not on. So it never
happened because the doctor took them to the infirmary and
ended it, no questions asked. It happened a good few times
over the years. Sex will always be and so will babies. Wim
didn't say a thing for weeks and that baby grew. Then she
spoke up and said Dilke was the father and guess what? She
was out of here before you could say jack-knife. I said to
myself, 'That's strange, the other girls have abortions but
when Dilke's involved the girl gets sent out. Dilke's got a
weak spot after all!' Later I heard she went to a home in
Manchester. Later still the Father told us she was not coming
back. She was allowed to keep her child. So I had my idea,
helped by Linnie who never forgot that the baby she had,
had been taken from her after she signed a paper.

One day Linnie said she was with child. That was my child.
And I was happy and sad at once because I knew now I had
to get Linnie out, and to do the thinking for her. I said,
'Linnie, if you do what I tell you that child will grow to be a
man or woman we can be proud of. If not that child will
never know life and will be taken from you in the infirmary.'

She said, 'Arthur, you tell me.'

'Number one,' says I, 'you tell no one, not a single living
soul.'

'No, Arthur,' says she. And she never did. The weeks went past. I knew the longer our secret was kept the better. One day she is out with me and says, 'The girls know but I didn't tell them. They can see now. Look.' And she takes my hand and puts it on her tummy where our child was. Then I knew that my Linnie and I had no more time left. I said, 'Stop the chair!' and she did and she knelt down by me. There was others about so she pretended to adjust my straps. 'Linnie,' says I, 'you must do what I tell you even if it's hard. You are my dreamgirl and have made me a man. Now my time to help you has come but you must listen.' I looked at her beautiful face and I thought, I must remember this for always. Then I thought, she is in my heart for ever already, I will not forget. Then I said, 'Linnie, if you say you're with child by me they will take you to the infirmary and take it out of your body. But if you say you are with child by Dilke they will send you away and you will have that child. So that's what you must say.

'Linnie listen. When that child is born he's ours and you're to protect him for ever. You never sign paper ever ever ever. Not ever. You say, "He's my child and I'll keep him." If you sign paper it will be like killing him. So your man says you must never ever do it.'

'Yes, Arthur.'

'They will tell lies to make you sign but your man never tells no lies. He says you must never sign.'

'Yes, Arthur.'

'One day that child in you will ask about me. Now listen, Linnie. It won't do any good knowing what I am or where I am. It's not fair him knowing that I'm this . . . So you never tell him. Except say that I did my best when I could, and that I was lucky to find my dreamgirl.'

'I want a boy for you, Arthur.'

'One day, if you can, you write and say it was all right. I would like to know. I will die content knowing that. You write to the Father and he'll tell me. And if you could come and show me my child I would be happy for ever. I would know I did one thing right in my life.'

'Arthur. You're the best there ever was. When we were wed by Frank I promised you a gold ring for the sun to shine on.'

'Now it will never be, Linnie, but we have something better.'

'It would have been good.'

'We got to say goodbye, Linnie, and my heart is dying.'

'You said one day the Skallagrigg will come.'

'One day he will.'

'Frank will look after you till then.'

'Yes.'

She got up from kneeling and pushed my chair under the trees of the glen and I said, 'Look!' but had no need to. She had learnt how to see those trees and the leaves that come back green each and every year.

When the walk was done my Linnie took me back in and that was the end of it. She went and told them and must have done what I told her to all right. Two days later she was gone to Manchester and the Dilke was hopping mad and I heard nothing more for five years except what the Father heard, which was enough. Linnie had a boy and she was free. I was proud to have helped make life.

So that's the true story of how I used my brains to get Linnie out of here. I hope Linnie was happy, and my boy too. I would have liked to see him as a man, but that will never be. Today he would be in his thirties. I hope he's loving like his mum and has brains like his dad. But if it has to be just one of them, I hope it's loving. That's the best thing for a growing boy; love.

When he was 'talking' Arthur's face was animated, and his hands moved jerkily on the sheet and over Frank's hand as Frank spoke in his turn, interpreting the noises his friend made. Arthur's clear eyes smiled on Esther, and watched her right hand as it took down his story. She smiled, too, for she noticed that he persisted in remembering it all as if he had been called Arthur, though surely in real life Linnie would have known him as Eddie. Perhaps, after all, he had revealed his true name to Linnie. Perhaps, he just chose to remember it that way. She started to ask him but gave up the attempt because he seemed so tired.

Indeed at times he would let his head fall back on the pillow and Frank would say, 'Arthur says, hope you're getting it all down. He's not got strength to remember again. Hope so.' He was reliving the past to be rid of it; he was passing on what he had seen and learnt as if he sensed his time was done. And when he had had enough he would let his head roll to the right and, looking past

Esther, stare out of the long infirmary windows to the leafless trees dark and silent in the glen.

But there was dread in Esther. For as Arthur got near the end of his story he seemed to grow weaker and she was beginning to suspect that the will to live had somehow left him, and that, as Frank had long feared, his silence to the Skallagrigg would be the ending of him.

SIXTY-ONE

It was the end of April and the pink and white spring blossoms in the front gardens of the great Victorian houses in Woodstock Road were beginning to open.

Tom had come to stay, summoned by Helen from London, because Esther's work on Arthur's book was over and she seemed a little down. He had taken her for a walk in the sun, into St Edward's School grounds, and walked her in familiar silence, staring at frog-spawn in the drainage ditches by the canal. He eyed the cantilever bridge suspiciously.

'Amh, I don't like work,' he said. 'Not much. When's Richard coming home?'

Richard and Kate were in Australia again, as they had been several times these past months, setting up ComputaBase's Singapore-based operation.

Their absence was, by tacit mutual consent, for the best: out of sight was out of mind. Despite her New Year resolution Esther found it easier not to think of her father and Kate together.

As for Richard, the world beyond Esther was opening up, and each trip to the Far East brought release.

Of them all perhaps only Kate saw the coming confrontation, and dreaded it, for she feared that, when it came, Richard's guilt and Esther's personality would make it impossible for Richard to make the break. A fear compounded by her own sense of guilt at coming between father and daughter, and her knowledge that, finally, she would not keep them apart. Yet to her personally Esther was now sweetness itself, writing the occasional letter and keeping her informed of progress on the Skallagrigg. But in these letters there was never any mention of Richard, and Kate was the first to see – perhaps even before Esther herself – that Esther's strategy was moving towards silence, the kind of silence that Arthur had imposed upon the Skallagrigg so fatally over the last few years.

In recent weeks Helen had been up to Herstorne alone, since there was little Esther herself could do. The ostensible reason was to continue research through the Herstorne archives – a slow painstaking business in damp basement rooms – but Esther was aware there might now be more to it than that.

Before the last but one trip Helen had gone to a cupboard and found, deep in its recesses, a pair of old-fashioned walking shoes. She had polished them up and confessed, a little bashfully, that James Freeman had asked if she might like to join him for a walk on the moors.

GO FOR IT!!!!! Esther told Helen.

'And what does that mean?' asked Helen.

HE OBVIOUSLY FANCIES YOU.

'Don't be so ridiculous, Esther. We're old-age pensioners.'

DOESN'T STOP YOU BEING PASSIONATE PENSIONERS!

'It's just a pleasant friendship,' Helen protested. 'James probably likes to go walking with someone else. I expect he goes with lots of people. Why, together we're aged nearly a hundred and forty so there's certainly not going to be any hanky-panky.'

Esther laughed outright at this.

DO YOU WANT SOME ADVICE?

'Not especially, young lady. But I expect you'll give it just the same.'

HERE IT IS THEN: DON'T LET HIM KISS YOU ON THE FIRST DATE!!!!

'Esther! And anyway, as a matter of fact, I'm not so sure I agree,' said Helen with a twinkle in her eye.

Their relationship was one of real friendship and deep affection. Getting to know Esther and having her to live with her had made Helen younger and much happier. She liked the contact another human being brought her. As for the effort of looking after Esther, it was barely effort at all, so well provided were they with a team of helpers organized and paid for by Richard. Her recent trips were possible because the helpers took over, caring for Esther full-time. They were both lucky, and they knew it.

Esther's future was now well-planned. She had gained a place at an Oxford college to read mathematics, starting in the coming October. For the summer vacation, after she had taken the examinations in computer science, she accepted an invitation from

Annette Roskill of Laydale Hospital to go and stay there and report on how computer technology might be applied to individual patient needs. She had not wanted to go especially, but it was a real job for a real wage, and Annette had been persuasive. Soon, too, Arthur and his three friends would have moved out of Herstorne into a new villa provided for them at Laydale, and perhaps there were more things Esther could do for Arthur, for whom she had developed both respect and affection.

By then too, surely, they would have found out the truth of the Skallagrigg and the story of Arthur would have been resolved.

Yet Esther, like Tom, was discontented. There were uncertainties, and she felt uneasy: about Tom who looked pale, about the coming three years at Oxford, about herself. Walking with Tom was nice, but she looked at the pink blossom on the trees and wished, sometimes, that she had something more to look forward to than work, and research, and being clever.

The correspondence with Daniel Schuster had reached a plateau of easy flirtation, of silly dreams, and she knew it would have to be stopped, promising herself that in the next letter she would tell the truth. But to have a dialogue with just one man was light, and fun, and brought her so much pleasure that she had not the courage to end it. When June comes . . . when the summer vacation starts . . . in September. No! When he says for sure he's coming over, *then* I'll tell him.

The new term started at the College of Science and she got on with her work steadily. She was not worried by the examinations because the final result was on the continuous assessment of work and she had got alphas throughout the course. Now that the search for Arthur was over, and the little book he had dictated finished,* she was spending more time on completing the 'Dunroune' game for which Daniel was doing some graphics. His letters usually came with packages of his software and floppy disks, for now they used the same computer to make their work compatible. Esther Marquand's world was her computer room in Helen's house, the trips to the college, walks with helpers or Tom, and evenings with Helen, when Helen was not gallivanting off to Herstorne to meet her new beau.

*

* This was eventually published by MENCAP (London), 1993.

In mid-May Helen came back from her latest trip with anything but a light heart. Arthur was weaker and the hospital staff were worried about him. Somehow, since dictating his life to Esther he seemed to have lost some vital spark. It was as though the book was a tying of loose ends, and, that done, he had nothing left to live for.

Three days after her return James Freeman sent a card to Helen. It read: 'Arthur grows weaker and we are worried for him. He says little now and Frank never leaves his side. I asked if he wanted me to try to contact Linnie but he shook his head and Frank said no.'

Esther read this with despair and surprise.

DOES HE KNOW WHERE LINNIE IS?

'I think he did when she first left Herstorne. He has lost touch with her but feels sure he could track her or her son down. But he's very conscious of Arthur's wish not to be in touch and respects it.'

IS THERE ANYTHING MORE WE CAN DO? IT SEEMS RIDICU-LOUS THAT WE CAN'T TRACE ANY MEMBER OF ARTHUR'S FAMILY.

'It would be simple if he would talk about it, but whenever anyone raises it with him he says no.'

I DON'T BELIEVE HE MEANS IT.

'Well, that's what he says.'

I STILL THINK A NEWSPAPER ADVERT IS BEST. PUT HIS NAME IN BIG LETTERS AND ASK FOR PEOPLE TO CONTACT A TELE-PHONE NUMBER WITH INFORMATION.

'Which paper my dear?'

A NATIONAL PAPER.

'It's very expensive and probably a complete waste of money. "Lane" is a common name.'

IT'S BETTER THAN DOING NOTHING.

'We're not doing nothing. I have been sitting in that dreadful basement weekend after weekend getting nowhere. But I'm sure there'll be something there. Perhaps I'll go up again this week if you don't mind being left alone.'

But in the event Esther dropped her studies and they both went, since, a few hours after this conversation, James Freeman called and said that Arthur had got even weaker.

They left the following morning, drawn by some instinct neither understood. They had both become embroiled in a drama on to whose stage they had long ago walked and whose final act they sensed was now coming.

They found Arthur in a smaller ward with just four beds in it. His bed was unscreened – Frank had said he did not like being closed in. The staff had wanted to move him to Grisedale General Hospital but he had not wanted to go, and no one could say that the care given him there could be any better. It was not as if there was anything physically wrong with him, except a general weakness and lack of will to live.

He was pale and his face seemed thin and gaunt, still with the constant movement of the extreme athetoid. He had the appearance of a man under extreme stress and his eyes were troubled.

When Esther came in with Richard Vause and Helen he turned and stared at her, opening his mouth weakly but saying nothing. His lips jerked this way and that, but his eyes smiled a little. Frank sat on the other side of the bed holding his hand.

Esther did not know what to say or do, and was scared. There was about Arthur no peace now, but rather a sense of loss and grief. His eyes seemed frightened. Somewhere down a corridor a man shouted and another laughed. Life beyond that room went on. There was a high window, arched and old, and though the room was brightly painted and there were poster pictures of wildflowers on the wall, nothing could disguise the fact of what the room had once been like. High arched windows, barred, no sunlight, cold bleak walls.

He stared now at the windows above and his lips moved, sometimes in spasm, sometimes in some semblance of speech.

Eventually Esther typed up, CAN YOU LEAVE ME ALONE WITH JUST ARTHUR AND FRANK? Helen, Richard Vause and the staff nurse retreated.

There was a long silence, but for Arthur's jerky breathing, before Frank suddenly said, 'Skalg's got to come now.'

'Nah,' whispered Arthur, and then much more softly, with gentleness in his eyes for Frank, 'Nah.'

'Got to,' said Frank. 'Father's said prayers for him. Christ Jesus will send him for you.'

'Nah,' whispered Arthur.

'Got to,' said Frank again, his voice screwing into a whine as he began to cry. 'Must now. Silence must end.'

DO YOU WANT THE SKALLAGRIGG TO COME? asked Esther in her way. YOU DID BEFORE . . .

'Skyagree koh?' she said.

Arthur's eyes turned from the high window to her.

He struggled to say 'No' but could not manage it.

'Will come now,' said Frank. Arthur's eyes turned to Frank.

WHO IS THE SKALLAGRIGG? asked Esther.

Arthur's mouth opened and he struggled to find a way of stopping their questions, his free hand restless.

'Skalg's to come now,' said Frank firmly. 'Time now. Long time over.' There were decades of waiting in his voice.

As Arthur tried to look towards him Esther said again, WHO IS THE SKALLAGRIGG? I MUST KNOW SO I CAN GET HIM WHO . . .

Arthur's eyes turned up towards the window. The sky was dimming to a lovely mellow evening.

'Got to now,' said Frank. 'Arthur knows Skalg's to come.'

And Esther could sense the terrible struggle in Arthur, the desperate fight against what she and Frank both wanted. Then as she began to ask yet again he moaned a curious cry of despair and reached up one hand towards the window as he had done long before and they heard him whisper 'Skyagree . . . Sky . . .' and his mouth weakened into tears which rolled down his cheeks. Frank held his hand and Esther whispered, DO YOU WANT HIM TO COME AND TAKE YOU HOME, DO YOU WANT . . .

For a long time he just stared, tears on his face, staring back to what he had lost. Then, with a final sigh of despair Arthur Edward Lane found he could fight them no more. So he nodded as best he could and whispered, 'Yeh.'

Then again, more loudly, *'Yeh, yeh, Skyagree, me.'*

'Tell Skalg to come, say to come,' said Frank.

'Yeh,' said Arthur, grinning suddenly. Ruefully. *'Yeh!'*

Esther brought her chair even nearer to him.

WHO IS HE, ARTHUR?

'Ess says who Skalg is,' said Frank.

Arthur was silent and Esther knew she must drag it out of him.

IS HE YOUR FATHER?

Arthur was still and silent and Esther was unsure if he understood, but she pressed on.

IS SKALLAGRIGG YOUR MOTHER? NOT A MAN?

Arthur somehow pulled his hand from Frank's as if he needed to be separate to tell them who the Skallagrigg was.

IS SKALLAGRIGG A FRIEND?

Arthur whispered very softly and Esther did not understand. He said it again for Frank: 'Arthur says more than a friend.'

IS SKALLAGRIGG YOUR NANNY? YOUR DOCTOR? YOUR SISTER? YOUR BROTHER?

And suddenly Arthur's face and mouth were quite still.

YOUR BROTHER?

Arthur barely moved his mouth, but then his head swung round to Frank and he strained and said a word or two.

'Arthur says he's more than a brother,' said Frank.

Esther spoke again: IS HE ALIVE?

There was a long silence.

'Ooh yeh,' said Arthur with complete certainty.

WHERE SHALL WE FIND HIM?

But Arthur did not know that.

YOU MUST HELP US, ARTHUR. WHAT IS HIS NAME?

His eyes fixed on her and then travelled to the window and suddenly Frank leaned towards him, gripping his hand again. Arthur was weeping and his mouth was wet.

'Me,' he said. 'Me, *me, me.*'

Frank looked up, straightened his back, and he said, 'Arthur says his name's Arthur. That's the Skalg's.'

Esther looked at him. 'The same?' she said, puzzled.

'Me,' said Arthur again. Then he lay back and nodded, the strength gone from his face and a curious peace settling there as if, after so long, the problem of finding the Skallagrigg was someone else's.

But all Esther could do was stare at him, at his tired blue eyes and his short grey-white hair, and the lines in his face, and say to herself, 'More than a brother, more than a brother, more than a brother.'

'Arthur's to sleep now,' said Frank. 'Arthur's tired. Skalg's to come for Arthur soon now.'

But Esther tried one last question.

WHEN WERE YOU BORN, ARTHUR? WHEN?

For a long time he lay silent and staring. When were you born?
Something in the question had stilled him and Esther knew she
was near a truth he had tried to escape from but never could, not
even by surrounding himself with the deepest silence.

WHEN?

And then . . .

WHERE WERE YOU BORN?

Again something stilled in him and he turned and looked at
her and spoke so softly that she could make nothing of it at all.
Frank leaned a little closer and Arthur spoke again to him. Then
once more, until Frank said slowly and clearly, 'August the thirty,
nineteen-twenty.'

30 August 1920, Esther typed on her screen.

Arthur looked at it and eventually said, 'Yeh.'

Then his eyes drooped but he carried on talking, as if to himself,
his hand tightening on Frank's as he said words so whispered and
slurred that Frank leaned right over him saying, 'Again, again.'
Whatever it was Arthur wanted it said and he spoke on until at
last Frank straightened up and looked over to Esther.

'Arthur says he was first, Skalg after. Arthur first. Best boy.
Oldest. Skalg was second. August thirty, nineteen- . . .'

Then all was still in Esther's mind and she knew the long search
for the pattern to the Skallagrigg was over and that Arthur spoke
truly when he said the Skallagrigg was more than a brother: of
course, he was more, much more.

'Skyagree me. *Me* Skyagree,' whispered Arthur.

And Esther Marquand understood at last: the Skallagrigg was
Arthur's twin.

And Arthur saw that Esther knew, and he was pleased.

WAS HE . . .? she asked, waving a slow hand over her body, and
Arthur's. Was he spastic?

'*Nah!!!!*' shouted Arthur. Adding, 'Ooh nah!' with love and pride
in his voice.

Frank could only look troubled and whisper, 'Skalg must come
soon. Arthur wants him now.'

With a date to work on Helen Perry-Wilcox knew exactly what to
do. The Register of Births, Deaths and Marriages was in London

and she wished to leave at once so she could be there first thing in the morning. But finally she agreed to go on an early train, so long as Esther could be looked after at Herstorne.

WHAT HAPPENS IF YOU FIND A BIRTH CERTIFICATE?

'I'll have a name, and with a name I can trace a marriage. And with a marriage I can trace an address.'

MAYBE HE'S A BACHELOR.

But Helen would not listen to doubts. She could no longer sit still and watch an old man die apart from his family.

'It's a chance worth taking.'

ASK DADDY TO PUT AN AD IN THE PAPERS. HE CAN GIVE THIS NUMBER TO RING.

'Really, Esther.'

GOT A BETTER IDEA?

'There's the Salvation Army, they trace people; or the police . . .'

TAKES AGES I BET. I DON'T MIND PAYING FOR AN AD FROM MY MONEY.

Helen sighed. 'I'll call your father then, but . . .'

IT'S WORTH A TRY.

'We'll try it if my approach fails. We'll know by tomorrow evening anyway.'

By noon the following day Helen phoned Herstorne with some news. The birth certificate had been traced: Arthur had been right, the name was the same, almost. *He* had been christened Arthur Edward Lane, and by some fancy of the parents, his twin brother had been christened Edward Arthur, a simple reversal.

'Arthur and his brother were born at Apsham Common House, Aisley, near Blackpool, which is not so far from Grisedale. Obviously, someone should try and contact that address – perhaps James will do it, if Richard Vause thinks that right? Meanwhile I shall press on through the years and see if I can trace a marriage certificate. It is rather a long shot but one never knows. It's better than damp basements.'

But in the event it was not Helen, or James, or Richard Vause who found Edward Arthur Lane, but the Salvation Army. For, despairing of ever finding a marriage certificate (she discovered afterwards that he married in his mid-thirties and if she had only continued through the files of two more years . . .) Helen had phoned their bureau of missing persons and asked for advice.

A man, calm and efficient, took the details. He took the number of the London friend with whom she was staying. That same evening he phoned and said, 'Miss Perry-Wilcox, I think we have some good news for you.' They were not empowered to give much information over the phone, these matters were delicate and needed a certain care and etiquette but . . .

'It seems that they have a record of everyone who contacts them,' Helen told Esther and Richard Vause excitedly over the phone, 'and one of the first things they do is check and see whether the person being sought has also made an inquiry. Well . . . Edward Lane has. He first did so in August 1948. He did so again at frequent intervals until 1956. The last time he contacted them was in 1972 . . .'

GO ON!! typed Esther, kicking her legs in anticipation.

Richard Vause did not need to relay that down the line.

'Naturally they are not just going to give me, a stranger, a telephone number and so they will try to reach him at his previously known address . . .'

DO THEY SAY WHAT THAT IS?

'Esther wants to know . . .'

'I know what Esther wants to know,' said Helen, 'but if she'll just be patient. They will try to reach him, explain what they have found out, and probably suggest he calls me or Richard Vause. I think technically they would be happier if it was Richard, since Herstorne is where Arthur lives. They will let me know if he is going to call.'

IT'S BEST ISN'T IT IF WE DON'T TELL ARTHUR?

On that they were all agreed.

At just after eleven the following morning Helen phoned again. Edward Arthur Lane had called and established contact. He had said little on the phone but asked a lot of questions. He sounded an intelligent and cultured man. He had been warned by someone at the Salvation Army of the need to proceed cautiously. Reunions were stressful things. He had asked if it would be possible for Miss Perry-Wilcox and Esther Marquand, since they seemed the key people, to visit him and put him in the picture. Soon. Please.

RICHARD, ASK WHERE HE LIVES!

Richard Vause did so.

'Cambridge,' said Helen. 'I could be there later today.'

'So must Esther be,' said Richard Vause with pleasure, 'if I have to push her myself.'

But he did not need to do that. At midday one of the social workers attached to Herstorne set off with Esther for Cambridge by car, and at half past four they met Helen near Cambridge's market square.

A few minutes before five o'clock they turned into the elegant tree-lined street where, for the past nineteen years, Dr Edward Arthur Lane, former Regius Professor of Music at Cambridge University, Emeritus Fellow of King's College, founder and chief conductor of the Royal Cambridge Choral Society, honoured teacher, scholar and player of church music, had lived and worked; and waited, as he had waited his whole life, for something beside which all honours and success were but the dust of a moment's passing – reunion with someone he loved but who was separated from him; someone who called him Skallagrigg.

SIXTY-TWO

Edward Arthur Lane opened the front door of his substantial late-eighteenth-century house as Helen pushed Esther's chair up the tiled path towards it.

They both stared at him more in shock than surprise, for his eyes, his face, his hair were all the same as Arthur's. Even his smile, even the set of his head to his body. As Helen went forward to shake his hand, she had the extraordinary feeling that she was about to shake the hand of the man they had left behind in an infirmary bed at Herstorne.

Behind Edward stood a woman, rather taller and younger than he was, with a fine warm face.

'This is my wife Alice,' he said, and then: 'Well! Well! Please come in. I have so much to ask you.' He took Esther's hand in his own and said, 'I understand I have to thank you for finding Arthur but I doubt if words will ever be enough.'

With that he led them into the house, through an elegant hall and into a large rectangular sitting-room lined with books and paintings, at one end of which, near some conservatory doors, was a grand piano, its lid up and music open, ready for playing. There was a music stand next to it, and a black violin case on the floor.

Alice quickly brought in a tray of tea things as Helen explained, as succinctly as she could, how it was that Esther came to track down Arthur Edward Lane.

At the end of it she said, 'And the first thing we would like to know, Mr Lane, is why your brother calls you "Skallagrigg".'

Edward looked at Alice and, for the first time, allowed himself to laugh outright. It was strange to see, for his mouth, the way his eyes wrinkled and his head jerked a little was like seeing Arthur again, only more clearly, as if the spasms of his cerebral palsy put before him a veil of confusion which was now suddenly lifted.

'Yes, there is a great deal to talk about. But first things first. Does

Arthur know? About your finding me? No? Well now, I think he
would like to. As a matter of fact I think he does know really, I
think he has always known the important things. But I would like
to phone Herstorne Hospital and talk to the Administrator, to let
Arthur know that I will be coming tomorrow.'

'Tomorrow?' said Helen, surprised.

'Oh yes, indeed, I would go down today but we'd arrive late and
that would be silly. We have waited fifty-seven years for this reunion and one day more won't hurt. Mind you, one day more
than that I could not bear!' He laughed again, happily. 'I want to
know everything, everything.' And then, more seriously, 'Is he
very ill?' but before Helen could answer he added, 'I rather think
not. Just weary. Tired. So tired. I know how he feels!' Helen gave
him Herstorne's number and he made the call as Esther imagined
Mr Vause walking the long corridors of Herstorne bearing the best
piece of news, surely, that any patient had ever received in all the
hospital's history.

When Edward Lane had finished talking to the hospital he came
back, sat down, and very simply told Esther and Helen the grim
story of how he lost touch with his handicapped brother.

The twins' father, Anthony Henry Lane, was an inspector of
education who had started his career as a teacher in Manchester
and whose first inspectorate was in the Blackpool area. Their
mother, Hilary, was the daughter of a Methodist minister; a pale,
thin, intense and under-educated woman.

She gave birth to them soon after the family's move north to
Ainsley from Manchester, and Edward believed that the severity of
Arthur's condition was not immediately apparent. Neither parent
ever talked to him about it and what little information he had he
gained later from a servant who had become the twins' unofficial
nanny. There were no other children.

Cerebral palsy certainly was not diagnosed, a task made more
difficult by the fact that but for Arthur's slow feeding and slight
floppiness nothing was overtly wrong with him. Only as the
months passed, and then the years, did his handicap become
more obvious and by then Hilary Lane seems to have been in a
severe and continuing state of post-natal depression, quite unable
to cope with the implications. The father was unsympathetic and

obsessive about his work – away for long periods visiting isolated schools.

Edward afterwards remembered only a cold and lonely household, with a mother who was distancing herself from the realities of Arthur's condition and beginning to neglect him. She was unable to deal with the one servant they then had, incapable indeed of looking after herself. She was, in effect, profoundly depressed and in need of help.

She never got it, and the marriage, never warm, became steadily worse. It was the father who first realized that something was seriously wrong with Arthur, probably when he was about two, and that his wife was incapable of caring for him, and so he employed a local woman, a Mrs Garce, who was widowed and childless.

She was a big broad woman and her main virtue was her strength. She was by nature a bully and quite unsuitable for a child like Arthur. But she seemed to resent both boys, talking of Arthur as a 'cripple' or 'idiot', slapping him if he messed himself or was slow to take his food. He had, of course, to be fed.

But here Edward found he had a role, because Arthur would accept food from him: from the age of four Edward learned to feed his brother, and loved to do so. Feeding Arthur was his first memory.

'I did not understand Mrs Garce's treatment of him, it made no sense,' Edward told Esther and Helen that first long evening in Cambridge. 'Arthur's nature was always to try to do his best and I never thought of him as anything but intelligent. But I also learned never to say so, for all three of the adults in that house attacked me if I did.

'Once when I said, "Arthur says . . ." my mother began to hit me and my father had to pull her off. "He's an idiot, he's an idiot," she kept shouting. I think that was the moment I understood she was not well.'

With Mrs Garce, Arthur used to cry continually. He was afraid of her, and very often cold because she did not understand that being unable to move normally he got cold easily. But the moment Edward went to him he was quiet. The two boys needed each other, and finally Mrs Garce realized this, and, finding her job was much easier if she exploited it, let them be together, though they were separated the moment either of the parents appeared.

After that attack, which occurred when the twins were nearly five, Mr Lane realized that his wife needed more help in the house. It was then he made Mrs Garce housekeeper and hired a girl as a maid. That was, as Edward put it, 'when happiness came into the house'.

The maid was the daughter of a labourer on the Apsham Estate and her name was Rachel Burrington.

'I remember the first day she came and hearing her singing round the house and Mrs Garce telling her what to do and be quiet about it. Her coming gave Mrs Garce status, and Mrs Garce was the kind of woman to make the most of it. I did not see Rachel those first few days, I just heard her busy and talking sometimes, with a full warm country voice. When I met her I liked her immediately.

'Then suddenly one day she appeared upstairs at the door of the room where they kept Arthur, to do some cleaning. I was near Arthur's bed and I turned when the door opened because I thought it might be my mother, so I must have looked frightened. I always felt I should protect Arthur and that I could never do it well enough.

'Rachel's first words were, "Why, I never knew you two were twins, I was never told that!" and she grinned, came straight over to Arthur and touched him affectionately. I remember he looked at me in total surprise. And he was even more surprised when she said to him, "You can help me clean this room by holding on to this little brush while I do some sweeping with a broom." He looked at me again, excited, and he held that brush as best he could and when it began to slip, because his grip was never much good, he called to me to help him.

'Rachel turned to him and said, "Didn't say you could talk neither," and I said, "Arthur knows the words I know."

'"That's a lot then!" she said, and I suppose it was.

'She was the most naturally loving person we had ever met and she seemed to understand instinctively the importance of talking directly to Arthur, and how we liked to be together.

'Mrs Garce did not seem to mind the time she began to spend with us because Arthur was so much better behaved. The crying stopped and he stopped messing himself. In fact, Rachel said she would make him a nice pair of flannel shorts if he did so, and he did.

'Rachel used to walk over the common and every morning she would bring some wildflowers she picked for us boys on the way and tell us their local names. I think Arthur's favourite was bird's-eye primrose – "Bonny bird een" she called it. Arthur loved to take them in his fingers and raise them to his face, to smell and nibble at them.

'By midsummer of that year she had taken us over and began taking us for walks on the common. It was the first time, and the only time, anyone took us out together in the country. By then Arthur was chattering away, though not in a way anyone could understand. Sometimes I thought I understood but his speech was not good. He could not manage "Rachel" though he always screamed out with delight when she first appeared each day. "Edward" was "Ehag . . ." or something like it. He did his best, and I began to understand the importance of speech to him, sensing that if he could manage at least some communication people might believe he was intelligent. I was beginning to realize that something might happen to him and that he had to prove himself. Mrs Garce had talked openly of him being "put away" and the fear of that was a gathering cloud. I think now that the only reason he was not put away sooner was because, however ineffective my mother was, she did not really want to lose him.

'By now I was going to the Ainsley primary school and learning to read and write. When I came back in the afternoon Rachel would encourage me to sit with Arthur and tell him all I had learned. He learned quicker than I did, and had a better memory, so I was conscious when I was at school that I was having to remember for him and that he would want to know everything when I got back home. I did very well as a result.

'He learned to read and it seems incredible now but neither of my parents ever knew this, not even my father.

'I know now that one of the defence mechanisms the parents of handicapped children use is simply to block off the reality of their child, not really to see him any more.'

Edward's voice was lower now, and his eye contact with them less frequent. He was beginning to live the past he had started describing so objectively, and to feel again the terrible loss he was building towards.

'That summer Arthur and I were happy with Rachel and she took us out a lot simply to get us out of the house and away from the adults. Nobody objected: probably they were pleased. I must have grown more confident because I began enjoying myself as other children do – climbing trees, chasing through grass, playing hide and seek with Rachel; Arthur was always watching, laughing and enjoying it too. I was always conscious that what I did was for him as well.

'Arthur had a wheelchair, a canvas thing, but it was not easy to push over rough ground and so the man who came in to do the gardening made us a cruder one with thicker wheels which worked much better. I was allowed to push that and Arthur loved going fast down hills in it. He was strapped in by Rachel.

'He began to get me to do things which I myself would have been too timid to do. For example, there were some plum trees in the orchard of a nearby house and he got me to scrump some for him. Arthur got stung by a wasp from one of them and I felt terrible, but Rachel said it was his fault in the first place for encouraging me.

'She also revealed that he was the first born, the elder, and this rather confirmed a feeling I always had that he was the one in charge. I was there to help him, he was the one with the brains. Whatever I did I did for Arthur, because he was unable to do it for himself. But you must not think he was selfish or demanding. We simply worked together: it happened that I had mobility and he had not.

'We lived near the Apsham Estate and used to go for a walk which took us along the wooden fence which ran along part of its boundary. It was made of sturdy palings cut into rough points at the top. We used to peer through the fence at the estate fields beyond, and in the winter when the trees were leafless you could just see Apsham House itself in the far distance.

'Rachel made up stories about the people who lived there and how they were kind to everybody, but you were only allowed to go to them through the gates on the far side of Ainsley, and by special invitation printed on a white card. Her father had gone to the House when he had a problem and they had been very kind and helped him.

'One day we found a gap in the fence where some boys had broken one of the palings. Arthur wanted me to creep through and although I was scared I did so for him and ventured into the field. Rachel saw me and called for me to come back.

'"You're a proper scalliwag you are!" she said, and she gave me a hug. "Arthur isn't, he's just a good boy!" she added, knowing very well that he had put me up to it. We all laughed. It was one of those happy sunny moments of childhood.

'That evening at home Arthur tried to speak and he said "Skyagree" and touched me. It took me a long time to understand what he was saying. Eventually I said, "Are you trying to say 'You're a skallagrigg'?" and he laughed and nodded. I think he knew I had got the word wrong, which made it even funnier. But "scalliwag" wasn't the kind of affectionate slang my parents or Mrs Garce used.

'From then on I was "Skyagree" or "Skallagrigg" if I said it myself – and I used to sign cards or little notes for him like that. Rachel called me "the scalliwag", using it when I had done things Arthur had put me up to. She intuitively understood the importance to us that some of the things we did, we did as one. So really "Skallagrigg" was me, but it was me in the unique context of Arthur. From then on that was always his special name for me and when he needed me to help him he would use it.

'I liked buying him presents with the little money I had, but it was hard getting anything he could do something with. But one day I got him a silver whistle of the kind used by football referees and we made a loop of wool and put it round his neck – it had to be wool so it would break easily if it got caught. It took him weeks but eventually he learned to get it to his mouth and blow it, and that was the first proper communicaton he had. One blow was yes, two was no, a whole lot meant he was glad to see me! If he knew I was coming he would try hard to get it to his mouth, and I would pause outside to give him time. In such ways did we love each other.

'My mother's family came from Cornwall and that was why she owned a cottage down there near Helston, which is on the south coast between the Lizard and Land's End. We used to go down for a fortnight's holiday in the summer every year and we boys enjoyed that. My father realized how useful it was having Rachel and she

came down with us in our last year together and we had a happy
time. The cottage looks out on to the notorious Racks, a graveyard
for ships. Arthur used to sit in his chair watching them, especially
fascinated when the tide was coming in over them and the sea was
rough. One day that summer he blew his whistle in a different
way, urgently, and I ran out to him. A boat was heading for The
Racks out of control. He "told" me to go and tell someone and I
ran all the way down to the village and lives were saved.

'Later I was praised for it and I felt guilty because I did not tell
them Arthur had been the one to see it. I have always felt guilty
about that.

'We still own the cottage; it came to me after my mother died. I
have not been there for years though we let it out each year.

'That summer holiday came to an end and when we came home
there was talk of a special doctor coming to see Arthur. We knew
it was important but we did not know why. My father said, "He's
nearly seven now," and I guessed from something Mrs Garce had
said it was something to do with him being put away.

'Rachel became very serious and one day she said, "The
doctor's coming to look at Arthur tomorrow and he's got to be
very good with him and show him what he can do. He's got to
show him he can talk and understand things. It's very important,
Edward, so you've got to tell him to be good." I remember she
was almost crying. I think she knew already what would probably happen.

'But I was confident because I knew I could explain to the doctor
about Arthur learning everything I was learning at school, and
that he had a few words and total comprehension. And I thought
he could demonstrate the whistle, which was his greatest physical
achievement.

'We made a plan, pathetic in retrospect, which was that Arthur
would blow his whistle when the doctor came as he blew it for me:
as a welcome. We thought that was clever and showed that Arthur
could do sensible things.

'I was downstairs when the doctor came in a car, and he was
not the doctor who usually came, but a specialist from Lancaster.
He was old and dressed in a suit and he did not smile. When he
started up the stairs to Arthur I heard the whistle going and saw
the doctor's face, and my father's. They were not pleased. And I

could see that from their point of view Arthur was simply making a racket, and I began to die inside for him.

'When they got to the room the doctor said severely, "I don't think we need that noise do we?" and my father took the whistle away. I saw the smiles and confidence fade from Arthur's face. Rachel had got him all ready: brushing his hair, putting him in his best clothes. I could see he was afraid. I could feel his fear as my own. I think he knew already what was going to happen. Even today, so much later, I can hardly bear to think about it.

'For a time the doctor sat in a chair and simply watched. Arthur and I looked at each other wondering what to do.

'"Can he speak at all?" he said.

'I said he knew lots of words but could not speak them.

'"Can you say your brother's name?" he asked Arthur suddenly. He spoke very loudly as if he thought Arthur was deaf.

'I began to explain that he could not say "Edward" but we had another name, but the doctor indicated that I should say nothing.

'Arthur said, "Skyagree" and grinned at me.

'The doctor repeated, "Can you say your brother's name?" and Arthur looked helplessly at me. I said, "That is his name for me."

'Then Arthur tried desperately to say my name properly, his mouth straining, and I felt I was watching someone who has one last finger-hold on a cliff edge and is straining to pull himself up.

'"Mmm," said the doctor, not seeing that he was trying. Then he said to my father that people close to such cripples often imagined they were more intelligent than they were.

'"Arthur's more intelligent than I am," I said quickly. "He knows all my school lessons."

'"Really?" said the doctor. He sat in his dark suit looking down at Arthur. The doctor had shiny shoes on, tightly laced. He looked arrogant and cold. All my life I have hated only one person and that was him.

'"He can do sums," I said.

'"You never told me that before," said my father. My father was never there to talk to.

'"Can you?" said the doctor to Arthur. His gaze was unbelieving and Arthur slowly reached down for his whistle, because he could blow a sequence of numbers on that. He had forgotten it had been taken from him. For a moment he looked at me and then began to tap his left foot over which he had some control. One tap, two taps, three taps . . . though it was hard to see.

'"He's counting with his foot," I said.

'Then Arthur went backwards – five, four, three – but when I told them what to look for they did not seem to want to see.

'The doctor produced a shilling from his pocket.

'"How many pennies makes one of these?" he said.

'Arthur started tapping out with his foot – he knew the answer was twelve. But before he got to twelve the door opened and Mrs Garce came in. Arthur froze and the doctor lost interest.

'All this time Rachel had been standing by the door.

'The doctor said, "I would like the boy undressed," but when Rachel came forward to do it the doctor said it was best that she and I now leave since those closest to such a child could "coach" them. That was the word he used. So Mrs Garce was told to do it and she had not undressed him for months. He hated her doing it as she was impatient and made him tense.

'When she went to him I saw him spasming up. As I was taken away by Rachel Arthur began to call out, "Skyagree, Skyagree." I began to cry because I knew I was letting him down. I wasn't fighting for him as I should have done. I couldn't . . .'

Fifty-seven years later Edward Lane began to cry again as he remembered that scene when his twin brother had been assessed by a doctor who simply did not know his job. But when Alice got up to comfort him he shook his head, waved her away and continued; he wanted to tell it right through to the end.

'Rachel must have seen that I was beside myself and took me outside. It was a lovely September afternoon. We must just have sat and waited but after a time I felt a sudden fierce and terrible calling and I knew instinctively that Arthur needed me. From what I have read since then I know that it was the same instinctual telepathy parents feel for children and, the evidence suggests, twins sometimes feel for each other.

'I got up, and ran back to the house, ignoring Rachel's calls. But Arthur needed help and it was like a rope pulling me. And as I climbed the stairs I could hear him screaming "Skyagree, Skyagree, *Skyagree!*" I ran to his room and pushed open the door and saw the most terrible sight I have ever seen.

'That man had got Mrs Garce to undress him so that he was

completely naked. The doctor was holding him up by the ankles, upside down in the air, and they were simply staring at him, while he, completely humiliated, was calling to me to stop them.

'I went straight in and hit the doctor, not, I'm afraid, very effectively, and the next thing I knew Mrs Garce had slapped me and pulled me from the room. My screams were Arthur's and his were mine.

'Outside the room stood my mother in a dressing-gown. She looked at me with complete loathing and suddenly and quite viciously slapped me and pushed me towards the stairs. I ran from her in pain and shock, covering my ears from Arthur's screams, and outside over the common to the wooden fence. I found the gap and ran into the field inside. I had some idea I think of running to Apsham House and getting their help. But by then Arthur's calling in my head had stopped, and with its passing my courage left me. I felt only a sense of failure and mounting loss.

'A few days later the doctor wrote to my parents with his verdict. Much later I saw the letter. In essence it said that in the interests of the health and mental well-being of the normal twin, myself, Arthur should go into care. The problem of looking after him was going to get worse as he grew, and he should be somewhere equipped to deal with his special needs. In the doctor's judgement he had little significant educational potential, but that which he had would be best catered for in a proper hospital, used to children and adults in his condition. He had connections with one or two asylums and could use his influence to persuade one of them to find a place for him.

'My father, perhaps in discussion with the doctor, decided that the sooner the move was made the better. Our seventh birthday, which was less than three weeks away, seemed a good date to choose.

'My father was at least open about what was happening, and told Rachel and me. I told Arthur and we knew we had little more time together. We knew somehow that the parting would be for a long time. We did not think it would be for a lifetime, just a long time. I think we accepted it as a condition of our childhood that we would need to be apart. We also assumed that one day, when I was bigger, I would come and get him back again.

'Those last few days we were very close; Rachel made sure of

that. I had started to learn the piano then and Arthur sat and
listened as I practised. He had a naturally good ear and thumped
his foot when I made a mistake – not just of note but of timing.
One piece I learnt, one of the early Czerny practice pieces, I at last
got perfect to his satisfaction. He liked me playing that.

'It was 1927 and an Indian summer. We managed somehow to
forget the coming separation for most of the time, but the day
before our birthday, when they were to take Arthur away, I impulsively decided I was going to escape with him myself. It was
after lunch, and Rachel had left us to play in the garden. I put
Arthur in the chair the gardener had made and we headed off
across the common. It was a lazy afternoon, and no one was
about, and I was saving my brother from the evil that was coming.
But it was such a lovely day, so warm, and we grew so interested
in other things – the fruits of autumn, and some crows at a rabbit's
carcase – that we began to forget our bold intentions as we
wandered about from one thing to another as children do. Arthur
always loved the countryside, his ears found things for me to listen
to, while I saw things to show him. Together we were one person
really, and that was why what they did to us was so cruel.'

Edward was silent, and Alice quietly got up and closed the doors
of the french window. They had arrived in late afternoon. Now
evening had drawn in and the sky outside was dark. Alice went to
make some more tea, and while she did so Edward Lane got up and
sat at the piano and played for Esther and Helen the little Czerny
piece Arthur had helped him to learn.

HE LIKES MUSIC, keyed up Esther. HE WANTS A HI-FI MORE
THAN ANYTHING.

'Does he?' said Edward smiling. He was beginning to believe at
last that very soon now he would see his brother again.

Edward continued the story: 'We found ourselves finally at the
wooden fence around the Apsham Estate and I knew Arthur
wanted to do at least one wicked thing himself, so I dragged him
through the gap.

'"The people at the House could stop you being taken away!" I
said.

'"Nah," he said. He knew it wasn't possible. But he made me
understand that he wanted to be taken into the middle of the field
and left alone there for a little. I think he wanted something special

to remember. So I took him into the long grass, and I remember we stopped where there were some late poppies still in flower. A scatter of red among the yellowed grass. He wanted to lie there and I left him, and walked back to the fence and climbed through the gap. Above the field there were swifts feeding high against the sky and I knew that Arthur was watching them too.

'I don't know how long he lay there while I sat on the edge of the field beyond the wooden fence. But the time came when I knew he wanted to move. When I reached him I knew he had accepted that our "escape" was over and that we must go home.

'That night I climbed into Arthur's bed and we held each other all night. We were saying goodbye. I remember that I said, "I'll remember my lessons to tell you when you come back," and he "told" me to be good and learn the piano well. We whispered deep into the night as little boys do. We were storing memories.

'They came for Arthur in a black van at 11.00 sharp the next morning. Rachel had given us a birthday cake at nine and put Arthur in his favourite clothes including the flannel shorts, and she looped his whistle round his neck.

'"You be good and work hard at the school-work they give you and you'll be back one day," she said. I think we thought he was going to some kind of special school. It was easier to believe that.

'My father had gone to work. My mother was in the house and briefly said goodbye but did not kiss him. Mrs Garce stood on the steps and I stood near the door of the car and watched the men put him into a special seat. It was too big for him. Rachel kissed him, told him to be a good boy, and I said goodbye. I wanted to put my arms around him but the straps were awkward and the man was not nice. He said to Mrs Garce, "Best to get it over with quick, it's kinder." I had one last look into Arthur's eyes before they closed the door. He was telling me to be brave, but he must have been so afraid. Rachel held on to me tightly as the black van's engine was started and then it turned and they took him away down Black-horse Lane and up the hill through Apsham Wood past the wooden fence through which I had taken him the day before.

'I was not allowed to visit him, or told where he had gone. I wrote an occasional letter to him which my mother addressed. I don't know if they ever got to him. A few months later my father got a promotion and we moved back to Nottingham. I knew that

Arthur was unhappy. Sometimes, at the most unexpected times, I could feel him calling for my help. It was almost unbearable. Rachel did not move with us, and some time then my parents parted and I was sent to a local boarding school. But I did not do well and when one of the masters talked to me about it I said I missed my brother.

'It was soon after that that my father came to see me during term. I knew something was wrong. We sat in one of the class-rooms and he said he had some bad news for me. I felt a terrible dread.

'He said, "Arthur has died. He was in no pain and it was peace-ful."

'I said, "When?"

'And he said, "Last week."

'Then he reached out and put his arms around me, which was the first time he had ever done so. He smelt of mothballs. "Do not be too upset, it is for the best. He would have had an unhappy life."

'My first reaction was one of total anger and bewilderment that Arthur had not "told" me. I had no reason then to disbelieve my father so I supposed it was true: Arthur was dead. But why had *he* not told me? It made no sense. Indeed, the only conclusion I could come to was that there was some dreadful mistake and that he was still alive. I think, incidentally, that my father told me this lie in a misguided attempt to make me forget Arthur and do better at school.

'From then on for a long time I blocked Arthur out of my mind and simply worked. I could face neither the possibility of his death, nor the instinctive sense that he was still alive. I blocked him out because I could not cope with anything else.

'It was probably two years later, while I was still at school, that I woke suddenly one night with that same powerful sense of painful calling I had felt on the day of Arthur's assessment by the doctor. I did not rationalize it, or even say "Good, then he must be alive after all": I simply lay in bed hearing him calling and knowing I must go to him in my mind but not knowing quite how. I was lying in a dormitory and found myself spasmed up as he often had been, and I felt so weak that I could barely move. I knew that he really was near death, because I was. I tried hard to think of something to make us strong, and I knew I was fighting for both of us. Then I remembered that day by the wooden fence when Rachel had called me a scalliwag for climbing through into the Apsham Estate field, and how Arthur had been happy that I did it and I began to "talk" to him, creating the image of the fence and saying if he could only crawl to it, and get through it or over it, the Skallagrigg would be there – I would be there. He had to stay alive to get to me. I needed him, he was the stronger, he always had been, he could not leave, he must know . . . and one day I would come for him as we had agreed, and I would take him home again, home being where I was. Suddenly the fence and the field were gone and I was by him, looking into his eyes which were my own, and I was touching him, and he knew I was there as I knew he was, and neither of us could leave the other alone on this earth.

'Then I was back in my dormitory, the weakness receding, and I knew Arthur was all right and that I had found the strength to go to him, and a great peace and sense of security came to me. I knew he was alive and that my father had lied.

'But for many years after I never felt that confidence so strongly again. I would never deny that my twin brother had died if the subject came up in the family, and I never questioned my father about it. Arthur became part of my secret world, though for a long period in my adolescence I blocked him out, I chose to believe him dead.

'Even so, quite unpredictable moods came on me sometimes – waves of happiness or misery – and I think now I was responding sympathetically to Arthur's different states. In retrospect it is significant to me that it was always he who sent out the call, and I who responded. I never called him. But there came a time when I had to.'

Edward was silent and suddenly smiled and his head rolled back rather oddly on the settee in which he sat. Afterwards Esther realized it was the way Arthur held his head in his ward bed sometimes.

'You know,' he said in a quite different and very relaxed voice, 'he knows I'm talking about it all now. I just know he knows.' Esther glanced over at Alice and saw she had tears in her eyes.

'For ten years or more there was silence on my side and then the war came. I was just the right age to be recruited, though by then I was studying music at the Royal College. Organ and violin.

'I went into the army and was soon seconded to one of the battalion's bands. In 1942 in North Africa I was caught in action – several of my colleagues were killed and I was quite badly injured. I was conscious and in pain and believed I was going to die, indeed I could feel myself sinking towards death. The pain deepened. I began to call to Arthur, quite instinctively. During this there was another raid and I was suddenly very frightened. I began to shout out to Arthur to come to me.

'Then I heard him calling from a distance and "saw" the wooden fence, and he was asking if I had forgotten that he couldn't walk, could barely crawl; had I forgotten? If I could come and help him to get over the fence he would help *me*. I said I couldn't because I was too weak and he said that I must try, I couldn't leave him, there were so many things still to do which I must do for him because he couldn't do them himself. I said, "What things?" and he said, "What do you love doing, think of all those things," and I began to tell him, and he was listening from beyond the fence he could not climb, and I was finding the strength to get nearer to him, nearer and nearer while I told him about my music, and my life and my friends and the good things I had had. As I got nearer to him we began to be as we always had been, brothers playing and creating a happy place within a difficult world where the sun shone on us and I became less afraid, less in pain.

'Then I was through the fence and with him and safe. I don't know how long we were together like that but it remains one of the most vivid moments of love and peacefulness that I have ever known. Then, just as on that last day together in childhood, he took the lead and indicated it was time to go now and he must leave and I must be strong and live for both of us. Then his presence seemed to fade and the reality of my wound came back to me and I found myself lying in the ruins of a house, the fingers of one hand caught above me in the laths of a broken wall as if it was a fence.

'What I felt most was not the pain of injury but of loss, of terrible loss; and I made the resolution that if ever I returned home alive I would search for Arthur and find him.'

It was late and Edward Lane was weary. His wife got up to sit next to him. They looked across the room at Esther and Helen and both smiled. Edward looked as if he had been on a long, long journey. Helen briefly described the incident in the chapel with

Arthur in 1942. Edward nodded and said, 'Yes, yes,' not in the least surprised.

'I got back to Britain finally in 1947 and I did start looking. By then my mother had died and my father had remarried. He was completely unhelpful. I wrote to all the long-stay hospitals I could locate in the north and simply asked if they had a patient called Arthur Edward Lane. I thought it would be easy but it proved impossible to trace him. A few replied, most did not. I followed up with visits to some. They were generally very unhelpful. I tried further afield. No luck, nobody had ever heard of him. Of course it did not occur to me that he might have been listed under a different name. How could it? And if it had, where would I have started? I began calling the Salvation Army from time to time.

'The feelings of calling occurred occasionally, and at about the time of my marriage to Alice there was a particularly strong one. I am sure that about then Arthur was in love, or involved with someone. I hope I am right . . .'

Helen and Esther nodded. 'Yes, he had a girlfriend,' explained Helen, 'her name was Linnie.' Edward smiled and continued his story.

'After my marriage I was not perhaps as energetic in looking for him as I could have been, nor was I really certain he was alive. After all, the experience in North Africa had been in extreme circumstances, and like a dream. It was the kind of thing that could have just been imagination, a psychological trick on oneself. Also, a lot of us wanted to forget the war, and its experiences. In any case my career was developing and 1927 seemed a long time ago, another world.

'So time passed and my calls to the Salvation Army grew more and more infrequent. Perhaps, after all, Arthur was dead. And yet, sometimes, always unexpectedly, I got those sudden inner callings that were as if he was talking to me. They disturbed me and yet were a comfort. But somehow I was beginning to dread that I might find him, as if then it would be proof I had not tried hard enough. I even began to resent him. Then, suddenly, in the early sixties, there was silence. Arthur disturbed me no more.

'When my father died in 1970 it was our job to go through his papers with his second wife. My mother had died years before. It was then I came across that doctor's letter. But there was no other

trace of Arthur at all, except a birth certificate. It gave the time of
birth and, as Rachel had said, he was the first born.

'We went back to Ainsley one summer and tried to contact
Rachel but we did not find her. The wooden fence was still there,
or parts of it, and the house too, surrounded by a lot of modern
buildings.

'Sometimes since I have been plagued by periods of acute depression and people around me have been kind. My work, or rather
ability to work, has been affected, but the quality of work has not
suffered. The sense of love that Arthur gave me has grown in me
over the years. I know he has been silent, and I know in my heart
he has been waiting. I have sometimes felt that I have lived for
him, even down to the sense that my career would have been his:
I'm sure he was more musical than I was.

'Recently, in the last few months, I know he has been ill. I have
been ill with him. Sick in my heart. Alice has known and without
her I would not have survived.' He reached out a hand and held
hers.

'I have been afraid to find Arthur because it has been so long. I
feel I should have found him years ago. Recently I have known
more and more he needed me and strangely I very nearly called
the Salvation Army people. When they called me I was not surprised. I do not accept that this was how our lives were meant to
be, but I must accept that this is what they *have* been. Each of us
has found some kind of peace, and now we are ready to see each
other again. He knows I am coming. He knows.

'It was a terrible thing our parents did and it blighted two lives.
And yet . . .' He stood up. Over the piano on the wall was a crucifix,
and Esther noticed Alice wore one.

'It makes you wonder if there is a God,' he said.

THAT'S WHAT ARTHUR SAYS, typed Esther.

'Does he? Does he believe?'

NO.

Edward laughed.

'Two sides of the same coin,' he said cryptically. And then,
after a pause, he added, 'I thank God this time has come and
that Alice is here to share it with me. Now tell me about his
girlfriend Linnie.'

Esther started to tell it as Arthur had, and Edward, though tired, watched as the words came up on her screen and came to understand something of what his brother was.

I HAD A DREAMGIRL ONCE AND HER NAME WAS LINNIE, SHE WAS THE SUNSHINE TO ME AND SHE MADE ME A MAN . . .

Linnie's name came up again the following morning, during a discussion they had before they left for Herstorne. Esther had wanted to know whether Edward Lane ever experienced any of the telepathic communications that seemed implicit to the Skallagrigg stories. This led to them comparing notes on dates and events, and to an informal compilation of the evidence which, much later, the Chicago Institute for Sibling and Twin Research collected in its exhaustive report on the Lane twins.

As in many other examples of long-separated twins, there were remarkable parallels in their lives. Apart from some obvious and easily explicable parallels (both were very musical, both wore their hair in a similar, odd, close-cropped way, both had had chest and bronchial problems throughout their lives, both wore a single gold ring on the same little finger, both had identical fillings in their teeth) there were some stranger similarities. The periods of illness in their life were virtually identical, the mysterious war-time experience witnessed by James Freeman in Arthur had a direct parallel in Edward who was seriously injured that day in North Africa, Edward's wedding to Alice took place in the same month as Arthur's 'wedding' to Linnie, Alice miscarried in probably the same *week* as Linnie conceived, the rape of Arthur by Rendel was at the same period (it is undatable) as a strange assault by two men on Edward . . .

But there was one other detail, inconsequential in itself but statistically so unlikely that even the researchers, long used to 'coincidence' in such cases, marvelled at it. The Christian names of Arthur's dreamgirl Linnie were Carolyn Alice; and of Edward's wife they were the same, but reversed: Alice Carolyn. And, unusually for that period, in both cases the 'Carolyn' was spelt with a 'y'.

SIXTY-THREE

They drove north the following morning, travelling in two cars since Edward and Alice would be returning to Cambridge, and Esther and Helen to Oxford. The social worker who had brought Esther down had gone back with the Herstorne van the night before.

They journeyed slowly, gently, stopping from time to time. Nobody wanted to hurry such a reunion. When they reached the Forest of Bowland Edward Lane suggested that Helen and Esther went on ahead; he wanted to dawdle over the last bit, thinking and taking his time.

As she drove away Helen smiled and said, 'I think these last few miles are going to take him quite a time. It can't be easy.' Esther grinned, but she was not sure why. For an aging gentleman, Edward suddenly looked as nervous as a boy on his first day at school.

Helen and Esther arrived at Herstorne in mid-afternoon and found things subtly changed. Richard Vause had put on a dark suit and the staff had put fresh flowers in Arthur's ward. They seemed excited and nervous too, as if they were about to be inspected.

Frank had insisted that Arthur be dressed in a shirt, and, as a result, Arthur had insisted on sitting in a chair. So now he had trousers on as well, and sat near the open french windows with the veranda outside. He was a little pale, but much brighter than they had seen him for weeks.

Eppie and Norman had put on their best clothes, and Norman's hair had been flattened with Brylcreem and combed neat with a parting.

So, all ready, they waited, trying to get on with other things; only Arthur was peaceful and smiling as if, like his brother earlier, he wanted nothing rushed. He just stared out of the windows down to the glen.

Helen had been right. It did take Edward a long time to reach Herstorne from where they had left him and Esther had been waiting for nearly half an hour at the front of the hospital when, at last, his car turned through the gates and parked.

Richard Vause had told her she could have the honour of taking Edward to the infirmary with only Frank there apart from her and the two brothers. Introductions to hospital staff could wait until later. No doubt Frank would decide when Eppie and Norman were to say hello.

The hospital seemed suddenly deserted as if no one wanted to disturb the peace. Even Helen had made herself scarce and Esther trundled her wheelchair across the tarmac as Edward climbed carefully out of his car, and went round to open the door for Alice.

I'M TO TAKE YOU, Esther announced.

Edward was pale, Alice smiling.

'Where's Helen?' she asked.

IN THE OFFICE PROBABLY WITH MR VAUSE. THROUGH THE MAIN DOORS.

'Well, I'll go and find her. I'll come along later.' And she discreetly left to let Edward make his reunion alone.

In the ward, Arthur was calm and very content. Frank was uneasy, fiddling with Arthur's straps, occasionally offering him a drink and brushing his hair until Arthur protested, and Frank went out on to the veranda.

The sun had swung round the building and now shone on the veranda and into the windows on one side of Arthur's chair. It lightened the room, and brought out the lines of Arthur's old face, and seemed to make his eyes shine.

Meanwhile, Esther proudly turned her chair towards the main entrance, Edward at her side.

'Could I just look at the building?' asked Edward, anxious to delay the moment of meeting.

WE COULD GO ROUND BY THE GARDENS.

'That seems a pleasant idea.'

Esther nodded and, turning back into the sun, started leading him round the building. She remembered how, in one of the stories, Frank had come back across the grass after his period away from Arthur.

IT'S NOT FAR, typed Esther.

'I feel most strange,' said Edward.

DO YOU WANT ME TO DISAPPEAR?

Edward laughed, a little nervously.

'No, you're my guide.'

And so it was. Edward Lane paced slowly along at the side of
Esther's chair, across the asphalt with the lawns stretching off to
the right until she saw the veranda of the infirmary wing where
Frank stood, watching.

Slowly they came, and Frank stared, not moving. Then Esther
saw him turn and say something through the open doors, and
look back.

ARTHUR'S IN THERE. THAT'S THE INFIRMARY, Esther typed.
Edward mumbled, looking ahead.

As they approached Frank turned from them and went inside.
Then as Esther stopped her chair and Edward climbed the two
wooden steps on to the veranda, she saw Arthur's legs and feet
being pushed out into the sunlight. And then his hands on a plaid
blanket over his lap. And then his head and his face and his eyes
smiling and his mouth excited as Edward took a few steps and was
there before him, looking down upon him, the afternoon sun across
them both.

Frank, behind Arthur's chair, said, 'Skalg's come now, from the
grass.'

As he said this Edward put one hand on the chair's side, knelt by
it and, whatever he had planned, he could say nothing. Instead he
helplessly reached forward, and, as his tears began to come, Arthur
whispered, 'Skyagree, Skyagree' and, reaching up his hooked and
spasmed hands, cradled Edward's head to his chest to let the long
years of separation fade in the sunlight of their reunited love.

Later, after Frank and Esther had helped them talk, and a staff
nurse had discreetly brought them some tea, Alice Lane came and
met her brother-in-law.

She too cried, and then so did Arthur, holding her hand and
looking into her eyes; she kissed him more than once and said it
was the happiest moment of her married life to see Edward 'completed'. Then Arthur reached out to hold his brother's hand and
look at his wedding ring and show him the ring Linnie had given
him so long before.

'That's Linnie's ring,' explained Helen to Alice, for she had not mentioned it in her account the evening before.

'They were wed by the cross,' said Frank suddenly. He had been silent until then, sitting in the background. Now he came forward and sat nearer them.

At the far end of the ward Norman and Eppie appeared, staring and grinning shyly.

'Skalg's come,' said Frank loudly. 'Say how do you do.'

Eppie laughed nervously, Norman loomed shyly, looking at the floor, unwilling to come forward despite all persuasion.

Arthur spoke and Frank said, 'Arthur says that's Norman who has been good to him long years, and this is Eppie who is a good friend.' Eppie came forward and shook Edward's hand vigorously, not letting it go. Then he turned to Alice and hugged her saying, 'I'll kiss you,' but not doing so.

Frank said, 'No, that's Skalg's girl. He can kiss her, not you.'

'No,' said Eppie, laughing shrilly: ha ha ha.

Arthur grinned at his brother who grinned back. Then Arthur spoke and Frank says, 'Arthur's tired but wants to show you his home if Staff says yes.'

Staff did say yes and so, like some ancient state visit, the little party set off and saw a part at least of the place that had been Arthur's home for fifty-seven years.

Months later, when visits had been made and the excitement had passed, Esther revisited Herstorne. She had travelled up initially to visit Laydale, where she had some computing business to discuss with Annette Roskill, and Helen had driven her on over the moors to see Arthur and his friends.

They took some cakes and, in the holiday atmosphere that had come to Herstorne under Richard Vause's enlightened regime, there was an impromptu party out on the lawn.

By then Arthur was fitter, his face tanned and his eyes alive with fun once more. Esther knew he had something to tell his friends, something important which Richard Vause had told him earlier, so their visit was well-timed.

She knew much of what had happened. Most important, how James Freeman had revealed that he had kept track of Linnie and, after she had died in 1976 aged about fifty-five, he had kept track of her son Peter. Never betraying Arthur's desire for privacy, but just making sure he knew where he was.

Arthur had repeatedly said that he wanted to keep his existence from his son for his son's sake, but, after a trip to Cambridge to stay with Edward, Arthur admitted that he would like just once to see his son grown up. He was thirty-three by then and the only people who knew were James Freeman, Edward and Arthur, Helen and Esther.

There is only one record of the incident by Esther and it is in a last story which she added to her book of Skallagrigg stories. It was never published with the rest of the stories, and yet, in its own way, it is a completion.

As they sat laughing and having tea that sunny afternoon at Herstorne, Eppie said, 'Tell us a story, Arthur, old pal,' and Arthur grinned and looked at Frank.

Frank said, 'Stories finished now. Skalg's back.'

But Arthur sat thinking, and a hush came over the gathering as if they knew that for one last time he had a story to tell them. Then he smiled at Eppie and began to talk. Esther suddenly realized that she was witnessing the telling of a Skallagrigg story, and that Arthur was telling it as if it happened to someone else and she began to record it on her keyboard. The story was his way of telling his oldest friends what he knew would mean so much to them.

A special day dawned and Frank lathers up Arthur and gets a razor from Staff and squints his eyes and does his job. Arthur's never been better shaved in his whole life and his cheeks pink and shiny like new.

Eppie says, 'Going out for the day then, old pal? Ha ha ha ha ha.'

'Shut up,' says Frank, 'got to think.'

But Eppie's right. That's the day Arthur's going to the Skallagrigg's home for the first time all the way on the busy road with big lorries where you can't see the load 'cos it's covered in steel boxes.

Frank puts Arthur's best suit on, and his white shirt and red tie.

Arthur speaks and Eppie says, 'You don't look too happy Arthur, what's the problem?'

Franks says, 'Arthur says he wants his favourite shirt not the smart one. Not comfortable. But he's wrong. Going to Skalg and going smart.'

Arthur grins and winks at Eppie. Sometimes there's no stopping Frank.

At eight-thirty Frank says, 'You can take Arthur down to the front now, Norman, Skalg'll be here.' So Norman does, pushing Arthur like he's pushing gold. All the boys are coming to wave goodbye for Arthur's weekend away.

Skalg comes and he's with his dreamgirl Alice. Says Frank, 'Arthur doesn't like too much milk with his cereal. Arthur doesn't mind hot water in the bath, doesn't like cold. Arthur's clothes in the bag. Arthur's not to look into the sun. Arthur's . . .'

Alice smiles. Arthur knew a smile like that once. It's a smile of love. Alice has a special surprise for Frank which Arthur has arranged with the Skallagrigg.

'Oh,' she says with her eyes wide, 'but you're coming, Frank. Can't do without you!'

So that is a surprise for Frank and all the boys laugh and Frank's pleased because he was beginning to look miserable at Arthur going off by himself. Frank likes to keep an eye out for Arthur.

The journey's long but passes in no time. Skalg stops halfways for wees and tea in a big place called Granada. There's enough food there to feed an army, except there is at least three armies of people there off coaches and cars. It was hot queueing but Arthur doesn't mind. He has a doughnut, Frank has a scone and the Skallagrigg has ice-cream. Alice has nothing.

There's a special lavatory for the disabled with sparkly white tiles and rails all round.

Then they come to the Skallagrigg's home. Well! There could be a book about the beauties of the Skallagrigg's house which Alice has made like dreamland. There are thick curtains on all the windows and carpets in every room pink and green and grey. Even on the stairs. There's more books than Arthur's ever seen and one has the Skalg's picture in. There's shiny glasses in a cupboard and a telly in a cabinet and doors open on to a patio with roses up the walls and red flowers in tubs, and apple trees. Alice makes tea and brings it out on to the patio and there's a special cake with candles and the words in icing WELCOME HOME ARTHUR and Arthur cries.

Then Alice goes into the kitchen and cries. And Edward walks in the garden and cries. Then Arthur laughs and speaks and Frank says loudly, 'Arthur says tears don't stop us wanting to eat the cake!' Then Skallagrigg says, 'We've got something for you, Frank,' and he gets it. It's a prezzie isn't it, small and wrapped in a pink ribbon. Frank opens it and it's a silver watch. Now that's something Frank's wanted all his long life, a watch, and he can't believe his eyes. He holds it up, lays it down, listens to it, tries the strap, and then puts it on. Says Frank, 'This is the happiest day of my life.'

The Skallagrigg says, 'No man has ever had a better friend than you've been to Arthur, not ever in all of time. Arthur would not be here but for you, Frank, and that makes you special to us. You will always be welcome.' And Alice gets up and before Frank can stop her she gives him a kiss and Frank blushes and looks uncomfortable.

When tea's done the Skallagrigg says, 'Now, Arthur, this is your weekend. Is there anything special you want to do?'

Arthur speaks and Frank says, 'Arthur says the first is to be with you and the second is to hear you play music and third is to meet your friends.'

The Skallagrigg laughs and says, 'We're doing the first, and we have arranged the second for this evening, and the third will be, so that's easy!'

'What's this evening?' asks Frank.

'We're going to a special concert.'

Arthur looks worried. He knows that in public he can't always stop spasming and his mouth makes noises and he can't help that.

'Will there be lots of people?' asks Frank for Arthur.

Edward grins and says, 'I thought of that and I know what's in Arthur's mind. There's nothing to worry about.'

Well! That evening was special. In King's College Chapel where Arthur has heard carols from at Christmas on the radio. They arrive and there's a notice saying NO ADMITTANCE TO THE PUBLIC.

They go past that and into the tall high splendour that is that chapel. Frank's had one shock already now he has another. He's never seen an altar of golden rails and shiny wood like he sees there. He even lets go the handles of Arthur's chair to stare.

In front of the altar is some gilded chairs for the orchestra, with music stands, and a bigger one in front where the conductor's to be. In the aisle is some chairs for the audience. Not many though.

Arthur speaks and Frank says, 'Arthur wants to know where the audience is.'

The Skallagrigg says, 'There's not to be many of them. This is a special concert for special people.'

'Who?' asks Frank.

'You're one for a start, and then Arthur's another. And Alice is a third. There's only three more and I expect they'll be here soon.'

A few minutes later who should come in all the way from the hospital but the Father all dressed up and looking smart. And with him he's got Helen and Ess and they're grinning fit to bust.

Everyone says hello and Frank says, 'Arthur wants to know something. Where's the orchestra? Where's the conductor?'

'I'm the conductor,' says the Skallagrigg. 'And if you settle down I expect the orchestra will come along.'

So there was a hush, and no one knew where to look there was so much light and colour to feed on, and in come the orchestra. They were dressed to the nines, the men in black jackets and trousers, the women in black dresses. But there was more than an orchestra, there was a choir as well. There was over one hundred people and many of them came up to Arthur and shook his hand and said, 'We know your story and we love Edward. This is our gift to you both. He has brought happiness to many in his life, tonight we will bring happiness in the way we know best.'

So they get into their places and the Skallagrigg stands up and says, 'This is a special concert of celebration. It's not to be stuffy, it's not to be formal. We did not think Arthur would like that. Also he's with friends so if he wants to sing or get Frank to move him around or finds his mouth makes noises nobody will mind. In fact we might prefer it then we can do the same! The college has been very kind and allowed tea to be served afterwards, so relax.' Then he turned to the orchestra and choir and said, 'Too much chattering at the back there!' just like a schoolmaster and then there was a hush, deep as deep can be. But before they could begin Frank stood up with his hands on the handles of Arthur's chair. He's never been in a chapel and not said a prayer and that was why he had been thinking.

'I want the Father to say something to Christ Jesus,' says he.

The Father goes to Frank's side and says, 'You say something for us all, Frank.'

'Don't know what.'

'We don't mind waiting while you think.'

That hush deepened more while Frank thought. Then he looked up at the golden cross and he said, 'Thank you for Skalg. Thank you for Arthur. Thank you for Ess. Thank you for here. Thank you, Christ Jesus, for what you give us each day and tonight and tomorrow to come. Bring good things to all who are here and to Eppie and Norman our friends who cannot be. You give us all happiness and that is enough. So thank you.'

Then Frank sat down and, after making sure Arthur was comfortable, he said, 'O K to begin now, Arthur's ready.'

That music was like nothing ever before nor ever will be again. There was quiet and there was loud; there was trumpets to begin and trumpets in the middle; there was a hundred voices and there was one voice; there was deep and there was high. In some the organ almost bounced Arthur's chair about, in others it was like sweet rivers on a summer's evening. If beauty ever stops still for a moment then it stopped that evening in King's College Chapel and was with them all. They played Bach and Monteverdi, they played Fauré and they played Britten. Some the Skallagrigg explained, some he didn't. Some was new for Arthur and some he knew. And Arthur knew that the Skallagrigg was saying with the help of his friends that the long years were over now and that bad time was gone.

At the end the Skallagrigg played the organ for Arthur, brother for brother, and none knew where to look so much beauty was about. Then the trumpets came again, and all the orchestra and all the voices, raised on high to say thank you for how that evening made the world all right.

After there was some drinks and chat and many signed that programme for Arthur and a picture was taken of Arthur and Edward in front of all those people and the high arched windows of the chapel behind.

Before they left the Father asked to speak to the Skallagrigg alone, which he did for a short time then they all left into the night. Helen and Ess and the Father were staying at a hotel and left Arthur with the Skallagrigg.

When they got back Alice made tea and Arthur and the Skallagrigg talked into the deep night until poor Frank could hardly keep awake. There was so much to say, so many photos to look at, so much to remember and some finally to forget. It was the light of dawn that sent them to bed. But before they went the Skallagrigg had something to say.

'I want you to think carefully about this, Arthur. It's your decision alone. Yesterday Father Freeman got important news. He found out where your son Peter lives and it's in Birmingham. He respects your wish that your boy doesn't know but wants to know if you still think that. He could arrange a meeting. He says you know what best to do but he felt he should tell you. He would have told you himself but didn't want to in the Chapel, so he left it to me.'

Then was Arthur silent thinking of all the fors and all the againsts.

'You think as long as you like,' says the Skallagrigg.

Arthur speaks and Frank says, 'Arthur says that it would be wrong to disturb his boy's peace now. What would he feel if he found out his Dad was a spastic? That wouldn't be fair. But Arthur says he was thinking what Linnie would have wanted and she would have wanted him to see their boy grown up.'

'He's not just grown up, he's married,' says the Skallagrigg.

'Arthur would like to go past his home and see where he lives. No harm in that.'

That happened weeks later. The Skallagrigg pushed Arthur's chair the last bit. Both their hearts were beating hard when they went into the street where Peter lived. House by house looking at numbers, door by door and little front gardens. They hardly dared look as they went past the blue door with Peter's number on it, all shut, but sneak a look they did. Arthur would have liked to see beyond it! But he was proud that Peter had a little home of his own. He must have been a clever boy to have that. They went past, right to the end of the street and then turned round for a second look, crossing over to the other side 'cos it was easier to look without seeming nosy. Arthur will always be glad they did that because as they drew near, that blue door opened and their dreams came true. There was a man there and he was the right age to be Peter. He came out and looked up and down and then called out, 'Come on, Martin! Get a move on.' Then into that front garden comes a little boy like Arthur and the Skallagrigg once were in a cub's uniform, green and yellow and badges down the arm.

The man and the boy were laughing about something. Arthur wanted to stare and stare but didn't dare and nor did the Skallagrigg, so he pushed by on the other side, wondering if that could have been Peter, and if that was then that boy Martin could have been Peter's son, Arthur's grandson. That would be a turn up for the books!

Well then they heard steps on the pavement behind them and that boy's voice and they were being overtaken. The man and the boy went by, the man holding the boy's hand. Arthur hardly dared breathe. The boy had badges for knots, swimming and fires on his arms. They were chattering about a camp they were going on some time.

As they passed the man did not look round but the boy lingered for a moment and looked back at the man in the wheelchair who was Arthur. And when he did that Arthur and the Skallagrigg saw his eyes, and those eyes were blue and kind and Arthur knew them to be the eyes of the only woman he ever loved. They were the eyes of Linnie all right and in that moment Arthur knew he had been blessed to see into the eyes of his grandson once in his life with the Skallagrigg at his side. And that was a great moment and what Linnie would have wanted.

The Skallagrigg stopped the chair and they watched Peter and Martin walk away from them down that road, hand in hand, like a good father should be with his son.

'I'm glad I lived to see this day,' said the Skallagrigg.

'Yeh,' said Arthur happily. They watched until Arthur's son and his grandson turned the corner and were gone.

After that Arthur was silent for some days and peaceful. Then he said to Frank to get the boys as he had something important to say. Ess had come with some cakes and so that was a good time to give good news.

Arthur spoke and Frank says, 'Arthur says that long ago he called out for the Skallagrigg to take him home. The years went by. Ess came and then the Skalg and we went to what had been my home once. Was no more. That was gone. We went to the fence and that was gone almost all. The Skalg said that father was gone and mother was gone. Then Arthur went to the Skalg's home where he lives with his dreamgirl Alice and it was good. But it was not Arthur's. Was Skalg's. Then he saw Peter's home where Martin is who has blue

eyes like Linnie. Then he thought, 'Why can't Skalg take me
to my home?' Then in the car coming back to Herstorne he
thought, 'Why am I happy to be returning?' He stares out at
the scenery and he has the best thought he could have had.
Then Arthur says to himself, 'My home is where my friends
are and where I am loved day by day. By Frank. By Eppie
who laughs too much. By my good friend Norman who helps
me. That is a better home than many have and I am content.
Sometimes the Skalg will come and that will be good. Often I
will think of what makes me proud, which is Peter and his
boy Martin even if knowing them can never be. But most I
will be glad to be here with Frank and Eppie and Norman,
and the memories we have, good and bad, which is what our
life has been.'

Then Frank said, 'Arthur has one more thing to say and it is
important, so listen. Then he is done. Arthur says that Mr
Vause is a good man and has our needs in his heart. They
will find us a villa at Laydale and we can choose our own
colours for the walls and have a carpet if we want. And a
broom and a place for rubbish and a garden which is ours.
Our life in a ward will be over. We can have a party and
ask the Skallagrigg to come and the Father and Ess and
that Helen and others too. We can have a telly and music
and meals in if we want. At Laydale we will have this home
for us and in it no dilke will shout never not ever. And on
the walls will be pictures of places we like and people we
know. This will be our home and it will be the best there is
because we worked for it through long years. Once there
were bad times and there was Dilke. But we forgave and
the bad times went. Now Dilke is not ours to worry over
and we have better things to do.'

Says Eppie, 'When?'

Says Frank, 'Soon. Six months. Arthur says before
Christmas. Then will Herstorne be no more and our home at
Laydale ready.'

'What do you say, Norman?' says Eppie. Ha ha ha ha ha ha
ha.

Norman grins and shakes his head and then nods 'cos he's
happy.

Frank looks at his silver watch and says, 'Time's gone quick.
Story finished now. Arthur's going in.'

These days Norman pushes because Frank's getting old,
so Frank walks at Arthur's side and holds his hand. Eppie

goes ahead and opens up a door. To right, to left, above and
back the old hospital stretches. It's almost over now and the
hospital will close and the boys will leave and start their
home at Laydale.

Arthur looked at his friends and his friends looked at him, and
they seemed to see no one else there then. Norman got to his feet
and took the handles of Arthur's chair and gently began to push it
across the grass towards the hospital. Frank walked at his side
holding Arthur's hand. And Eppie, laughing, ran ahead as best as
his age allowed, to open up a door and help them slowly in.

PART V

THE RACKS

SIXTY-FOUR

The resolution of the mystery of Skallagrigg's identity, and Edward's reunion with Arthur, seemed to leave Esther Marquand in a state of anticlimax and approaching crisis which the job at Laydale Hospital that summer did nothing to ease.

She was in conflict about her handicap and Daniel as a letter written in July 1984 shows: 'There is something about my life that I find difficult to talk about.' But 'One day I hope I can tell you the truth.'

It was a time of reflection, discussion and argument for Esther. But most importantly she was beginning to see everything in terms of gaming, even the problems of suffering which her work exposed her to. After a visit from James Freeman, during which he must have discussed the nature of suffering with her, she wrote to Graham Downer:

> It wasn't what he said about the problem [of suffering] that impressed me so much as the way he said it. I'm beginning to see that it's not what we say that matters but what we are. Actions speak louder than words. I seem to be discovering what everyone else knew already, and Alan [the chaplain to Laydale] says the only way of learning is through experience. Funnily enough that's what a book about computerized learning in the US by Papert says and I'm excited by the idea that games can be learning experiences and *that* may be their main function for patients in a hospital like this.

Writing to Daniel on the same theme she adds this significant comment:

> I'm beginning to think that computer games as we know

them so far are very limited in their value, whatever
their appeal. I'm sure kids playing them could be doing
better things with their time – I know increasingly the
last thing I want to do is sit in front of a screen all day.
Why do so many able-bodied kids want to do it? Because
something is wrong in what society offers them, that's
why. Sometimes I get quite angry about this!

Here Esther seemed very near to confessing her handicap.
In another letter to Daniel in early August she writes:

I've been toying with 'Dunroune II' [a development of a
game she had already worked on] but really think
there's no point in such games. There's a complete lack
of originality in them now and the amount of
imagination needed to create them, and play them, is
nil – although everyone is eager to create the illusion
that they're imaginative. I would like to make a game
which makes people really think and make decisions
about real issues. I've started to return to that favourite
subject of mine, 'Skallagrigg', and have decided to make
it a six-level game with some genuine problems – ethical
and philosophical – for the player to sort out, as well as
the usual puzzles. Puzzles bore me now anyway! I'm
going to incorporate a game of chess into one level and
am thinking of something similar to the Japanese game
'Go' on another level – not so easy I suspect. Graham
Downer has access to work being done at Cambridge on
chess-playing programs so that will be useful.

It was a time of intellectual challenge and change for Esther,
when she was independent of home and yet in a safe environment.
Then suddenly, at the end of August, when Esther was nearing the
end of her time at Laydale and had only a few weeks before she
was due to return to Oxford to begin study for her maths degree,
her letters to Daniel ceased. He wrote at the beginning of September
asking for a reply concerning some programming ideas for
'Dunroune'. Then a week later more urgently, concerning a change
to 'Tom's Game' for which there was a deadline, adding that he
was coming to England in October for a computer exhibition at

which *CODA*, the magazine he wrote for, was participating. He asked if he could expect to see her.

But Esther remained silent. The crisis with her father which she had feared for so long had come.

In mid-August Richard Marquand and Kate paid a flying visit to Harefield, and from there to Laydale. The waiting and indecision for them was over. They had found a home in Sydney they liked and told Esther that they intended to get married in September from Kate's family home. Expecting resistance they came to persuade her to fly out for the wedding with Helen and Marion.

But Richard had travelled into silence. Esther would not communicate with him or even look at him. Anger, upset, pleadings, threats . . . none made any difference at all. Her hand did not move on her keyboard to bring up words on the screen. Kate tried to talk to her. Silence for her as well.

'This is ridiculous, Esther, I *know* you know that.'

For a moment then it seemed that Esther would talk but something hardened in her and she did not. 'Oh, Esther,' said Kate bending down and kissing her, 'if this is all part of some grand selfless scheme to make your father forget you it won't work.'

But it had.

A few days later Richard Marquand left England without a single word from Esther. He was an angry man. He knew, and she knew, that there was no threat against her he could carry out. He could hardly withdraw her allowance or the help he gave through Helen. No one could be forced to talk. His last words to her were, 'I think it's just damned discourteous, whatever the reason is. But I suppose it's just an example of adolescent behaviour these days. Very normal, Esther! Well, when you come to your senses I hope you will agree to come out and see us, and that had better be soon because you can't go through three years at Oxford without seeing us. You can't just live with Helen all the time. Oh it's so bloody ridiculous!'

Kate shooed him away, fulminating, and they went to see Helen in Oxford to make sure that the necessary financial arrangements for Esther's continuing support were adequate, while back at Harefield Richard reminded Marion and Jeremy in Hill House that if Esther needed their help they were to give it and that Marion

should visit her within the next few weeks just to make sure that,
the silence to himself and Kate apart, she was all right.

But Esther, whatever she herself may have thought, was not all
right. She was on the verge of real depression. Perhaps it had
begun with the inevitable anticlimax of completing the Skallagrigg
research. No doubt it was aggravated by the growing conflict
within her over the inherent falsity of the correspondence with
Daniel. It was probably completed by Richard and Kate's 'sudden'
decision to marry.

Certainly, soon after they had left for Australia, Esther's silence
deepened dangerously. Helen picked her up from Laydale in the
final week of September, and first noticed it then. Esther was pale,
withdrawn, unenthusiastic about the coming term at Oxford. On
the journey back to Oxford she seemed close to tears and that
evening did cry, for no reason that Helen could understand.

IT'S NOTHING. I KEEP SAYING IT'S NOTHING. I'M JUST SAD.

'Is it your father's marriage to Kate? You could still go out.'

THAT'S NOTHING TO DO WITH IT. IT'S NOTHING. I'M SORRY,
I DON'T MEAN TO UPSET YOU.

But Helen *was* upset, and as the days passed without the depression improving she was increasingly worried. Then there was
a telephone call from Daniel Schuster. He really did need to hear
from Esther, he was coming over, he must know . . . His voice was
exasperated and not as friendly as the first time he had spoken to
Helen. Helen was apologetic but evasive.

I KNOW I KNOW I KNOW I KNOW, declared Esther afterwards.
She *would* write to him.

She began going daily to services at a nearby evangelical church
called the Church of the New Word. Strange, bland young people
with white shirts and ties came to pick her up; they treated Helen
with kindly indifference, as if she was a harmless heathen. At
Esther's bidding one of them stuck a multi-coloured cross on
Esther's door with the slogan CHRIST IS ALIVE underneath it. The
sudden tears, the paleness, the introspection continued. Helen was
deeply concerned.

She summoned Tom from London for the weekend before term,
and Esther brightened a little.

I'M GOING TO WRITE TODAY TO DANIEL SCHUSTER AND TELL
THE TRUTH, she announced.

'Mr Postman will come to the box,' said Tom, 'and we'll be there first!'

Well, thought Helen, that's something positive.

I'M LOOKING FORWARD TO STARTING MY MATHS DEGREE, continued Esther.

Even more positive, thought Helen, though Esther seemed to regard it all as little different from going to the theatre or for a day out in the country. It was true, Esther seemed to have made the minimum preparation, saying that it was best to wait and see what her tutor and lecturers said they expected of her.

NO POINT GETTING WORKED UP ABOUT IT.

'This isn't like the College of Science, dear,' warned Helen. 'It's a degree in a difficult subject. There'll be some very intelligent people doing it. You really must . . .'

PLEASE STOP WORRYING, HELEN. I'LL BE ALL RIGHT.

'Well, I do worry,' said Helen with pursed lips.

HOW'S YOUR BOYFRIEND IN THE NORTH? asked Esther to change the subject and with something of the old humour in her eyes.

'Esther!!'

Esther did write to Daniel, but failed to tell the whole truth:

My dear Daniel,

Please don't call or visit me when you come to England. This isn't because I don't want you to – just the opposite in fact. I long to see you and to be close to you. You know that. You're the only person I've ever been able to 'talk' to properly about what interests me, and you understand what I am doing. But there are things I haven't told you which I must tell you because otherwise I would feel guilty. I know when I do it will be the end of our relationship and I don't want it to end. So that's why I'm delaying I suppose. Will you give me more time? Please? This is why I have been silent. Also I have not been all that well. The Laydale work took it out of me, and also I am into 'Skallagrigg' again and this time it's exhausting. I can see a way of doing it but I'm afraid to follow it through. Oh I need to talk to you about it. I hate doing everything alone. I'm *dreading* starting at

Oxford even if it's meant to be a great honour. But I can't
avoid it for yet another year. Daniel, I'm sorry if this
letter is upsetting but I'm not happy at the moment and
it's best if I delay writing the truth. I love your letters,
and all you say, and I know that if we could have met
and you could accept me for what I am, which isn't a lot,
we could have made something of it. But that will never
be now. I will write soon.

Tom pushed Esther down Woodstock Road to the postbox
holding this letter and said, 'Shall I, Amh?' as if he understood its
importance. Perhaps he saw the upset and loss in her face.

She nodded bleakly and Tom, after his usual peering in the dark
slit, pushed the letter in and listened for its fall.

'Where to Amh?' But he knew, and after a moment of her
silence said, 'Gone now. To Skalg in Amercky.'

'Nah, Toh! Naaahth Skyagree!!'

But Tom did not reply. Amh had once said that the Skallagrigg
would come for her and he believed her. Arthur's Skalg had come,
hers would.

Esther's term started but she made no attempt to get involved in
any activities at St Anne's, her college. She was in any case a non-
resident, unusual for a first-year student but necessary in her case.

Helen had organized an efficient rota of helpers, supplemented
by Esther's friends from the Church of the New Word. Helen stayed
uninvolved, feeling as Margaret would have done that Esther had
best make her own way without an elderly woman in tow.

But the brief period of activity and better cheer that accompanied
Tom's visit and the start of term faded. Esther slumped into deeper
depression and Helen wrote to Richard and Kate in Australia,
sensibly warning Esther she was doing so.

'I'm sorry, my dear, you know I worry about you and do not
approve of this unwillingness to contact your father. Well, as you
have not written to him I have and I have told him that in my
judgement you are rather depressed at the moment. No one expects
these years to be easy, but the kind of upset and crying you seem
to be going through does not seem to me normal and you seem to
make things worse for yourself. I expect I sound dreadfully old-

fashioned but there it is. This "silence" business is plain rudeness in my book.'

I KEEP SAYING NOTHING'S WRONG. I'M WORKING HARD. I DO GET UPSET. THINGS ARE UPSETTING.

'What things? It's better to talk about them. Is it Daniel?'

IF YOU MUST KNOW, PARTLY.

Esther allowed herself one of her old grins and Helen relaxed. This was an improvement.

'Partly?'

ALL RIGHT THEN, I'M WORKING ON A NEW GAME.

'I thought you said you were working at your degree. I *wondered* what you were doing at that computer all hours of the night.'

THE ACADEMIC WORK IS EASY AT THE MOMENT. I CAN SEE IT WON'T BE LATER AND I'M NOT SURE I'M DOING THE RIGHT THING.

'Esther . . .'

BUT.

'But what? And what game?'

CAN'T TALK ABOUT IT YET.

Helen groaned.

'I'm glad I never had daughters of my own,' she said. 'I doubt if I would have the patience.'

Esther laughed.

IT'S NOT TOO LATE. I BET OLD JAMES FREEMAN WOULDN'T MIND!! AND MEDICAL RESEARCH IS PUSHING BACK THE FRONTIERS FOR CONCEPTION ALL THE TIME.

'Don't be so absurd, Esther,' said Helen trying not to smile.

But talk eased Helen's mind and a few days later she wrote more encouragingly to Richard.

If what Esther was suffering from was depression, it was not the kind a conventional counsellor might easily have understood. The truth was that she was, by degrees, beginning to immerse herself in the world of 'Skallagrigg'. Now that the reality of Arthur was established, she was beginning to fabricate a myth out of it, bringing together the loose strands of ideas for other games she had expressed from time to time to Daniel, and in her own diary.

It was as if she recognized that she could not hold on to Daniel by deceit and must very soon lose him, and was now creating the vast and complex world of labyrinths and puzzles of 'Skallagrigg' as an escape. As the weeks went by she became more and more immersed in it, pushing back the frontiers of her imagination into levels and sections whose horrors were darkness and suffering and to which she could not then see any end.

Indeed, Esther Marquand was beginning to create something which no one could have helped her with, nor rescued her from. But it was taking her to edges of suffering and extremities of emotion, of which tears were a small part, and her sense of loneliness and persecution were obstacles she had to overcome. This world she was making was her reality, while the degree she was studying for, the world of the college, the students, Woodstock Road, even Helen, finally even Tom, she was casting out into unreality. She must already have made the key decision for 'Skallagrigg' that the journeyer – the player – would have to become successively more severely handicapped if he or she was to reach the end of the quest. The game was becoming a journey into nightmare, of terrible self-acceptance, and the options the successful player would have to make would be ones towards self-abasement, humiliation, weakness and physical destruction in order to gain a spiritual victory. The method and the goal of the game were radically different from any similar role-play fantasy then devised.

The darkness and gloom that had beset Esther, and which concerned Helen so much, were the inevitable consequences of Esther's creativity, and alone and so far unaided she was pursuing it with a courage and tenacity which now, when only the game itself remains, seems simply remarkable; but which at the time, to those around her, must have seemed obsessive and grim.

The degree to which she was wearing masks in her day-to-day life is shown by a private comment she made about the Church of the New Word, to which, so far as Helen could tell, she was utterly devoted. Esther wrote in her diary of 10 October: 'Nonsense, what they say and believe is nonsense. They're so *nice* and *normal* that they can't see how vile they are. I mock them by going to their services and letting them push my chair. I laugh at them by simpering my agreement to their naive little Christian messages and weak philosophies. Helen's worried that they're a sect taking my mind over, well let her! If they could follow me into 'Skallagrigg' they might have a chance of getting to me. But I leave them standing at the entrance to the First Level. I feel terrible thinking these thoughts. God forgive me! But I go to their services because I can't work all the time, they ferry me there on the days my helpers have off, and I want to use them in some way in the game.

'In fact everything is going into the game now, everything I have felt and known. And I feel so lonely for Daniel who is the only one who could understand what I am doing. I know it is good good *good*. It's the best thing I have ever done and probably will ever do. I am putting all of me into it. One day Daddy will be proud of me. But It will be too late then and I am so lonely now. Sometimes I cry for no reason.'

A week later she wrote: 'Am obsessed by Arthur's son and grandson. Is he right not to tell them the truth?? I'm putting it into 'Skallagrigg', the only way I can deal with anything now. *Should* he tell them? Have they the *right* to know, whatever the consequences? If Daniel was handicapped like me and there was no chance of us ever meeting, what would be wrong with both of us feeding a fantasy about the other?? Tom is in 'Skallagrigg' and his bloody tomatoes. Got to have humour in it somewhere. I am going for six levels but players won't have to work their way through all of them. Maybe I'll make it seven. The Buddhists say that some people can cut through the seven stages to perfection in one lifetime, like Milarepa. Well, some players will be able to cut through the levels and get to the heart of 'Skallagrigg'. It grows and grows in my mind and is awesomely beautiful and I feel so lonely looking at it, feeling it, like a pioneer in a deserted land. Just to have Daniel there. Sexual fantasy!! Can't escape that. But I imagine him making love to me. Nearest I've ever got is randy Andy Moore touching me up. I didn't mind. I'd like it if I didn't get so shy about it in reality. But in 'Skallagrigg' anything is possible and I can walk and run and they can't stop me. I can make love too. But only Daniel. I must write to him now and tell the truth as I promised and see where that takes me in the game. I shall be so sad knowing it is over between us for ever: possibility feeds fantasy; impossibility feeds nothing. Or maybe . . . fantasy feeds fantasy, an acceptance of reality feeds truth. That's the key to it and 'Skallagrigg'. That's what the journeyer will need to grasp to reach the end. I *will* write that letter.'

Winter came early to Oxford. A miserable wet November with
sudden squalling winds. Esther stayed indoors and worked ever
harder at her game, which at that time was text only. Even more
bitter weather came and the central heating was turned up. Lecture
attendances fell, helpers were surly, the clapping and singing at
the Church on Sunday had a desperate air as hail beat at the
window. Esther was beginning to be silent to the world.

Helen summoned Tom again. One of the first things he said was,
'Mr Postman, Amh?'

'Yeh,' she said. Tomorrow morning.

'OK, Amh.'

So that day, a Saturday, feeling the calm of the condemned for
whom there is no reprieve, Esther finally wrote to Daniel. It was a
long letter, and it told the truth. It described her spasticity and
what she was, and what she could never be. It explained how
she had made a fantasy of him, and how in her mind she had
walked with him and made love to him, and run with him by
the sea. Those who have played 'Skallagrigg' and read this letter
now know that her work on the game to that point was a
necessary preparation. Without it she could not have seen herself as objectively as she did. Towards the letter's end she
wrote:

> I have been very lucky to have been loved so much. By
> my father, by my grandmother, by Helen, by Peter, by
> Tom. And you have been a good friend by cor-
> respondence. I feel I have betrayed your trust in me, as I
> have betrayed the love of so many by what I have
> become. I don't know why Helen is so good to me,
> putting up with me, and all the others too. They never
> complain and I have taken advantage of them.
>
> If you could have seen me as I am inside, Daniel, I
> think perhaps you could have loved me. I have delayed
> writing this as long as I could because I know that when
> I have finished it, I will not be able to work on 'Skal-
> lagrigg' any more. I needed you at my side, even if only
> the fantasy you. I needed to know that one person in the
> world would understand. So I'm sending all I've done
> with this and you can use it as you will. Please never

write to me or refer to it again. Make it your own, my gift
to you. There's so much to do that it's not much of a gift.
It needs graphics which I can't do and you can. There
are parts of it so beautiful and grand. But I can't go on
without you, and I can't have you, and I have betrayed
whatever it was we had and lived a lie. Please forgive me
and remember me. I would have loved you my darling
with my heart and my soul and my poor body. But if you
were here I could not even say your name. Daniel,
Daniel. I can type it (not write it and you never
questioned that, bless you) and it is beautiful to me. Oh
my dear forgive me.

Love Esther

'Toh! *Toh!*'

He came running and took the printout of her letter, and the
mass of printout for 'Skallagrigg', and some floppy disks on which
her programs were, and packed them up carefully. He put an envelope label into her printer and she printed out Daniel's name and
address and he stuck it on the package. And then some stamps.

'OK, Amh?'

Miserably, Esther allowed herself to be pushed down the road to
the familiar postbox. Tom went through his usual peering-in
routine. He liked posting letters.

He pushed the package into the slit.

NO NO NO NO NO NO NO NO NO NO DON'T, TOM, NO.

'What's wrong, Amh?'

'Nah,' she said beginning to cry. 'NaAhAhAhAhAhAhAh,' and
she did cry as she thought of him receiving it, and his hatred of her
for lying, and his disappointment, his terrible disappointment. And
then of the fact that she was not beautiful and never would be, and
he imagined she was. Then of the fact that to have had one person
in the world who had thought her worth knowing: one person
who cared. Just one.

'Nah,' she said finally, her face setting hard. *'NAH!'*

So Tom pushed her back to the house, back into her room, hid
the offending package with its truthful letter in a drawer and
Esther wrote another, briefer, final note:

Dear Daniel,

I said I would write and now I am doing so. I have misled
you and I feel deeply guilty about it. Nothing I can say or
do will erase the lies I have, by implication, told. The fact
is that for a long time now I have had a relationship with
someone else. It has had difficulties but now these are
resolved and we are to get married over the Christmas
vacation. I love Peter very much and am glad we are
taking this step. I would be grateful if you do not reply to
this, or make any attempt to contact me whatsoever.
Leon Sadler will deal with any outstanding matters
about games and that will be the end of it. I have only
ever loved one person and now I want to be his wife,
bear his children and make him happy.

Please forgive me and forget me. I would be grateful if
you could destroy all my letters or send them back so
that I can. I have destroyed yours and am sending back
the disks you have sent which have material on them.
Please do not write or communicate with me. I have
behaved badly but I was unsure of my own mind. Now I
am to live with the man I love and am very happy and I
hope one day that such happiness will come your way.

                    Yours affectionately, Esther Marquand.

The letter was put into another stamped addressed envelope by
Tom, who took her immediately back to the postbox. Cold, sure of
herself, indifferent now, her face a mask, she asked Tom to help
her put in the terrible letter herself and she did so, and heard it
flutter down into darkness beyond recall.

She returned to her room and got Tom to tidy her workspace. All
the 'Skallagrigg' material was put away, every last trace. Her study
books came out. A new programme of work was stuck on her door.

'Skallagrigg' was abandoned. The dream of Daniel was no more.

I'M MAKING A NEW START, declared Esther the next day.
I SUPPOSE EVERYONE GOES THROUGH A BAD FIRST TERM. I'M
SORRY I'VE BEEN SO FOUL.

Helen looked very relieved.

AND ANOTHER THING. I AM GIVING UP THE CHURCH OF THE
NEW WORD. IT'S ALL NONSENSE. FROM NOW ON I SHALL BE A
GOOD ANGLICAN AND START STUDYING FOR THE PRIEST-
HOOD!!! BY THE TIME I'M FIFTY THEY MIGHT JUST HAVE GOT
ROUND TO ORDAINING WOMEN! SORRY, JOKE.

They both laughed, but there was a terrible strain about Esther's
face and a desert around her heart, which she ignored. For the
days following, and then for two or three weeks, when the postman
called or the telephone rang she expected it to be Daniel. That she
could not have borne. But the danger period passed, and unpleasant November gave way to icy December.

She agreed to go to Australia for Christmas. The sun would do
her good. She would start talking to her father again. The crisis
was over.

Then on 13 December Esther was confined to bed with what
seemed merely a bad cold. Three days later she worsened rapidly
and influenza was diagnosed. A week later the doctor began to
visit daily and on 23 December, the day she would have flown to
Australia, Esther was taken slowly down Woodstock Road by
ambulance. She had pneumonia and was very weak.

'She appears to be in no danger,' said the doctor, 'but with
someone like her it is wise to take the greatest precautions. We
cannot know what reserves she has. Spastics sometimes . . .' He
raised his eyes to heaven, and shrugged.

Helen called Richard Marquand in Australia and he flew back
on the first available flight which, at that busy time of year, was
just after Christmas.

Esther was no better, and lay in bed very weak and with dark
circles under her eyes.

'She seems very fatigued quite apart from the illness,' the doctor
said. 'Has she been under any special strain, or working too hard?'
Richard and Helen conceded that both perhaps were true.

For a few minutes after his arrival Esther had seemed pleased to
see Richard but then, as if remembering herself, she had turned
her head from him and continued her silence. This, more than
anything else she had ever done, upset him. To Helen she would
talk, but not to him. Nor did she talk to him once during his three-
day stay.

By mid-January the crisis seemed over but she was still too weak even to contemplate returning to college. There were long-distance telephone calls between Richard and Helen arranging for Esther to be moved down to Hill House where Marion and Jeremy had trained staff to look after her once the Radcliffe was satisfied she could be released from hospital. Helen was reluctant, but her house was not suitable for convalescent nursing. There was, the doctors stressed, no question of Esther going back to college that term.

So as winter set in, and the snow and ice came, Esther lay in a room in Hill House, able to look over to the lawns and leafless apple trees of Harefield's garden, where once, when she was a girl, she sat with her father, and Tom was a herd of wild elephants in the distant undergrowth. Where once too they had believed that over the wooden fence the Skallagrigg waited, and one day they might find the strength to reach him.

Spring came but Esther remained weak, not in body now so much as in spirit. When the sun shone they were able to take her out on to the patio of Hill House and sometimes down the path and into the garden of the now empty Harefield. But her face was pale and her eyes were lost, and the energy and life she once had had gone, and seemed irrecoverable.

Helen visited every few days; Tom came. Arthur and Edward sent a card from Cornwall where they had gone for an early holiday. It was a picture of The Racks. In March Kate flew into Heathrow and came to see her and saw that it was as if Esther had given up on life.

'You're not well, you know, not at all. I wish you'd come out and see us when you're a little better. The change . . .'

WILL DO ME GOOD?

Esther's sharpness was still there though she typed the words slowly now.

'Mmm.' said Kate. 'It will, you know.'

OK, typed Esther, but quite spiritlessly. Kate had the impression that Esther would have agreed to almost anything she suggested.

'You'll really come? You won't make excuses?'

NO I WON'T.

'In May or June, then. I'll tell your father. He will be pleased.'

Esther did not respond but stared round instead at the garden where the bright cerebral palsied children whom Hill House cared for played and laughed and drove their wheelchairs far too fast. Sometimes they glanced up to where she sat watching through the long days. To them Esther was an old person, and ill, and she worried them with her pale face and sad dark eyes.

In April Tom came again, with an Easter egg for Esther. His journeys were always adventures to him and he arrived proudly, an air of the explorer about him. He was allowed to travel alone, always by train or bus, and had very strict instructions about where to go and what to do. Helpers always met him because otherwise he wandered off and got lost. He carried relevant addresses and telephone numbers in a plastic pouch round his neck. Ever since the time he had gone from Harefield into Wycombe by himself and been picked up by the police he knew that getting lost was naughty, and caused people trouble.

'Don't get lost,' he said. 'Never, not me. Best boy now.'

So his visits to Esther were a source of pride, and he would describe the journey to her in great detail.

But now even with Tom she rarely smiled, and this upset him. Yet still he visited.

So that Easter he came and gave her his present.

'Open it for you, Amh. It's an egg. Chocky yum yum.'

Her dark eyes did not respond.

'Amh, you're iller.'

'Nah . . .' she whispered.

'Yes, Amh,' said Tom, 'you are.'

He took her for a walk into the grounds of Harefield. The garden looked uncared for. Tom's old tomato beds were bare. Someone, from the church presumably, had pulled down the old wooden fence and replaced it with high solid fencing, new and creosoted. They could no longer see over it.

Esther said nothing.

'Amh . . .' began Tom. But he did not finish and he fell into silence and worry.

He took her back and Marion gave him tea, and then he said goodbye to Esther and was taken by Jeremy to Wycombe station and left on the platform.

'Bye, Tom,' said Jeremy.

Afterwards he reported that Tom looked subdued and did not give him his usual hug.

Jeremy left and Tom sat forlornly waiting for his train. As it came in he got up and stood watching it uncertainly. Then he ran down the platform and into the public toilets and hid from the train, as if it might have arms that would pull him into the carriage. The train left and Tom stood in the smelly semi-darkness of the toilet crying and looking at the plastic pouch with the address of the Centre, to which he was meant to be returning. Somebody would be meeting the train at Marylebone.

'Not going back,' Tom whispered. 'Going to find Skalg for Amh.'

Tom came out of the lavatory and walked up to a guard standing on the station.

'Oxford,' he said.

Tom was directed to another platform where he waited. Someone put him on the train and when they asked if he was being met he said, 'Yes,' nodding his head.

At Oxford he walked off the train and through the ticket barrier unchallenged. Perhaps they thought a Down's syndrome youth does not travel alone and so someone else had his ticket.

Oxford station is two miles from Helen Perry-Wilcox's home in Woodstock Road but it took Tom four hours to make the journey there, by which time police in Wycombe and London were looking for him. No one thought to look in Oxford.

When he finally arrived at Helen's house it was in darkness. She was away for Easter and the house was empty. He rang at the bell for more than an hour, crying and unsure what to do.

It was dark and cold and he must have been very afraid. The light of passing cars caught him, but no one noticed. Somehow he found the courage to go round the dark scaredy side of the house to the back and peer in at the french windows of Helen's garden room. They were locked and above him the branches of trees scraped in the April darkness and noises that were danger surrounded him. Yet he groped his way down the garden to the shed where he knew she kept her garden tools. He found a spade. He carried it through the dark back to the french windows and he broke the glass and was able to get in.

At that moment, a next door neighbour, hearing sounds and suspicious, called the police. Perhaps Tom knew he had little time. He went to Esther's room, turned on a light, searched her drawers, and found what he was looking for.

'Skalg in Amercky,' he said. And on the packet he himself had packed, addressed to Daniel Schuster, he painstakingly wrote PLEASE COM TOM. He found he could not open the front door and so had to go back out into the darkness and make his way to the front. As he walked away from the house towards the postbox a police car flashing blue lights went past him, stopped and began to reverse. He began to run.

The police found him, crying by the postbox, his hands empty as he said, 'Sorry, sorry, sorry,' for something that had required more courage than any ever knew.

'But, Tom, why?' they asked later.

But Tom only smiled and said, 'Mr Postman finds Skalg for Amh. Needs her Skalg now.' Of the packet he was silent, and of its contents he had no recall. Just that it was addressed to Daniel and Daniel was Amh's Skalg. She had said so once. She had. And now her Skallagrigg must come.

SIXTY-FIVE

Mr Postman travels in many forms. He is a dark recess in the Woodstock Road. He is a shelf in the central sorting office near Oxford station. He is the replete companionable canvas bag which jolts off into the night in a royal red van. He is the freezing cold of a cargo hold 23,000 feet above the Atlantic. He changes uniform, changes accents, and he travels by road, by air, across deserts and mountains, until he arrives on a shelf in the small, warm and lively post office of Hanniman Beach, California. And from there, mid-morning, Mr Postman bumps down the rough track which is Hanniman Beach's oldest road, and he delivers a packet to a mailbox, marked 'Schuster'.

That mailbox reverberates to the sea's roar and sometimes in winter salt spray is blown on it and corrodes the metal. Sometimes, too, Schuster doesn't show up to collect his mail at the bottom of his property even though he's in his house, because he's like that. Working. Or asleep at strange hours.

Then when he does, often as not, half the mail is junked into a trash can outside the back door.

This day he does show up, and he looks at that packet and its brief message on the outside in black felt-tip pen: PLEASE COM TOM. He looks at the postmark and the English stamps. He feels it, wondering. Oh he knows who it's from, but he's still wondering. He walks on down to the beach and he sits in front of the great incoming Pacific rollers. Windsurfers, made tiny by the great seas, go back and forth across the bay, but he does not see them. Slowly he opens the package.

First he reads the letter, quickly and only once. Then he peers in at the floppy disks and the printout, which he pulls out and studies. He gets up and turns back to the house, the wind nagging at his baggy jeans and sweatshirt and carrying off the sand his trainers kick up.

He goes indoors to a computer room, big, impressive and well-ordered. He puts one of the disks in a disk-drive, keys in commands, and watches as titles come up. He leans forward and studies them before keying in more commands. He gets a pen and clean pad and puts it by the keyboard.

Three hours later Daniel Schuster stretches, stands up and goes to make himself a coffee and stares out of his kitchen window. He does not seem to register much, like the fact that the wind is getting up, or that he has been occupied so long that the tide is almost in. He turns back to his computer room and leaves his coffee untouched on the side.

Darkness falls. A single light goes on in the house. Schuster is still at his computer. The clear pad he started out with is now full of numbers and writing. One word across the top, underscored again and again, stands out. It reads 'Skallagrigg'. He makes a call and returns to the screen. Twenty minutes later a car pulls up, and a man gets out, opens the front screen door, whistles, and shouts 'Hey, Dan. OK?'

It's the pizza man. Daniel's having a supper or maybe a late lunch; or, more likely, a late late breakfast. Carrying a can of Schlitz he comes out on to the front veranda, sits down on a step and eats his pizza. The phone rings twice but the answering machine handles it. He lives alone, no one visits, just the sea twice a day; receding for the time being back over the sands which gleam grey in the dark. Daniel Schuster is thinking. He gets up and goes back to his computer.

Outside the starry darkness deepens. Inside, Daniel's eyes are alight with excitement though he looks tired. His hands and fingers move smoothly over the keyboard, and he's on to his third or fourth page of notes. He has found a bigger sheet of paper and with a felt-tip pen seems to be drawing a labyrinthine map, adding information wrested from the screen from time to time.

Deep night and the wind has died. Schuster is asleep in a chair. In his hand on his lap is a typed letter from Esther Marquand. His face has dried where the tears were.

Dawn. Sun. Sun getting warmer. Rolling seas but calmer today. Just a dull distant roar. Across the beach windsurfers walk, fun boards tucked under their arms, rolled sails over their shoulders. On the shore above them the sun rises above a beach house where a boy-man sits on a veranda sipping orange juice. He has shaved. He looks rested and at peace. He sits and watches as they assemble their boards, turn to the sea and ride expertly into it, dagger boards looped over their forearms. Their shouts are as distant and light as the gulls riding the bay winds.

Schuster gets up, goes back into the house, rummages in a desk for a passport, money and credit cards, throws a few things into a bag, locks the house up and goes out to the separate garage. He opens up and there is a Mercedes two-seater, very new. Slung across the roof struts of the garage is a windsurf board, an old model and dusty, wrapped up, unused for months, maybe more. And a high performance sail. Schuster does not look at them. He drives the car out on to the road, closes the garage, and he sticks a scribbled note on the mailbox: 'Jimmy, keep my mail back for a week.' The sun rises high in the sky as the car turns towards the freeway and heads for Los Angeles airport.

Esther Marquand sits silent in the garden of Hill House. An opened letter is on her tray from St Anne's College. What are her plans for the coming term? She can hardly bear to look at it. It is warmer today and the sun has cleared the beeches at the bottom of the garden and shines across her pale face.

She turns the chair and slowly travels down the asphalt path towards the garden of Harefield. Somebody shouts 'Hi, Esther!' and for once she turns and does a wave as best she can.

She's feeling good: well, better. She'll write to Helen and thank her for . . . for what? For coming down so often. She'll do that. She'll write to her father and say the trip to Sydney is still on. She'll . . .

'Esther!'

It is Marion's voice calling from the Hill House veranda. Esther stops and turns her chair. Marion stands on the patio looking down at her with a strange excited expression on her face. At her side stands a man, or nearly a man. He is tall and sunburnt and his hair is loose and boyish over his forehead. He wears brown-rimmed glasses.

Marion starts down towards her, the man following. He is looking at her.

'Esther,' says Marion. And her voice is receding into an echo chamber and far far away Esther's breath is coming short and her chest tightening in fear and apprehension. 'Esther,' ESTHER, ESTHER. The man is staring and uncertain of her. He has come to see her and she knows who he is.

'Nah!' Esther begins to shout. 'Nah!' and she is in the nightmare of trying to get away but being unable to move fast enough.

She turns her chair to shield her body from his gaze that comes from behind those glasses because she cannot bear that he can see her as she is. 'Nah!'

'Esther!' and Marion reaches her, the man lagging behind uneasily, and Marion says, 'This gentleman has come to see you. His name . . .'

I KNOW HIS NAME I KNOW I KNOW DON'T LET HIM SEE ME, MARION, DON'T.

'It's all right,' says Marion softly. And then more gently, 'It'll be all right.'

Then Esther turns her chair and looks at the ground where the man's feet are. He's wearing trainers. She looks up at him but now he barely looks at her.

He smiles uneasily in her general direction.

'This is Esther Marquand,' says Marion.

The man's hands are gawky, awkward, in fact the whole of him is suddenly awkward. He's thin. Tall. Angular.

'I'm Daniel Schuster,' he says.

Only Marion smiles and there are lights in her eyes.

'I'll get you both a cup of coffee,' she says and leaves them to it. There is silence.

'Tom sent the letter you didn't send,' says Daniel. His voice is quick, nasal, quite strong.

'Oh,' says Esther.

'And the floppies. The printout.' He pauses as if uncertain how she is reacting, or even if she can hear. He is not looking at her directly, but somewhere in the region of the right handle of the chair. 'Skallagrigg,' he adds finally, in explanation.

'Yeh,' she says less tensely. He hasn't run away. He hasn't said he thinks she's ugly. He hasn't reacted to her at all. Not one tiny bit, and Esther is schooled in the minutiae of other people's reactions. If anything, he sounds annoyed.

'Can I sit down?' he says. 'I'm tired. It's a long way to come for a cup of coffee.' He sits down on a garden bench. Esther registers that he has a sense of humour.

'So that's Harefield,' he says, looking past her. Marion must have explained. He sits uncomfortably.

'Yeh,' says Esther. There is another long silence. He suddenly leans back and relaxes.

'You bet they're not going to remember us by our conversation,' he says.

'Nah,' she agrees.

Then he leans forward and looks into her eyes for the first time. He looks very serious.

'There's a hell of a lot of work to do on that game of yours.'

'Yeh,' she says.

Daniel looks around to see if Marion is coming with the coffee.

'Is there somewhere here I can take a shower?'

'Yeh,' she says.

'Levels Two and Three are confusing. Level One's brilliant. Level Four is just amazing.' He suddenly laughs, puts his hands behind his head, leans back and repeats, 'Just *am-aze-ing*! I did some outline graphics ideas on the plane. They're in my bag in Mary-Anne's office.'

MARION, types Esther. He quickly registers the screen attached to her chair.

'Yeh, yeh, now listen.' He leans forward conspiratorially. 'You better have a Minion in reach of this place because we are going to work, you know? W–O–R–K.'

Marion brings the coffee on a tray.

DANIEL WANTS A SHOWER, types up Esther.

Marion smiles. For the first time in five months Esther has colour in her cheeks.

'Soon as you like,' says Marion.

'I'm much obliged Mary-Anne,' says Daniel. 'I hope it's no trouble.'

'It's a pleasure, Mr Schuster. My name's Marion,' says Marion.

But Daniel misses that one because now he is on his knees looking at Esther's keyboard.

'Very, very cute,' he says, marvelling.

THAT'S THE ORIGINAL SADLER KEYBOARD. THE SCREEN'S HIS AS WELL, explains Esther.

Daniel immediately disconnects and unstraps it without a by-
your-leave or thank you, to take a better look. He pores over it
obsessively.

'Mr Sadler did this? I hope I meet him this trip.'

The shower is forgotten. Daniel reconnects Esther's keyboard
and checks that it works.

THANKS A MILLION, she types.

Daniel grins boyishly. He looks less tense. He sips his coffee.

THANK YOU FOR COMING, she adds.

'Thanks for asking me, Miss Marquand.'

Esther giggles.

'You know something? "Skallagrigg" is quite a game,' he says,
the seriousness back in his eyes. Worry and gawkiness have
returned. Eventually he says, 'I felt really nervous about meeting
you.'

AND NOW?

'Scared,' says Daniel.

They stare at each other. Esther's hand moves.

I AM TOO, types Esther and she looks down at her hands. I'M
SORRY I LIED.

'It's OK,' says Daniel, 'it's the game I've come about.' And with
a curious sense of disappointment Esther sees that it is. His eyes
wander here and there restlessly as he talks. He hardly seems to
see her.

Her coffee is beginning to grow cold on her tray.

'Hey, I'm sorry. Have this and we'll talk. I'll talk. You type.'

When Marion looks back at them Daniel is helping Esther to her
coffee and spilling it down her chin as, at the same time, he talks
incomprehensibly about computing.

Marion goes into Hill House and telephones Helen Perry-Wilcox.

'When were you coming today? For lunch? I suggest you delay
it for a day or two. Why?' Marion laughs. 'You'll find out,' she
says.

She goes and finds Jeremy.

'What is it?' he asks. Marion looks joyful and she goes over to
the window.

'Come over here for a moment,' she says, 'I want to show you
something out in the garden.'

*

Money did not seem to be Daniel's problem, although in appearance he was casual and student-like. He had hired a smart car at Heathrow and on his wrist he wore an expensive-looking digital watch. He said that he had rented a room in a motel.

Quite what they made of him there was hard to guess. His trainers, which were his only footwear, were worn down and cracked. His jeans were faded, though clean and of good quality. He wore a baggy short-sleeved shirt with a yellow-and-black lasso and saddle design all over it. He carried with him a well-designed, small rucksack, blue and red and with the logo ROCKEE down its side.

With everyone but Esther he was so awkward in manner and slow of speech that silences seemed interminable in his company. He had the gangly awkwardness of a growing boy, and under his thick glasses his eyes were narrowed and strained as if he was peering into bright sunlight. His hair was straight, dark and carelessly cut, with a white streak at the back as if a splash of bleach had caught it. His eyelashes too were blond.

He seemed barely interested in the world about him, except that small part which he happened to peer at, and which, for the time being, seemed to be Esther.

When Marion asked him if he wanted some supper – he had been sitting in the garden with Esther ever since their introduction – he said, 'That's great,' and returned to his notes. When she interrupted him again and asked where he was staying he peered up at her, dug into the back pocket of his jeans, and took out a hotel reservation card.

'Crest Motel on the freeway,' he said.

'Isn't that very expensive?' she asked.

'Could be,' he said. 'Seemed good.' Adding drolly, 'Plenty of space for my toothbrush.' He looked at Esther and she grinned back and looked, a little smugly, at Marion as if to say, 'Isn't he witty?'

YOU COULD HAVE STAYED IN HAREFIELD. NOBODY WOULD MIND, WOULD THEY, MARION?

'Er, no,' said Marion.

The following morning Daniel appeared suddenly at the garden entrance to the dining-room, peered in at the surprised residents of Hill House who were having breakfast, and hurried over to Esther.

She greeted him with a brief nod and blushed. He stood over her, a little awkward because everyone was staring.

The two girls who served and the sixteen resident children had no idea what to make of Daniel. There was a hushed excitement in the room.

'I've got to fix some things,' he said to Esther. 'Take till noon. You look at this. OK?' He put some sheets of paper down among the bowls of cereal and dishes of marmalade. Then he was gone out into the garden the way he had come before she had had time to nod and say, 'Yeh!'

By two o'clock that afternoon Daniel Schuster had installed two complete Minion systems in Esther's room, complete with double disk-drives, a configured Diablo daisy-wheel printer and an extra large monitor screen.

By two-thirty he had made up special leads allowing Esther to input to both computers from her Sadler keyboard.

By three, Marion, having put up no resistance to this sudden invasion of Harefield, felt she ought at least to watch over its initial phases and was completely lost. Esther and Daniel were in a huddle before the big screen and two small monitors as he explained to her the special commands and capabilities of the graphic program builder he had bought and which was held in one of the drives.

Marion, concerned for Esther's physical and moral safety with this strange, monosyllabic young American, had decided that whatever the attraction between them was, it was, for the time being at least, entirely of the mind.

'If she gets tired she's to stop!' said Marion.

But she was waved away from the darkened room by both of them. As she left the otherwise empty house to return to her duties in Hill House the only sound she heard was the plasticated rattle of computer keys.

At five there was a call on the Hill House telephone for Daniel Schuster. The voice was American and it said he was calling for Minion and left an Uxbridge number. A few moments later Daniel peered through the office door and asked myopically if he had had a call. He took the number, picked up the phone, and without asking, returned the call. Marion understood the 'Hi!' and the 'Ciao!' but nothing of the computer jargon in between.

'Say, I'm sorry,' apologized Daniel, peering around and starting to leave.

'Does Esther want tea? Do *you* want tea?'

'She needs to go to the john,' said Daniel. 'I should have told you before.'

The following day the Hill House staff noticed that Daniel's car was parked in Harefield's drive from early morning.

'How did he get in?' Marion asked Esther over breakfast.

I TOLD HIM TO TAKE ONE OF THE KEYS. And then: IT IS MY HOME. I MEAN, I CAN HAVE WHO I WANT THERE.

'All right, calm down.'

I AM CALM. VERY. She giggled, for the first time in months. And her eyes were brighter. And she looked as if she wanted to live again.

SORRY, she typed. DIDN'T MEAN TO SNAP.

'It's all right, Esther,' smiled Marion.

DO YOU LIKE HIM?

'Yes, I think I do. But what are you doing with him?'

PROGRAMMING A GAME.

'Oh,' said Marion. 'Helen's coming over today.'

GOOD.

'Will he have had any breakfast?'

I DON'T KNOW. COULD WE TAKE HIM SOME?

'He could have it here. Everybody's very curious to see him.'

HE'D PREFER IT THERE. HE LIKES WORKING. WHEN'S HELEN COMING?

Helen came in the afternoon, and Esther and Daniel took a break from their world of semi-darkness.

'This is rather a surprise, Mr Schuster . . . er, Daniel,' said Helen. 'I mean, your coming like this. I mean, after Esther's less than enthusiastic responses to your telephone calls. Isn't it?'

Helen found the going tough. Daniel seemed slow of speech and awfully *young*.

'It's a pleasure to meet you,' he managed to say eventually, gulping down his tea before she had finished pouring her own. Then, to her amazement, he helped Esther to hers. Marion had refused to say anything about him on the telephone and now she saw why. It was hard to formulate exactly what he was: youth or adult, ungainly or strong, morose or simply shy.

After ten minutes of tea he continued to sit with them as if under sufferance, and Helen might have felt that she was intruding except that Esther was so clearly delighted to be able to show off a young man. Under the glory of it all she had changed completely. Her face was flushed, and she kept darting little affirmatory glances at Daniel, who peered down at his hands, and looked uneasy. The only information Helen had had was that he was tall. He was also restless, with the kind of energy that spills tea into saucers, and crumbles biscuits into fragments. Yet when he was doing things for Esther he had a curious grace and tenderness, as if he had been doing them for a long, long time.

'What are you doing in there?' said Helen, indicating the general direction of Esther's room.

SKALLAGRIGG. DANIEL'S WORKING OUT A SCHEME FOR GRAPHICS. WE SHOULD HAVE DONE THEM TOGETHER FROM THE BEGINNING SO IT'S HARDER THAN IT SHOULD BE.

'You met Arthur,' Daniel told Helen suddenly.

'Yes, I did. I was there when . . .'

'I'm going to Oxford to see the Bodleian stack rooms. Level Four of the game. I'll need a ticket, Esther says. Could you get me one? I would like to see Herstorne and meet Arthur and his brother. That'll be the next trip.'

'Yes, of course . . .'

'Have to be tomorrow morning. I'm flying back tomorrow night. My week in the office.' He explained that he worked a week a month for *CODA*. At the moment he was holed up at his home in Hanniman working on some database software.

'This is a quick visit then Daniel,' said Helen, a little ironically.

DANIEL'S COMING BACK NEXT WEEK FROM NEW YORK. HE CAN STAY IN HAREFIELD CAN'T HE? THE MOTEL'S OK BUT . . .'

'Takes a while to drive over in the morning. Traffic. Just like Los Angeles. Forget it!'

DANIEL LIVES AT HANNIMAN BEACH. IT'S FAMOUS FOR WINDSURFING.

Helen had seen that sport on television.

'Do you windsurf, Daniel?' she asked reasonably.

He looked down and was silent. Curiously so.

'Nah,' he said, just like Esther. 'Not any more. Had an accident. I've retired.' There was an uncomfortable silence.

'Why exactly have you come, Daniel?' asked Helen at last, feeling she should ask a few parent-like questions on Esther's behalf.

'Because Esther's making a game that's very original. I wanted to be in on the act. Also she's stupid and thought that her handicaps make a difference to my involvement and that really riled me. So I came on over. They don't make a difference.'

He looked up and straight at Helen for once. 'Anyway, without them she wouldn't be making this game, would she?'

'I suppose not,' said Helen, feeling that she was beginning to like Daniel.

'How long are you coming for on your next visit?' she asked.

'As long as it takes, I guess. I need a break from Hanniman. It's been a tough eighteen months out there.' He kicked his trainers on the floor and then crossed his legs and leaned back, reminding Helen of a young giraffe.

'I want to meet Mr Sadler. We've talked on the phone about Esther's games.'

'Oh, are they successful?'

'You can bet they are. Esther's got quite a following, except no one knows who she is. We thought that was cute PR, now I know differently.'

'You design games don't you? Esther's shown me. Have you got a following?'

'Yes, I guess I have,' he said seriously.

The next evening Daniel Schuster flew out of Heathrow, and the morning after that a bunch of twenty-four roses arrived for Esther Marquand at Hill House. Among them was a card, and on the card was a message.

'Keep working,' it read, 'and next time you write a letter to a man in California get on and send it. See you soon. Daniel.'

Daniel Schuster returned two weeks later. This time he wore a neat grey suit, a classy white shirt and a red silk tie and carried a brief-case. He was driving a different hired car. He greeted Marion apologetically.

'I came straight from a meeting in New York,' he said. 'I didn't have time to change.'

Helen, who had come over to see Esther that morning, appeared at Marion's side.

'You look very smart,' she said.

'Smart?' he said. 'I am smart. You mean neat. Where's Esther?'

'Working over in Harefield,' said Helen smiling. 'She's in a bad mood.'

'That's great,' he said cryptically.

'I hope we'll see more of you this time,' Helen said quickly, as Daniel turned to walk the few yards into Harefield's grounds.

'Yeh, sure,' he replied unconvincingly. From behind he seemed even taller and thinner than before: perhaps it was the suit and polished shoes which clicked smartly – neatly – on the asphalt. The streak of white hair at the back of his head gave him a punkish air.

Ten minutes later Helen saw an odd sight. It was Daniel pushing Esther in her chair out into Abbey Road. He was taking her for a walk and he was talking; and as he turned her chair into the road his hand rested briefly on her shoulder as if to make sure she was quite safe.

Helen stared after them long after they had gone out of sight, for the picture of them together had triggered a memory and she was trying to place it. And then it came.

It was not of something she had seen, but of what she had been told. Of how, after that final Skallagrigg story Esther had collected, Norman had pushed Arthur back across the grass to Herstorne Hospital 'as if he was gold'.

What Helen had seen was Daniel Schuster pushing Esther as if she too was gold.

Helen stepped out on to the driveway, and walked slowly down to the road. Daniel was already a long way off with Esther, walking in his rapid jerky way as if there was not enough time for everything he wanted to do.

Helen walked into Harefield's front drive. The great copper beech was still leafless, but its buds were spiking and the sinewy branches rose green-grey into the late spring sky.

She walked round the side of the house into the garden. The lawn had had its first mowing the day before – ordered by Esther it seemed for Daniel's return. To Helen the day, suddenly, seemed beautiful. The air, chilly that morning, was now warm and made her heart spring-light and yearning.

She felt an unexpected joy, and a sureness, as if youth was

about her, alive and self-centred and purposeful. She thought suddenly of Brian, who had died in this garden, and of Margaret who always sat rather stiffly in it, sternly protective of her granddaughter. Now Esther was growing up at last and walking out with a young man.

Helen wondered by what chance of circumstance she herself had won the right to be so intimately *here*, and happy.

A day or two before Esther had explained the game she and Daniel were making, saying it was to do with levels and mazes; puzzles and problems, from which, said Esther, the player would have to break free to find the Skallagrigg.

Helen found herself standing on the lawn looking back up at the house which, for a time, had been home to Richard and Esther, and later a home to Kate, and a family place for Margaret and Brian. A second home for Tom.

To her right she heard the children in Hill House coming out into the garden. Sometimes they drifted into Harefield's garden, exploring where once Tom and Esther must have explored when they were younger. Well, Harefield would be one with Hill House one day and how benign it looked, how pleased.

And she . . . Helen folded her arms across her chest for a moment, her neat dark cardigan across her shoulders, her face lined, her hair shining and grey-white.

Circumstance and choice, Esther had explained, were what guided a player through the game.

IT'S UP TO THEM. PEOPLE HAVE TO KNOW HOW WEAK THEY ARE BEFORE THEY KNOW THEY'RE STRONG. THAT'S WHAT ARTHUR LANE SAYS.

Helen thought of Herstorne.

'Without me she would not have got there and found Arthur. Yet without her, nor would I. That's the kind of circular paradox that Esther's making a game of,' she told herself.

A look of amused determination came across her face, and then she smiled.

She walked up to the patio, into the kitchen and through into the hall. Esther's door was open, the curtains drawn, a computer's disk-drive humming. A computer screen was lit up with green numerics on it. Helen did not venture further into the room.

She opened her handbag and taking out her diary selected a

number from the few listed in it, and dialled it. Before the telephone started ringing at the other end she took a seat.

The telephone was answered.

'Hello, James,' she said, 'this is Helen.' She smiled a little while he spoke a greeting.

'Yes, it's a very lovely day here too. Summer's round the corner.' He spoke some more and she nodded her head familiarly.

'James,' she said after a pause, 'I would very much like to come and see you. Yes. That's right, I'm inviting myself up to see you. Because . . . there are things I wish to share with someone of my own age. Mmm? I'm sixty-five.'

James Freeman spoke a little more. Helen finally cut him short with a slight laugh. 'A few years at our age is nothing.' He said something and she laughed outright and said, 'As to when, my dear, I'm not quite sure. I rather think I'm needed here for a few weeks. Daniel Schuster has come back. But very soon. I just wanted you to know I wish to come. Tomorrow I might not have had the courage to make this call. But today . . . well . . . today seems to be a very happy one.'

They talked a little more and then Helen said a soft goodbye.

As she did so she heard Daniel Schuster laughing at the front of the house.

For a moment she hesitated, turning towards the door to open it for them, before thinking again and turning back to slip out through the kitchen into the garden and across the grass to Hill House. And in that spot in the labyrinth or the Level or the maze or the corridor or the great open space where she had been, another passing by might never have known she *had* been; while a third, old now, waited beyond the wooden fence, and heard her steps loud enough to know that she was coming at last.

SIXTY-SIX

Four weeks later, at the beginning of June, Esther announced that Daniel was taking her away for the weekend with Tom.

Helen was not in the least surprised. There was about the pair of them a delightful inevitability, and if they looked ridiculously young to be going anywhere alone together, that was because life itself was sometimes ridiculous.

'You know perfectly well I have to sound extremely cautious on behalf of your father,' said Helen.

NOTHING WILL HAPPEN. TOM WILL BE THERE.

'That doesn't fool me,' said Helen.

DO YOU WANT TO COME TOO THEN TO MAKE SURE WE DON'T GET UP TO ANY 'HANKY-PANKY'?

'No, my dear, I don't. But you can tell me where you are going and how.'

DANIEL'S HIRING A CAMPER VAN AND WE'RE GOING TO A CAMPING SITE IN SOUTH WALES NEAR THE SEA.

'You seem to have it all organized.'

DANIEL'S ORGANIZED. VERY. HE MAY NOT SEEM IT BUT HE IS.

'I think he seems a very organized young man indeed.'

I THINK . . .

'I know very well what you think about Daniel, my dear, and I prefer not to be told.'

WE MAY STAY LONGER THAN A WEEKEND.

'Decisions about college and so on are going to have to be made very soon.'

Esther looked bored.

THIS TRIP IS FOR MY HEALTH. WE'RE GOING TO DECIDE THINGS AFTER THAT.

'What things?' asked Helen, cautiously.

THINGS.

Then Esther added unconvincingly: ABOUT THE GAME. But her eyes were shining.

'You know this is quite ridiculous.'

I DON'T THINK YOU THINK THAT BUT FEEL YOU'VE GOT TO SAY IT.

Helen looked at her for a long moment and then said, 'As is often the case, Esther, unfortunately, you are right. Please ask Daniel to phone me when you get there and if you are staying longer, and send me a postcard.'

THANK   YOU.   XXXXXXXXXXXXXXXXXXXXXXXX   AND OOOOOOOOOOO THAT'S KISSES AND HUGS. I THOUGHT YOU WERE GOING TO BE DIFFICULT.

'Be careful, my dear,' said Helen gently, hugging her close. 'The difficulties may yet come.'

The calls came, but it was the postcard that was exciting. It was a picture of Pen y Fan, the highest mountain in the Brecon Beacons.

> Daniel and Tom got me to the top of this and the
> weather was perfect. It took five hours and some army
> trainees helped with the last bit over the rocks. Daniel is
> being boringly good so don't worry about my well-being,
> physical or moral. The camper is fine but a bit cramped.
> Tom's been very happy.
>
>   Love Esther

Daniel had written it out to her dictation. He had added: 'Don't worry, we're looking after her. Daniel.'

That night Helen Perry-Wilcox booked a personal call to Kate Marquand in Sydney. If there was going to be a storm, then everybody should be prepared for it.

Three days later, they came back looking happy and healthy and full of their adventure, and Helen knew that there would be a storm, and soon. Esther had a little silver ring on her left hand, an engagement ring. And Daniel had one on his. Tom just wanted to talk about mountains but Helen made them tea and said, 'Now then, my dears, I think we had better talk rather seriously. Tom, you had better leave us alone for a little.'

In a bid to stay in the room with them, Tom changed the subject from mountains to Daniel and Esther.

'Daniel's getting married,' he said. 'So's Amh.'

First there were telephone calls to and from Australia. Then Leon Sadler suddenly appeared at Helen's house, despatched by Richard to interview Esther and Daniel, a job he himself refused to do. Then Helen had yet another private talk with Esther. Then Daniel and Esther confounded everybody by going off, completely alone this time, for a weekend in the hired camper van.

Then, furious, Richard arrived. He said a brief and cold hello to Daniel, who shrugged. He ordered Esther to Harefield, but she refused to go while Helen refused to get involved. Kate arrived. Esther was silent, utterly. Except for one thing.

WE ARE GETTING MARRIED ON 24TH JULY IN THE PENTECOSTAL CHURCH IN WYCOMBE.

This was Marion and Jeremy's church. Richard had a row with Marion which, given her peaceable nature, one might have thought almost impossible. Jeremy came to her side and they told Richard with a good Christian niceness which infuriated him that they hoped he would come to the wedding. It would be a happy God-loving day.

'Bugger God-loving days,' shouted Richard more than once, his customary calm quite gone. 'Esther's meant to be studying at Oxford.'

Kate talked to Daniel.

'He's very nice, Richard, and I think he's sincere. I know they're young, I know all the problems but you can't *stop* them, so . . .'

'It's utterly ridiculous. I can't even begin to enumerate the problems. To start with he's only twenty-four and she's barely twenty. It's so *silly*.'

Leon talked to Daniel.

'He's very very bright, Richard. He's also rather well off. He has written several of the most successful American interactive computer combat games. He's highly thought of by *CODA*. He's been offered jobs by Apple and Digital. You can't fault him as a prospect . . .'

Wait. They could *wait* for Christ's sake, was Richard's next tack. His only tack perhaps.

JULY 24TH, insisted Esther. EVERYBODY IS WELCOME. I'M SORRY DADDY IS UPSET. IT'S PREDICTABLE THOUGH ISN'T IT?

There was about her now a simple pleasant calm, tinged, it must be said, with that youthful smugness which comes from the knowledge that there is little the older generation can do to stop the younger generation doing what it intends to.

'Where are they going to live? What does his family think of it? Has he got a family? What the hell's he doing it for? Oh Christ!'

Kate told Helen that never once since she had known him had Richard been even fractionally as angry as he was now. And no, he wouldn't be going to the wedding, assuming there was one. That at least was certain.

'I think he hopes that they'll get cold feet and call it off. "Coming to their senses," he calls it.'

'Well!' said Helen, who felt guiltily responsible, though in her heart she could not think of one reason, unless caution be a reason, for opposing the wedding. Esther and Daniel were as obviously in love as a couple of their age could be, and they had the inestimable advantage and strength which a shared faith gives.

'But why so soon?' asked Kate finally of Helen, for Esther did not seem able to give a sensible answer.

'I think it's practical,' explained Helen. 'I think they are working together on this game of Esther's and perhaps other things, and they find it a great interruption having other people around to look after Esther. Daniel seems quite happy to do it, and Esther has not the slightest embarrassment about it. But I think they feel that unless they were married it wouldn't somehow be right. I mean toileting, bathing and so on. It is rather bizarre. And it's no good trying to tell youngsters of their age to be careful, or warn them of the potential problems, because they won't see them will they?'

Kate laughed.

'You're a very special, lady, Helen, and I think the Marquands were very clever to have discovered you!'

'I'm rather afraid that if this wedding takes place Richard will never talk to me again.'

'It is very hard for him. I think he's a little jealous, and the silence between them has made him very angry. He's used to having his own way. And naturally, and quite rightly, he's desperately worried that Esther's going to be let down when Daniel realizes what he's let himself in for. I mean, you would have to be a saint. And, too, there are all the ancillary problems like children and so on. Are they intending to have any?'

'That is something for them to tell you, surely . . .'

'At the moment Esther barely communicates with me. She just looks so damned pleased with herself.'

'Yes, I know,' Helen said. 'I've thought of all the problems as well, and I am worried. And yet, there's something about them, Kate. I sometimes think what matters to them is the mental rapport they have over computing, and nothing else. Frankly I think they have hardly any physical relationship at all. They just want to get on with their work, and marriage is the most efficient way of getting on with it.'

'Couldn't they just live together?'

'Wouldn't be Christian would it? Though they are not very overt about it I think that matters to them both.'

The marriage of Esther Marquand and Daniel Schuster took place on the morning of 24 July 1985, in a modest church service. The bride was in a white cotton dress, with the flowers of summer entwined in her hair. The bridegroom was in a dark suit. The weather was fine.

Kate was there, but not Richard. Helen came, and Tom in a smart jacket. A single friend of Daniel's was there, but no family. Leon was best man.

After a brief and shy reception, Daniel helped Esther into the single extravagance of the whole day – the special German-made camper vehicle he had bought, and in which they were to spend their honeymoon.

'Where are you going?' they were asked.

North, they said. To see the Yorkshire Dales which Esther had passed through with Helen on her own first trip north and now wanted to explore with Daniel. And then over the Pennines to visit Laydale and possibly Herstorne because Daniel needed to see them as part of his design work on 'Skallagrigg'.

SEE YOU THERE? PLEASE! Esther asked Helen happily.

'Are you sure you want . . .' doubted Helen.

YES!

'But it's your honeymoon. You won't want to see anyone.'

WE'LL WANT TO SEE YOU. AND JAMES XXXX!!!!
'Esther!'
Then, changed into more casual clothes, the flowers in her hair taken out by Marion, Daniel and Esther drove away, and their few friends waved them goodbye. And good luck.

'But somehow, it wasn't quite right. There was something lacking. I think Esther was sad Richard was not there. And I thought the service somewhat bland. Well-intentioned, of course, James, but bland.'

Helen had finally gone to see James Freeman, and had booked herself into a small guest-house in Bowcraile, the village in whose church she and Esther had first met him. She had timed her trip to coincide with the planned visit to Herstorne of Esther and Daniel.

Helen and James Freeman had had two gentle days of walking and talking and, in their quiet way, had enjoyed themselves. Helen found his company interesting and peaceful; and he smiled upon her, with her, and seemed happy to have her at his side.

They were sitting now in his kitchen, a big old-fashioned room with a wooden dresser painted green, a panel of disused servant bells high up one wall, and a rough old door opening out over a stone step into the garden. Scarlet pimpernel and mint grew prostrate among the cracked flagstones outside, and caught the sun. The rooms inside were, as Helen had once been told, very spartan, all polished clean and minimally furnished.

Helen had brought him some flowers, and put them in a white ceramic jug in the deep windowsill.

Daniel telephoned to say that they were coming to Herstorne from Laydale, where he had met Arthur at last. They were all coming up to Herstorne for a day out – Eppie wanted to travel in the camper van. Edward, who was also visiting, would bring the others in his car.

So Helen had been busy making picnic things, and put them ready on the sideboard in neat plastic containers.

'I haven't been up to the hospital for some weeks now,' said James. 'There's no one there but a caretaker and demolition men. They're taking down one of the annexe buildings and boarding up the rest in case of vandalism. No one is quite sure what they're going to do with it.'

'And you, James? What are you going to do?'

'You speak as if I'm a young man. I'm retired. I'm going to sleep I expect.' He chuckled, but when the laughter faded from his eyes they seemed to hold a patient loneliness, as if his God had not quite fulfilled him but still held out the promise that he might.

'I expect they'll want to go up to the hospital when they all arrive – I imagine Esther's young man will. So we'll take our picnic up there. We could walk.' James spoke slowly, his voice rough. His hands, bent and swollen at the joints, were not still.

Helen had explained about Esther and Daniel's work, and how the game they were making was based on the search for Arthur and the Skallagrigg.

'Daniel told me he needed to see the place for himself if he was to create some graphics for the game. Something to do with atmosphere.'

'None of that left now, just dust,' said James. 'But at least the chapel's intact.'

They arrived together in the late morning when the sun was hot. Norman pushed Arthur, Eppie laughed and showed the Father the camper van. Norman and Frank had a drink of water.

The rest had a quick cup of tea and admired James's old garden. They would none of them be staying long. Edward had to drive Arthur and his friends back to Laydale and then set off for Cambridge that evening. Daniel and Esther had decided they had had enough of the north and were spending the final part of their honeymoon in Cornwall. Edward had offered them his cottage near Helston.

'Better than a campsite, you know,' said Edward, 'and I think the police won't allow you to park that great thing of yours even if there was room in the narrow roads. Gets very busy, Cornwall. But the cottage is a lovely spot.'

Frank said, 'Arthur says it'd be good for a honeymoon with the sea and that. He enjoyed it with Edward.' The two had gone down earlier that year.

They decided to visit the hospital and then have their picnic in the glen. So, slowly, they did. They greeted the caretaker, a man they all knew, and then wandered around the buildings whose doors the caretaker opened for them.

But the Father was right: there was little atmosphere now. Just the shell of a building, and sunlight at the windows. The wards were empty now, the offices bare. An odd chair here, a broken lightbulb there: but the windows were uncurtained, the place echoing.

Even the basements had been cleared, and the corridors swept. Nothing remained.

A little disconsolate, they drifted at last to the chapel which James unlocked. It was warm from the recent hot weather and filled with sun. There was no cloth now on the altar, no cross. But the brass rails were there, and the nineteenth-century stained glass, the reds, blues and yellows of whose panels were thrown in sunlight on the tiled floor.

They said little, but huddled in a group staring, as if looking back to a world that once was. Finally Edward broke free of them to look at the organ. It was unlocked.

YOU COULD PLAY IT FOR US, Esther said.

The caretaker went off to turn on the electricity.

They sat on the warm benches while Edward, with Arthur watching at his side, played them a few pieces, bringing the old familiar place alive again. The sound filled the arches and reverberated to the ceiling, seeming to raise dust which floated lazily in the shafts of sunlight.

Their mood changed. The chapel built with such piety, the scene of such frequently futile worship, now witnessed simple pleasure.

Frank stood up and went to Arthur's chair, took its handles in his hands, and eyed the barren altar.

'Good to say a prayer,' he said, 'please.'

James nodded at Helen. He was in ordinary clothes, but stood up, went to the rails and turned to face them.

'Perhaps just a short prayer.'

A BLESSING ON OUR MARRIAGE, typed Esther.

'Could you, sir?' asked Daniel.

It seemed a natural thing to do. Daniel pushed Esther's chair forward a little and quite unembarrassed kneeled at her side. He took Esther's hand in his.

James Freeman came to them and made a brief general prayer, then, speaking slowly, said, 'The Lord be with you.'

'And with you,' said Helen, Edward and Daniel.

'Yes,' said Frank.

James looked from Daniel to Esther and smiled.

'Daniel and Esther, you stand in the presence of God as man and wife to dedicate to him your life together, that he may consecrate your marriage and empower you to keep the covenant and promise you have solemnly declared.'

There was another pause. James stared about the chapel and behind Esther's chair to Arthur and Frank, Eppie and Norman. All but Arthur and Esther were standing.

'Marriage is given, that husband and wife may comfort and help each other, living faithfully together in need and in plenty, in sorrow and in joy. It is given, that with delight and tenderness they may know each other in love, and, through the joy of their bodily union, may strengthen the union of their hearts and lives. It is given, that they may have children and be blessed in caring for them and bringing them up in accordance with God's will, to his praise and glory.'

James Freeman paused again, his head dropping as he seemed for a while to study the tiles on the floor and think about what he had just said and so make others think. Then he said very clearly, 'This is the meaning of the marriage you have made.'

After that he led them in general prayer, ending with, 'Heavenly Father, by your blessing let these rings be to Daniel and to Esther a symbol of unending love and faithfulness and of the promises they have made to each other; through Jesus Christ our Lord. Amen.'

'Amen,' said Frank, grinning for once, and clapping his hands. Adding, 'under Christ Jesus in the glass! Where's the flesh of bread and blood of wine?'

James Freeman looked up and grinned at Frank.

'Not today, Frank.'

'OK,' said Frank.

The chapel was hushed, all were quiet. Esther looked as fragile as a poppy and Daniel so young. Two innocents made strong by love and faith. James Freeman turned from them to face the altar, and said a final prayer. His voice was shaking and Helen sensed that he was greatly moved. His prayer was one of thanks, of great thanks finally, as if the years had turned and turned, and somehow now all was right again. The chapel was at peace. Its work was done.

They sat in silence for a while, as Edward played them a final gentle voluntary. Then one by one they rose and walked out into the sunlight and down to the glen for their picnic.

Behind them the hospital buildings were lost in heat haze, all shimmering as if they were a mirage, insubstantial; an imagining.

DO YOU WANT TO GO BACK INSIDE? asked Esther of Daniel after they had eaten and lain in the grass.

He shook his head and said, 'I've seen what I needed to.' He stood up and stared up the slopes to the distant buildings. Then he turned away. They were all restless to leave.

When they got back to James's house none of them wanted to linger. Edward got Arthur and his friends into his car and they left with shouts, grins and waves. Daniel made Esther safe in the front of the camper van and slowly turned out into the street. They waved and the shining vehicle turned down the hill and was gone.

'Good luck!' shouted Helen. She felt like throwing confetti. It was as if, only now, after their marriage had been blessed in the hospital chapel, that they were really together as one.

Then she too felt she had better go, to get a good start down the motorway. James said that that did seem a good idea.

Helen wanted to help him clear up the picnic things.

James said that was not necessary, he would do them when she was gone. He was well trained.

Helen said she supposed he was. James dug up some mint for her garden. Helen said she would let him have copies of some photos she had taken.

She put a few final things in the boot of her car.

'Well, then, I had best say goodbye,' she said.

There seemed little else to say.

Impulsively she gave him a quick kiss on the cheek. His hands began to rise to hold her, just briefly, but then fell back. Too uncertain and shy.

There were last-minute suggestions of meeting again, of a visit to Oxford, of having a happy summer of good weather and gardening; then Helen turned her car out into the High Street and drove away, alone.

She drove slowly through the Trough of Bowland, utterly miserable. Hot, too, for the sun had been out all day. The roads were sticky with melted tar. She turned on to the motorway, driving slowly on the inside lane: Birmingham 106 miles.

Oxford. Her house. Esther gone now. They hadn't even decided where they would live. She felt utterly alone. The miles passed slowly, and she hated each one of them for it brought her nearer . . . what? Nothing. An empty house. An empty life now. Oh dear, suddenly she knew she was going to miss Esther.

She thought of James's house. She thought of the blessing he had given in the chapel. She thought of that strange suffering he bore and of moments during the past two days when that lost look had left his face. Up on the moors it had gone. They had both been surprised how far they walked and how good they felt.

Helen looked at her eyes in the car mirror. They were troubled. She thought of James. He was troubled. She thought of their goodbye: so uncomfortable and awkward. So silly really.

She pulled into a service area and had a bad cup of coffee and a sugary bun. She wandered into the motorway shop and stared uncomprehendingly at the world's headlines, and the garish books. She went back to her car and sat staring at the key which she barely had will to turn.

But then she did, firmly. She drove on to the motorway without a second look at the hitchhikers holding placards: B'ham and London and Oxford.

'No,' she whispered. *'No!'*

She drove fast down the motorway in the outside lane. At the next junction she slowed, crossed to the inside lane and on to the slip road. Up to the bridge, round the roundabout and then down, down on to the motorway, back back back *back* the way she had come.

Her eyes were troubled no longer.

An hour later Helen's hands were shaking as she brought the car to a stop. Her legs were shaking too as she opened the door and carefully got out of the car. She smoothed her summer skirt and slowly walked round the side of the building to the back. The kitchen door was open, just as it had been the first time she and Esther had come. She saw James through the window but he did not see her. He was sitting at the plain kitchen table, his back to the door. The picnic things were where Helen had left them. He looked as if he had been sitting just like that ever since she had gone; as if he had been sitting there decades longer than that.

She went to the door, looked in.

'James,' she said.

He turned round and saw her and she saw that his eyes were as vulnerable as a child's. He got up and came forward, unsure of himself or her.

Helen looked at him and suddenly her strength, which had carried her through so many decades, seemed finally gone.

'I felt so terribly alone driving on the motorway,' she said simply. 'I could not face that any more.'

Helen Perry-Wilcox and James Charles Freeman reached out and held each other close, together on the threshold that is as old as time.

SIXTY-SEVEN

November rain drove over the bleak cliffs facing The Racks and in wild noisy flurries against the windowpanes of Edward Lane's cliff-top house. Inside Esther stared back out, her hair wet and her cheeks red with cold wind and spray.

Through the splattered windows she watched great waves crash down upon the rocks far below, and white horses race across the darkening sea.

'Yeh!' she said as Daniel sat down with her and placed two steaming mugs of cocoa on her tray.

'Me first, too hot, then you.'

ME JANE, typed Esther. YOU'RE TALKING LIKE TARZAN. UNFORTUNATELY YOUR GLASSES HAVE SALT ON THEM WHICH SPOILS THE EFFECT.

Daniel smiled, totally relaxed. Here, in their own world, away from everyone, he was himself.

'That was a helluva good walk. Didn't you get cold at all?'

A BIT.

'You said you weren't cold.'

THAT WAS BECAUSE I KNEW YOU DIDN'T WANT TO TURN BACK.

'You should have had a blanket to cover your legs.'

IT WOULD HAVE GOT WET.

Daniel drank his cocoa, brooding pleasantly. His hair was wet too, and his cheeks pink.

They had been at the cottage since they had first come down in August; Edward and Arthur had encouraged them to stay on. They liked it, found they could work well together there, and Daniel had begun to adapt it to Esther's special needs. Edward had wanted them to stay there free, but they preferred to pay a rent, if only a small one.

It was more house than cottage, though attached to one end

was a cottage, disused and damp. The whole property stood in the centre of its own square half-fenced, half-walled garden at the top end of the rough road that dropped down to Gribber Bay. Further down were a few more cottages, mostly holiday letting properties; with the coming of winter all the visitors had gone, and Daniel and Esther were left in magnificent isolation.

The house directly overlooked The Racks, with the wide expanse of sandy Gribber Bay to its right. The only landmark on the high undulating cliffs was the memorial cross to the Rinsey lifeboat sunk on The Racks in 1911. Tom would go and stand on the cliff top staring at The Racks shouting, 'All hands lost! All hands lost!' It was a line he had learned from a television film about treasure ships and pirates. It was ideal for Esther and Daniel, who were focused on their own small world.

In October, Tom had moved in. Daniel found he needed help, and Esther had long worried about Tom's unhappiness working in London. Apart from helping them, they soon found that Tom's natural friendliness and interest in gardens got him a few odd jobs around Gribber, which gave him pleasure and a sense of belonging.

They had begun to work again on 'Skallagrigg' even during their honeymoon and, now they were established, Daniel was pressing on with a suite of database programs for a major graphics studio in Los Angeles. It was clear that Gribber could only be temporary, perhaps a year or two, but Daniel was happy to leave it like that, and travel to America when he needed to. They could always get extra helpers from the village, which had taken to them, or Esther could travel too. All in the future, all yet to come.

Now it was winter and they were staying where they were. Daniel's major project, apart from programming, was getting the side cottage habitable for Tom, so that he could have a little place of his own. They felt this extra privacy was necessary to him and themselves.

Daniel, used to living alone, had found it hard at first to be as regular as Esther's needs demanded, but had soon adapted. They all worked regular hours and had regular meals, with a bias to unprocessed and raw foods. There was a health-food shop run by Viola, the girlfriend of the man who had the council concession for windsurfing on the beach. His hut had a board on it: 'Gribber

Sailboards Ltd. Prop: E. Garratt.' The 'E' stood for Edmond but he
was unfriendly and brusque, preferring to be on the beach or out
boarding, fighting some battle of his own. Daniel and Esther called
him 'the Windsurf Man'. Viola laughed about him and said he was
not as bad as he seemed, adding cryptically, 'People come to the
West Country for their own reasons, don't they?' and looked at
Daniel in a meaningful way. Sometimes Esther was aware of her
own innocence, and Daniel's, and knew they still had things to
find out about each other; but it was the kind of risk she liked.

They had made the big sitting-room at the southern end of the
house overlooking the bay into their bedroom. Here Esther worked,
her computer and printer and other equipment housed on a unit
Daniel had built. He was so naturally talented with his hands that
whatever he made looked good and was finished well. The floors,
which had odd steps here and there, had been ramped, and some
doors widened, so that Esther could take her wheelchair where she
wanted.

Daniel liked to work in isolation, and had made a study for
himself upstairs above their bedroom. He moved restlessly about
above her, which she liked, for it made her feel close to him without
intruding. There was a small guest-room upstairs too and a
bathroom. They had converted a scullery downstairs into a toilet
and shower-room for Esther, though it was rather small and
against building regulations.

Daniel was already good at handling his money, using an account-
ant and lawyer in Los Angeles. Esther was less interested in this
than he was, but she had always had Leon Sadler acting for her,
and he had used her father's professional advisors as back-up.
Daniel was more aware than Esther of the marketability of the
work they were doing, but it was not something Esther ever became
involved with or needed to. She was well protected. The main
thing was they had no financial worries, and for the time being
seemed happy to live in what others would have felt obscure and
uncomfortable isolation.

Ironically, the people in Gribber took to them partly because
they assumed they were poor and, therefore, romantic. There was
something engaging about the trio up the cliff, who went for walks
across the sand in the worst weather and seemed to enjoy it and
not catch colds.

It was Daniel's pleasure to take her to places she had never been, nor expected to, as if to confound people who might think Esther was too handicapped. On their honeymoon, for example, he had taken her up Snowdon in the wheelchair, and down a slate mine the following day. The sea he had avoided, but in a fairground they came across he took her on the Big Dipper, which made her feel sick.

'Normal,' he said, unsympathetically. 'Didn't you say you wanted to experience everything?'

On Gribber Bay he heaved her, chairless, to the top of Crag Rock, a massive piece of cliff that had fallen down on to the shore and which the sea swirled round at high tide.

'Nah!' Esther had protested, laughing.

But she was getting to know her Daniel. She went where he went, and he went everywhere. If the chair, now battered and worn, could not make it, he unstrapped her and carried her himself. And with Tom in tow it became even easier.

At first she had worried that she hampered him from doing things, but this made him angry.

'I wouldn't do anything at all without you,' he said.

Which was true, and she slowly began to see that somehow he lived through her, as if her helplessness gave him strength. He found security in her, and she wondered about that and thought it strange. But as the winter nights had drawn in, and they had sat together talking more, she had begun to understand how much he needed her. And why.

It had after all been rather a mystery, his sudden arrival and attachment to her. That it was love she did not doubt; but why does an able-bodied, clever young man fall for a girl like me, she wondered. Why?

She noticed that at night sometimes he had troubled and fitful sleep, and as she lay beside him and heard the interminable wind outside she felt something similar inside him: nagging, fretful, unresting, never at peace.

It was to do with the sea, whatever it was. He sometimes liked to go off alone and she could see him standing out on the bay before the great rollers, endlessly watching them. Or over on the cliffs, his eyes narrowed against the harsh wind, watching the seas break on The Racks and on Starke Island, their furthest seaward point.

WHY DON'T YOU EVER GO SWIMMING? she had asked him
when they first came, for he seemed always to want to sit up on
the beach or rocks with her, spending his time getting her comfortable.

Then early one evening in late September as dusk was falling,
they had had an argument. Nothing much, just a build up of days
of frustrating work for both of them, and he had gone down to the
beach.

Tom came in to announce matter-of-factly: 'Dan's in the
water.'

For a moment her heart jumped. She got to the window and
saw him out beyond the surf, but she could tell even at this distance
he was enjoying himself. The seas thundered down upon him as
he surfaced and resurfaced. He came in with the waves, dived back
in, rolled, and let the surge of water push him up the beach towards
his clothes.

He was in for twenty minutes. When he came out he picked up
his clothes, put his shirt and trousers on without drying himself
and started walking back. The only other person on the beach was
the Windsurf Man, who came over, pointed to the surf, waved his
hands about and said something aggressive before Daniel turned
away from him. An argument.

PUT ON THE KETTLE, TOM. THE KETTLE.

'Tea, Amh?'

'Nah.'

'Coffee, cocoa, soup?'

'Yeh!' Soup.

When Daniel came in she saw their argument was long forgotten. His hair had dried streaky with salt and he was laughing.

'The windsurf guy told me it was dangerous. I asked him had he
tried Hanniman? He said no. I told him to stuff the Gribber surf up
his ass.'

DANIEL!

They laughed and Daniel had his soup, and Esther felt that she
had got to know him a little better. The violence of the sea and his
love–hate of it was the key to something important.

After that evening he seemed released from previous constraint
and swam regularly. Esther marvelled at the way he dived into the
waves and came up beyond them, and at how sometimes he stood

sideways to the undertow in the shallows and the backflow of water sprayed up against his straining thighs.

She noticed that after these swims he liked to make love, and did so more freely than was usual between them and with fewer words, picking her up beneath him so she felt tossed and turned as if she was the surf and he was angrily riding it again. His skin tasted of salt and she liked that.

But the truth was that their sex life was not as exciting as she had hoped. They made love and all *that*, but it was the comfort of his body she liked rather than the sex. She was pleased that he seemed pleased, and wanted to kiss and touch her. He insisted that she was naked beside him beneath their enormous duvet. But it was not quite how she had expected it or as relaxed. But this doubt was barely formulated because she had no criterion to judge by and knew only what film-shows and books said and surely they were exaggerated, weren't they? All that screaming, that oh oh oh oh ohing. No. Theirs was gentle, except for after the sea bit and that made her giggle. But then he said nothing, and she felt he felt embarrassed by his own vigour.

I DON'T MIND, she tried to tell him. I LIKED IT LAST NIGHT. But he did not talk about it and so neither did she.

They *had* talked to a doctor about babies, just in case. The risk of getting pregnant was there it seemed – in *that* at least she was normal – but it was probably less than average. Her periods had always been a little irregular and sometimes missed altogether and that made the chances of conception lower. But the doctor was not very clear about it, and he seemed vague about the possibilities that if Esther did conceive she might give birth to a damaged baby. The problem, he seemed to think, was more likely to be in a slow delivery because of her weakness, and that might carry extra risks.

But that was all academic. After she tried two different kinds of contraceptive pill which made her feel tired and irritable they used a cap, which he inserted for her. Perhaps it was that that made their sex seem, well, dull. Not that he minded performing such personal services (as the doctor had put it) because it seemed part and parcel of loving her. But it all felt a little dutiful.

There had been an incident before winter set in which made her think more about his life in Hanniman and realize there were things to find out. It was in October, on a day when the wind was steady but the sea only calmly swelling. One of the Windsurf Man's board-hirers drifted off towards the rocks. It happened from time to time and usually they would jump off the board and swim back along the shore, arriving exhausted; or a bad-tempered Mr Garratt sailed out to them and talked them back in.

Daniel would watch them, predicting the ones who would have trouble. He could tell by the way they got back on to their boards fatigued, and then started falling off more frequently. He said that the Windsurf Man should be more careful to whom he hired boards.

That Saturday Daniel saw a man drifting along the shore and having trouble getting going, and forecast another casualty. But he seemed worried, and stayed watching. The Windsurf Man was up a ladder painting his hut against the winter gales, and did not seem to see. Daniel watched.

IS ANYTHING WRONG? asked Esther.

'Maybe, maybe not. Difficult to say. He doesn't look right. Looks too tired too soon. I'll just . . .' He put on some shorts and went down to the shore. The Windsurf Man had disappeared altogether. Daniel stripped off his shirt and walked out into the surf. He dived through the waves and started swimming steadily towards the man, using the current to drift himself down to him. Esther saw Daniel rest on the man's board and the man squat down. The man slipped into the water and Daniel climbed on to the board. He stood on it for a moment and promptly fell off. Then he got on again and this time he seemed more sure-footed. He watched the man swim to shore, a distance of perhaps a hundred and fifty feet. The man was pushed in by the surf, scrambled up on to the sand and turned and waved. The Windsurf Man came down the beach and, as usual, had an argument. His client shrugged and pointed at Daniel.

Daniel turned the board across the wind and began a sudden run out to sea to gain length along the beach so that he could bring the board back ashore well clear of the rocks. Esther knew what he was doing because he had often explained it to her.

As he attempted to tack to bring the board back round he fell off. She could see anger in his body as he climbed back on board, and then an ungainly squatting as he turned it, with difficulty, in the choppy seas. The wind looked stronger out there than inshore. He stood upright again, held the uphaul in one hand, looked to shore as if to check his position, expertly raised the sail and, leaning into the wind, steered a direct course back to shore. The board left a wake as it rode through waves and finally he cut it expertly through the surf and brought it to shore letting the sail fall with a thump in the sand.

The Windsurf Man came down ominously, looking for another argument. Daniel patted him on the shoulder and for a moment Esther thought there would be a fight. Two stags meeting before the wild sea. Daniel turned away and waved, knowing Esther would be watching. Behind her window she raised her hand. She knew he could not see, but knew he knew she was doing it. A moment of silent, distant intimacy.

That night she got Daniel to tell her about that surfing accident he had mentioned once to Helen. It was off Hanniman Beach. He was windsurfing with his oldest friend who was called Jon. They both got tired. They had drifted too near to rocks and the winds had freshened. His friend's mast-foot had broken, the most common cause of serious failure in a sailboard. They were carrying spare rope and jury-rigged a mast-foot. They swapped boards because Daniel was the stronger and his friend had got cold. So Daniel took over the rigged-up board and, finding it hard to steer, drifted even nearer the rocks. Jon stayed behind, watching over him. The wind changed and strengthened and Daniel got a run, which he took advantage of and set off for shore. He heard a shout behind and thought his friend was shouting his pleasure. But he was not. He had come off by the rocks and must have hit one.

Daniel afterwards thought he remembered his friend's call, a memory surely fabricated by guilt and doubt: 'Help, Dan. Help!' But he had not helped; he had raced on.

By the time he had sailed back on his crippled board it was too late. The board was drifting among the rocks, his friend had gone. Daniel ditched the damaged board and, regaining the working one, searched with others and the lifeguards until night fell. There was nothing but the swelling sea.

They found Jon two days later, fifteen miles away, near Malibu. At the funeral his friend's parents would not even talk to him.

Daniel Schuster cried for the first time since Esther had known him, the night he told her this story. Behind the loss of the friend

was the loss of parents. His mother rarely saw him after her divorce
and when he was sixteen he had a terrible adolescent argument
with his father.

'He said I didn't need him, never talked to him, only to my damn
computers. I went on a long vacation with Jon and when I came
back, Dad had found a woman and gone. I knew where he was, I
visited, but really he had rejected me. And then I lost Jon.'

So Esther knew why he had found it so easy to attach himself to
her. She could *not* leave, so he was safe with her.

But she felt instinctively that the sea was where the final un-
reconciled loss had been and she began then to sense that it would
be in the sea that they would find the last graphic inspirations for
'Skallagrigg'. The game had to be more than just Edward and
Arthur's loss and reunion, it had to have something of its makers
in it as well. The first levels had been easy, and were forming
steadily. But from Level Five it was getting harder, and would have
to do with herself and Daniel, and the sea that never ceased to roar
at the cliffs beneath their cottage. These thoughts swirled half-
formed in Esther's imagination as that winter set in and she lay
naked beside Daniel, as Linnie with Arthur, as Kate with Richard,
and remembered that once she was a child and thought like a
child; and knew that now she was adult and must give up childish
ways. Levels levels levels levels: she began to feel herself going
deeper, and to know that, where she was going, faith, hope and
love must abide, those three; but the greatest of them would be
love, and she would need Daniel wholly at her side to finish
'Skallagrigg'. She heard his troubled breathing and touched his
thigh, knowing that he was not whole yet. Fearing that when he
was, he would be ready to move on and not be handicapped. Yet
though she feared it, she knew that that was the essence of the
journeyer's end in 'Skallagrigg' and she must find a way to reach
it.

SIXTY-EIGHT

In need and in plenty, in sorrow and . . . in sorrow.

Esther's problems with Daniel began immediately after his return from a brief trip to America in February.

He had wanted her to go, and when she had said no he had not wanted to go by himself. But she insisted, feeling that the visit would do him good, and so he left and she and Tom went to stay with Marion at Hill House.

When he came back he did not want to be met at Heathrow; he had a cold; he seemed discontented. Esther had never known him ill or morose for very long, but on the long drive south to Cornwall he was shrunk and silent, and suddenly everything seemed dark and vulnerable.

Nor would he talk in the weeks that followed, and gradually the atmosphere in their house, once intimate and loving, turned starkly lonely for them all. Outside the chill winds raged in on bitter seas, and the rocks of The Racks seemed bigger, darker, and ever more threatening. While behind The Racks loomed Starke, its bleak heights besieged by sea, its great central cleft a channel for white surf and waterfalls of dark green seawater.

Marion had warned Esther that marriage was not always easy, and she had read as much. But now she knew that 'not easy' meant desperate, when every little thing seems soured and tense.

It was not what he did – he still did everything for her, and never reproached her for it at all – but how he did it. In silence, sometimes a little unkindly. They stopped talking about their work, sometimes he seemed deliberately not to read what she put up on her screen. But worst of all, when they were in bed at night they stopped touching each other.

Helen visited at the end of February and guessed that something was wrong.

She let Esther talk a little but wisely felt it best to make no comment. Marriage was likely to be difficult, especially for a couple as young as these two, and with the special problems Esther had.

But Esther's evident misery seemed to Helen such a *pity* and she could think of no advice to give but to be patient. She resolved to write cheerful letters, and a more serious one to Kate in Sydney. But then they would have to make their own mistakes.

One thing at least: they certainly worked hard, and Daniel, whatever his present moods might mean, could hardly have done a better job on the house.

Helen left, and the long days of winter dragged by. Gribber Bay was empty but for the occasional walker and his dog, bent against the wind; and the Windsurf Man, who now came down and took his board out into the sea wearing a bulky black dry suit. Often he was the only life they saw all day, and he looked malevolent. For he was an angry man and took it out on the sea, standing out there on his board sometimes, balancing against the uphaul and staring at the broken, deadly water of The Racks. In the days when he had been talking to her, Daniel had told her that no one had ever sailed through The Racks, or round Starke Island at their far end.

'The Windsurf Man's obsessed by them. Believes they are the greatest challenge to windsurfers in British waters. Bull*shit*. It's just a case of getting the tide and wind right. The problem would be coming back, since what's right one way would be wrong the other. You'd finish under the east cliffs without room to make a tack to a point to make an angle to shore. Not nice.'

Daniel had noticed that even the very good windsurfers who sometimes sailed in the bay never ventured near The Racks. Perhaps it was the Rinsey lifeboat monument, looming up on the cliffs near their house, that warned people off.

The silences continued into March. Sometimes Esther tried to get him to talk but he would not; he just stared at the questions she asked and shook his head and said it was 'nothing'.

DO YOU HATE ME? she asked him. IF YOU WANT TO GO YOU CAN, I CAN LOOK AFTER MYSELF. I CAN HIRE HELP. I WOULD PREFER IT IF YOU WENT. ALL YOU DO IS SIT THERE AND SAY NOTHING AND THEN WORK AND WORK AND WORK AND THEN GO OUT. I KNOW YOU'RE MISERABLE. WHERE WERE YOU YES-

TERDAY EVENING FOR FOUR HOURS? JUST WALKING?????? I
HATE YOU. NO I DON'T I'M MISERABLE. I FEEL LONELY.

WE DON'T HAVE SEX ANY MORE AND WE'VE BEEN MARRIED
LESS THAN A YEAR. I BET THAT'S A RECORD. MAYBE WE DID
GET MARRIED TOO QUICKLY AS DADDY SAID. ARE YOU BORED
WITH ME?

'*No!*' shouted Daniel. 'It's not you.'

WHAT IS IT THEN? DANIEL, PLEASE TALK.

But when he did not, and he was gone, Esther cried because she
knew that she had tackled it all wrong, and it *was* her fault. What
he needed were her arms around him and support, real physical
support, and that was one thing she could not give. And she hated
that, and the feelings of jealousy she had. What *did* he do when he
went off by himself for so long?

So the seeds of jealousy and doubt, despair and inadequacy were
sown.

But at least routine kept them close. They shopped in Helston;
they went to church on Sunday. He took her out for a walk most
days, whatever the weather, even if they had not said one word to
each other. They slept in the same bed even if they did not touch in
any real sense. They ate the simple healthy meals that Daniel and,
increasingly, Tom made. They worked. They survived, miserable
and confused, not yet knowing that *that* was all so many others
do.

Spring came suddenly, sun across the cold grey sea, green
shoots in the sheltered Cornish lanes. They both heard good
news: 'Dunroune II' was second best seller among computer
games in Britain, and fifth in America; 'Dunroune I' continued
to sell well. As for Daniel, he was summoned to London and then
back to New York to consult about a major programming contract to do with a graphics package. They were both making
money.

'They complain because I live out in the sticks but, hell, I
wouldn't be producing if I lived near city lights,' Daniel said. But
Esther sulked: she did not like his use of the exclusive 'I'. Daniel
sulked: he did not like her taking everything the wrong way all the
time. Misunderstandings. Rows and arguments. Tension.

Tom finally moved into his cottage in March and a social worker
. visited. She seemed very impressed and he made her a cup of tea to

show he could do it, and counted out some money to show he could shop for himself.

Daniel went to America again and Esther opted to stay where she was. Daniel was against it but Esther was firm. She wanted to be mistress in her own house, even if she had to rely on Tom and outside help. She did not want to be a visitor to Hill House once more. The social worker arranged for extra help to relieve Tom in the evenings. He too had his own life to lead.

Without Daniel the little house seemed suddenly peaceful, and during the fortnight he was gone spring advanced rapidly. She found, quite unexpectedly, that she wanted to work once more on 'Skallagrigg', entering at last into the elusive Level Six, and finding that in its labyrinths and mazes she was putting some of the questions and doubts that had arisen over the last year, and taking the journeyer into the deeper regions of helplessness in which, she saw, she had herself been journeying. It was there, in the valley of the shadow as Frank had once called it, that the truth of 'Skallagrigg' would be found. But she knew she had not herself found it yet, just that it was coming.

In those two weeks she went back to the despair she had known in her first term at Oxford, when Helen had so often found her crying. She did not know why or how, but after the tears were over she was deeper into the labyrinth she was making, ever deeper.

One day Tom found her like that and he said, 'Come on, Amh. Walk. Like before. Come on.' He ignored her protests, strapped her into the manual chair, and took her out into the wind down to the bay. But there the soft sands defeated him, and he did not have the strength or skill to push her chair across them. They needed Daniel for that, and he was not there.

Esther knew she would need Daniel to take her on into the final stages of the game, and she knew she loved him and sat in her chair staring across the empty sea-swept sands she could not traverse, wishing he were back.

For Daniel's return she got Tom to buy some sweet-smelling spring freesias and put them all over the house. For each one she had a slip of printout saying 'WELCOME HOME'. The air was warm that day, the sea benign beneath their windows.

He came back changed. Still silent, but not angry now, just sad. He would not talk, except to say that he was into a new health routine and was going to go jogging every morning and evening. And he did, first thing and last thing, across the sands and back.

For his birthday Esther and Tom made a special trip to the health-food shop and talked to Viola.

CAN THE WINDSURF MAN KEEP A SECRET?

Viola laughed. 'Edmond's whole life's a secret. He never talks to me.'

Esther wondered how she could love him then, but dared not ask.

'What secret?' asked Viola.

I WANT HIM TO HELP ME BUY A SAILBOARD FOR DANIEL.

'That's a lovely idea.'

I ALSO WANT HIM TO HELP ME GIVE IT TO HIM . . .

'Yes?'

HE'S NOT VERY FRIENDLY.

'Who, Daniel?'

'Nah!!' They laughed.

EDMOND ISN'T!

'That's just him. I'll see to it.'

Which she did, and since Esther so rarely spent money she decided to buy the best. The Windsurf Man was reluctant, thinking it might be a waste of money, since such boards needed very good sailors.

THAT'S RIGHT. THAT'S WHAT DANIEL IS. HE'S DONE IT IN CALIFORNIA.

So it was agreed and kept secret. But the Windsurf Man had his own conditions. Did Daniel have a harness?

WHAT'S A HARNESS?

Did he have a buoyancy aid?

WHAT'S THAT?

Would he carry safety equipment?

PLEASE INCLUDE EVERTHING NEEDED. WE DON'T WANT TO LOSE HIM!!

The Windsurf Man nodded seriously, and got the best that money could buy.

Esther woke at dawn on the morning of Daniel's birthday, her plans laid and now beyond her control. She heard Tom's door

outside open, and the soft crunch of his feet on the track. She
waited for Daniel to turn and stir and for the alarm to go.

She closed her eyes and feigned sleep, stirring only slightly as
Daniel quietly got dressed in shorts, tracksuit top and trainers, and
left.

A few moments later Tom came in and got her out of bed, sat
her in her chair and pushed it to the window.

The sun was already slanting across the sands and she saw
Daniel turn from under the brow of the slope and out across the
bay. The sands were red-warm, the grass on the cliff above bending a little in the breeze. Rolling waves came steadily in as the
yellow windsock on the Windsurf Man's hut filled with breeze.

She watched Daniel run out from the shadows of the cliff, past
some solitary stacks and into sunlight. Ahead of him, on the sands
and caught by sun, where earlier Tom and the Windsurf Man had
laid it, was her present.

The sail was red, green and yellow, and loose, for if it had been
tightly rigged it might have caught the wind and blown away. The
board was white, the dagger board retracted. On the board Tom
had placed a birthday card. From this distance Esther could not see
it, but Tom said, 'We did it, and me. On the board. Will he go
there?'

Below them Daniel was turning up above the high tide mark as
he often did, passing the board below him on the wet shore, and
running on towards the distant end of the bay. Esther was not
worried. He often took that route, returning along the wave-line
and sometimes running into the surf to send up spray which caught
the spring sunlight. Sometimes too he took off his trainers and ran
out into the water to swim a little.

He turned in the distance, and started slowly back on the softer
sand, gradually approaching the board. Yard by yard he came
until he stopped by it and looked down.

She saw him pick up something and knew it must be the card
and she whispered its message as if he might hear it as she would
have spoken it, had she ever been able.

I LOVE YOU, ESTHER. HAPPY BIRTHDAY. I LOVE YOU.

She saw him look up towards her and knew, though she could
not see, that he was smiling. He knew she was looking. He walked
round the board. He felt the sail, lifted the board. Examined the

dagger board. He went round the sail and worked on the rope, leaning against it and tightening it. He checked the uphaul, the thick rope used to heave the sail out of the sea to power the board.

He picked up the buoyancy aid and checked the contents of the little sack on the back of it. Esther had trusted the Windsurf Man implicitly: spare rope, chocolate, two flares, a knife and a few other things. She imagined Daniel looking at them and smiling at her thoroughness and she hoped there was everything he would have wanted. He put the buoyancy aid on.

Then he fitted the sail to the board and raised it, to let the wind swing it to the far side. He pointed the board to the water and slid it into the surf, then pushed out into the waves.

He did not attempt the difficult shallow surf start but swam the board out through the waves until he was able to climb on to it and attempt to raise the sail. He fell in, the board swung out of position, he tussled with it and made a further adjustment to the sail. Its colours were bright on the grey sea. Up above the high tide mark appeared a van with boards on its roofrack. Early-morning surfers. But Daniel was first. He repositioned the board to wind and wave, pulled himself up on to it, and then suddenly, quickly, before another wave surged in, he had raised the sail and was leaning with it to the wind and the board, magnificent, powering forward out into the sea.

Back and forth he went, falling sometimes, but she could tell from the way that his body moved that he was happy and released. She did not even notice the orange juice Tom had brought her but simply watched as the sun rose on Daniel's birthday and he began to discover anew the sea he loved.

Towards the end, he sailed nearer The Racks' side of the bay, but inshore of them, and almost out of her field of vision. She saw that he was getting tired. She saw him make one last run out to sea, pause at its turn and let the sail fall. He stood balancing with the uphaul and staring off over the water of The Racks towards Starke, the broken water frightening even in these calm winds. For how long he stood there she could not say. But he stood just as the Windsurf Man stood sometimes, staring at something he feared but whose challenge he could not ignore.

Esther felt a stab of fear; the colour of the sail, the strength of Daniel, no match for the dark oppression of the great waters he

had briefly looked towards. Then he sailed back, and she had a
vision of him in the years coming: young, alive, fit, happy, so
much energy, so many good things to do. And she had the courage
to feel then that it was not right, it would never be right for such a
one to be for ever attached to her. It was too much to ask for any
love. Not this. And she saw more nearly what the truth of 'Skallagrigg' might finally be.

All spring and summer the sailboard was Daniel's escape from the
burden she was to him. He never said anything, but she could
sense it in the lightness of his step as, his duties done, and his day's
work complete, he would 'just go down for a quick sail'.

She watched him make friends down there, she watched him
recapture his skill to a point where no one who sailed there, not
even the Windsurf Man, sailed as well as he did. She saw the new
sails he bought to complement the one that came with the board.
A small storm sail, a great regatta sail. On each of them he had the
logo DEL placed in poppy red, her favourite colour. He bought a
small fun board and began to wave jump with it so that people
stopped to admire.

She travelled with him to north Cornwall for the West of England
Sailboard Championships, and saw him take second place in the
Open Class, the only American contender. The sailboard press
called him Dan Schuster, and said he was sponsored by DEL
Programs. D for Daniel, E for Esther, L for Leon. She liked that.

Yet, strangely, he never seemed to talk to the Windsurf Man,
who often sailed in the bay at the same time as he did. Both, too,
often stared out at The Racks and Esther felt a growing despair.
Their own relationship was still silent and strained. Both were
waiting. 'Dunroune III' was finished and in September he went to
the States again, this time for three weeks. Tom stayed alone, and
Esther was taken to visit Helen and James in Herstorne.

She opted to come back early, sensing some crisis was forcing
her back. Daniel too returned early. He always returned restless
and discontented, and sometimes she wondered if he would come
back at all.

Patience. Time. Each week, each day, each hour to live through,
hoping that change would come and they would find what they
had lost.

WHY WHY WHY WHY WHY WHY WHY DO YOU STAY?

We have not made love for more than four months, she would have shouted if she could.

No one's a bloody saint, they could both have said.

He would leave the house – always making quite sure that she was comfortable and Tom knew where he was – and go down to the beach and sail away his anger to gain strength for another day.

Then a strangely ominous thing. At the end of September Daniel was offered a trip in a fishing boat and took Esther. He put a lifejacket on her and they laughed and he seemed excited. He wanted her to see what Gribber Bay and their cliffs looked like from the sea. They chugged comfortably along at the foot of the ominous cliffs along whose tops she had often been taken. From below they looked massive and full of danger. Fulmars flew stiffly in and out of cracks, there were dark inaccessible caves where cormorants stared, the seas swelled up and sucked down around them. A dangerous place. They saw a blue door, paint worn but a white plastic handle still in place, jammed by some heavy sea into a crack of rock.

'It's been there all summer but it'll be gone with the first gale,' said Daniel's friend the boatman. 'Nothing rests long here.'

Esther could smell the fresh salty smell of rocks and sea, and then in the distance they saw The Racks.

The boatman's brows furrowed and he pursed his lips. The boat swung out to stay seaward of Starke, whose harsh outline approached. Though the seas were as calm as ever the rock seemed to have a quality that attracted violence: its vertical faces and overhangs sent up spumes of spray, and water drained back down its sides like river rapids. Gulls circled at its top, and Esther saw that the great cleft was bigger than she had thought, splitting the rocky island almost into two.

Daniel asked if they could circle it but the boatman refused, taking them instead only part of the way and pointing out the vicious broken water between Starke and the next skerry.

'It's as far as I dare go. Not a place to dawdle is it?'

Esther shuddered to see it: among the rocks scattered between Starke and the shore there was barely a single stretch of water that was not churned, whitened or maelstromed by the cross-currents and the winds.

But Daniel was fascinated.

'It would be possible get a sailboard through it,' he said, more to the boatman than to her.

'Aye, they've no draught to speak of. But you'd have to be quick, when the tide's high as now. And the winds would need to be sou'-sou'-west if you've a sail because the reaches between the rocks fall wrong any other way. And then how do you get back? Need a southerly for that and look where that would take you – right to the foot of the monument cliffs.' And he pointed to the lifeboat monument, and their house, and the grim black cliffs awash with white water at their base. 'Hard to climb ashore from there!' said the boatman.

'You could stop on Starke until the wind changes,' said Daniel.

'You're joking,' scoffed the boatman. 'Couldn't get on, couldn't get off. And you could be there weeks. A man got on before the war in flat calm. A couple of times since I've heard fellers have done it, one drowned. The Royal Navy put a man on top with a helicopter in the seventies. Had a devil of a job getting him off when the wind changed. And *that* was to southerly. Dangerous rock here. The sea drives you on it and cuts you to shreds.'

But Esther saw Daniel's eyes were excited and understood the purpose of this 'treat'. As the boat chugged safely back into Porthleven she felt sick at heart to see Daniel had eyes for nothing but The Racks in the distance, and the occasional random spumes of spray that shot high in the sky round Starke.

WHY WHY WHY WHY WHY WHY WHY WHY DID YOU EVEN TRY?

For inevitably he did. After an argument, on a windy October day, when the Windsurf Man was already out on the edge of The Racks, obsessive as well, Daniel suddenly tacked towards them and was gone in among them and lost in foam.

It took him twenty minutes to get back out and once his board struck rock and, oh oh oh, she thought he was lost. Then he was round, expertly up and out again to calmer waters, and coming back to shore.

Exhausted. His eyes frightened. His feet and legs cut where they had hit rock. Hardly able to climb back up the road to the cottage. The Windsurf Man staring after him and shouting, so Esther heard.

'You're fucking mad, Schuster. Don't expect me or anyone else to come and get you because we won't.'

'Because you can't!' Daniel shouted back. Two stags.

'You're an idiot, Schuster, but that's not surprising.' The taunt, Esther knew, referred to Tom and herself. She was glad Daniel ignored it as below him Edmond Garratt mumbled on into the wind about Americans and idiots, and respect for the sea.

WHY WHY WHY WHY WHY WHY WHY, she shouted on her screen, because she thought she had lost him.

He tried again two weeks later, but she didn't see him that time. Tom told her. And when he came back his wet suit was torn through to his skin and there were bloody scratches across his back.

DID YOU HAVE THE HARNESS ON?? WHY WHY WHY WHY NOT?? DANIEL, WHAT'S WRONG WITH YOU?

But she knew what was wrong. It was despair. There was something in him that wanted to die and it was to do with his friend dying, his father, herself; and 'Skallagrigg'. It had to do with all that.

November came again, and with it the gales. They secured themselves, and began to talk about leaving the following year. Maybe things would be better nearer London, or even in the States. Except for Tom; he was happier than he had ever been, slowly making his way with the villagers. He helped Viola in the shop sometimes and in their greenhouse; he had the job of cleaning out three cottages; he was fitting in.

These odd jobs brought him money which he put in a post office account. He would be all right, and they . . . could move when the present jobs were finished. Yes yes yes yes, YES YES YES YES?

'Shut up about it for chrissake.'

CHRIST DOESN'T COME INTO IT.

'Oh piss off.'

YOU KNOW I CAN'T.

Outside the wind seemed to whine with their strange rows, and the seas to surge with their anger.

DON'T GO SAILING JUST TO MAKE ME SCARED.

'I won't.'

PROMISE.

Silence.

PROMISE NOT TO TRY THE RACKS AGAIN. YOU'LL BE KILLED.

'Sorry, Esther I didn't mean to scare you. I don't know what's wrong. I hate myself when I'm like this. It used to be . . .'

MAYBE WE'RE TOO CLOSED IN ON OURSELVES. IT'S MY FAULT. CAN WE MOVE WHEN SPRING COMES? CAN WE GO TO AMERICA? CAN WE? TO HANNIMAN, TO MAKE IT OUR HOME? DO YOU STILL WANT TO BE WITH ME?

Daniel cried. The wind howled. She could not wipe the tears from his cheeks. Rain slipped down the window panes for day after day.

PROMISE YOU'LL NOT TRY THE RACKS EVER.

Finally he said, 'I promise.'

But with that promise she felt something in him die. Some life leave him. But she knew that she was nearer now, near to the seventh level, where hope has gone, where Arthur had learned to live, and where in the loss of hope a journeyer may find a final strength.

Yet still she pleaded, PROMISE PROMISE PROMISE.

Better half a man than none at all.

Except that, at night, when Daniel was so fitfully asleep and she heard The Racks roar, she knew she did not believe it for one second, not with mind, or spirit, or body. Better be no man than half a man.

While day by day, night by night, The Racks surged and threatened outside their window, mocking the promise she asked and the promise he made.

SIXTY-NINE

'Amh! Amh! *Ammmmmh!!!*'

It was Tom, but she could not hear his voice. Just saw his mouth outside in the darkening wind shouting shouting and pointing down to the sea. His eyes were scared and his hair whipped and wet with the gale.

'*Amh!*' He was inside now, the door left open, the house wild with wind. He was running and she knew what it was.

'It's Dan in the water. He's drowning, Amh.'

All day the wind had built up to the gales that had been forecast. Force six, force seven, force eight, and the sea had responded with white fury, the tide rising and pounding the rocks, the sea boiling with rushing surf for the half mile of The Racks.

Daniel had tried to work and so had she. Tom had been silent, afraid. Then at two-thirty, when Esther could already see dusk coming, Daniel went out to look.

'It's calming, the wind's dying back.' There was hope in his voice. It was November, but still he went out boarding, and so did the Windsurf Man; madness. Yet her heart raced to see them starting across the wet sand, into the surf and magnificently through the rolling waves. She was mad too.

Yes, the sea had calmed. It was cold-looking now, and mean, the rollers sweeping in, the surf a poisoned yellow. Driftwood on the shore; black broken seaweed scattered on the sand.

Don't go out today. Don't go out. Please don't . . . she tried to stop herself saying it.

DON'T GO OUT, DANIEL PLEASE DON'T.

'Esther!' he shouted at her angrily. 'It's all right. Anyway, what the hell, I'll go if I want to. I never promised that! Even you wouldn't want that.'

Now Tom came, wet and panicky, and she knew her fear had reason.

'Toh . . .' But Tom knew what to do. He lifted her into the
manual chair and then quickly put the big cagoule over her, easing
her head through it. Then out into the dark afternoon to the road
by the lower part of the cliff where they could see the eastern end
of the bay near the cliff base.

Daniel was far far beneath her, only thirty feet from the cliff base
rocks where the sea was churned like milk. The sail was in the
water, and he was too, one arm across the board, the other holding
the mast-foot. Curling waves bore down upon him and lifted him
and the board and tried to tear the sail from his grasp.

'Toh!'

'What Amh?'

Take me closer. Closer to the cliff.

Tom obeyed, and she saw Daniel more clearly. He was on the
board now, balancing precariously in the vicious seas which surged
about him, and which drifted him relentlessly towards the rocks
out of her sight beneath the cliff. He had taken his buoyancy aid off
to get at the sack on its back. He had taken out the spare rope. The
mast-foot must have broken.

She watched him begin the difficult job of lashing up the mast-
foot, the wind trying to pull him off the board, making it hard to
catch the ends of the rope, lifting the sail clean out of the water
and over the board on top of him. He was in the water again, the
lashing asunder, starting all over again.

While, above, Esther could only watch.

Oh dear God, he is fighting for life and he is mine and I cannot
help him please, please be all right *Daniel*!

'Daaaahnh . . .' but she could not even shout his name.

As he tried to set sail once more she knew something was wrong.
The sail was not uphauling correctly. She could tell by his sudden
foot change. The sail was off-centre, the rope not tight enough to
hold it full centre. But it was coming up and up out of the water
and he was leaning it into the wind and then moving, a few
inches, a foot, three feet, white wake, front splash, out clear of the
cliff. Clear of danger.

No. He would need to tack back to avoid the first rocks of The
Racks and he was having trouble getting movement from the sail.
He said, he had said it was difficult with a temporary mast-foot.
Now she saw why. He had no subtlety against the wind. He

dropped the sail a little and then somehow swung the board towards the shore, nearly falling in. But he had drifted too far to get a clear run back to the shore to their right. He was heading straight for the cliff again. He dropped the sail, turned back towards The Racks, and tried the whole manoeuvre again.

The rollers ran in, broken up by The Racks. Streaming in, and she could tell that he was tiring. He tacked and came back in, but he was still further off-course. Above them the sky was a livid grey and getting dark. The wind was harsh on their faces. Ahead the sea raged, white horses raced. Spumes of water shot vertically where incoming waves crashed against rock. Starke was foaming at its base, and waves seemed sometimes to engulf it. Daniel was small and weak and being tossed upon the sea, and she could feel that he was uncertain and afraid.

But then, as if he sensed her desperate thoughts, Daniel dropped the sail and stared briefly back to the shore. He was too tired, he could not swim back. And yet; and he turned away again and saw ahead of him the only line he could take with the unmanoeuvrable board: a line straight into the heart of The Racks.

She saw him stand and stare, one arm on the uphaul, the other loose at his side. She followed his gaze and saw the seas that no board sailor had ever run; no boat ever survived. Rock after rising rock, the rush back of broken water, the onslaught of angry waves criss-crossing, maddened, with the dark rising of the besieged Starke Island beyond.

She saw his body wilt, and that his spirit was dying. She saw he was afraid. She saw he was giving up. Either way, either way he could not go.

He turned his head, his legs bending to keep balance, and looked up at last, as she knew he would, towards the cliff. As he did so she struggled one white arm out from under the cagoule that he might see her, and as best she could she began to shout.

'Daaaanh . . . yeh. Yeeeeeeh!'

Yes. Yes to The Racks. Yes to surviving. Yes to being loved. Yes to life. Oh *yes yes yes yes*.

'Yeeeeeh, Daaanh . . .'

Suddenly his body gained a stillness on the board as all about him moved. He had seen her. He could not have heard her, but he had seen her and he knew what she must be trying to tell him. Yes. Yes, yes, *yes*, now . . .

He raised a hand to her, turned back to lean into the wind, raised the sail and looked up to take a final line. He pulled the wishbone expertly into his body, he let the wind fill the sail with a snap so powerful that its sound was carried up the cliff to where Esther watched and urged; and then, suddenly gathering speed, Daniel Schuster began a run straight into the centre of The Racks' violent seas. One fall, just one, would be all. He leaned back until his back itself was touching the racing water and he looked forward, steering right and left as best he could, through one great wall of water, seeming almost to leap over a group of skerries, on and on and on into the dusk until all she could see was the luminescent spot of his sack moving, dodging, hidden beneath troughs, obscured by spray, the sail hidden by great seas, on and on towards the rising hell of Starke.

On until she could see him no more, and he was lost, lost in dark seas. On she stared, unbelieving, waiting, hoping, praying; beseeching whatever gods there were to let him find a place to gybe or tack, and an escape route out across the bay. Please, oh God, please.

A minute, two, five minutes, ten. Esther and Tom watched. But he was gone.

'*Toh!*'

Back towards the house, turning terribly from where he had been and Esther thinking, thinking. Cold now, calculating. Viola. Quicker to go there than to get Tom to phone. Down the rough track, fast Tom fast, quick quick quick.

Viola was in. She took one look at the two of them and knew something was terribly wrong.

'Amh says it's Daniel. He's sailed in The Racks. Now he has.'

Viola raised her eyes to the skies behind them, and the gloom of evening all about, and said, 'Sailboarding?'

Esther nodded.

'The Racks?'

'Yeh.' *Do* something. People are so slow. Please, now.

Viola called the police and they called the coastguards and then the nightmare started, when everybody did everything and nothing could be done. Launch Rinsey lifeboat? Where? For what? Search

The Racks? Has he got flares? When was it? The Rinsey coastguard saw nothing. Can't launch there at night, not in the day in these conditions. So many people, in boots and yellow sou'westers, the police in bright red jackets, with flashing lights, telephone calls, cups of tea, and always, always the wind battering and the sea's cruel empty roar.

'What is it, Esther?'

WHAT IS IT??

For three hours they had done nothing but take her back up to the house, get her keyboard and screen so she could communicate, and get an account of what had happened again and again and again.

I TOLD YOU WHAT HAPPENED. CAN'T YOU DO SOMETHING?

'We're doing everything we can, madam, I promise you. Royal Navy helicopters in Penzance are on alert but obviously, in the dark, in these seas . . . I'm sorry.'

Viola had come and made some soup. Packet soup, the kind Daniel liked. Oh God, there was cold ice through her body, oh dear dear, my dear dear, my darling. Think think think think think think. Never in her life had Esther wished so much that she was able-bodied. The world was mad around her, and she unable to do anything at all. But then if she had been, what would she have done? Rush into the sea? No no no no. Think, think.

Tom, despite what the police and Viola and everybody else tried to say, would not leave her side. Ready to do only her bidding. Amh was thinking now, not angry with anyone now, just thinking. Amh knew what to do.

'Toh!'

'Yes, Amh. Who, Amh? *Who?*' She had raised her hands in their language. She wanted him to make a telephone call.

TELL TOM TO PHONE THIS NUMBER, VIOLA. NO. TOM. NOT YOU.

It was Helen's number, and Helen answered.

'It's me,' said Tom. 'It's Amh. Amh's here.'

'What's wrong, Tom?' Helen could tell something was.

'Daniel . . .'

He told her, and Viola explained the details. The police spoke to her. Walkie-talkies spoke as well. The place was a chaos of noise.

'Can I speak to Esther, please?' said Helen finally. They put the phone to Esther's ear.

'I'm driving down, my dear, they all sound mad. I'm coming now.'

'Nah.'

'Yes, my dear, oh yes.'

Nine, ten, eleven. Five hours from Oxford. Two in the morning she would be there. Please come soon, Helen. Please. Esther felt so useless and alone.

I WANT TO GO OUTSIDE.

'Amh wants to go out on the cliff.'

I WANT TO.

'It's best not, Esther,' said Viola.

'Better not, ma'am,' said the officer.

WHY NOT?

'Best not,' he said firmly, looking at her body all spasmed now and tense, looking at the rain against the windows, and listening to the wind. 'Nothing she can do,' he said to Viola as if Esther wasn't there.

Somebody else turned back to Esther and spoke loudly, as if she was deaf, 'It's all in very good hands.'

'Amh wants to . . .' insisted Tom.

'Don't want you going over the cliff edge do we, son?'

HE'S TWENTY-FOUR.

'All right?'

They would not let them go out, and the most she could do was to retire to the bedroom with the lights off and peer out to sea, where there was nothing much to look at as the night was dark.

'Look, Amh!'

It was Starke. Searchlights from the air, briefly. A naval helicopter. Possible because the wind had eased marginally, but still very dangerous. Marvellous men, the navy pilots.

Then the light again out at sea, and the briefest of glimpses of heavy seas and the harsh silhouette of Starke.

Minutes and then an hour. And then the police coming in. Oh dear God, no.

'We understand they have sighted a board. No sail, just a board. On Starke, stuck in a cleft. I'm afraid there is no sign of anything other than that.'

YOU MEAN THEY CAN'T SEE MY HUSBAND?

'Exactly.'

WHICH SIDE IS THE BOARD?

'North side. Shoreside.'

Esther's face changed.

IN A CLEFT. THE BOARD?

'They said so. But it's an impossible place and control pulled them off. You know, those pilots would go anywhere if they could. But . . . I'm sorry, we'll just have to wait for daylight.'

HE'S THERE ALIVE.

'Yes, we can hope so.'

HE'S UNDER THE BOARD. HE'S ROLLED UP THE SAIL TO PRO-TECT IT. HE'S WAITING. HE'S THERE. I WANT TO GO OUTSIDE NOW!!!

'Better not,' said the policeman so gently she wanted to scream.

The Windsurf Man appeared. What the hell's going on? For the first time ever Esther was pleased to see him. Sanity in his anger now.

Esther explained, and asked for support for her theory.

'If he had got to the far side of Starke he would have gone on out into open sea where it's safe, so it sounds as if he couldn't get round,' said Edmond Garratt. 'Staying there is what I'd do. But . . .'

GET OUT GET OUT, Esther suddenly told everyone. Oh please God, let him be alive. Silent, pale-faced, desperately tired, Tom stayed with her and Viola got everybody out to the kitchen.

Eleven. Midnight. The wind worsening. The vigil darkening. Esther wanted the window open. It made her feel nearer.

'Yes, Amh.'

Cover my papers, Tom. Yes. Put the duvet right over them. Yes. Otherwise the wind will blow them.

The window was opened. Just wild darkness and the sea's roar outside. But Esther felt closer as she stared into the distance where Starke was until her eyes hurt. She felt he was there, and that he was living, and with each surge of sea, and crash of surf she felt him holding on and desperate, and her body suffered too the pulling and sucking and battering of sharp rock and cold.

The night deepened further until later she felt a hand on her shoulder.

'Esther. My dear, my dear . . .' The police had told her what had happened.

I WANT TO GO OUT, HELEN. MAKE THEM LET ME. THEY CAN'T...

Helen did. Indomitable, turning on the stupid police and Viola standing overweight and useless.

'Mrs Schuster wishes to go outside, which I can understand. And she will do so now.'

ON THE BEACH IF THE CLIFF'S DANGEROUS.

'On the beach.'

So down they went, taking the back track through the village to the front as the normal track was dangerous with the tide running unusually high.

Wrapped up, and with a vacuum flask, Helen organized Esther, Tom and herself on the beach while the police and Viola and others waiting for dawn were told to stand a little way off. Esther sat facing the sea, watching the surf caught by the shore lights, her eyes never leaving the spot where she imagined Starke was.

HE'S ALIVE, I KNOW HE IS I KNOW. THEY SAW HIS BOARD HE'S...

The dark night of Esther's soul deepened and she fell into a terrible silence, not noticing the gale while Tom held her chair safe, nor feeling the salt spray carried sharply on to her cheeks.

Then she began to talk to Daniel, sweetly urging him, telling him, loving him. You are alive, you are alive, you are, you are, you are, and gradually she felt nearer to him and knew that he was alive, but that he was dying. Each heavy sea, each terrible surge was at him, tearing at him in the darkness but hear me, hear me, my beloved, remember remember remember, and she began to talk to him as once Edward talked to Arthur when he was dying in a ward, as once Arthur went to Edward who was injured, out into the darkness, over the wooden fence, willing him who was her all, her everything, repeating words again for marriage is given that husband and wife may comfort and help each other and she who could not run, who could not walk, who could not speak, who could not even sit up without support, could *can can* send out comfort now, and strength, and faith, out to her Daniel who had seen her on the cliff-top and who knew she would be waiting and watching over him.

The police watch changed. Tom sipped tea. Helen sat down on the beach. Neighbours gathered in the dark like gulls on the shore. All knew that her husband was long dead. All knew that no man could survive such seas. Why, by morning, the board, if that's what it had been, would have been ripped from its cleft on Starke and washed far away. The sail would be nothing but ribbons. Silly bugger. Poor sod. Nothing to do but wait for a sorrowing dawn and see the ritual through.

Three o'clock. Three-thirty. And several there sensed a deepening of some darkness then, as if Esther was projecting her own sense that now was the hour when men weaken, now now the sea's crashing surges would be too great for a tired hand to keep its grip, now, *now*.

TELL THEM TO TURN SOME CARS TO FACE THE SEA WITH THE HEADLIGHTS ON. TELL THEM, HELEN.

Pointless really, but it was something to do. Four cars were turned on the front and their lights put on. But all they seemed to do was to lighten the sands and make the sea's surf seem even more dangerous as it caught the lights.

IF HE CAN SEE THE CAR LIGHTS IT MIGHT HELP. HE'LL KNOW I'M HERE.

'Yes, my dear,' whispered Helen. 'Yes.'

A strange shape rose in the violent water just off shore, caught by the lights. A coastguard turned a beam on the surf. A rectangular shape was turning and toppling and rushed ashore. A door. A blue door, complete with a handle.

Esther had seen that door before. The boatman had said a winter gale would force it free. This was the gale.

Four o'clock, the worst darkness yet. Daniel, Daniel, Daniel, over and over she spoke his name to the darkness, for now she sensed he needed her, now he must survive; turn one way to life and the other to death. One way to life, that was the choice, and will be, but she was sinking now, she could feel him sinking, he was turning and she must tell him not to turn that way. Daniel, Daniel, but her strength was failing and she felt such love for him as her eyes began to close on him and she to drift, too tired now, Daniel, you must, you must, you must.

'Amh!!!!'

It was Tom but he had no need to shout more.

They all saw it, high over the sea, high high they saw it, all the watchers, a shooting of light, distinct, just visible, before it burst into red light hanging for a moment then sinking away in the wind. A red flare whose brief light caught Starke in its colour. It was Daniel's flare.

'*Daaaanh . . .*' and she knew he was speaking to her, telling her; she knew he would live. He had saved it for her. Daniel was telling her his choice. Yes yes yes yes.

HE WILL LIVE.

There was a flurry of excitement, people ran, police and coastguards spoke, Royal Naval controls crackled. A red flare over Starke. Yes the subject had a flare. Possibly two. Subject's wife uncertain.

But the wind was wrong for helicopters, it was veering southerly, the worse possible. Hard to take off, let alone . . .

Dawn? The merest glimmer.

GET THE WINDSURF MAN. TELL TOM. HE KNOWS. GET HIM NOW. DANIEL IS ALIVE.

The Windsurf Man, Edmond Garratt, came at the first glimmer of dawn.

HE'S ON STARKE AND HE'S ALIVE. THERE WAS A FLARE.

'I know. A helicopter will try and get him off,' he said.

HE'S PROBABLY WEAKENING. HE'S BEEN THERE TOO LONG. HE'S ROLLED THE SAIL AND GOT IT UNDER THE BOARD.

'You can't know . . .'

HE TOLD ME WHAT HE WOULD DO, she lied. HE'LL TRY TO COME BACK ON THE BOARD.

'Don't be daft.'

HE WON'T BE ABLE TO TURN IN TO SHORE. The boatman said that. THAT'S WHY HE HAD TO GO OUT. HE'LL MAKE A RUN THROUGH AND THEN HE'LL BE IN AN EVEN WORSE POSITION THAN LAST NIGHT. AND HE'LL BE TIRED.

'I . . .' The Windsurf Man looked uneasily at Helen. 'Shit,' he said. 'He should never have fucking gone out.'

WHY DO YOU GO?

Edmond Garratt was silent.

'What can I do?'

BE READY WITH A BOARD.

'If the wind dies they'll get him off.'

IS IT STILL SOUTHERLY?

'Look, if it makes you happier I've been ready with a bloody board since last night at nine when I heard. If I can do anything *I will* go out, Mrs Schuster.'

PROMISE?

He laughed.

'Get stuffed,' he said, and left.

It was the most comforting conversation Esther had had all night. No; for months. Beyond the rudeness she saw strength and fear, and a man getting ready for a fight, who recognized that she too was fighting.

Within half an hour of the flare not only had dawn come, but so had a television crew. There were more lights on the front. Then a helicopter flew round the bay head and over the wild sea.

Though the tide had receded the seas still rushed high up the sands, full of driftwood and plastic bottles, seaweed and rubbish. The beach was littered with flotsam, and the blue door. Crowds watched as the helicopters hovered over the island, and some huddled round the police car to try to hear any news. Many had trained binoculars on the distant outline of Starke.

Then news. The board *was* there. Life was there. But unreachable, caught too low with these winds and seas for a lift to be made. Too dangerous. They would have to wait.

THERE IS NO TIME. DANIEL'S TIRING NOW. THERE IS NO TIME.

Helen could only stand with her, stare out to sea, touch her, and feel her helplessness and strength.

HE IS ALIVE, HE IS.

The helicopter seemed to hover and try, and something hung from beneath it, but then it swung suddenly away. People drifted up the track to the cliff to get a better view, and so did the television crew. The police kept a radio interview man clear of Esther's group.

'I'll go to see when Daniel comes,' said Tom, leaving her at last. And he went up the cliff to get a better view. It was the first time in twelve hours that Esther smiled.

HE IS ALIVE, HELEN, BUT THEY MUST BE QUICK.

Behind them there was an argument. The Windsurf Man was telling a radio interviewer to piss off.

'Why are you in a wet suit? Are you going out there?'

'Fuck off.' The police got wind of it.

'No heroics please, sir. We don't want two casualties.'

'You haven't any yet, chum,' said Edmond Garratt, telling them where to go as well. He brought his board down to the high tide mark. And then went back to his hut and sat inside it.

The sky lightened, and the seas with the change of tide, but the wind was as bad as ever, and out over The Racks the seas still raged. Starke was white with water, but the helicopter came back, fighting the winds, dipping down but then shying away as huge waters spumed dangerously up towards it.

NOW NOW NOW THEY MUST.

But they could not, the man on Starke was too low for them, the overhangs above him too difficult for him to make the climb.

The helicopter veered away. There was a long pause of uncertainty. The dawn lightened further. Heavy seas raced up the beach. And then, over on the cliff they heard a cry, not one but two or three, and down that track Tom started to run, heavy and ungainly and shouting so she heard his voice, 'Amh! Amh! Amh!' And there was the flash of bright sail in the raging base of Starke and someone with binoculars said, 'He's trying to sail himself off,' and Daniel Schuster freed the board, turned it into an impossible sea, leaned into the wind, raised the sail and started the long run home.

Unnoticed, Edmond Garratt took up his board, carried it quickly down to the surf, and before police or coastguards could stop him, beach-started out into the great waves, black to their grey, strong to their strength, out beyond them as the wind picked up the spray from the front of his board and hurled it back towards the shore.

Out beyond the surf he went, out to meet Daniel. Tens, perhaps hundreds saw it: a windsurfer launching from the beach into the rough sea, out through the waveline and then turning across the bay to the cliffs under the monument, to wait for the other coming through The Racks. They saw Daniel coming, fighting each yard of the way, tired but surer now, white water courage, not one stretch of calm, not one single place where a fall meant anything but death. On on on he came while high overhead a helicopter followed him, its roar answered by the sea's.

Nearer now, the sail visible sometimes to Esther where she waited on the beach, dipping in troughs of white water, lost behind black vicious rocks, until at last it was clear and alongside the Windsurf Man.

Few knew what they were doing down there beneath the cliffs, tossed and turned by the waves. But Edmond Garratt had taken out a spare mast-foot and they calmly dropped sails and cut Daniel's rope mast-foot. They put the new mast-foot on. Then they turned the boards and tracked out again to get a run to the beach. Above them the helicopter hovered, navy men in orange lifejackets leaning out.

The two boards turned towards the shore and at the last moment before the surf Daniel waved his helper on because once he had lost a friend who had let him go ahead. He did not want to repeat the pattern.

So Edmond sailed in first, hard hard up the beach; and then came Daniel, his coloured sail gleaming wet with spray, his face set with tiredness and cold, his arms and legs lacerated and white with immersion; but his body strong and alive.

When he put foot on dry land he ignored the many who came to him, but went straight instead to Esther, and people stayed back while he kneeled in the sand, wet and cold, and she reached out her weak arms and took him to her. 'You were waiting. I saw the lights. I was helpless but I knew you were waiting,' he whispered. 'I kept saying Skallagrigg, Skallagrigg endlessly because I was helpless.'

Yes yes yes yes yes. 'Yeh,' she whispered, that's it, that's what is.

The salt taste of his face, the salt thrill on her tongue, then and later when they were alone, might have been sea, or it might have been tears. You are alive, Daniel.

'Yes, yes, yes, yes,' said Daniel; and she was his world, and he was hers, and where they were the storm was gone.

SEVENTY

Twelve months later, a child was born to Esther and Daniel Schuster. They named him Robert Brian Martin. Robert was for Daniel's grandfather and Brian was for Esther's. Martin was Esther's special wish – it was the name of Arthur Lane's grandson whom he saw once so briefly in the street of a Birmingham suburb. Martin is my name.

Esther was not strong, not before the pregnancy, not during, and not after, and the doctors watched worriedly over her for she was weak and had problems throughout.

She was not an easy or predictable patient and they warned her that she would not be strong enough for a natural birth and must have a Caesarian.

DON'T LET THEM, DANIEL, I WAS BORN THAT WAY. And her hands wandered hopelessly over her body and her eyes were frightened. Few mothers knew so well what an abnormal birth can mean.

'OK, Esther, but it'll be up to you. I'll be there to see no quick decisions are made.' They did not want to be harried in the pressure of the moment into agreeing what Esther did not want.

Daniel sat with her when labour started and watched over her, urging her on: 'If you don't do it soon, I'm going windsurfing' (which only made her laugh and lose all concentration); and 'Relax and imagine you're there already, think of something else, think . . .' – and though the labour was almost critically long, with Daniel's encouragement Esther succeeded giving birth the natural way.

No mother ever asked with more feeling than Esther, 'Is he all right?' Eyes smiled down at her, voices said 'yes', but it was Daniel's quick nod that meant most, and she began to believe it when they put her baby in her arms, and helped her hold him.

They warned her she might find breastfeeding difficult. Daniel was annoyed and a more sympathetic nurse was found who relaxed Esther until she did manage to breastfeed, if only for a few weeks and in some discomfort.

But that was all the easy part. Now she had to watch as others did the work she wanted so to do, and suffer the frustration of being given her child as if she herself was a child.

'Mummy wants to hold you now, Robert, Mummy wants . . .' The nurses were so tactless in their tone of voice. Substitute 'Baby' for 'Mummy' and their meaning was plain.

Even getting mother and child out of the hospital was difficult, because they wanted to hold them far longer than other mothers. Finally Daniel came with a suitcase and a helper, and they were out within hours.

Yet what happiness then in their house for a time. Tom was a godfather, Helen and James came down, and Kate made a special trip.

But her father she would not have, and it seemed he did not want to come. Their silence continued. Seeing them, seeing the house, made Kate worry. Daniel looked tired, Esther looked fragile, her skin pale and her eyes dark. Sometimes she cried. She was working at her computer too hard as a compensation, Kate ever after believed, for what she could not do for her baby. But she *had* to work she said; she was finishing the game 'Skallagrigg'.

So she turned her back on Robert and what she was unable ever to do for him, and entered the final levels of her game.

While outside Tom, healthier than ever, marched busily up and down the Gribber track, round Gribber's steep narrow streets, doing his jobs, being made welcome, showing those who would look at it the photograph of Robert he carried in a plastic bag.

Social workers visited the Schuster house frequently, looking askance at the odd arrangements but unable to deny that they worked. The place was orderly and clean, the helpers all gave good reports, the baby was healthy if a little small. In fact, they concluded, the baby was well cared for. It was Mrs Schuster who gave cause for concern.

'What is it that she *does*? She's very intelligent. But what is all that equipment for?' The local health-care workers did not play computer games, otherwise they might have understood.

'They make games.'

'Games?'

'For computers.'

'Oh.'

'And they're quite successful apparently. Quite well known.'

'Ah.'

Esther had got to the seventh level of 'Skallagrigg' but though she worked long hours, she advanced only slowly. The social workers were right: she was not well. Depression. To be expected really. So at case meetings in Penzance they agreed to keep an eye on her.

They planned a trip to California in June, when the baby would be six months old, hoping they could leave him for two weeks while they both had a break. Everybody said that's what they ought to have. But when the time came Esther did not want to go and the doctors, reluctantly, were against it too. She was *weak*.

The sun that year was strong early, but though she sat out in it, and they took her walking over the bay, still she looked pale. Time, said the doctors, and rest. Don't work so hard, no need. But Daniel could not stop her, and nor did he wish to. He knew, as Kate did, that she worked because she could not do anything for her baby. She refused to play the game the helpers tried of pretending to make decisions.

'What feed would you like Robert to have today?'

YOU DECIDE.

'What jumpsuit?'

YOU DECIDE.

'He smiles at his mummy.'

HE SMILES MORE AT YOU AND DANIEL.

To play that game was to live a lie; not to play it was to suffer those little glances that others gave which say, 'You're not a loving mother.' But oh she was, but had not been given the means to express it. Perhaps Esther was able to enter the final seventh level of 'Skallagrigg' because she was now experiencing ultimate helplessness – that of a parent who cannot help her child. The helplessness her father felt; and her mother, once a girl running over sands, would also have felt. And she felt angry, and controlled it; and frustrated, and controlled it; and helpless and useless, and wrote that into a game that others might know and value better what they had and she had not.

So Daniel went to Hanniman Beach alone, and while he was there he made a video of the house and beach so that she might know what it was like before she was well enough to go herself.

When he came back they had a film show and she saw his home. The veranda, the postbox with 'Schuster' where that letter came, the stretching beach and Pacific waves which swept in and in; and little things – his bedroom, pictures of his parents, his aunt, a cat he once had. He videoed the Daniel she did not know. Over it all shone the Californian sun, and the sounds of sea she knew so well, but lighter and more airy than that other western shore.

She watched, and smiled, and held his hand, watching Tom hold Robert and proud of what she had made.

IF ANYTHING HAPPENS . . .

'Nothing will happen.'

IF ANYTHING . . .

'Esther! Not that again.'

DARLING, IF ANYTHING HAPPENS WILL YOU PROMISE TO TAKE ROBERT TO HANNIMAN? PROMISE? PLEASE? DON'T STAY HERE, DANIEL, NOT IN THIS COUNTRY. TAKE HIM THERE.

And Daniel could not speak.

At the end of the summer they took her back into hospital for tests. Severe anaemia, general fatigue, lassitude. After three days she begged Daniel to take her home because she felt lonely and missed Robert's noise and the sound of the sea. She missed Tom. In hospital she always felt like an object.

But the doctors said she must stay another two weeks for observation. Post-natal depression? Possibly.

PLEASE TAKE ME HOME, DANIEL. I MISS THE SEA. I WANT TO WORK.

'They say you're depressed.'

I AM. I HAVEN'T FINISHED 'SKALLAGRIGG'. YOU'D BE DE-PRESSED. ALSO IT'S NOT VERY NICE NOT BEING ABLE TO HELP WITH ROBERT. HE CRAWLS BETTER THAN I DO. HE'LL BE WALKING SOON.

'Jealous?'

Esther grinned. She could laugh at herself, sometimes, but it was always a risk, she had a low breaking point.

I FEEL IT'S ME DOING IT. YOU'RE NOT JEALOUS OF YOUR OWN CHILD.

'You would have been if it had been a girl.'

Tears welled up in her eyes and she whispered, 'Nah.' She would have liked a girl.

'They say you've got to work at getting better. Have a change, forget *work*, let me arrange a holiday in the sun.'

NOT YET, DANIEL. SOON MAYBE SOON.

But he did: an old-fashioned spa holiday in Germany, just the thing. They went. It rained. Esther grinned.

JUST MY LUCK.

'Just *my* luck you mean!'

LET'S GO HOME.

Somehow they both felt it was where they should be. Time was not theirs to waste.

Winter brought dark despair and in its long weeks Daniel grew up. He got up at night for Robert, he cared for Esther, he made decisions for all of them, he learned to love and to live day by day. He felt helpless before her weak helplessness, and though the work on 'Skallagrigg' tired her, they now did it together, as they began to create the extraordinary marine graphics at which journeyers who reach the final passages of the game marvel. Enormous seas, dark electronic rocks, the roar and hish of waves more gargantuan even than any he had known in that long night of survival on Starke.

They created a journey through locations of land and sea such as no computer game had shown before, and few have equalled since; where mazes move, and where the journeyer must shed his very hope of life to find the true way forward.

It was in this period that Daniel got Esther to write down her account of the search for the Skallagrigg. which meant her life.

YOU MIGHT READ IT!!! ALL MY SECRETS.

'I might one day,' he said. 'And it'll help me and others make sense of "Skallagrigg".'

WELL, I MIGHT THEN, she said. MAYBE.

So she started, telling of her foster-mother Mrs Dillard, of the Ealing Centre, of Peter, and of the day her father came and, with Peter's help, she got him to spell 'Skallagrigg' for the very first time. Of Eileen, of Netherton, of all of it day by day she wrote, and

Daniel saw that the depression did not deepen, but rather eased as she put her story down. Until at last she began to write of him, to him, and of her love and dream of him, her desire for him. She was passing her life's dreams to Daniel and Robert.

DON'T READ TODAY'S, she sometimes said, but he rarely did. She was writing it for herself, to find out what had happened and to take her mind off the present reality which was that Robert was daily growing, and daily advancing past her.

It was at some time then that she became concerned again by the problem of Arthur's son Peter, and his grandson Martin. Was he right to keep his existence from them? Originally she had thought not. But increasingly, as she saw her own son reach for her and gain enough strength to pull himself up, or pick something up which she could not; when she saw him begin to feed himself not much less effectively than she, she realized that there were profound problems in her raising a child. The books on handicapped parenting denied it, and they had smiling faces on cheerful covers, but the wheelchairs grated and the children, she noted, were never quoted. It was a problem and one, she felt, no family should have to face.

Yet what when that same child grew up? When I was a child I spoke like a child . . . I reasoned like a child; when I became a man I gave up childish ways. For now we see in a mirror dimly, but then face to face. Face to face. Wouldn't anyone be proud to know their parent was an Arthur, with all his humour, intelligence and humility? Wouldn't any grandchild, like Martin? Esther wrote to Arthur on these lines, and Edward wrote back for him explaining that he had not changed his mind.

Yet had he the right? Esther believed that somewhere in all our pasts is handicap, and often in our present. Here, now; daily in the papers. Parents whose psychological handicaps were more severe by far, and more damaging, then palsy, Down's syndrome or spina bifida.

That winter Esther worried about Martin's rights, and decided, perhaps wrongly, that he deserved the opportunity to know his own past, however slight that opportunity might be. So she began to build some clues for him into the game, hoping that the greatest clue of all was there already: Skallagrigg, the name. For if he did not know that, if Linnie had not passed it on to his father, and his father did not pass it on to Martin, then why should he ever notice a game called 'Skallagrigg' or think to look in it for clues to something more?

So into the final levels she put anagrams and questions, puzzles and number series which played on the name Martin and Peter as son and father, and on Skallagrigg as grandfather. If such handicap existed, she asked in her game, what rights have children to know? And on what might such rights be based? Read, mark and learn, make your choices. Life is usually a self-made maze whose walls are fears and prejudice, a maze through which there is no perfect route, whose final stages demand acceptance of weakness, not display of strength, where you must accept that one day your child may lean over and take the spoon from your hand, without your having the strength to resist. In the end strength lies in acceptance, hope is in truth not fantasy; peace cannot be in craving, but in the giving up of desire.

So, in her last dark winter, Esther pursued these final reaches to the Skallagrigg. Tiring now, worn, and the growth and health of Robert a bitter-sweet thing, for in his discoveries of strength and his successive expression of ever more complex needs, Esther confronted her own final helplessness. She had made a child who was of her life but she could do nothing for him.

There came a day in the new spring when Robert Brian Martin Schuster walked, and when he did he walked past Esther, from one side of the room to the other, ignoring her call. For that too he had learnt: that she had no power. And Esther had to watch, as she had always watched, and always would.

Daniel always remembered the day Robert first walked: it was the day that Esther seemed nearly mad, staring out of the window at the sea with a despair so deep that when he held it he was holding ice.

Yet somehow, she found the courage to tell him: IT'S ALL RIGHT, IT'S BEST I FACE THE TRUTH. LEAVE ME, I WANT TO WORK.

So she did the final work on 'Skallagrigg' and made a game that others might learn to value what they had, and to know their body's worth and find the joy in the simple things that she could never know.

In May she was weaker and spent a second period in hospital.

But this time Daniel responded to her pleas, and, over-ruling advice, quickly brought her home. Helen came, and helpers from Hill House. She worked one last time on her game writing instructions for Daniel and making him understand that the final imagery would be the sea they had shared, its violence and its calms, and The Racks would be a dominant motif. He must make graphics that spoke not just of the fear, but of the love and faith that had given him strength to live through a night of hell, and come back to her, and life. But journeyers must have the choice of turning one way or another, to decide finally if they had finished and reached the end. Only they would know; her game was to help them know. Her game was the Skallagrigg who waited in the middle of a field, where poppies blew. Who, if players found strength to reach him, or perhaps her, would reach out and hold their hand. Not as one more powerful, but as one whom the journey had taught them was an equal, so that they could stand side by side: Arthur to Edward, Helen to James, Brian to Margaret, and, perhaps, Richard to Kate. In that confession of need, which came through the racks of helplessness, whose passage Arthur and Esther knew, lay the discovery of Skallagrigg.

So Esther worked, too weak finally to key in the commands and strings of code but only 'talking' on her screen to Daniel.

DO YOU UNDERSTAND, MY LOVE? YOU KNOW WHAT TO DO AT THAT LEVEL? YOU KNOW IT WILL BE SO LOVELY THERE. YES YES YES.

DO YOU REMEMBER JAMES AT HERSTORNE WHEN HE BLESSED US? DIDN'T YOU FEEL OUR MARRIAGE REALLY STARTED THEN? DIDN'T YOU...

Daniel sat holding her in bed, both naked, her pale skin almost transparent against his health, and he nodded, feeling she was giving him a love so strong that it was to be for Robert, so that he might know his mother loved him and never feel a loss, as Daniel had, which can destroy a life, and others too.

At the end Helen had to protect them both from doctors and helpers and social workers who might, through kindness, have invaded them. The social workers wanted to take Robert away for a time but Helen stopped that, sitting him instead on his parents' bed so he could jabber to his mother and touch her face, even scramble on her weak body to catch her twisted hands in his sound ones and laugh in the security of her love.

When night came, Helen shooed Daniel to his wife and, whatever convention might say, suggested that if they wished to hold each other, that was only right, however weak Esther was.

Until she had strength only to smile and be close and whisper words, words so powerful that they could only be of love. So finally faith, hope, love abide, these three; but the greatest of these is love.

Then a night came in June when the dark seas whispered and the winds began to die. When the waves slowed and the sea was calm, stirring at the rocks but gentle until all fell still. And Helen, who had sat up and could not sleep, walked out on the cliff and stared in the night to a distant horizon where sea mirrored sky, and sky was the sea, Arthur to Edward, one to another.

Inside, Daniel lay asleep in the bed with Esther in his arms. Outside the dawn brought light across the sands where once they had gone laughing, and known more love in an hour than many ever know.

When Daniel awoke he seemed to remember Esther whispering and touching, words that have no spelling, touches that have no name, and he had fallen asleep to them, and woken to them. She had found strength to give them to him always. He kissed her once again, and knew she had no need to whisper more. Nor ever would again.

Esther Schuster, formerly Marquand, died in June at her home on the cliff above Gribber Bay. They said that perhaps the life there was too hard for someone with her disabilities; that having a child was the wrong thing. They said all sorts of things. Daniel and Helen never said anything.

She was buried a few yards from the tower of Gribber's parish church. Today the white stone at her grave is beginning to weather with the salt sea wind.

On the day of the funeral they were there, her family and friends who loved her, and many from the village. And Tom.

During the service Tom stood at the front with Daniel and Robert. On the far side was Richard. Tom wore a new jacket he had bought for the midsummer dance with his own earned money. Edward Lane came but Arthur was unable to, for he was ill. So Frank was not there either, but Eppie and Norman were. And Graham and Tony Downer and Betty Shaw.

Tom stared about during the service, and looked sometimes at the light oak coffin. He liked the flowers on it. He grinned about. He was restless but said nothing. He was glad when they went outside to do the burying but he cast no soil down.

Instead, it seems, he took Richard by the hand and led him to the churchyard wall and peered over it to a field of corn where poppies were beginning to bud.

'Amh likes them,' he said.

'Esther's gone now, Tom,' said Richard.

They saw Tom put his arms around Richard and comfort him. Tom tried to cry because everybody else was, but no tears came. It looked more as if he was grinning which he did not intend. So then he stood aside and took Richard's hand again and busily pointed past the church down towards the sea. From there The Racks looked nearly benign, and beyond them the sea stretched out to a blue horizon.

Tom said, 'Richard?'

'Yes?'

'Amh's all right now. Amh's coming back.'

Richard smiled, but Tom knew that smile: it was Esther's when she didn't believe him.

'Ooh yes,' Tom said, 'Amh is.'

SEVENTY-ONE

We started with Arthur, and Esther and me. We set out in pursuit of the truth of 'Skallagrigg'.

I started because I found a game whose name was one which my father had once told me his mother had mentioned. His mother was named Carolyn but her friends called her Linnie. She was my grandmother but I do not remember her.

When I was just adult I was shown that game and I played it, though it took me many years to reach into its deeper levels. When I finally did so I found a message for me alone: find the truth of the Skallagrigg and you'll know what to do. So I got to meet Richard Marquand, and Daniel Schuster, and I got to read Esther's papers. I have written what I could with their help, and sometimes without it. It was too late to meet Arthur or Edward or Helen or James Freeman. I came down here to Gribber Bay and was allowed to spend the winter in the house where Daniel and Esther lived.

Tom is still alive and lives next door, but it is impossible to come to Gribber and not meet him. He works in the old-style market garden that Edmond Garratt runs with his daughter; he beach-combs for drift wood; he does jobs for people who own homes on Cliff Road which they desert over winter. People here say that Gribber would not be quite itself without Tom.

Tom could not remember much of Esther and nothing at all of Skallagrigg.

What he does know is that Esther's coming back one day. At the least opportunity he will take your hand, point to the sea, and say, 'Amh's coming back.'

There aren't many in Gribber now who know what he means, or who Amh was. But Tom believes it and always will.

'Amh's coming back,' he says again, grinning, his hair nearly gone now, and what is left nearly white. When he grins his eyes screw up behind thick glasses, and his cheeks seem so shiny they reflect the sea.

One of his jobs is to look after this house where Daniel and Esther once lived. Edward Lane left the property to the Marquand Foundation, and it is a holiday home in the summer for handicapped children from Hill House. Tom is caretaker, and they all know him, and his shelves are full of cards from them. He cannot remember all their names.

At Christmas he has cards from America; from Daniel and Robert, who is Tom's godson, and Robert's daughter Mary. Since Mary was born thirteen years ago they have sent a family photo every year and Tom keeps them in an album with pictures of plants from horticultural catalogues.

'My friends in Amercky,' he tells you. 'Daniel and Robert and Mary.'

He grins, and he likes you to look several times. He never shows a photograph of Esther, and perhaps he has not got one. He looked at some I had and said, 'That's Amh.' He pointed to her grey chair and added, 'She's all right now. She's coming back.'

I was allowed to stay in the house this winter to finish my account of how Esther came to make 'Skallagrigg' and this I have now done. There's more, I suppose, of the programming and how Daniel completed the graphics before he would leave Gribber Bay, and how the game was marketed and gained recognition as a classic sometime during the nineties.

When Daniel finished the work on the game he fulfilled his promise to Esther, and took Robert back to the home that she had only ever seen on video.

Windsurfing must have been in the Schuster blood. Robert learned it as a boy and is one of America's best, though he is now in his thirties. Naturally Mary learned as well, and I understand that she has recently started winning junior championships. I remember with pleasure how, in the early days of my research on 'Skallagrigg', I stood on Hanniman Beach and watched Daniel coaching his granddaughter then nine. Esther would have been proud of that.

So I came to this house and completed my work in the room where Esther worked, and heard and saw the seas she knew. It's a good place. I finished a month ago and sent off what I had done to

Richard in Australia and Daniel in California, asking the Marquand Foundation if I might stay on here. They agreed.

Since then I have wondered again as often before precisely why Esther should have broken her promise to Arthur and told me who I was, if only so obscurely that the chances of my discovering it were slim. But she did, and I did, and I wonder why. I hinted at the start of this account that when I first met Richard Marquand, and saw that he had never really come to terms with Esther's handicap or her death, I began to think that Esther was making a trade. The knowledge she had given me for a favour I could do her, which was to heal, or try to heal, the rift that she created and which still remains between Richard Marquand and Daniel and his family. Richard saw Robert only at Esther's funeral; he never met Mary. Perhaps, if Esther had lived, things would have changed. But Richard blamed Daniel for her death and so the rift deepened.

Last week I felt my time here was coming to an end and I walked across the bay to Crag Rock, where once Daniel perched Esther and she laughed, and I sat and thought how strange it was that since those days none of them had been back. One of the marvels of the game she made is that Esther gives players – journeyers – great freedom in what routes to take. So I sat on the rock and stared out towards Starke and made my choice: before I turned my back on Gribber, and on the story of the Skallagrigg, I would do for Esther what I think she wished me to do.

So I telephoned Daniel and I said, 'Please come, Tom,' the words Tom once used. To his credit he laughed: he recognized the quote. I added, 'Tom's getting on. He'd appreciate a visit.'

Daniel said he had read what I had sent him. Right through. There were some things he had not known, some he disagreed with, and much that moved him.

'When do you want me to come?' he asked.

'Soon,' I said, 'very soon.'

'Any special reason?' he asked. I hesitated over whether to admit that I intended to ask Richard Marquand to come as well. I decided not to but I think he guessed. 'We'll all come,' he said finally. 'Next week. OK?'

Two days ago he called me here, the telephone ringing early in the morning and getting me out of bed, and confirmed his arrival for two days' time.

Which was strange but somehow not unexpected; Richard is coming then as well. He had said to me at the start of our research, 'If you ever find the Skallagrigg, let me know.'

So after I first spoke with Daniel I sent Richard a cable which read, 'I have found the Skallagrigg' and gave my number and address in Gribber Bay.

Kate called.

'Please come,' I said simply, because it is the best way. A short while later she confirmed they were coming.

Last night Kate called from Harefield, asking me to meet them at Penzance Heliport at noon today. I'm going over with Tom in an hour or so. Neither side knows the other will be here. In fact, I'm not sure if Daniel will be here by then. He just said it would be some time today. I think Esther would have giggled at the adventure of it all.

We picked up Richard and Kate, Tom and I. Richard is nearly eighty, and frail, but he holds himself erect. Kate is also erect, but much less fragile. She is very protective of Richard.

When we first saw them Tom was immediately shy and took my hand. At first he recognized Kate but not Richard, but when Richard spoke he remembered his voice. Then he went to him and hugged him and said, 'Amh's coming.'

Richard wept a little. Tom hugged him. Kate kissed them both. They shook me by the hand. They did not know, and have not guessed, who Arthur was to me. Esther would have wished me to stay silent. As I drove Esther's father back to Gribber I felt that only then, after so very long, was I finally near the end of my own quest. I felt that she had known that in this reconciliation of people who are not mine, and with whom in truth I am quite helpless, I would see the truth that I had sought.

So, we picked them up and drove them to Gribber Bay. I had booked them all into a motel in Helston. I felt it was a risk worth taking.

'Do you want to go to your motel first?' I asked them.

'Oh, well, I'm not sure we are going to stay the night as well,' said Kate carefully. 'The service back to London is very good.' Keeping their options open; Esther would have liked that too. 'Why not take us straight to the house in Gribber Bay.'

So I did, but nervously, knowing that Daniel might be there.

But he was not, just a hired car, full of suitcases. He had arrived and gone off somewhere.

Tom showed them his cottage and made us all a careful cup of tea. It was a lovely day and Tom took us, as I knew he would, out on to the cliff to see The Racks and stare down at Gribber Bay. There were a few people about, and windsurfers as there always are.

Tom said, 'I can beachcomb and get wood,' and pointed down the length of the bay.

Richard smiled and leaned on Kate's arm, and she shaded her eyes as she looked down over the sea.

I think she noticed the sudden change in Tom before I did. His face seemed to go serious suddenly, and his mouth hung open. He took a step forward from us to get a better view down to the sea. He turned to look at us as if for support, and then turned back to stare.

'What is it, Tom?' I asked.

'It's Amh,' he said pointing. 'That's *Amh*!!'

We all saw her out on the sea at our end of the beach. Just below us. She was thirteen, slim, her hair dark and sleeky wet. She was in a blue wet suit and wore a harness. She was on a sailboard holding the sail expertly, launching the board at speed through the incoming surf. Several others on the beach were watching her. One was Daniel and another Robert but I don't think Richard or Kate saw them then.

They were watching the girl Tom said was Amh as she rode the board out into the sea. She leaned our way into the wind, jumped one wave and then another, spray flying, body perfect, alive with youth and life and joy.

She reached a far point in the centre of the bay, The Racks safely off to her left, and then she turned and we saw the sun on her face. She was laughing, happy and so full of pleasure. She *was* Amh. She leaned yet further out and started to drive the board hard back towards the shore.

'It's Amh come back,' said Tom again.

It's Amh come back.

How does an old man open his heart to so much? Richard just stared, expressionless, but his hand was tight on Kate's arm and she close to him as they watched that young girl sail on the sea below.

'You know who she is?' she whispered at last. The wind was on their faces and in their white hair; and their eyes held tears.

Richard turned to her and nodded, and then turned back to stare, for he did not want to look anywhere else but at the girl who was of him, his great granddaughter, the girl who was of Esther, a girl such as Esther herself might have been. While Kate looked at Richard, and in her face was relief and delight in the love and pride, so long delayed, she saw, beginning now to come to Richard's eyes.

'Will you go down to the beach to meet her?' she asked.

'Yes, yes,' said Richard with an old man's impatience, and waving away any other help, they made their gentle way down towards the beach. As they did so, Daniel saw them at last, and spoke quickly to Robert before both stared up at the cliff path and started up to meet them.

While Tom ignored them all.

'Amh!' he was shouting, *'Amh!'* as he ran clumsily past Richard down the track, past Daniel and down the sands towards the waves.

As she approached the waveline Mary Schuster seemed suddenly to see him standing there and dropped her sail to stare. A Down's syndrome man, bespectacled, aging, nearly bald, grinning, waving, jumping up and down with excitement.

Then she raised her sail and leaned to wind and powered through the waves to the shore where Tom stood waiting.

I wondered what a girl so young would make of Tom. I need not have worried. Wet with spray and her eyes alight, she brought her board in and jumped off, letting the sail drop with a thump as board sailors love to do.

She ran to him.

'It's Tom, isn't it!'

But he could only stare and whisper shyly, 'I said you'd come.'

She laughed and went to him and put her wet arms around him, to give him a hug. Then, taking his arm, she walked him up the beach to meet them all.

I saw Daniel turn and Richard go to him. I saw Kate reaching out to Robert. Beside the sea the rift was healed.

But the last thing I saw, before I turned away and left them for ever to their privacy, was Tom, as proud as ever he had been. At his side was his beloved Amh standing as she had never been able to before in all his life, and she was holding his hand with love, as Esther would have done. In their reunion I saw the Skallagrigg.

FOR THE BEST IN PAPERBACKS, LOOK FOR THE

In every corner of the world, on every subject under the sun, Penguin represents quality and variety – the very best in publishing today.

For complete information about books available from Penguin – including Pelicans, Puffins, Peregrines and Penguin Classics – and how to order them, write to us at the appropriate address below. Please note that for copyright reasons the selection of books varies from country to country.

In the United Kingdom: For a complete list of books available from Penguin in the U.K., please write to *Dept E.P., Penguin Books Ltd, Harmondsworth, Middlesex, UB7 0DA*

In the United States: For a complete list of books available from Penguin in the U.S., please write to *Dept BA, Penguin, 299 Murray Hill Parkway, East Rutherford, New Jersey 07073*

In Canada: For a complete list of books available from Penguin in Canada, please write to *Penguin Books Canada Ltd, 2801 John Street, Markham, Ontario L3R 1B4*

In Australia: For a complete list of books available from Penguin in Australia, please write to the *Marketing Department, Penguin Books Australia Ltd, P.O. Box 257, Ringwood, Victoria 3134*

In New Zealand: For a complete list of books available from Penguin in New Zealand, please write to the *Marketing Department, Penguin Books (NZ) Ltd, Private Bag, Takapuna, Auckland 9*

In India: For a complete list of books available from Penguin, please write to *Penguin Overseas Ltd, 706 Eros Apartments, 56 Nehru Place, New Delhi, 110019*

In Holland: For a complete list of books available from Penguin in Holland, please write to *Penguin Books Nederland B.V., Postbus 195, NL–1380AD Weesp, Netherlands*

In Germany: For a complete list of books available from Penguin, please write to *Penguin Books Ltd, Friedrichstrasse 10 – 12, D–6000 Frankfurt Main 1, Federal Republic of Germany*

In Spain: For a complete list of books available from Penguin in Spain, please write to *Longman Penguin España, Calle San Nicolas 15, E–28013 Madrid, Spain*

Callanish

As the iron bars close round Creggan, the captured eagle, his heart begins to die.

But inside the cages is Minch, a female eagle, who is determined to teach Creggan not to forget about freedom. And outside is Mr Wolski, the Zoo's sweeper, a man haunted by the horror of captivity – his own and the birds'.

When the time comes Creggan and Mr Wolski are ready for the final struggle towards Callanish.

Brilliantly imagined, spare and tensely plotted, *Callanish* is dedicated to Goldie, the eagle who escaped briefly from a London zoo in 1965.

'A fascinating book of rare insight and understanding' – Virginia McKenna

A CHOICE OF PENGUIN FICTION

A Fanatic Heart   Edna O'Brien

'A selection of twenty-nine stories (including four new ones) full of wit and feeling and savagery that prove that Edna O'Brien is one of the subtlest and most lavishly gifted writers we have' – A. Alvarez in the *Observer*

Charade   John Mortimer

'Wonderful comedy . . . an almost Firbankian melancholy . . . John Mortimer's hero is helplessly English' – *Punch*. 'What is *Charade*? Comedy? Tragedy? Mystery? It is all three and more' – *Daily Express*

Casualties   Lynne Reid Banks

'The plot grips; the prose is fast-moving and elegant; above all, the characters are wincingly, winningly human . . . if literary prizes were awarded for craftsmanship and emotional directness, *Casualties* would head the field' – *Daily Telegraph*

The Anatomy Lesson   Philip Roth

The hilarious story of Nathan Zuckerman, the famous forty-year-old writer who decides to give it all up and become a doctor – and a pornographer – instead. 'The finest, boldest and funniest piece of fiction which Philip Roth has yet produced' – *Spectator*

Gabriel's Lament   Paul Bailey

Shortlisted for the 1986 Booker Prize
'The best novel yet by one of the most careful fiction craftsmen of his generation' – *Guardian*. 'A magnificent novel, moving, eccentric and unforgettable. He has a rare feeling for language and an understanding of character which few can rival' – *Daily Telegraph*

Small Changes   Marge Piercy

In the Sixties the world seemed to be making big changes – but for many women it was the small changes that were the hardest and the most profound. *Small Changes* is Marge Piercy's explosive new novel about women fighting to make their way in a man's world.

Family Myths and Legends Patricia Ferguson

Gareth was just beginning to believe that he really enjoyed his relatives these days. And then Gareth's grandmother turns up in Gareth's hospital – and he is up to his upwardly-mobile neck in family once more. 'Great funniness and perception, and stunning originality' – *Daily Telegraph*

The Beans of Egypt, Maine Carolyn Chute

Out of the hidden heart of America comes this uncompromising novel of what life is like for people who have nothing left to them except their own pain, humiliation and rage. 'It's loving, terrible and funny and written as deftly as stitching on a quilt . . . a lovely, truthful book' – *Observer*

City of Spades Colin MacInnes

'A splendid novel, sparklingly written, warm, wise and funny' – *Daily Mail*. *City of Spades*, *Absolute Beginners* and *Mr Love and Justice* make up Colin MacInnes's trilogy on London street life from the inside out.

Fiddle City Dan Kavanagh

'Scary insider's data on the airport sub-world, customs knowhow and smugglers' more sickening dodges are marvellously aerated by bubbles of Mr Kavanagh's very dry, sly, wide-ranging and Eighties humour' – *Sunday Times*

The Rachel Papers Martin Amis

A stylish, sexy and ribaldy funny novel by the author of *Money*. 'Remarkable' – *Listener*. 'Irreverent' – *Daily Telegraph*. 'Very funny indeed' – *Spectator*

Scandal A. N. Wilson

Sexual peccadilloes, treason and blackmail are all ingredients on the boil in A. N. Wilson's, *cordon noir* comedy. 'Drily witty, deliciously nasty' – *Sunday Telegraph*

FOR THE BEST IN PAPERBACKS, LOOK FOR THE

A CHOICE OF PENGUIN FICTION

To Have and To Hold   Deborah Moggach

Viv was giving her sister, Ann, the best present she could think of – a baby.
How Viv, Ann and their husbands cope with this extraordinary situation is
the subject of this tender, triumphant and utterly absorbing story.

Very Good, Jeeves!   P. G. Wodehouse

When Bertie Wooster lands in the soup, only the 'infinite sagacity' of
Jeeves can pull him out. 'A riot . . . There are eleven tales in this volume
and each is the best' – *Observer*

The Good Apprentice   Iris Murdoch

At Seegard there is something rich and strange, with the power to change
people's lives – for better or worse. 'Iris Murdoch is here very much at her
formidable, myth-making best; inventive, comic, moving' – Elaine Fein-
stein in *The Times*. 'A heaving, sprawling headlong spiritual thriller' –
Observer

Internal Affairs   Jill Tweedie

The bestselling author of *Bliss* has fashioned a mordantly funny novel
from this most unlikely subject – the effects of family planning on a third
world country. 'A delight . . . an original and constantly entertaining
novel which did, with embarrassing frequency, make me laugh out loud' –
Standard

The Garish Day   Rachel Billington

A sweeping, panoramic novel of spiritual and sexual crisis. 'Rachel
Billington's marvellously readable novel . . . is a real treat. Telling insight
and poker-faced humour' – *Daily Mail*

Charlotte's Row   H. E. Bates

With its superbly realized industrial setting and cast of memorable characters, *Charlotte's Row* is one of H. E. Bates's best novels in which he reveals
his deep understanding of the ambitions and dreams of ordinary men and
women. 'He is the Renoir of the typewriter' – *Punch*

A CHOICE OF PENGUIN FICTION

The Enigma of Arrival   V. S. Naipaul

'For sheer abundance of talent, there can hardly be a writer alive who surpasses V. S. Naipaul. Whatever we may want in a novelist is to be found in his books . . .' Irving Howe in *The New York Times Book Review*. 'Naipaul is always brilliant' – Anthony Burgess in the *Observer*

Only Children   Alison Lurie

When the Hubbards and the Zimmerns go to visit Anna on her idyllic farm, it becomes increasingly difficult to tell which are the adults, and which the children. 'It demands to be read' – *Financial Times*. 'There quite simply is no better living writer' – John Braine

My Family and Other Animals   Gerald Durrell

Gerald Durrell's wonderfully comic account of his childhood years on Corfu and his development as a naturalist and zoologist. Soaked in Greek sunshine, it is a 'bewitching book' – *Sunday Times*

Getting it Right   Elizabeth Jane Howard

A hairdresser in the West End, Gavin is sensitive, shy, into the arts, prone to spots and, at thirty-one, a virgin. He's a classic late developer – and maybe it's getting too late to develop at all? 'Crammed with incidental pleasures . . . sometimes sad but more frequently hilarious . . . *Getting it Right* gets it, comically, right' – Paul Bailey in the *London Standard*

The Vivisector   Patrick White

In this prodigious novel about the life and death of a great painter, Patrick White, winner of the Nobel Prize for Literature, illuminates creative experience with unique truthfulness. 'One of the most interesting and absorbing novelists writing in English today' – Angus Wilson in the *Observer*

The Echoing Grove   Rosamund Lehmann

'No English writer has told of the pains of women in love more truly or more movingly than Rosamund Lehmann' – Marghanita Laski 'She uses words with the enjoyment and mastery with which Renoir used paint' – Rebecca West in the *Sunday Times*. 'A magnificent achievement' – John Connell in the *Evening News*

FOR THE BEST IN PAPERBACKS, LOOK FOR THE

A CHOICE OF PENGUIN FICTION

The Ghost Writer   Philip Roth

Philip Roth's celebrated novel about a young writer who meets and falls in love with Anne Frank in New England – or so he thinks. 'Brilliant, witty and extremely elegant' – *Guardian*

Small World   David Lodge

Shortlisted for the 1984 Booker Prize, *Small World* brings back Philip Swallow and Maurice Zapp for a jet-propelled journey into hilarity. 'The most brilliant and also the funniest novel that he has written' – *London Review of Books*

Treasures of Time   Penelope Lively

Beautifully written, acutely observed, and filled with Penelope Lively s sharp but compassionate wit, *Treasures of Time* explores the relationship between the lives we live and the lives we think we live.

Absolute Beginners   Colin MacInnes

The first 'teenage' novel, the classic of youth and disenchantment, *Absolute Beginners* is part of MacInnes's famous London trilogy – and now a brilliant film. 'MacInnes caught it first – and best' – *Harpers and Queen*

July's People   Nadine Gordimer

Set in South Africa, this novel gives us an unforgettable look at the terrifying, tacit understanding and misunderstandings between blacks and whites. 'This is the best novel that Miss Gordimer has ever written' – Alan Paton in the *Saturday Review*

The Ice Age   Margaret Drabble

'A continuously readable, continuously surprising book . . . here is a novelist who is not only popular and successful but formidably growing towards real stature' – *Observer*